FLOWERS OF FATE

Book 2

DARK RAVEN CHRONICLES

by

Steven Hutton

BODDINGTON & ROYALL

Flowers of Fate

Published in Great Britain
by Books Illustrated Ltd

This paperback edition published 2018
1 3 5 7 9 10 8 6 4 2
Text and illustrations copyright © Steve Hutton

ISBN: 978-1-9164203-1-1

This books is a work of fiction. Names, characters, places and
incidents are either the product of the author's imagination or are
used fictitiously. Any resemblance to actual people living or dead,
events or locals is entirely coincidental.

Printed and bound in Great Britain by
CPI Group (UK) Ltd, Croydon CR0 4YY

BODDINGTON & ROYALL

www.**DarkRavenChronicles**.com

*'For Freya, Scrappy, Moses, Pierre, Ollie,
Maggie, Peter, Stan, Mouse, and finally Isabelle*

*Now you are spirit cats, and the heavens
are your gardens.'*

Broken Thread

Under oceans and mountains her lifeless body passed, carried by fate's river to a lost place where ghosts of treachery readied her welcome.

His will had been defied. The Patternmaker had commanded a thread be broken and with it a life should have ended, but his order was disobeyed and the weave's perfection was defiled.

At first it passed unnoticed for such a thing had never happened before, and so creation continued as it always had. But before long, the Patternmaker became aware that the weave wasn't as it ought to be. He scrutinised it and finally perceived the unbroken thread and it enraged him.

As his rage cooled he was able to look closer and so finally understood. The Timekeeper, the great spider who wove fate within a cosmic hourglass, was the cause of his fury. The unbroken thread was a witch and the Timekeeper had gifted her life over death in the name of pity. He knew the wrongness must be corrected and if his loyal servant could no longer be trusted, then he would send an assassin to mend the weave, slay the great spider and take his place. The thread must stay broken this time. The witch must die.

CHAPTER ONE

Bridge under the moon

'The final secret is that there is no mystery. In this way man is initiated into the cult of the material world. He is encouraged to amass wealth and practise indulgence because he believes there is nothing beyond. Thus, imagination is replaced by fear of death, which in turn becomes his prison.'
Knights Illuminata

'Thrice be the glory of the threefold way.'
The Book-of-Nine

"It's a bad business." Captain Platt exhaled and took the telescope from his eye. An outcrop of rock shaped like the prow of a ship dominated the valley, and at its summit sat Leonhard castle. It coveted a commanding view of the Dreisam River, which swept westwards through miles of empty forest to the town of Frieburg.

Platt looked again. It was gone midnight, but the full moon made the snowy landscape look bald. This was going to be as dangerous as any daylight raid he'd ever undertaken. A narrow bridge spanned the river, carried by thirteen arches, each with a cluster of dead branches around its foundations, testament to heavy autumn rains. Now though, it was February and the cold ran deep and bitter and left the river as a fragile highway of ice. That bridge was wide enough for a horse and cart, but it would be a delicate job to get a kraken over it.

"A bloody bad do." He clicked his teeth and swept the telescope towards the castle where turrets bristled like arrowheads. The moonlight would help, but it might just as easily betray them. The bridge crossed almost two-hundred yards of open water: the knights would be exposed like players on a stage, and the castle's countless brooding windows were the audience.

He snapped the telescope shut and slid back down the slope into the woods, to the smell of horses and men. He heard the jangle of bridles and bits as his fifty squires hurriedly wrapped them in cloth to muffle the noise. "No guards," he said to Black, his lieutenant.

"Almost too good to be true." Black peeled back his hood to reveal a face battered by warfare.

"Aye, I agree, but it's a bad do."

"All war's a bad do sir," he grinned. "Shall I send a message to the gathered knights that we're moving out?"

Platt considered, nodded once, and the raid was on.

Minutes later he heard the hammer of hooves as the messenger set out. He knew this would be decisive. If they failed tonight then six-hundred years of British control would pass to foreign hands and whoever controlled the Illuminata shaped the world. Platt was part of a force that comprised only eight knights and fifty squires and they had to take a castle and hold it ransom. Those knights and their giant krakens had been lifted in by airships two nights prior under the cover of a blizzard. They were hidden in the forest nearby with their furnaces idling ready for the signal, but first they had to secure the castle and Leonhard's family. Of course the knights could march right up to it and pound it to dust, heaven knows they were powerful enough, a coal-fired kraken stood over twenty metres high and weighed one-hundred and twenty tons, but then there'd be little left to ransom. "A bad do," he muttered to nobody.

The other squires were already mounting up, with their gleaming bayonets concealed in black cloth. He took his horse's reins and patted the mare's nose. The rags around her feet made her look comical, but they were vital. They planned to ride across the frozen river and iron hooves on thin ice wasn't a good idea.

How had it come to this? he wondered again as they set off. Their greatest knights had been utterly wiped out in just one battle. They set out to conquer a coven of witches and only a handful of them had lived to tell about it. The small force assembled here in Germany's Black Forest were the survivors of that ill-fated assault last October.

Platt took his place at the head of the line feeling like the chief mourner. Nobody spoke and even the horses seemed sullen. They would ride two miles west and cross the river where it swept around the valley and out of sight. Once on the opposite bank they'd ride back through the forest and take the castle's defences long enough for their lords to march over the bridge. In light of what had happened to the British last October, the Leonhard family were now Europe's strongest Illuminata family and most likely to take the title of Knight Superior. Platt's orders were not to let that happen. This was their last chance to keep power firmly in British hands.

They rode single file, with Platt leading the way. His own knight, Sir Thomas Kent, would be leading the charge and so Platt led the squires according to tradition. As they rode away from the castle he couldn't help looking back at the fortified crag, convinced enemy eyes were watching already.

Twigs crackled under their muffled hooves, until the sound gave way to the crunch of gravel and he knew they had arrived at the tributary feeding into the river; the place they would cross. He slid down from his horse and led her to the edge of the ford. Through an opening in the trees he could see the frozen river ahead, laying silent and still like a corpse. He imagined his men out there as dark silhouettes and wished the astrologers hadn't planned this assault for a full moon. "Black!" he hissed, "take my horse." He passed the reins, and stepped out of the woods on to that bright river of ice. His shadow suddenly appeared at his feet, making him twice as large.

"Easy goes it sir," Black whispered.

The ice against the bank was rock solid, but with each step Platt knew the water under him was growing faster, colder and deeper. Nails on his soles gave him purchase and after twenty paces he turned back and was mildly disconcerted to find there wasn't a trace of his men in the darkness.

They might just pull this off after all he thought.

He took the bayonet from his Martini-Henry rifle and stabbed at the ice a couple of times. It was hard as army oatcake, but he still didn't trust it, he never liked a mission that depended more on God's will than good planning. He knew God, and knew what a fickle master he could be. He crept back to his troops and claimed his horse from Black. "Ice seems sound." He pulled a scarf up over his face.

"Will it take fifty horses and men though?" Black was dubious.

"We'll soon see."

"Good luck sir," he bid him, then raised his own scarf as Platt led his horse and the squires out across the river.

None of them saddled up: it would have been impossible to escape the horse if it fell through the ice. Instead, they walked single file and a horse's length between each to spread their weight. Platt's horse paced out onto the ice after him and her muffled hooves boomed like a hollow barrel and he winced. "A bad do," he muttered again.

One by one his men followed, provoking ominous growling sounds from the ice beneath their feet. The further they ventured the more vulnerable he felt. His horse plodded after him blissfully unaware of the danger below or awaiting them at the castle. Leonhard kept only a dozen troops and while the staff were numerous Platt didn't think servants and cooks would give them much trouble. They would kill the castle guard, then find Leonhard and his family while the knights advanced over the bridge, and hold it from Leonhard's own knights when they finally showed up. Platt thought the man a fool for having them garrisoned so far away: just four months ago spies reported that Leonhard had moved them twenty miles west towards Frieburg to spare the cost of shipping coal further up river. The castle and the family would be theirs for ransom and the price would be enough gold to rebuild the British garrison, and a signed pledge that Leonhard would renounce his claim as Knight Superior. It was a scoundrel's plan but all was fair when it came to feuding bloodlines.

"Krast!" Platt had damned the man a hundred times over. If not for the former Knight Superior's disastrous assault this leadership struggle would never have arisen, and as much as he admired his own knight, Kent was merely a lad thrust into top position because everyone above him had been suddenly killed. The inexperienced lad had been talked into leading this covert action by a senior who was right now tucked up in his feather bed in London: namely Victor Thorpe.

"Bloody Krast." Platt breathed a cloud of vapour and through it he saw the opposite bank and its welcome covering shadow. He picked up his pace, anxious to be out of the moon's staring eye. As soon as sounds of scraping ice turned to crunching gravel again he puffed a sigh of relief and then counted the men through, letting out a huge breath when he got to fifty. The first major threat was over.

Black came to his side holding his pocket watch. "Made better time than I thought, God's on our side eh sir?" He sounded pleased.

"God has a nasty habit of changing sides when it suits him." Platt shot him a sideways look but saw only the white crescents of his eyes in the gloom. From here it was two miles to the castle. He sent two scouts ahead and mounted his own horse. "Black, tell the men; masks up and no chatter."

"Aye sir." He went to spread the message as Platt watched his two scouts vanish into the darkness.

They arrived back at the bridge without incident, and Platt made ready. "Black, when we get to the castle take half the men and find Leonhard, the rest of us will deal with the castle guards."

"Understood sir."

"And remember, don't fire the cannon until the guard is dead and Leonhard is caught." That was the signal for the knights to advance, and Sir Thomas Kent would be leading them.

Maybe it was because he'd rebuked God's less than honest nature not long since, but just as Platt's words left his mouth God changed sides – and a cannon fired from the battlements. He saw the silent muzzle flash followed by a rumble a second or two later. There was a stunned moment when nobody said anything and all just stared in horror at the insignificant puff of smoke drifting away from the castle. "It's a trap!" he barked, secrecy redundant now. "You!" he grabbed the closest squire. "Back over the bridge, tell the knights not to advance, it's an ambush!"

Black had already drawn his sabre and his men did likewise. "God's had a change of heart sir." He sounded thrilled.

"Squires!" Platt shouted and they raised their sabres. "Take the castle or our knights'll be cut down. For your lords!" He was already spurring his mount out of the woods and onto the track, while his chosen messenger was now half way across the bridge, racing to where the knights would already be stoking up their krakens. "A bloody bad do," he cursed again.

Together with Black, he led the troops towards the castle in a rattle of hooves and flying grit. Trap it might be, but he knew heavy cannons would be trained on the bridge and what pretty targets their knights would be. This had gone from a capture mission to a rescue mission, and it was their own knights in need of rescue.

Amazingly, despite the thunder of the charging horses, Platt heard a single shot ring out and he knew instantly that his messenger was dead. He wheeled his mare around and sure enough saw his man sprawled on the snowy bridge, looking like an ink smudge on a blank page, and his bewildered horse trotting away. The knights would still be advancing.

"Black, lead them on!" He spurred his mare away before his lieutenant could reply and made back for the bridge. The moon flickered between trees as he charged onwards, and then behind him he heard the inevitable volley of rifle fire as Leonhard's ambush closed in around the rest. A sardonic smile parted his lips. They'd been soundly outmanoeuvred, but the least he could do now was save the knights from disaster. If the family arms were captured it would mean shame and a crippling ransom to regain them. He kicked at the horse's flanks until his heels were sore.

The trees thinned and the moon spilled across him and there before him was two-hundred yards of bridge, empty except for a fallen squire, but while that was bad enough, it was the colossal figure emerging from the forest that drained the air from his chest. The last of Britain's knights had begun their advance, led by the inexperienced Sir Thomas Kent.

"Back!" he shouted, in vain. "Back!" He spurred his horse on, vaguely aware that marksmen might add a second body to the one already lying there, but unable to stop himself. The foremost knight was his own. He saw Kent's banners fluttering over the kraken and he could imagine the lad's sense of pride as he marched his war-suit. Proud but doomed.

Kent's kraken gleamed in the moonlight. Its helmet resembled an Egyptian god, but as magnificent as it looked it would soon be just cannon fodder.

The kraken's huge feet made the bridge shudder and behind it, through a fan of smoke rushing from its furnace chimneys, he saw the rest of the knights forming a column. "Back!" he screamed impotently, just as an artillery shell droned overhead and punctured the icy river, sending a shaft of water high into the air.

Inside the kraken's cockpit Kent sat surrounded by levers and dials and watched as a squire raced towards him across the bridge. "Platt?" Thomas Kent, a young man of seventeen with a straight nose and a sensitive face, squinted through the visor and knew something was wrong. Then the river to his left exploded like the blow from a whale as the first barrage rained down. "They're firing on us!" His voice had that uncertain edge of a youth not yet a man. He looked around the cockpit, wondering if any of the controls could tell him what to do now. Platt was less than a hundred yards away, swinging his arms wildly, gesturing him to retreat.

Kent snatched the communicare and ordered his knights back. "Retreat back to the forest, evacuate the bridge!" A cluster of shells hit the river sending up an icy wave as the moon continued to stare down stupidly, exposing their blunder in startling detail. "All knights, full retreat!" he ordered, but the communicare just crackled in reply and he wondered if anyone had heard.

A shell landed only feet away. The noise was deafening and debris pelted the hull. His kraken rocked and lurched and he had to heave on the controls to stabilise it. Outside, he saw Platt was now horseless and laying in the snow. A shell had severed the bridge, leaving only a treacherous drop into the river. There was no possible way forwards, and he began an about turn but almost instantly rammed into the knight behind. His machine juddered hard enough for his teeth to snap down on his tongue and he was thrown against the cockpit, smashing a pressure gauge with his brow and drawing blood. Regardless of the damage he forced the machine around. Metal screamed against metal as his kraken came face to face with the leering gargoyle helmet of Sir Horace Butterworth behind. "Retreat Butterworth, bloody retreat!" he shouted. Blood mingled with sweat and he saw his column strung out along the bridge and now behind them, emerging from the forest, came Leonhard's own knights. "Dear God!" he flapped. This was going to be a slaughter.

Platt climbed to his feet, tipping a shower of broken ice from his clothes. The river around the bridge churned with ice, and across its broken span he saw Kent try to turn his kraken, but the huge machine butted against the knight behind. It had nowhere to go, and instead just teetered on the brink with its metal feet ripping at the crumbling masonry. The forest behind was no longer black. He saw tell-tale sparks rising from the chimneys of the German knights now marching out of hiding. "They're trapped." Platt knew there was only one way this night could end. Behind him, back along the track to the castle, he heard desperate shouts, the clash of sabres and pop of rifle fire. Black was still pinned by the ambushers and Platt was stranded literally in the middle. He staggered to the bridge's edge, horrified by the sight of Kent's kraken perched on its lip moments from falling. "Sir! The bridge!"

Six files back, one of the British krakens was hit by cannon fire and exploded like a firework, illuminating the whole valley. Brilliant sparks showered up from its severed neck and Platt saw its lion-helmet peel slowly away and tumble into the river with a huge splash. The knights at the rear were pinned by the emerging German knights and worse still they had their backs to the enemy.

The leading German piloted a kraken fashioned like a glaring eagle. It was absurdly simple for him to march right up behind the last knight in rank and punch a hole right through its chest. The furnace ruptured and burning coals showered out like blood. The huge machine instantly sagged to its knees and Platt rocked on his feet as it crashed to the ground. Along the length of the bridge the entire column of knights were clumsily trying to turn, like lumbering giants walking the plank. He pulled his rifle from his shoulder, how it would help he had no idea but it felt better to hold something than just watch centuries of British tradition be torn down. "Treacherous bastards!" he screamed, forgetting all was fair in family feuds, and let off a futile round. Muzzles flashed in rapid succession from the castle, shells screamed down, battering the river and he looked up to see Kent's kraken slide from the crumbling bridge. For a moment it seemed as if the huge machine was undecided, carefully considering its options, then it swooned into the river. "Sire!" He dropped his rifle and backed away.

The kraken fell gracefully, trailing Kent's family banner, which ironically showed a stag nimbly leaping a river. It vanished from sight and a second later a wall of icy water spewed up and thunder rolled around the valley. Platt was smacked from the bridge by the wave and landed in the river. The cold was instant and brutal. His chest seized and his lungs shrivelled. He tried to call out, but Kent's kraken was just a steaming wreck, rolling and gurgling amongst the ice and breathing frothy bubbles as it sank.

The current tugged at his legs and he scrambled at the ice but his clothes were heavy and his limbs were wooden and powerless. "Sire!" he gasped, and then vanished as the current took a liking to him. He spluttered up a moment later, flailing at anything and clung to the kraken's gauntlet, but the metal was smooth and his hands were as stone. "Sire!" he cried again, but the current pulled him away to be its plaything. Water closed over his face and poured death into his lungs. *A bad do*, he thought.

Suddenly the ice was above him and he looked up from under it. Shells streaked overhead and the moon winked down at him seeming to laugh, then the current carried him away and the black and the cold became eternal.

CHAPTER TWO

A necessary evil

'If evil wasn't necessary, God wouldn't have invented it.'
Unknown

A mere ten days later a small group of men met at the stone circle on Salisbury plain. On one side was Wilhelm Hieder, a representative of Europe's Illuminata families including Leonhard's, and on the other was his British counterpart Lord Victor Thorpe, who had instigated the Platt mission at the behest of the British bloodlines.

They arrived in carriages, exited without ceremony, and even shook hands, as if a hostile British force had never been trespassing in the Black Forest just over a week ago. Thorpe, a tall, well-built man bordering on sixty with a sharp nose and cold eyes, removed his gloves and regarded his opposite. His bushy moustache concealed his mouth, making him rather expressionless and hard to read. "I suppose you know why I've summoned you?"

"All of Europe knows," Hieder shrugged, then scrutinised the grey February skies. "Doesn't the sun ever shine here? No wonder the British are so repressed." His excellent English was dressed with a soft Bavarian accent. He was tanned and rather podgy and so looked distinctly out of place in this snowy landscape. Thorpe thought he would look more at home as a eunuch in some desert harem. The two men circled the stones at a lazy pace leaving their carriages and retinues.

"I thought they'd be bigger," Hieder patted one of the great stones. "Strength is so often a bluff. Nothing is ever what it seems eh?" he smiled at Thorpe even as he insulted him.

"I don't suppose you've had the chance to come here before." Thorpe's reference wasn't to do with Hieder's travel experiences, but rather the grand tournament. "It's been over six-hundred years since there was a tournament here, and with good reason. Imagine it: six centuries of supreme control." He walked a little taller, but Hieder just shrugged again.

"Nothing remains the same forever, and your 'supreme control' doesn't change the present, and the situation is this," he stopped and folded his arms, no longer looking like a soft old eunuch, but a mean bulldog with the scent of blood. "You initiated hostilities to prevent Count Leonhard making his legitimate claim as Knight Superior. Fortunately our informants learned your plans." He pursed his lips and shook his head. "And now your brave knights lie at the bottom of the Dreisam River."

Thorpe glowered at him. Spies had put paid to their mission all right, but he didn't think Hieder would be so smug when he showed him his parting gift today.

"And now that your plan has failed," Hieder continued, "you show no shame in calling upon an obscure tradition that demands no further hostilities until June 21st, when our differences be settled not in conflict, but in a tournament according to laws of chivalry." He smirked at this last word.

Thorpe nodded and let Hieder's indignation sail clean over his head. "That's about the long and the short of it yes."

Hieder threw his hands up. "But you have no fighting knights left! Nor any krakens to field them in. If he wanted to, Leonhard could march into London and what could your six-hundred years of total supremacy do to stop him? I tell you; nothing, that is what!"

"Indeed," Thorpe replied coolly, "and that is the very reason we called upon the Constantine-truce. I agree it might stick in your throat, but as Britain is still the controlling nation, implementing the truce is legitimate." His smile was as cold as the weather. "And Leonhard will respect it."

"Or?" Hieder's arms refolded themselves. Thorpe believed it was more to keep his hands warm than look defiant.

"Then we will have to find other ways to fight Europe." He started away, giving the stout little Bavarian chance to grasp his threat. After ten paces Hieder caught him up.

"Are you mad!"

Thorpe paused to light a cigar. The wind was fresh and it took him three attempts and all the while he was aware of Hieder's rasping breaths. At last when the tip was glowing red he took a puff, savoured it, then smiled at him. "Britain's enjoyed much experience of war and if nothing else it's good for the economy, so please don't believe for a moment we won't. It's the tournament or Europe-wide war, your choice." He stalked away trying to conceal his anger. The British had only four months to manufacture more krakens and train their youngest knights. Europe's best chance was to accept the tournament and both of them knew it. After a while he heard Hieder catch him up.

"Mr Thorpe," he sounded amiable now, "let's not make any mistakes, Leonhard relishes the chance of a tournament. The pomp and socializing are much to his taste, but you cannot win. You know this don't you? Your days are over my friend. Your finest knights will come here in four months and they will be broken and the title of Knight Superior will pass to Leonhard. He even has the backing of the other families, the French, the Portuguese, the Spanish, all of them will field knights under his banner. You're outnumbered and outdated, rather like these relics." He nodded to the stones.

Thorpe turned and looked at the impassive stones around him. He reached out and touched one, but felt nothing. It was said they had been built by the Romans, the Druids, and even a race of giants, but he knew the truth of it. The 'Henge had been built by witches, and that thought kindled the old flame, the one that burned bright enough to keep the bloodlines bound through even war and treachery: their hatred of witches and desire to seize their knowledge. "I look forward to meeting the Count again in June, the English summers can be quite pleasant you know." He reached into his overcoat and drew out a scroll. It was only small, but it was a legally binding notice. "Signed by the Queen-Empress herself. If June 21st comes and goes and none of Leonhard's knights arrive, then war shall be declared."

Hieder sighed, reached out and took it and in doing so acknowledged the contract. "Until June then Mr Thorpe."

They walked back to their waiting carriages through a curtain of drizzle and watched a bank of fog roll in across the lonely plain. Thorpe's men looked up from their positions and raised their rifles uneasily. "At ease," he commanded.

Hieder headed straight to his own carriage, eager to see this day over with.

"Oh, Mr Hieder," Thorpe called pleasantly, "before you go there's something I'd like you to give the Count, a gift as it were."

Hieder raised his eyebrows. Perhaps he'd been too harsh on these cheerless British, he thought. Thorpe smiled and clapped his hands. At his signal a man loomed up out of the thickening fog leading a horse harnessed to a cart. Thorpe's men silently moved up to flank him and kept their rifles ready. The horse came to a stop in front of Hieder and his escort. On the trailer were three unmistakable human shapes wrapped in grubby sackcloth, bloody ones at that.

"We're returning these to the Count," Thorpe took a pace forwards and his guards cocked their rifles, prompting Hieder's men to do the same. "We found them where they ought not to be. No wonder the Count knew those knights were coming. And now we're returning them. Be so good as to thank the Count for his gift, but tell him we have no liking for spies." He flicked cigar ash across one of the corpses.

Hieder looked at the trailer. Now he knew why their agents hadn't contacted them for a week, but he kept his face neutral. "That won't be necessary," he gestured for his men to lower their weapons.

"I'm sorry we're unable to return them in the same condition they arrived." Thorpe toyed with the edge of the sackcloth. "But spying on Goldhawk can be a rough business and on occasion things get broken."

Hieder just shrugged again. "Keep them. Broken or otherwise, the Count has plenty more." His threat was as delicate as the drizzle. With that he climbed into his carriage making the springs complain and slammed the door. His guard detail filed towards their own carriage and its team of impatient horses. "I hope the British summer is all you boast Mr Thorpe. Until June!" He thumped his cane on the roof and the carriage departed for Southampton to the tune of snorting horses and the whip of harnesses.

Thorpe watched him leave and then took a last puff on his cigar, tossed it down and twisted the heat out of it with his foot. "Hun bastard," he muttered.

If Europe had indeed gathered under Leonhard's banner then Britain's days were truly numbered. He turned and looked back at the stones.

"The days of the British are over my friend," Hieder's words came back to him.

"Only if we play by the rules," Thorpe thought aloud, "only if we play by the rules." The Illuminata stole secrets from defeated covens, which had allowed them to dominate the course of civilization, but there was one area of magic they were afraid of and here they at least agreed with witches. Anyone who sought to exploit Ruination was damned. But now perhaps the Illuminata were desperate enough. "I should thank you Leonhard, you leave us no choice," he muttered, as if absolving himself of the calamities to come.

"What do we do with these sir?"

He looked to where his captain stood by the dead informants. "Dump them in a ditch. The crows will eat anything – even froggie spies." He twitched a smile and made for his carriage, anxious to be back to London. He wanted to speak with the head families and get his plan underway, and he had just the man in mind to see it through. *Galen,* he thought and smiled. *Yes, now is finally the time, Galen, your hour has come.*

Ask any witch of Britain if they know Goldhawk Row and they'll either blush with anger or blanch with fear. Since witches first devised spells to protect the Earth, others have hunted them and the Illuminata have done very well from stealing their secrets. Goldhawk Row, a plain brick building by the Thames with sturdy railings and dark windows, was the headquarters for the British Illuminata. It was now April and the trees decorating London's parks and gardens were putting on their finest spring foliage, but Goldhawk was devoid of such greenery and so it remained grey and sombre.

It might appear invulnerable, but Goldhawk had suffered a very deep wound. Its fighting units lay in tatters and the former Knight Superior killed in action. The battle for Kittiwake-coven had cost them dear, but the worst had come in February when their last hope, Sir Thomas Kent, had sunk into the Dreisam River. The first thing Britain had done was to order a truce, which would last until the summer solstice, a law that reflected the order's ancient esoteric roots.

June 21st this year saw the golden jubilee of the Queen-Empress. It was an excellent omen and it would also provide a suitable distraction. Attention would be fixed on celebrations in the capital while the bloodlines could fight their grand tournament in private.

During this uneasy peace, preparations were underway to construct barracks at Wellesley Hall on Salisbury Plain which would host the tournament, while London was putting Thorpe's last gambit into motion, and a very risky one it was too. They were racing against the clock and it had taken two months just to locate their chosen man, but they only had themselves to blame. It was they who had exiled him in the first place. After weeks tracking him down, he finally arrived from India and all he was given was a dusty little room tucked away in the library where he would live and work. Hardly a welcome fit for the man charged with saving the British Empire.

Goldhawk's library filled the building's voluminous roof space, but its contents wouldn't count as light reading. There were over twenty miles of shelving, housing books on witchcraft and esoteric law. The windows were blacked out and the library was off-limits to most staff. Today there was only one man on the upper floor amongst the books: the specialist Thorpe had called in. He had set up his rough sleeping arrangements in a small ante-chamber close to the library's entrance. Adjoining rooms contained confiscated artefacts such as wands, lightning-staffs, witches' ashes in sealed urns, bones and body parts. There were stout cabinets crammed with arcane specimen jars, where mummified creatures languished in vinegar. Creatures resided here that no Londoner had ever seen, magical creatures said not to exist; fairies, drummon-toadies, water-sprites, embryo mermaids, unicorn horns and severed human hands that had once served a terrible master in the bowels of the earth. There seemed no end to the bizarre collection, and that was part of the appeal for the Illuminata's equally strange guest. He loved the smell of preserving fluid and old books. Being close to death soothed him.

The man known only as Galen was forty-six years old, but his hair was still soot-black and he had disconcerting pale eyes that saw more than just surface deep. He was moody and spoke little, but when he did the listener might detect a soft Irish lilt, but he was not from there. His frame was lean and his breathing rapid and shallow, as though something inside burned him up, and he was dogged by a faint but persistent cough.

He sat composed on a rough wooden cot, and there was a lantern by his side despite the fact it was only noon. The room's only window was tiny and daylight appeared reluctant to pass through it. He hadn't been home in years, then four weeks ago a telegram reached him instructing him to come to Goldhawk as a matter of urgency. Now the organisation that exiled him had provided him a room and an interesting proposition.

He wore a satchel at all times, guarding a special book; the Book-of-Nine. In his hands he gripped a black cane that had an unpleasant greasy shine to it. He had no need of a cane, he could walk perfectly well, but he had plentiful need of the creature living inside it. "Elios," he said as he stroked the wood, and the creature inside purred at his touch.

"She's there," Elios informed him. She rarely left the confines of the strange walking cane.

"Sophie," he said sadly, cleared his mind and went to that place he had visited since childhood. Inside the cane, his companion sensed his inner journey and knew what to do. She opened a door into a place that was the antithesis of Earth, both disturbing and bizarre, where natural laws were turned on their heads. In this place everything was upside down and back to front. Galen stared into the wilds of Ruination.

The landscape of Ruin languished under a baking sun that gave no light, populated by creatures with no purpose or logic. Blind fledglings sat on heaps of their dead siblings and gulped down scaly worms bigger than themselves. Hairless dogs ate and regurgitated themselves over and over. Multi-jointed fingers sprouted through the earth like trees, and rivers of lead ran across the landscape like buckled railway lines. Embryo piglets in amniotic sacks drifted through the skies followed by a hurricane of flies. At the heart of this madness stood a huge figure as tall as a mountain, blindfolded and clothed in millions of rotting flowers. It ponderously worked the handle of an organ-grinder that spewed time into the universe in a glorious never ending song. Time was the slow death of everything, from stars to starlings. The gigantic creature was known as Àeon amongst his followers. He was Ruination incarnate.

It was said by many that creatures from Ruination were 'evil'. They were only half right. Àeon gave creation the gift of time so that it might crumble and allow new life to follow and although most agreed death was frequently tragic, few would argue it to be evil. Àeon had found Ruination a lonely place and so he populated it with beings of his own making, his own thoughts given life. But it was the emanations from Àeon's subconscious that brought Ruination its reputation as the abode of demons. When he dreamed, as all beings must, his subconscious creations sometimes escaped Ruination and found their way to Earth. This is how Galen and other Book-of-Nine cultists understood Àeon's world. It was the ultimate hope of each adept to fathom a spell that would make them immune to Àeon's song, to live free of time itself. Immortality was not just a dream for men like Galen.

"My lord," he muttered humbly and looked away. It wasn't right to look at the overlord of Ruination, but then again he only ever had eyes for her. "Sophie," he whispered.

A young girl wearing a long christening gown knelt by a pool of molten lead with her back to him. He couldn't say for sure, but she looked to be cradling something in her arms. Her dark hair fell down her back like a sheet of undertaker's satin. He felt that same old loneliness when he saw her. She seemed so close but she was a universe away. Beside her, wiry saplings with translucent skin and pulsing veins reached out and caressed her gently. Other strange creatures had gathered close, likewise besotted. He had the profound sense that she was beloved by Ruination and that made him jealous. The denizens of Ruin sensed him looking through the barrier, but sweet Sophie never did. If only she would turn to look at him, just once.

As always she hummed a little nursery rhyme. *"Little Miss Muffet sat on her tuffet, along came a spider and sat down beside her."*

Spiders, Galen thought. He had heard this for decades, if only she would say his name instead. While he grew old in this world, she had hardly aged. She was still a child, but they were twins born of the same mother at the same hour. He lost her when she was just days old, she was taken by something not of Earth. A creature known as a crib-robber had swallowed her and slipped away between the gaps in reality taking her to where she was now, but for what purpose nobody, not even Galen, knew. The bond between twins was strong enough for him to look through the barrier however, although tantalising glimpses were all he could steal. "Sophie." He felt incomplete without her. They were one child divided in the womb, but perhaps she didn't even know he existed. *What if she doesn't even want you?* That horrible possibility had haunted him his whole life. *What if one day, when at last you find a way to bring her back, she sees just a broken old man and doesn't even know you?*

"*Galen.*" A voice shook him from his melancholy. It was beautiful but tragic, like a dying bride. It was Elios again. "*Turn away now, they're beginning.*"

He opened his eyes and the vision vanished. "Until next time Sophie," he sighed. "And of course gratitude to my ever patient Elios," he patted the cane. Without her, he wouldn't have been able to see his lost twin. "Now, what is it these scoundrels are about?" He brought his mind back to matters of the day and using talents outlawed by the Illuminata, and aided by the mysterious Elios, he listened to a private conversation between two men several floors down.

John Doulton stood looking along the table. Daylight fell through the windows and turned the polished mahogany silver. The huge table accommodated thirty-two chairs with an ornate carver at its head presiding over the entire room. If anyone was in doubt as to the chair's rightful occupant there was a crest above it showing a swan encircled by a crown. It was the arms of the family Krast and the chair stood empty because Krast was dead and the family disgraced. When all the feuding was over the Krast arms would be replaced, but who the Illuminata's new ruling family would be was a question that cost Doulton his sleep. He tried to imagine the Leonhard arms on the wall and he shuddered.

For a while he stood and looked out at Westminster Palace across the river, and thought of the man sitting upstairs in the library and marvelled again at how they were desperate enough to consider using him. He heard the door to the meeting room open and turned to see Virgil Lyle enter. He was a squat balding man in his early fifties who always wore a sour expression, but his loyalty to the Illuminata was total.

"Good day Mr Lyle. Touch of spring about the day wouldn't you say?" It was April, but London looked as grey as ever.

Lyle blinked behind his thick glasses and his chin receded into the folds of his neck as if the comment had offended him. He always reminded Doulton of a leathery tortoise, but there was nothing slow about his wits. "Little to celebrate, spring or otherwise." He moved quickly to the head of the table, stopping to straighten a chair that was a fraction out of line. "Have you forgotten our situation? I for one don't relish spending my life working for pig-herding Prussian overlords." Lyle disliked his colleague, thinking him an idealist. He especially disliked his moustache and suspected he wore it to make himself look older than his thirty-one years. Fate, in the shape of Lord Thorpe, had brought them together to rescue the Illuminata and under normal circumstances the Master-of-Arms wouldn't have anything to do with the Squire's Marshall, especially one who'd inherited the title and never seen battle. Lyle was senior and delighted in his new found importance and he never let his other half forget it. "I trust you've read the brief Lord Thorpe and I prepared?"

Lord Thorpe and I, Doulton thought with disdain. *They sound like a royal couple.* "Indeed. First and only name is Galen. Aged forty-six, exiled these last twenty or so years to Amsterdam, then Istanbul and finally India."

"Repatriated," Lyle corrected, "not exiled."

"The same thing isn't it – he didn't want to go."

His mouth puckered in disapproval. "Whether he wanted to go or not, he had his orders."

"Indeed," Doulton agreed wearily. "And has anyone briefed Galen of our position?"

"I took the liberty of speaking with him this morning. He knows the full picture." He wiped a testing finger over a chair looking for dust.

Without telling me? Doulton disliked being shut out. "And his verdict?"

"He retired to consider, we shall hear all he has to say when he arrives." He glanced at Big Ben across the Thames, "Which will be very soon now."

"Maybe while he's at it he can shed some light on what really happened to Krast at Kittiwake-coven last October."

"Isn't that obvious?" Lyle squinted at him, daring him to say otherwise.

Since October, feeling against witches had run at fever-pitch and few stopped to ask what had really destroyed their knights that day. "There are lots of unexplained factors," Doulton reminded him.

"Such as?"

"Well, since when did any witch have the power to turn men into ash, or steel into powdered rust? Even the horses were picked clean." He had studied the battle report too.

Lyle regarded him suspiciously. "I see you're one of those liberals that likes to forget just how foul witches are."

"All I'm pointing out is that there were no survivors, the only ones who made it back had fled before the final assault."

"They didn't flee, it was a tactical retreat," he fumed, "tactical retreat!"

"Either way, we have no eyewitnesses, and I for one am not certain it was witches that finished those knights."

"We'll make them all pay," Lyle promised, ignoring him. "Both the rats hiding in their covens and the European bloodlines. Galen's skills will bring them all to heel." He stormed over to the windows and stood staring moodily at the river.

"I still think using a cultist is asking for trouble. His allegiance isn't clear. Making an accord with these creatures is madness, even witches won't have anything to do with them."

"As you've said many times. But thankfully Lord Thorpe understands solutions such as the ones you support won't work. 'Treaties and cross-family marriages', stuff of fairy tales." He made a 'tut' sound.

Doulton flushed with anger. "It might have saved a lot of men's lives."

"Men? We have plenty of those, don't fret about saving them."

"I'm glad Captain Platt isn't here to hear that," he said icily.

"I was referring to the lower ranks," he blustered.

Doulton collected himself. "I still don't like what this Galen stands for."

He shook his head. "We've no knights of fighting age left. Galen agrees we're vulnerable, not just to rival families but to witches."

Because he practically is one. Doulton kept his thought private. "So Thorpe's set on employing a magical solution to our dilemma?"

"I didn't say that," he retorted.

"Then why are we letting a magical adviser save our skins?"

"He's an esoteric expert, not a witch." He didn't like his repeated use of the 'M' word.

"Let's hope you're correct. His credentials are vague to say the least. I'd not even heard of this cult before."

"The Book-of-Nine is known to very few."

"Wasn't it Krast who had it dissolved? Didn't he think research into Ruination made them dangerous?"

Lyle folded his arms. "Perhaps you forget that the tournament is just over two months away?"

"Our factory in the north is making new krakens. Do we really need this Galen?"

"Consider his role a safety net."

Doulton leaned forwards and spoke in a low voice. "What if he can't control the things he lets out of Pandora's box eh?"

His mouth twitched. "Nonsense, Lord Thorpe has the utmost faith in him, as do I."

Doulton sank his hands into his pockets and paced idly back to stare at the Krast arms. "And if Galen can wrest control of the Illuminata back for us, I understand that you'll act as mentor to our next Knight Superior; Albert Kent, the two-year old brother to Sir Thomas. You'll be holding the reigns of power for quite some time."

His eyes narrowed. "Your meaning?"

"Nothing, other than I hope you're ready to be a father."

Lyle scowled as he decided whether or not his motives were being questioned. Doulton looked on with a fixed smile and wondered. Something told him that was his real reason for complying with Thorpe's plan. After all, what man of sane disposition would seek the advice of someone like Galen? The Book-of-Nine was outlawed because its members had sought communion with Ruination. Galen, for all rhyme and reason, walked with demons.

"They're right to be wary." Galen sat on the bed staring into space, having heard every word. He had also read the battle report from Kittiwake-coven and was moved to tears. How he wished he could have seen that massive Ruinous incursion. Alas, they would have lived only a few days, but such a spectacle must have been sublime. He rubbed his brow where a headache brewed. Listening in on people was hard work.

"Lyle has his own motives," Elios observed.

"Don't we all," he smiled wearily.

"Please be careful dearest Galen."

"Am I in peril?"

"Yes." She feared for him. Creatures of Ruin were strange and savage but they were children compared to the men downstairs. *"Men are such strange beasts Galen, they think one thing and say another and never see it as a broken way to live."*

"Elios dear," he patted the cane, "perhaps you're right. I don't trust them either."

"Can it really be done?" she asked. *"Can they recruit Ruination to their cause?"*

He thought for a long time. "Not the way they think."

"The others failed."

"I know," he sighed heavily and listened to the sun warm the roof tiles, making soft cracking sounds. He watched a dandelion-fairy briefly land on the skylight before flitting off again. There were very few fairies in Goldhawk Row. Maybe they disliked seeing their kin in pickling jars, he thought.

"I don't want you to end up like Clarence Forster." She sounded afraid and with good cause.

"Forster?" He'd almost forgotten the man.

Ruination had a strange effect on men. It whispered the ridiculous and the insane and before long they began to see sense in its ramblings. Galen had seen cultists lose their heads obsessing over ideas that were patently mad, and there was no better example than Forster.

He hadn't been there in that opium den in Amsterdam that night. Forster had retreated to a back room and put his final plan into action. He'd caught a Ruinous beast, a crib-robber. It was only a small one but nevertheless it was no mean feat. It had taken Galen six years to find one himself. Forster had become convinced that he could physically enter Ruination if the crib-robber *devoured* him. He'd taken a fast acting poison, leaving orders with the other Niners to dismember his corpse and feed it to the crib-robber, where upon he would reassemble himself in Ruination.

He placed a bell on the altar and promised his followers he'd ring it when he was whole again on the other side. The crib-robber ate well and died shortly after from his poisoned flesh, but if Forster put his mangled corpse back together on the other side he was keeping quiet about it. Forster was never seen again and the bell remained silent.

There was a murmur of disquiet amongst his followers however. They believed that he had in fact succeeded and found the song of Àeon, the secret to life outside of time, but was jealously guarding it. What Galen found most shocking was that a good number of his disgruntled believers wanted to repeat the experiment and go there themselves, ready to drink the poison and have their body chopped into dog meat for a crib-robber. Ruination did just that, it ruined things, chiefly men's sanity.

"Forster had a few loose marbles to start with," he smiled without humour. The story still gave him a chill.

"He began with the best intentions and a strong will and mind."

"Don't we all Elios." His head flopped back against the wall with a long sigh. "Don't we all."

CHAPTER THREE

Fairies of the Cold Coast

'You ask what is the greatest spell, the one that could transform our world?
The greatest spell is the simplest and yet the hardest: the act of forgiveness,
and there is no one harder to forgive than one's self.'
'Higher Forms of Magic - a witch's meditations on daily life'
Author unknown

We're told by those who can't prove it that only humans possess a soul. Long ago however it was held that all things had a soul, from pebbles to snowflakes, feathers to leaves, and at the end of its life each soul was escorted to Evermore by a patron fairy. Thus there were fairies for animals, stones, berries, moonlight, fog, hail, bird-song, and everything in creation.

Despite magic's slow demise, it's said that the strongest witches can still see these souls and the fairies that protect them, which is not the gift it might sound because by and large fairies are not a pretty sight, and the fairies of the Cold Coast are very wild indeed. While April might herald spring elsewhere, here on the Cold Coast far beyond Britain's realm it was still a month haunted by winter.

Neet crawled over the ice along with other frost-fairies. It had been washed up on the black sands like scattered jigsaw pieces and now he and his fellows clambered over it using their hooked limbs like crampons, or flitting about on their stunted wings. A weak sun floated above, more like the memory of the sun than the real thing. "Poor harvests, always poor harvests," Neet complained.

As each crystal melted the frost-fairies collected their souls, and once laden with them they would journey to Evermore and release them so that the ice could live again as raindrops. Each soul paid a goodwill tithe for the fairy's service and it was this spiritual food they thrived on. Long ago there were more souls than they could manage and harvests were good, but that was before the Cold Coast had been damned and now fairies fought over lean pickings.

"Miserable ice," he muttered as he worked. He often wondered why he couldn't have been a sunflower-fairy and live somewhere hot. "Always cold and hard."

Each species of fairy looked different to the next. Neet was no bigger than a wren and his grey flesh was pulled tight over his stick-thin bones. His limbs ended not in hands and feet, but in a single sharp hook, while his bulbous head dwarfed his spindly body and blades of bone swept back from his brow like a jagged crown. Shrewd little eyes, framed by sharp forward pointing ears, sat above a tiny snub nose while below that lurked a mouth packed with sharp teeth. Few people would describe a frost-fairy as pretty.

His acute senses alerted him to something and he stopped and peered along the beach. His eyesight lagged behind his incredible nose but he detected the body of a woman lying on the sand. Her hair was braided into a ragged plait, skewered with sodden feathers and she might have been young or old; he couldn't see her face. A trail of belongings snaked out behind her. He saw a satchel, a white staff, a soggy cloak and a pointed hat. Her right arm was thrust out and in it she clutched a stick.

"Shipwreck," he concluded, and quickly dismissed her as just another bag of gristle dumped by the tide. Starving he might be, but in lieu of soul-tithes, fairies ate only living flesh and then only the unfortunates who accidentally slept in their territories. A lost sheep had entered such a fairy-ring two winters ago and that had been the last mortal food he had eaten. *Gulls never go hungry,* he thought sourly. Maybe he'd be a gull in the next life if he couldn't be a sunflower-fairy. "Drowned sailor, not so tasty but better than empty belly," he sighed.

His work was ice not corpses, and he was ready to turn away when he saw her move. Her hand, the one clutching the stick, twitched. It was difficult to say from this distance but he would swear the stick was a wand, although it looked a strange wand, it was black and almost as long as her arm. "A drowned broom-rider?" he chirped in his scratchy little voice.

He stared intently and caught a glimpse of the stick's magical signature, like iron-filings around a magnet, but it was the scent that sealed it, the unmistakable scent of copper and roses the hallmark of magic. It was a wand and wands were only carried by witches. *Or by people foolish enough to steal from them. And maybe the broom-rider isn't gull meat just yet?* he wondered. *No broom-riders on the Cold Coast for many long years.* As he pondered this a cunning idea began to grow in his mind like an icicle.

He cocked his head and blinked his pin-prick eyes then checked his companions, who were busy snapping at one another. One of them named Tet scuttled close by and without thinking he lunged at him with his fearsome teeth. "Mine!" he snapped. "Neet's! Neet's!" He defended his paltry harvest by shrieking his name.

"Tet!" the interloper retorted, swiped with his lethal hooks and rattled his wings menacingly.

It was an age-old display Neet had seen many times. He hurled himself at the intruder, aiming for his scrawny throat. Tet twisted away in a flash but his upper arm ended up between Neet's jaws. He screamed and scrabbled, raking at him and leaving puncture wounds in his scalp before struggling free. Neet let go and spat a mouthful of blood after him, and Tet scurried away to lick his wounds, abandoning his harvest of just one soul, which was quickly snatched away by one of the others. Neet felt a pang of shame but it quickly vanished. Instincts demanded survival. It was all he'd known since the Cold Coast had been blighted and if he'd ever been more than just a beast it was forgotten.

He quit harvesting and sprang into the air, landing on another raft of ice from where he studied the strange woman. Sure enough there weren't any bone-fairies around the corpse. If the witch was dead they would be undoing the body and breaking it down. "Even half drowned witches know magic," he plotted. "Enough to put Valgard's monsters back where they came from?" No, that was naïve he thought. No witch would willingly fight the monsters that ruled this land. He thought back to the time when the last witches had been driven away, and the monsters they kept in check so long were left to wreak havoc. The local farmers had no idea of the harm they were doing when they forced them out.

"Endless poor harvests, endless growling bellies. Valgard's bastards," he muttered, and then cast fearful eyes sky-wards hoping Valgard hadn't heard him. As he watched, the witch began to move and already he had plans for her . . . whether she liked it or not.

She felt something coarse prickle her cheek and realised she was lying on a beach and when she blinked, her eyes felt gritty and the daylight made them throb. She never imagined death would be like this and she was dead, of that much she was certain. She had watched her own death approach with each passing heartbeat, woven by a spider within an hourglass until she had no heartbeats left. She saw her life-thread cut with her very own eyes, so she must be dead. What other explanation could there be?

Dead she might be, but fool she wasn't. The dead weren't supposed to think or feel and so she tried to ignore the world around her and just carry on being deceased, but it teased her with sensations; the gritty sand, the tang of salt-air and the soft breeze. *Has there been a mistake?* she wondered without looking up.

Perhaps the gods hadn't troubled to notice her small death and so instead of being a real corpse she was left stranded halfway as a thinking, feeling corpse. She felt guilty, believing any moment she might be caught and punished for not being properly dead, so she lay still and she tried to forget the cry of seabirds, and the touch of her sodden clothes and just get on with being dead.

No matter how she tried though, she couldn't resist the call of the living world. She rolled her eyes upwards and the blurry view hinted at a horizon of grassy dunes with snowy mountains beyond and behind her she could hear the heartbeat of the tide and a gull's lulling song.

Dead people shouldn't feel these things, she thought, and began to suspect something horrible: that she wasn't really dead.

After a while she lifted her head and swallowed and it felt like a stone rolling down her throat. The first thing she saw clearly were her own hands, but they looked unfamiliar. Her skin was flawless but the flesh on these hands was sickly pale, which made the numerous cuts and scratches look even more vivid. In her right hand she gripped a wand almost as long as a sword and as black as the surrounding sand, but she couldn't remember how it came to be there. Why would she need a wand? Only witches carried wands. Just who was she? As she lay there, vague memories began to circle like wolves and something told her these memories had sharp teeth and that she deserved to be bitten.

Valonia. The name fluttered through her mind and was gone. *Am I Valonia?* she wondered.

Just as she registered this one of those circling memories rushed forwards and took a bite. *You're dishonouring your coven. Just look at yourself, sprawled in the dirt like a beggar thrown out of a tavern! Get up before anyone sees you, you're supposed to be a witch of high-rank!*

"A witch of high rank?" she mumbled.

You used to be until you sold your sister and brother witches, and even your gods to the enemies of magic.

As if that was the signal they'd been waiting for they charged. Painful memories burst from dark corners eager to exercise their jaws. She saw Kittiwake-coven and her rival Kolfinnia. The gifted girl called Rowan. The deities Hethra and Halla and how she betrayed them in a disastrous attempt to serve them. Her faithful attendant Farona, who went into the earth to save Hethra and Halla from the Illuminata. A warrior witch named Clovis, and a tower of rock concealing the great spider known as the Timekeeper. Then lastly, her own reckless bargain with him, exchanging her own life-thread for Kolfinnia's so that her rival might live.

You betrayed them to their deaths!

"No," she pleaded, "leave me be, I'm dead!"

You'll never finish paying.

"I paid with my life!" she cried to the empty shore, "isn't that enough?"

No, the voice chuckled, *you'll carry it through every life you'll ever have, right until the end of time itself.*

"It's not fair!" She waved the wand as if trying to swat the memories away, but one after another they tore at her. Her failings and treachery were revealed to her all over again and right then, Sunday Evelyn Flowers, a witch of high rank and solstice queen of the Regal-Fox coven, wished with all her heart that she really *was* dead.

Doulton watched with distaste as Galen demolished his meal. From the look of it he was making up for years of poor living and it wasn't just his table manners he found revolting. Amongst the cod heads, pigeon pie and damson pudding, was a boiled hare and Galen attacked it with relish. The hare was an animal associated with witches and never served at Goldhawk, but of course that's why he ordered it. Its milky eyes regarded Doulton accusingly as Galen hacked at it with his cutlery. He knew from his studies that witches eschewed meat and Lyle was right in that respect; Galen wasn't a witch or a knight, but something in between.

Doulton had taken an instant dislike to him. He arrived late, wearing a scruffy black suit and a long black army officer's coat stripped of its finery, and its only adornment now was a neat bullet hole just above the heart. He wore a straggly neck tie that looked like a withered spider, and in another breach of etiquette his battered bowler hat sat on the table. He carried a stout black stick that looked like a ruffian's attempt at a gentleman's cane, and he was moody and mumbled most of the time, which Doulton believed was deliberate. *He's taunting us because he knows how badly we need him,* he thought, and as if he'd heard him Galen looked up and smiled.

"Lord Thorpe is most grateful you came Galen." Lyle made it sound as though there had been a choice in the matter.

"Aye, I'll bet. Rest assured I can deliver what you gentlemen seek."

Lyle beamed as if this solved everything.

They were sitting at the long table under the watchful eye of the Krast arms on the wall.

"You've read the battle report?" Doulton asked.

"Aye," he coughed and wiped his fingers on a napkin.

"And?"

"And what?"

"Your verdict on our current problem." He was growing impatient.

Galen leaned forwards. "The same force that brought you down will rebuild you," he tapped a finger to his nose.

"Witches?" Lyle's look of disgust was almost comical.

Galen shook his head. "Knights and witches have their own rules." He reverentially patted the black leather satchel around his shoulders.

"This is the Book-of-Nine, the workings of Ruination, and your solution lies within: because it has no rules."

Doulton eyed the battered satchel. "Teachings banned by the Illuminata and shunned by witches, it seems you stand on neither side."

"That's as maybe, but help, either shunned or forbidden is your only choice. So do you want my assistance or not?" He put aside his fork. "And before you answer, think on this; your promise of a pardon's all well and good, but I've lived long without it. I can pack up and be away, there'll be no bad feelings, but I'll leave it to you to tell Lord Thorpe why I've taken my leave."

Doulton didn't want to think about what Thorpe would do to them if they failed to keep this character happy.

"Your task is simple," Lyle ignored his blackmail, and gestured to his satchel. "Use that to create a device that'll stop the European bloods."

He sat back in the chair, looking smug. "I never thought I'd see the day when the great Knighthood would stoop to cult worship."

Lyle cleared his throat. "I would say that sometimes we must make deals with the devil, but that would be a touch too close to the truth."

Galen smirked. "So you agree that by engaging my knowledge you've thrown the rule book away?" He sounded like a barrister cornering a witness.

Doulton looked at the sinister satchel. *Just what forces are we playing with here?* he thought uneasily.

"By the power invested in me by Lord Thorpe, I accept," Lyle declared.

"A wise move," Galen complimented.

"But is it safe to tamper with these forces?" Doulton shuffled in his seat. "Safe?"

"We require an effective response to the European challenge, with no lasting consequences," Lyle elaborated.

"Other than your continued domination of the globe?" Galen toyed with the bullet hole in his coat.

"Well, of course," Doulton smiled. "But can you commune with these intelligences and control them? This talk of 'no-rules' is unnerving."

"Ruination is a misunderstood realm full of wounded and impossible souls, but in some ways they're identical to man. They'll help us if we can offer something in return." He rubbed his fingers, as if counting money. "We give, we get back."

"And what would such beings want?" Doulton was fascinated despite himself. "Surely not money?"

"Ha!" he barked in amusement. "Yer a sauce Mr Doulton, that's for sure. No, they want what all living things want: to survive."

"How do you mean?"

"Most Ruinous creatures are too primitive, too abstract to negotiate with, but there's a small number of stronger and quicker ones, and I'm confident they might."

"You spoke of survival," Doulton offered.

"Beasts of Ruin don't belong on Earth, and if trapped here they soon die, like fish out of water. Although there are some exceptions."

"And what makes them so different?" Lyle struggled to control his frustration. He had believed Galen would just wave a wand and fix their problem.

He took up his fork again and chewed thoughtfully. "They're changing. Growing more intelligence."

Doulton didn't like that at all. "You mean to imply they're evolving?"

Galen raised his eyebrows. "Well done, that's exactly what's happening."

"Are we about to be overrun?" Lyle sounded offended.

"No, these evolved strains are very rare, but they're intelligent enough to know that once marooned here they can't return to Ruin, and so they seek safe places to hide."

"And they'll help us?" Lyle hounded.

"They're intelligent enough to know that they need a safe haven. In theory, if we can offer them one, they might help us in return."

"In theory?" he said sharply.

"Theory is all I have for now," he smiled ruefully, "I haven't found one of these 'evolved' Ruinous creatures yet. Nobody has."

Lyle's mouth dropped open. "The solstice is just over two months away!"

Galen just smiled. "You're at liberty to seek another solution."

"That won't be necessary," he huffed, and pushed his glasses back into position, "but I trust you have everything you need and can begin right away."

"Almost," he coughed, then sipped some water. "I understand there are prisoners, witches taken last year."

"And what of them?" Doulton asked warily.

"I want them." He pushed the half eaten meal away.

Doulton saw the hare's head rock lazily as though urging him to refuse. "For what purpose?"

"They're to be saved for my experiments."

"Why?"

"I might need them, that's all."

Doulton had no liking for witches, but he wasn't happy about handing them over to this man. He was about to say as much when Lyle overruled him.

"Consider it done. Just make haste that's all."

"What!" Doulton exclaimed.

"The decision's made," Lyle said firmly. "They're hostiles, not even prisoners of war."

"So we use them as some kind of sacrifice to cement an alliance with Ruination? Gallows and firing-squads are all well and good, but this is indecent!"

"Don't be so melodramatic!" he sneered. "Nobody's talking of sacrifice, you speak as if *we're* the bloody witches."

"I see you two gentlemen have much to be discussing," Galen smirked, and stood and planted his bowler on his head. "I'll be away. No rest for the wicked."

Doulton glowered at him. "And where do you intend to start? Remember, you're to notify us of your whereabouts at all times."

He leaned on his cane, looking like a con-man. "Don't go fretting, I'll be out looking for this solution you need so much."

"But where?" He rose from his chair and planted his hands on the table.

Galen regarded him coolly, and twisted his mouth as he tongued a scrap of meat from between his teeth. "To a place where the ground's soaked in blood and fear Mr Doulton, that's where you'll find your salvation." He plucked the scrap from between his lips and flicked it away into the fire, then he nodded to Lyle, turned and left.

Sunday lay curled on the sand and hid behind her hands and cried hot, miserable tears for a long time. At last, when the grief abated she could hear something other than her own pathetic sobs, something more than equal to her torments. It resonated through the sand and flowed into her weary heart like rains on parched earth. It was a distant heartbeat, or rather a *pair* of hearts beating in unison. "The twins?" she whispered. Hethra and Halla, the great serpent-twins of oak and holly were safe and that could only mean Kolfinnia had prevailed. She just hoped that Kolfinnia and little Rowan had survived and her sacrifice hadn't been futile. "The twins are safe," she smiled weakly. Tension drained away, but her relief was tainted by the fact that she had been the one who put them in mortal danger to begin with.

She struggled up onto all fours and immediately felt nauseous, as well as undignified. The old Sunday would have been dismayed, but this was quite a different witch to the one who had dazzled with her beauty and high-handed manner. The way she felt now she'd be lucky to earn a glance from the passing gulls. "Like a dung-pushing gardener girl," she laughed faintly, remembering a certain young woman she had once been very cruel to.

When the dizziness passed she clambered into a kneeling position. The wind tugged at the feathers in her hair and her face was streaked with war paint. When last she dressed, she dressed for battle, not expecting to survive. Still gripping the mysterious wand, she pushed her tangled hair from her eyes and surveyed the place where fate's river had delivered her. The first thing she saw was a piece of home. Her white lightning-staff gleamed against the sand like an exclamation mark. "Strike!" In her self-pity she'd forgotten her thunder-sprite. She reached out, but her fingers stopped inches from it. "Don't be gone, not after all this, don't you leave me as well Strike," she prayed.

Thunder-sprites were born when lightning stuck a tree. Magical law decreed that the sprite was always male and for generations witches had paired up with sprites, cutting a staff from the ravaged tree that the sprite could live within and empower with flight. When a witch died the bond was broken and the thunder-sprite returned to his home in the storm clouds above.

She'd died, but *not* died, so was her staff now lifeless? The answer was just inches away. At the thought of losing him she remembered how she'd been curt or impatient with him, yet he had remained loyal throughout and now fresh tears stung her eyes. "Don't be gone!" She clutched at the staff, raking furrows in the sand. "Strike?" She gave it a firm shake. "Strike!"

"Miss Flowers?" His voice was barely a breeze in her mind.

Relief deflated her and she held the staff like a child with a cherished toy. He should be gone she knew, the laws of contract between witches and sprites were immutable. Something huge and powerful was at work and even if that power was her champion, its greatness scared her.

"Where are we miss?" He sounded exhausted, but the word 'we' was wonderful.

"We've been washed ashore. I've no idea where, but it's not Britain and not anywhere warm either." She glanced up at the grey sky then along the ice-strewn shore. "There's ice all along the coast and the sand's black as night." Far inland she saw a towering cloud that could have been ash or smoke. This was a very strange place she thought. She looked around nervously, convinced something was taking an interest in her conversation, and wished Strike would appear.

"I saw the battle unfold from up high," he said dreamily.

"The battle?" She suddenly forgot the cold and her wet clothes. "You saw what happened?"

"I don't know how long I drifted." He seemed oblivious to her questions. *"I was becoming cloud and hail again, being one with the thunder-heights, when I felt,"* he groped for words, *"the world turn backwards."*

She chewed her lip as she considered this. "He changed his mind; the great Timekeeper, who else could have done such a thing?"

"Miss Flowers, why did you want us undone and separate?"

She flinched at the sadness in his voice and now she was relieved that he remained hidden. "I didn't want us undone, but understand I had to make things right, or at least try."

"I watched you die in the Timekeeper's cavern, I watched you die and I felt more alone than I knew was possible." He sounded more confused than accusing.

Without knowing why she glanced sideways. A stranded piece of ice drew her attention, and she felt a shiver. "What happened Strike?"

She spoke quietly, wary of watching eyes, imagined or otherwise. "What happened after the Timekeeper broke my thread?"

He heard an unfamiliar note of humility in her voice. *"You fell miss,"* he said simply. *"When your thread broke I rushed upwards and I saw you fall into that river that ran through the cave and it carried you off into the darkness."*

"The river of fate," she said solemnly.

"Then we were separated and I couldn't sense your heart in the world any longer and I knew you were dead."

"And then?"

"I saw the battle as I ascended alongside other sprites cut from their witches." He meant witches who had died and unlike her hadn't been granted a second chance. She cringed with dishonour. It seemed that even dying wasn't enough to pay her debt. *"The battle was awful miss,"* he continued.

"Later please," she stopped him, knowing she must hear it eventually and hoping for the courage to do so. "After the battle, what do you remember?"

"I drifted with other sprites and rode thunder-heads. I began to unravel and dissolve and then . . . then the world felt re-made, and I began to fall faster and faster until I found myself back by your side," he finished humbly, as though there were no other place for him.

"And I'm glad," she said and then did something he'd never known in the ten years they'd been a pair. She kissed the staff and it was meant for him.

Neet watched all of this with great interest. Once or twice she looked in his direction but didn't see him. In fact he had shadowed her all afternoon and seen something miraculous in her soul-sign.

Every human soul took the form of a tree floating above the head like a crown. On rare occasions the tree was uniform, but most carried branches bearing differing leaves and fruit. Although Neet didn't fully understand the symbolism he grasped that a tree in blossom showed a soul at peace, a bare tree indicated a soul who was mean or cruel and a twisted tree bore witness to a soul who was cunning. Sometimes there was no tree at all, just a dormant seed. Neet had seen many human souls down the centuries but nothing like hers.

The tree above her head was not unusual, some branches were verdant, some bore fruit or blossoms while others were naked. It was the trunk that took his breath away. It had been cut clean through the middle separating the roots from the crown, it could mean only one thing – she had travelled to the place of death and returned. Somehow she had defied the first command of the universe and now as he stared at her strange soul, he felt both awed and fearful of her.

Now she was gathering berries, but she stopped, looked in his direction and frowned. For a moment he daren't move, convinced she sensed him. Eventually she shivered and looked elsewhere. "Knows when eyes are watching," he chirped approvingly. He was still fascinated by her soul, it was against all natural laws, like a sun that radiated dark light. The longer he thought about it the more convinced he was that she could defeat the monsters that haunted this coast. "This broom-rider might free us. Good harvests for all, no more rat or half-drowned sailor to chew on, soul-food fit for fairies." He looked to the leaden sky and thought what he dare not say, *She'll fight your children Valgard. Fight them and kill them.*

The waves rumbled like thunder and Neet imagined he heard a rumble of disapproval from the vindictive god who blighted this coast, and he cowered.

Not so very far away, one of Valgard's 'children' slid open an eye. His sleep had been disturbed. Even though he was entombed beneath a glacier his ears caught the tail end of the echo. It had sounded like Valgard himself, the war god he served unquestioningly. He listened to the choir of running water and the ragged breathing of his two companions in the dark, but the echo was gone. He yawned and a thick purple tongue rolled from his cavernous mouth along with a foetid vapour.

He sank back into his stupor and stretched, disturbing a carpet of bones and rusted armour. The armour had once belonged to Norse kings and warriors. He had no need of armour however, for there wasn't a weapon in the world that could harm him. He slept and dreamed of battle but as always there was a stranger in his dream, a ghostly and elusive memory. It danced between the bloody spear-tips and hid behind the battered shield wall from where it whispered to him, but the message was lost in the storm of steel and screams and even his sharp ears couldn't catch it. The dream was always the same, and in it he almost remembered that he had once been a man.

Chapter Four

An assassin in the weave

'Without flaws, creation remains perfect but dead.'
Witch saying

Later that afternoon, Lyle met with Thorpe to discuss his meeting with Galen. It would have been easier for him to simply attend, but Thorpe appeared reluctant to have direct contact with the former exile. Being a man of the Illuminata's banking elite, Thorpe had no chambers at Goldhawk. His domain was the Bank of England, and so Lyle's office was the venue for their informal chat. "Have you had much to do with him sir, Galen I mean?" Lyle was curious as to how he knew of the cultist.

Thorpe ignored the question. "Is he the man for the job?" He took a cigar from the box on Lyle's desk and lit it.

"As a fellow I found him boorish and insolent, and his table etiquette is no better than that of an ape."

Thorpe smiled and waved his match out before throwing it into the hearth where a fire crackled. He took a considered draw from the cigar before answering. "Just the sort of man we need."

"He strikes me as a bit of a pirate sir," Lyle said unhappily.

"Even better!"

"He says he'll be about London tonight looking for a place where he can make some sort of unearthly contact with these forces he claims to command."

"Oh, did he indicate where?"

"Just said something about 'blood and fear'."

"Plenty of that in London." Thorpe sucked on the cigar and the tip glowed blood red. "I'll have a couple of my men keep a close eye on him."

"You think he's working for the French or Germans?"

"His loyalty is to himself." Thorpe studied his cigar for a moment. "I don't approve, but I can live with that. No, what I'm afraid of is our special fellow winding up in the docks with a blade in his back. French spies put paid to Kent's assault, they could do the same to our man."

"I suppose so sir." He shifted in his chair and the leather groaned; it sounded melancholy.

"You don't sound happy Virgil?" Thorpe peered at him through a haze of smoke. "Don't like breaking the rules eh?"

"The Knighthood has never entered into a pact like this before, I'm wary that's all. Doulton on the other hand is plain frightened." He removed his glasses and polished them briskly. He never passed up the chance to diminish Doulton.

"Don't tell me you're afraid of imps and hobgoblins?" he taunted.

Lyle replaced his glasses and looked serious. "The forces commanded by witches are based on science and can be rationalised, but this is different. Galen's proposing we go a step further. 'Uncharted waters' he called it."

"At my insistence," Thorpe reminded him.

"The principle's sound sir!" he backtracked. "It's just that Galen strikes me as a bit of sham."

"There's nothing to fear Lyle, and do you know why?" His moustache bristled as his mouth twisted in amusement.

Lyle shook his head.

He clenched the cigar between his teeth and went over to the fire, pulled his overcoat from the stand by the door and retrieved a paper package. It looked quite heavy and when he threw it towards Lyle it landed on his desk with a hefty thud. "Something I borrowed from the bank. Open it."

He pulled the packaging apart and inside was paper, but not just any paper, these were banknotes. He thumbed the rare notes in amazement, noting their high value and authenticity. Each note was marked as worth ten-thousand pounds.

"You hold the best part of one million pounds in your hands!" he boasted. Lyle made a small choking sound. Thorpe grinned and let him relish the sensation, then reached over and snatched the packet out of his lap. "Watch." He held it up for a second, then tossed it into the fire. It landed with a whooshing sound and a shower of embers.

Lyle sat in bewilderment as the first notes began to curl and blacken. It would take some time for the entire package to be destroyed. One million pounds gone up in smoke. Goldhawk must have the most expensive chimney soot in the world, he thought.

Thorpe watched him carefully then threw his half-smoked cigar into the flames as well. "I'm not afraid of witches or sham cultists like Galen. Oh, I concede they may be able to conjure a few impressive tricks, but that," he pointed to the money burning in the grate, "that is real power. Those pieces of paper can start wars of bring down empires. Now you tell me, which is more terrifying: goblins and trickery, or the power of paper?" He slipped his coat on, amused by Lyle's stunned expression.

He cleared his throat nervously, still looking towards the grate. "Will that not be difficult to replace sir?"

"Just pieces of paper," he smiled then slipped out of the door leaving Lyle's office to be warmed by the price of a nation.

The afternoon hours passed in the same way the creamy foam vanished into the sand after each wave. Sunday explored a little, and thought the coast was bestowed with the same kind of beauty as a spider's web: magnificent but dangerous. Rugged cliffs ran northwards and a few gulls glided around their battlements, but she was glad of their company because their heartbeats filled the loneliness a bit. Inland, she saw a column of dark cloud reach for the sky. It hardly moved and finally it dawned on her that it wasn't cloud, but ash and smoke. It was either a volcano or a very big fire.

"What kind of land has ice *and* fire at the same time?" she pondered, looking from the cloud to the icy shore. "And is this winter or summer?" It was gloomier than midwinter in Britain. *Couldn't I have started anew in Athens or Paris?* The thought tempted a smile.

She wanted to discuss these things with Strike, but he was sleeping. She still wasn't sure how long they had been separated ('dead' was such an impolite word) but something told her that it wasn't long, although it might have been decades and the Timekeeper's act of kindness had left her stranded in an age yet to come. She also learned something odd about herself. She used to be right handed, now she was left handed. It seemed that crossing from life to death and back again had subtly changed her, and she worried what other small changes she might discover.

"Do I even still look the same?" She pressed a finger to her nose and mouth, convinced for a moment that she had a new face and found herself scared senseless by the idea. Her head was battered by such thoughts, and so when a more mundane thought popped up it was like a breath of fresh-air. *God-oak, I'm so hungry*, she thought and her stomach growled approvingly.

"At last you're listening to me!" it seemed to say. *"You're not amongst the dead and it's time to start living again, and living folks need to eat."*

She looked around the shore knowing there would be edible creatures, but like all witches she found the idea of eating flesh contrary to true witchcraft and so followed the Pythagorean Principle. Coven-gardeners encouraged plants to bear fruits right through the winter, it was known as 'calling' and she could manage that providing she could find fruiting plants to start with. But right now she longed for a fresh loaf hot from the oven and such thoughts set her stomach growling like a dog. "I hear you," she said impatiently, and headed into the dunes carrying her scant belongings and the strange wand, not really knowing what she had in mind but glad to be on the move.

By dusk she had a small fire crackling and she sat in the dunes eating roasted seaweed and fungi. The meal was dour, and though at one time she'd have wrinkled her pretty nose at such fare, right now at least it filled her stomach. Tomorrow she could make a better effort of collecting food she told herself. Throughout her meal she pondered the Timekeeper.

"What made you change your mind?" She stared into the fire, listening to the wind. "Did you send me here or was it chance?" She suspected the great spider didn't deal in chance and after seeing him work she had the horrible feeling that no such thing even existed. The wind didn't see fit to comment either way and she sighed and nibbled a few crow-berries. "I hope Kolfinnia escaped," she murmured and suddenly had a vision of fires, krakens, and witches hurtling into battle. "I'm glad they won," she added fiercely as she recalled Hethra and Halla's soft but definite heartbeats.

Burning wood popped in the fire and embers sailed upwards. The glowing specks drifted up to be doused by the night. She followed their trails and saw clearly the constellation of Arinidia the spider. It all seemed so contrived that it made her dizzy. "Spiders in the sky and under the earth," she whispered. Arinidia twinkled back but remained silent. "You changed your mind. Untold lives are yours to weave and you've never changed your mind before. Why now?" Arinidia dimmed for a second as if admitting something. "Did meeting Kolfinnia and I change you in some way?" The fire crackled loudly again, perhaps in answer, or perhaps it was just chance and nothing more.

"Perhaps so?" The Timekeeper murmured to himself. The great spider sat within his towering sand timer. Although far away, he held Sunday's thread and read her every thought. "Yes, perhaps that is just what happened." He looked around his empty cavern and remembered when two witches came here and brought something new to his world.

His cavern was dark and empty. It had been that way since creation was spewed from the star-dragon's belly and he saw no reason to believe it would be any different when the star-dragon devoured creation again, but until Sunday had come he didn't know that empty could also mean lonely, and black could also mean lost.

He wove the thread of every living creature, but had never encountered any of them until Sunday and Kolfinnia ventured to his cave, and he saw for the first time that although their lives were as short as a raindrop that falls to earth, within it they experienced a richness unknown to him. He also saw that with the cutting of each thread came great fear.

There was fear on Sunday's face when she stood before him ready to die so another could live, and he began to wonder at the 'why' of it all. Why did the Patternmaker order him to weave terrible events, why did he favour a tapestry woven in blood and misery?

From then on when he ended a life he wondered if each thread deserved to be cut, and what of those rotten threads that persisted nonetheless? He did something then that he had never done before and would never repeat. He disobeyed fate and he did it for himself as well as her, the brave but flawed witch who came looking for redemption. He took her severed thread and joined it anew so that this little raindrop might enjoy the fall to earth a while longer and for a while he wouldn't feel so alone in the darkness under the earth.

But disobedience brought retribution. He felt galaxies lurch under the Patternmaker's wrath and braced himself against the inevitable punishment and asked himself over and over: *Will I obey this time and let her fall, or will I make a stand?*

It was a question he still didn't have an answer for.

By nightfall her clothes were dry. She wore all she had because the night was cold, and she retrieved her silver fox pendant from her pack, a reminder of her coven. She loosened her hair, removed the feathers, said honorary spells for Hethra and Halla and now she sat by the fire idly running fingers along her lightning-staff, toying with each knot and wondering how to awaken Strike. Normally she would command him but *that* Sunday betrayed the twins and she couldn't bear to think that person still lurked inside her. If she could only be *that* Sunday and no other then she might as well curl up and give in right now. She coughed nervously. "Erm, Strike are you sleeping?" She stole a glance around the darkening shore. The sinister feeling of being watched had dogged her all afternoon. "Strike, if you can, I wish to know about the battle at Kittiwake, what did you see?" When he still didn't stir she called him by his formal name, "Lightning-Strikes-Lonesome-Ash, will you speak with me please?"

The staff trembled softly. *"Miss Flowers?"*

"Strike," she sighed, "I'm sorry to wake you but I have to know something . . ." She didn't have the fortitude to listen before, and she wasn't sure she had it now but the uncertainty was unbearable.

To her relief he materialised, but with some effort, emerging from the staff rather than leaping from it. Like all sprites he was raven-sized and covered in blue feathers. His body was more ape than bird, although his face was hawk-like, and a pair of broad wings fanned from his back.

He stretched and clambered down next to her. He had been her companion since she was ten years-old, yet she had never really noticed the fetching way his long ears swept back or the noble set of his hooked beak. His azure feathers were like scales and to her shame she only noticed now that one on his right shoulder was green not blue, like a birthmark. *How could I never have seen that?* she thought sadly.

Even though he sat hunched and tired, just looking at him reminded her of the thrill of flying. He had carried her into battle and out the other side, and she owed him so much but had given him so little.

She felt strangely shy, as though he was her mentor, and she was trying to frame her words when he spoke first. "They lived Miss Flowers, if that's what you're wondering." He just stared into the flames.

"Kolfinnia and Rowan? You're certain?"

"Yes, Kolfinnia was shot, and dying."

"That's when I left them and went to the Timekeeper," she said quietly, remembering that awful day.

"But she lived miss, Kolfinnia lived thanks to you and that meant Rowan had cause to go on living too."

She felt a satisfied glow. "And where are they now?"

"I can only tell you what I saw miss, where they are now is beyond me, but all the witches left the field of war before they came."

"The knights."

"No, the others."

She frowned. "Who else could have been there?"

"There was another army that day neither witch nor knight." He stopped, reluctant to go on.

"Strike, I have to know."

He sighed. "Janus opened a passage to Evermore for everyone to escape along, but just after, when the knights finally surrounded the stones, *they* came in answer to the twin's terror."

The 'twin's terror' had been Sunday's doing and she knew what was to follow could be laid squarely at her door. "Go on," she said, bracing herself.

"I saw little by then," he looked down at his clawed feet. "I was so high and everything below was tiny and meaningless, but they passed me as I rushed upwards. They carried decay with them."

Instantly she knew he meant Ruination. "An *army* of them?" In all her days she had only encountered one Ruinous creature: an emissary of the Gorgon's Veil which had taken residence inside a rotten yew. The confrontation had lasted only moments but it would stay with her always.

"Thousands descended after the witches escaped." He paused, and his next words were like the closing of a tomb. "Not a single knight left the hill."

She swallowed. "But the twins are safe now aren't they?"

"Oh they're safe." He looked concerned, imagining he had upset her. "The twins are safe Miss Sunday."

She winced. "Please, from now on just call me Sunday." She felt burdened by his servitude, recognising that she had made him that way. "I don't suppose you know where we are?" she sighed, changing the subject.

"Sorry miss." Each time he used that word it was like seeing the chains of ownership she'd forged around him.

For a while they sat in silence with the fatigue and darkness thickening around them, until finally she asked her terrible question, the one that festered in her soul like a worm. "Do you think me wicked Strike?"

There was a long pause.

"You acted with the twin's best interests at heart," he said quietly, and she smiled at his diplomacy.

"My idea of 'helping' cost many lives."

"One of which was your own miss," he reminded her. "We faltered. We paid. It's over."

"*Me*, not *we*," she corrected. "It was all my doing."

"I could have said no."

"Why didn't you?"

He hung his head, unsure what to say. He had complied through loyalty but also because he feared to disobey. If she was wicked then he was a coward. "A sprite should obey his witch," he said at last.

"Very well, it's over. And we have a new start," she added, trying to sound cheerful. She pulled her cloak away from the fire where it was drying and drew it gratefully around her shoulders. Above her, Arinidia was covered by its own cloak of clouds. "The spider sleeps," she observed, "and so should we."

She patted the staff. He hopped onto it without looking at her and melted away into the wood. She lay on a simple mattress of dune grass surrounded by a dusting of snow, curled herself around the staff, soothed by his gentle hum from within and the fire's glow, and surrendered to sleep. Within moments she was dreaming of dark rivers and weaving spiders.

Neither sleeper had noticed the mushroom-ringed hollows scattered amongst the dunes. In fact neither realised that they slept inside such a ring – a very dangerous thing to do and a witch ought to know better.

Each ring was fairy territory and fairies guarded them jealously and even fought over them, but mortals were always welcome because it was well known that anyone who slept within a fairy-ring did so at their own peril. In more civilised parts of the world, fairies let sleepers go if they could answer riddles or grant favours, but the fairies of the Cold Coast had suffered years of famine and they were *always* hungry. Riddles had as much use here as a napkin for a starving man.

Neet had stayed close the whole evening and as soon as she carelessly entered the ring he knew that trouble was brewing. "Stupid meat-bag witch!" he hissed for the hundredth time, unseen and unheard. "Cabbage-headed broom-rider with useless sprite, no good dead, only little good alive." He flitted around in agitation. Unique soul or not, he was starting to think that she wasn't going to be worth the effort of saving. Even if he pulled her from the ring before the others came to feed he reckoned she must be so witless that it might be a mercy for her to end up eaten. "Walk into open oven if told, stupid broom-rider?" He was convinced that humans loved mayhem so much that they went out of their way to create it.

He looked on helplessly, thinking against the clock. When her sleep reached a critical depth her aura would change and fairies would be drawn in their hundreds and he couldn't enter the ring and warn until then either. There weren't going to be any haggles about who owned this territory, this was going to be a free for all. He scrutinized the darkness and saw glowing souls, but so far no other fairies. "Meat, meat," he clacked his sharp teeth. He'd taken his share of flesh down the years. His impulse was to join the coming frenzy, he was hungry enough, but he had plans for this witch. He was more than a little ashamed of the savage creatures they had become and he needed her help more than a bellyful of flesh. "Awaken witch!" he urged, hovering inches away, waiting for the right moment.

She was standing in front of that enormous hourglass again, staring in terrible fascination at a silvery thread. Any moment now that thread would snap and she would die, already she felt pain burning in her chest where a healthy heart counted down its last beats. She held the black wand, and now she remembered its real name. This was Valonia's wand, the wand that had called Britain's surviving witches to Kolfinnia's new coven, the coven she betrayed. This wand was hrafn-dimmu – dark raven. *Die,* she thought, *sleep forever with the debt of shame paid.* She hoped the guilt would end when her heart stopped but an unknown voice cried out in her dream.

"Awake!" the voice commanded. "Awake now!" But she was committed to the exact opposite.

Let me sleep, sleep always, then I'll have paid in full. The pain in her chest intensified.

"Awake stupid witch! Awake or be dead!" The voice grew angry. The pain in her chest burned like a branding iron now and the shrill little voice seemed to shriek right into her ear. "Wake or be eaten, stupid pointy-hat hag!" it screamed.

She bolted from sleep. The dream vanished and her eyes flew wide, but the burning pain in her chest followed her and when she looked down she screamed.

A tiny fairy armed with snapping jaws and multiple legs had clambered through her clothes and lay against her breastbone where it was suckling blood. She screamed and snatched at it in panic, ripping it free before hurling it away and that's when she finally noticed the mushrooms hidden by the snow and realisation crashed in on her: they'd trespassed into a fairy-ring. "Fairies!" she screamed.

"Run!" someone shrieked, and she saw the owner of that shrill voice. A fairy with silvery skin and a bulbous head hovered inches from her face like an angry wasp. Behind him circled a horde about to drop like a net. "Run stupid witch!" Neet screamed.

He might have been friend or foe, there was no time to think. Instead, she swatted him aside with a satisfying smack then rolled on to her belly towards her lightning-staff and grabbed it just as hundreds of fairies descended like a plague of locusts. "Strike!" she screamed, but her cry was drowned out by buzzing wings and chattering jaws.

She felt a brief jolt from the staff as Strike awoke then she was smothered by a blanket of biting mouths. Many landed on her clothes, but her exposed skin burned instantly as tiny teeth sank in. It was like being hit by a hail of fire. "Strike!" she screamed again, almost gagging as a fairy tried to crawl into her mouth.

"Meat, meat, meat, meat!" the cry went up and thousands of sharp little mouths took up the chant. Fairies from far and wide had come for the banquet. They bit at her calves, her hands, her neck and ears or set to work gnawing at her clothes to reach the warm meat beneath. Her hair teemed with them and their delighted squeals rang in her ears and their fluttering wings purred against her face.

Her thoughts were scattered and desperate. Had she been brought back to life just to die in such a horrible fashion, was fate *really* so cruel? And wasn't there a part of her that believed she deserved no better? "NO!" She dragged herself towards the boundary only a few feet away, if only she could cross it.

Fairies jostled one another to reach the tenderest places, which slowed them long enough for an angry thunder-sprite to come to his senses, but Strike was weak. He needed her strength as well. *"Both of us!"* he screamed, loud enough to make her teeth shake.

She rolled on to her back trying to raise her staff, and in doing so exposed her belly and a frenzied shriek went up. Fairies crawled up her legs and she clamped her knees together, but the swarm was relentless. Strike shouted something, but it was garbled by her panicked mind. Fairies burrowed into her clothes, looking for sensitive places, and that awful feeling of violation gave her the outrage she needed. "GET OFF ME!" She swung her staff, pouring all of her fury into it and Strike answered.

Lightning flashed. Night instantly became day, but not the gentle light of summer. This was harsh and blinding, like bleached bone under a baking sun. There was a horrifying howl as hundreds of fairies cried out and an instant later thunder crushed every other noise in the world. The biting cloud was swept away and countless charred bodies were flung into the darkness like dead leaves. Thunder rolled out to sea, followed by ringing emptiness in her ears and a darkness only the blind knew.

She lay crumpled inside the fairy-ring, clutching her staff. Charred little bodies drifted down and littered her clothes, and blood trickled from countless small wounds, but shock kept the pain at bay for now. "Strike?" she whispered hoarsely. The only sound was her racing breath and the thunder's dying echo. "Strike?" she pleaded.

"I watched you die once, that was enough for me."

She heaved a groan of relief at the sound of his voice, but it was what he said next that made her both smile and cry.

"Sunday," he said.

The Timekeeper knew disobedience brought retribution and finally on the day Sunday Flowers was complete again it came. It was April, some six months after her life had ended. He had hidden her renewed thread a short way ahead in the future to protect her from the Patternmaker, but he'd found her. He kept one of his eight eyes on her thread like a protective father, and so when it quivered he instantly knew something was wrong. Something had woven her into sleeping in a fairy-ring. "Unwise," he muttered, "and unkind, such a grim way to die." Now his unanswered question came back to him. *Do I let her stand or fall? And is it right that the Patternmaker alone commands fate?*

They were coming to kill her, but this wasn't his doing. There was an intruder loose in his hourglass. He had to make a snap decision. She'd brought light to his dark world, and now the moment had come he found that he couldn't do it, he couldn't let her die like this. "NO!" He defied fate once more and began weaving a rescue.

He needed to find a soul to aid her and by Oak there were precious few threads where she'd ended up. The coast was barren and the best he could find was a selfish fairy with schemes and plots in mind, but he would suffice. He counter-wove against the intruder's pattern with blinding speed, sending Neet to awaken her before the swarm descended and with no time to spare he averted disaster. She awoke, fought back and survived.

The thread's distressed harmonic died away and the Timekeeper listened, but for now it was quiet again. "It seems we're not alone," he said to the darkness and scanned the forest of strands before examining Sunday's thread more closely. Sure enough there were signs of sabotage. Tiny teeth marks showed where something had almost chewed clean through it. There was an assassin inside his hourglass and he felt real anger for the first time. "Is this to be a contest between us?" he asked the universe. Silence was his only reply.

"You ask for a flood that kills tens of thousands and I give you such, can't we let this one concession stand in the name of pity?"

At the word 'pity' the forest of threads trembled as if an unseen wind had passed through them. Clearly the Patternmaker wasn't in the mood for concessions today.

"Must you send assassins to my glass to play havoc with the threads of life?" He had never spoken so boldly before and he fully expected an angry response, but none was forthcoming. "Then I await your next move my Lord." He settled down to weave the lives of many, obeying the very being who now plotted against him. He began to weave love, death, disaster, triumph and tedium for millions of souls, but he kept one eye fixed on Sunday's thread knowing she had become the gambit in a game neither of them wanted to play.

Meanwhile, in one of the glass's many dark corners, the Patternmaker's chosen assassin curled up in a nest of threads and awaited further orders and its next opportunity to strike.

CHAPTER FIVE

Market day

'How is man able to do these terrible things? I tell you: he is born broken.
It is the quest of everyone who passes through this life to repair this flaw and
become a complete and compassionate soul. There is no higher purpose.'
'Higher Forms of Magic - a witch's meditations on daily life'
Author unknown

Jonas hefted the sack over his shoulder and made ready to turn home.
It had been a poor day and he was glad to be done. He knew the ghost
stories about this coast but reasoned that fewer people meant more
birds, and not being a man who feared god or ghost he'd set out on his
stout little Icelandic pony at first light to hunt puffins. He expected cliffs
teaming with birds ready for the breeding season, but they were strangely
empty, just random individuals which made netting hard work. He
brought five sacks but was leaving with only two dozen of the colourful
little birds. He swiped his net at the grass in frustration as he walked back
through the dunes to Helti, his mare, then remembered that a broken net
wasn't the best way to end a bad day's hunting and controlled his temper.

"Helti," he called, but she didn't turn. She was still tethered to the
rickety fence of an empty farmstead, but she just stared out to sea with
her ears pricked, and suddenly he felt cautious. "Helti?" he said again, but
softly this time. As the light failed, the stories about this coast felt more
real. "Hey girl, what's taken your interest eh?" He lay the sack down and

its canvas top yawned open revealing the dead puffins, their once cheery faces now looking like funerary masks. He kept walking, but treading quietly. The horse flicked an ear in his direction but still didn't turn.

He was just a few paces away when she whinnied softly and he froze. Something down on the beach had spooked her. The setting sun had painted her fiery orange and he briefly spied the shape of something huge and black reflected in her wild stare, something on the beach just out of his view. "Easy girl, we're riding home now, soon be back." He tried to soothe himself by soothing her, with little effect on either of them.

He loosened the rope, which dropped like a dead snake, and he half expected her to bolt but she remained transfixed, as if spellbound. "What's down there?" He felt a destructive fascination, and edged closer to the crest to see for himself.

He kept low, not wanting to be seen, but through the long grass he had the tantalizing glimpse of that large dark shape reflected in Helti's eye. "Is that a boat?" he asked no one, and palmed the grass aside, and smiled a pirate's smile. There was a dead sperm whale lying deflated on the beach. It hadn't been there this morning when he arrived, if it had he would have saddled Helti with as much blubber as she could carry and left without a single puffin. *Why didn't this happen when I arrived!* he groused, already calculating how much he could slice before dark. He didn't relish the idea of roughing it in the ruined farm, but the trail back was over treacherous moors where pot-holes could snap a horse's leg like matchwood, not a place to be in the twilight with a heavy load. "Damn!" he spat and was ready to tether her when she whinnied again and this time he saw what had really scared her.

Something moved just behind the whale's flank, something as tall as its ribcage and covered with dark fur. He could see what might have been its shoulders as it lumbered back and forth. At first he thought 'bear'. He knew Iceland had no bears, but occasionally a polar bear might drift across from Greenland, but this creature was black not white. Helti stamped a hoof, making him jump. "Hush girl!" he hissed and looked back to the dead whale.

The dark shape stopped moving. He heard a series of sharp breaths and his heart froze: it was sniffing for their scent. He felt panic rise in his gut like a bad meal and reached for Helti's rope, but this time she didn't whinny, she screamed and bared her teeth. Without thinking he turned back and saw it.

The moment it appeared from behind the beached whale his brain and eyes had a major disagreement, neither crediting what the other was saying. It still looked like a bear, but what bear walked on two legs, and what bear had claws that looked like scythes? It was the rubbery strands of blubber dangling from those claws that finally set him to flight. But Helti bolted first.

"Helti!" He watched in disbelief as she galloped away through the dunes with his kit bag bouncing against her haunches, and inside was his only knife. He scrambled up and sprinted for the farmstead, hoping to find anything to use as a weapon. He was only yards from the door when a creature just like the one on the beach emerged from behind the crumbling building, but tawny, not black. Dumb with terror he continued running towards it, trying to understand what he was seeing. *There's more than one?* It was his last cohesive thought.

He watched in slow motion as its huge arm swung towards his head. His eyes rolled towards its face and he saw that he'd been right, it was a bear, but it was also a man, then its paw crashed against his head and the world span like a dervish. Jonas felt the wind whip through his thinning hair. Heaven and earth rolled violently and then there was a thud. Suddenly he was looking at the world from a crazy angle. Ten yards away he saw a headless body sway on its feet and then topple to the ground and he realised that it was *his* body he was looking at, and the monstrous creature was already stooping to devour it. *How?* he muttered, but no sound escaped his lips.

The world flickered and dimmed. He was still trying to understand what had happened when his life ended, and his severed head joined the dead puffins in his own sack, all of them gazing blankly up at the sky.

Before he left for the night, Galen sat down to make some notes. Outwardly he was just a man scribbling in an old book, but this was an auspicious hour. No initiate had ever finished the ninth chapter, and so his hand wasn't quite steady as it moved the pen across a page he had waited twenty years to begin.

April 25th 1887

He stopped and scrutinised the date for any esoteric significance, but the letters and numbers just stared back at him giving nothing away. He swallowed and then began in his most careful script.

'Tonight I shall pursue my most promising lead so far in the hunt for that rumoured 'evolved' strain of Ruinous beast, thus far dubbed 'valkyries'. I have concluded, after years of searching the most deplorable haunts of man, namely the battlefields of Europe, that there are even greater pools of horror and slaughter and it is there, not on the battlefield, that I now believe I shall enjoy my best chance of encountering and communing with these elusive beings.'

He lay his pen aside and read the passage again, wondering what additional text he might add after tonight's expedition. He pulled on his long coat, pressed the bowler on to his head and took up his cane. "It's a lovely night for a stroll. Would the good lady Elios care to step out with me?"

She trilled at his humour and together they set out for a night around London, like a distinguished couple bound for the theatre.

The men he passed in the corridors of Goldhawk Row had an air of apprehension about them, and with good reason. Their champions were dead and only clerks, devisers, and correctionals remained.

"They know their days might be ending." Elios thrived on defeat and Goldhawk was thick with it.

"Nothing lasts forever, not even this lot." He paced along making hardly a sound on the polished marble, and through the huge doors and out into the London night. The cool air carried the river's perfume, which was stale and damp, and the river itself glistened under the Albert Embankment's modern electric lighting. Galen had no liking for it. He believed it was against natural laws to light up the night, and besides it might scare away the very creatures he was looking for. He looked out across the Thames to the houses of Parliament, or more exactly to the great clock whose hands bore witness to the slow death of everything.

"I noticed you didn't tell them of Sophie," Elios enquired from inside the cane.

"No. If they think my investigations are for their benefit alone then we'll get more out of them." He began along the embankment just as Big Ben chimed ten o'clock. It was a beautiful night and he was in no hurry, his destination wouldn't be quiet until at least midnight.

"Are you glad to be home?" she asked from nowhere.

"This won't be my home until Sophie's back at my side."

"My dearest," she sympathised, *"one day you'll bring her home, I know it."*

"Only if I discover the missing laws in the Book-of-Nine." He gripped his satchel and felt the book's comforting weight inside. "Without them I'm trapped here growing old and she's trapped there ignorant of me."

The mysterious Book-of-Nine was named for its number of chapters, explaining Ruination and how to commune with its creatures. Each initiate made a copy of the book by hand, but in all copies the ninth chapter was always blank. It was the hope of every initiate to discover the reputed missing laws and record them in that empty chapter, but so far nobody in the cult's twelve-hundred year history had come close. The missing chapter was saved for the final revelation: how to cross at will between Earth and Ruin, and negate Àeon's song, the emanation of time: The key to life without death.

"I envy you, you've walked there, in the meadows of Ruin." He thought of the blank pages. If Elios had been full-blooded Ruin instead of only part Ruin she might have been able to help him fill them.

"Part of me, only part of me," she insisted and as always he couldn't tell if she was relieved or regretful. Elios was a complex and unique creature, half Ruinous and half something else. *"If you find what you're looking for will you abandon them, or will you stay and finish what they've asked of you?"*

"Abandon? Do you believe I owe them a favour or two?" he admonished gently.

"Of course not, they treated you so unfairly, as did your former master. But will you leave without a word when you have what you want?"

He considered. "That will be for my master to decide."

"When will he come do you think?"

"When he's good and ready," he scowled. He was anxious about seeing him again after so long.

"And in the meantime?"

"In the meantime I'll play along until I find what I want. After that, every witch in Britain can dance naked through Goldhawk and rut on the Knight Superior's bed for all I care."

He'd nurtured his bitterness for two decades. When the order had come to disband the Book-of-Nine, there were just seven initiates. He had no idea what had become of the others, maybe the Illuminata had killed them, but he escaped to continue the cult's aims, and it was one obscure account that drove him on. A former initiate long dead, named Harrow Caul, claimed to have seen one of these 'evolved' creatures and even started the ninth chapter. The sighting dated to over seventy years ago, on the battlefield of Waterloo where almost fifty-thousand men lost their lives. Caul had scouted the battlefield in the aftermath looking for traces of Ruination. And he saw one. He found it by accident, lurking in a crater lined with corpses. According to Caul it had looked grotesque, but clearly female, and it hovered over the dead in fascination, drawn to the horror. For this reason he dubbed the creature a valkyrie, but when he called out to it, it had fled.

Galen knew that terrible places were like lamps to moths for Ruinous creatures and Europe steadily collected more and more of them. Death on a huge scale was rare in nature, but cannons and rifles had been steadily changing that. Now there were numerous places where death overflowed on an unnatural scale, making the creatures drawn to them stronger and more intelligent, forcing Ruin to evolve. If the Illuminata disliked the concept of their evolving, they only had war to blame.

"Can you feel it?" Elios sounded animated.

He couldn't, they were still too far away, but she could and her Ruinous half grew excited. "Blood and fear." He knew they would find both in abundance. Considering where they were headed, how could they not?

"An ocean of it. It's just what you've been searching for."

For years he wandered battlefields searching for the valkyrie race, but although the slaughter might have been catastrophic he always arrived too late and found only residual traces like an empty bed growing cold. Finally the truth had dawned on him and he could have kicked himself. There was a place where terror had soaked the fabric of the world for centuries, a place where almost two million souls fed the earth with their spilled blood each year, and it was right in the heart of the capital. He had to hand it to the church, their doctrine was so convincing that even he'd grown accustomed to thinking they had no feelings. But the church was wrong. He could almost smell the manure and fear, and he smiled. Smithfield market was getting closer.

He ambled through the back alleys towards Blackfriars bridge, paying no heed to the ruffians prowling the dark streets. He didn't see the city as Londoners did, he saw it as a witch might see it. He detected fairies in their thousands, and above he saw faint glowing lines where keddy-potts had flown by, singing a lament for green things as they went. London bristled with magical beings and mostly the kind that thrived on decay, but whereas a witch would look with wonder, Galen was a reductionist. The magical creatures he saw were a phenomena designed by the universe to serve man, that was their sole purpose. If he caught a fairy and dissected it, its cries were without meaning in the same way a rusty gate might complain when opened. He had opened plenty of magical creatures and never once believed their pitiful cries were anything more than a 'rusty gate'. He saw a blossom-fairy tending a fallen apple core in the gutter, and the tracks of water sprites left in muddy puddles, he heard the song of kelp-harpies in the Thames, but none of these things moved him. They were the mechanics of nature and nothing more.

Such thoughts sent his mind back to an early attempt he'd made to interrogate a Ruinous creature. It had taken years of trying, but finally he had caught a crib-robber, the very kind of beast that had taken Sophie. He walked on, seeing London through the filter of the past.

"And I ask again," he demanded, "how do you travel between Ruin and Earth at will?" He turned the tap on the vacuum pump, drawing yet more air out of the bell jar. The crib-robber convulsed and collapsed further, now it looked little more than a deflated balloon.

"Ruin, yes travel to Ruin," it gurgled. This had been its stock reply for hours. He was starting to think it was too primitive to say anything further.

"How do you cross between worlds!" he shouted.

"Travel to Ruin." Its huge mouth pulsed, open then closed, open then closed, and it flapped its filament arms against the glass.

"Wrong answer, yer fiend," he sneered and increased the pressure. The creature quivered and its arms trembled. He released the lever and allowed a little precious oxygen back into the jar. The crib-robber gulped it down and pawed at the glass. "There'll be more of that if you answer me. Tell me: how do you pass between worlds?" His hand hovered over the Book-of-Nine ready to write.

"Ruin, yes, travel there," it gasped.

"Agh! Yer stupid beast," he spat. He might as well ask a pigeon how it flew. He jerked the lever again, cutting off the air entirely. "Yer deserve death." He tossed a sack over the jar, so disgusted with the thing that he couldn't even be bothered to watch it die. He sat with his arms folded and his back to the jar and fumed over his missing Sophie, not hearing the pathetic scraping coming from under the sacking, it was nothing more than a rusty gate.

As he stepped onto Blackfriar's Road a rat darted from his approach and a voice startled him out of his daydream.

"Four fat 'uns for a penny sir?" He looked down at a middle-aged woman sat on the kerb with a wooden tray of whelks in her lap. "I'll lets yer have four for a penny." Her speech was slow and heavy with gin. She held the tray higher in an attempt to make him part with his money. He looked down at the tray of whelks. They were poor specimens, rather like their vendor. Weary eyes peered up at him from under a bonnet strewn with withered flowers. He plainly saw that she suffered a chronic illness and the feeble gaslight made her look even more sallow.

"Have you enjoyed a good night's trade Madam?" He pushed his bowler back and smiled down at her.

"Trade? I dunno sir, but I've enjoyed a good night's hospitality that's for sure." She grinned and he had no doubt tonight's earnings had gone straight into a publican's pocket.

"She's dying Galen", Elios understood. *"Disease is all around us."*

"I know," he murmured, "all of London's dying." Sure enough there were mortis-fairies hovering around the woman. Three of them crawled through her wiry hair, while others clung to her clothes like orphaned pups.

"What's that yer say?" Her head wobbled on her shoulders and she made to stand, but only managed to tip the whelks into the road. "Bugger," she slurred and set about scooping them back onto her tray. He swept aside his coat, knelt and retrieved the wooden pepper box and placed it back on the tray which stank of vinegar, and took a good look at her. She stopped what she was doing and tried to focus on him. "Whelks, four for a penny," she enticed him again, but she sounded forgetful.

"I've no belly for whelks right now my love," he said with peculiar regret.

"Then what yer wants?" She sobered a little, wary now. "I shall scream," she warned without conviction.

"Galen, she's in pain. I can taste it." Elios sounded distressed but also excited. She was right. Ruin clung to her like the smell of hard spirits.

"Then out of compassion let's make it quick," he agreed.

"Make what quick?" The woman pulled her tray closer to her chest. "What you got in mind? I shall scream for a constable!"

He heard voices not far off, but doubted anyone would come. The city's morality was as sickly as this woman. He raised his cane and she fell silent and her mouth trembled. "Don't be afraid Madam, you'll thank me when you're on the other side."

"Other side of what?" she uttered, and he thought it ironic that in the moment just before she died she looked truly alive.

"Of the spiral my dear." He gently touched the stick to her heart and Elios gave her the gift of Ruin. She flinched once, then her hands slid from the tray and the whelks tumbled back into the road and she slumped against the cobbles. "Safe journey," he stroked her thinning hair. "Elios?"

"That was beautiful," she sighed.

"Did she satisfy you?" The mysterious Elios didn't reply, but from her delighted humming he knew she'd fed well. Such thoughts made him feel hungry and he reached out and plucked a whelk from the road, then gently placed a penny in the woman's open palm and curled her dead fingers around it.

He walked dreamily towards Smithfield, across Blackfriars bridge and through the web of alleys around Ludgate Hill. The streets were growing busy as publicans ejected drinkers for the night, but Galen walked through them oblivious.

He passed the Old Bailey where human cattle were sentenced to death not far from their four-legged counterparts at Smithfield, and arrived at Newgate Street just as the clock in St Paul's churchyard chimed midnight. They were only a short way from Smithfield now and the smell of dung grew sharper.

"Can't you feel it? It's like walking through a river!" Elios strained like a tethered dog.

"Blood and fear," he promised and hurried towards the heart of it. The ninth chapter would soon be complete and Sophie would be his.

The river of fear soon became a human river, as the alleys around Smithfield were still busy at this late hour. Galen pushed his way through gangs of drovers, butchers and hawkers. The cobbles were slick with dung and the air bitter with urine. Most of the animals arrived at Smithfield via the underground railway, but plenty were still driven through the streets although today's arrivals had already been rounded up and dispatched to the rings. The cane trembled in his hand as Elios grew more excited and she gasped as a boy hurried past pushing a wooden cart loaded with pigs heads, followed by a barking dog.

"Bugger off!' The lad lashed out a foot and sent it yelping away. One of the pig heads splashed into a pool of slurry, and he cursed and yanked it up by its ear and hurled it back amongst the others where it landed face down.

"Is it all you were hoping for?" he asked discreetly.

"Galen the fear here eclipses anything we found on the battlefield." She sounded jubilant.

"That was my mistake."

"We were both wrong," she soothed him.

He knew valkyries were drawn by fear and he'd blindly believed like the rest of the world, that animals had no soul so therefore no feelings. Searching for valkyries where dumb animals had died didn't make sense, yet here at Smithfield what he'd begun to suspect was vindicated. Here was an ocean of horror that had accumulated over the centuries. The manure might get cleared away, but the fear just got thicker and thicker.

"Is that it up ahead?"

At the end of Giltspur Street lurked a dark shape like a fortress. Smithfield Market.

"I fancy it must be." He couldn't see clearly, the air was smoky. He pushed through the crowds and they came out into West Smithfield and his heart almost sprang into his mouth. "Elios," he gasped, but she was speechless with wonder as both of them gazed at a sight only their eyes could see.

Smithfield Market loomed out of the haze of fog and filth. It was a citadel surrounded by bone-boiling houses and gut-scraping quarters. At each corner of the huge building was an octagonal tower and a yawning gateway in the middle of each wall. Galen saw only the south west tower from where he stood, but it wasn't the building that arrested him, imposing though it was, rather the fairies that flocked around it.

"Dear Àeon. I've never seen so many!" He clutched his cane, while Elios could only manage a stifled gasp. Mortis-fairies without number circled Smithfield like a gigantic tornado, reaching from the flickering gaslights and into the night black. Souls had been dispatched here for over a thousand years, their total numbers must have been astronomical, but it wasn't just animals. Heretics and political prisoners were executed here. Swindlers and coin forgers had been boiled in vats of oil and witches ended their days by rope and blade. Smithfield was man's temple to death right here in the heart of the world's most powerful nation. No wonder mortis-fairies were drawn here in plague proportions. "The years I wandered looking for such as this," he said, close to tears. "They have to be here, they *have* to be."

Ahead, drovers and handlers mingled with the cattle in a confused mass, lashing at them with sticks, driving them towards the rings, railways and killing pits. He ignored the shouts, barking dogs, whistles, bells and the animals' wretched cries and pushed his way through the crowds, gazing up at the tower of mortis-fairies, which shimmered like a beacon calling him home.

CHAPTER SIX

A drawing in the sand

'All art has power – why else would this world trivialise it?'
Eustace Corning 1791 - 1864

They spent the night on the shore but Sunday hadn't slept. Now they walked along mile after mile of black sand, but at least the sun was shining.

Where are we going? she wondered. *And why on earth are we here of all places?* She touched her wounded cheek for the umpteenth time and sighed. It was petty but she wanted to ask how it looked, probably no different to the other fairy-bites she suffered, but in her mind's eye she saw an ugly scar. Thinking about it kindled some of her old vanity, which disturbed her. But on the other hand was it so shameful, she was only human after all? Things had been so much easier when she'd been selfish to the bone. She plodded on, confused and weary, but at least she had Strike. He rode her shoulder and the touch of his soft feathers made her feel safe. "Strike?" she asked casually.

He'd seen this question coming and prepared a tactful answer.

"Do you think these bites'll fetch an infection?"

"No, they're not deep enough." He gave his head a firm shake.

"They feel deep enough."

"Give them a week or two and they'll be gone."

"This one hurts more that the others," she pretended, prodding her cheek.

"Well, it looks no worse than the rest."

"How *does* it look?"

He peered at her closely, getting his first good look at it. "The scab makes it look worse, it'll vanish, trust me." He considered a moment. "Actually it's shaped like a tiny hourglass." He said it to lighten the mood, but quickly regretted it when he saw her amazed expression.

"An hourglass, like his?"

"Well, vaguely," he played it down. "One hourglass is the same as another."

"I suppose it'll leave a scar." She shrugged as though it didn't matter, then scratched at her other bites.

"If it does, let it be a reminder. We were lucky to come away with our lives." He liked this new Sunday and didn't want her slipping back into old habits.

"You're right. We'd have died if . . ." Suddenly something she'd forgotten came back to her and she stopped.

"Problem?"

"Last night – there was a fairy!"

He frowned. "There were thousands of the little buggers."

"Language Strike!" She'd never heard him curse before.

"Sorry," he muttered, embarrassed.

She covered her smile. *I'm left handed not right, and Strike's finding his feet.* This really was a new start.

"There were lots of fairies is what I meant," he apologised.

"But there was one in particular. It warned me just before we were attacked." She looked around the shore. "God-oak, I'd forgotten!" She pressed a hand to her brow as the memory unlocked.

"What kind of fairy?"

"I don't know, I'm not good at fairy species, but it wasn't pretty. It was greyish and had thin arms and legs."

"Hmm, no such thing as a pretty fairy," he growled, "and this might not be the best time to say this but I've felt that something's been following us all morning."

"You think it's the same one?"

He leaned closer and spoke into her ear. "I've heard a sound on and off."

"What kind of sound?"

"The whine of tiny wings, never far away. If there's anything sprites know about, it's wings." He ruffled his own to make his point.

"Wings." She knew he was genuine, that was part of the mystical bond between witch and sprite, and since her resurrection she felt it keener than ever.

"He could be close, might even be sat on my shoulder." Although joking, the idea made her uneasy.

"Fairy-kind never do anything without a price."

"Well, this one sounds like he's after the fee for his good deed."

"I say pay him in pain."

"That's fighting talk," she smiled.

"If you don't mind me saying," he added meekly.

"I don't mind, but no, that fairy saved us. Sleeping there was one of the most stupid things I've ever done." *Apart from my note,* she thought shamefully.

"So, we just wait for him to declare himself on his terms?"

"No, I think fairy-kind have enjoyed the upper hand for long enough." She rammed her staff into the sand and Strike flapped to its tip and sat there, alert. "Show yourself, we know you're following us!" she shouted, then set her fists against her hips and straightened. She stood perfectly still with her eyes attuned for movement. The wind played with her hair, but nothing happened.

"Cat and mouse. Cloak and dagger," Strike muttered.

"Do you wish me to command you, drag you bodily from the fairy realm?" she warned. "I can do it!" She went to draw her wand, left handed of course, but instead of clasping her own she found the black wand had mysteriously found its way into her hand. *Hrafn-dimmu, Valonia's wand,* she thought, proud to hold it.

Strike pricked his ears. "I hear wings."

"I know you can hear me," she continued.

Silence, except for a mocking gull close by.

"Then we do this the hard way," she sighed, and bent and collected four pebbles of equal size. "I'm told this can be painful, that it can leave a fairy with a sore head for a week," she called as she made a show of casting the spell. She pressed each pebble into the sand making a square of about a yard along each side. "I've never tried it before, and I hope I get it right, because if I don't," she paused dramatically, "there's a chance you'll be turned inside out, or end up with your wings sprouting from your nostrils. And I wouldn't want to hurt the fairy who so graciously rescued us last night."

Silence span around them.

It's got colder, she thought, and saw her breath and knew he was right there with them. "Very well," she said regretfully. "Strike, keep watch please while I work." She lay the tip of the black wand against the sand within the pebble square and immediately caught the whine of tiny wings and jerked around. Strike heard it too and flashed her an anxious look. "The spell begins," she called, and then making sure not to step into the square she began to draw.

Neet watched with mounting unease. He was sitting right under their noses, by Sunday's feet, but his attention was fixed on the picture she was drawing in the sand. It was a crude likeness of him and even though he appeared only briefly last night, if she had a good memory it might be enough. "Cunning, nasty, ungrateful witch. After saving her life!" He clacked his jaws. "And ratty lightning-sparrow, thinks he's kinder on the eye than any fairy? But ugly fairies would've made meal of them if Neet hadn't been there." He groused on and on. The first part of his plan had gone well, but now she was going to expose him prematurely and spoil everything. She etched the outline of his spiky wings, and as she did he felt a tugging sensation in his belly. *No!* he panicked. Her spell was working.

She closed her eyes to enhance the memory, trusting to draw without looking, and sketched his hooked limbs with a flick of the wand. She included every detail she could remember, adding slit nostrils and small eyes, and as she did the buzz of angry wings grew louder, until she heard Strike's surprised gasp followed by a soft growl. She went to add more detail, but the wand hit something solid, rousing a spiteful little cry.

"Sunday!" Strike barked, and she opened her eyes. There was a fairy inside the sand square: the one from last night.

Instantly she held the wand over it so that he couldn't fly away. The tiny creature writhed and twisted on the sand, erasing her sketch and all the while screaming, "I'm trapped! Kill her! Kill her!"

Strike landed on her shoulder but she barely noticed, holding the wand was like keeping the lid on a pan of boiling water. An unseen force kept trying to push her arm up.

"Come to my aid, kin folk!" the fairy shrieked. "The broom-rider's out to make spell fodder of us all! Clip your wings and pull your teeth, squeeze every last drop of fairy blood for cauldron wickedness!"

"The longer he goes on, the more fairies he'll bring down on us," Strike whispered anxiously.

"He's bluffing," she groaned, the spell was hard and her arm burned with the strain.

"Help me!"

"Stop it," she insisted.

"Help me fairy kin, kill the broom-rider!"

"STOP NOW!" she boomed, and the fairy froze and even Strike flinched.

It looked up at her unblinking, and she was amazed that such a small creature could project such anger.

"Stop now," she commanded more evenly. "Nobody's coming to your rescue, you know that as well as I do." She squatted down for a better view of him. "If any fairy answered your call, they'd be tearing *you* apart, not me."

Neet crawled into an upright position and just glowered at her. His bluff had failed.

"You're outside your own territory aren't you?" she asked sadly.

He sat stony and silent, but she was right. He'd not counted on her knowing so much about fairies. She was sharper than he guessed.

"Territory?" Strike asked.

The strain of holding the wand lessened, but she kept it in place, just in case. "Yes, fairy folk are very territorial. If an intruder's caught in another's area they're dealt with severely."

He saw what she was getting at. This fairy couldn't call for help because the others would attack him not help him, the only thing keeping him safe was staying in Sunday's shadow, where her magical signature masked his own. "That's how he'd slipped away from his own territory," he guessed. "He's alone and he knows it."

"But where are my manners," she softened, "we should thank you for last night."

Neet sat in the middle of a mess of sand scratches and said nothing.

"It would be easier if I knew your name? I'm Sunday Flowers," she said after he wasn't forthcoming. She displayed considerable trust, for names were powerful tokens amongst magical creatures. "And this is Strike, my friend."

Strike felt a silly lump in his throat at the word 'friend'. She'd never called him that before.

The fairy made a harsh little 'tick' sound.

"I'm sorry?" she said mildly.

He rose into the air and hovered eye level with her. "I said Neet, my name is Neet!" he shot back.

From so close she could see that he had a strange kind of beauty many would call bizarre. "Then Neet, we owe you a great deal, is that why you took the risk of following us, to let us say our thanks in person?" Her baited question was smooth as silk.

"Followed you to escape at last, saved you that I might go back," he replied cryptically.

She was struck by how angry he sounded, and recognised that hardship was his soul-mate. "If I release the spell, will you flee?" She knew he couldn't, but he nodded once and she slowly withdrew the wand. "You put up quite a fight," she complimented as she rubbed at her sore wrist.

"Enjoyed much practise," he said quietly.

She lowered herself onto the sand and lay her staff across her lap. Strike perched on her shoulder, watching everything. "You're not like most fairies," she observed.

"Most fays don't live the way we do on the Cold Coast."

"Is that where we are, the Cold Coast?"

"Only this coast," he gestured with a withered arm, "but men call this land Iceland."

The name instantly struck her. *Valonia was from Iceland, that must mean so is her black wand,* she thought. She and Strike exchanged a meaningful look. "My thanks again, I wasn't sure where we were."

"I know, I saw you washed ashore. Homeless and lost." Again, he was entranced by her soul, he was so close now he could reach out and touch it.

"Tell me more about this place, why are you so eager to leave, it's quite a risk isn't it?"

"Hard place this. Hard, cold and haunted."

This last word caught her off guard. "Haunted? By whom?"

"Not whom, not since they stopped being men. Haunted by 'what' is better asked witch-Sunday." He snatched a look around the shore. He might have been on guard for enemy fairies but she guessed something else frightened him.

"You came to warn us of these ghosts, last night?"

"Came to spare you the sting of fairy teeth," he agreed evasively.

"And what else?" she asked shrewdly.

"Followed you to escape at last, saved you too that I might go back," he repeated.

"You've said so already, but it doesn't make sense," Strike interrupted.

Neet span his way. "Killed many of my kin last night thunder-sprite, but I see a strong sprite and that's to the good, strong you'll need to be."

"For what?" Sunday asked angrily. "And no more riddles, or I'll let the fairy folk hereabouts enjoy something different for lunch." She tapped a finger against her wand.

He made a whimpering sound and shook his head, but the glint in his eyes never softened. "This coast wasn't always haunted. Not always cursed, but if the haunters –," he almost said something then corrected himself. "If the haunters go away fairies can live as fairies were meant, like before, long ago."

"Ahhh," she smiled without humour, "if the haunters are *defeated* you mean."

"Huh!" Strike barked. "Like I said, fairy folk never do anything without a price. No prizes for guessing who'll be ridding this place of its ghosts."

She regarded Neet coldly. "We owe you, I don't contest that. Although it would have been nice to think we were saved by kindness, and not just profiteering."

He just glared at her.

"You said they were once men? Tell us exactly what haunts this coast," she demanded.

He drifted to the sand and squatted there, gently pawing at the ground and began. "There are three of them. Once men of war from an age ago, hundreds of summers since when men rode the seas in dragon ships and fought with steel."

In his sleep he heard his name spoken, or more precisely his nature, for his name was long forgotten. Someone somewhere was speaking of him . . .

"There are three of them. Once men of war from an age ago, hundreds of summers since when men rode the seas in dragon ships and fought with steel."

He didn't know who this narrator was or why he wished to tell their tale, but it left him deeply unsettled. Last night they had killed again on Valgard's behalf and his dreams had been violent and dark as always, but amongst the jumbled memories of battle he remembered one fight in particular. It was his last as a mortal man.

King Halfdan had usurped the throne and his forces were killing any who refused to swear allegiance to his kingship. It was just a matter of time until they came to his village and on the last day of summer they came: two hundred men. He led the doomed villagers against Halfdan's mercenaries, but they stood little chance.

He and his two trusted companions had the villagers form a shield wall in the narrow gorge and there they faced the approaching enemy. His forces numbered just fifty farmers against two hundred warriors, but time was their purpose, not victory. While they held Halfdan's troops the villagers would escape.

He remembered them advance, drumming their swords against their shields and screaming curses. He watched in horror as the tide of warriors crashed against their shields, and axes and blades lashed down like rain. Their left flank buckled almost at once, and men were hacked to death. They had broken through and their loved ones would be forfeit. It was then in a moment of utter desperation that he and his two companions offered their souls to Valgard if the war god would gift them victory, and so he had, but he soon came to know that it was truly a curse.

The last memory he had as that of a mere man was of a beautiful woman, but now he couldn't remember who she was or why she might be important to him. In the next instant he was no longer a man but a beast as terrible as a bear with a hide like steel that no weapon could pierce. The three of them slaughtered Halfdan's troops to the last man, tearing them apart and delighting in their screams, but in doing so their own folk were so terrified that they fled, leaving them to a life of wandering and fighting, and the black rage was their constant companion. It suffocated their memories and they became monsters of fury and all shunned them, except for ruthless leaders bent on conquest like Halfdan. They fell into the service of such men and earned rich rewards, but the more they killed the more monstrous they grew until in the end they no longer resembled men at all and every waking moment was filled with anger. Valgard had ensnared them, and the power that had saved them had driven away everyone they knew or loved.

"There are three of them. Once men of war from an age ago, hundreds of summers since when men rode the seas in dragon ships and fought with steel," Neet began his tale.

"Men of this island?"

He nodded gravely.

"Vikings?" Sunday did the maths in her head. The Viking age ended some eight centuries ago.

"They worshipped gods of fighting and thunder," he shot Strike a glance at this. "And men who fought well, found favour with him," he jabbed his chin upwards.

She looked to the sky. "Him?"

"Him!" he hissed. "The god of war."

"There are many gods of war," she sighed ruefully.

He glanced around and then whispered quickly, "Valgard."

She shook her head blankly. There were more names for war deities than days in the year, it was a sad reflection on humanity's prime obsession.

"Think he's not real?" he challenged.

"I'm sure he is," she sighed. "But tell me why these three are so important to him and why they linger here."

"He likes to watch." He looked skywards again, convinced they were being watched right now. "Likes to watch men fight and kill and best of all to die. The strongest of the strong he makes gifts to."

"What kind of gifts?"

"Power of course!"

"What kind of power?"

Neet groaned. "Power to kill better than the rest stupid witch-Sunday. Power to resist weapons of steel. Power to terrify!"

"Why would Val–," she stopped herself just in case; "why would *he* bestow a gift like that? It sounds more like a curse."

"He likes to watch," he repeated.

Slowly it dawned on her what he meant. "He makes men into monsters so he can be entertained by bloodshed?"

"Something tells me these three gentlemen still live close by," Strike muttered.

Neet nodded. "Sleeping the years away until he calls them."

"Tell me more, and no riddles Neet, I need to know." She sounded business like and Strike had the uneasy feeling that she was readying to help him.

"The berserker rage some call it. Men who turn into bears, but not real bears as the gods of nature made, men-bears of the kind *he* favours. Bears on two legs and claws like knives." He waved his own small arms in comparison. "With a lust for war that can't be sated, they fight until the ground oozes blood and no warriors, not even their horses remain!" he chuckled, sounding like a tiny chain rattling. "But not always men-bears, those they only become in the very worst of the battle. They can change, become almost like true bears or eagles or even orca, to make war in the air or sea. And worst of all, they cannot be harmed, all steel breaks against them. Axes, swords, spears, all lie in pieces. Even magic weapons fail against them."

She swallowed and wished the sun would come out. "You've seen this?"

He nodded.

"There was a battle here?"

"No. Battles were always across the sea. That's where his favoured children fought, going from land to land wreaking havoc, but when they came back here and there were no more wars, what then eh?"

"Who was left to fight then?" Strike interrupted.

"In this land?" he shrugged, "no warriors, but farmers, woodcutters, weavers and other folks, oh yes, plenty left to play with. The old witches here kept them at bay, kept the people safe, but people don't trust broom-riders and they forced them away. Then the monsters took this coast for themselves."

Sunday and Strike swapped horrified glances. *Why did we have to end up here of all places?* she despaired and looked around, and what should have been obvious from the start landed on her like a brick. The grassy mounds scattered along the coast were abandoned farmsteads. She hadn't really seen them at first, they were so overgrown and caved in, but now they seemed to rear up like gravestones, and she felt like a fly in a web and suddenly thought of the Timekeeper. "He made them kill the ordinary folk of this land, but why?"

It was Strike who answered. "Because it pleased him to watch."

Neet growled an agreement. "And with that souls began to depart these lands and fairy-kind began to know famine. And we've known it well ever since." He concluded his tale with a snap of his jaws.

She was sickened, not to mention frightened: somewhere close by lurked three ancient and invincible monsters. She looked down at the sand where Neet had struggled and saw the unmistakable shape of a spider in the scratches. *Is that you my Lord? Is this your will, that I stop these things?*

"Sunday?" Strike whispered.

"A spider," she murmured. "Look, a spider." She pointed at marks that might have been legs.

Neet watched in puzzlement, but Strike knew exactly what she was driving at. "At a pinch it could be, but even so, it's just a shape," he tried to reason. "It doesn't necessarily have meaning."

"A witch sees the world as full of meaning." She stared down at the image. The Timekeeper had left her a cryptic message she was sure, and maybe this was why she'd been sent back. Her atonement wasn't complete.

"Sunday?" He was getting worried.

She cast him a sideways glance and smiled sadly. "I think we have our answer."

"You can't!"

"I'll go alone if I have to, but I'd rather you came. You're free to say no."

He once obeyed through fear and helped her make a terrible mistake, but now he had a better reason: friendship. "Very well," he nodded, and she regarded him so tenderly that he almost blushed.

She looked down at the crude image in the sand, it was all the proof she needed. "Tell me how to find these monsters, Neet"

"You'll help?"

"I think I have to." *I'm sorry Strike,* she thought, and hoped her sense of guilt wasn't going to get them both killed for a second time.

The three of them set off, but flying this time. She understood now that this coast was uninhabited and even if it wasn't, people would be looking out for worse things than a lone witch. "How far?" she shouted over the wind

"Up to the island-mountain-glacier, through the woods of Thor," Neet squeaked from her shoulder. He took cover from the buffeting wind under her pointed hat.

They left the dark sands behind, crossed the dunes and inland over a wilderness of stunted birch to the glacier known as Eyjafjallajköull. It looked like a huge white shield and below it Valgard's monsters were sleeping, protected by hundreds of feet of ice. "How are you faring Strike?" She dropped low enough to feel the birches brush her feet as they raced by.

"I'm here," he answered starkly.

She knew he didn't approve, just like the time when he helped her deliver her treacherous note. She said no more and hoped this wasn't history repeating itself.

Since meeting those two special witches last autumn, the Timekeeper felt that a little of their humanity had rubbed off on him. For starters he'd begun to marvel at some of the Patternmaker's commands. He plotted events in the world that were beautiful, but then in the same instant he might order something cruel and destructive. These things had never occurred to him before, they just 'were'. There was one command he still resisted however, and that was the cutting of Sunday's thread, but despite his feud with the Patternmaker the weave continued.

The millions of small events that shaped the world ran their course as always, but today had seen a few other more interesting patterns woven amongst them. A flash flood in a remote part of South America created – albeit for only a day – the greatest waterfall on Earth. Unusual weather systems in Asia resulted in swans gathering in a flock two-thousand strong, while in the far north the last survivor of an Arctic expedition had chanced upon a frigate and so been rescued. The Timekeeper discovered that he was a sentimentalist and enjoyed a happy ending, there were so few of them though. It had been an interesting day, but the weave never stopped and he worked thread after thread.

"Interesting," he almost smiled as he selected a thread. As soon as he began to weave he knew who it was. "I am glad to see all is well Kolfinnia." It was like a snippet of gossip and he was secretly delighted to catch up with her again. The young witch was busy with her new coven and he felt a rush of gladness for her. It was soon extinguished though, and his pleasant day took an ugly turn when another familiar thread quivered and he quickly drew it close. "Sunday and Strike," he called aloud. "Your assassin is persistent."

He knew it would try again, but this time rather than sever her thread the intruder had given it a gentle nudge, so softly that he hadn't detected it. Her fate was set and he couldn't turn her back. *Curse this wretch,* he fumed. "Be bold and show yourself!" His voice rumbled through the cavern. The threads trembled but the intruder remained hidden. He listened so intently that he could hear the stalactites growing, but the assassin was adept at hiding. "I will find you, and I will have you!" he vowed. Then keeping one eye on the forest of threads he took a closer look at Sunday's.

It was entwined with that of a fairy, ironically the very one who saved her last night, and now she was tangled in a plot to confront three lethal monsters. "Oh Sunday," he lamented, "you should keep better company. Fairy-kind are less than honest." He knew the secret killer had manipulated Neet into leading her towards danger. "Very subtle my lord. My compliments!" he called and a succession of droplets dripped from the cave roof and tinkled against the glass, sounding like applause. *Yes, very subtle, getting the fairy to unwittingly lead her to death,* his thoughts raced. There had to be a way to save her, he just had to find the right thread. In the outside world Sunday flew onwards to where Valgard's monsters lay sleeping. *A countermeasure is here somewhere,* he thought frantically, and from very close he heard the assassin's faint laughter. "I'll have you," he promised, and when he did he would wrap it so tight that it would burst before he even sank his fangs into it. His legs blurred and his eyes darted back and forth as he traced every thread surrounding Sunday; seagulls, gnats, foxes, fairies, each and every living thing around her right then, looking for one that could help. Finally he found it and unexpected it was too. "Ha!" he exclaimed and began weaving. "Help can come from the most unlikely sources."

Sunday was heading for a confrontation with the war god's champions and she wouldn't stand a chance, unless she made a lucky discovery and made it quick. The taunting laughter fell silent and a baleful rumbling filled the cavern, but he was too distracted to worry about the Patternmaker's chagrin. Sunday was airborne. Now if only he could encourage her to veer off a little, there was something forgotten on the lonely moors that might even the balance and he knew just how to deliver his message. "Better luck next time my Lord," he said with bald sarcasm as he wove a delicate knot, entwining Sunday's fate with the those of her unlikely rescuers; a humble cloud, a flock of geese, and a black wand.

CHAPTER SEVEN

The lonely song

*"Our very identity is built around the supposed uniqueness of
man's soul. Can you imagine how the world would crumble
if we finally confessed this was not so?'*
Corthus Jorum, 11th century Knight-Superior

Although the glacier concealed a terrible secret, Sunday was awed by it.
She had lived almost her whole life at Regal-Fox, surrounded by woodland
and meadows. "Do you see it Strike!" she grinned.

"Almost worth coming all this way for. It looks like a sleeping giant."

"Look to the north!" Neet directed her attention to the vast, grey cloud,
churning over the glacier.

"Is that a storm?"

"The worst kind," he cackled, "storm from under the earth, a storm of fire."

"A volcano," Strike guessed.

Banking towards it she got a better view. Magma churned in a fissure half a
mile long, like boiling soup, showering the glacier with debris and belching
a huge ash plume shaped like a fist. "They'll never believe this back home,"
she shook her head in amazement and thought of Regal-Fox and then
remembered that it no longer existed, the Illuminata had seen to that.

Her sadness spilled over into Strike. *"There'll be plenty of other witches to tell
when we get back,"* he consoled.

"I won't fail you this time." She kept her thought just for him.

"I know. Let's hope our luck doesn't fail either," he worried.

She was about to answer when the wand around her waist jerked sharply. "What in Oak's name?" She reached down to make sure it was still there, and just as her finger closed around it, it jumped again, forcefully enough to pull her arm with it.

"What's the matter?" Strike asked.

"Something very odd's going on."

"What's odd?" Neet piped up, catching only her half of the conversation.

"It's Valonia's wand, it's acting very strange."

"Never mind, just keep going!"

Just then hrafn-dimmu twitched again.

"It's agitated." She looked around for danger but saw nothing.

"It's a stupid stick, how can it be alive, ignore it," Neet demanded.

"No!" She pushed wind-blown hair from her face. "Raven's wand sailed the length of Britain to find a new coven, it's as alive as you or me."

"Stupid stick," he whined and hid deeper in her hair. She didn't enjoy him so close nor listening to his insults.

When hrafn-dimmu bucked again it was stronger than ever, and she looked about in confusion, and her sign wasn't long coming. As they flew onwards, a voluminous snow cloud, the unmistakable shape of an hourglass, slid out from behind the ash plume. The harder she looked the more she saw until she could almost discern its incredible occupant suggested in the curves and shadows, and there and then, she knew. "Strike, that cloud – its shape!"

"I see it," he said warily, *"don't read into it."*

"He's trying to get our attention. It's him!"

"Only perhaps."

"Nobody wants your attention, just fly faster witch-Sunday!" Neet peeped out from her hair.

"Not yet!" She slowed and scrutinised the miraculous cloud, hovering high above the glacier and shielding her eyes with her hand. "The shape's incredible, it can't be wholly natural."

"Even if you're right, what could it mean?" Strike hoped whatever sign she imagined, it was telling them to ditch this foolhardy plan.

She shook her head. "What's the purpose of a divine omen if you can't decode it?"

"Time's against us? Time to stop? Time to go home?" Strike guessed, he particularly liked this last one.

"Please my Lord, you brought us back from Evermore, don't play with us like this," she prayed softly.

"There!" Strike alerted. *"Movement."*

She continued staring up at it, wondering if she was going mad, reading signs in clouds and scratches, but then she smiled. "Yes! They're geese I think."

"So what's the significance of that? Are we going to pelt these monsters with goose eggs?"

"It means something, I know it does!"

"Sunday, it could be just a cloud with some geese . . ."

"But it's not." She felt excited. It was like watching the pages of a magnificent book open before her eyes. "When the geese pass, we'll follow them, that *must* be it."

"No, we'll not follow the stupid geese! Men-bears that way!" Neet waved at the glacier.

"There's more at work here than just your problem," she chastised him. "We'll follow the geese first and then head back."

He buzzed in annoyance, "Wild goose chase is all this is. I told you that —"

"There'll be NO discussion about this," she interrupted. He gave a sullen growl, and Strike was glad to see a bit of the old Sunday come back, least ways when it came to dealing with Neet.

The geese passed over in a rush of wings, flying in tight formation. She counted twenty-two of them and read numerous meanings into that, foremost of which was a date, October 22nd, the day Kittiwake-coven fell and she met the Timekeeper. "We have to follow them Strike." They turned away from the unique cloud in pursuit. "Keep an eye out for signs."

"What am I looking for?"

"I don't know, anything that jumps out at you."

"Understood." If he couldn't dissuade her he could at least help.

"Who you following witch-Sunday," Neet complained, "silly geese?"

"Not that it's any of your business, but I think the geese were sent by an old friend."

"But men-bears are that way," he snivelled again.

"We'll turn back as soon as I'm satisfied."

He kept his peace and curled up against her neck where she felt chilly indignation radiating from him.

The geese continued, closely followed by Sunday, and her keen eye was rewarded with the sight of a narrow valley in the featureless plain below. The geese made a sudden racket as they passed over and hrafn-dimmu jerked again for good measure. "Calm yourself, dark raven, I get your point," she patted the wand. "Strike, the valley's our target."

"Leave it to me," he agreed, beginning a cautious descent.

She watched the geese slip away, wondering where they were heading, before turning her attention towards the ominous looking gorge, suspecting their own path would be a lot darker.

"Not good place this," Neet looked out from under her hat. "Bad smell to it."

She didn't say anything at first, then she caught a delicate scent on the breeze, rotten flowers and warm blood. "Ruin," she hissed.

Neet made a whining sound. "Noooo! No not good witch-Sunday, turn back!"

"I can't go back, and you'll have to accompany us." The valley opened wider, and looked even blacker against the wintry landscape, like a wound that had split open and then flooded with nothing but bad dreams.

"This is like flying into open jaws," Strike warned. *"You're sure this is where we're meant to be?"*

"I'm sorry Strike."

"Same old stubborn witch," he grumbled.

"I heard that," she smiled.

They dropped into the trench, the sheer walls of which were cloaked in moss and seemed to soak up the sunlight and throttle it. Ahead, there was a dark and tangled forest, but large trees this time unlike the sparse shrub elsewhere and the whole place was deathly silent, even the volcano lost its voice.

"Slow and steady," she advised. They floated quietly towards the forest, which choked the whole gorge ahead, and the smell of Ruin grew stronger. She could feel Neet trembling on her shoulder.

"Witch-Sunday," he said as his bulbous head swivelled side to side.

"Yes?"

"There are no fairies here," he revealed with a mixture of dread and wonder. "Not a single one!"

She couldn't see them anyway, but his fear was certainly genuine.

"Sunday," Strike growled, *"this isn't right."*

But she had the utmost faith in the Timekeeper and had even begun to see him as her own 'dear champion'. *"He wouldn't have sent us unless it was urgent."*

"Maybe . . . if he sent us here at all."

They drifted along the fissure and now the smell of Ruin was so thick it was like a mist in the air, and no wonder for these weren't really trees at all. "Oak and holly save us!" She pressed the silver fox pendant to her lips. "Oak and holly save us," she repeated. They halted only feet above the corrupted ground where boulders were entombed in moss. Ahead of them was a wood, but without a single natural tree. "Dead-walkers," she whispered. Trees of Ruination that weren't trees at all, but parasite creatures whose seeds had a taste for flesh.

"I never thought there were so many in the world!" Strike was so astounded he forgot to be afraid.

She nodded mutely. Dead-walks were rare yet here was a wood full of them. They were tall and slender, and their limbs spread like arteries rather than branches. They were leafless and their ebony bark was smooth and had a distasteful organic sheen to it. "But why would they gather here?" Her knuckles whitened as she tried to squeeze all the luck out of her silver fox.

"I don't know, but I think we'd stand a better chance fighting those berserks than this lot." Strike kept the staff charged, ready to bolt.

"It's the song," Neet murmured dreamily. "The song brought them here."

"What song?" she asked.

He hummed sleepily, "Such a song!"

"Neet, what's the matter?" She craned around, and saw the back of his head. He was staring into the wood, fascinated by the blackness between the trunks.

"Something's in there, singing in the heart of the black," he pointed.

The darkness looked so solid she imagined they could slip into it as easily as a pool of ink, never to be seen again. "Do we have to go in there and find whatever it is?" She looked up at the gash of sky between the chasm walls, hoping for a sign, but this time there was nothing.

Strike didn't share her conviction. *"So what next. Do we just sail right in there?"*

She didn't reply, something had set her thinking. "Neet, are you afraid?"

"Who can be afraid with such music?" he sighed.

"Don't the trees frighten you?"

He closed his eyes as he listened to the song emanating from the blackness. "We should go and join the dance forever," he surrendered.

"I don't hear anything?" Strike wondered if Neet was playing a trick.

She closed her eyes and listened. Strangely, although she faced a horde of creatures from Ruination, she found that she wasn't afraid. In fact, the longer she sat there the more peaceful she felt. "They're all under a spell," she sighed without opening her eyes. "They've gathered here from far and wide. Perhaps Neet's right, we should go and join them."

The dead-walks swayed and their trunks groaned contentedly.

"Join them," she repeated absently.

"Sunday!" Strike buzzed a current through the staff.

She jerked, and blinked a few times, "Strike?"

"You drifted off, whatever's in there you need to fight against it!"

"Sorry." She rubbed her eyes. "There is something singing in there, and it's powerfully hypnotic." She dropped the fox pendant back into her shirt. The touch of cold metal revived her, but Neet remained entranced.

"Let him be, we'll get some peace at last," Strike recommended.

"I don't think the trees are a danger. They're enchanted by the song."

"We go in then?" he posed.

She stroked the hourglass scar on her cheek and took a deep breath. "We go in – and find the source of the song," she decided, and then advanced into the wood, heading for a gap in the trees that was so dark it could have been a wound in reality.

Galen had returned to Goldhawk in the early hours. The night's events had been extremely disturbing, and he returned feeling dazed. He heard a bell peal five or maybe six, but couldn't be sure. He undressed and crawled into his bunk, still stinking of Smithfield, and wrote his first sentence in the ninth chapter.

The early hours of April 26th 1887 shall be remembered in history, for last night I, Galen of the Book-of-Nine, found a valkyrie.

He returned the special book to the satchel and lay there exhausted, but with his mind spinning. Last night had been a trial. The market had been manically busy and so he sneaked down into the lower levels where trains brought animals and left loaded with carcasses. In one of the service tunnels he found a little respite and sat down trying to tune into the esoteric vibrations. The air buzzed with mortis-fairies and other varieties, but it was valkyries he'd come to find. He took a trinket from around his neck: a gold ring bearing the cult's seal. He never wore it openly, but liked to feel it against his skin. He stroked its embossed crest, which showed a square at an angle like a diamond, with a circle in its centre. The symbol of the Book-of-Nine. "Are we soon to unlock your secrets number nine?" he said to no one.

The four sides represented the Book's eight chapters, each side having two faces; the outer being the material world, and the inner the esoteric world. Four sides, two faces on each, a total of eight. The circle was the missing ninth chapter, and all initiates carried such a ring.

He slipped the ring back into his shirt and curled up in the dark. In his state of meditation an old memory crept out of hiding. It had been a long time ago, before Elios, before he called himself Galen even. It had been before his exile, when he had travelled willingly. He was a boy of only fourteen and had set out to find a coven that would accept him, but they all rebuked him because of his fascination with Ruin. In the end he found a lone mentor in Rome and befriended him, then accompanied him over much of Europe, but kept his motives secret. His name had been Rang-Shaa, and he was an Indian mystic.

When Rang-Shaa had identified himself as a 'servant of the twins', Galen knew he was a witch, albeit a lone practitioner. He endured months of drivel about the sanctity of life, mastering basic spells and living a vegetarian life to convince the old man he was genuine.

At last, after nine months, Galen broached the subject of Ruin. They were sitting by the sea in a small Italian port. Rang-Shaa had made him go there to visit a holy mountain where he could meditate. After four days of this and eating nothing but wild olives Galen decided he was tired of pretending. "How does one send the Ruinous fiends back to their own world?" he asked with just the right note of empathy.

Rang-Shaa creased his brow as he thought. "And why would a witch send Ruinous souls home?"

He was being tested. "To return them to their own realm, in compassion for their plight." Rang-Shaa studied him and smiled. Galen began to suspect he was mocking him. "Isn't it?" he pressed, growing impatient.

"Only you can know that," he replied mysteriously, then he put his pipe back in his mouth and looked out across the sea, with Galen's questions forgotten.

His patience snapped. He slapped the pipe from his mouth, grabbed the scrawny man's robes and hauled him to his feet. "How am I supposed to be a true witch if I can't fight the forces of Ruin?" he snarled.

"But you have never desired to be a witch," he replied softly. The old man had known his motives from the start.

Galen exploded, and landed a fist in his face. Rang-Shaa hit the floor in a cloud of dust, dropping his staff and Galen snatched it up and began lashing him across the head, landing brutal blows until his arms ached and the old man lay still. He dropped the stick and backed away, listening to the old man's breathing grow weaker and his moans grow quieter. He'd never killed a man before and he cupped his hands over his ears. "It's just a rusty gate, nothing more. A rusty gate," he insisted, then fled.

He might not have learned the way into Ruination, but he learned something almost as valuable: guilt and compassion could drive a man insane. If he was ever going to learn to live with what he'd done he knew he had to do away with them.

There was a timid knock at the door and he looked out from under the blankets. "Who is it?" he groaned.

"Beckingstaff sir," came the reply, "Mr Lyle asked me to come find you."

He scratched at his stubbly chin, unsure if he'd slept at all. "Tell him I'll be down presently," he answered groggily.

"Very good sir," Beckingstaff said and marched away.

For a moment he lay there and listened to London coming awake outside. Although the library was on the top floor, sounds painted a vivid picture of the city; dogs yapping, cartwheels on cobbles, ships sounding their horns. London was stirring and he must do likewise. He reached under his bunk and stroked the walking cane. "Elios?"

"Mmmm?" She was exhausted from last night.

"I'll meet them myself, stay here and rest." He got to his feet, ignoring the aches and pains of middle age. *How long do I have?* he wondered. Would he be an old man by the time he solved the ninth chapter, would Sophie want a twin brother old enough to be her grandfather? He scrubbed at his hair, then slowly gathered his clothes from the floor and poured himself into them.

"You're hoping for a breakthrough aren't you?" Doulton regarded his colleague over his copy of the Morning Standard and took another sip of coffee.

"I'm sure he'll have something for us," Lyle insisted without conviction

Neither of them was happy though. Galen slipped away last night without reporting it. He could have assassinated the empress for all they knew or circled London on a broomstick with his britches around his ankles. Wherever he went, Doulton just hoped he'd been discreet. He looked at his pocket watch again just as the door creaked open and Galen slouched through. "Ah! Good morning to you," he beamed without getting up.

Galen just scowled. Lyle was on his feet, offering him a chair and shoving plates of eggs, bacon and toast towards him before he'd even sat down.

"I see perhaps that one is not at one's best in the morning," Doulton smiled and caught Lyle's angry glance.

"My dear chap," Lyle sympathised, "you don't look to have slept a wink."

"You could say that, not sleep worth winking at least ways." He piled an assortment of foods on his plate and Doulton looked away as he gulped down black pudding, eating and drinking like a navvy, gradually slipping into his Galen persona.

"I trust you're rested enough to indulge us with your findings?" Lyle offered the sugar bowl and Galen plucked three cubes from it with his dirty fingers and dropped them into his tea with a plop.

"For certain," he boasted.

"Pardon the early start," Doulton said modestly, "I didn't realise that you'd be away *all* night, I applaud your tenacity."

"I know what you think, that I've been out whoring or gambling your funds away," he accused as he plastered butter on his toast.

"No, not at all!"

"I take my duties seriously. I've as much desire to find one of these creatures as you."

"And did you?" Lyle added hopefully.

There was a stiff silence as he chewed thoughtfully on his toast. Both leaned closer, and he chewed slower to prolong their torment, because it amused him. "Yes," he said at last.

They swapped electrified glances and then shuffled their chairs around to face him. "You found one you say?" Lyle insisted.

"My suspicions have been proven. There's a place close by that's perfect, and these creatures can't help but be drawn to."

"But did you actually catch one?" Lyle insisted.

"Mr Lyle!" He replaced his cup with a rattle. "The aim isn't to catch one, they're not dumb beasts. I'm out to forge an alliance with them."

"Yes I'm sure," he hurried, "but you saw one though?"

He placed his hands on the table and looked at the fireplace and all its finery and ornaments and thought how flimsy they were. A breath away was another order of life that could swallow this empire whole, and last night after twenty years of searching he finally saw one of the new order of Ruination. "Yes I saw one."

"Where?" Doulton whispered.

He shook his head ruefully. "I'd been a fool. I spent years searching when the answer was right under my nose. Blood and fear are the key, but I forgot."

"Forgot what?"

"That both can be found in our own backyard, not just the battlefield." He looked sad, reflecting on the lost years.

"So where in London is fear and blood found in abundance?" Doulton had the horrible feeling he meant Goldhawk Row.

"Smithfield," Galen said simply.

Lyle's brow creased. "The market you mean?"

He nodded, noting their confusion.

"Blood aplenty I grant you," Doulton said warily. "But fear? The only things that spill blood there are dumb animals."

He nodded vigorously. "Aye, just as I always thought, and that was my undoing. But an idea set in my head and it wouldn't be shaken, death and blood are all the same to Ruination, but especially fear."

"Fear? You're telling me that beasts 'feel'?" Doulton smirked.

Galen rocked his head in confirmation. "I could have found it right from the start."

"But beasts don't have the capacity for feelings." Lyle sounded indignant. "They don't even possess a soul, the notion is ridiculous!"

"All I can tell you is that fear and blood have soaked Smithfield for centuries, and it seems that valkyries are drawn to it." He ruptured an egg yolk with his toast, then smeared it around his plate before leaning over to eat.

"Valkyries?" Doulton asked. "You mentioned that before."

"The creatures we're looking for," he mumbled through his food.

"Wagner's maidens of battle and bloodshed?"

Galen didn't answer, but continued to shovel food into his mouth.

Lyle looked down at the top of his head, still wrestling with his news. "No," he said at last. "No I can't believe that. The good Lord made animals dumb for man's sake. They're not equipped with the same emotions as us."

"Tell Ruination that."

"We seem to have a theological conundrum on our hands," Doulton smirked.

"Take this seriously!" Lyle growled.

He looked away, trying to conceal a smile.

Galen wiped his mouth. "It's not a problem. We won't be discussing our findings with the archbishop will we? Why should we care if beasts feel or don't feel. The point is what we're looking for is there at Smithfield."

Lyle blinked a few times and settled back down. "No, I suppose you're right," he simmered down.

"So, what did it look like?" Doulton took a sip of coffee. "A beautiful Norse maiden perhaps?"

Galen's smile faded and he coughed into his napkin and took a sip of water. The two men waited for him to compose himself, then he began to recount what had happened at Smithfield just hours ago.

After waiting in the lower tunnels with no success, he made his way back into the Pandemonium above. The market heaved with bodies, both four legged and two, all presided over by the gas lamps' infernal glow. The ground wasn't in sight, it could have been cobbles or a Persian rug for all Galen knew. He'd come here expecting the day's trading over, but he'd underestimated London's taste for flesh. Today's trading had ceased and now tomorrow's had begun with hardly a pause between.

Trying to barge through was useless. He was bumped and jostled and more than once light fingers explored his pockets. He wasn't worried though, he had nothing worth stealing. Carts loaded with split carcasses, trotters, tongues, and glistening organs trundled past, their drivers cursing and cracking knees and shins to get folks out of the way, but he was frustrated. What he needed was an overall view. He clambered up onto one of the stanchions where girders supported the roof, and found himself head and shoulders above the crowd.

Together, he and Elios watched intently, ignoring the shouts, squeals and constant bleating. Sometimes he saw scuffles break out as men disagreed over prices, or animals tried to run for it, but the crowd was too dense and it concealed these little dramas as quickly as it offered them. The hands of the clock moved steadily onwards and still he watched, looking for something that only he might see. He saw both worlds at once, the material and the esoteric. Mortis-fairies passed over the crowd in dark clouds. On occasion they flew close to inspect him, but they were like bothersome flies and he had no regard for them. Neither did he have any regard for the animal souls that roamed Smithfield. Sheep, pigs, cows, goats, horses, geese and hens circulated the market in confused flocks. Their violent end had shocked them into remaining earth-bound and so they failed to move on. Galen thought any beast too stupid to know it was dead deserved an eternity of wandering, and that didn't just go for animal kind. There were lost people here too.

Suddenly an almighty riot went up, making his hair stand on end. The mortis-fairies fled in terror and the animals kicked and cried and men were generous with their sticks as they laboured to bring them back into line, not realising that a valkyrie walked amongst them.

"And then?" Lyle asked, transfixed.

"It was the result of twenty years of searching." He'd forgotten they were there.

Lyle scowled. "Well?" he jabbed him. "What happened?"

He framed himself, and continued.

It emerged from one of the girders, and Galen saw the iron was badly corroded. It had been hiding inside, and the metal had prematurely decayed as a result. At first it was just a shadow drifting through the crowds, but it moved with purpose, flitting between animal pens. It had been drawn out of hiding by its need to be close to death. Galen felt a tear run down his cheek.

The blackness yielded for a second and he caught a glimpse of the creature within. It was tall, at least twice the height of a man, and it had clothed itself in what looked like skins to hide its nakedness, but where the skins were torn he could see its form beneath and it was wraith-thin. Its face was hidden by a hood but he plainly saw that its arms were basically human if elongate. It caressed the piles of split mutton lying on a cart in fascination.

Then Galen coughed, hardly enough even for Elios to hear, but the valkyrie froze and then slowly turned his way. From inside the blackened hood, something scrutinised him and he felt as if his soul was being dissected. Elios whimpered, feeling it too, then it slowly raised those bony hands and lowered its hood.

It was Sophie, his lost sister.

"What did it look like?" Doulton asked as they reached the pivotal moment.

He'd got to the hard part now, the real reason he hadn't slept. For it to have mimicked her face the creature must have actually seen his twin. They wouldn't understand and he didn't want to explain. He coughed, took a sip of water, then lied, "It was an ugly hag of a monster. I never want to see such a face again."

"Excellent!" Lyle poured him a fresh cup of tea. "Can you return, and establish a parley with this creature, tell it we want to help it?"

"I'll go back tonight, but to commune with it directly I'll need the place emptying."

"That's a tall order, lots of people come and go there," Doulton cautioned.

"Some sort of danger or atrocity, something that'll close the place down for a while?" he pressed, "it's vital."

"It's difficult to arrange such things." Doulton shuffled uneasily.

"But you can do it?"

"We're the Illuminata, we practically own London," Lyle interrupted. "Leave that to us. Shall we say two days time until we can make Smithfield all yours?"

"Two days then," Galen agreed, "and I want to see what krakens you've got in barracks."

"What for?" Doulton asked bluntly.

Lyle scowled at him, then turned to Galen. "I'll have a driver take you to Hobbs Ash."

Galen smirked. "I thought a train ran straight there for Illuminata seniors only."

"Alas, no longer. There was an incident at Hobbs Ash last October and the line was destroyed."

"But the krakens are still stationed there?"

"Oh yes, all ten of them," Doulton said with ironic pomp.

"Ten?"

He nodded slowly. "Reserve machines that didn't see service."

"And what of the machines used in that 'great assault' of yours last year? You've got them at Hobbs Ash haven't you?" He sounded unduly anxious.

"A handful yes. None are operational, but they're at least recognisable, the rest were turned to powdered rust."

Galen knew the machines had been touched by Ruin. "That'll be perfect," he smiled and helped himself to more breakfast.

In all her years she never would have believed that she could come this close to Ruin and live to tell about it. They passed right into the tangled dead-walks. The shadows congealed into an impenetrable fog and the creatures' branches brushed against her as she glided by. She saw with revulsion that each was tipped with a delicate fingernail. "They're all under the spell," she repeated, stupefied.

Neet said nothing, but just hid in the cover of her hair while Strike piloted the staff and kept his mouth shut.

How long have they been here? she thought. *And what could sing an enchantment so sublime that even these fearsome creatures are subdued?* As she wondered, the sheath containing Raven's wand snagged on a branch. She reached around to secure it but a moment later and it happened again, and she stopped the staff.

"What's wrong?" Strike asked.

"It's him."

"The Timekeeper?"

"Maybe." She looked around. "What are you trying to tell me?" She stroked the wand-sheath and slowly edged forwards again.

The wand had belonged to Valonia. Was it possible that the mysterious singer was in someway connected to her? Sunday had learned the hard way that fate could be incredibly cruel, but it could also be incredibly contrived. Vast cogs and wheels seemed to mesh neatly together, bringing disparate events into harmony and the expanse of the mind that created it was so huge that she felt insignificant.

"You are far from insignificant," a voice sounded.

It was the last voice she had heard before she died. It was the great Timekeeper. "My Lord?" She halted again, and listened. Without realising, her hand touched the tiny scar on her cheek. "My Lord is that you?"

"Sunday?" It was Strike.

"I heard a voice, I'm sure it was him."

It was fair to say he was worried; clouds, geese and now voices. *"Him or not, let's find this thing and get out."*

He was right she thought, this wasn't the time. "Agreed," she willed the staff forwards again. "Find it and get out."

Before long she realised that the dead-walks weren't swaying randomly, but in unison, as if following an unheard melody or sharing a single intelligence, and it was the most sinister thing she'd even seen. Some of them had risen up on their gnarled roots, although they weren't really roots at all but jointed legs like those of a crab. They stood there, gently pulsing back and forth, with branches held high in worship. All around her came the creak of undulating trunks and swishing branches and a peculiar ticking sound that was eerily regular, almost like language.

"Are they speaking to each other?" she thought with a shiver.

"Maybe they're singing along to the tune?" Strike's remark had a sinister plausibility.

The darkness was broken here and there by drifts of snow and up ahead she could see the creatures were gathered around a clearing. "The song maker's in there," she realised.

Almost as if under a spell of her own she reached out and caressed one of the dead-walks. Its trunk was black and smooth like whale skin and as soon as she touched it she felt the weight of ages push down on her and knew it was Time, the gift of Ruination. Her fingers slid across the trunk and the sensation was gone. No witch had come so close to these things and lived to tell about it, and not for the first time she wondered if the Timekeeper was somehow protecting her. "My Lord?" she named him in a whisper, but her only answer was the sigh of swaying branches. "Dear champion?" she tried again, but the voice remained silent.

"It's there," Strike interrupted. *"Look."*

She saw a small mound in the clearing's centre. "What is it?"

"The source of the song."

She finally arrived at the inner circle. The trees here seemed to be the oldest, as their trunks were thick and their branches clothed with strange growths like lichen, but she knew no earthly organism would grow on these trees. She gazed around, feeling like a mouse amongst sleeping cats, and she saw something that would stay with her for the rest of her days.

The largest were so entranced that even their primal instincts were subdued. Under hypnotic relaxation their trunks had yawned wide to reveal their innards. It was vulgar, obscene even, but she found she couldn't look away.

"Sleeping with their mouths open." Strike's comparison was disturbingly apt.

The dead-walks had splayed their trunks and their fleshy innards pulsed with bluish blood. Her gut instincts told her there was something indecent about it. "We should go," she whispered, but just then a strong pulse swept through them and they arched ecstatically, splaying even wider, and her gaze drifted downwards and she saw what she dreaded. Embedded in its gullet was a human skull. She knew there would be one in each and she closed her eyes as the horror washed over her. "They're the people they grew from." She flattened a hand to her mouth, afraid she would be sick.

"Find it and get out," Strike brought her back.

She nodded, sending tears down her cheeks, and pressed on into the clearing. The darkness retreated and she saw the sky again. "Be ready," she warned and slowly dismounted.

Her feet touched down into perfect snow, indeed, there weren't even any animal tracks. Strike hummed inside her staff, while Neet was so silent and still that he could have been just a pebble on her shoulder.

Now she was closer the song rang in her ears and if she wanted she could have stayed and danced forever like the enchanted horrors, but she knew better. She bit her lip, and stepped nearer. There was a cluster of rocks like a small cairn, and at the centre of it a small wooden figure was jammed between the stones. "Is this it?" she asked, looking around, half expecting to see the Timekeeper suspended from a branch. It was him who had sent them here, and now she realised why. This relic had quelled a host of Ruinous creatures. She would have to use it to bewitch the berserks, *not* fight them. "Thank you my lord," she bowed and stepped up to the cairn.

She saw now that the figure was carved from a branch or root, but certainly not from any cursed dead-walk. It was perhaps twelve inches high, with the lower legs carved into a single spike jammed into the cairn. Rags sewn around it gave the impression of clothes. Its arms were just stubs, part of the wood's natural growth, and its hair was a tangle of rootlets. It wore a head-dress of crow feathers, beads and buttons. Its face was just two little pinhole eyes, and a knot in the wood resembled an open mouth and she couldn't decide upon its expression. Was it singing or crying? She reached out a trembling hand and then stopped. "Who made it, and why did they leave it here?"

"Who cares, grab it and go!"

"If I take it, what will happen to the dead-walks?"

"They'll awaken, be ready for a very fast departure."

"Neet?" she asked, but he was as helpless as the trees. "Useless bloody fairy," she muttered. "We mean you no harm little soul," she addressed the doll. Her fingers curled gently around it and as soon as she took hold two things happened simultaneously.

The first was hrafn-dimmu came fully awake. It filled her head with its memories of this strange place and immediately she knew what the figure was and why it was singing. The revelation was staggering and she was about to share it with Strike when far away the second event happened – the assassin struck at her thread again.

Inside the Timekeeper's glass the intruder had waited patiently. Even creatures from Ruin had threads, and hidden from the spider's gaze it curled tightly around one and bit just hard enough to awaken it.

Sunday grasped the doll and briefly became a bridge joining it to Raven's wand around her waist, completing the circuit. Hrafn-dimmu recognised the doll at once, and jerked like a firing bow, delivering its revelation. "Strike!" she blurted, "the wand *does* know this place, it used to be –"

She didn't finish.

From behind, there came a terrible sound like timbers splitting in a storm, followed by an inhuman scream that banished the trance in an instant. The dead-walks awoke. The largest instantly snapped their trunks closed with a wet clapping sound and the ticking escalated to a racket like hail on a tin roof. They swayed their greasy branches in fury and tore themselves out of the ground. Turf and rock erupted where their legs unfolded and a wall of black trunks advanced.

Neet yowled in fear, waking from the spell and finding a forest of living branches lunging for them, and Strike yelled a warning, *"Let's go!"*

She ripped the doll free of the cairn and was on the staff in a second, but fleshy branches lashed out and groped at her legs. She screamed and swung the little figure, using it like a knife, and it glanced off a branch, screeching like nails on a blackboard. "Strike! For Oak's sake get us higher!"

The horrible ticking became an incessant drumming, and Strike roared and drove forwards. Branches lanced out and clawed bloody lines down her legs. Neet darted from under her hat and sank his teeth into one limb that had anchored around the staff. As they climbed higher it spooled out like a length of intestine, but still it clung on, stretching and stretching. "Neet! Neet!" he screamed and did what the Cold Coast had taught him to do. He attacked.

His powerful jaws snapped closed and bitter ooze flooded his mouth. He spat it aside and mauled it again, and the dead-walk yielded. Its umbilical arm snaked away and the staff shot forwards, but the forest wasn't ready to let them go so easily. As one, each tree released its cargo of seeds and there was a tremendous noise like a string of firecrackers, as countless pods exploded, and in the next moment Sunday was plastered with hundreds of the tiny crawling things. "What the hell was THAT!" she screamed.

"Seeds!" Neet wailed. "Hungry seeds everywhere!"

Like blood sucking ticks, they began to scuttle over her body towards their goal.

"Oak no!" she moaned in horror. If just one seed invaded her, then one day there'd be a dead-walk splaying its vile branches to reveal her glistening skull. That thought almost started a landslide of panic.

"They're all over us!" Strike cried in disgust.

Seeds were crawling over her hands and scaling her bare legs. She wanted to scream, but she kept her mouth welded shut, knowing if they crawled past her lips she wouldn't stand a chance. They were already crawling upwards, through her hair and towards her face and once there, as every witch knew, they only needed a tiny opening and the horrific germination process would begin.

"We have to stop!" Strike yelled, *"We have to stop and get them off right NOW!"*

Neet did his best, trying to snap them in two, but even he wasn't immune. They'd just as eagerly force their way into his shrunken little body, and before long he had to stop helping her and fight for his own life.

As they careered crazily through the sky, Sunday raced to come up with a plan as well as hold on, and all the while Strike and Neet were either screaming in disgust or shouting things that didn't help. She puckered her mouth tight and clamped a hand over it, but instantly she felt them squirming between her fingers. *What do I do! What do I do?* She couldn't think straight, never mind fly straight.

Not far away the volcano showered the glacier with magma and she had an idea. It was dangerous to the point of madness, but she'd rather die that way than end up as a birthing womb for a dead-walk. The plume drew closer, and what she saw on the glacier's surface sealed it: hundreds of fractures resembling a giant web. She put her trust in him, turned and accelerated. "Neet!" she screamed through her hand, "hold on."

"What are you doing?" Strike stammered.

"Just let me fly!"

Now it dawned on him. *"No! are you utterly mad!"*

A seed wriggled into her ear. Soon they'd be inside her and she would be as good as dead. Neet burrowed into her clothes snapping at the living seeds as he went.

The fire drew closer, but she was a solstice queen and fire was her element. She had once perfected a spell to walk unharmed through the coven bonfire, intending it as a show stopper during Regal-Fox's solstice ceremony. Now she had a better use for it. But a volcano was hardly a bonfire. She thought of her delicate thread so far away and what manner of death would break it this time. Ignoring the crawling swarm, she recited the spell and readied her will.

Magma began to rain down around them, while the air grew baking-hot and choking sulphur poisoned her every breath. She saw lightning flicker inside the plume and knew she would rather die in there than be eaten from the inside. The volcano's fury filled her ears, and her fingers buckled under the seeds' supernatural persistence. *I won't fail you Strike,* she thought, and they plunged into the ash cloud and vanished.

The Timekeeper watched in horror as they were engulfed. He had commanded no such thing, regardless of what she believed. It was almost certainly suicide. "SUNDAY!" His cry echoed around the cavern and behind it he heard the assassin's satisfied laughter.

CHAPTER EIGHT

Wrecks of glory

"'Magic is alive, it is a living force and like all living things it evolves.'
'Higher Forms of Magic - a witch's meditations on daily life'
Author unknown

The disused railway station of Hobbs Ash stood by the Thames, overlooking the Battersea Reach on one side and defended by an inlet known as the Chelsea Creek on the other. The area was under heavy guard and looked impregnable, but if anyone could have seen it before last October they wouldn't have recognised it as the same place.

Where the grand station stood was now a mass of scaffold so dense that the building beneath was totally buried. The peripheral buildings were also undergoing repairs and there were deep pits filled with rainwater where the ground had been rent as if by an earthquake.

All of this devastation was caused by one lowly witch named Ada Crabbe. The Illuminata had used her in a highly experimental machine designed to transform matter, but she had thoroughly sabotaged it. She had paid with her life, but said farewell to this world in a cataclysmic explosion that had kicked them right in the seat of their pants. No wonder the men at Hobbs Ash harboured a deep hatred for the few remaining prisoners. They were all witches, the very ones Galen had in mind to use in his negotiations with the valkyries.

Duty-warden Topp hurried through the army of labourers. "Good day to you sirs," he saluted.

Doulton and Lyle made lazy salutes in return, while Galen stood to the rear clutching his cane and just observed. The carriage ride had been bumpy and left him feeling queasy.

"Lads are working double speed I assure you sirs." Topp led them off at a brisk pace, swinging his arms like a toy soldier, and Galen had the impression that Topp, a tall wiry man in his fifties, never took time off, and likely bathed and dressed according to a timetable.

"We've not come to see the repair work." Lyle pulled his gloves on as he walked. "Mr Galen here is our resident expert and needs to inspect the krakens."

Topp shot their 'expert' a glance, noted the scruffy man in a bowler and huffed something under his breath. "Might I remind you sir that our best devisers have already looked them over and their fighting days are over. I'm sorry if the trip has been a waste of your expert's time." He made 'expert' sound more like 'dung collector' and Galen smiled. He liked irritating people.

"That'll be for Mr Galen to decide," he sniffed.

"The place looks no better than last month," Doulton grumbled as he pulled his collar up. The weather was chill for April and the clouds had a wintry look about them.

"We're doing our best sir," Topp declared.

"What are those over there?" Galen pointed towards the docks where huge iron spheres sat inside an engine shed. They were as tall as houses and armed with long spikes.

"Prisons sir," he said, stating the obvious.

Galen frowned. They looked fearsome, impenetrable even, and not just physically. When he tried to assess what was inside he drew a mental blank.

"It's as though they're alive and guarding their secrets," Elios noted, taking a dislike to them also.

"You won't have been around to witness all the drama last year will you?" Doulton explained. "Those were the prisons for witches, they were built to be counter-esoteric."

"Resistant to magic?" Galen was mildly impressed.

"To a certain degree," Lyle added, "a captive would find their curses and evils suppressed. You can take a good look later. But first we'll take you to these krakens." He politely shooed him forwards as if June 21st were only days away.

"Resistant to magic?" Elios sounded disgusted.

Galen regarded the ugly machines. *"They can't have been that resistant, the covens got the upper hand didn't they?"*

"And here we are sirs," Topp waved a hand at the grand station where the krakens were housed. "Now if you'll permit me I'll be about my duties. I wouldn't want you coming back next month and finding the place still in a mess." He offered Doulton a withering look before marching away.

"Insolent chap," he muttered, then turned to the others, "right, let's be about it." He led them into the damaged station, through a maze of scaffold where the racket of hammers and saws was constant.

They followed to where the last krakens stood, all ten of them. Even the huge machines looked small in the cavernous space. They stood in ranks, patiently awaiting new knights to come and pilot them. Their paintwork was immaculate and they were all armed with crushing claws and helmets fashioned like fabulous beasts. Galen knew from experience that when their banners were hoisted they looked even more formidable. It seemed impossible that anything could stand against them. "These are the reserve machines," Lyle went on, "they never saw battle."

"And the rest?" Galen enquired.

"Just between us, what you see here is the total fighting force left in these islands." He sounded embarrassed. *And if Leonhard's spies already know that, we'll be the laughing stock of Europe,* he thought dismally.

"Our principal forge factory in the north is building new ones as we speak," Doulton added hastily. "In fact we have almost fifty close to completion." He didn't add that they were short on knights to pilot them, or the sections took weeks to assemble.

"Before June 21st I hope?" Galen was enjoying their discomfort. "And I suppose you'll be training up your finest young gents to pilot these new walking war machines eh?"

"Something like that." Lyle wanted to tell him to mind his own business.

"You should pick men who've learned to fight, instead of just chase foxes and gamble," he smiled. "Then you'd show witches a thing or two."

Lyle forced a smile. "We're investing all our hopes in your skills now."

"Best get to work then," he winked.

They passed the proud-looking machines, and came in sight of a second group of krakens, these held upright by chains and pulleys. They looked like diseased beggars in comparison and Galen immediately veered off towards them.

"They're the ones recovered from Kittiwake-coven," Lyle explained. "Galen? Where the hell you off to? I just said they're broken!" he shouted after him. Galen ignored him and continued towards the battered wrecks. "Where the hell's he going?" he scowled.

"Don't ask me, I didn't invite him here," Doulton sighed. Without waiting for a retort he hurried after him. "You needn't bother with them," he shouted, "none of them are operational."

"Aye, I know," he called over his shoulder.

Doulton caught him up. "But they don't work, they never will again. They were salvaged from the battle."

"Where's the rest?" Galen looked around, "I thought the task force comprised the whole garrison, but there can't be more than a dozen here am I right?"

"It did comprise most of the garrison."

"So as I say – where's the rest?"

"The rest couldn't be recovered."

"In what way 'couldn't be recovered'?" He tapped his cane against his leg impatiently.

"There were virtually no physical remains." His tone was grave.

"Ruined," Galen surmised. He pulled one of the tarpaulins aside for a better look. Underneath there was the suggestion of a foot. It stood as tall as he did, but the steel claws were horribly bent and the paintwork blackened. "They put up quite a fight didn't they? I'll bet they thrashed your lads good an' proper."

"They slaughtered many good men that day," Lyle brooded. "Made a lot of widows and fatherless children. They're anarchic vermin."

He thought of Rang-Shaa and all the other witches who'd rejected him down the years. "Aye, vermin," he agreed quietly. "Thing is though," he said, putting his own anger aside, "the krakens you've got here, they weren't just toppled by angry witches. They've been touched by something else all together."

"Ruin," Doulton muttered fearfully.

He let the tarpaulin drop and moved further into the stockpile where the shadows were deep and the smell of soot was thick. They made to follow, but he raised a hand. "No need, I'll find my way." He vanished into the shadows, cane at the ready. "Elios?"

"Those men are such fools," she despaired.

"Doulton's quicker though, I'll have to watch out for him," he warned.

Wreckage lay all around. He couldn't make out where one machine ended and another began. Some stood upright supported by chains, but mostly it was just a confused tangle of body parts. All of them were charred and deformed by great explosive force. A lion-sculpted helmet stared at him from the gloom. It had exploded from the inside like corn heated over a fire, making it ugly and misshaped. Its bronze finish had partially melted and globules clustered around the eyes like tears. "You've seen better days my lad." He patted the lion's nose and peered inside the cockpit where the knight had fought, and ultimately died. It was such a blackened mess that the incinerated knight might be still in there for all he knew.

He pressed on, and ran a hand over a great armoured fist. The fingers were as thick as a man's waist, and curled around the hilt of a shattered sword in a kind of death grip. Rivets trembled past his fingertips and he was able to hear the faint sounds of battle, of witches and knights screaming in fury as they exchanged blows, magic against steel. At last he stopped. "Are you ready then my sweet?" Confident of his privacy he held the cane across his forearm and waited for Elios to appear. She emerged warily and crawled on to his waiting arm. As always her beauty fascinated him and he smiled at her lovingly. "It's time for you to catch up with a few old friends," he twitched an eyebrow at the broken war suits. "They've been Ruined."

She raised her head and sniffed, then smiled as if he'd brought her a romantic gift. "Take me to them." And so they set off to find a suit of armour fit for a valkyrie.

Fire was everywhere, but Sunday saw only boiling night illuminated by the occasional lightning bolt. Comets of glowing magma shot past in endless shoals, red-hot cinders swirled in a blizzard, ice roared as it boiled to steam and the noise was like the end of the world. Without the spell's protection they'd have died instantly.

The dead-walk mites weren't so fortunate. Unprotected, they blistered and crackled, swelling to the size of chestnuts until they burst with a shrill scream. She felt their empty husks sweep past her and little by little that awful crawling feeling vanished.

"I can't see!" Strike cried. *"Are we heading up or down?"*

She dared to open her mouth a crack. "Straight on, just go straight on!" she screamed, burning her throat in the process. Any second now they should pass into clear air again, or so she hoped, the spell wouldn't last much longer. Then the blackness turned crimson.

Smoke gave way to devastating heat, and in the crater's forge-like heart she saw the impossible. What witch had ever flown through the hell of a volcano and witnessed such a thing? She could think of none and for a moment she was almost glad she'd come here.

"What in oak's name?" Strike exclaimed.

"Witch-Sunday!" Neet screamed right by her ear, "Look!"

Lava-trolls waded through the boiling lake, hurling blocks of magma at one another in trials of strength, roaring and bellowing. They were towering creatures with ponderous limbs like basalt columns and wrinkled skins of congealed magma. One of them looked her way and for a split second she connected with the earth-mind and its billions of years of history. She saw the very beginnings of the Blue-orb and even Hethra and Halla descend from the stars, bringing the dream of life to a barren world.

An instant later, Sunday penetrated the ash wall again and the divine vision was gone, and the air became a seething black ocean once more, punching out wave after wave of pumice. She clutched the doll, and its ethereal melody cleared her head, and at exactly the same instant the air suddenly cleared and there was daylight and the snowy fells once more. Ash and lava continued to rain down, but in a diffuse shower. They were out the other side.

She released the spell with a giant gasp like a diver surfacing for air. Without its protection the heatwave caught her up and she gagged on the residual fumes and began to cough and retch. Her eyes started to stream, so badly that the world became just a blur, and Strike's screaming only added to the confusion.

"Too low!" he yelled.

She rubbed ash and tears from her face and finally saw their plight. The ground zoomed towards them like a pure white page to put their mark on and she just hoped it was snow and not solid ice, otherwise today was going to end with a crunch.

The tips of her boots skimmed the snow and that was enough to send them spinning. She uttered something very unladylike, then the staff cartwheeled away with Strike screaming inside. The world spun head over heels, and all she could do was close her eyes and hope. Her throat was so dry that she couldn't even scream. There was a brief moment of flying free that actually felt rather wonderful, then she hit the ground in a cloud of powder-snow and the breath was ripped from her chest and her teeth cracked together.

Neet, fortunate creature that he was, simply fluttered safely down to earth. By the time he landed, Sunday and her staff had rolled to a stop and both lay unceremoniously in a crater surrounded by a shower of snowflakes. He regarded the witch with a kind of dazed despair. Since finding her yesterday he'd had to save her from being eaten, then suffered the indignity of being summoned, then entered the Ruin forest followed by a flight through a volcano. He was beginning to pity Valgard's berserks. "Your life always so dull witch-Sunday?" He shook his head and swept ash from his arms and legs.

She pushed herself upright and melted snow dripped down her face. "Aren't Sundays meant to be dull?" she coughed, then spat a mouthful of cinders. "Strike?"

The staff twitched once, Strike staggered from it and flopped down looking bewildered, and with his wings hanging limp. "We've landed?"

"Safe and sound," she helped him onto her shoulder. He swayed a little before finding his balance and then he looked back at the fuming volcano on the horizon.

"We came through that?" he asked, not quite believing it.

"We did. The dead-walks didn't," Neet said flatly, flicking one of the dead seeds from Sunday's cloak.

She reached up and brushed ash from Strike's feathers. "You flew like a hero," she praised him, then began coughing again.

"I did didn't I?" he smiled back, looking rather muddled.

She wiped more grime from her face then turned to the volcano, thinking of the incredible creatures at its heart. "Did you see them, the trolls I mean?"

"I saw them."

"I saw the twins," she confessed.

He swayed a little at this. "Then you're blessed."

"Forgiven maybe?" she hoped.

"Only you can do that." He regarded her thoughtfully. Her eyes looked sore and watery, and her face was streaked by snow and ash. It was fair to say she wasn't the solstice queen he remembered, and he was glad about it. "Life's got more interesting since we died hasn't it?" he said from nowhere.

She stared at him, then burst out laughing.

"Lot of fuss for stupid doll," Neet grumbled, settling on her satchel and pawing at the flap. But stupid or not he desired to hear that beautiful song again.

Neither heard him, they laughed together and right then Sunday felt she could take on a dozen berserks.

Her thread remained intact and the great spider dared relax again. Neet had a point: Sunday took a lot of looking after. "There are millions of lives to be directed," he shouted. "Millions bereft of their fate while we wage our petty struggle. Can we not let this one thread be?" He listened for an answer that he knew would never come. He could snap her thread and have done with it, let the Patternmaker win, but she called him 'dear champion' and what kind of champion betrayed such trust? She had come to him in the dark and showed him that life had value, not just a place in the weave. He couldn't abandon her. "Do you hear me?" he demanded, and even the assassin was still. Maybe the great planner of fate was considering his offer he thought. He sat poised over his garden of threads, as he waited for his impossible answer.

Finally a wrathful voice boomed around the cavern, followed by the rasp of silk as something slithered away into hiding. His stare shifted instantly in its direction, but he saw nothing. The Patternmaker had refused and his assassin had slipped away again.

"Very well," he said quietly and set about his proper duty, but there was only one thread he was interested in and he found that to him it was worth all the others combined.

"Back Galen," Elios clambered up onto his shoulder and pointed, "the feeling is strongest over there."

He ducked and squeezed between a kraken's legs. "This way?"

"Yes, keep going, it's getting stronger."

He stepped through oily puddles and crunched over a carpet of bolts and sheared rivets. "This one?" It was one of the few standing upright, but bound with so many ropes that it looked like an Egyptian mummy. It soared away into the gloom, but when he touched the battered metal even he could feel it.

She hummed contentedly. "Yes this is the one, it was closest to the black storm when it came."

"Aye, but not too close, otherwise there wouldn't be enough to fill a snuff-box." Touching the machine gave him a clearer picture of what happened. Ruin had finished what the witches begun. He glimpsed wild beasts of Ruination descending from a tear in the sky and ripping the life from everything they found; men, horses, plants, and even the very molecules in these machines. The worst affected were turned to dust, Ruined you might say, while the ones on the edge of the incursion survived, but their ionic structure had been altered.

Elios climbed down onto the kraken's foot. As soon as she touched it she shivered. "Yes the metal remembers, it should be altered enough to hold a valkyrie."

"Good, then we're done here."

"No wait, I want to see," she insisted.

"Very well, but no dawdling."

She felt for the steel's memories and listened to the story of that terrible day. She saw Ruinous beasts in their thousands and gasped in amazement.

"Elios?" He stepped closer.

"A moment, there's more."

The witches fled and the black storm engulfed the knights, then she saw something that caught her by surprise and sadness swept over her. The witches flew with thunder-sprites that were healthy, robust and full of fire, the way she longed to be. Distressed, she turned to hide her face.

"Elios, it's taking too much from you," he insisted and offered his arm, and reluctantly she climbed along it and back to the cane. "You're tired my sweet," he fussed her.

She smiled, knowing she was more than just tired. The awful black cane was her home and prison. She remembered the thunder-sprites she'd seen, but said nothing, and feeling defeated she slid back into the cane and he breathed a sigh of relief.

"Witches," he growled. They could have shown him the way to Ruin years ago. They had thunder-sprites full of vigour, while Elios paid dearly for her unique nature. No other thunder-sprite had ever been born through striking a dead-walk, and because everything in Ruin was upside down, aside from being the world's only Ruinous thunder-sprite Elios was also the only ever female one.

Thorpe went to Goldhawk as soon as he received Lyle's report later that day.

"We need to clear the place out sir, and I thought a murder enquiry might buy us enough time." Lyle poured his senior a brandy as he relayed Galen's demands, namely Smithfield all to himself.

Thorpe slid the glass from the table and swirled the amber liquid as he thought. "Aren't you forgetting something?"

"Sir?"

"For a murder enquiry you'll need a murder." He took a sip and found it adequate, then returned to his cigar.

Lyle had considered this and wanted to prove his mettle. "Someone lowly, a prostitute perhaps?"

He sniffed disparagingly. "Plenty of those thrashed around Smithfield, no it'll need to be more shocking."

He thought for a while. "Something Galen said; that this thing he's looking for will likely come if there's an atrocity."

"Atrocity?"

"His words sir, not mine."

"Huh, simple murder not good enough eh?" Thorpe looked pensive for a moment before nodding to himself. "I know the man for the job."

"And who shall be the, erm –," he floundered.

"I'll make some enquiries, we'll find the right medium."

Lyle found the word perfect and so finished his brandy with satisfaction.

"I shall return tonight at eight o'clock." Thorpe downed his drink in one gulp, tossed his half smoked cigar into the hearth and saw himself out.

The door closed with a muffled click and Lyle wondered. Right now Thorpe would be choosing someone to be their 'medium'. He looked at the clock, it was just before two in the afternoon. Between now and eight someone would die and they wouldn't even know it.

They stopped by a stream and the first thing she did was soothe her throat with a cool drink. Next, she carefully picked every dead seed from her clothes then shook them vigorously, before finally scrubbing the ash from herself and her staff. She dressed again quickly, but her clothes still reeked of sulphur.

"So why all such fuss?" Neet moaned again, "Stupid doll nearly killed us all."

"It wasn't so stupid when you were under its spell," she shot back.

"So what makes it so special?" Strike asked.

"We'll soon see: the wand knows." She drew hrafn-dimmu and held it flat across her palms. "This wand began life here."

Strike arched his eyebrows. "You mean we didn't just end up here by chance?"

"Chance? I don't know if there is such a thing. Hrafn-dimmu was on the verge of telling me when the dead-walks attacked."

"It was?"

"And what does speaking-stick say of speaking-doll?" Neet huffed.

"Let's see." She ignored his sarcasm, sat down with the wand and held it firmly, closed her eyes and listened to its tale.

The dead-walk forest had not always been there. Long ago it had been home to a coven of witches. One of their number was a girl named Valonia. The black wand was hers, and she named it hrafn-dimmu; dark raven. She carried hrafn-dimmu all her life, but in the end she made a gift of it to her finest pupil in the hope that together they might save Britain's covens. Her hope hadn't been in vain, Kolfinnia prevailed and the Illuminata were defeated. Then Sunday had come and claimed it to save it from their enemies. By chance or design, she became its new companion, not owner, because every witch knows a wand cannot be owned for it is a living thing and life is not property, but hrafn-dimmu hadn't forgotten its home. Just days ago Sunday had come ashore close to Valonia's original coven, now abandoned and left to the wilds. The witches had been forced out long ago, but they had unknowingly left something behind.

When she was eleven Valonia had been instructed by her coven-mother to place magical dolls called way-bewares, around the coven. Each sang a song of warning, keeping unwanted visitors away. When Valonia's coven had finally fled, they hastily collected the spell-dolls, but one of them was left behind.

It continued the song of warning, but alone now. The song pushed living things away, and wild animals gave it a wide berth. Years passed and the way-beware grew desperately lonely. It had the merest suggestion of a consciousness, but that was enough, and a small miracle happened on the lonely moors of Iceland without a soul around as witness. The way-beware 'evolved.'

If a song of warning made living things avoid it, then it would sing a new song it decided, one so beautiful that creatures would flock to it to listen and the little doll wouldn't be lonely any more. The way-beware's song was so beautiful that even the most dread creatures, emanations from the mind of Ruin, fell under its influence. They gathered from the corners of the Earth, because the most frightening are often the most afraid and needy for solace. This is how magic evolved, and the doll sang until one day hrafn-dimmu came again after so many years, bringing its new companion. They had need for the way-beware's magic, and with a little help from a weaving spider, they found the last survivor of Valonia's old coven.

She held hrafn-dimmu tenderly, and wiped a tear from her eye. Now she knew the truth, and the way-beware's story touched her heart. "Thank you," she kissed the wand gently. This is why she and Strike had been washed ashore here. She'd taken the wand to keep it from the Illuminata, and she'd been holding it when she died. Without a companion or purpose it had done the only thing that made sense: it had gone home, taking her with it.

"Does it tell us of the doll?" Strike hopped closer.

"Oh yes," she nodded, "it's called a way-beware. It was left behind long ago when the witches fled and its song calms the soul."

"And what of the black wand?"

"Hrafn-dimmu." She regarded it. "Yes it began life here too, this was Valonia's coven."

"Of Wildwood?"

"The very same." She stroked the wand respectfully.

"Hmm," he considered, "now I see what you mean about chance, or the lack of it."

She looked at him and neither of them smiled.

Now they had one journey left: to find Neet's monsters and stop them. Neet seemed little interested in the way-beware, now safely tucked in Sunday's satchel. She had lulled it into a peaceful sleep with a simple spell and would awaken it when it was needed, which would be very soon now. She hoped it would enchant Viking warriors as well as dead-walks. "Time we were off." She checked the sun. It looked frail at this latitude and dusk was not far away.

"Shouldn't we wait until dawn?" Strike wondered.

"No," Neet interrupted, "now is best."

Strike flashed him an angry look.

"We'll go now," she agreed quietly, and held the staff out.

Strike twitched his wings and sighed deeply.

"You're allowed to say no," she reminded him.

"Wouldn't dream of it." He climbed up and vanished into the wood.

"Neet," she said as she mounted, "direct me as we fly." He buzzed up on to her shoulder and clung to her hair. "Not so tight," she complained.

"Witch-Sunday never happy," he snipped back.

She said nothing, but as she secured her things her mind turned inwards. *This land is full of relics,* she thought, *lost wands, ancient warriors and lonely dolls.* Suddenly she just wanted to be back at Regal-Fox, with Farona fetching and carrying for her, and tending her beautiful hair, and with a warm fire and a warm bed to look forward to. But her home was gone and the silver fox around her neck was just another relic.

Neet settled on her shoulder, still muttering, and then the staff began to move, curving upwards higher and higher until the little stream was just a glistening thread. The volcano rumbled away to the north, disgorging black smoke, but Neet directed her back to the glacier, looking for a special opening that would lead to the terrible sleepers under the ice, but this time they had a special weapon.

"In there," Neet whispered even before they landed, and gestured to a dark hole in the glacier's flanks. They touched down on to slurry and mud. The first thing she saw were footprints and the first thing she felt was woe. She shivered at the sight of the cave entrance, cascading with melt water, and sapphire blue within. The barren floodplain was encrusted with boulders, and huge paw prints tracked haphazardly through the mud. Whatever made them walked on two legs. *"Neither man nor beast,"* Strike noted.

"They've awoken again." Neet clicked his teeth in apprehension.

She held the staff like a spear and now Strike appeared. Quickly he hopped onto her shoulder, eyes alert. "The moment of truth." Her voice dropped to a whisper. She opened her satchel, took the way-beware and woke it from sleep. Almost immediately Neet fell under its magic.

"Where did it learn such a song?" he asked dreamily.

"It's a long tale Neet." Now she understood the way-beware's power, she hoped to defeat the berserks without bloodshed, chiefly without *her* blood being shed. She pushed the way-beware into her belt, then she took her knife. "Neet," she declared, and he buzzed from her shoulder and hovered before her looking worried. "I think it best that Strike and I go on alone."

"If you think so," he agreed quickly, and looked away shamefaced.

She couldn't find it in herself to be angry with him. What could he do to help anyway? Very little she suspected. "If we don't come out of that cave Neet, the spell protecting you from the local fairies will end and they'll find you."

He regarded her stonily. "Maybe small price to rid the Cold Coast of his curse."

"You'd do that for your kind, when they'd kill you if they found you?"

He looked away, angry and embarrassed, and she saw that she'd been wrong about him, he wasn't quite the selfish creature he appeared.

"We're all taking a risk." She acknowledged his bravery without flattery and he looked grateful. "And so, I want you to take this just in case we don't return." With that she reached up and cut a lock of her golden hair with the knife. "Wear it until you get home, it carries the same spell that's shielded you so far and it'll continue to do so regardless of what happens to us." She had wanted him to show her the faded-realm, just a glimpse, but now the parting had come asking felt awkward and she let her simple request slip away. "And if we don't come back you'll have something to remember us by," she finished sadly, and reached out, careful not to touch his beating wings, and gently tied the lock around his neck where it hung like a scarf and glimmered in the evening light.

Neet stared in bewilderment, first at the gold around his neck and then back to her sapphire eyes. He opened his mouth to speak, but nothing came out and she could see he was shaking.

Without a word, she took her staff and followed those enormous footprint towards the gaping ice-cave. Neet wanted to call her back, tell her that she didn't have to do this. Life on the Cold Coast wasn't so bad and a hard life was better than death, which is what she faced inside there. When he first met her she was just a stranger he had no regard for and so he had tricked her into this bargain. Now though, he wore her hair around his neck because when she looked at him she didn't see the wretched creature he believed he'd become, she saw something of worth. "No witch-Sunday," he whispered to her receding back, "come back." But she was too far away to hear and he didn't have the heart to follow.

The cave loomed over her and she looked so small. In a second she'd be inside, following the tunnel down under the ice to where monsters slept on a bed of rotten armour and bones. He looked down again at the golden strands around his neck, a tear welled up and clouded his vision, and when he looked up again the witch with the broken soul had gone.

CHAPTER NINE

Sleepers in the ice

'Let sleeping dogs lie'
Traditional saying

Twice she fell while navigating the ice tunnel, both times flat on her rear. "I'm glad Neet's not here to see this," she complained, and rubbed her numb backside and picked up her staff again.

As they followed the tunnel neither of them spoke much. Sometimes the passage narrowed, or became so low that she had to crouch, or it curved out of sight and she dreaded what might be around the corner. It always led gently downwards however, and all around them was translucent ice and the tinkling echo of running water. The ice looked static, but it creaked and groaned like ship's timbers making her feel very anxious.

"I can hear the way-beware," Strike said quietly to her mind.

She looked down at the satchel. "Just as well, if it stops singing we're in big trouble."

"It's distracting. Is there a spell that'll stop it, just for the time being?"

"Yes – it's called will-power. Just try to ignore it." She crept forwards, wary of slipping, wary of the cave collapsing, and wary of what they'd find at the end of the tunnel. It seemed there was much to be wary of these days. "Oh Strike," she sighed, "where did it all go wrong, am I going to pay forever?"

He didn't like her melancholy. *"Do you remember that solstice feast two years ago? It was your nineteenth birthday."*

Her brow furrowed as she thought.

"That senior witch visiting from Shorewell-coven had a coughing fit when he saw you in your solstice dress."

Even without seeing him she knew he was smirking. The memory came back and she smiled. "I thought his eyes were going to pop from his head!" she whispered, trying not to laugh.

"Fair's fair, it was a very revealing dress."

"I learned later that someone had to give him a tonic to calm his nerves."

"Cruel thing to do to such an old man."

"Not so old Strike," she said shrewdly, "he still knew where to look even if he didn't approve." She smiled as she remembered her old life. Seduction and envy had been her tools, now here she was with a bruised backside and covered in fairy bites, creeping into a frozen tomb to fight monsters simply because she promised Neet, and all out of guilt.

"It's not guilt." He caught her unprepared, reading her thoughts. Sometimes a witch and a sprite could be too close.

"It's not?"

"No."

"What then?"

"Honour," he said simply.

"You think I'm honourable?" she laughed gently.

"Through and through."

"Fine mess all this honour of mine has landed us in."

"You wouldn't have it any other way though."

She inched forwards, hand against the ice to steady herself, and smiled. "No, I wouldn't."

On an island surrounded by a lake of blood sat Valgard. Lovers of glory liked to imagine he was the god of war, but he was so much more. His shadow loomed over the murderer waiting in the alley, the husband with cruel fists, the slaughter house, and the judge with warrants of execution. All of them fed Valgard.

He comprised a huge and shapeless mass cloaked in countless millions of crows. They swarmed over him, flapping and squabbling, and pecking at his carrion flesh beneath. Their numbers were so dense that nothing of him could be seen. Valgard was a mountain of living, seething blackness.

The mountain lurched, crows scattered then descended again, jostling for the best places. Valgard turned to the north, and two red pits opened at the mountain's summit as he looked towards something that had disturbed him. The fiery orbs stared out, withering all in their path, stripping away all matter and time until he saw the cause of his consternation. A witch had come to steal his champions.

The lake began to churn and boil. Its surface heaved and a thick crimson mist rose up. His thunderous roar cracked the sky and turned oceans to stone. The crows screamed and cackled and Valgard called his berserks to the fight.

The ice underfoot gave way to rock. They'd reached the glacier's foundations and found themselves in a honeycomb of ice tunnels on a bed of scoured basalt.

At least it's easier walking, she thought, even though her footfalls crunched loudly on the gravel. She dipped under an overhang and came out into a large chamber and the smell immediately made her throat clench. It was the stink of rot and animal filth. They'd reached their goal.

Her staff began to tingle as Strike powered up and she groped for the way-beware. Any moment she expected attack, but all she heard was her own breathing and her hand fumbling in her satchel. As soon as she grabbed the way-beware she held it up like a shield and raised her staff. Strike provided illumination and the staff glowed pallid blue. Now she was trembling and the fear began to trickle into her bloodstream, soon it'd be a river unless she controlled it. *I died once. I can do it again,* she thought coldly.

"I see nothing," Strike warned.

She took a step into the chamber, straight into a puddle of frigid water. The cave was enormous, stretching away into the shadows. Weak light filtered down through the ice, but there was no sign of Neet's monsters. *"More light,"* she commanded, and the staff's brightness increased.

Another step into the unknown and her foot scraped against something metallic. She looked down at a litter of sword hilts, misshapen with corrosion. Shards of rusty metal lay between them and the meltwater was oily and the colour of tanned leather.

She looked from her feet towards the centre of the chamber and saw helmets encrusted with rust nodules, rotten planking that might have once been shields, and of course bones: thousands of bones. It all looked untouched and ancient, or so she thought until her gaze fell on something clearly out of place. A flurry of small black and white feathers spilled out of a sack and amongst them she saw a puffin's head peering out. Its colourful beak was still vivid, as though the little bird didn't know it was dead. Next to it she saw a severed human head. Mercifully it faced away and all she saw clearly was a balding pate with a tissue of wet hair clinging to it. This had happened very recently. "They've risen again," she heard herself say. Finally her gaze strayed to a black pit lying at the cavern's centre and her heart shunted in her chest. "Dragon!" she exclaimed and jumped back a step. Before them was a snarling face with bulging eyes.

"Wait!" Strike commanded.

She expected it to lunge, but after a moment's disorientation her senses clicked. A carved dragonhead loomed out of the pit. The head was crude, being little more than a blunt curve with ugly eyes like those of a suffocating fish, and a gaping mouth of sawtooth fangs. The long neck was decorated with an angular criss-cross pattern that looked as though it had been carved with an axe rather than a fine chisel, and it disappeared down into the dark pit below. It was the decorative prow of a Norse longship. "I thought it was alive," she expelled a long breath.

"Was it from their ship?"

She just shook her head vaguely, but if the cavern held more than just bones, if this dragonhead was a token of their past then part of these terrible monsters must still be human and that gave her hope. "They're in there, in the pit." She advanced with the way-beware, stepping deftly through the weapons, past the dead birds and the lost head whose face she didn't want to see. Melt-water drizzled across her, it was freezing cold but she burned with fear.

"When I strike, the first bolt will blind them, be ready to close your eyes," Strike instructed.

"Only if we have to, remember I want the doll to subdue them." She crept closer. Blackness seemed to radiate from the pit in waves, carrying the smell of disease and savagery. The dragonhead loomed over her and she could see tiny icicles hanging from its open mouth like whiskers. The wood was hacked and studded with broken arrow shafts. It looked so fierce and ageless that it could have been Valgard himself. "Please, sing for me now,"

she whispered and pressed a kiss against the way-beware.

She advanced inch by inch through bones and blades until the edge of the pit lay at her feet and she could go no further. She readied herself and leaned over. Light spilled from her staff and illuminated its putrid walls, then down across the rocky floor revealing a pool of liquefied bones. But nothing else.

It was empty.

"Strike, where –"

"Hush!"

She stood perfectly still and listened. The way-beware's song drifted through her head, but other than that she heard nothing except for running water and the volcano's distant rumble.

"I hear breathing," he warned.

She stiffened, then concentrated and let her ears sift the silence for clues. The cavern seemed to give up its secrets begrudgingly, but soon she sensed it too: the sound of breathing from close by. It sounded like stones being ground together. The hairs on her neck stood on end and she swallowed a dose of fear and turned slowly to face Valgard's champions. There was only one place they could be. She raised the staff higher and craned upwards. Above her was a forest of icicles, each as thick as her waist, and nestled amongst them, like roosting bats, were three huge dark shapes.

Valgard's berserks stared down at her.

He dreamed of battle. Clontarf, Ireland, many centuries ago. A bloody day that was. He and his two companions broke the enemy shield-wall. Ireland's finest warriors were torn down by his hands, except these were not his hands. He saw huge claws where his fingers ought to have been. The brave attacked, but their swords broke against him, while others cowered or prayed for mercy, but all met the same fate, and brave or cowardly they all screamed the same in the end. The dream was ghastly, and always close by was Valgard's poisoned laughter, but today Valgard did not laugh.

Today there was music in the dream and it was so ethereal that the screams and clashing weapons melted away. Under the influence of the strange melody he was calm, rested and utterly at peace. Far away he heard Valgard call them to battle, then grow angry and roar in fury, but it mattered very little. The fight raged around him, but he was separate from it. Then he saw her.

She walked through the storm of weapons, oblivious to the armies slaughtering one another, and not a single man gave her the slightest notice, but she took his breath away. She was the most beautiful woman he'd ever seen. Her eyes were glacier blue and her hair fell to her waist and shone like gold. She drifted through the horror untouched by it, and he could see why: she clutched a miraculous doll to her chest. When he listened to the doll's song he remembered that he was a man, he even knew his true name again. All he wanted in the whole world was to follow forever and listen to that song. It was all that made sense, all he was born for. He turned to look for his companions. They had seen her too and they rose from the blood and filth to follow. Valgard howled in fury but even he was forgotten.

Three pairs of eyes stared down at her from the blackness above. "Strike!" she uttered, and raised her staff.

"No the roof will come down!"

He was right, she realised, and instead thrust the way-beware up in front of her. "Please sing, please sing!" she stammered.

The eyes above sparkled with cold intelligence and they were fixed, but not on her. They followed each tiny movement of her hand, or more precisely, the wooden doll she clutched in it. She swept the way-beware left – they followed, she moved it right – their eyes tracked it. "Halla's teeth! Strike, I think we've done it."

She didn't know it, but the berserks were hers the moment she stepped into the chamber.

"But now what?" he urged. *"What in Oak's name do we do next?"*

She suddenly realised that she had command of three terrifying monsters, and she didn't have a clue what to do with them.

While Sunday faced monsters under the ice, different but equally dangerous monsters were finalising their plans elsewhere. London had its own dark caves and Lyle's office at Goldhawk was the venue. Big Ben chimed eight and Lyle opened his office door for Victor Thorpe.

"This woman." Thorpe handed over a clipping from The Times and breezed past him. It was cold in there tonight. Lyle hadn't bothered lighting a fire, thinking he'd be away soon and something about their business made him want to hide in the shadows.

He took the clipping, pushed his glasses onto his nose and saw that it was dated three weeks ago. "Charlotte Anne Pilling of Love Lane, Guildhall," he read, "charged with causing a disturbance of the peace at Smithfield in February this year after instigating rowdy discourse with drovers over the alleged mistreatment of their beasts." The article went to say how she was a regular around the market, championing the birds and beasts and drawing attention to their plight.

"You'll need to lure her there," Thorpe ordered. "Woman has a weakness for dumb beasts, takes up against anyone she sees hitting the brute things." He shook his head in disgust.

"She'll have a full time job at Smithfield," Lyle joked politely.

"Just get her there tomorrow night."

"How shall I get her there sir?"

"Use your wits man! She's under the delusion beasts suffer, exploit that weakness. Just get her there tomorrow night."

"I'll do it right away, sir." And from the look on Thorpe's face he knew he'd better come up with something quick.

"Kollip has been briefed, and he knows what to do." Thorpe was already putting his gloves back on, ready to leave.

"Kollip?" Lyle didn't want to second guess him, but Kollip, the former Illuminata surgeon, wasn't altogether reliable. It was said that opium had an unwholesome grip upon him and although he'd do anything to fund his addiction, his behaviour was erratic.

"So long as the devil keeps a clear head he'll have no problem completing the job," Thorpe argued.

"I'm sure you're right sir, but –"

"But what?" He paused from lighting yet another cigar and fixed him with a cold stare.

"He's known to be a little indulgent."

"Atrocity, you said. Who better to perpetrate one than Kollip? The man's a perfect fiend." He gave a throaty chuckle and the cigar between his teeth wobbled as he lit it.

Lyle swallowed nervously. "I take your point sir."

Thorpe made for the door through a haze of his own expensive smoke, then turned back. "You are up to this aren't you Lyle?" he crackled without warning.

"Certainly sir."

He grunted a reply, then saw himself out. Lyle watched him leave and then looked at the newspaper clipping. *A convincing lie to draw an unknown woman to her death,* he thought. It was going to be a long night; he looked at the empty hearth and wished he'd lit a fire after all.

By nightfall, Galen rose and slipped into the Goldhawk library, taking his satchel and lantern. He left Elios sleeping. She'd been distant all afternoon and he had a shrewd idea it was the images of thunder-sprites that had set her brooding. She was dear to him, but she was prone to moodiness and fussing, and right now he wanted a little peace to make his notes. The library's locked doors proved no obstacle and he passed them without any magic at all, just an old fashioned pick-lock.

The library was dark and the silence gave the books more presence. They seemed to be humming away quietly in the background. He lowered the lantern flame because he loved the dark, and he walked contentedly, clasping the strap of his satchel. "You ought to be jealous ladies and gents," he addressed the books, knowing the one he carried had no counterpart here. The Book-of-Nine wasn't welcome, not even here amongst glorification of torture and executions. Witches didn't want him or his book, and neither did the Illuminata. As he walked he ran a finger along a highway of leathery spines listening to the books tell their secrets, until he heard a scratching sound coming from the darkness ahead, and he stopped. He dimmed the lantern further, edged silently around the corner and saw a tiny tree-fairy sniffing and scratching at the lowest row of books, and a cruel smile spread across his face. "You're a long way from living trees little 'un," he murmured quietly.

The fairy didn't hear him.

He stepped closer. "Only pulped, dead wood around here," he smiled.

It continued investigating the books unaware of him, touching each in turn with its rootlet arms, drawn by the presence of so much wood, but confused that it couldn't find a single tree. It rattled its wings, which were brown and veined like sycamore seeds and twitched its ears, which were broad and furred like beech pods.

Galen raised his foot slowly and silently. The fairy fluttered along oblivious, alighting here and there, still looking for trees that weren't there. "They're all dead my friend. Everything here's dead. Let me help you fit in."

His boot came down, and a harsh thud echoed around the library followed by a crunching sound. He twisted his foot once to be sure, then gave a satisfied nod and moved on. Lantern light briefly glistened over its remains, but nobody at Goldhawk would ever know. Only the very few can see fairies, and only the books would remember its passing. He continued, with the fairy forgotten and before long he found a quiet alcove where he could sit. He laid out his writing implements, turned the lantern up, dipped the pen and began.

Excerpt from the Book-of-Nine

Elios is disturbed. She laments not being of true sprite blood. I say little, but it worries me that she does not appreciate her Ruinous heritage, which I must confess I wish was stronger in her. Unbeknown to her, down the years I have encouraged her dead-walk nature whilst subduing her thunder-sprite instincts. These deceits are essential for me to benefit from her insights. These matters aside, there is better news today. I have located a number of krakens infected by Ruination, which might hold a valkyrie. Many questions remain, but if a valkyrie can be brought here and if the machines can withstand their touch then we have the beginnings of a valkyrie army. I almost pity the fools that arrive for the tournament expecting a match of honour and gallantry.

'Fools' he looked long and hard at that particular word. There were fools all over he thought. Plenty in the Illuminata and plenty in the Book-of-Nine, crucially though, was he one of them? He sat back and wondered. Many had tried to solve the ninth chapter had paid with their sanity, now here he was walking the same path as some of the Niner's most notorious cultists.

Isaac Cornell, for instance, went to great lengths to collect the bedding and garments of infants taken by crib-robbers. After years of searching he slid into a failure-induced dementia. The last Galen heard he'd made a set of clothes from all those soiled rags and wore them constantly in the belief they could protect him against the effects of time.

"Ruin takes its own price," he said to himself.

He had given a lot of thought about what to do if his plans failed and Sophie was denied him. But there were compensations if all went wrong. He toyed with a fanciful idea, smiled coldly, then took his pen and added a few additional lines.

If I cannot finish the ninth chapter all is not lost. I have the beginnings of my own army do I not? The question occurs; who would be the valkyries' chosen Knight Superior? It would be a privilege to bestow this title upon my absent master. It is my one burning desire to see him pleased by my efforts.

He closed the book and picked up the lantern. "Knight Superior of the Book-of-Nine," he smiled, thinking his master would appreciate it also.

Chapter Ten

The straw lady

'Even the most insignificant commoner's life can be of profit to the Knighthood,
whether it be given freely or taken by force.'
Alexandrus Marrium, 2nd century Knight Superior

She backed out of the cave without taking her eyes from the roof,
holding the way-beware like a crucifix warding off evil.

"What do we do?" Strike blustered.

"I'm thinking, don't rush me!" But if she had any ideas they were
hiding. She ducked under the ledge and into the tunnel, only there did
she dare to turn her back. A heavy thud sounded from the cavern behind,
followed by two more, then the scrape of gravel, the splash of water and
the distinct click of claws on rock. "They're following." She was horrified
and exhilarated. The plan was working, but she didn't want to see them
emerge and so she turned and started back to the surface. For no rational
reason she kept the way-beware held high, making sure whatever was
following could still see it. For a while she walked on in silence, until
there came the sound of something large grunting in effort and the hiss of
coarse fur sliding against ice. They'd breached the cavern's narrow mouth
and were in the tunnel with her. As if to prove it a burst of foul odour
wafted after her.

"Please sing, please sing," she chanted softly, knowing the way-beware was
her only protection. Strike said nothing but the staff was hot with his anxiety.

It percolated through into her and she fought to keep her pace steady and ignore her instincts, which screamed at her to run from the sound behind, the sound of lumbering feet and breath like a steam engine. "Please sing, please sing," she moaned over and over.

Time, as the Timekeeper would tell you, is a very fickle thing. Sometimes it runs, gallops, even skips ahead and other times it crawls or stands perfectly still. Sunday firmly believed time had simply died. The journey was endless and each time she turned a corner she half expected to be back in the berserks' cavern, caught in some infernal loop.

She slipped once and fell to her knees, but kept her deathly grip on the doll. There was a deep rumbling growl from just over her shoulder, sounding almost like an exclamation. "It's all right!" she chattered nervously. "The doll's fine!" *What if it stops singing?* she thought as she clambered up.

"If that happens, aim for the roof, I'll do the rest and the tunnel can collapse behind us," Strike promised, and she was glad one of them still had their wits about them.

The blue in the ice seemed to intensify and she knew that meant they were nearing the surface, but she still didn't have a plan.

"Leave the doll, they'll sit round it like dunces until they rot," Strike suggested.

She snatched a glance at the little way-beware. Its song was so lonely yet so hopeful. It had waited years for company and all it found were wicked trees and fierce monsters. "No, it deserves better." She couldn't abandon it. Anything that knew loneliness had feelings.

"Then lead them to the volcano. Magic or not, I'll warrant the deep fire will finish them off." His suggestion was so cruel, yet so perfect that she reeled at the callousness, then in the next instant she found herself tempted.

"I don't know, Strike . . . I just don't know." But what other choice was there and could she knowingly lead these creatures to their death? They were really men after all. The entrance lay ahead and she could see daylight. One way or another she had to think of something fast.

So many times he had passed under this frozen gateway, and always to spill blood in Valgard's honour, but now he saw so much more. The beautiful woman led them, and the sky beyond was dusky red. In his years of constant rage he had never thought to look at the sky, but now the sight of it was almost as beautiful as her. He turned to look at his companions and sure enough they followed him, just as in life when he had been their chieftain. The sky beckoned and he felt the excitement of freedom.

Neet fluttered a little way from the tunnel, then changed his mind and flew back again. He'd tried to leave a dozen times, but just couldn't. "Stupid witch-Sunday," he cursed, not meaning a word of it. He reached up and touched the hair around his neck, and wondered again if she would ever appear. Then he worried about more immediate things, such as what would happen if those hostile fairies could see him. Only the talisman around his neck kept him safe, but that wasn't the only reason to treasure it. "Witch-Sunday," he moaned softly, "please come back."

On very rare occasions the thing we want the most comes just when we need it, and Neet was privileged to have one of those moments right then. Sunday appeared at the mouth of the cave, walking slowly and purposefully, carrying her staff in one hand and the way-beware in the other. He felt a burst of gladness, but the look on her face told him to postpone the celebrations. "Witch-Sunday!" He flew closer, then the smell of offal and fear-sweat rolled out of the cave like a cloud and he knew what was following her out into the evening light. "She claimed them!" She was taking the disease out of the Cold Coast like a surgeon cutting away a bad limb.

She shot him a warning look and he sank below a rock, barely peeping out to see. The dark cave mouth moved as if it was alive, and he thought his eyes were playing tricks, until he realised the undulating blackness wasn't shadow, it was *them*.

They lumbered out from under the ice, following Sunday. She looked pale and under a spell of her own, but one of terror, then Neet felt the way-beware's miraculous song in his ears and the dread ebbed. He watched as if it were three graceful unicorns following her rather than Valgard's cursed champions. He gasped in awe, not seeing the way they walked upright with pendulous arms trailing massive claws, nor did he see the foamy ropes of saliva painting their jaws or the matted fur rippling over immense muscles.

The sunset sky called to him, it was a hazy pink but whether it was blue, black or red he knew he could lose himself up there. The constant clamour of battle and

Valgard's booming voice were gone, and now he longed to fly. He gestured to his companions and they too had the same look of longing. The girl with the special song and the golden hair had freed them.

"They're right behind us!" Strike looked back and regretted it at once.

"I've an idea," she swallowed. It wasn't much, but it was the best she had. "On my command we fly, but not too fast."

"Clear, then what?"

Her eyes flicked sideways and she caught a shadow to her rear, close enough to touch. "Then we –"

Suddenly there was movement behind, fast and deliberate, and the shadow lunged.

"Sunday!" he bellowed.

Without thinking she threw herself forwards just as something black swept over her and blotted out the light. "NO!" she screamed, convinced claws and jaws were about to shred her, but what she saw left her speechless.

She lay looking up at the sky and three huge eagles rushed past only feet above her. They were close enough for her to see their smooth talons and the evening sun gleam across their bronze feathers. Their passing sounded like a gale, and the downdraught from their broad wings lashed at her face and swept her hair across her vision and for a moment all she saw was a haze of blonde.

"They're leaving!" Strike shouted.

"What?" Confused, she swept her hair from her eyes and saw he was right. They had transformed and now they were heading skywards. Their leader had dazzling white tail feathers and his two fellows flanked him. "They're going!" She looked from the eagles to the little way-beware with amazed reverence. "You did it," she whispered and the doll regarded her as though it was all in a day's work.

Strike appeared and landed on her chest, staring after the berserks, now soaring into the sky. "What did it do to them?" He looked from the eagles to the way-beware in her trembling hand.

She shook her head. "I don't know, but I'm grateful."

Neet landed close by looking stunned. "You sent them away."

Strike climbed down as she sat upright, and dusted snow and gravel from herself, and regarded the way-beware. "He did, not me." She straightened the doll's ragged little cloak.

"Then Valgard's curse is gone?" he asked hopefully.

"I think so, yes." She stood and Strike landed gently on her shoulder and together they stared up at the birds, now just ragged black oblongs in the sky.

"They're gone," Neet whispered again.

"So what *was* your plan?" Strike asked.

"Oh, doesn't matter now, but it would've worked."

"Always so modest," he smiled.

"As a solstice queen should be," she joked, then tossed her hair prettily.

The sound of Neet's laughter made them turn. He was pointing at thin air. "Look, look!"

They couldn't see the cause of his delight. It's said only the very strongest witches can see the souls of grass and stones, but Neet could. Valgard's curse was like a cloud that was now passing and souls began to shine like stars, glinting from pebbles, snowflakes and moss. "Souls in their hundreds." Neet gazed all around, seeing more and more emerge from their long hibernation. "No not hundreds, in their thousands! More than thousands!" He zipped back and forth, giddy with joy. "How much more comes after thousand?"

Sunday looked around at the darkening landscape. The only living things she could see were themselves. "The faded-realm is something for your eyes only Neet." She felt a touch of regret and reached up to caress Strike's feathers.

Neet thought of the gift he carried around his neck. Maybe there was something he could give her in return. He whisked onto her other shoulder and sat by her ear.

"You wish a ride home?" she asked, misunderstanding.

"No, that much I can manage, but first see the world as fairy-kind do." He clambered closer to her ear and whispered something, and she felt his little teeth gently rasp her skin.

His words unlocked a long dormant part of her brain and it was as if the world around her bloomed. Souls appeared around everything; motes of dust in the evening sun, sparkling grains of ice, the clouds above and even the air had a shimmering cast to it as the countless oxygen molecules revealed individual souls. Fairies had begun to come out of their haunts to marvel at the spectacle, and she saw moss-fairies, birch-fairies, mud-fairies and a host of others. It was like watching a world being reborn. Her hand went to her mouth and a tear ran down her cheek.

"Sunday?" Strike looked concerned.

"Oh Strike I wish you could see this!"

"Won't work on sprite kind," Neet said abruptly, it was only witch-Sunday that had a place in his heart.

As quickly as they'd appeared the souls began to dissipate, fade and then vanish altogether.

"They're disappearing!"

"Can't last for long, must be a fairy to see them always," Neet said blandly.

"But I don't want it to!"

"Then learn the proper spells and see the faded-realm." His tone was formal now. He didn't want her knowing how special she'd become to him.

"Fairies," Strike shook his head in disdain.

Neet floated from her shoulder, and drifted into the air.

"The curse is ended?" she asked, as if Neet's vision weren't proof enough.

"It is ended," he agreed.

"Then I suppose the time's come to leave."

"Where?" Strike muttered absently.

"Home."

"Home?" They didn't have one anymore, but the idea of looking for one sounded good. "Long flight back to the isles of Britain."

"Dangerous too. And where do we go when we get there?" Sunday shook her head.

There was a waiting silence begging to be filled by one name.

"Find Kolfinnia?" Strike said cautiously and waited to see her reaction.

"Maybe," she whispered. She wasn't ready yet to face the young woman she'd betrayed.

"Ahem," Neet coughed, "you'll take him?" He jabbed an arm at the way-beware. "Fairies get little work done if he stays and sings." It broke his heart to think of never hearing that song again, but it was for the best.

She regarded it anew. "He needs a home too. His last coven left him here by mistake." An idea began to form in her mind. The witches who'd placed this very doll had fled Iceland, and one of them had founded a new coven, none other than Valonia of Wildwood. The doll belonged to her, or at least her next in line if she was no more. There were so many unanswered questions about last October's great battle. She looked around, as though a dream had ended, feeling there were a million things to do. Regal-Fox witches including Alfred Berwick, her own coven-father, had been captured. If she needed a new purpose this was it. "We're going to London Strike."

"London?" he asked, incredulous.

"There'll be survivors taken captive."

His eyes narrowed. "And you mean to break them out?"

"If I can."

"Would this be anything to do with the 'note'?"

She said nothing, but her cheeks burned.

He coughed awkwardly. "I'll fly with you 'til the end, you know that, but," he lowered his voice, "but there'll come a time when you can't pay anymore." She just frowned at him.

"If you can't forgive yourself you'll keep finding new ways to atone until you just get yourself killed."

She looked blankly across the hills and out to sea, not knowing what to say. The captives at Hobbs Ash had been taken long before her terrible sin, but that didn't lessen her guilt.

"And perhaps no kindly spider to bring back life eh?" Neet said at last. They both looked at him, stunned.

He hovered inches from her face, staring at the hourglass on her cheek.

"How much do you know?" Shamefaced, she raised a hand to the little scar.

"Not so much." He didn't want to know her past, or how she earned a broken soul.

"Sunday, saving them won't save us," Strike advised gently.

She turned to look at him, admiring the way he said 'us' when he had nothing to repent. "Those prisoners aren't there because of us, I know, so helping them isn't atonement. It's justice. Can you imagine the fate they'll suffer?" *Or have suffered?* she was helpless to wonder.

He considered before speaking. "Alfred Berwick."

She nodded. "Susan Lilly, Martha Kelly, Jack Clay." She could add many more names. "They're Regal-Fox witches, *our* witches."

He knew she was right. They had to do something. "So, London it is."

She smiled, grateful again for the chance to know him better.

"Land of Britain that way," Neet waved an arm at the horizon, half wishing that he could go with them.

"Take care of that," she pointed to the lock of hair around his neck, "don't let it get scruffy or tangled. I don't want fairies to think I have hair like a scarecrow. I'm a witch of high rank you know." She gave him a mysterious smile.

"Wear it always," he said with utter conviction.

"Britain?" Strike reminded her.

"First things first, I haven't had a decent meal in months." She looked westwards, along the empty coast. "Come on Strike."

"Where?"

"Shopping," she winked.

Lyle stood sheltering under his umbrella and watched the chaos boil over at Smithfield Market. The night was wet, windy and downright foul and the common folk who worked there were no better.

Late last night he instructed a runner to deliver a note to the Pilling woman's address, then he fretted the whole day wondering if it would work and what Thorpe would say if he failed. Now from the look of it the note had worked doubly well. Smithfield had been emptied, the trading folk were outraged and apprehensive, and Scotland Yard were already at the scene. He saw constables struggle to eject the last ruffians and hold back an army of others wanting to get out of the rain and get on with trading, butchering or swindling.

Lyle was thrilled that one small piece of paper could cause so much disruption and he thought back to Thorpe's example with the bank notes. "Paper is power," he nodded and checked his pocket watch. In another five minutes he would lead his team of Goldhawk men in, order the Yardies out and Galen would have the place to himself.

Inspector Lord pointed his lantern back into the sow-pen where the dead woman lay and shook his head in disbelief. He'd policed London for over thirty years and thought he'd seen every example of man's inhumanity to man, not to mention inhumanity to women, children and animals. Until tonight that is.

"Right enuff place forrit sir," Barclay, his constable, muttered.

"Is the Chief Inspector on his way?" Lord asked.

"Aye sir."

"When was she found?"

"Just before midnight," Barclay checked his notebook.

Frank Lord stared around at Smithfield market. It should have been heaving, a typical Thursday night you might say, but everyone had been removed, which had been a major operation in itself. Two of his constables had been assaulted, which meant more paperwork on top of everything else. The market echoed with mournful bleating and raucous squealing of penned animals. Beyond, he could hear shouts of outrage from the packed streets as hundreds of sellers, drovers and poultry men stood in the rain. To make matters worse the night was wet and wild. Lord sighed heavily, knowing it was just a matter of time until tempers frayed and more fights broke out.

"It's ugly out there sir," Barclay looked towards the west-gate. "Lads will have their work cut out."

"Not so dainty in 'ere," Lord muttered. He raised his lantern again and looked down at the woman and wondered if there really was a heavenly father. If there was he worked in mysterious ways indeed. Two local butchers had confirmed her identity. They even jested she should have been served up with cress and pickles.

Charlotte Anne Pilling was the middle-aged wife of a local tailor. She came regularly to Smithfield out of pity and the traders knew her and generally despised her, calling her the 'sheep-lady' amongst other less flattering things. She tried to offer the animals what little comfort she could in the way of fresh water and kitchen scraps. She was often seen arguing with the drovers, and twice she'd been assaulted, but she continued. Until tonight. Charlotte Anne Pilling hadn't just been murdered, she'd been taken apart.

She lay half naked in a mound of filthy animal bedding. Her dress had been torn open and lifted up over her face, making the indignity even harder to witness. Strands of straw floated in a mire of blood, which looked bottomless under the flickering gaslight. Whoever had killed her had then gone to work on her, opening her up and painting a picture of horror with her innards. Now there was little difference between her and the rows of split pigs dangling from the stands up and down the market hall. If someone put a chalkboard over Charlotte Anne Pilling with a price per pound on it nobody would have noticed the difference.

"Butchered," Lord uttered in disbelief. He just hoped her death had been swift and she hadn't been alive when the killer had begun his madness.

"As I say sir, right enuff place forrit," Barclay said absently. He seemed unmoved.

"Any evidence?" Lord asked vainly.

"A note." Barclay held up a square of paper. Lord took it carefully and opened it up. "In her coat pocket."

Lord unfolded it and read it. The type could have been from any of a thousand typewriters. It was anonymous and scant help at first glance.

Dear Mrs Pilling, I understand that you have a hope of aiding the abused beasts at Smithfield. I represent an influential group of devoted Christian-fellows and also desire to strike a blow against the dreadful conditions endured by God's four legged creations. We must be discreet, but if you wish our assistance I shall gladly meet with you. Ten o'clock tonight. Smithfield's west gate.
Yours respectfully
A friend

"A friend." Lord felt his age tonight. Had someone played upon the woman's compassion, lured her here and gutted her? But how had the killer struck, butchered her and then vanished in such a bustling area without being seen? *It's as if he's a ghost,* Lord thought soberly. He checked his own watch and saw it was just past 1am and he looked around at the west gate wondering what had transpired there a few hours ago. Who had she met here and what happened in those missing hours? Was she killed here or elsewhere and why? From what he'd been told, any one of

Smithfield's workers had a reason to kill her. "I've seen enough, pass me that cover-all." He snapped his fingers and a rough blanket was pressed into his hand and he immediately draped it over her. Even the dead were entitled to dignity he thought.

"Sir?" a voice called, and he looked around. Miller, another of his constables, was shaking the rain from his overcoat, looking apologetic.

"Is Chief Inspector Able here?" He couldn't understand what was keeping him.

"No sir, but there's a few other gentlemen and they've come about erm, another matter you might say," Miller fumbled.

"Spit it out Miller," he demanded.

He jabbed a thumb over his shoulder to where nine or ten men had gathered at the police cordon. "It's them sir, they say they'll be taking over for now."

Lord saw that they were all wearing dark overcoats and looked very official. "Taking over?" He didn't know whether to be angry or grateful.

"Bloody hell they won't," Barclay growled, looking roused at last. "Who in God's name are they?"

Lord didn't answer, he was already striding towards the newcomers. Barclay and Miller fell in at his side, and he balled his hands into fists. He wasn't in the mood for departmental politics and if it was the newly commissioned Special Branch he'd tell them to take a running jump. But from this distance the only man he recognised was Chief Inspector Able, his own superior.

"Inspector," Able waved him close and led him a little way off. He looked shaken, and spoke quietly. "These men are taking command of the investigation."

Lord looked them over. Nine men in dark overcoats, all of them dripping with rain, all with the same lean, sentiment-less faces, and a tenth man in a shabby suit and battered bowler hat. He could have been the killer for all Lord knew. "On what authority sir?"

"Orders direct from Whitehall," Able looked afraid.

He blinked in surprise. Whitehall intervention could mean only one thing. "They're from Goldhawk?"

He nodded gravely. "They think this is connected with, erm," he floundered. Being a devout Methodist, he found dealings with Goldhawk uncomfortable. "Something to do with the occult," he finished quickly.

"A ritual murder?" It made a twisted kind of sense. Lord looked back at the Goldhawk men. Last year London had reached melting point after an occult assassination sparked hysteria, and the city was only just returning to something like its grubby self. "It would explain a lot," he mused. "But that doesn't make them criminal investigators sir, when does Scotland Yard get to start the investigation proper?"

He shrugged impotently. "That's not for me to say, my orders are to keep the public out until Goldhawk have finished."

Lord sensed his humiliation. A Chief Inspector was being given orders from men he didn't even know, and all they trusted him with was crowd control. He straightened. "A crime like this demands a proper investigation, not mumbo-jumbo spiritualists and amateurs." He found himself half wishing Special Branch would turn up and start treading on a few toes.

"Frank," Able gripped his arm tighter, "do this for me, just let this one go. Let 'em get on with it. Then they're out of our hair."

"Have you *seen* her sir? Have you seen what's left?"

He nodded evasively. "I know it's a bad 'un Frank."

You don't know the half of it, he thought and turned to look back down the gloomy aisle, to where a kindly lady lay in tatters. "And will Goldhawk be telling Mr Pilling how his good lady wife finished up tonight, or are they trusting that particular duty to us?"

Able looked down at the floor where his own sad reflection gazed back at him from the slurry. From somewhere close by a ewe bleated softly. "Be about your duties Frank," he mumbled and his hand dropped from his arm. It wasn't just Inspector Lord who felt old tonight.

"Wait here until we summon you," Lyle instructed Galen. There were still uniformed constables around and Goldhawk business wasn't for the likes of them. The police waved them through and he headed towards the murder scene with Doulton by his side and a lantern in his hand. The remaining Goldhawk staff followed like a line of mourners. Lyle was uneasy, and not just because of what they might find. He'd carried out Thorpe's orders, but failed to tell his junior the finer points. Doulton was under the impression they'd find a neatly done in woman of ill repute.

Meanwhile Galen stayed put, watching them with great interest.

"This might be important," Elios advised.

"We'll soon see," he agreed, and within moments he'd cast a spell that made their secrets his.

"Our man made quite an impression," Lyle commented from the corner of his mouth.

Doulton hardly heard him for the rain assaulting the roof and the incessant cry of penned animals. "Not too much of an impression I hope, we only need the place closed, not city-wide hysteria." But he gathered from the market folk that something drastic had happened here tonight.

Francis-Joseph Kollip was a former Illuminata surgeon with an addiction to opium. He did what was asked and took the money. It was a tidy relationship, but Doulton had a bad feeling as he walked towards Kollip's handy work. For starters there was way too much fuss over a throttled prostitute and the atmosphere around Smithfield was tense. He hoped to God that the deranged old bastard hadn't gone too far. He had met him once some years ago and was still haunted by his blank stare. He'd never met such an empty man.

'A tidy, quick job, not too nasty, just enough to buy us some time to work unobserved.' Lyle had assured him everything would go smoothly. They passed a row of handcarts loaded with skinned cow heads and the animals' bulging eyes and blank stares reminded him of Kollip.

Lyle arrived first. "Good God," he groaned, but in exasperation not sympathy. Galen wanted an atrocity and by heaven he got it ten fold.

"Well?" Doulton reached his side, saw the carnage and the wind left his lungs in a rush. "No! This isn't what we agreed!"

"Keep your voice down," he growled.

Doulton had the distinct feeling of being trapped. "I want Kollip bringing in," he simmered. This woman hadn't simply been killed, her humanity had been stolen.

"What for?" Lyle peered into the pen, mildly curious.

"Isn't it bloody obvious. Look at what the maniac's done!"

"He's done what we asked of him." His tone was cold. "He caused a distraction and closed Smithfield."

"We –," he began, then checked himself and started again, "I didn't ask for this!"

Lyle turned on him. "*We,* that is to say you and I, were instructed to clear Smithfield, and dispatching a life to that end was considered legitimate."

"No, no it was not, we said —"

Lyle grabbed him and pulled him close. For a small man he was remarkably strong. Doulton could see veins pulse in his neck and his eyes betrayed a hint of fear. "The time to wrestle your conscience is passed. Now I've no more liking for this than you, but what's done is done and *you* are part of it." He shoved the taller man away and they stood regarding each other like a pair of gunfighters.

"It shouldn't have been like this," Doulton fumed. "That fiend!" He looked accusingly in Galen's direction.

"Would it have suited you better if he *hadn't* indulged himself after he'd strangled her? It wouldn't make much difference to her, she'd still be dead."

He couldn't think of a reply, and simply clenched his fists and thought how satisfying it would feel to hammer one of them into Lyle's face and the other one into Galen's.

"A word of advice," Lyle removed his spectacles and polished them, "dispense with the delusions, death is death, it's no good trying to put a pretty face on it to appease your morality."

Doulton thought on this for a moment and remembered what Galen had said about places of 'blood and terror'. Everyday they put a pretty face on death by reminding folks that dumb beasts didn't have feelings or souls. Galen's fixation with Smithfield however proved otherwise. He was going to retort with this but he was too weary.

"Now, let's get on," Lyle dismissed his worries and beckoned to Galen, still waiting patiently by the west gate.

He raised his cane in reply, then began towards them without any sense of urgency.

Lyle pushed his spectacles back into place. "Regardless of the means, we have privacy and time to work. I suggest you let him get on with it, else her sacrifice will have been in vain."

He made it sound so noble that Doulton felt a humourless smile pull at his mouth.

Galen stepped through the correctionals and joined them, tapping his cane in the palm of one hand. "Lots of rumours flying around outside gentlemen."

He looked past them, towards the sow-pen. "Tailor's wife with a soft heart for beasts, gutted like a Christmas goose. You certainly don't hold back do you?" He coughed a little laugh, then removed the bowler and tipped droplets off it.

Doulton stiffened. "Tailor's wife?"

Lyle just shrugged, he might as well know the truth of it now. "Easy mistake to make."

"We agreed, a prostitute!" he hissed. But what difference did it make? He was equally guilty and she was equally dead.

"Either way, Smithfield is ours." Lyle checked his pocket watch. "No time to lose, it's a bit of a mess in there I'm afraid."

Galen glanced at the sow-pen again. "No, it's perfect."

Doulton turned away, furious with them, but mostly with himself, and feeling this assignment was getting out of control.

Inspector Lord watched from a distance while the Goldhawk 'experts' stood around, seemingly doing very little. Then they began to disperse, but the scruffy man in the bowler lingered next to the pen when Charlotte's body lay. Lord patted the coat pocket where the killer's note was hidden and swore to do all he could to bring her murderer to justice.

"Ow much longer yer gonna be?" someone outside yelled. "Am catching my death out 'ere!"

That sparked another wave of shoving and shouting. Lord groaned and got back to his job of keeping the mob from tearing each other apart, and so he didn't see the bowler-hat-man slink into the sow-pen and out of sight.

Doulton, like the others, had been casually dismissed by Galen. "Bloody commoner thinks he owns us," He stamped his feet against the cold and wet. It was now past 1:30 am and by rights he should be in bed. His mind drifted to the rewards that awaited if they succeeded, and the daydream helped him forget the murder. He didn't like the way Galen worked to his own agenda. He had been promised a pardon but so far nothing about Galen struck him as being the kind of man who wanted a pardon. "What's your real game?" he wondered, looking towards the sow-pen, knowing the crafty little sod was in there, probably doing something very unsavoury to the late Mrs Pilling. He took another sweep of the emptied market hall, and confident none of the others were watching, he crept back. *Just doing my duty*, he told himself. That made him feel more useful. He edged closer, hiding behind a pillar from where he could see what was going on.

"Elios?" Galen stroked the cane.

"I'm here," she answered.

When certain the others had gone he slipped inside the sow-pen. It crawled with mortis-fairies, but he ignored them. He wasn't a monster and he was sorry for the way this woman had died, but he needed an atrocity to draw the valkyrie and the more terrible the better. "Sorry my dear," he looked down to where Charlotte's face was shrouded by her petticoat. "But Sophie needs me, and I've no intention of growing old and dying like the rest of mankind."

He clambered over the rails and into the adjacent pen where he could see through the planking. He found a space in the straw and settled down, then took out his watch and lay it in his lap. He saw nothing but straw and stained petticoat through the slats, but it was enough. He stole a deep breath, held it long enough to turn his face red then let it go along with all his distractions. Focusing as taught, the only sensations in the world became the touch of his fingers on the cane, and his reward was a view of Sophie.

"Is this wise Galen, the creature might appear any moment?"

"Not now," he said curtly. He rarely disagreed with her, but the memory of the valkyrie wearing Sophie's likeness had haunted him for three nights. He had to find it and question it.

He looked through the lies of the material world and there she was, his beloved but detached twin with her back to him, holding something he couldn't see. Creatures of Ruin flocked around her and he felt jealous again. "All this I do for you," he whispered, but she didn't turn. She never turned.

Elios retreated into the cane's depths feeling wounded. She also had reason to be upset. The images of flying thunder-sprites had troubled her, not that he could understand that. He could at least wallow in his hurt, but each time she imagined what it must feel like to fly, the Ruinous part of her, the awful dead-walk she struck so long ago, arose and terrified her into submission. She was two minds in one and not strong enough to beat her Ruinous half, and so wrapped in her pain she didn't feel the valkyrie's proximity until it was right on top of them. *"Galen!"* she quailed.

His eyes snapped open and the vision vanished.

"It's close by!"

The first thing he noticed was the utter silence. The crowd still clamoured outside, but inside the market each and every animal had simply frozen with dread. The mortis-fairies squeaked in alarm and took flight.

He heard straw rustle and smelled decaying wood and spoiled milk. He rolled his eyes towards the gap between the planking, scared that even the mere sound of his gaze might be enough to frighten it away.

"It's her," Elios whispered at the back of his mind.

At first all he saw was straw and petticoat. Then movement, but not the creature itself, rather the air disturbed by its presence. He saw eddies waft and curl, driven by the movement of something behind the darkness, all centred around the Pilling woman. He detected long fingers tracing the contours of her wrecked body as something studied her with great fascination. He noted the time on his pocket watch. It was 01:42am. "That won't help you my friend," he whispered softly.

There was a pause, and the darkness in the sow-pen seemed to solidify as something considered his words. A voice drifted through the air between them. "But the Ruin is so exquisite."

He trembled. There was no way he could know, but that voice was as he imagined Sophie would sound: lost and beautiful. "It's not a place you can hide in."

"It is not?" There was great regret in the voice.

"No," he managed.

"Then I shall die here."

"No, there is another way." He was so close now.

"And can you show me this other way?"

He tried to control his excitement. "Are you alone here?"

"No there are more of us." She was so honest that he almost pitied her. This creature, however terrifying, had a lot to learn.

"How many?"

"Nine so far, but others may come."

He smiled, the number was perfect. "I can help all of you and I have a token here of my good will." He drew a shard of metal from his pocket. It was a fragment of kraken armour from Hobbs Ash, one tainted by Ruin. "Follow the scent to its origin and I shall meet you there and show you this safe place I speak of."

"But time is short." The voice sounded resigned to defeat.

"How long have you been here?"

"I cannot say."

"How have you survived thus far?"

"There is Ruin all around, red-rivers without end." She looked longingly at Charlotte, admiring the craft of her death. "This would be such a pretty home to live in. But such places cannot sustain us so we hide in the world."

He knew she meant the physical environment, but whatever they hid inside they Ruined before long. He wouldn't be surprised the hear of unexplainable damage around Smithfield, ruptured water tanks, sagging walls or badly corroded metal.

"You are the first to see me," she added and her tone was so flat he didn't know if she found that good or bad.

"Most men do not see the way I see."

"Men come and go here all the time, and yet they do not see."

"I see you," he stressed again.

"No. They do not see the fear. Are men ignorant of this?"

Fear? he wondered, trying to make sense of her words, then it finally dawned on him. "Don't be alarmed, the beasts don't feel."

She made a hissing sound and that caused his skin to tighten. "Would I be here if they did not?" she accused, wondering how any creature could walk through this place and not see the fear.

He winced at his blunder. She was new, innocent even, and if she developed a sense of empathy then his chances of controlling her would vanish. "Men see the fear," he lied, "but they cannot change it and so have learned how to walk through life without being hurt by it. I can show you how to do the same."

"Is this true?"

"On my honour."

There was another long pause. Even the rain sounded far away. "It makes no difference. I will still die here," she added wistfully.

"No! I can give you a safe home." He thought of living krakens possessed by valkyries. "This is my token." He pushed the metal between the planking and heard it drop into the straw.

Nothing happened at first, then he heard the scrape of metal against concrete and the rasp of straw as the shard was accepted, followed by gentle crying.

"Why are you so sad?" His tone was so tender that Elios felt a pang of jealousy.

"The beauty fades so fast." The air moved around Charlotte where the valkyrie caressed her corpse, but it was fast losing its potency and soon she would flee.

"Then be away, but remember my token and come."

There was a long pause. The darkness became inert as the valkyrie considered. "I will come," she said at last.

He heard the whisper of straw as it made to leave. He felt such sorrow for it having to flee from one place of horror to the next. "Wait! before you go," he dared to press his face against the rail, "was it you I saw three nights ago?"

Another considered silence. "I saw a man," she recalled, "his eyes were different to the others, they saw beneath."

"That was me!"

"This man carried a shard of dead-walk."

"I carry the same, even now." He gripped the cane in proof.

"Inside lived a hybrid," she went on, "not of pure Ruin, but neither the creature it was meant to be. A mistake."

"A mistake," he agreed without thinking, making Elios gasp in outrage. "Yes that was me, but I have to know; the face you wore – where did you see it?" *And are you wearing it now?* he thought but dare not ask. There was a long silence and something about it suggested the valkyrie was calculating rather than reflecting, but he brushed his suspicions aside.

"I saw it when I was just a shadow on the great plains of Ruin, a lost girl by a river. I copied her face. She had something never seen in Ruin before."

He frowned, not sure what she meant.

"She brought joy," the valkyrie elaborated, with a dry gasping sound that could have been laughing or crying.

Joy? For a moment he felt offended. How could his beloved Sophie find happiness without him?

Deep in the cane Elios felt flinty satisfaction at his hurt.

"Could you take me to her?" he demanded.

"I cannot return myself, what makes you think you can travel to Ruin?"

"I have spells and teachings, but the most potent are missing, maybe between us we could discover the missing secrets and both travel there."

"Why would a creature of blood and bone wish to be in Ruination?"

"The girl you saw, whose face you wore, she means much to me. I wish to bring her back, and in doing so I might be able to return you there." He put the stress firmly on the latter.

"Ah, is that all," she said blandly, "and if I agree to help you will there be more red-rivers?"

He saw the tendrils of darkness swirl as her fingers moved over the spilled blood and he grasped her meaning. "Red-rivers," he smiled, what did man do best if not unleash red-rivers? "More than you can dream of my lovely."

There was a long pause, then a soft rustle of straw. The smell of sour milk and worm-ridden wood vanished and he knew the valkyrie was gone. For now.

Doulton heard murmurs but saw nothing either enter or leave the sow-pen. The rest of Goldhawk were nowhere to be seen, including Lyle. He moved closer, took cover behind a cart and peered out, but Galen wasn't there. The crafty sod had slipped over the sidings and was lying in the adjacent pen. He could just see his shabby brown shoes. "What the hell's he doing?" He rested a gloved hand on the cart and leaned forwards. He could just make him out through the slats and he appeared to be talking to his walking cane. "I ought to have guessed!" he smiled. Their esoteric expert was a first rate madman. "That should be enough to get the fool dismissed." Wearing a satisfied grin he crept closer.

"We made contact!" Galen slumped back in the straw. "We actually made contact!"

"Well done," Elios said coldly, and without being invited she materialised.

"Elios! This isn't the time or place!"

"Afraid I'll be seen?" she retorted. The effort drained her, but she spread her wings to show how angry she was.

"Of course!" He glanced around and tried to usher her back inside.

"Why?" she demanded. "Ashamed to be the companion of a half-breed mistake?" She was sickly, but she was proud, and did her best not to cough or tremble.

He stiffened, then relaxed. "Of course not my love." He reached out and gently stroked her feathers, knowing just how to handle her. "I ought to have thrashed it for what is said, but then it would have fled and our whole mission would've been finished." He made a marvellous job of being indignant on her behalf . "I hate to see you dismayed like this. That creature couldn't hold a candle to you."

She softened and her wings drooped. "As I say, well done," she repeated, sincerely this time. Now the valkyrie had gone, the penned animals began to low, bleat and squeal once more and the sense of the banal was completed by the rain drumming on the roof. She sat for a moment thinking. Her feathers looked dull and papery under the gaslight and she wore a worried expression. "I don't trust it," she said quietly.

"It's early days."

"No, it's hiding something."

"You can't know that."

"It knows more about this world than it pretends."

Her fussing was starting to irritate him. "She's the first of a new race, she can't know subterfuge and deceit."

"Are you already so enthral to it?" She looked scared for him. "It's quickly captured your heart. What if it can't help you find a way to Sophie, will it still have a claim on you?"

You're just jealous because it's so much stronger and purer than you. His own anger caught him by surprise.

She saw something in his eyes, but outside the cane she couldn't read him clearly. "Be careful Galen, please."

"Of course. Now, you know how worried I get when you're outside." He held the cane up for her.

She regarded it, and thought of the valkyrie. Both of them were trapped by their nature in some way, but something told her that the valkyrie had a better chance of escape that she did. Without a word she vanished into the dead-walk's rotten core and nurtured her worries.

Big Ben chimed three as they arrived back at Goldhawk and Galen hurried towards the library in a great rush. He was so preoccupied that he didn't notice Elios's mood. She had been silent since leaving Smithfield, but he reckoned she had simply drifted off to sleep. He gathered his writing tools, left the cane under his bunk and departed to record tonight's amazing events before they lost their clarity. As he left he pulled the door closed, but the latch failed to lock. He ignored it and headed off into the library to be alone.

Elios heard him leave and wondered why after all their years together he wanted privacy now. The last few days had been a turbulent time, but the most distressing had been his failure to defend her. A 'mistake' the valkyrie had called her and he had agreed.

Sophie, she thought again and felt a pang of resentment. Maybe it was the upset or the anger, but she did something then that she'd never done before. She emerged from the cane at her own bidding and without him present.

The black silk rustled and Elios peeped out at the empty room. It was a small room but it looked large and menacing without Galen, in fact she'd never seen the world without him being there. For a moment she just wanted to hide again, but resentment drove her on. "Mistake am I?" she sniffed. With that she emerged from the shadows under the bunk and was totally free. After a moment to gauge her surroundings she crept into the centre of the room, stretched her wings and gave them a brief flutter. *Galen wants his privacy, and so I'll have mine,* she thought churlishly. The feeling of breaking some unwritten rule was as thrilling as it was frightening. "Galen?" she whispered, knowing he wouldn't hear. "Galen are you there?" she asked, bolder this time, growing comfortable with the silence.

"No Galen here," someone said.

She squeaked, spun around and saw a fairy. It was only small, about the size of a mouse, sniffing its way along the floorboards. Its crescent-shaped scales glistened in the moonlight.

"No Galen," it said again and peered at her, curiously at first, then more cautiously. "Moonlight is mine!" it growled, buzzed its wings, and puffed itself up threateningly.

She relaxed. The creature was a moon-fairy gathering the moonlight souls floating through the room. "I have no need of your silly moonlight," she replied stiffly. "Take all you wish."

"You are fairy?" He sniffed the air for her scent. If she didn't want the moonlight then in his book that made her a friend.

"No, a thunder-sprite." She said it before she even had time to think, and then a great realisation came to her. Her Ruinous half wasn't there, it was still inside the dead-walk. She panicked for a moment, as though she'd stepped out of her very skin. "I should be back," she blurted and scurried towards the bunk.

"Back under the bed?" he chuckled. "But don't sprites live in the thunder clouds or by the side of witch-folk?"

The fairy's words stopped her and she turned. "Not all sprites live that way," she replied indignantly.

"No witch ever came to find you then?" he asked, kindly.

"I have a splendid witch if you must know, for I'm a thunder-sprite worth finding." She ruffled her wings, feeling rather insulted. *Galen would baulk at being called a witch.* She found the thought mischievous and exciting.

"The Galen man?" The fairy blinked his large round eyes. "Nights and nights I come here when the moonlight falls, but I smell no broom-rider in this place." He seemed confused.

"Galen is not a common broom-rider, he is so much more."

"But sprites and broom-riders go together, this is the way it's always been." He sat down and pondered this. "So you do not fly?"

His question was like being jabbed with a needle. "Only when I wish," she lied.

"Nothing like the thrill of flight is there?" he grinned. "To fly is to live yes?"

"Yes," she agreed weakly. "To fly is to live." Suddenly she felt faint.

Galen had always advised her against leaving the cane. She should go back right away, and she glanced towards the bed. Under the bunk the cane looked like a coffin, tailor made for her.

"Come to bed little Elios, you are sickly and weak but I can give you peace. Come and rest inside me forever." Sometimes she hated the foul stick, but always she needed it.

Without realising, she turned back and heard the terrible truth fall from her mouth. "No witch ever came for me. Only Galen would suffer me. I cannot fly and I was not meant to be." The words were spoken aloud at last and she almost believed the world would shatter.

The fairy gave her a hard look. "Have you ever tried to fly?"

It was a simple question, but one that startled her. She was about to answer when she heard footfalls. Galen must have forgotten something. "Be gone from here if you value your life!" she hissed.

He snatched a few last souls from the air, offered her a sympathetic look, then swept up towards the open skylight and away. Elios scampered under the bunk and plunged into the dead-walk. The door opened and she saw Galen's feet. He marched over to the desk, retrieved something and left. This time the door closed fully and clicked shut.

Inside the cane Elios slowly joined with her dead-walk mind, changing from the lone thunder-sprite into the uniquely Ruinous sprite and as she did many of her worries and concerns simply melted away. It was a beautiful, cathartic moment, but something the fairy had said couldn't be so easily dismissed.

"Have you ever tried to fly?"

Who was it that said no witch would come and claim her she thought? She hid these dangerous ideas from her dead-walk side, knowing the answer was too disturbing. She wanted to think more about the fairy's words, but now she was one with the cane it seemed to matter less and less. She finally rested and dreamed. She dreamed of flying through mountainous thunderheads and spiralling the stems of forked lightning, and the fairy was right, the thrill was like nothing she'd ever known.

* * * * *

The shackles of fury had been removed and he owed it all to the young woman with the enchanted doll. The whole sky was his kingdom and the land below was his own treasure chest to enjoy at will. His companions sailed at his side, and he remembered something that he'd forgotten in the haze of Valgard's curse. He was Eirik Thorvaldson and the three were brothers from Sogne of Norway. Eirik, Karl and Harger.

The first signs of something wrong were so subtle he didn't see them. The way-beware's song waxed and waned depending on what direction he travelled, like a bad gramophone recording coming and going.

He banked east, and the morning sun dazzled him and he felt a brief stab of irritation at it. Below he saw a river cutting its way through the miles of black sands, but it didn't gladden him, instead he found the network of rivulets messy, which also inflamed him.

Miserable barren wastes, he dismissed the sight that had enchanted him just moments before and then, as if his anger was ballast, he felt heavier. It took enormous strength to keep himself airborne, and the only way to find that strength was through fury. *Bastard earth!* he cursed. *Bastard sky!* Everything was his enemy and he wanted to destroy the earth for being too far away and the sky for being too empty. The way-beware's song was doused by a rumbling laughter he recognised all too well. *No! To hell with Valgard the liar!* He wrestled the darkness and summoned all the best things he could think of, but before the might of Valgard his life looked puny.

It was his wife Freydis that saved him. He saw her face as clearly as the mountains below. Her hair was golden and her eyes were calming blue, just like the girl with the magical doll, and for a moment he could think straight. That's when he realised that the doll's song had dwindled to barely a whisper. "The song!" he cried to his brothers. "The girl with the doll, find her for Odin's sake or we're lost!" Anger coursed through him like an infection and his words were melting into snarls. "Find her!"

Valgard's laughter almost split his head and the sky turned fiery crimson, except for one distant speck on the horizon. It remained calm blue and there was the faintest echo of the song from there. It was his lighthouse on a sea of death and he aimed for it with all his strength, towards the way-beware; the one thing that could keep them from descending into the berserker rage once more.

CHAPTER ELEVEN

The scarred cherub

'Of course they're afraid of us, of course they imprison us, because if everyone knew the truth of magic nobody would have to toil or suffer ever again.'
Ardella Blake, founding witch of Night-Wood coven, Dorset

It was almost dark when they reached the outskirts of Reykjavik, the only sizeable town in Iceland. Even from a distance Sunday thought 'town' was rather a grand word for it, but when she saw twinkling lights from afar she decided this was close enough. They stopped in the middle of a lava plain, and she was searching vainly for a place to shelter when she spotted a white fox and was so delighted that she went for a better look. The shy animal had gone, leaving a scattering of delicate paw prints, but beside them she found a mossy hollow in the lava that the snow hadn't reached. It was the perfect place to camp and she wondered if the fox had been sent by a certain someone.

So far, the weather had been calm but cold. She found just enough wood to light a little fire. The moss grew in fat cushions as soft as any mattress and she lay by the fire wrapped in her cloak and with a canopy of stars as her companion, but before long duty beckoned. She started with sleeping spells for Hethra and Halla, and now she was busy with a transmutation spell, the very kind the Illuminata had spent centuries trying to synthesise.

In her hand she held three rusty nails recovered from a ruined farmstead, and she concentrated on the spell. It was hard and not many witches her age could manage it, but as Neet observed, she was a strong broom-rider. Strike knew not to bother her right then and so he sat enjoying the night while she rocked gently, muttering the song of iron, asking it to change from iron to silver. She said they were going shopping, but not even a witch could do that without funds.

Eventually he heard a deep but satisfied sigh and he turned to see her holding three bright spikes of silver in her palm. "A clever witch never goes without," she smiled, but looked tired. The spell had taken a lot of effort, as had their encounter under the ice.

"Only if there are merchants to spend the silver on," he noted, "but while you've been busy with the metal of the moon goddess, you've been missing the show. Come and look before it fades."

She crawled over to join him and saw a ribbon of green light in the night sky. It glowed, and undulated like a living thing, but made not a sound.

"We saw them plenty from the thunder-heights," he reminisced about his ancestral home, "it's an even better view from up there."

"It's beautiful enough from down here."

"A good omen." He nodded, satisfied.

Without a word she retrieved her cloak, fed the fire and sat in the entrance to the hollow and watched the lights with him, hoping he was right.

She regarded herself as well travelled, she was almost twenty-one after all, but trips to neighbouring covens in southern England hardly counted as seeing the world. It struck Sunday that she had actually led a rather sheltered life at Regal-Fox. With this in mind she didn't know what to expect of Reykjavik and maybe because she had no expectations she found it charming.

"Why are the roads so muddy?" It made sense for Strike to stay hidden and she used her staff like a walking stick.

"Same reason there's still snow on the mountains and no greenery yet, winter lasts longer here." She squelched through the narrow streets carrying her few belongings.

The colourful timber buildings were quaint and despite the harsh conditions they looked cheery. They huddled together as if sheltering from the elements, while the narrow streets were awash with mud and scored by cart tracks. Every building sported the Danish flag, which was so common that it seemed to outnumber the locals, as did the population of ducks and seagulls. Where the buildings weren't timber they were turf or corrugated iron, but even these had a rude comfort about them. The only building that wasn't wood or turf was the white-washed governor's residency. All in all the town had a frontier feel about it and she found that she actually liked it.

She did her best to look inconspicuous, and to that end she wore her most ordinary clothes and kept her magical tokens hidden. Even so, more than a few eyes turned her way, especially when she stopped to stroke the stout little ponies tethered to rails and posts. "Strike," she said from the corner of her mouth, sensing curious glances, "do you think they know I'm a witch?" She wasn't sure how the locals felt about witchcraft, but from what Neet had said she doubted they'd throw a party for her.

"No, it's probably just the Sunday-effect."

"Sunday-effect?" she repeated, ducking in to an alley between crooked buildings. A group of young men on the dockside had been very interested in her.

"Yes, you know, that strange effect you have over people."

"Do I?"

"Yes, but it seems to work mostly on men."

It took her a moment to realise, and she smiled, happy to know she still had some of her old magic.

The silver nails had been chopped into smaller pieces. She bought practical supplies, which wasn't hard as each merchant's establishment had a brightly coloured pennon outside. New clothes were high on her list, but nothing fancy. She bought men's trousers as they were more suitable for staff-riding than dresses. Another item that took her fancy was a large square of oil cloth which would make a good shelter if she had to sleep rough, and a brass compass that had a lucky feel about it. In a second-hand pile of clothes she picked out a black dress and other garments she could alter later. *Reduced to rummaging through people's cast offs,* she thought, and smiled at the irony. To disguise her lightning-staff she tied on the bundles as she bought them and carried it over her shoulder.

"What's the idea?" Strike objected.

"It helps the overall disguise."

"So I have to travel disguised as your wardrobe?"

"Strike dearest," she teased, "if I had my whole wardrobe it'd break this staff."

She examined a map in the town library, a small wooden building adjoining the even smaller hospital, but crammed wall to wall with books. The Icelanders it seemed were fond of reading and even though the words on the map were unintelligible, Britain's crinkly outline made her heart ache. The librarian directed her to a merchant who could sell her a copy.

"So when do we leave?" Strike felt like a bird on the eve of its migration.

"Not until tomorrow, I need to find a bed for the night, get a solid meal, study the map."

Her interest wasn't all practical though. In the window of one small house she saw a ginger cat sat between pots of carnations, enjoying the gentle sunshine. She tapped the murky glass and smiled at it, the cat blinked at her unimpressed, but another face loomed up too. The cat's owner turned out to be a widow who supplemented her living selling trinkets carved of driftwood and she deftly ushered Sunday into her one room dwelling to meet her handsome cat, but mostly to interest her in her wares. Sunday was reluctant to use her silver for trinkets, but when she saw the crafted items laid out on a square of white lace she was immediately taken with them and bought a wooden comb and two hair pins, both carved to look like arctic foxes.

"Foxes, Strike, isn't that just perfect!" she said later when she had a moment to admire them properly.

"I'm glad you bought them for a magical reason," he quipped.

"Don't be such a grump, I've been through a lot, I need a little pampering."

They stopped by a pond in the town square noisy with ducks and gulls, and she began combing her hair. Maybe it was breaking some obscure local custom, but passers-by were more than a little curious. Even so it felt wonderful to straighten all the tangles and before long it was its lustrous gold again and she pushed the fox combs into places and fastened a black headscarf to complete the look. In many ways she could pass as a local. "What do you think?" she asked from behind her hand.

"I think you've told all of Iceland that you're here," he grumbled.

"It feels good to have a little normality back," she sighed.

She was right he thought, and so he complained no further.

The idea of sailing home also occurred to her. With enough silver she could buy herself a passage on a steamship, but there'd be a lot of questions asked on a long sea voyage, and those questions would multiply the closer she got to Britain. She asked around the wharves, but most of the steamers were heading to Nova Scotia or Norway. A ship named 'The Kittiwake' had left two days ago bound for Norway via the Faroe Islands. The name immediately seized her, it was fate for sure, and she wished she could have at least completed that leg of the journey in a comfortable cabin. It was disappointing but at least it settled the matter. They were flying home.

They continued to hunt through the town for useful items and as the day passed she began to suspect that the white fox she'd seen last night wasn't the only helper sent her way. All across town she met useful people or stumbled across useful items by chance. She bought a few ounces of powdered sulphur, a spell ingredient hard to find back home, and the owner of the trading post turned out to be Danish and have a good grasp of English. He was a kindly old man who was surprised to learn that she wasn't Icelandic herself. "But this!" He indicated her hair. "You are a local girl!" he smiled as though he knew some secret about her.

"I told you Strike," she thought triumphantly and he just chuckled in reply.

As it transpired, the shopkeeper knew of a seamstress who took in lodgers. Sunday needed a room and Asbjorn was always glad to have the extra money. Her small two-story dwelling was easy to find, it was painted red and the house was named Tofa, which she later found meant 'fox'. Asbjorn was a small woman who might have been eighty but looked somehow ageless. She wore her grey hair in a tidy plait, and had broad cheekbones and delicate almond shaped eyes.

While there, Sunday explained she was happy to eat anything so long as it was only vegetables. Asbjorn didn't speak English, but when Sunday eventually clasped her hands as if in prayer, she understood in a roundabout way that something akin to religion was the reason. When meal time came Sunday gorged herself on potato and barley stew and lots of bread while Asbjorn sat by the fire and kindly mended some of her tattered clothes.

When Asbjorn had gone to bed in the small downstairs room that served as both kitchen and bedroom, Sunday took her leave and went to her room upstairs. There she lit a lantern and a small fire in the hearth, and began plotting her journey.

"It's such a long way," Strike said again as he looked at the endless open water between Iceland and Britain.

"Mmm," she worried. In truth she was deeply afraid. "But we can cut it into segments. Look, if we go from here to this place," she tapped a finger on a collection of islands, "the Faroes, that's the halfway point, and then here," she moved her finger, "Shetland. Then we're in Britain and practically home."

"You make it sound so simple."

"Come on, we beat death, dead-walks and berserks, what harm's a little water?" she tried to cheer him, but there was a long silence between them as they thought of the trials ahead. Spring could still be a stormy time, there were fog banks and gales to consider, not to mention the numbing cold. "Maybe this wouldn't be such a bad place to settle down. I look like a local by all accounts," she joked to hide her fears.

"You wouldn't be happy," he said truthfully.

She nodded, knowing the urge to simply go home might cost her life. "Tomorrow it is then."

They slept little that night. She lay under her blankets listening to hail blast and gust against the tin roof and the dying fire crackle in the grate as she thought of her coven, a home that no longer existed. In the still of the early hours, when the darkness was total and under cover of her blankets she whispered a prayer to her 'dear champion'. "You gave me so much. My life was renewed and with it the chance to be something better, but now I have to ask another favour of you. If it's within your power I'd humbly ask you to watch over the threads of Sunday Evelyn Flowers and Lightning-Strikes-Lonesome-Ash a little while longer. Just long enough for us to get home . . ." she trailed off. If she had to die she at least wanted it to be a place she knew, that was her most basic desire right then. "Please look after Strike if I should be no more," she ended and dried her eyes.

Beside her, silent and still in his staff, Strike listened and thought it cruel that the dangers that had brought them closer could ultimately separate them again.

Before dawn she was awoken by a soft knocking at the door, Asbjorn had prepared her a meal. She might not speak English but she could tell that this young woman was embarking on a very significant journey. Sunday took enough porridge to be breakfast, dinner and supper in one huge meal. Strike had made a weak joke about carrying all that extra weight, but she knew that behind his bravado he was as scared as her.

At first light they began. She paid Asbjorn double the rate then hugged her farewell before she walked down to the harbour and looked out across the sea. The early light seemed to grow from the land not the sky, and the sea glowed faintly as a prequel to dawn while to the north the faint fingerprints of the aurora were fading as night dwindled.

She stood with her assorted belongings bundled around her. All her clothes were put to use, and she wore everything she had, making her look stocky. Hrafn-dimmu and the way-beware were safely folded into her clothes and she was as ready as she'd ever be. The sky took on a delicate pink glow and the distant mountains shimmered white. It was perfect flying weather. She ought to have chosen a quieter launching spot but Sunday was still the exhibitionist, and besides, if hrafn-dimmu's tale was right then Iceland hadn't seen a real witch in many years. Something told her she owed it to Valonia.

She was ready to start when fate threw her one last surprise. By chance she noticed a document pinned to harbour master's office. It can't have been there more than a week or two old because the paper was crisp and the ink still sharp. The language mystified her, but the date at the top made perfect sense.

April 18th 1887

April the following year. She and Strike had been dead for almost six months. She digested this news slowly, wondering what had become of all those people she cared about.

"Six months?" she grappled with this, and maybe because of it she decided that being seen to leave wasn't enough, she was going to announce their departure. "Come on Strike, let's go home." She pulled the black scarf up around her face, turned and looked down the rickety wharf, slick with fish guts and littered with ropes.

She raised her staff and inside Strike waited, ready. He heard her scream and sensed bewildered faces turn their way. Next came the thump of boots over the wooden boarding as she charged towards the open water. Why she chose those words she'd never really know, but they became her name and cause in the months ahead and before summer was over all of London would come to know it. "Blackwand!" she cried and launched herself out over the frigid water.

The harbour master peered from his office window wondering who was screaming at this early hour. Fishermen looked up from repairing nets, not believing what they saw; a figure on a staff sailing across the calm waters of the harbour and then banking around to soar across the lava plains beyond. The figure vanished behind a row of turf huts, and the oldest men and women of Reykjavik briefly remembered tales of witches long ago and felt the echo from a past-age catch them up, but then like the broom-rider, it was gone.

It was only three in the afternoon but Doulton needed a drink. He helped himself to a sherry from the decanter as he waited. Lyle walked in, cast a disapproving look at the sherry glass and sat down behind his desk with a weary sigh. "Make this brief, I've much to do."

He finished his sherry in one gulp and thudded the glass down. "Galen's mad."

Lyle rolled his eyes as if he'd been told the sky was blue and made to stand again.

"Hear me out," he said angrily, "I saw something at Smithfield the other night."

His brow wrinkled and he lowered himself back down. "What exactly?"

"This is what I've been trying to tell you." He leaned forwards, hands on the desk. "Where's Galen now?"

"At Hobbs Ash, why?"

He looked around the room and lowered his voice, "I don't trust him."

"Get to the point, Doulton."

"I saw him talking to a creature at Smithfield."

"A valkyrie?" This was something concrete to tell Thorpe and he looked excited.

"I'm no expert, but no, I don't think it was. For starters it was small, not much bigger than a crow, and it had wings and feathers."

"Sounds like a crow after all," Lyle said sarcastically.

"It wasn't a bloody crow!" He was starting to feel silly for bringing this up. "It was blue for one thing and it had arms and legs."

"Could still be a valkyrie," Lyle enthused.

"Will you listen to me, it wasn't one of these valkyrie things."

"And how do you know? You said yourself you're no expert."

"Because it appeared from that cane of his and when they'd done talking it vanished back into it."

"And what were they discussing?" Lyle asked, serious now.

"That's the hard part, I only caught snatches, but they seemed to be in disagreement about something, of that much I was sure."

He stroked his fleshy chin. "He's got his own secrets, if there's something living in that cane then as long as it's working with him and not against, then leave it be I say."

"So why hasn't he revealed it before?"

"Galen communes with forces best known to him. Leave him to it, questionable or otherwise."

Doulton just looked to the window and the bright sunshine outside. "You saw what he ordered done to the Pilling woman. Would you call that 'questionable'?"

He shuffled in his chair, trying to look repentant when really he didn't give a damn.

"He's working without boundaries," Doulton continued. "And what do we know about the Book-of-Nine really?"

Lyle's face set like cement. Thorpe had been the one to invest in the cult's help and he was touchy about criticism to say the least. "We'll see just where his allegiance stands tonight."

"Ah yes," he smirked, "his grand parlour piece. He's going to bring a valkyrie to Hobbs Ash isn't he?"

"So he says, yes."

"And if it doesn't show up?"

"Then I'm sure Lord Thorpe will give him the heave-ho," he lied.

"Really?"

"Yes, without a doubt." Lyle stood up and rounded his desk. "Now, I've plenty to do before tonight. I want you to check the security arrangement for Hobbs Ash."

"Right away." Doulton was already hoping that Galen would fail, and the fraudster would be shipped back to whatever flea-pit he'd crawled out of.

Lyle ushered him to the door with pretend patience and saw him out, but once the door was closed he leaned against it and tapped his lip. How was he supposed to implement Thorpe's plans when his second in command was a chronic worrier? And if Doulton believed Thorpe would actually send Galen away then he was the mad man.

Excerpt from the Book-of-Nine

Mr Lyle of Goldhawk arranged the timely demise of one Charlotte Anne Pilling, in the shape of a note luring her to Smithfield. Once there, Francis-Joseph Kollip, whose life is embittered by addiction to opium, did what many men would quail at and ended her life. Kollip's work was so grotesque yet so artful that the valkyrie could not help but be drawn close. While the Pilling woman's death was regrettable, it was essential, and beside her butchered body I instructed the valkyrie to follow the scent of the Ruined armour to its origin at Hobbs Ash – tonight. But Elios is less than happy. I have taken to making my notes in private while she rests. I fear she is made envious by the attentions I lavish upon the valkyrie, and although she is admittedly half-Ruinous herself, I find myself weary of her more female delusions and worries.

Galen finished with astronomical observations that might be relevant to the valkyrie's appearance and aid future cultists. The sinister book then vanished into the satchel and he left the small supply room where he'd gone to work in private. The afternoon was wearing on and there was still plenty to do. He ambled across Hobbs Ash towards the grand station to see how work was progressing on the valkyrie's new home. He had taken a look earlier that morning and left something important in the Ruined machine, and now it was time to collect it.

"Top work Mr Topp," he beamed at his own joke, but Duty-Warden Topp had heard them all in his time.

"I'm sure sir," he replied politely as he escorted Galen into the old station.

Everywhere he saw hard work, sweat and sparks, or lumbering shire horses pulling supply wagons. He trailed along behind Topp, enjoying the boom of metal echo around the huge building. A series of wooden frames had been erected to screen the back of the station. Hundreds of yards of tarpaulin had been nailed in place creating a featureless barricade of dull fabric, because what would happen tonight wasn't for the eyes of mere navvies. The canvas parted, they slid through and Galen felt the very air change from dirty to pure and blessed. "A temple fit for a valkyrie," he smiled.

"Laid out just as you asked sir," Topp indicated the wrecked machine. It had taken two days hard work but every piece of wreckage was laid out, right down to the last spring and rivet. It had been painstaking, and as far as Topp could see, utterly pointless.

"Just right," Galen nodded and dismissed Topp with a wave. He walked around, appraising quickly but thoroughly, and finding it to his approval. The metal giant lay in the centre of its exploded innards like an autopsy specimen and hundreds of chains and pulleys dangled over it like a shower of petrified rain.

He picked his way through the debris towards the helmet, which had taken the brunt of the attack. It resembled a cherub of the kind common in Renaissance art, with flowing hair and rosebud lips, and finished with copper plate that was meant to be kept scrupulously bright by daily polishing. Below the regiment badge was the personal identification name. It was obscured by burns, but it should have read 'Victorianus'.

The cherub's head had been deformed by a terrific blow, leaving the face twisted and troll-like and the sumptuous lips sneering rather than pouting, while cracks decorated its face like razor slashes. He wiped a finger over the copper finish. It hadn't seen polish for months and now it was green with oxide, while trickles of rust had seeped through the joints and looked like fresh blood. He reached the cherub's scalp and the cockpit hatch and pushed his upper body inside to retrieve what he'd come for. He grasped the cane and called to her.

"Galen?" Elios sounded upset.

"Are you rested my sweet?"

"You've been gone so long," she ignored his question. *"It is strange being left alone. I felt lost here."*

"Aye, I missed you also, but surely it's worth it. Don't you feel gladdened for being here amongst your own kind?"

"In part." She wasn't so sure Ruin was her own kind. The last few days had been very confusing.

He sensed her reservations and knew just what to say, "I'm glad you're back by my side, I'm half the man I am without you."

"*Really?*"

"Cross my heart and hope to die." He drew a finger across the bullet hole in his coat. "Now, is there anything we've forgotten, any detail we've overlooked?"

"*Does everyone know the time it will arrive?*" she reminded him.

"One forty-two in the morning, precisely." He had memorised the exact moment the valkyrie had appeared at Smithfield. He suspected it was very literal, and two days exactly meant 01:42 tomorrow morning. "That's when it'll come."

"*And if it doesn't like the chariot you've chosen for it?*"

"Then the Illuminata can pickle its ugly carcass for their museum." There was such conviction in his voice that she felt a surge of happiness.

"*Then we can leave the Illuminata to fight their own causes?*" She just wanted to wander the dark corners of Europe, with him all to herself as it used to be. "*Who cares if they stand or fall as long as we're together.*"

"A very romantic notion," he smiled, "but I'll have to play along with their demands for a while longer."

"*But you owe them nothing!*"

He sighed. "I've got all the funds and apparatus I need, there's never been a better time to find Sophie, as long as I continue the pretence that I'm saving their skin."

She suddenly felt spiteful and wanted to tell him to forget Sophie. Why would a child lost in Ruin wish to come to Earth, a place she'd never known, and live an immortal life with a brother she'd never met? But she kept her peace, although not quite well enough.

"Elios," he suspected, "what's that you're thinking in there? Don't forget I know you my dear. Love has no secrets, remember."

"*Is that so?*" she said primly. "*Then what am I thinking now?*" She accessed her Ruinous mind and summoned a host of the dead-walk's memories, memories so abstract and horrible that even he couldn't face them.

He flinched at the alien thoughts, which were like sharp edges against his mind. "Enough!" He rubbed his aching brow. "Your point's taken. You're as good at giving a fellow a headache as any other woman."

"Please, don't assume you know my every thought, they're not yours to read at will, but should you just ask me then they're yours for the taking." She didn't like having to use hard words against him.

"Spoken like a true woman." He put their little spat aside, patted the cane affectionately and continued his inspection.

"Where is he?' Doulton asked wearily.

Topp glanced around at the barricade. "In there sir."

Just at that moment the canvas parted and Galen walked through, brushed dust from his coat and came over. "Ah, Mr Doulton. I need to see the prisoners."

"What for?"

"Don't worry son," he rolled his eyes, "Mr Lyle says it's fine and correct, and he's the one in charge after all." He tapped him dismissively on the chest with his cane.

Doulton thought of the creature hidden inside the loathsome stick and swatted it away, disgusted. "I'll have to check with him about that."

"Lead on Mr Topp please." Galen ignored him.

He looked to Doulton for his consent, aware of the younger man's humiliation. Doulton managed a flustered nod and turned away angrily. "This way sir." Topp turned on his heels and clattered over the concrete.

Galen shot him a smug look, then followed him towards the sinister prison machines and their miserable captives.

The prisons had also been screened off, but their hasty barricade had seen a whole London winter pass by and now it was streaked with algae, and tattered canvas hung like skin, giving glimpses of the machines inside. "This way." Topp disappeared between the canvas.

Galen followed, and immediately reeled at the machines. They were like huge cannon balls that had grown spines, and each had a forest of chimneys sprouting from its crown, and to cap it all it was said they were magic-proof. There were eight in total clustered beneath the engine shed. Galen thought they looked like fungi that had sprouted in the dark. Their original colour might have been black but it was hard to tell now because they were all desert-red with rust. Gentle smoke drifted from their chimneys, showing their systems were still generating power. They were dubbed 'iron-spiders' by their crews, but each had a name plate on the hull bearing such stirring names as Valour, Temperance, Honesty, and even Mercy.

"Best start in here," Topp gestured to the nearest. "This one's ready for decommissioning, and the inmates will be moved to one of the others."

Galen followed him to the foremost machine, which half jutted out into the elements through a gaping tear in the canvas. The corrosion on its hull was so thick that it looked like a skin disease. He saw the name plate read 'Freedom', and thought of Sophie. "Ironic name," he commented.

"I'm sure you're right sir." Topp didn't see anything ironic about it. The way he saw it, keeping witches imprisoned protected freedom.

There was a wooden gantry leading to a small hatch in the hull and Topp began to climb the rickety stair towards it. Galen followed, trying all the while to read the machines, to collect any sense of the occupants, but all he could gather were garbled feelings.

"I'm scared Galen," Elios shivered inside her cane. *"These machines are wrong."*

"I feel it too," he agreed silently, unsure if she meant the machines or the morals of locking people away. *"We'll make our selection and leave. We won't dawdle."*

At the top of the gantry Topp pulled on a chain by the door and almost right away it opened with a shriek of rusty metal. "Taylor," he acknowledged as he stepped past the doorman; a lad of seventeen with a fluffy moustache and who'd never fired his rifle once.

"Sir," he said briskly and just blinked at Galen, who silently stepped past him and into the metal guts of the aptly named 'Freedom'.

The corridor was wide enough for a man to pass through, so long as they didn't mind stooping under the succession of girders. The smell of burned rubber and warm wiring pervaded the whole machine. "We have a total of sixty-three prisoners here sir," Topp declared as he navigated the claustrophobic corridor.

Galen did the maths in his head. Six and three, the magical nine. "A good number," he remarked.

"Had more of them until they made a run for it, close on twelve hundred. They'd have been secure enough if not for the accident."

Galen knew it was no accident. Thanks to Ada, the place had gone up like Fawkes himself on a bloody big bonfire.

"A few were recaptured," Topp smoothed over the defeat.

"And the rest got clean away."

"I suppose so sir."

He waited to see if he would elaborate, but he seemed tight-lipped about the episode.

"Galen," Elios sounded breathless, *"I can hardly breathe in here."*

"Just a little while longer," he thought back.

"The air is dead, there's no essence of magic here at all."

He thought her upset strange, after all, her dead-walk side ought to be in its element. He dropped a little way behind, and under the cover of his noisy footfalls, brought the cane close to his mouth to whisper, "What's troubling you really?"

"Don't you pity them?"

"Whatever for?"

"To be so cut off from the sublime and the magical?"

Sublime? Magical? he thought worriedly. These were strange words coming from a Ruinous creature, and he wondered if she was gaining the upper-hand over her dead-walk side. "I've never felt sorry for witches. And neither should you. Remember not a single one wanted you as their sprite." This usually won her over, but not today.

"But this is purgatory, the machine steals everything of worth. This is a spiritual vacuum." His indifference upset her.

"Then those we choose will be spared this fate. Shouldn't we be happy for them, like the poor lass selling the whelks?"

"I suppose so," she agreed reluctantly. *"But select quickly and let's be away. This place is like a tomb."*

Again, he thought this an odd sentiment for a creature that thrived on Ruin.

"How many do you need?" Topp asked, already reaching for his keys.

"I need three for tonight and probably more later."

"Any preference?"

"They just need to be real witches. I know the Illuminata can be a little pre-emptive in rounding up suspects. I've no use for lone hags that sell bottled piss as medicine. And they'll need their lightning-staffs returned to them for the test."

"Whatever for?" Topp hardened.

"It's for the test."

"As you say sir, but one old witch caused a lot of mischief here last year. She didn't even have matching shoes let alone a wand, and you want to give 'em back their weapons?"

"I've taken that into account, I know how to make them cooperate."

"Even so," he muttered. "It's a big risk sir, if you don't mind my saying so."

"I don't mind at all, but the fact remains that they'll need to be able to defend themselves. I need witches with a bit of fight left in them." He tapped the cane against his palm impatiently. "Remember these orders come directly from Lord Thorpe."

Topp grunted something under his breath. "Then best start here." He halted by a metal hatch with a tiny glass pane. "He's still got fight in him, although his name is anyone's guess."

Galen looked through. In the tiny cell he saw a crumpled young man with shoulder-length dark hair sat cross-legged on the floor as if deep in meditation. He looked dejected and filthy, but not beaten. "Open the door," he ordered.

Topp located the right key and obliged. The door opened loud enough to make Galen wince, but the young man never looked up. He stepped into the doorway and looked down at his opposite. He reached out with the cane and touched the lad's shoulder. He never moved, but Galen could tell he was aware of everything.

"He's a true witch," Elios vouched.

"I'm told you don't have a name, so I'll be calling you 'witch'," Galen declared coldly. "What was your coven, witch?"

The lad, whose name was John Fold, looked up. Galen saw defiance in him, but defiance down to its last reserves. "Nine-Maidens, of Worcestershire," he said flatly.

"I knew nine maidens in Worcestershire once," he licked his lips, "sweet lasses all of 'em. There wasn't a thing they wouldn't do for a new shiny penny."

Fold regarded him with a mixture of anger and pity.

"And would you be willing to serve me?"

"I serve the twins of Oak and Holly alone," he stated.

"Oh aye, the twins of Oak and Holly, dragons with pretty scales and wonderful dreams. You still peddling that old tripe?"

"You're right, their dreams can't be that wonderful if there's a walking heap of shit like you in the world," he smiled up at him.

Galen burst out laughing. "I like that son," he patted the satchel around his shoulders, "I'll be sure to write that down for posterity." He backed out of the doorway still chuckling and nodded silently to Topp, "He'll do." The cell door closed and they moved on.

"Two more to go my sweet," he promised her, and Elios readied herself to assess their next test subject.

Later that afternoon a series of blunt telegraphs shot between Lyle and Thorpe. Knowing Thorpe was an impatient man, he kept it brief. He sat down, composed himself and typed out his message:

DOULTON HAS RESERVATIONS ABOUT OUR DUTIES – ADVICE PLEASE.

"For better or worse," he muttered and sent the message. The machine rattled and juddered as it sent his words across London, to the Bank and into Thorpe's ear. He twiddled his thumbs pretending not to be tense, and waited.

He took a deep breath and looked out of the small window, towards the pinnacles of Westminster palace and imagined a witch flying through the sky. "It'll never happen Virgil," he promised himself. Once the tournament was done and Europe knew its place, he would be mentoring their new Knight Superior until he reached the age of inheritance. He was just relishing this pleasant daydream when the telegraph jerked into life. He jumped, and yanked the roll of paper from the machine. It read one word.

EXPLAIN

He read it three times and each time it looked to be shouting at him. 'Explain.' He rubbed his chin, knowing Thorpe was waiting at the other end, probably tapping his foot impatiently. He quickly rattled off a reply that sounded concerned but not worried.

DOULTON BELIEVES GALEN CANNOT BE TRUSTED AND

WISHES TO RETURN HIM TO CONTINENT. CONCERNED
DOULTON HAS NOT THE FORTITUDE TO FOLLOW YOUR
PLAN.

In under a minute the machine began to print Thorpe's reply.

IF D IS RETICENT THEN DEVISE SOLUTION OR BE
REPLACED. END

"End," Lyle read aloud. It would certainly be the end for him if Doulton continued to make a fuss. He knew he couldn't reply. He would be seen as a man floundering. It was time to show Thorpe what he was made of, time to show some initiative. He took the messages to the grate, put a match to them and in seconds they were gone. He had to get tough with Doulton, and he suspected that if Galen's valkyrie actually turned up tonight then things were going to get very tough indeed.

Someone somewhere is looking after us. Sunday thought this many times over the last six hours.

The north Atlantic was as still as a millpond and a fresh tailwind pushed them along. Fulmars glided past her on their stiff wings, utterly content on the open sea. The sky was clear and the sun was actually warm enough to coax a sweat. She pulled down her mask and loosened the scarf, letting the sea-air cool her body. She took the compass from around her neck and checked their bearing. So far the crossing hadn't been just good, it had been enjoyable. So easy in fact she kept expecting things to go wrong, but there was just the calm sea and the endless blue sky. "It's magnificent Strike!" she called, pulling the headscarf away so her hair fanned out around her shoulders and back.

"We're half way to the first stop-off point, the Fairy Islands!" He was very pleased with their progress.

"Faroe," she corrected. "You're flying marvellously by the way."

"And you're doing a marvellous job of just sitting there!"

She grinned, happy in his company and happy to have the sea all to herself. It was easy to forget that she was heading for London and all its dangers. She took a swig from her canteen and a pinch of bread, while keeping one hand firmly on the staff. As she chewed she gazed at the glistening waters speeding past. Occasionally she saw the streamlined shape of a dolphin, as sunlight dazzled and flashed across the surface. The effect was hypnotic and she could easily lose herself to it, and so she didn't see the plume of steam on the horizon until they were relatively close.

"Steamer!" Strike warned.

"What?" She looked up sharply. "A ship?"

"Not a problem unless it's a war ship."

"Indeed." She checked the compass. "It's roughly on our bearing."

"Can we avoid it?"

"It would mean a wide detour, more flying."

"I can manage."

"No, you've done enough. We'll get closer and see what she is. If she's not a battle cruiser we'll pass."

"In a hurry."

"Of course, but it'll give the crew something to talk about."

"You enjoy being a spectacle don't you?"

She laughed, "I won't wave to them if that's what you mean." She pulled her mask up again and they accelerated, heading for the distant steamer on the horizon.

They trailed the ship at a respectable distance for some time. By now the sun was languishing close to the horizon and this was the part she dreaded most. The idea of overshooting the Faroes and sailing out into the black set her stomach quivering. The steamer was some half a mile distant now and she was already close enough to spot tiny lifebelts along the rail and the churning waters at her bow, but no sign of guns. "Can you see anything yet Strike?" she shouted over the wind.

"Wait, I see a name."

She strained to see, but her eyes were nowhere near as keen as his. "Is it a naval vessel?" she asked anxiously.

"I think," he paused, *"I think yes, it says Kittiwake! Yes it's Kittiwake, do you know what that means!"*

"Of course!" She punched the air in triumph. It was the steamer that had left Iceland two days ago bound for the Faroes, but clearly delayed for whatever reason. Somebody was looking after them for sure. "Are you thinking what I am?"

"A free ride?"

"Absolutely! Keep us a little way back, when darkness falls we'll get aboard and tuck ourselves into one of the lifeboats. We'll snooze the night away and be in the Faroes by dawn!"

"And then to Shanty-land!"

"Shetland," she corrected. "We're as good as half way home!" She looked up at the dusky sky and the friendly line of smoke wafting along behind the Kittiwake, and shook her head in wonder. Today had been a miracle and she was sure she had her dear champion to thank for it. "Thank you," she whispered to the sea, knowing he was down there somewhere. "Thank you." She wiped a wind tear from her eye and smiled.

"And you are more than welcome," the Timekeeper replied from his empty cavern far away. He seldom got the chance to weave fine weather in that part of the world. All day he'd kept an eye on her, expecting the Patternmaker's assassin to strike while they crossed the sea, it was the perfect chance, but nothing had happened. The Patternmaker continued to send down his instructions on how fate should be woven and the Timekeeper continued to weave as though there wasn't any hint of a dispute between them, but the occasional whisper of silk somewhere in the glass proved otherwise. The assassin was still close, but he knew it couldn't hide forever. *I'll have you yet,* he swore silently. Although his mind was vast and intelligent, he took a spider's form because it was perfectly adapted to manage the weave. But on occasion he also *thought* like a spider; with implacable patience and iron logic.

He set about keeping the rest of the world on track, there were plenty of other threads besides Sunday Flowers, and each must be attended. There were so many threads in fact that he didn't spot three rather unusual ones following Sunday, just as she followed the steamer. Three threads that were neither man nor beast, although in a peculiar way they were both at once.

They had changed from eagles and taken the form of enormous killer whales, and as they ploughed through the ocean they sent a wave of dread before them, forcing seals deeper and shoals of fish into frenzied flight. All three were fleeing Valgard's curse and racing to catch up with their one hope of salvation before they lost its scent forever.

The Timekeeper continued to weave, but deep in the silken forest a tiny grub lay still and dormant. It had taken orders to rest and build a cocoon. When the Patternmaker decreed, it would crawl into its cocoon and change, then it would emerge and challenge the Timekeeper head on. Fearsome the Timekeeper might be, but there was one creature yet more formidable. Soon the assassin would slay the great spider and fate would have a new master.

CHAPTER TWELVE

01:42 am

"Ruinous creatures adopt shapes that reflect the well-being of the world and, as man has done much to upset that well-being . . . well, the rest you can work out for yourself."
Valonia Gulfoss - founder of Wildwood-coven, Cumberland

By midnight Galen was satisfied that everything was as ready as it could be. He slipped behind the barricade and into the restricted area, and once there he went from Galen the rogue to Galen the cultist. His eyes hardened and he walked taller, and he scrutinised the shattered kraken for any mistakes.

In the world on the other side of the barricade men bustled about their duties, but here it was still and quiet. The night was cold and his breath rose in clouds, turned golden by the sodium lamps. The dead kraken lay in the centre of a brilliant pool of light and the chains above it swayed gently making an eerie melody that appealed to him. Occasional moths fluttered past, but otherwise all was still. He paced around the giant with deliberate steps, tapping his cane as he went. "Soon my broken friend you'll live again, and your new master won't be any privileged gent, she'll be a lady."

"If she comes," Elios added.

"Oh she'll come, she's desperate." He fished for his pocket watch, sprung the case and saw it was now ten minutes past midnight. He set the watch to chime at 01:42, or as near as the old instrument would allow and then lay it gently between the kraken's feet where it looked like a gilded clam.

"What if this valkyrie thing —"

"She's not a thing," he interrupted, "kindly remember that."

"My apologies," she flinched, *"what if she cannot help you?"*

"She will."

His blunt reply drew a line under her worries and she said no more on the matter.

He knew without looking that someone had entered the restricted area. "Yes?" he asked without turning and heard someone clear their throat in annoyance.

"I don't like talking to a man's back." It was Lyle.

He fixed his public smile and turned. "Forgive me, lost in thought."

Lyle forced a smile then looked serious. "I thought it prudent to bring the test subjects across."

"Best keep them in the wagons for now, and have the surgeon look them over, I want to be sure they're in reasonable health, to put up a good fight you understand. Oh, and Mr Lyle . . ."

He turned back, with his hands in his overcoat pockets.

"Make sure Topp knows to return their lightning-staffs and wands. I trust they're still kept in the confiscated items vault?"

"Oh he knows all right, he's been cursing you all afternoon," Lyle grumbled.

"I hope he has!" Galen saluted with his cane.

"What's he doing behind there?" Doulton rubbed at his eyes. For the second time this week he found his sleep ruined in the name of duty.

"I don't have the faintest idea, but would you really want to know? You saw what he had us do at Smithfield." Lyle stressed the 'us' just to remind him. He stared ahead at the canvas, but all he saw were bright points of light like stars where it was punctured and torn.

Doulton checked his own pocket watch. "Just over an hour to go, and if this all turns out to be some cheap charade he's on the next boat back to the sub-continent."

"I suppose," he mumbled, remembering his lie. But if Galen's valkyrie didn't come tonight then Thorpe would simply make him try again, no matter what Doulton believed.

"Sir?" They looked around to see Topp a discreet distance away. "Just to let you know the prisoners are here." He looked to the station opening where three wagons stood like funeral hearses, and each had an armed escort of thirty men.

"Who's first?" Doulton muttered uneasily.

"Galen wants the lad from Nine-Maidens," Lyle explained. Their eyes turned to the barricade, which billowed like a heaving lung and the collection of differing sheets made it look like a patchwork of skin grafts. Doulton gave an involuntary shudder and checked his watch again. Soon, Galen would either conjure a valkyrie or be packing his bags, and he knew which he preferred.

He sat on the floor with his back against the cherub's smashed face, legs outstretched before him, gently tapping his toes. Each tap was perfectly synchronised with the second hand of his watch thirty yards away.

Elios felt his fingers play along the cane and knew what was expected of her. He wanted to see Sophie again, but tonight she didn't want to help him spy on his lost twin. *Sophie!* she thought angrily, everything always came back to Sophie, the lost girl who was so perfect. But how special could she be if he'd never met her?

Galen asked again, and for an instant she considered refusing, but just as she thought this her dead-walk self rose up in anger. *"Let him have her, you crippled slut,"* the voice hissed. *"Why would he want you? A broken sprite that can't fly, an outcast amongst your own, a freak with no home or family. If you love him, then let him see his beloved."*

She cringed at the voice, and in a state of confused subservience she yielded and opened a window for Galen, who sat unaware of her turmoil. She worked her magic aided by the dead-walk's rotten heart and the veil between worlds thinned.

Galen felt the gauzy world of matter melt away and reveal the true world underneath. The place where Àeon created time itself. He saw her straight away. There she was, lavishing her attention upon something out of his sight. His Sophie, unaware of him, unloving and distant, and he swore to bring her home kicking and screaming if he had to. She had half of what was rightfully his. "Sister," he said, but like a man promising revenge.

He gazed long at the girl with the black hair and white dress, listening to the tune she hummed. Her voice was gentle but distant, like a whisper on the other side of the world. *"Little Miss Muffet sat on her tuffet,"* she chanted over and over. *"Along came a spider and sat down beside her. . ."*

Along came a spider, he thought. Why did that always give him a shiver? He wasn't in the least bit afraid of spiders.

He would have watched her forever if something hadn't disturbed him. It was the sound of his pocket watch chiming. His eyes flickered open, Sophie vanished and Elios swam towards his touch.

"The watch has spoke Galen."

He climbed to his feet and looked around. Lyle and the rest must have also noted the time because there wasn't a sound from behind the barricade. He looked around, not sure what to expect or where she might appear. "Please," he whispered to the ether. "Please Àeon send her to me."

Elios and her dead-walk self listened as one, differences momentarily set aside.

He couldn't see them, but he knew hundreds of eyes were staring at a wall of tattered canvas ready for his signal. The chimes began to distort and lose their melody as time killed them as it kills all things. "Great Àeon, please let her come," he whispered again. Single haphazard notes drifted up from the pocket-watch like memories from a dying man and then they stopped altogether.

Silence.

He looked around, chilled by his own sweat. His mouth was dry and his pulse was racing. If she didn't come Sophie was lost. He stared intently at the dead kraken. A few stray moths fluttered around the dangling chains, driven insensible by the lights. He watched closely, but not knowing why, and then they began to fall. In a second there were dead and dying moths twitching on the concrete and he knew the valkyrie was there with him. "Thank you," he whispered to Àeon and clutched his satchel tight.

On the other side, where men stared at an empty screen, Lyle felt his skin prickle as the temperature dropped. Now his watch said 01:43. "Topp!" he hissed and gestured to be ready with the first of the captives.

Doulton suddenly understood that Galen would be with them for a while longer yet, and it was only now that he realised that he hadn't wanted the creature to come because now they had to feed it. He looked at the prison wagons and wondered for the first time if this was right.

Lyle saw his unease. "Remember Smithfield," he cautioned quietly. "We can't turn back now."

He wiped his brow, then stuffed the handkerchief into his pocket. He didn't want to see the stain, it would be too easy to imagine the stain on his own conscience.

Galen crept along holding his cane in one hand and stroking the battered metal with the other. The kraken's clawed feet drew closer and he knew that just behind them, out of sight, was his pocket watch and the valkyrie. It seemed only natural that she be fascinated by time. He halted at the tip of the foot, hiding in its shadow and letting her sense him and understand he meant no harm. He heard a series of sharp sniffs and scratches, but daren't look out.

"This device?" The voice drifted towards him like smoke; the same voice he heard at Smithfield.

"The watch?" he asked softly.

"Watch," she repeated, grasping the word. "It measures the music of Àeon?"

"That's right," he smiled at her phrasing. "It measures time, the song of Àeon."

"It reminds me of home." She sounded melancholy again.

"But I promised you a new home, isn't that why you've come?"

There was a pause as the valkyrie considered. "You also promised red-rivers," she reminded him.

"And I have brought you just that. And this machine, blessed by Ruination, so that it might hold you indefinitely, will you not try it out?" he tempted, as if he'd bought her a new gown.

He heard metal scrape against stone. She'd picked his watch up to inspect it and he felt absurdly honoured. "I have hidden in places around your city, but before long they are Ruined and I must find new ones. Fleeing from place to place is weakening us. This machine, it is the safe place you spoke of?"

"Yes."

Another long silence. He was about to speak when she asked him another question out of nowhere. "What is your name?" She caught him off guard, and for a moment he floundered.

"Don't tell her your true name!" Elios almost screamed.

He steeled himself. If he declined she would leave, but if he told her she would have power over him. There was only one option. He readied himself to believe that 'Galen' had always been his name. He took a deep breath, made himself believe the lie and then spoke. "Galen," he said quickly, "and yours?"

There came a rasping sound and he had the horrible idea she was laughing at his deceit. "None was ever given me."

"She's lying Galen!" Elios moaned. *"Send her back while we still can!"* But he ignored her.

"Then may I be so bold as to lavish a name upon you?" he asked chivalrously.

"If it pleases you," she agreed indifferently. Any name he gave her would have no power over her.

His mind raced as he groped for a suitable name, then he thought of the machine she would crawl into and inhabit. The name on the chest plate was blackened and barely legible. It had read 'Victorianus' but now in its damaged state it read 'V...or...us' and the name fell into place. "Vorus." He named her.

"What does this name mean?"

"To conquer and triumph. It is inspired by our Queen-Empress."

"Then it is fitting, and I shall gladly wear this armour." She sounded more confident than she had at Smithfield and a tiny part of him wondered, *Should I send her back?* But he didn't, and so the inevitable calamity took another step closer.

"Blast it! It's almost 2am," Doulton snapped his own watch closed. "I say we drag him out of there."

"He'll signal us when he's ready. Until then nobody moves," Lyle glared at him. "He'll signal us when he's ready," he repeated quietly, then folded his arms again and stared ahead at the barricade.

There was a tingling in his palm from the kraken and he knew the valkyrie, now named Vorus, had entered the machine and was easing herself into it like fingers into a glove.

"Galen I'm scared," Elios whimpered.

"Not now my sweet." The sensation in his palm vanished and the metal suddenly felt dead. "Vorus?" He wondered now if the machine had failed. "Vorus can you hear me?"

There was only silence, but another moth spun to the floor, trembled and died and he knew she was still in there. Suddenly he heard metal scrape against metal. It was an ugly sound, like a confession, and it rang through the whole station. Something was moving. He ran towards it, ducking between the great metal feet and around the war-suit's opposite side, and came into the bright sodium lights and skidded to a halt in amazement. The fingers of the right gauntlet, so damaged that they ought to have never moved again, were gouging at the cement as the hand tried to clench into a fist. "Oh my dear," he gasped, "you do learn fast!"

"What was that?" Doulton jumped and dropped his snuff box, spilling the contents over his shoes.

"Topp!" Lyle barked. The scream of metal was deafening now. "Topp, bring up the first one!" He thrust a finger towards the prison carriages and Topp set off at a run as Lyle turned back in dread fascination towards the barricade, wondering just what the hell Galen had summoned.

Galen backed up giving the kraken room. The sinister cherub head rocked slightly, then slowly began to rise on its broken neck, squealing and grinding at it went. A few errant sparks joined the hovering moths above, which fluttered away as the machine grew higher. "Dear Àeon!" He watched in wide-eyed wonder.

The huge figure was trying to sit upright like a wounded soldier, and the cherub's scarred face turned his way, but sat at a disconcerting angle, making the thing look calculating and intelligent.

"It's too late," Elios despaired, but she was drowned out by the mountain of rising metal.

It was like watching a landslide in reverse. Broken body parts and components that had no earthly way of adjoining were building themselves into a mound of metal, reassembling a figure, but not according to any blueprint of man. The scream of metal was as piercing as the penned animals at Smithfield. He watched as the huge barrel arms began to roll towards the shoulder sockets, and steel cables, chains and melted rubber hose threaded back into them like living veins.

"Bring up the first one!" Topp ordered. The horses were skittish, but they were tugged and whipped ahead against their will. Galen had specified them in a particular order, and inside the first wagon sat John Fold.

Meanwhile back at the kraken area, nervous infantry directed their rifles at the barricade, looking to Lyle and Doulton for orders and wondering if bullets were any use. The noise rumbled down the entire station and crashed off the curved roof like a wave. Doulton fancied all of London must be able to hear it. He looked down at his watch in a kind of dazed stupor and found that it had now stopped.

Vorus continued to gather her new armour, delighting in the sensation of movement and power and creating a machine driven by the will of Ruination alone.

Galen watched broken metal and bent springs twitch and roll upwards along the giant's deformed limbs, adding flesh to the steel skeleton. None of the components had a purpose or even worked, but the whole they created was magnificent. The giant twisted to one side and a massive hand boomed down onto the cement sending up a cloud of dust. It pushed itself up into a kneeling position, a feat no kraken based on human technology could achieve. Fragments continued to flock around it like bees around a queen until they found a place in the chaotic structure to serve the will of the creature within. "Beautiful!" He felt a tear run down his cheek, and in his rapture he certainly didn't hear Elios weeping inside the cane.

"Galen! Send her back!"

"Bring him up!" Lyle shouted over the racket and the first of the nine locks on the prison wagon were sprung, while the infantry made sure their rifles were ready. If this witch so much as moved a wrong muscle he'd be dead before he hit the ground.

The cherub stared down at him and he saw something that both amazed and honoured him. His pocket watch was now embedded in the copper of its forehead like the mystical third eye. This kraken's emblem was Time and he knew Àeon would be proud. His gaze fell from the pocket watch down to the cherub's eyes where an intelligence regarded him from behind the vacant sockets. "Yes Vorus!" he cheered. "Is this new home to your liking?" His words were crushed by a wall of noise, but she heard him and he felt her reply.

"My – new – home."

"Yes, your new home my dearest," he gushed, forgetting Elios.

Metal continued to swarm across her like ants, further adding to her bulk and menace. "This is not just a home Galen, this is," she paused, overwhelmed by the sense of power, "this is a fortress."

"You're safe now my sweet," he applauded.

"Safe?" she echoed.

Elios shivered. She thought Vorus sounded little interested in being merely 'safe'. *"It's not all it seems Galen,"* she moaned quietly.

The cherub helmet twisted slowly to the left, spraying a wave of sparks as it did, and Vorus regarded the sheet of material. "What is beyond?" she asked.

"What you asked for Vorus: red-rivers. I have brought three for you as a gift."

She laughed at that, and now she was enshrined in her new chariot she sounded almost seductive. "A gift for me?"

"Galen please!" Elios eventually did the only thing she might, she appeared physically.

"Leave him be you half-breed viper, he has no need for you!" The dead-walk tried to pull her back, or maybe it was just her paranoia.

She dragged herself from the cane with a weak flash of static, feeling dizzy from the effort. "Galen, it already has you under its spell. Please, go no further!"

"Elios?" He looked down at her in surprise, and took hold of her gently but firmly.

Inside the kraken, Vorus fixed her cold stare on the small creature in his hands. "Is this my red-river?" Her voice reverberated around the metal skull.

Elios bristled with fear.

"No, she is not for you," he said firmly, holding her to his chest.

"But there is life in her, as well as Ruin," Vorus said longingly. "Open her up for me and release the red-river Galen." The cherub regarded him with its full lips, dead eyes and patchwork of scars and it looked to be considering. "As a gift," she added, using his words.

"It learns too fast," Elios pleaded, "it'll outgrow you and it won't take long."

"Not *it* Elios, *she*."

"What does it matter! She's hiding something!"

"Nonsense," he kissed her brow and despite everything his affection still worked its magic and she felt calmer. "She's mine. She's not for you! Understood?" he shouted up at Vorus. "She's mine, but I have brought you other red-rivers that you might release and enjoy."

"Was that him? I swear I just heard him shout something, do you think he's in trouble?" Personally Doulton couldn't care less if the valkyrie skewered him like a cocktail cherry and sucked the marrow from his bones, but what if it got loose and he couldn't stop it? He took a step towards the barricade.

"No, wait," Lyle ordered. "No one's to go in there and nothing's to happen until he gives the signal. Nothing, do you understand!"

"Show me these gifts Galen." Vorus sounded excited. "The ones with red-rivers waiting to flow."

He didn't answer right away but instead turned to Elios. "You're tired."

"I have to speak my mind. Galen I don't trust her."

"We cannot stop now, for Sophie's sake, for my master's sake."

"Be cautious, that's all I ask, be cautious and don't let her ensnare you."

"And I will." He brought the cane up. "Best be inside, you're in no shape for this." He stroked a finger across her useless wings, and for a moment she could pretend that it was just them again, as it had been for so long.

She gave him a lingering look trying to decide if he was being honest, then still undecided she vanished, leaving him to face Vorus. "There are men behind this barrier that can assist you," he addressed the valkyrie. "It would be best if you didn't meet them on your knees."

The cherub helmet tilted questioningly.

"To be on ones knees is a position of defeat and shame," he explained. *Show them Vorus, show these blue-blood vermin what you can do,* he urged silently.

The kraken flinched. Clearly she understood defeat and she wanted no part of it, and so she clambered up onto her new feet for the first time.

The thunder of grinding metal began again and Lyle and Doulton looked in amazement at the terrible thing rearing up over the barricade. The rusted cherub rose into view and turned its empty eyes on them and every man there gasped in horror. "Dear God Almighty." The words dropped from Doulton's mouth. Suddenly men cried out and rifles were aimed at the rising monster.

"Lower your weapons!" Lyle screamed and flapped his arms. "It's not to be harmed! Topp, bring up the prisoner!" This was the signal Galen had prepared him for. Pulleys rumbled and chains rattled as the screens were drawn fully back and Hobbs Ash was rewarded with its first proper view of a valkyrie.

John Fold sat in the rear of the prisoner wagon and listened to the commotion outside. Whatever they promised, he knew there wasn't going to be a happy ending for witches tonight.

He had been here since last September and here he would have stayed if it hadn't been for the explosion a month later. He remembered it well. The memory of that day still painted a smile on his face even when things were at their darkest and he smiled now as he relished the memory of prison ships swarming with witches during the mass break out.

He made a break for it along with the rest, jumping ship and swimming down the Thames. It seemed inevitable that some of them would be recaptured, but of the hundreds that escaped they took back just a few dozen. He might have been one of them, but it did his heart good to see so many empty cells. "One old lass tore this place to pieces, let's see if I can't do better," he promised himself.

Keys rattled in the lock, the door creaked open and Topp looked in. "Out you get laddie." He stepped back and waved him forwards. He always called him 'laddie' because nobody knew his name.

Fold shuffled along the tiny bench, slid out and dropped to his feet. Chains rattled as he hit the cement and he wobbled before finding his balance, and despite everything he loved the feel of the night air after so long being locked up.

"Bring him," Topp gestured to two guards. Behind them was a wall of infantry, all with their rifles trained on him. One wrong move and he'd be dead. For a moment he considered feinting an escape. He'd get about a yard then fall to the ground with a score of bullets in him, but at least it'd spoil their experiment. If he did however, they'd go find another witch, and Topp had stated that they'd punish any escape attempt by killing five prisoners. Personally Fold thought they'd be better off, but their lives weren't his to play with and so he shuffled after Topp's guards who led him around the wagon. That's when he saw it, and it took incredible strength to hold onto his defiant face.

He'd seen krakens before, but never one like this. It was like a revived corpse. He swallowed and felt clammy, and only then realised that he'd stopped walking. Hands grabbed his upper arms and pressed him forwards, but he didn't want to get any closer to the undead thing.

The kraken stood looking down at him. There was a pilot of sorts inside, he knew that instinctively, but where as all krakens ate coal and belched smoke, this one was alive in a very different way. His gaze travelled up along its mangled limbs, scorched paintwork and mutilated hands, over the gaping hole in its chest where the furnace ought to be and up to its face and a small groan of fear escaped him.

It was a cherub, something he found creepy enough at the best of times, but its face was green with decayed copper and streaked by rust. With its pouting lips and chubby cheeks, it looked like a child with a cruel streak, the kind of little angel who enjoyed tormenting insects to death. He steeled himself, remembered who he served, and met the atrocity's stare directly. *Oak and Holly, just let me die well,* he thought.

A man came sauntering towards him and he recognised him from earlier. He wore the same bowler hat and shabby coat and Fold's dislike intensified.

Galen fixed his familiar persona and regarded him somewhat sadly. "Now then son," he tapped him with his black cane, "ready to tell me your name?"

"I'm a witch of Nine-Maidens coven," he said through clenched teeth.

"Nine ladies," Galen liked the number, but little else. "Then I'll just have to carry on calling you 'witch'." He made that sound sordid. "When I saw you last I spoke of an offer, that if you help me I'll help you."

Fold said nothing.

"You see my friend over there?" he continued, and raised his cane towards the kraken.

He regarded it again, and noticed something he hadn't seen before, the shoulders were slowly rising and falling. It was breathing. He turned back to Galen without a word. Jaw clenched, eyes stony.

"Well, I know that you see it, surgeon says you've got perfect vision," Galen smiled. "So let's just say that my offer is this; I'll give you back your lightning-staff and wand."

Fold almost gaped at him and then cursed himself for giving any reaction at all.

Galen saw it and smirked. "All I want you to do is take that staff and knock over that big ugly brute there." Again he pointed. "Now I know what's going through that head of yours," he tapped Fold's brow with his cane. "You're thinking you might just climb on that old broomstick and whisk away over London never to be seen again." He leaned closer and his voice was full of false sympathy. "Am I right?"

He let his breath rush out between his clenched teeth, but still he said nothing.

"Now I can understand you wanting such a thing, but make no mistake witch, if you do then I'll just have to find some pretty young witch lass and have her take your place." He leaned closer. "But maybe we'll pass her around the lads first."

Fold trembled with anger.

"I'll do it," he vowed, "all mockery aside I'll do it – and then I'll get another and do it again. Understand witch?"

Fold stared at his feet, mouth shut.

"Insolence is something I usually find hard to stomach, but I like it in you, it'll just make the red-river all the richer."

Fold had no idea what he meant, and he was glad. Sometimes ignorance really was bliss.

Galen turned to Topp. "Unchain him and return his weapons." With that he walked back over to Vorus.

Topp took hold of Fold's prison shirt and read his serial number. In lieu of his name they addressed him by this. "Bring up 0142's weapons," he called.

Galen stopped in his tracks and looked back. "0142?" he smiled contentedly. He liked neat little coincidences. Vorus meanwhile looked on expectantly and he could almost taste her impatience. He'd explained the deal to Fold and now he would explain to Vorus just what was going to happen and how to release the red-river. He was going to teach her how to be a killer.

"Vorus?" he pressed his hand against the kraken, and looked up at the cherub high above.

"Galen," she replied, by-passing the aural and speaking directly to his mind state.

"There's a man over there, a witch. Do you know that name?"

She thought for a moment. *"This is a new word for me."*

"Witches find creatures such as you and kill them," he lied.

"Witches." The metal trembled slightly and he guessed his remark had sunk in. *"They hunt our kind?"*

"They do," he lied again.

"And the red-river is inside the witch?"

"Aye."

"But there are so many men, so many rivers to unleash."

"No," he resisted, "the men here are not to be opened up, only the witch is for that. If you harm even one of these men they'll take this machine away from you. Would you like to go back to hiding in sewers?"

She was already dependent on this new feeling of security. *"No Galen, that would be awful,"* she confessed. *"Then I agree, the men here will remain whole, but the witch?"*

"The witch is all yours," he smiled, "but he'll resist you."

"Why?"

"Because he doesn't want the red-river to flow. He needs it to live. So he'll attack you with that staff he carries, but it can't harm you, do you understand?"

She pondered this. *"If he needs the red-river to live, then is it right that I release it?"* She sounded uncertain.

He knew he had to tread carefully. The valkyrie for all her power didn't have man's instinct to destroy. He had to instil it in her. "If you don't Vorus, he'll try to take away this safe place I've given you."

"No," she gasped. *"But then I would die!"*

"Indeed, that's why you must not let him. Do you understand?"

She thought this over quietly.

"Do you remember the beasts at Smithfield, and the woman in the sow-pen?" he manipulated, "do you recall how artful you found it?"

"Yes."

"Then take this witch, open him up Vorus, turn him into something beautiful and the red-river will flow. I promise he won't be able to harm you." He heard a churning sound deep inside the Ruined kraken, like a rumbling belly and knew she was ready.

Topp's men retrieved his staff and wand from the munitions locker resting on a carriage drawn by a shire horse. It was plate steel and must have weighed at least half a ton. A guard retrieved a roll of fabric from inside and brought it across. It had the number 0142 stencilled on the side, and right away Fold knew his lightning-staff was within. "Corn lad," he said softly and smiled. He hadn't seen Hail-Strips-Cornfields-Bare for over six months and if he had to die here he couldn't think of a better friend to have at his side. The roll was placed at his feet and the armed guards closed in.

"Off with those manacles," Topp ordered. "Now then 0142, on my order I want you to take this roll and open it. Inside you'll find your things. Mr Galen's told you what to do with them. If however, you try to do something he ain't asked you to do then my lads here will fire without hesitation. Understood?"

Fold looked at him directly. He was just a man doing a job because his life was so devoid of anything else, he couldn't hate him for that, but Galen was different.

. "They'll just fetch another if you do," Topp added softly. This young lad might be his enemy, but he still had respect for his enemies and as far as it went 0142 hadn't been such a bad prisoner. Fold twitched his head in the merest of nods and then Topp retreated to stand in rank with his men. "Make ready," he ordered and rifles were raised. "Prisoner 0142 will now retrieve his belongings."

John Fold knelt, anxious to see Corn again, and undid the knots with trembling hands. The rubberised material insulated and isolated the thunder-sprite from the outside world. Corn would have sunk into a state of stupor and remained inert all this time. He peeled away the cloth, feeling angry at it for hurting his sprite, and saw a piece of home inside. A tear fell onto the wooden staff, and as soon as he touched it Corn rose up to greet him.

"Johnny?"

"Aye it's me," he smiled. "How you feeling?"

"Like a rat in a trap, where are we?" he asked, disorientated.

"In a bad place, with a big dirty beast to knock down, can you manage?"

"I'll need time," he said faintly. *"Can you buy me some time?"*

"Anything for you." He had already formulated a crude plan. He just hoped that Corn could still deliver. He reached for his wand and fastened it around his waist, and now he was ready for anything, even death.

A shrill whistle blew and the experiment began.

"Behind the red line," Lyle ordered, and everyone including Galen gathered behind a thin line of paint on the cement. They formed a long file, each man wanting a good view and each rifle fixed on John Fold.

"Forwards," someone ordered.

Fold felt a rifle prod him in the back and he advanced towards the kraken. He walked on into the flood-lit arena, alone now and heading straight for the mountain of living metal. "You see it lad?" he asked.

"Seen plenty of 'em before."

"Not like this one," he said ominously.

Fold knew that no thunder-sprite could go from dormancy to battle in a few moments, but he didn't care, it was just great to have his old friend back even if it was just for a few minutes. There was only a hundred yards between him and the kraken and he walked on without slowing.

Inside her cane Elios watched intently. Her dead-walk half was excited, but Elios watched with a very different kind of excitement. The young witch carried a genuine lightning-staff and inside was one of her kind. She'd never been this close to another thunder-sprite before. *"Please be careful,"* she whispered, both to the sprite and his witch.

Galen frowned and looked down at the cane, he could have sworn it had changed. Just for a moment it had felt unfamiliar, but he thought no more of it and returned to the spectacle of Vorus's first kill.

Vorus looked down at the witch and saw only a fragile vessel containing a river of glorious red. Galen had told her to break that vessel to protect herself and in this war-suit she could do just that. The witch was fifty yards away now and he walked directly towards her without slowing.

Fold continued his last walk and each step made the terrible machine seem even taller.

"Let's just mount up and sod off!" Corn suggested.

"Can't. Others are ransom."

"Oh," he said simply. *"A good plan though eh?"*

"A rascal's plan," he smiled sadly.

"We'll just do our best." He might have been dormant for months, but he wasn't a fool.

"Did you know about the breakout?" He wanted to say something positive.

"No! I've been in that bastard locker for months!"

"They all got away, well almost all of them."

"And you're one of the almosts." He sounded sad for him.

"Makes little difference now." He felt oddly calm even as he walked into the kraken's shadow, and twenty yards from it he drew his wand and broke into a run.

Twenty yards from the kraken they all saw the witch charge and a chorus of whistles and cheers went up from the guards. "That's enough!" Topp barked and they fell quiet. He disliked the idea of an execution becoming entertainment.

Doulton pressed a hand to his mouth, suddenly feeling ill. Lyle snatched a look at Galen, but his eyes were shadowed by the bowler and his face looked carved of wood. "What's going to happen?" Lyle asked.

For a moment Galen just watched the tiny figure vanish into the kraken's shadow and wished he could enter Ruination just as easily. "You're going to see what the German and French knights will see this summer," he smiled thinly, "you're going to see the force that brought you down, rebuild you."

Over six months ago the Illuminata had turned his home into smoking ruins. Of the twenty witches that called Nine-Maidens their home sixteen were killed, the rest captured and now the only surviving member remembered his murdered friends, and in particular a witch named Anna, and raised his wand and raised his war cry as he sprinted towards his fate.

The kraken never shifted. It stood as lifeless as a scarecrow and he landed a blow against the right ankle, hoping to smash the mangled metal and topple it. The wand hit home. The spell of iron was released, weakening the molecules. He felt the wand hit its mark and a split-second later he felt a pressure wave boom through the station as the spell discharged. His chest throbbed with the sonic blast and he sprinted away from the falling giant, hit the cement and rolled to one side to avoid its death-dive.

He was up on his feet again in a flash and looked up through a mop of sweaty hair, but the kraken hadn't budged an inch.

Vorus watched from behind the cherub's blank face as the witch ran at her. "The red-river," she lusted. She could smell it inside the witch-man. Galen had told her she must break him open if she wanted to see it. Just then the witch was under her, out of sight and he lashed at the war-suit with a wand.

The spell hit, and the station rumbled in its aftermath and she saw the men behind the red line shove and push for a better view. The spell washed over the kraken like gentle rain and vanished in a second. Ruination had disarmed it and a hundred yards away Galen smiled. His theory had proved correct.

"You missed!" Corn shouted.

"No, it was a hit, I know it was!" Without hesitation, he made a second run, from the rear this time.

"Same ankle! It'll be weakened!"

He charged, expecting the kraken to turn any moment, but the huge thing just stood inert and vacant. The iron-fall spell hadn't worked although he knew he'd done it correctly. Something more insidious was at work here. Only feet from the machine he summoned a void-spell. If the iron couldn't help him the air might. He screamed in fury and stabbed his wand at the metal. The wooden shaft bounced off and sent a shock wave up his arm as the spell discharged. He ducked and sprinted a safe distance away before skidding to a halt to watch the giant fall over.

The kraken didn't move and it remained intact.

"No!" he groaned. The spell had failed and the cherub helmet turned lazily, screeching as it did, and looked down at him and he knew he would die here. "No!" he seethed, too angry to be afraid. "No, I hit the bastard thing, I know I did!" The spell should have created an intense vacuum, strong enough to crush the metal.

"It's resistant to magic," Corn finally realised. *"Let me try!"*

"You're too weak." He wiped sweat from his eyes.

"Neither of us is going to get any stronger if that thing gets a hold of us, let me try!"

"The ankle again?"

"Anywhere, just let me hit the bloody thing!"

He charged again. Now it was Corn's turn to see how well it stood up to a thunder-sprite. He screamed as he ran, angry that its pilot considered him so insignificant. "Try this!" he roared and swung the staff. There was a blinding flash as Corn made his strike and Fold carried on running, while behind him he heard thunder roll around the cavernous station. He flung himself to the floor then rolled to a stop, spun in the dirt and looked back. The kraken's left leg was a crumbling mess, pouring smoke and dropping huge, twisted chunks. "We did it!" he cheered.

"Magic-proof my arse," Corn growled triumphantly.

The huge machine began to disintegrate. One moment it stood implacable, the next it was a landslide and the noise was biblical in scale. Fold stood and screamed in victory, holding his staff above his head.

Doulton gasped a sigh of relief and lowered his head and rubbed his eyes, more to disguise his smile than relieve his fatigue. Galen had failed.

"Nice work," Lyle said acidly and turned to Galen. "Nice – bloody – work! Now what the hell do we do in June eh? What do I tell Thorpe!" he raged.

Galen stood tapping his cane against his cheek thoughtfully. "It'll be interesting to see how long it takes her to realise the truth of it, won't it?"

"What the blazes are you on about? That convict Jik scum just shoved a ramrod right up the backside of our best hope!" he screamed, and grabbed his coat lapels.

The guard detail stopped what they were doing to watch this new confrontation, it seemed to them that tonight's entertainments just kept on coming.

"Back to your duties lads," Topp shouted and they turned their rifles fully back on John Fold who was now performing a victory dance in front of the wrecked kraken.

"Well?" Lyle was nose to nose with him now. He felt humiliated and cheated, and he was well aware of Doulton watching with great interest.

"She's a new creature Mr Lyle," he said, not in the least bit ruffled, "she's still learning." He wriggled free, turned and gave him a confident smile. "If you'd been shot wouldn't you also take a while to gather your wits?"

Lyle balled his hands into fists, tired of his cultist-babble. "I want you on the boat to Amsterdam tomorrow, after that I don't give a shit where you go." His voice was quiet and deadly.

"No, I don't think your friend Thorpe will like that," he yawned.

Lyle grabbed his arm and spun him around and was ready to land a fist right in the middle of his face when he heard a terrible sound like nails scraping glass and every man there turned and looked back; every man but Galen that was. "Like I said," he smiled. "I don't think I'll be leaving just yet."

The kraken had barely fallen into a heap, when it suddenly began to move again. The cherub helmet sat in a sea of wreckage and it slowly juddered around to look at Fold.

"Lord Oak," he breathed.

The pouting face regarded him from its bed of scrap, and then a second later it began to rise on a spinal column of machine parts. Pipes and wire cables dangled like severed nerves and they whipped and groped around until they latched onto other components and dragged them towards the head, gradually rebuilding a torso.

"Dear Oak no!" he cried in frustration.

"Hethra's not with us this day," Corn answered.

One of its arms dragged itself over the floor and flipped itself over like an upturned crab. Metal screamed in a nightmare symphony and the cherub continued to grow higher as it collected its shattered body back into one whole. Pipes, cables, gaskets, cogs and steel juddered back into place and cemented themselves into an irregular, but immensely strong block. Vorus had learned. She had *evolved* and now she understood the magic in the witch's staff she could make herself resistant to that also, just as she had with the wand.

Fold looked back at the men far away in the ordered world behind the red line and his hatred of them spurred him on. "This is our last run," he stared up at the kraken's mocking face. It was almost whole again now. "And I know just where to hit it!" he spat, and charged again, but this time he mounted his staff and flew.

Elios was suddenly wonder-struck. The witch was flying. He made a wide circle to come at Vorus from the back, and swept easily over the concrete, climbing in height until he was level with its head, and there he dropped nimbly from his staff right onto the kraken itself. *A real thunder-sprite!* she admired, careful not to let Galen hear.

Fold landed on the kraken's shoulders and as soon as his feet touched down he knew there was something very wrong with this machine, something very wrong indeed. He swallowed his fear and edged closer to the doll-like face and still the kraken didn't move.

"Kill it and let's be done!" Corn shouted.

Just as he was about to swing the staff, the helmet screeched around to face him and suddenly he was looking into those dead eyes, and those full lips were close enough to swallow him whole. Now, at point blank range, he could see the golden object between the cherub's eyes was a pocket watch, and the hands steadily ticked away, counting down his life. Something inside the cock-pit shifted, he could see movement through the eye slits.

"Kill it!" Corn screamed.

"Is that a man inside there?" He felt confused and forgetful, under the spell of Ruin.

"Just kill it!"

"There's something alive in there," he murmured.

"Then whatever it is just kill it!"

Grinding metal shattered the trance. He blinked away the stupor and looked up to see a huge misshapen hand reaching towards him. "This is for Anna," he snarled and lashed at the vulgar face with all his strength and the next instant thunder and lightning filled the station.

"Dear God!" Lyle cried and flinched away. For a second he saw nothing but a blinding whiteness. He looked back at the kraken and tried to shake the after-image from his eyes, but his vision was too fogged to see what happened next.

Fold stood and looked at the staff in his hands with mute horror. His strike had not made the slightest mark.

"Resistant to all magic," Corn despaired, forgetting everything else.

The metal hand loomed closer and he knew the time had come. "I'm sorry Corn."

"I'll miss you too." He couldn't say anymore.

Time kills everything, and Fold's time had run out. The metal fist swung like a demolition ball and hit him full on.

Vorus brushed the witch aside with casual ease and he was flung through the air. She watched him spin to the ground and saw the impact of blood and bone against concrete. The lightning-staff broke under him, and there was a final flash as Corn was separated from the staff, as well as his earthly contract with John Fold, and he began his irresistible journey back to the thunder-heights.

The last witch of Nine-Maidens lay in a contorted heap looking up at the station roof. He saw lightning and knew it was Corn leaving this realm. A pane of glass high above shattered as he was pulled through back to his origins. There was a mournful cry and then he was gone. He watched shards of glass twirl down like snowflakes and listened to men shout and cheer from far away. *Best of luck Corn,* he thought. He wanted to speak but his lips wouldn't move and the sound he thought was thunder was in fact the approaching kraken. The glass roof was blotted out as its huge foot swung into view and hovered over him. *Anna,* he thought, knowing that was the last word he'd ever think and feeling that wasn't such a bad way to end things.

"Unleash the red-river." Vorus remembered what Galen had told her. She looked down at the dying witch, feeling pity for him because he wasn't as beautiful as Charlotte Anne Pilling, but she knew how to remedy that. Galen had shown her and like a child eager to win her father's favour she brought her foot down and the red-river flowed.

Doulton watched in horror as the kraken crushed John Fold. He just hoped he was already dead, but a muffled scream proved otherwise and in the next instant he heard a sickening crunch and thanked his lucky stars he was a hundred yards away.

Galen looked on while all around him Topp's men groaned and winced. It was no way for a dog to die let alone a witch, and when Fold screamed his last, some of them even turned away, but Galen never so much as twitched an eyebrow. To him, that final scream was just a rusty gate.

Chapter Thirteen

Good hunting

*'Those who live by the rule of the strong must one day expect to
fall prey to those stronger than themselves.'*
Traditional witch saying

Their steamer arrived into the Faroes in the dead of night and bumped
against the harbour bollards making the whole vessel shudder. Sunday had
no idea how long she'd been cramped up in the small lifeboat. Outside the
canvas she could hear men shouting in a strange language, ships' horns,
and booted feet marching back and forth.

"Fairy Islands?" Strike asked hopefully.

"Faroe," she whispered, "time we were on our way."

"Surely not flying in the dark?"

"Not flying, sheltering. We'll jump ship, and bed down somewhere quiet."

They slipped out of hiding and drifted away under cover of darkness to
pass what remained of the night in the company of sheep somewhere in
the hills around Tórshavn. Sunday had no idea what the Faroes looked
like, but it took her some time to find a level piece of land and she
assumed the islands were rocky and steep.

The worst stretch was over and so she slept deeply, but the next thing
she knew there was a rough snout pressing at her face and warm breath
that smelled none too pleasant. She opened her eyes and saw a curious
sheep peering in at her under the oil cloth. "At least the locals are friendly,"

she commented sleepily. The sheep looked startled at the sound of her voice and bolted.

Strike yawned. "And at least there aren't any hungry fairies."

"No, just hungry sheep." She scratched at some of her fairy bites, then pulled the oil cloth back from the large stones securing it. A flock of gulls and a few rabbits had gathered around during the night, enchanted by the singing way-beware. As soon as she sat up they swooped away and the rabbits darted for their burrows. "Sorry to spoil the show," she apologised.

Although early, it was already daylight, and she saw the islands for the first time and they were indeed steep and rocky. She combed her hair, took a drink and a bite to eat, which was the last of her rations, and checked the map and compass.

"Do you think there are any witches here?" Strike asked, looking around.

"Just one tired and damp one as far as I know." She checked hrafn-dimmu and the special way-beware, who was still singing quietly to himself in her satchel. "Time to be on our way."

"The Shanty Islands?"

"Almost," she smiled, "but I've a better name for them."

He blinked at her expectantly.

"They're the northern most bit of Britain, so as far as I'm concerned that makes them home."

"Let's go home then." He climbed onto the staff feeling well rested and vanished into the wood changing it from a dreary old stick into an object of true magic.

Then southwards to London and whatever fate brings, she thought and touched her scarred cheek. She threw her last crust of bread to the sheep thinking it'd make a pleasant change from grass, then confident everything was in order they were airborne in a second. Sheep ran as they darted overhead and clouds of seabirds rose up in squabbling flocks, then there was only the grey ocean again, and they were bound for Britain's northern isles and ultimately London.

Her first glimpse of Shetland came far sooner than expected. Again, the crossing was smooth and the weather wonderful, and again she said a silent thanks to her dear champion. The Isle of Unst was a wall of sheer

cliffs eroded into ledges teaming with birds. It was now late April and the
breeding season was in full swing. The cliffs she mistook as chalk from
a distance turned out to be a colony of gannets and for a while she rested
and watched birds diving for fish, and all those little dramas unfolding as
birds battled for life and death. Loath to leave but knowing she must, she
checked the map, which was now quite ragged, and set out for Lerwick
careful to avoid any fishing boats. Tales of mermaids and silkies might be
common enough but reports of a flying witch might reach the wrong ears.

In Lerwick she was amazed by the sight of seals languishing on the
rocks close to town, and a ruined but impressive broch standing next to
a small loch. Again, she swapped silver for food and other supplies and
even a night's lodging. In the upper story bedroom overlooking the quaint
stone houses with the sea lapping their foundations, she got to grips
with mending her clothes, studying the chart and making her plans. She
enjoyed a hot bath, and after dressing and fixing her hair with her special
pins she almost felt like a solstice queen again.

She walked Lerwick's narrow alleys dressed in a modest shawl, and
simply wandering at will, enjoying the relaxed atmosphere, content that
the worst was behind her. All that remained was the open water between
Shetland and Orkney, which she anticipated shouldn't give her too much
trouble. In fact there was a small island between the two where she could
shelter if conditions grew rough.

The harbour jostled with ships and boats, many of which carried
Norwegian flags, and Strike pointed out the 'Sunday-effect' again when
a good many of Lerwick's menfolk showed an interested in the young
woman with the golden hair. *"What is it about you?"* he grumbled.

"I've no idea what you mean," she laughed, enjoying the attention.

She stayed two nights in Lerwick, delighting in being comfortable and
snug; stark contrast to sleeping rough on a beach. At dawn on her last day
she was awoken by the tickle of a spider against her hand and knew it was
time to leave. She smiled at the significance of her little visitor and placed
it safely on the window sill. They left early without being seen, and even
before the sun had crept over the horizon they were riding the waves with
an escort of gulls bound for Orkney.

After many miles of flight Orkney loomed out of a thick sea-fret and so literally took her by surprise. The only warning she had was the clamour of seabirds, a whiff of guano and then before her were towering cliffs covered in nesting auks. The sight was staggering and she stopped to plant her feet on solid ground after sixty miles of open water.

"Orkney!" she laughed and collapsed into the grass, ignoring the heavy dew and the blowing wind. She devoured her last rations in one go, secure in the knowledge she could easily acquire more in Kirkwall. Strike shared her joy, but she could tell he was exhausted and so they rested there that night without going any further.

The following morning she spied a strange tower adjacent to a craggy and foreboding island. Her map told her it was Hoy and the tower was in fact an 'old man'. She landed on its windy crown and thought of another tower at the opposite end of Britain where she met the Timekeeper and where Kolfinnia had founded her coven. "Almost feels like home," Strike gazed out across the sea.

"Kittiwake *was* home for a short while," she agreed, then felt a great sadness.

"Wind in your eyes?" He pretended not to notice her tears.

She nodded mutely and tidied her hair.

"I feel rested now," he lied. "Would you like to go shopping?"

She offered him a fond smile. "First we'll need some rusty nails."

He looked baffled.

"Silver doesn't grow on trees." She pulled the scarf tighter around her neck. "Unlike brave thunder-sprites."

He wore a curious little smile as he studied her.

"What's tickled you?" she asked, puzzled.

"I was thinking of the day we met," he said with feeling.

She arched her eyebrows. This was a tale she'd never heard, largely because she had been too self absorbed to listen. "You know, I'd love to hear it." She sat down and patted the grass and he floated down from the staff, and began to tell of how a young witch had come to find a storm damaged tree. They sat together at the summit of the old-man, and she listened to a chapter of her life told from another view point. At the end of his tale she thought of the lost years, and as she stroked her scarred cheek a strange thought came to her from nowhere,

Dying was the best thing that ever happened to me.

A little silver again paved the way for another comfortable night's lodging, this time in Kirkwall. She ate her fill and enjoyed the luxury of a roof over her head. She slept with the window ajar, thrilled by the sound of the sea so close and in the morning they began their last, and shortest, journey across the waves. Indeed she could see the mainland and it stirred her to think her home was connected, albeit distantly, to those hills on the horizon.

There was no hurry and so it was almost midday when they left the final island in the chain that had begun in Iceland. In no time at all Orkney's pastures changed to waves and foam, then quickly changed again, this time to moors and heath. They had bridged the waters and arrived on the mainland.

We're home! The thought should have filled her with a triumphant glow, but she felt a strange foreboding. This wasn't just coming home. This was a return to the fight.

Caithness was a sea in its own right, but a brown and desolate one. The compass became her guide however, and she followed it with total faith. They tracked through the Highlands, keeping away from inhabited areas and sheltering the nights in dense forests. Maybe it was the singing way-beware, but often wild animals would come close, drawn by curiosity. Occasionally she glimpsed a shy pine marten or even a wild cat, but no people, for which she was thankful. Although she was still a very long way from London, she felt caution settle on her like a second skin.

They travelled onwards, day after day and finally the wilds of the north were replaced by fields. The stark mountains gave way to verdant hills, and pines and heather changed to oak and beech and the number of lanes, farms, roads and settlements began to increase. Eventually, weeks after leaving Iceland and with May blooms decorating the woodland, Sunday passed back into England. She was in her home country again and she didn't even know it.

In the two weeks that followed, an uneasy quiet fell upon Hobbs Ash. It had finally dawned on everyone that they had sailed into uncharted waters.

They had broken a long held taboo and raised a demon that was resistant to magic as proved by John Fold's tragic end, yet only Galen seemed to know what to do with it or want to be close to it.

The station became a heavily guarded cave, full of rumours and secrets, and the monster in the cave was named Vorus. She had become the Illuminata's new family member, but one so terrible she was kept hidden, and tended by the only man who enjoyed her company: Galen.

The canvas barricade was like the frontier between the world of men and the world of magic. It shielded Vorus from prying eyes and made the workforce feel less uneasy, they didn't like the idea of it watching them as they cleared the station's huge floor space to make way for the next phase of Galen's plan.

"They somehow look bigger flat on their back," Doulton observed, pacing around the shattered krakens. There were a further eight of them lying in a meticulous grid of body parts awaiting their new masters, or more accurately new mistresses.

"They'll put the fear of God into Leonhard," Lyle sighed happily and looked up to the glass roof.

They put the fear of God into everyone, Doulton shivered to himself.

"I should inform you that I received a telegraph this morning, regrettably Lord Thorpe has had to postpone his inspection," Lyle said from nowhere.

Thorpe showed a distinct avoidance of Hobbs Ash now. *Is he washing his hands of us?* Doulton wondered. "For what reason this time?"

Lyle sniffed at his impertinence. "He's chairing a gathering of families at his estate in the north and it looks like they'll be staying longer than first thought."

"But he still hasn't seen our prodigal son's achievements."

"He doesn't have to, he trusts us."

Doulton just felt that made things worse. "So long as he knows all we've achieved here."

"He knows," Lyle echoed. He sent daily telegraphs to Thorpe, understanding that the more sensitive the experiments became the more risky it would be for Thorpe to be seen coming and going. Leonhard's spies might be anywhere. "When Galen sows the other eight machines we'll have a fighting force nothing can stand against."

'Sows'. Doulton thought it an odd choice of word. 'Possessed' was more accurate. "Vorus still hasn't been tested against another kraken."

"She'll prevail I'm sure."

"Yes, but nine is still a pitifully small number, even for such as that thing."

"It's hoped Vorus and her kin will fight alongside the newly commissioned krakens."

"Oh," he said blandly. *What men of sound mind would wish to fight alongside demons?*

"You sound worried?"

"Uncharted waters," Doulton reminded him.

"It's Leonhard who should be worried." He clasped his hands behind him as he walked. "Nine is all we need to bring Europe back in line."

They reached the kraken's bull-fashioned helmet. The cockpit hatch was open, like a little door leading into its skull. Doulton had the absurd notion that if he looked inside he'd see the machine's thoughts and dreams. *Don't be so childish,* he told himself, and deliberately took a look to prove it. The helmet was empty and he shuddered to think about the thing that would crawl into it and give it life. "What are these things?" he whispered.

"Leave that to Galen," Lyle advised. "Once June's gone do you really think there'll be room for the likes of Galen in the Illuminata?"

"Well now you mention it, I suppose not."

"Keep a level head, and by June all of this will be over," Lyle assured him. In fact he made such a good job of sounding sincere he almost believed it himself.

Galen had changed, but so few people knew him anyway that hardly anybody noticed. He became sullen and more demanding. Doulton noticed however, and didn't like it, thinking Galen was a like a mean dog that had learned to slip his lead whenever he wished, and right now that mean dog gazed up at the kraken, knowing Vorus was waiting for her daily visit.

"Remember, be cautious," Elios had said this daily for the last two weeks.

He shielded his impatience. "I'm no fool. I saw her right about the prisoners did I not?"

"I know," she admitted.

"You think she can wrap me around her little finger eh? Well I promise she can't." After killing John Fold she was so ecstatic that she would have broken all their prisoners, but he didn't let her. He sent the others back to their cells unharmed, intending to use them as one would train a dog with rewards. They had sixty-two prisoners left, a considerable amount, but he had a lot of tricks to teach her. He couldn't waste them needlessly, and of course there were more valkyries to come, more to train. "I'm holding her reins I assure you."

"You said she learns quickly, maybe she's learned that Sophie's likeness has power over you?"

Just then he didn't care to hear his sister's name. "Let my ears know some peace!"

She immediately became silent.

"Forgive me," he mumbled, and set the cane down on a barrel.

"Go Galen," she said dismissively, *"go attend her."*

"Take some rest my petal." His fingers brushed the cane, and then he was gone and Elios felt like a child left alone in the house. She felt the change in him more keenly than anyone and knew Vorus was his new favoured lady.

When she was sure he was far enough away she appeared, confident she was alone. This was something she'd done more frequently lately, but she was always careful never to go far. She dropped to the floor, scampered around the barrels and looked out. Galen was sat cross-legged on the floor a hundred yards away beside Vorus. The huge machine was laid recumbent like a broken puppet so that he could speak intimately with the creature inside. "Vorus!" she hissed. How she hated the thing for stealing her Galen. She saw him reading to her. "Reading to the thing as if it were a child!" she shook her head despairingly, and it was that despair that compelled her to eavesdrop on him as he so often had to others.

He was reading nursery rhymes and fairy tales like a devoted father. Elios heard the 'three blind mice' followed by 'Snow-white' followed by 'Goldilocks' and each time Vorus excitedly asked him what were mice and what was porridge and a hundred other such questions, he patiently told her and she gasped at these mundane things. Elios heard a story about a fairy with a broken wing and all of a sudden her ears pricked forwards.

"Why could this fairy not fly Galen?" Vorus sounded sad.

"Because she believed all her life that she was broken dearest."

"But was her wing not sound and proper all along?"

"Indeed my love, but the important thing to remember in this tale is that power of belief."

"Belief?" Vorus repeated earnestly and Elios recognised her precocious tone, showing her beloved father how well she could study.

"Many that should fly are grounded because they believe their wings are broken," he explained.

Elios uttered a small cry and darted back into the shadows. He could have been speaking of her, not a fictional character.

"Have you ever tried to fly?" The moon-fairy's words came back to her.

"No," she whispered. "No, I never tried, because," she took a deep breath, "because Galen said I was broken." She sat on the cold concrete feeling breathless, and a moment later she crept back into her cane taking her newfound concerns with her.

Every step of Sunday's journey had been noted by the Patternmaker's assassin. It had lain dormant for a while, but always alert for further instructions, and now they came.

The Timekeeper was busy. He had created a flow of good fortune to aid Sunday's journey, which itself was enough to infuriate the Patternmaker, but now the most dangerous part of her voyage was done he'd withdrawn to attend other matters in the hourglass.

With this in mind the assassin shifted quietly towards its target. It found a clear view of Sunday's thread, but this time rather than assault it the assassin encouraged a subtle, even innocent, thought to reverberate through it. It was so subtle in fact that all the creature had to do was breathe against it, and it was such a natural thought even the Timekeeper wouldn't see it for what it was. The thought was: *I'm hungry.*

The assassin reached up and blew gently. Sunday's thread swayed minutely and the idea to stop for refreshment wound its way up from her subconscious and into her waking thoughts. A few seconds later, in the real world, her mouth was dry and her stomach rumbled.

The Timekeeper looked up from weaving, certain he'd heard something. After a glance at Sunday's thread, he saw she was quite safe, and carried on unaware.

The assassin waited for him to return to his weaving then slipped away back into the dark jungle of silk. Sunday would now stop where she hadn't planned to stop, and in doing so she would meet some very unpleasant people indeed.

"Strike, how about we rest a while? I'm really hungry." Sunday looked down at the acres of dark forest and longed to take a drink and eat her rations. Perhaps she might even risk stripping down and enjoying a decent wash.

"Hmm, can't we go a bit further? There's nobody around to see us, perfect chance to keep on flying."

"We've been flying since dawn, come on, I don't think we'll meet anybody down there."

"Very well," he agreed reluctantly.

"This is going to be wonderful!" she sighed, and was already tugging at her cloak and looking forward to a peaceful snooze under a tree. *What can go wrong?* she thought. After all she had her dear champion to watch over her, and so she dropped into the wild forests of Northumberland with little sense of caution.

Thorpe and his six guests made hardly a sound as they advanced through the bracken. Most of the trees were slender pines and so the shooting party enjoyed a far-reaching view, despite being in the heart of the forest. Thorpe's gamekeeper, a short man named Muldoon, went ahead and scared any birds and rabbits from cover and Thorpe and his guests did the rest. Least ways that was the idea, although nobody had fired a single cartridge in the last hour. They'd been shooting all morning and as a consequence most of the wildlife had either gone to ground or fled. Up ahead Muldoon raised an arm signalling them to hold while he went to investigate something. Thorpe took cover in the bracken where tender fiddlesticks were starting to sprout as May lengthened.

"What's he seen?" Albert Grant muttered.

"Soon see." Thorpe watched him dip out of sight behind a fallen tree.

"You seem preoccupied old man?" Grant observed.

He smiled faintly. "Next month is June, and you know what that means."

"Mmmm." He pushed his cap back and sighed heavily. As an Illuminata banking chief Grant knew exactly what that meant, and this week of shooting at Thorpe's estate was intended to let them finalise their plans. "The next few weeks will be sorely testing make no mistake, but in the end this might all strengthen the British claim over the entire Knighthood."

"I wish I had your optimism." Thorpe was beginning to wonder if Galen could dig them out of their hole after all. So far he'd created one solitary living kraken. Although he hadn't seen it himself he recognised it as a stupendous achievement, but one wasn't enough.

Grant slid the tweed cap from his head and mopped his brow. He might be short and overweight, but he was a crack shot. "Trust me, in a few weeks Leonhard will be no more lively than this girl." He reached around and lifted the plump vixen he shot earlier.

"Don't know why you keep that sordid thing," Thorpe disapproved.

"There's a space in the study, thought it'd look quite striking there."

"It's Muldoon," someone whispered. Thorpe looked to his other side where John Golding knelt in the grass. "There," Golding pointed.

Muldoon was standing by a tree, gesturing them to advance.

"Hope it's a deer," Thorpe grunted.

"Another fox would be nice," Grant smiled, "there's a space in the cabinet for two."

"Even better, we might come upon a few froggie spies," Thorpe anticipated.

The shooting party quietly rose from cover and headed to their next kill.

"There's a girl," Muldoon explained when they caught him up. "Juss lying under that tree yonder, sleepin' would you believe it!"

Thorpe's party was huddled behind a fallen pine. "A trespasser?" He leaned out for a better look.

"Not just a girl," Muldoon said gravely. "Looks like a Jik, and she's got a flying stick, right by that tree. I swear."

Thorpe immediately went to load his gun. "Gentlemen," he rasped, fumbling the cartridges as the anger began to rise. "Looks like we've found better sport than deer." Behind him he heard the rest gasp and mutter, while ahead he saw the intruder through the long grass, and just as Muldoon had said she was sleeping innocently in the shade of an oak. From this distance all he could discern was the flash of fair hair and a white staff propped against a tree. "Of all the nerve, just look at the brazen whore, lying there like she owns the place." He shook his head in outrage.

"Do you think they know about our meeting here?" Grant asked nervously.

"Huh! Why else would the spying harlot be here? Likely others close by, but we've caught this one napping." He turned to Muldoon, "You still have that rubber cloth?"

"Aye sir," he held up the sack.

"Tip those wretched things out and pass it over."

He poured out a dozen wood pigeons and handed it across.

"Right, we'll go and apprehend the spy. You head back and alert the guard and return with every man you can find. Where there's one there'll be more."

"Aye sir," Muldoon scurried away. Thorpe Hall was less than a mile away, he'd be there and back with reinforcements in no time.

"You think we're under attack?" Grant whispered fearfully.

"And if we are?" Thorpe bared his teeth. "There are almost one hundred soldiers and twenty family members at Thorpe Hall, and a vault full of weapons. If they've come looking for trouble by God I'll make sure they get it."

"But what about us?" Grant whined.

"Good God man," he sneered, "you've got a gun haven't you!"

"What do you want us to do Victor?" Harrison was older, but eager to help.

"Knew I could bank on you Charles," Thorpe smiled. "This is how we'll do it; you and Grant take this oil cloth and follow me. We'll sneak across there without waking the insolent bitch and you make sure you seize that white staff propped against the tree and wrap it in the cloth good and tight."

"You mean that's one of those the heathen devices the wretches fly on?" Harrison peeped out. He'd heard of lightning-staffs but never seen one. "They operate on some kind of electrical system don't they?"

"Indeed they do, and that's why the cloth will neutralise it, it's rubber coated."

"And without it she can't hurt us?" Harrison clarified.

"She'll be as tender as spring lamb."

He licked his lips, "This is better than squirrels and martens eh?"

"Nothing like the thrill of the hunt." Thorpe was actually glad. First they'd enjoy the hunt, then the delights of interrogation. "Everyone ready?"

"Ready," they replied together, and crept out from cover.

Grant was last, and he tossed the dead vixen into the bracken. Thorpe was right, it wasn't worth keeping and he'd lost interest in it anyway. The vixen tumbled into the undergrowth and lay watching the sky. Now they had a far more regal fox to play with, and the animal was just a meal for the flies.

She was dreaming. About what, she couldn't recall, but it was lazy and relaxing, just the rest she needed. And so at first the voice didn't really register.

"On your feet witch," it said.

Sunday stirred in her half sleep. "Strike?" she murmured. Her hand flopped out to her staff, but found only thin air.

"I said on your feet – witch whore." This time a boot jabbed her in the ribs.

Her eyelids fluttered open. She saw a haze of light, the blue sky and a ring of silhouettes surrounding her. Her eyes went wide and rolled full circle as she took in the grim faces staring down at her. Now she came instantly awake but said not a word. The dream's lazy comfort vanished and left her cold and trembling. *They know I'm a witch, these must be men of the Illuminata. Strike where the hell are you?* she groaned, while her hand still groped for her missing staff.

"On your feet," the man with the gun demanded for the third time, "and do so slowly or I shoot you and bury you where you lay."

Strike? she thought with rising panic.

"On your feet!"

She heard a firing pin being cocked, and she elbowed herself upright, her mind racing and eyes seeking her staff. Reluctantly she got to her feet, and still she didn't look any of them in the eye, instead her gaze darted back and forth. *Strike! Where the hell are you?*

"What's your name and what are you doing here?" the voice came again.

She forced herself to look up and saw a hard-faced man with a bristling moustache, pointing a shotgun at her. The twin barrels looked like staring eyes, both blank and emotionless.

"You can answer our questions here or back at the Hall, it makes little difference to me," he said, hardly moving his lips. He glanced to an older man at his side. "Harrison, search the Jik for weapons."

The man called Harrison must have been at least sixty. He had small eyes, ruddy cheeks, a nose made bulbous by years of drink and his breathing was too rapid to be healthy. He passed his own shotgun to one of the others and stepped up with a confident swagger that Sunday instantly loathed. He passed behind her and she flinched when hands began to explore her body.

"Make it thorough," the moustache-man ordered.

She heard Harrison's murmured reply from behind her, then one of his hands smoothed her right breast on its way to her waist. She gave an involuntary hiss and stiffened. His hands slid down her body keeping contact the whole way. When he reached her ankles, he repeated the journey in reverse and she thanked Lord Oak she'd bought trousers in Reykjavik and not a dress. The idea of his palms on her bare legs made her want to choke. His hands crawled higher and she thought of the invasive dead-walk seeds. He was making a very thorough job, and not in the name of security. She looked ahead at nothing, trying to ignore their amused faces and determined not to scream, even when he clutched her hips. He leaned closer, his gut pressed into the small of her back and his rough breathing filled her ear. His hands snaked their way around her lower belly and fumbled with her belt. For a moment she feared the worst was about to happen, but then her belt fell away and Harrison stepped back with a satisfied sigh. He'd taken her wands.

"Good man. And get the bag there Harrison," Moustache-man indicated her satchel by the tree. "And the rest of her rags." He jerked his head towards her cloak and the other belongings.

Strike? Dear Oak, Strike where are you? she pleaded silently.

"Name?" moustache-man demanded again.

She said nothing.

"Then let me begin; I am Lord Victor Thorpe. Master-at-Court to the Britannic bloodlines of the Knights Illuminata. I assume that means something to you?" He kept the gun level as he spoke. "And how many more like you can we expect to find trespassing here today?"

Again, she looked ahead but said nothing, racing to come up with a plan.

Thorpe just shrugged and took the belt from Harrison, glanced at it and passed it to Grant. "Keep hold of this, and keep it with the staff."

At the word 'staff' she jumped and looked around.

"Yes. We have your flying stick," he gloated. "And I assure you the demon inside is quite powerless."

The man named Grant held a long slender bundle in his arms and she knew it was her staff and by some foul means they'd subdued Strike.

Thorpe smiled maliciously. "We have devisers in the Knighthood that can undo a witch's artefacts and learn their secrets. Mayhap we'll put your flying stick under the knife and see what spills out?" The rest looked amused and their amusement turned to laughter when they saw the horror on her face.

Strike! By Oak if they've hurt him I'll curse this place till it bleeds! She felt tears of anger tumbled down her cheeks.

"The Jik weeps!" Thorpe declared sarcastically. "Almost as if she were gifted with human feelings." The men chuckled again. "Tie her," he ordered.

Someone out of her vision grabbed her arms and pressed them behind her back to fasten her wrists, and all the while Thorpe kept the gun's two black eyes locked on her.

"Now move witch." He waved the gun and the men closed in around her in a cordon making sure there was no escape.

She began walking, frigid with fear. Something hard pressed between her shoulder blades and she knew it was another gun. Ahead, she saw Harrison carrying her belt with the two wand-sheathes dangling uselessly from it. Tales told of the strongest witches, the Ragged-Brothers, who could cast spells with no wand at all, but by Oak she was just a young woman and she badly needed hers. *Strike,* she sobbed silently, *Strike I'm going to find you and together we'll get away from here!* How she'd manage such a thing didn't matter, it felt good just to think it.

As the party escorted their new catch back to Thorpe Hall, each man dumped their brace in the grass. Events had taken a far more interesting turn and the rabbits, squirrels and martens were instantly forgotten. She stepped over a mound of conies, careful not to trample them and a tear fell. The gathering moved away leaving behind a ring of dead animals, and for all the world the circle of trampled grass, ringed by bloodied little corpses, looked like a place of dark sacrifice.

Chapter Fourteen

A story fit for a queen

'If you believe it it's true.'
Traditional witch saying

Thorpe's estate was vast. It comprised two-thousand acres of moorland primarily for shooting and grazing, six hundred acres of managed forest and a further thousand acres of tenanted farmland. Thorpe Hall was the stone and mortar equivalent of the land; vast, and managed by an army of servants and grounds men.

Less than half a mile from the Hall, Muldoon arrived with twenty-five mounted troops. "Hall's on full alert sir, the Major is in touch with London as we speak."

"Good work Muldoon." Thorpe gestured to the guard captain, a clean-shaven young man named Bloom. He obediently dropped from his horse and marched over. "Captain, I want this spy taking to the round tower in the east wing, maximum security, there could be others close by." He squinted at the forest suspiciously.

"Aye sir." Bloom turned his attention to the prisoner expecting to see an old hag, but what he saw instead snatched his breath away. A young woman with fair hair and intensely blue eyes.

"About it Captain!" Thorpe snapped. He hadn't failed to notice her beauty either, but comely or not she was a witch-spy and he was convinced she'd been selected for this mission precisely because of that. Beauty could wreak havoc with men. *Cunning women, the serpent's sex, they've ever been the downfall of man,* he thought sourly. He would order London to dispatch a correctional and bring a chromosite creature to use on the Jik. *We'll see how pretty she looks after she's had her locks shorn and spent a few days under interrogation.*

Bloom mounted up and pulled his horse around, barked orders to his men and a half dozen of them dismounted and relieved the party of their dangerous charge.

The prisoner escort set off in tight ranks with Sunday trapped in the middle. Thorpe watched them head back and rubbed his chin thoughtfully.

"Victor?" It was Harrison.

"Where there's one there'll be more," he said moodily.

"Then they know about the tournament? Do you think they'll attack us here?"

The rest closed in and Thorpe looked around the forest and wondered. "A rescue mission?" he smirked. "No, witches are subversives and agitators, they won't fight in the open." He turned and put his hands on his hips. "Isn't that right?" he shouted to the forest. "No backbone, an army of spies and cowards!" His voice rang through the trees, startling a few birds, then the silence returned. Far off he could hear hooves clattering into the distance, but nothing else.

Harrison looked around at the tranquil forest. Thorpe was probably right, but he remembered Kittiwake-coven where their knights had been utterly defeated. "Let's get back Victor." He gave the taller man a friendly pat on the back. "Make a start on the Jik spy eh? I for one long to see her defrocked."

"Hmm," Thorpe rumbled. He fished a cigar from his jacket, lit it and then turned and walked back to the Hall.

Harrison breathed a sigh of relief, cast a worried glance around the others and trotted after him, glad to be leaving the forest behind. Things had changed and now he felt like the hunted rabbit.

The east wing's round tower was actually square, but otherwise it lived up to its austere sounding name. The lower ground floor was a cellar and above that on the ground floor was a disused scullery.

Sunday found herself shoved and pushed through small courtyards between the rambling wings of Thorpe Hall. The door to the round tower was already open to receive her, and six sentries were posted outside, all of them looked mean and scared, which she thought a very bad combination.

"Inside." Bloom pressed her forward, led her to a plain kitchen table and sat her down on a wooden chair. As he fastened her already bound wrists to the chair, she did her best to take in her surroundings looking for anything that might help her escape.

"Where are my belongings?" She tried to keep her voice level.

He finished tying her and stepped in front of her, looking mildly surprised. It was the first she'd spoken. "You are a suspected spy and as such you have no rights, your items are confiscated and now the property of Lord Thorpe."

She looked past him, assessing everything in the room. There was a stove, and a pot sink under the windows, but the windows themselves were barred and too small to crawl through. Cupboards stood around the edge of the room and the walls were covered in tiles the colour of washed-out limes, while those on the floor were red quarry tiles. There was a well stocked knife rack and a heavy set of scales, any of them might improvise as weapons she told herself. There was another doorway on the opposite side of the room that she assumed led into the main house, but the door was double bolted and the wood was seasoned oak, making it very strong.

"Did you hear what I said?" he asked.

"Those are my things, and I haven't done anything wrong," she asserted.

"That remains to be seen, Lord Thorpe will decide if you are what you say." But he knew Thorpe had already made his mind up. The six guards outside were joined by six more, three of who entered the scullery. "Watch her," he ordered, then with a last admiring look he went in search of Thorpe.

By now word had spread that a 'real live Jik' had been caught snooping around. Outside in the small courtyard she could hear men whispering and she glimpsed curious but cruel faces trying to peep past the guards as if she were a zoo exhibit. From what little she could see they all wore tweeds and could have been brothers to the men she'd met in the forest.

Strike, please where are you? she pleaded, and strained at her bindings.

"I wouldn't do that if I was you," one of her captors advised. He looked younger than her and lowered his rifle level with her head.

She sat in silence listening to her own thudding heart. A cuckoo piped up from somewhere outside and she wished with all her heart she'd never stopped in this cursed place. To land in her enemies' lap and be caught so easily, it made her think she deserved it for being so stupid.

Determined footfalls drew closer and Thorpe breezed into the scullery. The room emptied of guards and the door closed with a hefty boom. The sounds of birds and rustling trees were killed stone-dead, leaving just Thorpe's mechanical breathing coming from somewhere behind her, and the smell of stale tobacco. She thought it was just the two of them when suddenly Harrison slid into view. For a heavy man he was deft and agile. He dropped himself onto a chair on the opposite side of the table, soon followed by Thorpe who placed a canvas package on the tabletop and began to unroll it with deliberate slowness. She was disturbed to see they'd both removed their jackets and rolled up their shirt sleeves, as if ready for dirty work and she expected to see knives and other cruel devices in the package. Her heart leapt however when she saw her satchel and wands inside. Thorpe studied her closely before speaking. "These were found with you." He rubbed his hands on a handkerchief, implying her possessions were degrading. "Occult and pagan objects. Possession of these alone carries a heavy sentence of imprisonment. But I'm rather more interested as to why you were spying on my estate."

She bit her lip and looked at the tiled floor.

"London has been informed, and they're sending a team of correctionals with interrogation devices," he continued.

"Why am I being treated this way?" she asked primly, reckoning her best tactic was denial.

"Of course we could do away with the need for the chromosites if you cooperate," he ignored her.

"And I say again, why am I being treated this way?"

He smiled and shook his head. "How many of you are close by?"

"Why am I being treated this way?" she insisted stubbornly.

"Enough!" He slammed a hand on the table, making Harrison flinch. "You're no lost milking maid and don't pretend you are. Now answer my bloody questions, how many of you?"

She stared at him blankly.

"You were sent to spy on our preparations weren't you?"

Preparations for what? she thought. *Why are so many of the Illuminata's highest born men here of all places?* And right then, she decided to see what *she* could learn from *him*. She composed herself and relaxed, ready to plunge into this dangerous sea. "You've good reason to be afraid of us Mr Thorpe." She injected a little of the old Sunday into her voice, enough to give her words a playful edge.

He recoiled an inch. "So there are more! How many? Where?"

"I'm working alone," she looked him in the eye, "for now."

"And what have you found out all by your pretty little self?"

"I know about your plans," she bluffed.

"Plans?" he pretended.

She kept her mouth shut, letting him do the work.

"Do we have any plans Harrison?" he asked blandly.

She turned to Harrison, but the man didn't see her; he was studying her breasts and his face was as red as molten lava. *What a fool,* she thought, and deliberately arched her back, pulling her shirt a little tighter. She saw him blink and swallow and knew if it was just him she'd charm her way out of this place in a moment, Thorpe was harder though.

"Erm, no, no plans," Harrison mumbled.

Thorpe frowned at him, then looked at her long and hard before slowly drawing a pair of surgeon's gloves from his pocket and making a play of sliding his hands into them. For a while there was nothing in the room but the squeak of rubber. Without taking his eyes off her, he drew her satchel closer with a single finger, loath to touch it, undid the buckles, reached inside and drew out her possessions. Seeing him touch her cherished items was sickening. Her compass, atheme, lucky stones, polished shells, the wooden fox-comb. There was the strip of purple cloth she had worn at Kittiwake to show her allegiance to Kolfinnia's Flower-Forth witches, and next to that a golden coin from the Saxon treasure horde at Regal-Fox. Looking at them made her want to cry. "Explain this?" He held up the way-beware.

She looked at the little doll. It had survived countless winters in the far north and subdued a forest of evil creatures, but it looked powerless in his hands.

"Explain it," he demanded again.

"It's nothing," she whispered sadly. The way-beware's song drifted through her head and she could have wept for its innocent soul. "Just a trinket I made." She looked at her own feet and forced back the tears. *Dear champion where are you now?* she begged the universe.

Dear champion. The words floated through his world and he looked up feeling suddenly anxious. Immediately he scrutinised Sunday's thread.

"Very cunning!" The Timekeeper at last sensed her distress. "Making her land herself in trouble with such an innocent thought, but two of us can play at that."

If he could just pluck her out of there, or make every man at Thorpe Hall keel over with a sudden heart attack he would, but there were rules to be followed. Threads could only be helped or hindered by other threads, and not so far away he found three ideal ones. All he needed to do was send them a signal to come, and he knew just the man to send that signal . . . Thorpe himself would save her, merely by losing his temper.

"A trinket?" Thorpe examined the way-beware for a second and the room filled with a foreboding quiet. "LIAR!" he roared, and lashed the doll against the table. There was a sickening crack and her mouth dropped open in horror, expecting to see the spell-doll break in two.

The way-beware cried out, but only she could hear it. Its lovely song wavered and stilled for a moment, it didn't fully stop though, but continued like a whisper in the next room. *I'm so sorry,* she thought in despair. It was as much alive as Strike and it hadn't asked to end up here in the hands of this maniac. She couldn't stop the tears this time and she trembled with rage as she began to cry.

He had known his name for a short while but now he was forgetting again and he just flapped wearily through the skies with no sense of purpose. The chase had beaten them. The golden girl with the magical doll were lost and Valgard's orders had become harder and harder to deny. It was over and he was ready to sink into eternal rage again when a scream of pain rang out.

"The song and the girl!" he roared to his brothers, "they're close!"

"The girl is in trouble?" Karl felt he was waking from a dream, remembering his purpose all over again.

"And the singer is in pain!" Harger realised. "What do we do?"

"If the song dies we're all finished!" Eirik; his name was Eirik and now he knew exactly where the singer and the girl were, and both were in danger. And by all the gods he'd never felt more like fighting.

"What's your name witch?" Thorpe tossed the way-beware onto the table with a clatter and leaned forwards.

"I'm a witch of high rank." She refused to utter her name in this cursed place.

"And what 'rank' would that be?" he jeered.

"Summer solstice queen," she declared proudly, blinking tears from her eyes.

Immediately his eyes narrowed. "Summer solstice you say?" He nodded to Harrison, some wordless exchange passed between them and now Harrison looked worried.

"June 21st," she replied, proud to share her birthday with the sun's day.

Thorpe bunched his fists. She heard joints grind and rubber creak, and his breathing had become faster. "You know much about the solstice then?" His voice was quiet and dangerous and he got up and slid behind her out of sight.

"A great deal," she answered truthfully, but not in the way he believed.

Suddenly, his voice sounded beside her ear and she jumped. "You lying Jik!" he hissed. But he sounded unsure, afraid even.

"Every coven across Britain knows about the solstice." It was obvious that she'd hit a nerve, and again she spoke nothing but truth, but not in the way he understood it.

"Victor?" Harrison moaned.

"Get on the telegraph. Tell London it's worse than we thought. I want Galen to accelerate his plans with the valkyries and I want those correctionals here before dark. I want answers from this witch by dawn."

Galen? Sunday thought. Valkyries? Just what's happening here?

Harrison jumped to his feet and a second later he was out of the door.

She saw the guards again briefly then the door slammed and she was alone with Thorpe. He was still behind her, hands planted on the chair back. She could smell his sweat and his frustration. There was a silence as delicate as thin ice. Then suddenly he hauled the chair around so violently that she yelped in surprise and the chair rocked to a stop making her jaw snap shut. He gripped her shoulders and she looked into his cold eyes and saw nothing behind them but hate. "You're planning to attack the tournament aren't you?" he seethed. "Did Leonhard put you up to this?"

An Illuminata tournament! she realised. No wonder they were so paranoid, it must mean the Knighthood was in disarray, and despite facing torture she felt jubilant. Now if she could just escape to tell about it.

"Aren't you!" he roared into her face.

She smelled tobacco and onions, and felt spittle dash her cheeks. "Perhaps," she whispered.

He grabbed her jaw hard enough to make her teeth throb, and jabbed his fingers into the tender places under her cheekbones. "Is this the mark of your coven, or whatever filthy band of rogues you belong to?" He studied the hourglass mark on her cheek. It was so perfect that it looked deliberate. He appeared transfixed by it and his expression softened. "Time," he murmured absently, "time kills everything."

She just stared up at him, confused and scared.

He shook the vacant look from his face. "I wouldn't soil myself with you, but Harrison's less discerning. He might as well enjoy you now, because soon there'll be precious little left of you to play with." As if to prove it he struck her flat across the face. The slap echoed around the scullery and she drew a sharp, outraged breath.

Whatever's coming to you Thorpe you deserve it, she thought from nowhere.

"Perhaps you relish the idea of Harrison riding you?" he provoked. "Makes a change from rutting with beasts of the forest I suppose?"

"Please, don't," she gasped, anxious for more information.

Just then the door opened and Harrison swaggered back in. "Telegraph on its way to Goldhawk as we speak."

Thorpe grinned. "She's yours for the taking old boy."

"Really?" He suddenly looked like a child promised every toy in the shop.

"No you can't!" She heaved at her restraints and sobbed in fury.

"Then bloody talk!" he roared again and kicked the table sending it crashing into her stomach, making her grunt in pain. The way-beware rocked and its carved face turned her way.

Please, if you can do anything, please help me! she pleaded.

The way-beware looked like it was trying to tell her something very important, and if it could talk it would tell her to take cover. Big trouble was coming to Thorpe Hall.

Thorpe Hall was on maximum alert but Corporal Percy Hart still found time for a quick cigarette. Between furtive puffs, he kept a watch outside the main gates, but just because he was taking a crafty smoke didn't mean he had to be a sloppy soldier. Lord Thorpe had ordered them to secure the perimeter, but he anticipated a Jik rescue force would come from the forest, not along the road, and so Hart was the only man posted outside the gates.

"Hart?" a voice came.

He turned and skilfully tossed the cigarette away in one smooth move. "Sarg."

"Anything to report?" Sergeant Soaper peered down the long narrow road hemmed in by towering pines. It looked eerily empty, like a blank page awaiting a nasty story.

"All's quiet Sarg." Hart sounded bored.

Soaper ignored him and stood watching. Something was wrong but he couldn't say what.

"Sarg?"

Soaper watched a flock of wood pigeons take to the air four hundred yards down the track. They exploded from cover in a hurry to be away. "Nothing," he sighed and tried to tell his gut that all was well, but it wouldn't listen. He'd been a soldier for nineteen years and knew guts told the truth more often than eyes or ears. He turned and set off back to the main gates, when just after twenty paces Hart called him back.

"Sarg, something's moving down yonder."

He felt the hairs on his neck bristle, and in reply he spun on his heels and trotted back to where Hart now stood pointing his rifle down the empty road.

"Something moved down there," Hart elaborated.

"Where the birds flew from?"

"Aye, how did you know?"

"Guts," Soaper said simply and together they watched the road until their eyes began to throb. Then they saw movement. At first Soaper thought it was a deer. A large animal stalked out of the forest, but it was too far away to make it out clearly.

"Is that a deer?" Hart echoed his thoughts.

If it's just a deer why do I feel so bloody scared? Soaper thought uneasily. He was reaching for his field glasses when Hart stopped him.

"Bloody hell, there's two more." He squinted into the distance.

"They're not deer," he muttered, watching the shadowy creatures.

"Must be." Hart was as oblivious to the threat as a rabbit staring down the barrel of a gun.

Soaper heard a distant rumbling, almost like a growl. His gut knotted in response, then the things began to advance and something about their gait told him these were not grass-munching, doe-eyed deer. "Back to the gate, sound the bell," he said quietly.

"The alarm, you sure Sarg?" He was going to feel a clot for alerting all of Thorpe Hall to three deer.

"Get going," Soaper had already drawn his revolver and something in his tone made Hart's own guts quiver in alarm.

"Aye sir," he said shakily and hurried, then ran, feeling his rifle thud against his hip.

Soaper raised the field glasses and focused the wheel. "Someone's havin' a lark!" he gasped.

Three huge bears were ambling down the track. He lowered the glasses, rubbed his eyes and looked again, but they were still there. Without thinking he drew his whistle and gave a shrill blast, just as Hart began ringing the bell back at the gate. The call was taken up and in no time there were bells and whistles screaming and clanging all over Thorpe Hall, and men readied rifles and looked to the sky for the first witches.

He checked through the glasses again. Impossible though it was, the three bears that couldn't have been there were now running. And right towards him. He saw horrible details quite clear; fangs and claws glinting, and fur rippling over dense muscle. *They've escaped from a circus,* he told himself, but there was some unearthly intelligence about them. He dropped the field glasses and raised his revolver. "Fall back!" he bellowed to no one, then fired six times in rapid succession. They were only one hundred yards away, but he didn't stop to get a better look. He dropped the empty revolver, turned and fled.

"This way lads! Sarg is out there!" Hart dashed back out onto the track, accompanied by a dozen soldiers and all of them froze in horror.

Sergeant Soaper was sprinting towards them with his whistle still clamped between his teeth, making a shrill toot with every puff and running like the devil was after him.

"What the bloody 'ell is that friggin' thing!" someone shouted, clearly not meaning the distraught sergeant.

A tide of fur and teeth seemed to race in pursuit, ripping up the road as it came and it was quickly catching him up.

Hart watched helplessly as a shadow loomed up behind his sergeant. "Covering fire!" he ordered, dropped to one knee and began shooting.

"It's a bloody bear!" someone screamed in disbelief. "How did a bear get 'ere?"

"Just shoot!" he screamed again.

Soaper was almost fifty yards from the gate, still piping an insane tune on his whistle when one of the monsters crashed down on him like a wave. Claws and teeth flashed and with one last blast of his whistle, he disappeared in a mist of crimson as he was instantly torn apart. "Dear Christ!" someone yelled and every man there opened fire. The air was fogged by rifle smoke and bullets were tearing towards their attackers, but Hart still couldn't grasp what he was seeing. Thorpe Hall was under assault not by witches . . . but by three gigantic bears.

Harrison looked petulant. Thorpe had said he could pleasure himself with their beguiling captive, but now he'd begun his relentless questions again.

"I want to know exactly how you'll strike the tournament." He gripped her neck and pressed his face closer. "Or else," he glanced at Harrison meaningfully.

She coughed and nodded, ready to tell the most elaborate lies of her life, anything to buy her more time. His hands slid away, and he sat back slowly and perched himself on the table's edge. She swallowed, took a deep breath and got ready to tell a fabulous fiction. "There are at least two hundred of us," she panted, "and the French have –"

She was cut off by a ringing bell from outside. Harrison gasped in fear but Thorpe seemed oblivious. "French have what?" His eyes gleamed and his moustache twitched.

"Victor," Harrison interrupted. "That's the alarm, you think they're coming for her?"

He blinked a few times, then finally registered the racket outside. In truth he'd never expected an assault and he felt angry at being caught off guard. "False alarm," he growled. "Wait here and keep an eye on her while I go sort things out." He pulled a revolver from his belt and handed it over. "Bolt the door once I've left and if she tries anything, shoot her somewhere painful but not lethal." He cast a hateful look at Sunday. "We'll finish later," he promised, then stalked out through the door at the back of the scullery.

She heard bolts being drawn and the rattle of the latch then she was alone with Harrison, and still tied up. He bolted the door as Thorpe ordered and then looked down at the revolver, thinking of the treat he'd been denied. He could take it by force, but the bells and shouts of panic were a distraction. He heard a sudden volley of rifle fire and jumped. Even the witch looked afraid and it was the confused look of fear on her face that unnerved him the most. "Don't move," he warned her, but the revolver trembled in his hand. *This isn't a false alarm Victor,* he thought and found it difficult to look confident.

There was a storm of rifle fire again and more shouting followed by a gristly scream. Sunday gasped in genuine shock and Harrison clutched the revolver tighter, wrestling with the uneasy idea that the Jik was now the least of his problems. Sweat glistened on his brow and he wished Thorpe would hurry back.

"Close the gates!" Hart screamed and started to drag the wooden gates shut. They were solid oak and nine inches thick. The company jumped to action and in a second there were twelve men hauling the gates closed. Hart looked up from under a mop of sweaty hair and saw the three creatures still ravaging poor Soaper's remains, not that there was much left. A boot whirled through the air followed by pink glistening things that he didn't want to see. Then the gates thudded shut and blanked out the terrible sight, and Hart gasped a sob of relief. Locks and bars were slid into place and the world felt a saner place again. "They can't get through that." He retreated away from the gates not quite believing his own words. "Form line!" he ordered, taking charge without a second thought, and suddenly there was a wall of olive drab with rifles and bayonets directed at the main gates.

"What the hell were they?" someone muttered.

"Poor Sarg," Hart shook his head. He'd begun to think rationally again and figured they were wild animals escaped from a circus. Poor old Soaper got in the way and what they ought to do was put a few sentries up on the wall and shoot the damned things dead. Yes, that was the sensible thing to do, and he was about to suggest so when the gates rocked under a terrific blow from outside.

"They're trying to break in!" someone cried.

"Hold the line!" Hart snapped. "And don't be a burke, why would they want to break in for God's sake?"

"What if she summoned them, an' supposin' they're not natural?" someone else suggested.

"Who the bloody hell said that?" Hart looked around. Stupid ideas like that might get them all panicked.

There were a few guilty glances and someone was about to own up, when the gates rocked again and Hart heard the sickening sound of wood cracking, and the men moaned in fear. *They can't! They're just dumb beasts!* he told himself.

"They're coming for her – for the witch!" someone whimpered.

"Enough of that!" He could feel the fear spreading. The iron handle rattled and the gates shook, then all was still. He could hear a distant alarm bell and the rapid breathing of many scared men. Suddenly, something outside scraped against the gates. He jumped, and instantly felt foolish. "Just beasts," he muttered, but reached for the little crucifix around his neck just in case.

The sound of claws against wood turned to the sound of claws against iron. Hart heard a gentle 'tink-tink-tink' sound and absurdly imagined fairytale dwarves at their smithies and anvils. The line of rifles flinched and Hart watched in disbelief as the iron handle started to turn. It jerked and swung as something on the other side tested the mechanism. He raised his rifle just as the moving handle stopped, but he couldn't take his eyes off it. Not far off in the stable block he could hear horses whinnying in fear.

From behind he heard marching feet and turned to see Captain Bloom arrive with the rest of the garrison and felt a blessed wave of relief. He felt an even bigger sense of relief when he saw the gun team had brought up the two deadly Maxim guns and were setting them into position at the top of the courtyard gardens. "What's the situation?" Bloom ordered.

"Wild animals on the road sir."

"Animals?" He looked confused. "Not witches then?"

"Animals sir, bears would you believe it, they killed poor Sergeant Soaper." Hart pointed towards the stout wooden gates.

Bloom looked towards the fortified gates – at exactly the same instant they shattered.

Wooden wreckage and iron bolts exploded all around the courtyard, knocking men off their feet and making the ground tremble. Horses screamed and men cried out and Hart saw the iron handle spin past like a saucer, tear clean across the gardens and embed itself into the masonry by the front doors with terrible force. "Bloody hell!" he screamed, and accidentally fired off a round, which thudded into the ground inches from his foot.

A cloud of dust swept through the courtyard, obscuring everything and right in the heart of it Bloom heard a growling sound that turned his innards to ice. Hart yelled something and suddenly the air was full of gunfire and screaming. The dust cleared a fraction and Bloom stared in dumb terror at the three monstrous creatures that had smashed through the gates, and his revolver wilted in his grip. "Bears?" he gasped in bewilderment, but these bears walked upright, their claws dragged across the cobbles, and they towered over every man there. "Bears?" he mumbled again.

Hart screamed something again but Bloom just stood transfixed as the monsters tore into his men and began to kill.

CHAPTER FIFTEEN

Valgard watches

*'As species decline so too do their patron fairies, but others spread across
the globe like a plague. Everywhere I look I see fairies of steel and blood.'*
Arthur Telford, founding witch of Red-Shawl coven, Devon

Thorpe knew it was a false alarm. It had to be. Witches would never
take on Thorpe Hall in direct attack. He heard a volley of shots, then a
few random splutters then silence. The men probably got spooked and let
fly he reasoned. "Bloody lily-waving altar boys, the lot of 'em." He hurried
through the downstairs corridor past the numerous function rooms,
stopping to collect a weapon from the trophy room and within a minute
he arrived at the entrance hall armed with a shotgun and a foul temper.
That's when he heard what could only be described as an explosion.
He skidded to a halt on the marble floor as the whole building shook,
making the chandelier above tinkle merrily. "Damn the Jik, I knew it!"
he roared.

She had a rescue force tucked away all the while, and played them
for fools. The sound of the explosion rolled away, leaving behind the
unmistakable sound of battle. He ran through the main hall towards the
sound of gunfire, loading his gun as he did, but the gunfire turned to
screams, and the screams turned to cries of terror and panic.

"We'll bring back the old ways and torch the slut," he seethed as he
arrived at the inner door and heaved on it like a madman. He charged

into the courtyard, only to freeze in confusion. "What in the name of sweet God?" His mouth melted into a witless droop. The garrison weren't fighting witches, they were being slaughtered by monsters.

In one swipe Eirik felled three men. His claws split them open as easily as water-filled balloons.

"Dear Christ! Gun company!" Bloom ordered the Maxim units. "Gun company!"

He emptied his revolver into the thing in the smoke. It was like a bear, but enormous and unnatural. Sometimes it looked like a man and even made sounds like words. Behind it, he was stunned to see two others just like it, both were flailing their arms like windmills and mowing men down.

The Maxim crews signalled their readiness and Bloom wasted no time. "FIRE!" he bellowed and suddenly the two heavy guns exploded into life, drilling bullets directly into the tangled mess of bears and bodies in the courtyard. The air turned white with smoke and the noise was deafening. No beasts, wild or otherwise could live through such a barrage, but Bloom was taking no chances. If these were creatures aligned to witches it might take more than just a few rounds to finish them off. "Company, form line!" he issued, and finally the garrison fell back in a ragged line with their rifles fixed on the wall of smoke ahead. The Maxims continued to fire, pouring hundreds of rounds into the creatures who were now invisible behind the powder fog, but it wasn't enough, Bloom was going to add to their pain. "FIRE!" he ordered. Rifles blazed and he heard the monsters roar. *I'll have three heads pinned on the wall by nightfall,* he promised himself. "FIRE!" There came another volley, and then another and another. There was nothing left to shoot at other than a curtain of dense smoke, but the garrison happily obliged and the sound of the creature's agony was music to his ears.

"Cease fire!" he called at last and the shock of gunfire ebbed away leaving a ringing in his ears and a faint echo around the forest. All around, he could hear men coughing or groaning in pain, but the courtyard remained an arena of smoke and dust.

"Are they dead sir?" someone called out.

"We'll soon see." He reloaded his pistol as he peered into the smoke. He could see bodies lying on the ground, but nothing was moving in there. "Stand ready," he called, and a line of guns steadied in response. Men looked nervously to their comrades and the Maxim teams were busy reloading.

"They've gotta be dead – gotta be," someone declared from nearby.

Bloom looked around and saw Hart, rifle raised, wary for any movement. "Right you are Hart," he agreed, "they've got to be dead."

Valgard was pleased at last. His wayward champions might have disobeyed him, but ultimately they had found a battle unlike anything they had encountered before. Shields and swords they knew, but rifles and gunpowder were new, and Valgard watched in fascination as bullets tore into his disobedient children.

Just as the valkyrie struggled to adapt to a blow from a lightning-staff, now Eirik and his brothers had to understand the power of modern weapons. Valgard toyed with the idea of taking back the Berserker rage. Without it they'd revert to mortal men and die in an instant, but the thrill of the fight was too good to spoil. He would let them remain invincible – for now.

Thorpe edged down the portico steps until he was standing in a world of ordered flowerbeds, gravelled pathways and balustrades, but only seventy yards away Bloom stood in the middle of a battlefield. "Bloom?" he called, and saw the captain turn and raise his hand. The danger was passed. Thorpe relaxed and swung the shotgun over his shoulder, thinking he'd better get back to the Jik before Harrison humped her to death.

He lay in the smoke, amid a tangled heap of bodies. The weapons had hurt them, but they'd not suffered a single wound. It was a lesson, he knew. Now Eirik understood the nature of bullets and gunpowder, and they were no more of a threat to him than a blunt sword. Strength flowed through his limbs and the fighting fury rose again. The girl, he thought, she set us free but she's in danger. He had a vision of a man's face, a man with cold eyes and sunken cheeks, the very one who was harming both the girl and the singer of that enchanted song.

One of Bloom's troopers edged forwards. "Hart, fall back!" he ordered

Hart might be the kind of soldier that enjoyed a crafty smoke, but he had friends amongst the wounded and he didn't abandon his mates. "Just a moment Captain," he squinted into the mist.

"Damn it Corporal, that's not me requesting; it's a bloody order now shift!"

He muttered something, lowered his rifle, and took a few paces back to the ranks, but something wasn't right. His own men were staring past him in fear, and backing away.

A cry went up, "Get out!"

It finally dawned on him that something very nasty had loomed up behind him.

"Hart! Drop man, drop!" Bloom yelled.

He heard the scrape of gravel behind, and spun around just in time to see a massive shaggy fist come at him in a brutal upper-cut. "Captain!" he screamed, and in the next instant his head was popped from his neck like a cork from a bottle.

Bloom saw his head spin over the crowd like a watermelon and land in the ornamental fountain with a hefty splash. Instantly, rifles and Maxims resumed their tune of death, but this time Eirik was ready and so were his brothers.

Thorpe saw a monstrous shadow loom out of the smoke and a second later some unfortunate soldier's head went spinning. Instantly the guns began spitting death again. Creatures resembling giant bears charged out of the fog, snatched men off their feet, tossed them in the air like pancakes and gutted them in the same move.

He almost tripped over himself as he backed away, now fumbling for his gun. Bloom was shouting something over the racket, but Thorpe wasn't going to hang around and watch. These beasts were coming to rescue the Jik. He screamed in fury and fired off a wild shot before charging back towards their prisoner, as the battle for Thorpe Hall began in earnest.

The building rocked. That was the only way he could describe it. Harrison felt a distant wobble beneath his feet and a rumble of what might have been thunder, followed by a storm of gunfire. He gave an involuntary jump, then instantly swaggered to compensate, aware she was watching him. *Victor!*

he whined silently. *Get back here now!* He turned from the tiny window with its view of the adjacent outhouse and back to the witch, and it was her expression that really rattled him. Clearly, she had no more idea about what was going on than he did. "I fancy your friends are taking a thrashing young lady, I wouldn't like to be on the receiving end of that barrage." He forced a hollow grin, all the while staring at the door Thorpe had vanished through, willing him to return.

Sunday's mind whirled. She'd given up wondering what was going on and now she focused all her resources on exploiting it. While Harrison darted nervously around the room, she'd been busy inventing a fiction and now all she needed was a little dramatic licence to put it into effect. "Mr Harrison?" she sobbed, acting helpless.

He spun around. "What?"

"I think something terrible is going on outside."

"I can see that!"

"No, please, you don't understand." She pulled at her bindings and feigned terror, which wasn't hard under the circumstances. "Yes, I confess there were more of us, but only two I swear. But there's something else: it followed us here." Her voice crumbled and she managed a few tears.

It followed us here. The words were like a hook, and he was dragged along by it. "What do you mean something followed you?" He felt scared, then remembered he was the one with the gun. "And don't lie to me!"

"We were hiding in the woods not far from here," she panted, "trying to raise a creature of the Dark-Veil but the spell failed. It escaped and killed my two companions and now I think it's followed me here!" Where these lies came from she had no idea, but she had the absurd feeling that this is how the Timekeeper must feel as he wove the fictions people called their lives.

"Dark-Veil?" He shook his head, and she saw his fleshy chin wobble under his ruddy face. "Make sense you stupid girl!"

"It's hell Mr Harrison, the Dark-Veil is another name for hell and that's where it's come from. It'll kill every man here, please you have to untie me, only I can stop it!"

At the mention of 'hell' Harrison suddenly grasped the picture. "You mean there's a demon out there?"

"Of the worst kind," she nodded furiously, and just then there was a sinister lull in the shooting. The rumble of guns trickled away into a few random crackles then silence. "I think it's got inside," she moaned pitifully.

The scullery was almost vacuum-silent. Neither of them breathed as they listened. It was so quiet in fact that far away Sunday could even hear a clock ticking and the hum of a wasp against the window. "It's coming for us. Oh, what have we done!"

"You're lying!" he protested, hoping to God she was. "I don't believe a —"

A distant scream pierced the air and suddenly the guns spluttered back into life. He squeaked and clutched the revolver to his chest.

"Please Mr Harrison," she begged, "if you return my staff I can kill it!"

"And then?" he shouted, torn by uncertainty.

"I've no wish for it to take our souls there, to the Dark-Veil, I'd sooner remain a prisoner."

"Take us to hell?" he mumbled. It was all making dreadful sense now. This demon wouldn't be happy to just kill them, it would snatch their immortal souls away for Satan's imps to torture for all eternity. He suddenly had a vision of himself as a child with Beattie Fellows, his nanny. He was sitting in her lap listening to Bible stories. Even then he'd shivered at the thought of a timeless existence in hell, and clung to her. She'd pressed little Charles Harrison to her breast, which he'd enjoyed immensely, thank you very much indeed Nanny Bea.

"Sinners go to hell little Master Harrison," Nanny Bea had promised, *"where they suffer every torment known to man, forever and ever and ever."*

"Forever," he gasped, and another bout of fighting rocked the building.

"I can stop it." She yanked on the bindings. "But not like this. I need my staff before it's too late." She looked to the door. Regardless of her lies she knew something very bad would come through it sooner or later; Thorpe or some other demon, it made no difference to her.

"Hell," he whispered, then from nowhere he uttered, "Nanny Bea?"

"Mr Harrison, please!"

"I'll get Victor," he blurted.

The house shook again and somewhere masonry thundered to the ground.

"No, there's no time." She dragged the chair around to face him, making the legs screech against the flagstones. "He's probably dead already, please Mr Harrison . . . Charles –," she added.

He looked at her properly and blinked away his fear.

"Charles, let me go. I'll banish this demon. And I surrender to you and you alone." She moistened her lips, and gave him a meaningful and lingering look. "You alone . . ."

If Harrison hadn't been terrified he might have been a little more shrewd, but his biggest downfall was mans' oldest weakness. Here was a ravishing girl promising to save his neck and hand herself over to him afterwards. Two very appealing offers in one he thought. His flimsy morals never stood a chance. "Yes, Victor would concur," he muttered and tucked the revolver into his belt. He rounded the table and loosened the bindings, but only the ones keeping her fixed to the chair, her wrists were still fastened behind her back. "I'll save you Victor," he mumbled repeatedly. "Trust good ole Charles."

It's a start Sunday, she told herself, *it's a start.*

"On your feet," he commanded, pulling her up. "Now move." He retrieved the revolver, pressed it against her back and shoved her towards the door at the back of the scullery. She edged towards it, careful to look compliant. "Halt." He reached around to slide the bolts open, pressing himself up against her as he did. His face loomed over her shoulder and he grunted in her ear as he struggled. She could hear his rough breathing and smell his expensive perfume, and she deliberately added to his problems by turning her head so that her hair brushed his cheek and her lips were almost touching his. Of the two of them she noted that he was trembling the most.

I'll soon get you free Strike, I promise. Trust the Sunday-effect. The thought almost made her smile. The bolts finally surrendered and the door swung open to reveal a dark corridor and the sound of battle outside grew louder. "Where are we going?" she cringed.

"Victor's study. There's a strong-room there."

Where Strike is! she deduced with elation.

"Now move, but slowly." He shoved her forwards into the dark, towards the sound of guns and screaming, but she'd never been happier.

He stood, renewed and full of fury, and found an insignificant warrior had strayed too close thinking them dead. He swatted the man's head from his shoulders and then the thunder of guns began again, but they were impotent against him. He looked around, calculating strengths and weaknesses in a heartbeat, and then he saw him. Standing on the steps to the grand Hall was the man with the cold eyes who had dared harm the girl. He roared his war cry, the animals of the forest fled in terror, and he charged his enemy.

Thorpe heard a furious roar just as he reached the Hall's front doors. He turned back and saw one of the beasts break away and charge directly towards him. At first it ran like a bear then in one fluid move it reared up and ran on two legs. "Don't these bastard things die?" He heard the Maxims take up against it, but the creature kept coming. It hurled men aside and Thorpe knew in his heart that it wanted vengeance. "You'll have to catch me first," he taunted, and slipped back into the Hall. If bullets couldn't stop them, perhaps taking the Jik hostage might.

Captain Bloom saw one of the creatures charge directly towards Lord Thorpe. "C Company, it's heading for the Hall, after it!" he screamed and six men disengaged and ran to Thorpe's aid. Bloom turned his attention back to the disaster in the gardens and saw that it was hopeless. Just then he heard metal shatter against stone and turned to see one of the Maxims being torn to shreds: its crew either running for their lives or lying in tatters around the broken gun. "Nothing can stop them!" he despaired and as if to prove it a Maxim's mangled wheel skimmed overhead and smashed through the drawing room windows. A soldier's battered body sailed after it and smacked against the fountain with such force that the structure toppled and the dainty shower became a gushing torrent like a severed artery.

"Retreat!" he cried. It was time to get the guests away. They were his priority now. "A and B Companies!" he bellowed, "Evacuate senior staff!" Men broke away to round up Thorpe's guests, while he ordered the remaining soldiers to fall back.

They began a slow retreat up the tiered gardens, firing round after round into the monsters. Bloom skidded and wobbled as he backed up on a carpet of spent bullets and rubble. Little by little his surviving troops limped and hobbled back towards the Hall, firing as they went, then suddenly behind him he heard the awful sound of wood and glass shattering. "Dear Lord, no." He turned to see the proud doors to Thorpe Hall hanging like torn sails and C Company disappearing through in pursuit. One of the creatures had forced a way into the house after Lord Thorpe.

Karl felt bullets shower across his flank but he gave them no regard. Men swarmed around him, thrusting bayonets and screaming in fear and fury. The steel bent and shattered, but while these warriors were puny they at least fought with gusto and when their bayonets broke, they drew knives or clubbed him with their rifles. He almost admired them. Nevertheless, he sent one flying with a powerful blow and watched him land in the fountain, the rest he pummelled to the ground, or shook them senseless between his jaws, and Valgard watched in sheer delight.

Harrison heard the loudest noise yet, and he froze. Glass shattered and something large crashed to the floor, and it wasn't outside. It was in the house. "Victor!" he shouted down the dark corridor. "Victor, answer me!"

"It's in the house with us." Sunday's fear wasn't play acting now.

"What do we do?" he blubbered.

"The strong room. If I can get my staff I can kill it."

"Yes, the strong room," he nodded frantically, seized her collar and pushed her ahead like a shield. The corridor was narrow and functional and Sunday guessed it must be a servants' entrance. At the end, she could see a far bigger door.

That leads into the main house, she thought. If they ran into Thorpe her lie would be revealed, she had to think of something quick.

"Open it," he commanded.

"I can't, my hands are tied," she complained, hoping he'd release her.

"It's already ajar, just kick it!" He gave her an impatient shake.

She took his meaning. The door hadn't been closed fully and she reached out with her foot and shoved it. "If it comes I can't defend you like this," she struggled, "you'll have to untie me."

"Keep quiet," he hissed.

They stopped and listened. Sunday saw a large hallway with a grand staircase leading up through numerous turns to the upper floor. The wood was dark and sombre and there were stuffed animal heads staring blankly from the walls, and marble figures lurking in the shady corners.

"Victor?" he called out. The fighting seemed to have lulled again and his voice echoed around the huge staircase. "Anyone?" he called, louder this time.

It was Sunday that heard it first. A deep growling coming from one of the passageways, but it was far too dark to see anything.

"Victor?" he whispered.

"We have to get to Thorpe's study," she moaned.

The growling came again, closer this time, followed by the sound of claws tapping against the hard floor and her flesh turned cold. She knew that sound, but her mind just couldn't locate the memory, or didn't want to. From behind her she heard Harrison gasp, "Nanny Bea?"

She realised he was close to losing his wits. "Thorpe's study," she pleaded, "get my staff!"

"Thorpe's study," he echoed, and backed away, pulling her after him and they slowly retreated down the corridor.

A door creaked ahead of them and a sliver of light fell upon the floor and fattened into a rectangle as the door opened wider. Harrison made a tiny whimpering sound. "Victor?"

At first there was silence, but Sunday knew someone was listening. A tall figure slid into view. It was Thorpe. "Charles, is that you?"

She heard the wind rush from his lungs in relief. "Dear God, Victor."

Immediately Thorpe raised his gun. "What's the Jik doing out of the tower? Are you a hostage Charles?"

"Nothing of the sort." He stepped out from behind her and jabbed the revolver under her ribs to show what an efficient job he was doing. "She told me about the demon, only she can stop it!"

Now was the moment, she knew. Thorpe would tell him to stop blathering and drag her back to the scullery, but instead he flashed her a hateful look. "*Three* demons have come for her," he snarled, "and killed most of the garrison already."

"Three?" Harrison gasped.

Three? she thought, and her dread peaked. *Three, and the click of claws on stone. It can't be.* For a bizarre moment she felt that her terrible fiction had come real.

"She can kill them," Harrison pleaded. "We've got to find her weapons, and make her kill them."

"Oh I'll wager she wants her weapons back," Thorpe crept closer, red with fury, "and she will kill them I promise you that." He advanced with the gun pointed directly at her head. "I'll wager you'd delight in feeding them my head wouldn't you, Jik?" his eyes bored right into her. "Hold her steady Charles," he hissed, and the hand around her neck tightened obediently.

Strike please! she thought. But it wasn't Strike that saved her.

A tiny sound heralded his arrival: the soft click of claws on marble. An instant later a huge shape exploded from the shadows with a roar that shook the house. It seemed berserks knew cunning as well as fighting.

"Victor!" Harrison squealed and leapt back, pulling Sunday with him.

Thorpe turned and fired both barrels without thinking, catching the beast square in the chest and Eirik was hurled against the wall, shattering the oak panels. He recovered in a flash, and would have had Thorpe right then, but he was met with a burst of rifle fire. C Company had finally arrived to the rescue and the hallway filled with screaming and shouting, and firing and roaring.

"Nanny!" Harrison shrieked, turned and ran, dragging Sunday with him.

How did they find me here? Her thoughts raced as fast as her legs as she struggled to keep up.

Harrison sprinted along, pulling her behind and she could hear his terrified sobs. "Nanny Bea, I don't want to go to hell!"

The sound of fighting faded as they ran headlong through Thorpe Hall and just when she thought Harrison was running in blind panic he turned a sharp left into another room, swung her through the doorway like a sack of potatoes and slammed the door. They'd reached Thorpe's study.

Eirik saw the girl first. She was captive to some decadent man, but as soon as he saw her his lust to kill died away. Feeling calmer just being in her presence he waited, calculating how he could reach her. That's when the cold-man had appeared and as soon as he advanced on the girl Eirik's blood boiled and he charged.

Just when he thought he'd have that cold bastard's neck in his jaws, more men arrived and began shooting. Eirik saw the girl dragged away into the depths of the house. He knew he'd have to cut his way through the soldiers to reach her, and he wasted no time putting those fearsome claws to good use.

"Don't move!" Harrison bawled and threw her into a plush chair by the hearth where a fire blazed happily to itself, bringing cheer where there was only blood and mayhem. He kept the revolver pointed at her while he ransacked Thorpe's desk for the keys to the strong-room.

"I can get us out of here Charles I promise," she tried to soothe him. In his panic and armed with a gun she thought he was as dangerous as any berserk.

He nodded mutely and his chin rippled in response. "Get us out," he gasped, "yes, get us out." His eyes flicked between her and his own hand, which was hunting for the key and knocking all manner of items off Thorpe's desk. "Can you save poor Victor?" he asked between sobs.

I'd sooner feed him to the bears, she thought. "Only if you hurry, you saw him trapped by one of those evil things." If there was an abode in purgatory for those who told lies, hers would be as palatial as Thorpe Hall she thought.

While he ransacked the desk, cursing and sobbing, she stared around at Thorpe's study. Her gaze was drawn to the huge stained glass window which reached almost floor to ceiling, and almost every inch of wall space was taken by stuffed heads. She saw boars, bears, tigers, lions, alligators and a dozen different species of antelope, and even a fox, but one with snow white fur just like the one that helped her in Iceland. Now she was more determined than ever to escape and she tried her bindings again.

"Stop that!" he shouted, and waved the gun at her.

She blinked innocently. "I think I hear it coming!" she lied, "but I can't fight it like this!" She waggled her shoulders, indicating her tied wrists.

He ignored her and continued his search, outside she could hear more gunfire and screaming. She sat there trembling and her gaze was drawn back to the white fox and she wondered what was so wrong with men like Thorpe. *If I get out if this I'll pay him back for you,* she promised the fox silently. It just leered back at her with its cheap taxidermist grin.

"Found it!" he cheered, and snatched a key from one of the drawers.

More gunfire barked along the passageway outside. She flinched and looked to the door, knowing if Thorpe came in he'd either shoot her right there or at the very least make Harrison see sense and spoil her escape. "Please hurry Charles!" she grovelled. "Only magic can stop them!"

"Just stay where you are," he warned as he ran to the strongroom: a narrow iron door flanked on either side by deep bookcases. She heard the key scrape against the lock as he fumbled with it, then the lock mechanism tumble and Harrison grunt as he heaved on the door, then the blessed squeak of hinges. Strike was almost free. She got to her feet in excitement.

"Sit!" he ordered and waved the gun in her direction, and she obediently lowered herself back down.

An instant later he threw a tightly wrapped package on the floor at her feet then heaped another on top, it was her belt with the two wands fixed to it, and her heart boomed in her chest. He shoved the revolver in her face. "Open it!"

"My hands?"

Without shifting the revolver he fished a pocket knife from his jacket. "Hold steady," he commanded and pressed the blade against the bindings, while she longingly eyed the bundle on the floor.

I'm coming Strike, she thought, terrified Thorpe would burst in at any moment. The blade did its work and her hands slid away from one another and she gasped in sheer joy. "My staff, cut the bindings, then we're almost there." She rubbed her wrists and looked him directly in the eye. "Almost safe!"

His head wobbled in agreement, and he set to slitting the cords. Each knot popped open, and little by little the rubberised material flopped aside, and her throat tightened when she saw her beloved lightning-staff. They were almost free. "Now pick it up and kill those things!"

"Yes," she nodded meekly, "I'll go and stop them."

"No!" he shook his head firmly, "*We* will go, I'm not letting you out of my sight. You first."

She nodded and reached for her staff, with the revolver only inches from her head. Her fingers curled around it, and inside she heard a tiny buzz like a bottled fly. That buzz became a roar as Strike rushed up to her.

"Sunday! Where in Oak's name have you BEEN!" he almost screamed.

"No time!" Something in her voice stilled him.

"Trouble?"

"The worst kind."

Harrison watched her stroke the staff, eyes closed, concentrating. Now that salvation was at hand he calmed a little and had chance to admire her again, seeing through her clothes and appraising every contour of her body. "Very well, that's enough. Take the staff and do what you promised," he demanded, "you're my prisoner now."

Strike now understood the bare bones of their plight. She climbed slowly to her feet, careful to maintain the act of compliance. In her hands she held her lightning-staff and Harrison had no idea how vulnerable he was, how easily she could kill him. He'd be dead before he even knew what had happened, it would be so simple and satisfying. And that's precisely why she couldn't do it, she couldn't just murder him.

"Do it!" Strike urged. *"Kill the brute!"*

The staff hummed in her grip, sending shock waves up her arms. She'd never known him so angry. *"I can't, not like this."*

"What are you waiting for, Jik?" Harrison accused, not realising she was deliberating over his death.

"Sunday, there's no time for this!" As if underlining Strike's point, the clock on the mantel chimed the hour of three.

"Three bears," she whispered.

"What?" Harrison frowned. "Just get out there and kill them." He sounded arrogant now, and there was no mention of 'nanny'.

She made her mind up and fast as a snake she hit him right in the chest. There was a loud bang and he was flung over the desk bathed in smoke and sparks. He landed with a surprised squeak and a heavy thud, then she heard him roll over gasping and snarling. Rightly or wrongly he still lived, she made sure of that. "Jik whore, come back!" He staggered to his feet, clutching at his scorched shirt front. "You promised!" he wailed.

She snatched her wands and was already at the door when a bullet thumped into the wall and showered her with plaster. She yelped and flung herself through the doorway before he could squeeze off another shot.

He lurched out of the study after her, blubbering curses and threats. He'd been well and truly deceived and it burned him as much as her heathen staff. It had finally dawned on him that she wasn't going to save any of them. It was all lies, and worst of all somehow he'd have to explain this to Thorpe. He saw her lithe figure sprinting away into the gloom and fired three more shots. "Lying Jik BITCH! Send her to hell Nanny Bea!" He fired again into the empty corridor in sheer frustration, and now his revolver held one last shot.

Behind him he heard a deep growling and his heart fluttered. He turned slowly and saw a towering shape standing not four feet away. It held something glistening in one paw and he was glad he couldn't see it in the half light. He raised the tiny revolver and its one last bullet. The gun fired with a faint 'pop', without him even realising he'd pulled the trigger. It sounded almost comical, and when the echo died away he was still left with that towering shadow and the sound of its heavy breathing. "Nanny?" he whispered.

His answer was a massive fist. It smashed him through the wall of Thorpe's study. And on the other side a new head crashed through the plasterwork alongside the stags and antelopes, and joined them in gazing at nothing forever.

CHAPTER SIXTEEN

Fate's champion

'I knew without knowing how I knew. Such is fate.'
'The Tree and the Rosy Crown' Rudolph Gerten, 1670

John Golding and Albert Grant ushered them through the kitchens, making sure everyone was accounted for. Thorpe's guests had come to shoot, but now they were sport for other hunters, and Captain Bloom had ordered an evacuation, while the shrewd serving staff had fled as soon as the fighting started. "Where's Pinn?" Grant hadn't see Philleas Pinn, the banking magnate, for some time and was wondering if he'd received the order to evacuate.

"I don't know but if he's not here soon then he can take care of himself," Golding snorted just as there came another salvo of distant rifle fire.

The last of Thorpe's guests were hurrying through the cramped servant quarters and out to the waiting carriages. All of them carried what they could salvage and most of them still wore their tweeds. "What about Harrison, where's he?" Grant noticed.

"Last I heard he was with Thorpe." Golding didn't care either way.

"But Thorpe isn't here either!"

"It's his residence, let him sort himself out. Now come on, the horses are waiting," Golding had seen men torn apart by monsters that shrugged off gunfire like snowflakes; he certainly wasn't going to wait any longer. He stalked away through the kitchens where hares and pheasants hung from the ceiling, and ahead of him outside in the courtyard he could see men jostling to get aboard the carriages. Outside, the rear gates stood open and a track snaked away through the forest. "Bloody Victor," he growled again, "should've shot the harlot in the woods and had done with it."

Grant caught him up. "Just about everyone's in the carriages," he puffed. "Escort?"

"Ready." He jerked his head to a dozen mounted soldiers, whose horses looked nervy and stamped at the gravel, eager to be off.

I know how you feel, Golding agreed. "Right, we're ready."

"But what about Pinn?"

"Bugger him!"

"Wait!" someone yelled. "Wait for me!" They turned back to see Philleas Pinn scurrying along the servants' corridor towards them. The willowy man was carrying two large suitcases, and still wearing his ridiculous deerstalking cap and his spectacles hung askew on his nose.

"Shake a leg!" Golding shouted. "And drop those bloody cases, it's not a damned day trip to Brighton."

They watched with mounting agitation as Pinn caught his cases in the doorway and then dropped the cumbersome things. He muttered something and stooped to collect them.

"Leave them!" Golding's patience was spent. Already he could hear the first carriage trundling out of the courtyard and away. The clomp of hooves and rattle of wheels was like a siren song he had to follow. "Bloody hell!" he roared in frustration and went to Pinn's aid, if he didn't get the idiot out they'd never leave.

"There's no call for ruffians' language!" Pinn scolded him.

Golding got ten paces back into the kitchen, when the wall opposite exploded as something burst through it. Broken bricks, copper measuring ladles and mixing bowls flew through the air. Pinn saw something crash through, and emitted a shrill scream of horror. It was the largest bear he'd ever seen.

Outside, Grant heard the crash of falling masonry and breaking crockery, then Pinn's screams followed by Golding's angry shouts, and gallantly decided it was every man for himself. "Drive on!" he screamed at the last carriage and ran for the open door. The driver lashed the horses and they jumped. Grant was almost at the carriage door when there was a bestial roar from inside the house, the horses screamed and burst into an uncontrolled gallop.

"Hold it there, hold!" the driver howled, but the horses had other ideas and he was flung from the carriage and landed with a smack against the cobbles.

Grant watched in horror as the last carriage left Thorpe Hall at breakneck speed, crammed with senior Illuminata, but no driver. The open door beat back and forth like a laughing mouth and although he knew it was futile, he sprinted after it. "No, for God's sake don't leave me here!" He skipped over the fallen driver, and out onto the track. "Don't leave me!"

Without warning, the wall shattered and jugs and saucers flew through the air. A plate cracked against Golding's skull and he was hurled to the floor. Most of the debris missed Philleas Pinn however, because he was already on his knees trying to collect his fallen suitcases. He looked up to see a massive creature tearing through the wall as if it were nothing but a bamboo screen, and he screamed. He saw Golding knocked off his feet by a wave of rubble, and in reply he gripped his suitcases, thinking in a disjointed way that the harder he held onto them the sooner this nightmare would end.

Golding climbed up from the floor, skidded around, faced the monster and drew his revolver. The bear-thing bellowed in fury, still half embedded in the wall. "You're going to hell along with that Jik whore!" he laughed manically and opened fire.

Point blank range. Six shots. But it never even flinched.

"That's not fair!" he screamed. In a frenzy he bent and scooped up a set of kitchen weights. Cast iron discs flew across the room, but the monster just shook them away. It bellowed again, and Pinn, still standing with his suitcases, saw the cavernous mouth drop open wide and heard something almost human in its cry.

"Bastard!" Golding threw anything he could snatch. A wooden mixing spoon twirled through the air and bounced off the bear's nose, a handful of silver cutlery showered over it like snow, then a cream-jug glanced off its brow. Finally it struggled through the wrecked wall, and charged. Golding, having nothing left at hand, hurled his revolver in contempt. "Not fair!" he screamed again.

Pinn watched the revolver bounce off the monster's muzzle, just before the creature landed on Golding and all the brave words and bullets in the world couldn't change the inevitable. He vanished in a flurry of fur and a shrill scream. The next thing Pinn knew there were shreds of expensive tweed drifting down and the thing was shaking him this way and that, knocking tables and chairs around the kitchen, skidding and sliding across the blood-slicked tiles. An enamel cylinder rolled off the dresser and spilled a blizzard of oats across the floor. Pinn suddenly thought of Goldilocks and sweet bears that ate porridge and slept in quaint little beds.

He decided he'd seen enough now and quite calmly set off with his two cases still hanging from his numb hands. The door was only ten feet away. He could see the cobbles and the water trough outside and smell fresh air. There were no carriages, but Pinn knew that didn't matter. All he had to do was exit with his cases and all would be well. Behind him he could hear tearing fabric and muffled growls. "Goodbye dear Victor," he said merrily. "It's been a pleasure to shoot, but I really must be going."

The growling and crunching behind him stopped.

"Do give my regards to the Queen-Empress when you next see her." He reached the doorway.

There came the sound of claws on flagstones and heavy breathing.

"Perhaps I'll see you again for the glorious 12th, and we can bag a brace together," he chirped. "Farewell dear Victor!" He stepped out of Thorpe Hall and into the small courtyard.

He wasn't sure what would happen next but he knew something must. After all, he had his suitcases and he'd left the kitchen as he planned, but some part of Pinn's terrified brain understood that this fell short of an effective escape plan. "Erm, yes, now then?" His brow furrowed as it dawned on him that he hadn't been whisked away to safety nor had he awoken from a nightmare, and perhaps the suitcases weren't the magical talismans he'd believed. "Victor?" he called hopefully.

Behind him came the scrape of claws on cobbles and a bass growling sound. He took a deep breath and turned slowly.

The creature was like a bear, but much larger and it walked on two legs. Its eyes were small but they burned like branding irons and the claws were wickedly sharp and long. He saw its massive shoulders rise and fall with each breath. It took a step towards him. He backed up and dropped his suitcases and with them went his numbing sense of the unreal and the fear caught up with him in an instant. "Get away!" he shrieked, "off, you beastly thing, off with you!" He held up his hands and shooed the monster away.

Karl regarded him coolly, even curiously, and took another step closer.

"Get away, get away!" he gibbered and backed up in a trot. His skinny legs pumped up and down making him look like a puppet doing a jig. "Get away you horrible thing!" he screamed and slapped the creature right across the face, sending a spray of saliva from its muzzle.

Karl blinked in surprise and took step back. What was this screaming little creature, he thought?

"Be off!" he screamed and swatted it again. "Leave me alone!"

Karl had lost interest now, and in one contemptuous swipe he smashed Pinn into the wall, leaving just a dark stain and sending his deerstalker hat spinning away into the bushes. Then he ambled out through the courtyard, flattening those neatly packed suitcases as he went.

"Wait!" Grant screamed again. The driver-less carriage careered off in pursuit of the first vehicle, while the mounted guardsmen were too far away to hear anything or be any help. He wasn't ready to give up however and he sprinted after the runaway carriage sobbing and sweating in his heavy tweeds. "Please for God's sake!" he panted, feeling a stabbing pain in his abdomen. "WAIT!" But his cry came out as a dry gasp and he keeled over fighting for breath and began to sob. "No," he pleaded, and watched the carriage as it bounced along the road, lurched and finally toppled into a ditch. The horses ploughed into the ground, evoking a cloud of dirt in reply, then they righted themselves and scattered, dragging their broken harnesses behind them.

The carriage rolled onto its roof and the only thing Grant could see moving were the wheels, which continued to spin, literally going nowhere. He climbed to his feet and began to stagger along the road without a plan and without a hope. Behind him back in the courtyard, he heard a man shouting as though trying to shoo away a troublesome dog, then a short but telling cry, and knew he'd be next. "Treacherous jackals," he sobbed, "left me to die!"

He plodded on and drew closer to the carriage. It lay in the ditch, and the road was littered with expensive luggage. Some had disgorged their contents along the track. Grant followed a trail of laundered shirts, cigar boxes and lotion bottles, back to the crashed carriage. A hand groped out of the broken windows and he heard someone groaning and coughing. He stiffened and remembered his pride. "I trust you gentlemen can manage without my assistance," he sniffed childishly and wiped blood from his grazed cheek.

He knew it would happen eventually, and just as he drew level with the carriage it did. He heard heavy paws thudding behind him. A clot of fear seemed to crawl up his gullet. He couldn't breath properly and he felt sick. "Please," he moaned softly, "no please. It wasn't my idea to take the lady prisoner." There was no mention of 'Jik' any longer.

The clawed feet grew louder, and now he could hear wood-saw breath as well. It blotted out all other sounds completely. The world was filled by those marching feet and that steam-hammer breath. He wanted to run but his legs felt boneless and watery. *Soon I'll be dead,* he thought and cringed at the unfairness of it. He cast a hateful glance at the upturned carriage. "Bastards!" he whimpered and wiped the snot from his nose.

"Albert?" someone called, followed by a groan of pain. "Albert!" More urgent this time.

The marching feet and panting breath suddenly stopped, and he felt a spark of hope.

"Albert for God's sake," the voice wailed, "we're trapped in here, bring help!"

Those clawed feet began moving again, but this time heading towards the smashed carriage and the pleading voice.

"Albert, is that you? Anyone, please help!"

The monster had been lured away.

His heart jumped and everything changed. The road ahead wasn't the path to the executioner's block, but the road to freedom. He heard claws scrape on wood and someone inside the carriage call out, mistaking the sounds for rescue.

"Merciful God be praised!" Grant sobbed, and broke into a run as he heard wood splinter behind him and the first screams from the trapped men. He ran faster and the birds began to sing again, the sunshine found its warmth and the breeze was the most delicious thing he'd ever felt. He ran, shouting and laughing at the top of his lungs, and so he didn't hear the terrible chorus of screams back along the track as his former friends saved his life after all.

Captain Bloom was a brave and obedient solider, but even he tussled with his loyalty as his garrison were pushed further back and steadily picked off. No matter how hard they fought or how much ammunition they shot into the devilish things they just kept on coming. All around he heard men shout that they were low on ammunition and to make matters worse the two Maxim guns were now lying around the gardens in pieces, as were their crews.

He took cover behind a large ornamental urn and began reloading his revolver for the tenth or eleventh time just as Major Devon ran to take cover with him. The major had a bloodied nose, but otherwise he was unhurt. "Carriages and guests should be away by now, have you seen Lord Thorpe?"

Bloom stared at the older man. "No sir, he ran back into the Hall and I dispatched C Company to go after him."

"I've telegraphed the local reserves for reinforcement, there's nothing more we can do here. Call your men back and sound a full retreat, we're leaving."

This was music to Bloom's ears and he grinned despite everything. "Company!" he shouted over the creatures' roars. "Fall back!"

Sunday couldn't believe how wonderful it felt to have Strike back. He had become so much a part of her that having him again was like recovering from an illness.

"Curse me for not seeing it!" he despaired again.

"It's fine," she whispered as they crept through Thorpe Hall, which was now ominously silent.

"But I can't believe I was taken so easily."

"We were both taken easily," she reminded him.

"A sprite should always be alert," he berated himself. *"And where was I when you needed me most?"* He was growing angry again.

"Not now Strike," she hissed, trying to remember the way back to the scullery. Her belongings were still there, but most importantly so was the way-beware. "This way I think." She chose a passage that looked narrow and functional, just the kind of thing that would lead to a kitchen, or so she hoped. At last she came upon a door. "Pray it's open," she whispered.

"I have a key!" Strike rumbled.

She tested the handle. It turned quietly, the door opened a crack and she let out a huge puff of relief; it was the passage Harrison had bundled her along, the one leading from the scullery into the main house. "This is it." Escape was so close, and she felt a horrible certainty that everything would go wrong now, like the soldier who dies on the last day of the war.

She advanced on tiptoe hardly daring to breathe, wary of each door she passed, convinced Thorpe would leap out and finish what he'd started. She winced when a floorboard creaked and even her heart sounded too loud. The fighting had stopped she realised. There were a few alarm whistles and then all of Thorpe Hall had fallen quiet. *A sleeping house,* she thought, *with very bad dreams.*

At last she gripped the handle to the scullery door and pushed it open, staff at the ready.

"They won't catch us sleeping this time," Strike promised.

The first thing she saw was the table, then a wave of heavenly relief when her eyes settled on the way-beware and her other belongings. She knew then that she was complete again. A second later she was wearing her satchel with all her priceless things back safely inside and with the way-beware tucked into her belt. "Come on Strike, we're leaving."

She arrived in the saloon at a run and slid across the marble floor. The doors to Thorpe Hall hung wide where they'd been smashed open and there were shards of glass all around the floor. "Neet's monsters," she shook her head in disbelief.

"Just pieces of paper my dear," came a voice from the shadows. "It can be repaired in no time at all."

She knew it was Thorpe and the loud click told her he was holding a gun. Strike promised they wouldn't be caught twice, but now look at them.

"Drop the staff and turn slowly, I wish to see your pretty face one last time before I splatter it across the walls," he said warmly.

"*Let me kill him!*" Strike was desperate.

"*Not like this.*" There was one last piece of the puzzle and she was determined to uncover it. "*Trust me Strike. Trust the Sunday-effect.*" That was her last command to him. She dropped the staff and turned slowly to face him.

He materialised from the shadows with his shotgun pointed right at her, and unlike Harrison he held it rock steady. She knew he was going to kill her as surely as the sun was warm, and water was wet.

"My compliments Lord Thorpe, you fight well, but you'll have to put on a better show in June if you hope to defeat us," she smiled demurely.

He shook his head in quiet rage and grinned. "I have to hand it to you, witch-with-no-name, your friends have caused much mischief here."

"As we will again in June," she taunted.

He pursed his lips. "Perhaps, but you won't be alive to enjoy it, and I think Galen can devise a charm that'll thwart even your protectors." He made a play of looking around the saloon. "Who it must be said are not here to protect you."

Galen? He'd mentioned that name before, she thought. "You still don't understand. You *can't* kill me Mr Thorpe."

He stopped and his eyes seemed to double in size "Oh, what a delightful challenge my dear!" He emitted a dry laugh, which sounded like sand pouring from a tomb. Four paces away from her he pulled the trigger with the gun aimed directly at her head.

The hammer fell against a bad cartridge and there was just a soft click, nothing more. His eyes narrowed and he bared his teeth. His finger squeezed again and the second hammer struck home, but both barrels remained dark and silent.

She smiled at him prettily, but her lips felt numb. "You see Mr Thorpe? I am protected by more than just invincible warriors. Fate has chosen me to be its champion." It didn't matter that it wasn't true, this was a war of belief.

His jaw trembled and the gun slowly drooped until it slid from his fingers completely and clanged against the marble. The colour drained from him and he growled something in his throat, something hateful and furious. Veins throbbed at his temples and she saw crimson flush his cheeks. The awful growling continued and it took a second for her to realise that it wasn't Thorpe after all, the growling sound was coming from behind her.

She stared into his icy eyes, but he wasn't looking at her. In one of the saloon's decorative mirrors she caught a glimpse of them; great shadows, drawn by the way-beware. She touched the doll in her belt for luck. "It seems my protectors have arrived," she bluffed.

A smell like bad meat wafted through the saloon and she heard something large lumber towards her. The footfalls were confident and powerful. The last time she had seen them was beneath a glacier in Iceland. *I knew it wasn't over,* she thought without a shred of fear. *I knew they'd come back.* She bent slowly, without taking her eyes off Thorpe, who looked mad enough to be a berserk himself, groped for her staff, and clutched it tight.

"*Don't ever do that again!*" Strike raged.

"*I'm sorry.*" They were one, and the world was balanced again. "Now then Mr Thorpe," she enquired politely, "will I, or will I not be seeing you in June?"

He was shaking with terror and fury, and perhaps just a little more of the latter. At his sides, his fists opened and clenched pointlessly and his face was twisted with hate. He growled something deep in his throat.

"I'm sorry," she frowned. "I didn't catch that?"

"There'll be more knights at Salisbury than you ever dream possible, Jik whore." Now he began to shake with laughter, and spittle glistened on his lips.

Salisbury, she thought. *That's where the tournament is, the missing piece of the puzzle.*

"Sunday?" It was Strike.

She thought of the enormity of what she'd learned here today. "One last task," she promised her thunder-sprite.

Thorpe was so close that she didn't even have to move, she simply jabbed her staff and knocked him to the floor. He dropped to his knees with a crack and yelped in pain, while behind her she heard the berserks growl approvingly. He looked up at her like a man condemned, but just like Harrison it wouldn't have been right. "I wouldn't soil myself by killing something as pathetic as you," she sneered down at him, using his words. "You'll live today Mr Thorpe, but know that each breath you take from this day on was bought by my mercy."

He glared up at her, but was he was powerless. All he had was rage.

"Now hands behind you." She stepped to his back, careful not to look at the monsters in the doorway, and tore a strip from the hem of her shirt.

He stared down at the floor. A bead of sweat dropped from his nose and glistened on the black marble, and in its glassy surface he saw the three standing watch over their precious witch. He felt her nimble hands pull the cloth tight, and the knots she fastened were as tough as chains.

"On your feet and go to your study. Now!" she commanded. He stood, and now it was her turn to push him.

He began to walk with the staff pressed between his shoulders knowing there was nothing he could do. He shuffled along, a hostage now in his own house, stepping through smashed wood and broken plaster. Amongst the devastation Sunday saw a body hanging skewered on the antlers of a stag's head. It was Muldoon the gamekeeper and she wondered, not for the first time, if fate had a vindictive sense of humour.

When they arrived at his study she saw the rear end of Harrison's lifeless torso hanging out of the wall. She prodded Thorpe through the door and into his inner sanctum, careful not to look at Harrison's head, and shoved him towards the fireplace. There was still some life left in the coals, and that was enough. "On your knees." She didn't wait for him to comply, but instead hammered the back of his legs and dropped him. He landed with a grunt and stared up at her, and some of his confidence had returned now that her guardians weren't breathing down his neck.

"We have many witch captives, you know," he said smoothly.

Her heart clenched, but she remained defiant.

"And I give you my word that in payment for this outrage I shall execute a dozen of them in your honour."

Horror must have passed across her face because his eyes brimmed with satisfaction.

"He's lying," Strike calmed her.

She took a deep breath.

"Know that every scream they suffer before they die will be bought by your evil this day." Now he was playing with her words.

A groan escaped her lips, and Thorpe chuckled at her anguish. From the corner of her eye she saw the white fox inside its glass coffin and remembered her promise. *'If I get out if this I'll pay him back for you.'* Without a word she went to his desk, knowing anything she could take might be useful. She yanked the top drawer open. Inside lay a bundle of official looking papers. Without stopping to inspect them she grabbed the whole lot and stuffed them into her satchel.

He huffed as if he'd been expecting this from the start. "Stealing? Is this what this is all about? Fancy that, you murdered all those innocent souls so that you might thieve from me. May your own soul be damned."

She ignored him and went to the sideboard and tested the crystal drink decanters until she found what she wanted. He watched her with renewed interest.

"Finding solace in a bottle?" he taunted. "Too late you thieving slut, it won't bring back the good men you've butchered."

She slipped the stopper from the decanter and tossed it into the chair by the fire.

"And when you're good and drunk will you cavort naked with your beasts and celebrate the blood you've spilled?" He regarded her with pure disgust.

She let his foul talk go unanswered and went to the window, looked from the brandy bottle to Thorpe and back again. Without taking her eyes off him she tipped the spirit over the long velvet curtains.

His expression melted as it dawned on him what she was doing. "Lunatic whore!" he exploded, and struggled to his feet.

"DOWN!" She hurled him back against the floor with one blow. There was a brilliant spark and she heard Strike hiss in satisfaction.

He landed in a heap, with his heart fluttering with the aftershock. "You murderous gutter-whore!" he groaned, and writhed on the carpet trying to right himself.

She didn't stop to relish his hurt. Instead, she took the shovel from the hearth, scooped a generous load of coals from the fire and carried them over to the curtains.

He glared at her in disbelief. "You wouldn't dare," he gulped.

She looked at the white fox again, and now its leering grin looked more like a contented smile. "I made a promise," she pledged, not caring that he'd never understand, and with that she tipped the hot coals over the curtains.

He watched them roll down the material and plop into a pool of brandy at the bottom. There was a delicate 'woof' sound and a soft blue flame appeared. It snaked up the curtains in a flash and became fiery yellow as it bit harder and found it liked the taste. He wanted to rave and scream, but nothing escaped his mouth other than a dribble of saliva.

She threw the empty bottle into the chair, where it struck the stopper with a beautiful note, which seemed to stir Thorpe from his horrified trance. At last he looked at her, then back to the curtains still not quite believing what he was seeing. The fire was now licking at the ceiling. "I'll execute them all in *your* name," he swore.

She stood before him and drew hrafn-dimmu, Valonia's black wand, and she thrust it against his throat, pressing the tip deep into his flesh. He rolled his eyes up towards her and she saw enough hate in them to last countless lifetimes. "You asked my name this afternoon Mr Thorpe, and now I'll tell you – my name is Blackwand, and I've let you live so that you may tell all of London I'm coming." She pressed the wand harder. "This is your one simple task and I trust you have the wit to carry it out. Tell them all Blackwand is coming and she is unlike any witch you've ever fought."

His expression was marble-hard. "When I next see you, I shall kill you." There were no threats in him now, just facts.

"No," she said blandly, "the next time I look upon you Mr Thorpe you'll already be dead." She swiped him contemptuously across the face with Raven's wand, making him flinch, and then marched past him not caring if he ran or burned to death. He'd been given the choice, which was more than his kind had ever done for witches. Behind her, she heard the fire crackle and laugh like a monster set loose and the first wisps of smoke billowed across the ceiling and followed her out through the door.

The Timekeeper lay down Sunday's thread. It was the great spider that had ensured Thorpe's gun was loaded with defective cartridges. Yet again he'd foiled an attempt on her life, and yet again the Patternmaker's fury rumbled around the cavern. *This cannot go on,* he thought to himself. *All this hate and death for the cost of one single thread.* He thought of the mayhem unleashed at Thorpe Hall and all because the assassin had sent her there in the first place. "This cannot go on!" he called out.

The silence that followed wasn't entirely empty. There was the gasp of silk as the assassin moved again.

"This cannot go on," he muttered, but knowing that it would and suspecting that the Patternmaker was readying for a different kind of attack.

Buried deep in the threads of fate, the assassin-grub wriggled into the cocoon it had prepared and sealed the entrance. Inside, it lay still and began the lengthy transformation process. When next it emerged it would have no need of secrecy and the spider would be its prey.

CHAPTER SEVENTEEN

An unwilling gift

'Wise is the man who stops the falling stone
before it becomes a landslide.'
Indian proverb

". . . And all that remained of the wicked witch was a dark stain on the floor. She was never heard of again and so the valley at last found peace." Galen finished reading and closed the book.

"That tale was wonderful," Vorus enthused.

"Quite so my sweet. It's a favourite of mine too." He patted the cherub's gruesome face. The helmet rested on a bed of scrap because Vorus, true to her nature, preferred the machine in its collapsed state.

"Galen?" Her voice sounded like a bee in a cave.

"Yes?"

"When may I see the red-river again? It has been so long."

She asked him this frequently and now at last she sounded hungry enough. "Alas my lovely, I'm not permitted to bring you anymore witches until you help us in a small matter." He examined his cane and inside Elios listened to him toy with her.

"She's not a fool," she cautioned, but again he ignored her.

There was a scraping sound inside the helmet as Vorus shifted closer. He could almost imagine her peering out like a child at a sweetshop window and he smiled to himself. "It is help you need? I will help you, just ask."

"Those miserly buggers, Lyle and Doulton." He swiped the cane in mock frustration. "They've told me that they won't let you see the red-river until you explain more of your home." There was a considered pause and he just looked at the floor, waiting.

"They wish to know of Ruination?"

"That's so my sweet."

Inside the cane even Elios waited. Would answers to the ninth chapter really come so easily, she wondered?

"What of Àeon's world intrigues them so?"

He shrugged. "They wish to know what makes time itself."

"The song of Àeon makes time of course, didn't you know?" she laughed softly as if he'd asked her whether ducks like water.

He shouldered her gentle teasing and propped himself up on his cane, now looking like a seaside dandy. "Aye petal, you know that and I know that, but Lyle and Doulton are like blunt knives."

"Explain?"

"Not so sharp," he said, making her titter. His word play seemed so bright and clever to her. "I fear the only thing that'd appease them is to hear Àeon's song for themselves, but alas that ain't possible," he sighed, leaving a waiting gap.

"But Galen?" she sounded confused, "I know the song of Àeon, all creatures of Ruin know it."

He made a tiny choking sound, but was careful to hide his excitement. "Aye, they do but most aren't as clever as yourself, they couldn't remember it to say it aloud." He scrubbed at his neck with his handkerchief, "I'll bet my clever lassie can do it though?"

She gasped, "Yes I can, I can sing you the song!"

Elios listened intently, and hearing Galen from the viewpoint of a spectator she detected something horribly sham about his sweet talk. It was the way he'd spoken to her down the years. *No he loves me!* she insisted and for once her dead-walk mind seemed as doubting as her.

Galen feigned an amazed look. "My clever little buttercup! You can really sing me the song of Àeon?"

"Yes!" she offered, longing to impress.

The secret to life outside time lay within that battered helmet. The thought made him dizzy. "Vorus," he began. "I'll wager you sing like a nightingale, could poor old Galen listen to that sweet voice right now?"

He heard her take a breath, ready to sing for him, and he would have sworn the very earth slowed its orbit to listen.

"Galen!" Suddenly Lyle charged in, looking horrified and waving sheets of paper. Elios sensed the moment collapse like a burst balloon and part of her was pleased.

"How dare you burst in here!" Galen roared.

"This isn't a private room in a brothel!" he retorted, "we're at war!"

Galen rocked on his feet, and for a moment he had the bizarre idea that May had slipped by and June's great tournament was on them. Even Àeon's song was momentarily forgotten.

"Thorpe Hall's been attacked by some witch and her familiars!" Lyle stammered.

"And Lord Thorpe, was he hurt?"

"Safe thank God." He waved the papers. "Telegrams here tell all. You have new orders."

"From Thorpe?"

"Who the bloody hell else?" he panted, "Thorpe Hall's in the north of
—"

"I know it," he interrupted, snatched the telegrams and began tearing through them.

"A lone witch Thorpe says," Lyle added, "the vicious slut burned the place to the ground! Can you believe it!"

Galen screwed his eyes shut and pinched the bridge of his nose while in the outside world Lyle was still blabbering.

"And she had three familiars, demons or such like. They tore the garrison apart and nothing could kill them."

"Nothing?" His eyes snapped open.

"Nothing, and even worse," Lyle gripped his arm, "even worse, half the family members are unaccounted for and presumed dead!"

Galen said nothing, and continued to examine Thorpe's telegrams.

"A direct attack on the head families, the witches must know about the tournament!" Lyle panicked.

"But from what you told me the covens are broken and scattered?"

"Are you blind!" he shouted. "Look what one solitary witch did to Thorpe Hall! She promises to come right here to London with her demons, she promises a fight the likes of which has never been seen before!"

"The likes of which has never been seen before," he echoed and looked around at Vorus and bared his teeth. It was as close to a smile as he could manage. "Oh I'm sure she's right."

"Thorpe is explicit!" He swatted the papers in his hand. "More valkyries right away. When Blackwand gets here you're to hunt her down, understood?"

"Blackwand?" He looked amused.

"That's the only name she gave, what's it matter, we need more valkyries and now. Just kill the bitch and then we can get on with preparing for June." He hadn't believed the situation could get any worse, yet here was a terror-mongering witch come to rock the boat still further. "Kill her. That's your highest priority."

"Very well," he simmered down. The song of Àeon would have to wait, but he could exploit this situation. He looked across to the cherub's battered face and heard her excited breathing within. It seemed that Vorus would have her red-river after all. "Consider her dead, Mr Lyle," he promised.

She left with an escort of three eagles, and the last she saw of Thorpe Hall was a dark plume of smoke rising above the surrounding forest. *"Fine home coming,"* Strike added.

"I was hoping for something a little more cheery," she sighed heavily. Death and destruction seemed to follow her as surely as the eagles. "And now we seem to have a new problem," she glanced over her shoulder at them. They flew some miles behind and much higher, but she felt their presence like a weight in her chest.

"Why do you think they followed us all this way?"

"I've got a shrewd idea," she touched the way-beware in her belt. It was still singing, although subdued after Thorpe's attack. "One way or another, I'm glad they came when they did." She turned south west, intending to be as far from Thorpe Hall as possible by sundown. The wind whipped at her hair and she brushed it aside.

"We're changing course?"

"There's a place I want to see again."

"It might be best to put down for the night first chance we get, we don't want to be seen."

"What's it matter now? We have three invincible guardians . . . whether we like it or not." Again she looked back at the dark shapes following.

"But if we run into trouble they'll charge in and kill anything that moves."

"We'll stay well away from towns and cities."

"You know I was quite enjoying our journey, until today. Just the two of us."

She smiled. "So was I Strike."

He was quiet for some time before he spoke again. *"Things have changed haven't they?"*

"Yes," she confirmed sadly, "they have."

"So what do we do?"

"Fly 'til dusk and find somewhere for the night, it's been a long day."

That night she slept in the forests somewhere between Northumberland and Cumberland. The three were nowhere to be seen, but she knew they were out there in the darkness watching over her, or simply watching her. Either way she was too tired to worry and she strung the oil cloth between two branches and bedded down under it just as the first raindrops began to fall. "Reminds me of that horrible bloody thing they wrapped me in," Strike growled.

"Well, you can either sit under it with me, or stay out in the rain." She cleared some leaves for him.

"You think they're close?" He crawled inside and sat beside her.

"Oh yes." She idly played with her silver pendant and looked up, wondering what was lurking in the branches above.

"You're going to invite them in too?"

She cast him a puzzled look, then smiled. "There isn't enough space, besides I can't share my bed with strangers, a solstice queen has her reputation to think of."

He tried to smile, but failed. "You haven't told me what happened back there, while I was, you know . . . caught."

She lay on her side and pulled the blanket around herself. He came and sat against the crook of her belly and waited. She stroked a finger down his feathered chest and looked reflective. In her other hand she turned the way-beware as she regarded it. "Such a small and innocent life," she murmured.

"And yet it saved us."

"It saved us," she rocked her head in agreement. "Twice."

He snuggled against her and listened to the pattering rain. She took a deep breath and began her account, and listening to it again made her realise what a miracle it was that they'd lived through it. Her flesh crawled when she spoke of Thorpe and Harrison, and of being tied and interrogated, but in the end she'd learned more from them than they knew.

"How did you know his gun would fail?" Strike enquired. "Twice he tried to shoot you, point blank, and twice he failed."

She hadn't really thought about that, everything had happened so fast. "I can't explain. I just knew it would." But in her heart she knew an hourglass and a spider were involved. "He's been protecting us all along," she sighed, and traced the small scar on her cheek.

"Regardless of how it happened, it certainly wiped the smile from his face."

She smiled faintly. "I'll wager Thorpe is now spreading the word that there's a very powerful and very angry witch on the loose."

"He's not wrong." He wriggled closer.

"I thought it was the end for us today Strike."

In the dark she felt him grasp her finger. "I don't think we'll be allowed to go to Evermore just yet, there's plenty of work ahead."

"Plenty of work," she agreed. *Plenty to atone,* she thought. She held the way-beware tight, wanting to lose herself in its haunting song.

They curled up for sleep and the rain began to fall harder. Maybe hours passed, she couldn't be sure, but in the dead of night when she ought to have been sleeping and words seem to have more power, she finally gave voice to the idea that had chased them all the way from Thorpe Hall. "With them on our side nothing could stop us," she whispered.

"That's what worries me," Strike replied.

In the branches above, three eagles dreamed, but they didn't dream the dreams of eagles. They dreamed with the hearts of men.

Eirik sat oblivious to the rain, in a state of complete peace. They had found the miraculous way-beware at last and he vowed never to lose it again. He took his rest along with his brothers and dreamed good dreams.

He dreamed deeper and happier than he had in centuries. He dreamed of Freydis his long lost wife. She walked through their hay meadows around their farmstead. It was summer, a fine time for blooms and the weather was all it could be. He took her by the waist and gently turned her towards him. Having not set eyes on her in centuries he yearned to see her again, but when she turned to him he saw that this was not Freydis. It was her, the witch.

Eirik looked upon the beautiful young woman, but while her face was as radiant as the sun, he saw darkness all around her. She was heading for a war against monsters far worse than the ones they'd fought today and he understood it was a war she could not win. *Unless,* he thought.

"With them on our side nothing could stop us," someone whispered, and Eirik knew in his heart that it was true. He could not find his peace yet.

Galen found himself crossing Blackfriars Bridge again, heading back to Smithfield, but this time Lyle had insisted he travel by carriage. "This'll do," he thumped the roof with his cane and even before the wheels had come to a stop he was dropping out of the carriage and onto Ludgate Hill.

"Beggin' your forgiveness sir, but Mr Lyle was clear as day, 'take the gent to Smithfield' he said?" The driver looked worried.

"And I said this'll do." He slammed the carriage door and set off without even looking back. It was now nine o'clock in the evening and a passing shower had left the cobbles glossy and the air smelling fresh. There came a distant rumble of thunder and inside her cane Elios listened with a longing she couldn't explain.

"What shall I tell Mr Lyle sir?" came a worried shout.

Galen ignored him and walked on. The time had come to build their valkyrie army in earnest, but now there was this 'Blackwand' to be taken care of. "Where is she?" he demanded.

Elios sniffed for signs of Vorus. *"She is not far off."*

"We almost had it Elios, we almost had it," he growled and his jaw tightened. "Lyle blundered in at the worst possible moment."

"She will cooperate again soon, I'm sure," Elios encouraged, but thought it unlikely. In truth she thought Vorus was a deceitful wretch who'd bewitched her dear Galen.

"Huh! Will she?" he snorted. "She likes playing games, and now she knows I've a longing to hear Àeon's song she'd likely dangle it before me like a carrot."

"It might be prudent to keep such thoughts private Galen." She didn't trust Vorus. She might be closer than they knew.

"That arse Lyle! All his talk of Blackwand has set Vorus ashiver. The bitch is like a saucy mutt with the scent of blood," he grumbled. "I swear blood is like strong wine to the black-hearted fiend."

"Galen please!"

He simmered down and burned up his agitation with his brisk pace. "Where's she now?"

"Very close."

He scanned the narrow street, alert for traces. He had wanted to leave her at Hobbs Ash, but Vorus could find her sister valkyries far quicker than he could.

"She's following, but staying hidden."

"Aye, like a game of hide-and-go-seek."

"You yourself said she was like a child."

"Every child needs a beating now and again."

"Not this one perhaps," she warned him.

He drummed the cane against his palm as he marched along and his mind turned to other matters. They left Ludgate Hill and dipped into the alleys between Holborn Viaduct Station and Old Bailey. A few street sellers were hawking peas, roasted potatoes and whelks, another was packing up a tray of sheep's trotters and had plenty left from the look of it. "What do you make of this Blackwand?" he asked at last.

"What can I say, we have so little to go on?"

"Tell me what your gut says Elios."

"She wants something? Maybe revenge, or justice or atonement."

"The whole world wants that!" He sounded unimpressed.

A dog suddenly yowled nearby, and a roof tile slid from besides a chimney, rattled down and smashed in the alley below.

"She's here."

"Play time's hardly begun sweetness," he called, "come along for Smithfield's red-rivers. You like them don't you?" He stood watching the empty street. The light was failing and already a few gaslights flickered further up the hill. A young girl carrying a bundle of rags pattered past on bare feet and gave him a frightened look, he poked his tongue out at her and laughed when she broke into a run.

Vorus flowed through the world unseen by men. When she first found herself stranded on Earth long ago, she'd been terrified and desperate. Rightly or wrongly she blamed Àeon for her plight and she had nurtured that resentment ever since. Now that she had a refuge however, the world of men seemed an exotic festival.

The creatures of Ruination spoke of this place with dread. To them it was the abode of demons and until Galen had come and saved her, she had thought likewise.

Men couldn't see her, but many animals and magical creatures could. Fairies gave flight when she approached, some even spat curses at her. A pair of crows dive-bombed her, afraid for their young, and mice stilled inside their nests under the eaves. There were traces of Ruinous creatures too, albeit primitive ones. She saw a crib-robber's slithering tracks along the gutter, and she could even see where it had paused and tested each doorway, hunting for infants. Crib-robbers were one of the few creatures of Ruin that could pass at will between worlds, others weren't so fortunate. In one alley she saw mortis-fairies swarming over the remains of a korem-kor.

Galen, she thought. Her saviour was waiting for her, but her mood was playful. She lingered for a while on the roof tops, where chimney smoke hung like a veil, but wherever she stayed for long she Ruined. One of the roof tiles perished. The nail fastening it crumbled to dust and it wobbled. A small four legged beast below sensed her and yelped in fear, just as the tile plunged into the alley with a crash. The small creature fled, and then Galen called her name. She waited a while longer, delighting in his impatience, but when at last he mentioned red-rivers, she gasped and burst forth from her hiding place.

"Galen!" It was Vorus.

"At last, now where are you at eh?" It worried him that she'd learned to conceal herself so well.

"Can't you guess!" she trilled and flowed around him as a vapour.

He felt a breeze against his cheek and smelled stagnant water. "Ah! Very clever my shady lass." He looked down and saw the puddle by his feet. It was green with corruption and smelled of bad eggs, and in its depths he saw a shadow flicker. Vorus was hiding there. "Will you not show me your true self eh?"

Just like Sunday copying Neet's likeness, even the sight of her might give him power over her, but of course she knew this. All he'd ever seen was a glimpse that first night at Smithfield. "But I am naked dearest!" she laughed in his ear.

"Naked?" He forced a smile, knowing this was a game he had to endure for now. "But that's the best kind of lady."

"I will reveal myself in good time, but first where are the rivers of red?" The stench of spoilage from the puddle grew stronger.

He lifted his cane and pointed. "A short walk away, red rivers a plenty, and if you'll oblige, we'll find more of your lost kin."

"And offer them safe refuge?"

"They'll have houses as grand as your own."

The three set off, passing a horse pulling a cart loaded with coal and a gang of ragged children loitering on a street corner, but if any of the street-sellers should look up from packing their goods away, all they'd see would be a lone man wearing a bowler and carrying a cane.

Despite the earlier shower the evening was mild and somewhat humid, which made Smithfield even more overpowering. The stench was dreadful, so bad in fact that Galen couldn't pinpoint Vorus. "I'm in no mood for parlour games lass," he warned.

Suddenly he heard a racket of squealing pigs and he knew she was close. "Vorus, now's your chance, find your lost sisters and bring them."

Next to him, a burly butcher clutching a pencil and a scrap of paper, and wearing a ragged top hat gave him a shifty look. He turned his attention back to where a man was taking bids for a score of geese. Their featherless bodies were hung from a row of hooks like exotic fruits.

A breeze flowed by and Galen caught the smell of decayed roses.

"More of us," she sighed, speaking so quietly now that he heard her with his mind, not his ears.

"Aye, but be quick." He was anxious. Inspector Lord had been to Goldhawk asking about their progress on the Pilling case. He didn't want to be seen or recognised. "Find them and tell them to come."

Again the butcher offered him a curious look.

"Be quick about it," he grumbled and tapped his cane impatiently. Someone barged him from behind and he shoved back angrily, he hated crowds.

"Am I to think you're addressing me sir?" the butcher demanded at last.

They were pressed shoulder to shoulder, and Galen looked him up and down. "Nay sir, just thinking aloud," he rebutted and looked away.

He grunted in disapproval. "It ain't proper for folks to speak to themselves."

Galen ignored the man, but it seemed his challenger had other ideas.

"Some say it's the hallmark of the mad!"

"I'll wager they're right," Galen muttered. He smelled Ruination stronger than ever, and although he couldn't see them, the sheep in the opposite pen began to bleat in panic. Vorus was right besides him.

"Kill him for me," she murmured.

He blinked in disbelief and wondered if he'd heard right.

"I say, talking to yerself one moment and not having the decency to reply to others in the next?" the butcher sounded affronted.

"Kill him, like I killed the witch." Her voice was seductive and enticing. *"As a gift for me, then I might seek out my sisters."*

Might? Galen fumed quietly as the butcher babbled on beside him. He'd drop the fat man like a sack of bricks if it served the Book-of-Nine, but not like this, at another's command.

"Galen you can't!" It was Elios.

He said nothing, but she read a terrible certainty in his silence. He could and would.

"The whelk seller, remember her?" Elios tried to reason. *"She was dying, the mark of Ruin was all over her, but not this man, you can't make me do it!"*

"What's wrong? Cat got your tongue?" the butcher pushed the pencil behind his ear and tapped him with a cane of his own.

Galen stared ahead at the goose seller, who was now pulling the bird's wings out to display its meaty breast.

"Kill him for me," Vorus insisted. *"Make a gift of him to my glory. Or does Galen of the Book-of-Nine follow every word of the flightless runt inside his cane?"*

"Galen no!" Elios pleaded.

Galen looked up. The iron pillar just feet away was bleeding rust and he knew she was hiding inside it, watching him, playing with him. "Go find them!" he demanded, louder now.

"Find what?" the butcher scowled, and prodded him with his cane again.

"I have a cane of my own big fellow," he addressed him from the corner of his mouth, careful not to been seen talking to him. "And I can use it to prod just as well as you. Would you care to see it?" He brought his black cane up a fraction and he heard Vorus laugh softly and Elios struggle.

"I'd care more for you to move along sir, you've no better breeding than these beasts," he grunted then went back to his list.

"No please!" Elios was distraught.

"No witch would ever suffer you, but I did. Now show me your love," he growled and held the black cane up to the man's chest, exactly where his heart lay.

"Galen!" she begged.

"Obey me," he ordered.

"Obey you?" the butcher exclaimed. "I shall call for a constable sir!"

"Call to your God, it shan't change a thing," he promised, and pressed the cane to his chest.

As soon as it touched him Elios did as commanded, and Galen heard Vorus laugh and the animals bleat and squeal in dread. She made sure it was fast, to get the awful job over with. In one instant she Ruined his heart and the great muscle clenched one last time and stopped dead. His eye's fluttered and rolled to white and he slumped to the floor just as an alarmed cry went up from the bystanders. One or two went to the poor man's aid and Galen sauntered away as casually as he could. "Satisfied?"

"Very much, I knew you wouldn't fail me," Vorus sighed.

"You've had a treat my lass, now earn it and be about your work, we don't have all night." People flocked past him to see what the fuss was about at the poultry pen, while Elios waited, trembling and ashamed inside the cane.

"I will bring them to you," she pledged and vanished into the cavernous market.

Someone shouted for the superintendent and the crowd jostled to see who lay dead in a pool of filth and dung. Galen heard frantic shouts, which suited him just fine because nobody gave him a glance. Nobody that is except for one man.

He waited in the least distasteful place he could find; beside a cart loaded with straw, and he watched the man with the bowler hat and the cane. He'd been watching him ever since Charlotte Anne Pilling had been murdered, but he wasn't a police man, or a man of Goldhawk. His name was Benedict Collins and he was a witch. *Who in Oak's name are you, and what are you?* He kept his thoughts private, because even in the chaos of Smithfield a man like this one might hear him.

"Bastard reeks of magic," Wake, his thunder-sprite concurred. *"But he's not a knight or a witch, and that cane of his . . ."*

"Aye, it's alive," Ben growled softly. He watched the shabby figure disappear into the crowd. "But not in a good way." He crept out of hiding, pretending to hobble and using his lightning-staff as a crutch: the best way to hide it in plain view. He ran a hand through his fair hair and scratched his stubbly chin. Benedict Collins was only in his early twenties, but lurking in this awful place had aged him.

"Don't do anything rash Benny." Wake understood his conflict. *"Think of Charlotte."*

"They killed her I know it."

"Find out why and make them pay for it. Do both and you'll avenge her."

He nodded slowly, swallowed his anger and focused on his mission. He'd been sent to London to find out what the Illuminata were up to, and he owed it to his coven-mother to do just that. Kolfinnia was counting on him.

CHAPTER EIGHTEEN

The black flower

'Because in his heart man still fears the night he fears all that is black,
but black shields the innocent against horror, black is worn by those with the pure
desire to defend and protect.'
'Higher Forms of Magic - a witch's meditations on daily life'
Author unknown

The following morning was wet and a fine fog rolled across the forest.
After what she'd learned at Thorpe Hall, Sunday knew her short holiday
was over. June 21st would be a pivotal day and she had to get to London
as fast as she could, find other covens and muster a resistance. *A grand
tournament,* she thought, what an opportunity. But Britain's covens were
still recovering, would they be willing to fight again so soon? *Where are
you Kolfinnia?* She'd give anything to know where the hero of Kittiwake-
coven was right now.

"Troubled dreams?" Strike asked. He looked to have been awake for
some time and was busy preening.

"No dreams at all." She rubbed at her eyes and peeled back the blanket.
The damp air made it clammy and she was glad to be up. "Let's be off."

"No breakfast?"

"No anything, we ate the last of our supplies yesterday."

"Shopping then I take it?"

"Carlisle is less than thirty miles. But we can't linger, news of Thorpe Hall will be close behind us."

"Then we'll just have to stay ahead of it."

She yawned and brushed her untidy hair away from her face, before grabbing her boots and crawling out of her shelter, where she stood and stretched. "I'd love a wash – get rid of the filth of Thorpe Hall. Do you think it'll be safe to find a river and bathe?" She pulled her boots on, rubbed at her stiff back, turned around and stopped dead. "Dear Oak!"

"What!" He leapt out beside her. "What is it?"

She lifted a finger and pointed.

Three huge bears were sleeping peacefully around their makeshift tent, and from the look of it they'd been there all night. Dew sparkled on their fur, and now the danger was gone they looked like ordinary bears, but extremely large ones. Their claws were easily as large as kitchen knives and their snoring rumbled through the ground and tickled the soles of her feet.

"Yes, I think it's safe," Strike whispered.

"For what?" She daren't move a muscle.

"A bath."

They were bound for Carlisle, and while visiting towns had been a pleasure before, now she felt almost paranoid. She was resolved simply to get fresh supplies and leave again as soon as she could. She didn't want to be caught, nor did she want the berserks tearing the town to shreds. The fog shrouded them as they flew but made navigation tricky. Her plan was to find a quiet place to put down and finish their journey on foot, because people dropping out of the sky tended to get noticed. As part of her hasty disguise she tied her hair under a head scarf, and smeared a little mud over her cheeks hoping she'd pass as just a farm worker. Within ten minutes of leaving their camp she sensed them following. "My escort," she said with mixed feelings. Behind her were the now familiar eagles, although they were mere silhouettes in the gloom.

"How will you keep a low profile with those three trailing behind you?" Strike kept their flight roughly westwards. *"Folks bring horses to town, not bears."*

"I don't know, maybe we can leave them and the way-beware somewhere safe, then go back for them?" She glanced back again.

"Either way decide soon, the miles are wearing down."

"I know," she breathed, "I know."

The problem of what to do with the berserks settled itself. Just miles from Carlisle they simply vanished into the fog. "Let's just get on our way and leave them!"

She shot him a rueful look. "Strike, they followed us right across the North Atlantic." They had landed in a copse of birch trees.

"Hmm," he sighed, still peering up at the grey sky. "You don't think they somehow *heard* you and took their leave for a while?"

She'd been thinking just that, and it troubled her. "Maybe. I don't like the idea that they can hear us, *understand* us even."

"No, but if they can understand, then there must be more man than beast in them."

She considered this. "Could they become men again?" she thought aloud. This thought was followed by a distinctly darker one, *Considering what lies ahead would you want them to be?* She looked up at the grey sky and shivered. "Come on Strike, let's get this done and move on." Sadly, shopping had lost its thrill.

He didn't question her strange purchases and they stayed in the town for just one hour. He knew this because when they arrived the town clock struck ten, and by eleven they were heading away from Carlisle carrying their new belongings. Strike remained hidden all the while and never once complained about the added packages tied to the staff.

The relaxed feel of Shetland had been replaced with heavy sense of caution. The Illuminata knew there was a new enemy in their midst called Blackwand. Already she'd burned one of their strongholds to the ground and the berserks had spilled their blood. A good start some might say, but Sunday didn't feel anything good about it. *I just wanted to save witches held captive, not start a one-woman war against the Illuminata.* She plodded along forlorn.

"It's the same thing," Strike said from nowhere.

"What?" She halted.

"Rescuing witches. It amounts to the same thing as starting a war."

"Strike," she argued, "it's rude to pry on someone's thoughts." She carried the staff across her shoulder, and of course forgotten he could hear her every idea. She set off again, grumbling.

"Did you think you could just knock on their door and ask for them to be released?"

She bristled at his boldness, but it also proved how their relationship had deepened. "No," she said tartly, "but I didn't want to announce myself until I was ready, we've lost the element of surprise, and now they're readying for a fight."

"From what I heard at Thorpe Hall that's what you wanted?"

She stopped again. He was right, what could she say: that her brave words were just heat of the moment boasting? "Strike, I'm not sure, but . . ."

"When you put him on his knees and said that to him, that vile monster, my heart almost burst. I've never been more proud of you." Confident they were alone, he emerged and sat on the staff regarding her. "Never."

"Really?" She looked at her feet, feeling embarrassed.

"With all my heart . . . Blackwand."

She laughed. "I know, silly isn't it?"

"Not in the least." He looked deadly serious now. "Don't detract from it, else it'll harm the magic. That creature Thorpe is already afraid of you and that's half the battle won."

"You think I'm right then?"

"To risk all for our friends and break this great tournament of theirs?" The feathers around his neck fanned out and he looked fierce. "Without a doubt."

"Then we'll need their help." She didn't need to explain who *they* were.

"But do they follow the way-beware, or you?"

"That's something we'll need to find out," she muttered uneasily, and looked back the way they'd come. The track was deserted and the town lay someway behind them. "Come on, Blackwand's had enough of walking." She took the staff from her shoulder and Strike vanished. A second later the little track was empty except for a trail of footprints that came to an abrupt and mysterious stop.

The fog burned away and the day grew warm and pleasant. Mile after mile they flew and because the weather had cleared Sunday flew high to avoid detection. Even so, she found herself frequently looking up to greater heights and finally after some hours she saw three soaring birds.

She was flying at her altitude limit, heading south west away from Carlisle, and not to London but to a place she once visited before. Now she harboured mixed feelings about going back there, but the idea had grown in her mind and become like a shrine on a pilgrim's path and she knew she had to go.

For a short while it had been a venue for witches across the country, all of them gathered to meet an incredible lady of the magical realm: Lilain the hive-empress. It had been a time of celebration and socialising. Sunday had travelled there as Regal-Fox's envoy, and as the dazzling solstice queen she'd loved every moment of being seen and admired. It was the place she learned of Rowan's talents and met the feisty Kolfinnia Algra. It was the place Raven's wand had called home for almost fifty years. She was bound for the ruins of Wildwood-coven.

"There!" Strike called.

She peered down at the sea of evergreen spires. "Where?"

"There, I recognise the river!"

The staff banked gently and the sun flashed off the winding river. "The Appelier River," she grinned, and even though she knew returning would be bitter-sweet, she couldn't help but feel excited.

"This is almost like home," he laughed.

"Almost." She touched hrafn-dimmu. *But this really is home for you,* she added, but the wand remained silent and she read something lonely in that silence. They looped over the Appelier River, and back inland over dense forest towards Wildwood. The trees embraced them like welcome guests and memories flashed by, growing stronger by the moment.

"Keep left!" she advised and they weaved between huge oaks downy with young leaves. Wood pigeons scattered as they passed, butterflies danced in shafts of sunlight and she saw a pine marten scamper away under a log.

"Look!" he called. They saw a tattered spell-flag fluttering from the branches, then another. Even though they were faded, they stirred something in her heart. Here and there she saw lanterns hanging askew and she knew they were on the right track, but something told her this return was going to be hard on her heart.

An overgrown footpath flashed past before she knew it, then another, then the remains of a fence now tangled with young brambles. Forgotten buckets poked through the grass, and she saw collapsed huts and willow-fences strangled by weeds. Severed rope ladders and bridges dangled from trees like spider threads and then suddenly the trees thinned and sunlight bloomed, and they arrived at the gardens in the centre of Wildwood-coven. "Strike!"

"I know!"

But where's Valonia's tree? she thought with rising worry.

"There!" he cried, and she saw it.

A mountain of broken limbs in the middle of the clearing was all that remained of Valonia's tree and the cosy little house that had once rested in its branches. The spectacle was like hitting a wall. She slowed and at last touched down in what was once Britain's biggest coven. Not the richest or grandest perhaps, but certainly the most homely. "Oh Strike!" tears sprang from nowhere, "what did they do here?" He climbed up on her shoulder as she walked through the gardens, now home to weeds and thistles, and towards the devastated tree. "How could they?" She shook her head in disbelief, understanding now what Kolfinnia saw the last night she came back here. "I'm so sorry Kolfinnia."

Strike gently clutched her shoulder and hung his head in silent respect.

As she walked, memories played out and many were so ordinary that she'd forgotten them, but now as they lived again they seemed priceless. She saw Farona, her young attendant, trying to conceal his adoration of Flora, which at the time had nettled her. She disliked him even turning his eyes away from her for a second, but she enjoyed the furtive glances she stole from her admirers. At the time she revelled in them, but now the memories made her cringe.

Not everything she saw was to her shame however. There was a spot where she'd seen Valonia sit and read to children from visiting covens. She could still hear their laughter as she told them of Silver-Fist, the Lord of thunder-sprites and how he tricked the evil gods that haunted the young Earth. To the east was where she'd first met Lilain and been awed by her wisdom. Before she knew it, she was smiling wistfully and she could almost forget that Wildwood was just a graveyard of memories.

When she at last came to the old tree she stopped and looked upon the Illuminata's violence. It had been hacked down by krakens, leaving an ugly stump, and to ensure Wildwood's death they had bored holes in the stump and plugged them with borax-salt to kill it stone-dead. It was their policy to defile covens, to make sure witches could never again use them as sacred places. "What is so wrong with man?" she asked despairingly, looking around.

"I remember this very spot, it's where you and Kolfinnia first met," Strike murmured and she looked about her and suddenly had a vivid memory.

"You must be Sunday Flowers," Kolfinnia addressed the tallest witch, reading her name from the day's guest list.

"Correct," she answered in a velvety voice and lowered her hood almost ceremonially, revealing her face and immediately everyone there saw that she was magnificent. Her features were so perfect that she looked to be sculpted from marble and there wasn't a blemish anywhere on her fair skin. She openly appraised Kolfinnia's dress and hair with critical eyes, found her appearance adequate and smiled flatly in approval.

A very different Sunday Flowers once more looked around the gardens. Butterflies flitted between clumps of thistles, and grass sprouted where cabbages ought to be growing. There were baskets piled with rotten apple, and fallen rakes and hoes in a sea of ground-elder, buttercups and leathery looking docks. "These were Flora's gardens," she confessed, as if it were a crime. Now she looked she saw the clearing was fringed by scorched and fallen trees. "I heard about the battle here. The worst defeat in the Knighthood's history I was told."

"Until Kittiwake," he reminded her.

"Serves them well I say."

"Where are all the fallen knights?"

"They must have salvaged them." There wasn't a single piece of wreckage to be seen.

"Maybe it was wrong to come here," he pondered.

"No." She shook off the melancholy. "There's something I've wanted to do and I knew here would be a good place for it."

"Well unless it's something quick we'll be spending the night here."

"Oh, that wouldn't be so bad," she smiled faintly, and turned away from the sad sight of the ravaged tree and immediately froze. "Strike!" she hissed.

In front of her were three enormous bears.

Strike jumped. "I wish they'd stop doing that!"

They were lying like obedient dogs, with their paws out before them, regarding her closely. One of them was a little nearer than the others, and now she was closer she could see that he was slightly bigger and his fur was tawny brown. The bear to his left was darker, like wood-ash, and his muzzle was more slender, even elegant looking, while the last of the three was silvery-grey, his eyes were deep amber and his claws were almost ivory white.

Without looking, she drew the way-beware. All three lifted their great heads and their ears swivelled around. The largest bear, the tawny one, made some ominous sound deep in his throat. "You came for this?" she asked nervously.

Tawny looked at her impassively.

"The song is beautiful isn't it?" She knelt slowly in the grass. "This is why you came all the way to Thorpe Hall isn't it?" She reached out and pushed the little way-beware into the ground. And then she let go of it.

"What are you doing!" Strike spluttered.

"I told you. This is something we have to find out," she replied, never looking away from that huge bear. A butterfly landed on his ear and he flicked it away with a single twitch. He watched her so intently that his mouth hung slack, and she thought his expression was almost comical. "Now we'll see who you've been following all this time shall we?" She spoke softly and edged away from the only thing that had protected her so far from savage claws and teeth. "Is it me, or the little fellow there?"

"If I'd have known your love for danger I'd have paired up with another witch all those years ago!" Strike flapped.

"I have to know." She continued slowly away, staff at the ready. "First sign of trouble we make a dash for the way-beware."

The largest bear, the one she'd begun to think of as 'Tawny', looked from her to the way-beware and back again. She saw immense muscles flex under his fur, and for a moment he looked confused, but he didn't move from his place of worship at the way-beware's feet. She took another step away from safety, but still none of them shifted.

"They're not moving," Strike whispered.

"It's the way-beware isn't it?" she admitted softly, and the huge bear just blinked at her. She relaxed a little and straightened. But they all just lay before the way-beware like contented lambs.

"Looks like the Sunday-effect doesn't work on bears," Strike whispered.

"Hmm," she agreed vaguely.

"You're disappointed aren't you?"

"Not in the least!"

"Really?"

"Well, maybe. It would've been nice to think they wanted *my* company as well." She gave him a mischievous smile.

"Same old solstice queen," he smirked.

"I hope not," she sighed and her smile faded.

While the way-beware played nanny to Sunday's protectors, she set about the task she'd come to Wildwood for, but first there was one imperative job to be done.

"Kitchen ware?" Strike looked at the battered iron pan and the enamel mug she bought in Carlisle. "No wonder the staff was heavier!"

"I haven't had a decent cup of nettle tea in an age," she sighed happily as she added more kindling to the fire.

Strike took care of his own business too and preened himself thoroughly, as she finished her rest and set about more serious duties. It was now early evening. Only a few hours of daylight remained and so she worked fast. Aside from the pan and the mug, the next peculiar thing she retrieved from her pack was a small pot of Stockholm tar and a brush. "I hope you've noticed I was too polite to ask what these items were for?" Strike interrupted.

"I noticed," she sang without looking up, prying the lid open and dipping the brush.

"I also notice you're *still* not telling me what you're up to?"

"I noticed that as well." She concealed a smile and applied the brush to her white lightning-staff, which was mostly grey and dirty now.

"I notice you're painting my staff!" he blurted.

"Blackwand can't have a white staff!" she replied in mock horror, "how dreadfully unfashionable would that seem in London?"

"But my staff!" he complained and fluttered over to her side. "I hope you're not going to paint me to match it?"

"It'll be better protected than ever I promise." She meant the tar's waterproofing, but he took it very differently.

He watched her concealing the white and it occurred to him this was no vain embellishment. They really were heading for the world's largest city, where they'd fight the Illuminata on their home ground, more or less alone. "Black protects," he heard himself say.

"Yes, black protects," she agreed looking pleased. "All those years I sat through my spell lessons and I thought you were just dozing inside your staff," she joked.

He looked at her directly. "We're going to London to fight alone."

She lay the brush down. "Yes, but perhaps not alone?" She twitched her eyebrows to the three. Now they'd rolled over and lay in the grass belly up, fast asleep. They hardly looked like the demons that had torn Thorpe Hall apart

Strike wanted to say something light-hearted, but like the black paint creeping up the staff he felt a darkness rolling over the world. "I'd better let you finish," he said at last and flapped back up onto the fence post. She gave him a concerned look, thought no more of it and went on working.

Before long her staff was black, and she set it by the fire to dry. Now she concentrated on the garments she'd collected in town. Amongst the odd assortment Strike saw a pair of belts, ladies' gloves, a needle and thread and a man's overcoat, all of them black. She chose the dress first and cut it shorter to make a knee-length shirt. The sleeves were long and loose and she left them as they were. Her trousers were the comfortable ones she bought in Reykjavik, and now she tucked them into her boots which came to just below her knees and were fastened with strips of cloth rather than laces. The black coat she stripped of its sleeves making a long waistcoat, and she fastened her belt around both this and the shirt underneath, so her wands hung where she could easily reach them. The black headscarf she fastened around her neck where she could pull it up over her face when needed.

While Strike fed the fire and the darkness began to settle in, she took the off-cuts and piece by piece sewed them over her witch's hat. And so just like her lightning-staff she had a strange sense of rebirth as the white was slowly covered with black.

Blackwand is coming, she thought with a shiver and glanced at her sleeping companions. Incredibly, they slumbered so deeply that rabbits grazed around them and birds hopped across their flanks picking off insects. *But is it right to bring them along too, they're really men after all?*

When she was done her hat was midnight-black and bristled with ragged seams of cloth. She snipped the fingers off the gloves, thinking them more practical, and her cloak and other possessions she slipped into black sleeves made from the waste material and attached them to the two belts that now crossed her chest, where they hung against her back without hindering her. She collected jackdaw feathers, and when the time came she would braid them into her plaited hair. She adjusted her cherished silver fox pendant so that it sat high against her throat for all to see, and the final touch went to the purple band she'd worn at Kittiwake, which she tied around her left arm. "Strike?" She pulled the scarf up over her face and pressed the hat onto her head, collected her staff, and turned slowly. "How do I look?"

In the fire's gentle glow she looked to melt into the evening darkness. "Like you could stand with the night and nobody would see you."

"Just what I had in mind," she touched the special scar on her cheek. He said it would fade, but it hadn't and she was glad.

"Now you truly are Blackwand," he finished.

She looked at the bears. "All that's missing is the fight I promised."

He followed her gaze. "Somehow, I don't think that'll be a problem."

CHAPTER NINETEEN

Ben

'Witches owe Kolfinnia everything.'
Benedict Collins, Parting-Ways coven, Lancashire

Galen left Smithfield alone, or at least that's what he believed. Normally, he was astute enough to know when he was being followed but tonight he had much on his mind. Vorus was missing and he'd been made a fool of. He barged out of Smithfield, intending to take a cab back to Goldhawk, unaware that Benedict Collins was doing his best to keep up.

Ben lost him in the crowd but that didn't matter too much. Witches had ways of finding people that didn't involve plain old eyesight. For a better view he slipped outside, found a quiet alley and removed the stock from his pretend crutch. Once it was his lightning-staff again he ascended to Smithfield's rooftop world.

"Glad to be out of there," Wake flexed his claws and wings.

"Aye, it's a gross offence against the serpent-twins." Ben unfastened his long coat concealing his wand-sheath and satchel, and perched on the north tower's domed roof, which offered a good view of the shifting crowds. Up here they were hidden, and the stench was thankfully masked by chimney smoke. Wake squatted and watched the crowds shove and jostle. Beside him, Ben took some dried sage from his satchel and began rubbing it to dust between his palms. This was the spell to summon Harl.

"I wish we had more to report to the others." Wake watched the crowd intently.

"Aye, but if we say nothing they'll just think the worst."

"If only we knew what's in his mind."

"He's a slip and no mistake. Hard to follow, that one." They'd been trailing Galen for over a fortnight, trying to discover his agenda.

"And once we know we can set our minds to getting the last prisoners out of Hobbs Ash," Wake brooded.

"Aye," he agreed. It ate him up that witches were still captive, but until they had a clearer picture of the Illuminata's strategy they couldn't risk exposing themselves. That had been Kolfinnia's prime order.

Wake said no more, knowing he had to concentrate, and for a while he just sat there examining the sea of faces below, as the scent of sage wafted over them.

After perhaps twenty minutes there was a flutter of feathers and suddenly a large crow strutted over the roof towards him. This was Harl, one of the messengers who helped witches in the city to maintain contact with each other. "Blessings on you Harl." Ben dusted the sage from his palms, reached into his coat for pencil and paper and started to write. "Now then, I'd ask you to pass this note around the others. I wish it were better tidings, but so far –"

"Ben!" Wake hissed.

Witch and crow looked up, and followed the thunder-sprite's gaze. The shabby man with the bowler hat was weaving through the crowds below.

"Here we go again," Ben muttered. He scribbled over his first message and replaced it with another: *'Leaving Smithfield in pursuit.'* Lastly he added the date and time.

"He's getting away," Wake pestered.

"I know!" He rolled the note and Harl took it in his beak. "Good luck." Harl was gone in a second, and even Ben didn't know where to. It would be dangerous for witches to know each other's locations. He watched him vanish then turned his attention back to their quarry. *There he is,* he thought venomously, *Goldhawk's man of mystery.* He saw him weaving through the crowds, occasionally vanishing behind a cart, or smoke from one of the braziers, but he never lost sight of him. When his target vanished around the long curve of King Street, Ben judged it time. He launched himself from the roof and was flying through the black, soaring above Smithfield, and leaving a trail of sage dust.

They sailed from rooftop to rooftop, tracking their quarry. Ben hid behind a chimney stack, where the tiles were slimy and the smoke was bitter. The man in the bowler left King Street and backtracked along Snow Hill, until he reached Farringdon Road, where he hailed a cab. "At last," Ben muttered. A cab was easier to track. Now they could follow him some distance. When the cab disappeared around the corner, he dropped into thin air and flew.

"What will you tell Lyle?"

Galen didn't hear her, he was still too angry.

"Galen?" Elios persisted.

"Haven't I endured enough female prattle for one night?" he snapped. For a while he sat in silence, swaying with the rocking carriage as they trotted across Blackfriars Bridge. "I'm sorry," he said at last. "My anger should be saved for that maggot-hearted trickster." Vorus had gone looking for her own kind, and not returned.

"She'll have to return to Hobbs Ash," she reassured him, *"her kraken is the only safe place for her."*

"Hmm," he agreed distantly. Losing Vorus wasn't his real concern. What angered him most was her disobedience. "Thinks she has leave to come and go as she pleases, forgets her place, and what she owes me."

"What will you do if she resists you further?" She'd warned him of this from the start, but now wasn't the time to remind him of that.

"I'll dispose of her and start again."

"Kill her?" She was both pleased and shocked.

"I'll have that kraken of hers melted down, then we'll see how long she lasts living in broken walls and festering puddles."

"But what of everything you've been looking for: the ninth chapter and Sophie?"

"I'll find another valkyrie and we'll start again. I've been too lenient with her." Vorus had got the better of them tonight, and now they were the dogs being trained with rewards.

"But June 21st will not wait."

He let out a weary breath and massaged his brow. "How many times must I say this? I couldn't care less if Leonhard turns Buckingham Palace into a brothel, everything we're doing is for The Book-of-Nine."

"Perhaps so," she shot back, *"but if the British lose, then your experiments will come to an end."*

He looked out of the window, at the misty plane of the Thames, and wrinkled his nose. "Not necessarily, mayhap our new Germanic masters will be interested in a Ruinous army. I'll find a way to Sophie and Àeon's song yet, don't you worry about that."

The cab proceeded towards Goldhawk, to collect Lyle and Doulton, and then straight to Hobbs Ash, where Galen expected his unruly child to finally skulk home after her night of debauchery. Elios was right; she was growing wilful, and he still hadn't decided what to do about it.

Vorus flowed through the world, but not alone. She had two companions, and she guided them to where their own krakens awaited like living tombs. She was eager to show them to her dear Galen. What a surprise it would be for him, and what an insult to her father Àeon, snatching his beloved children from under his nose. To appease her twisted sense of justice, she would lure every last one of her sister-kin away from him as punishment for abandoning her.

The three valkyries streaked over a landscape of roofs and chimneys, spoiling all they passed. Bricks crumbled, beams sagged, babies cried out in their sleep, and nests of rats fell silent. Vorus was growing stronger, and even without her Ruinous shell she was a match for any of London's night creatures.

Away off in the dark she sensed a broom-rider of the kind Galen had warned her about. She felt it was her duty to make sure the wicked fiend couldn't take her cherished armour from her, and so she left her companions and veered away to tackle him.

Ben landed neatly in a deep trough between slated roofs, and watched the carriage trundle over Blackfriars Bridge. "He's heading back to Goldhawk." He looked east, where the sky was already a shade lighter. "We'll have to call off soon. Daylight's too dangerous to be flying."

Confident the carriage was far enough away, he broke cover and launched himself from the roof, making the tiles rattle and the gutter creak.

A hundred yards further, he landed deftly and crouched low. The air up here was dry and gritty, and there was an open skylight to his left. From inside, he could hear someone murmuring drunkenly.

The cab reached St George's Circus and turned down Lambeth Road. Ben chose his next vantage point; a church spire, and sailed across the open gap. Streets and buildings blurred past below, and he was almost at his goal when something hit them very hard.

"Ben!" Wake erupted.

He yelped as something slammed into them and hurled them through the air, and the next thing he knew they were spinning towards the jagged profile of the Bethlehem Lunatic Asylum.

Wake tried to pull them level. He had no idea what had happened, but suddenly he found he couldn't fly. Something had simply stolen the magic from the air around them. *"Ben!"* he tried to warn him, but even speaking was a terrible effort.

Ben saw streetlights blur into a whirlpool of shooting stars as they spun uncontrollably, and in the next instant he slammed into a steep roof.

He hit it hard enough to crack a few slates, and probably rouse most of London, and then he began to slide. Tiles flashed past, rubbing him raw and tearing his clothes. He clawed at them but he couldn't stop himself. He expected to plunge into the street below, but instead he splashed into a wide gutter between two adjoining roofs, sending up a wave of sludge and stagnant water. His forehead crashed against the tiles, gashing it and making coloured dots sparkle before his eyes. "Shit!" he groaned, and lay there for a moment, sodden and sore. A complement of broken tiles slid after him and thudded into his ribs making him gasp. "Bugger and shit!" He was angry now, as well as hurt.

He crawled up from the ooze and looked about, feeling blood trickle down his brow and along his cheek. Above him, he saw the sky was pre-dawn grey, but he couldn't see what had attacked them. He flopped against the roof and sat hunched over, chasing his breath. When he tried to flex his leg, it complained and he grimaced. He wasn't surprised to find his trousers ripped and wet with blood. Somewhere off in the distance he heard a dog barking and someone calling out. His landing must have made a real racket. "Wake?" Inside the staff he could hear the thunder-sprite groaning.

"Wake, talk to me!" He scrutinised it, feeling for damage. *No don't be broken!* he dreaded.

"What happened?" Wake asked groggily.

He gave a groan of relief. "For a moment, I thought you were gone."

"Something attacked us?"

He looked around. All he could see was a roof on either side of him and a wedge of sky above. It felt like being in a chasm. There could be any number of night-creatures out there with a grudge against a witch, he thought. "Come on," he whispered, "we might still catch him."

"Ben," he groaned, *"I don't think I can."*

"Can what?"

"Fly."

He was about to answer, when he heard something like a soft sigh. He looked upwards and his chest tightened. There was a dark figure watching them from the ridge. Quickly, it dropped out of sight into the shadows, and he heard tiles creak as it slithered down the roof towards them. "Wake, it's a thing of Ruin!" He pressed himself against the slates and readied his staff. The crawling thing stopped at the sound of his voice, but all he could see was shadow. *"Wake? Can you fight?"*

"I'll try," he promised weakly.

Just then the tiles rattled as it began moving again. He backed clumsily along the gutter, ankle deep in sludge. The thing halted. He heard it sniffing and its claws tick impatiently against the slates and he knew it was assessing them.

"Ben, something's wrong," Wake despaired, *"I can't make the fire."*

In all his years Ben had never known his or any other sprite lose their powers. Until tonight. Clearly, whatever was stalking them was something no witch had ever faced before. He drew his atheme ready to fight. If it came to it he'd jump from the roof and take his chances rather than let the thing catch him.

He heard the creature sniffing again, then came a rumbling sound followed by a hefty splash, as it skidded down the roof and into the gutter. He jumped, expecting an attack, but nothing happened and the sound of rippling water faded away. "Show yourself!" he demanded.

A stink like death under a hot sun rolled towards him carrying distilled futility; an infant's burial gown inside a sealed casket, a wedding dress hanging in shreds. That soft sighing drifted towards him from the darkness again, followed by a childlike tittering. He was certain of one thing: it had no fear of them. The smell grew more pungent as it advanced and the gutter water lapped at his shins.

"Ben!" Wake groaned. *"There's no fire in me, there's no point!"*

He suddenly felt icy cold, and sensed the thing was within striking distance. He raised his knife and useless staff in reply. "Come on then!" he challenged. Somewhere in the real world, the dog continued barking and a ship blew its horn.

Vorus studied the broom-rider in fascination. She could smell a delicious aroma and realised it was fear, but she could also hear her companions' desperate breathing. They were weak and if they didn't reach a refuge soon they'd die. "What is the delay! Safety you promised us!" one of them gurgled.

Vorus wanted to open him as Galen had showed her and drink in his final terror, but her new charges took priority now. Regretfully, the witch would have to wait until another time.

"Come on!" Ben shouted into the darkness, not caring if he woke the whole Asylum. "Fight me!" He brandished his staff. A solitary drop of blood fell from his chin and plopped into the gutter. An instant after, the water heaved and the shadows uncoiled with terrifying speed as it lunged. He roared and swung the staff blindly.

Filthy water spattered his face, followed by that awful smell. He crashed back against the roof, and as the wind rushed over him, so too did thoughts of despair and suicide. He swung again, aiming at nothing, but the creature had gone. He rolled onto his side and caught the tail end of some fast movement, like a black flash, and then they were alone. He lay there looking over London. Lights twinkled in windows and the sky was turning violet as dawn approached. Voices drifted up from below and the dog sounded a lot closer. "Wake?"

"I'm fine," he gasped.

"It's gone, can you fly?"

"What was that thing?"

"Never mind now. Can you fly?"

"Aye, now it's gone, Ben I'm sorry."

"No. It's not your fault, now come on." He staggered to the roof edge and looked out cautiously. Trusting his sprite, he climbed gingerly on to his staff, careful of his wounds, and soared silently out of the trough. They gladly left the stink of rot and death behind, all the while wondering what new creature haunted the London blackness.

Doulton inspected his pocket watch, and registered the unearthly hour of three thirty-eight in the morning. And still Galen hadn't returned. "You don't think someone's done him in do you?"

"I'll bloody do him in," Lyle fumed. Thorpe's telegrams mounted by the hour. All of them demanding to know what they intended to do about this so called 'Blackwand'. Each was more furious than the last, and this latest was the worst. "He's coming back. He'll be here by Monday afternoon." Lyle held up the accusing telegram. "That gives us less than two days!"

"You speak as if events at Thorpe Hall were our doing." Doulton kneaded his tired eyes.

"If we haven't got the bitch in gaol or dead by then it might as well be."

Doulton reached for the sherry decanter, thought better of it and settled for soda water. "She might not even come, perhaps it was all boastful threats?"

"The garrison dead and Thorpe Hall a smoking ruin?" he retorted. "That amounts to more than bluff."

The clock on the mantel chimed quarter to four and Doulton rolled hateful eyes towards it. "Lord Thorpe hasn't seen Galen's creature yet has he?"

He ran a hand over his scalp, harvesting a good amount of sweat. "I suppose it might placate him when he arrives. Pray it's enough."

"Perhaps Galen will return with better news. By Monday there might be more. . ." For a moment he wasn't sure how to describe them. "More than one of them," he finished and lowered himself into a chair and stared into the struggling embers in the hearth.

"All this and the Yardies too," Lyle sighed heavily.

"Yardies?"

He grimaced at his slip. "Yes, Lord, the Inspector from Scotland Yard." Doulton suddenly felt a chill. "What did he want?"

"What do you think? He came sniffing around about the Pilling case."

"When was this?"

"A week ago."

"And you didn't see fit to tell me?" Now he felt too hot. "Do you think he knows?"

Lyle rolled his eyes. "Think about it man; it's not their business any longer, it's our case. We decide the outcome."

"But still –"

"Disregard it," he curbed him. "Our business now is finding this Blackwand. And we have to work together." Thorpe had ordered him to bring Doulton to heel, or be replaced. This unpleasant thought made him turn to the decanter himself, but he never got his drink. Just then there was a knock at the study door. "Come," he demanded.

A steward entered. "Mr Lyle sir, a cab with Mr Galen is waiting at the front entrance."

"At bloody last!" He grabbed his overcoat and hat and charged out of the door, swirling the angry telegrams into a whirl as he did, closely followed by Doulton.

Doulton in particular found the ride extremely tense, largely because Lyle never shut up, Galen hardly spoke and that sinister cane of his was only inches away from him.

"Where's Vorus?" Lyle demanded for the third time.

Galen coughed behind his hand. "Even if she was sat beside you I doubt you'd know. You haven't the knack for seeing."

"That accursed creature is our prize weapon," he wagged a finger at him. "When Lord Thorpe gets here on Monday –"

"Thorpe's coming here?" Galen interrupted.

He mistook his concerns, and looked satisfied. "Yes, I thought that might finally rouse you. You've been too indolent by half. Now where's Vorus?"

"She'll be at Hobbs Ash," he lied.

Doulton sat quietly like a child between bickering parents.

"And the others? You departed hours ago with orders to retrieve more demons from Smithfield."

"And I have done just that."

"Another lie," Elios thought to herself.

"I sincerely hope so." Lyle squinted at him from behind his thick glasses, while Doulton squirmed at the word 'demons'.

Galen lazily drew the likeness of a spider on the dusty carriage windows. *'Little Miss Muffet sat on a tuffet, along came a spider and sat down beside her.'* He could almost hear Sophie's gentle voice. "I assure you, when we arrive at Hobbs Ash you won't believe your eyes," he said smoothly.

Lyle sat back and eyed him coldly, while inside her cane Elios marvelled at his audacity, and part of her actually believed that something incredible really was waiting for them at Hobbs.

Hobbs Ash was eerily quiet. It was barely five o'clock on a Saturday morning, and the only staff around were the guards. The three set off for the kraken hanger with Lyle in the lead. He hadn't slept all night and he was in a frightful mood. "Right, where is it then?"

Galen slouched along at the rear.

"Where's this spectacle, the one you claim will amaze us all?" He stopped and turned.

Galen said nothing and continued past him.

"You'll have to put on a better show than this when Lord Thorpe arrives," he barked after him, relishing the showdown.

At the mention of Thorpe's name something inside Galen stirred. He clutched his cane and entered the station, quietly dreading what he'd find there.

"It's your neck on the block, not mine!" Lyle shouted. He watched Galen vanish into the cavernous hanger and just then Doulton caught up with him.

"What'll Thorpe do if he can't deliver?"

Lyle tugged at his collar. "It's his neck, not mine," he repeated uncertainly and set off in pursuit.

Inside was cool and shady. Early sunlight fell like blades through the glass roof and both of them could just discern Galen's tiny figure marching towards the barricade at the station's rear.

"You're here bright and early sir?" a voice said, startling them.

Lyle turned to see Topp approaching flanked by two guards, one of whom restrained a mastiff on a chain. "Some of us haven't had the privilege of seeing our beds this night. Any movement in there?" He twitched his head towards the barricade.

"None. Been quiet all night sir."

Lyle nodded as though he expected as much and marched off. The rest fell in behind and before long their entourage swelled as more guards drifted over, drawn by the sound of voices. By the time they arrived at the barricade there were at least a score of them, but no sign of Galen. Without stopping, Lyle flung the canvas aside and marched through, and the first thing he noticed was the complete silence. "Galen?" He clapped his hands as if summoning a dog, and a dejected-looking figure stepped out of the shadows holding a cane in one hand and a battered bowler in the other.

"Vorus is resting," he lied.

"I don't doubt it!" Lyle laughed scornfully. "That monstrous trollop has enjoyed as little sleep as the rest of us. And what of her associates, are they sleeping too?" He swept an arm at the empty krakens. All of them looked like broken marionettes and suddenly the sense of defeat was tangible.

"Vorus is resting!" he asserted again. "She is resting and will appear at my beckoning."

"Then beckon her!"

Galen stood silent, and looked at the floor.

"As I thought." Lyle had him this time, he knew. "So this is our great weapon against Leonhard? Perhaps we'll be lucky and he'll die laughing at our inadequacy."

Galen turned slowly and regarded the mountain of broken arms and legs. They looked so much like his dreams.

"She isn't coming back," Elios said to him alone.

For a moment he didn't know what to say. He could no more admit he was wrong than a fish could breathe in air. *"She's out there,"* he said without conviction, aware that all of them were staring at the piles of rusted scrap he promised would be Britain's salvation. *"And so is my road to Sophie and the secrets of ninth chapter."*

Elios felt his sorrow and reached out for him. *"No matter what happens, I will always be at your side,"* she promised, and immediately felt two distinct sensations echo back from his subconscious; one was a flicker of gratitude, the other was disappointment that she, rather than Sophie, would be his lifelong companion. She suppressed her hurt and tried again.

"Galen, believe me when I say —"

Metal screeched as something in the scrap pile shifted and Elios felt her words and her hopes shrivel and die. Vorus was amongst them.

Galen took a sharp breath and looked up, Elios's tender words forgotten. Lyle and the rest took an instinctive step backwards. The mastiff whined softly and crept behind its master's legs.

"Vorus?" A crafty smile touched his lips and his teeth appeared like the sun from behind a cloud. "You've come home my sweet! And what's my little cherub been up to this fine night?" He slipped effortlessly into his play act. Elios cringed at how phoney he sounded, while the rest were fixed on the dead krakens.

There came the scream of juddering iron and suddenly the cherub's corrupted face began to emerge from the mess of machinery like Jonah appearing from the whale. "Galen dearest!" she purred, and how Elios hated her right then.

The cherub pushed through a tangle of plate steel, leaving grooves of fresh copper in her cheeks like angry scratches.

"Vorus!" he cheered, all his confidence restored, and raised his arms in welcome. He turned to gloat and in doing so found a parade of frightened faces gaping back at him. The racket continued unabated, and now new sounds joined the throng. More metal was on the move and without looking back he knew that Vorus had not come home alone.

A mangled bull helmet arose on her left while a rusted eagle ascended on her right. Broken arms and legs moved under their own will and began to build towering bodies for the new angels of Ruin.

"He's done it," Doulton gasped. "He's bloody done it."

The mastiff's whines became terrified barking and it practically hauled its handler away. A bronze bull and an iron eagle stared down at him as their skeletal bodies gathered more bulk. Sparks showered down like spring blossom as the wrecked machines slid and scraped over the concrete. Nearby, a barrel of solvent was toppled. Spirit poured across the floor and for an instant Galen saw the sparks reflected in its perfect surface, before they touched down and the pool ignited. There was a rush of flame and the krakens were engulfed. Vorus and her sisters continued to rise, undaunted by the fire, and resembling demons waking in hell.

"Clear everyone out," he ordered without turning. "This area is for me only." They were glad to leave. One valkyrie was unnatural, while three was downright terrifying.

At last only Lyle remained. He stood with his arms folded and watched the krakens rise fully. The cherub, the bull, and the eagle stared down at him. The spilled solvent was exhausted, leaving a sea of fine smoke and now the undead machines looked to be emerging from a mist. *"Quite the showman aren't you Galen,"* he conceded.

"You too," Galen waved him away without looking.

"Smug bastard," he retorted under his breath, and turned to follow the others.

Galen lost interest in everything but the valkyries. "Thrice be the glory of the threefold way," he whispered. Their army was well and truly underway.

Chapter Twenty

Sunday's choice

'The answer to every question you might ask already lies within you.'
Traditional witch saying

The night was clear and she slept in what were once Flora's gardens. *I'm truly the last witch at Wildwood,* she thought as she watched a shooting star fall to earth. Surrounded by so many sad memories, she thought it would take an age to drift off, but she was sound asleep within minutes and the night passed without her knowing.

The following morning she had an unpleasant wake up call: hungry midges were on the prowl. She felt them nipping at her cheeks, and she groaned and rolled over, not wanting to be up just yet. It came as something of a shock when she rolled up against something large and obviously alive. One moment there was nothing and in the next she had a face full of fur. Her eyes flew open and she jumped back with a cry, "Oak's-blood!"

The largest of the berserks, the one she dubbed Tawny, was sleeping contentedly by her side. She turned her head slowly, feeling like Daniel in the lions' den, and saw the two she named 'Ash' and 'Silver' had also come over during the night from their place by the way-beware. All three had curled up around her like a shield. "Strike?" She groped for her staff, never taking her eyes from the huge bear. "Strike?" Finally she clutched it and felt him asleep inside. *"Strike!"*

He groaned in protest and uncurled from his dreams.

She lifted her head above the wall of fur and peered around. As she expected, the way-beware was just where she'd left it. A flock of sparrows was gathered around it in worship, and if she concentrated she could hear its beautiful song, and she was pleased to discover that it was a little louder than before. For a while she had worried that Thorpe had wounded it. What she couldn't grasp was the fact that these berserks had chosen to sleep twenty feet away from it – next to her.

"Sunday?" Strike responded.

"Shhh . . . Strike look at this!"

In a second he was by her side and she caught a flash of his blue feathers from the corner of her eye. "So it does work after all!"

"What works?"

"The Sunday-effect."

She gaped at their impossible situation. *Right now this very spot's probably the safest place in the whole world,* she thought.

"Pity though," he added.

"What is?"

"You're irresistible to pin-tips also." He shook a thickening cloud of midges away from his head.

She got to her feet with minimum fuss, tiptoed through the sleeping warriors, expelled a whistle of relief and regarded Wildwood. It was beautiful but sad, and as she looked towards the spot where Valonia's tree once stood the coven gave up its final memory. It had saved the hardest for last, and now she was partly relieved that the great tree was gone because it would be too easy to replay the night she'd eavesdropped on Valonia and learned Rowan's secret. That had been the beginning of her downfall. "Some debts can't be paid," she sighed and turned away, back to the wild gardens and as she did she recalled an episode from her own coven gardens years ago when she'd been only seven years-old. It had been a lovely day and she'd been weeding with Connie Walsh, the head gardener.

There was a question that had been on Sunday's mind for some time and seeing as Connie wasn't as bad tempered as usual she hazarded a stab at it. She dusted the dirt from her hands and turned to Connie, who was deftly nipping weeds from between the peas. Sunday took the hat from her head and regarded it with a frown. The hat was the source of her puzzlement. "Miss Walsh?" she asked.

"Hmmm?" Connie didn't look up.

"Why is a witch's hat pointy?"

It was silent but for a few chirping grasshoppers. Connie regarded her through the young pea plants. In truth she found it hard to like Sunday. The child was precocious, but she put that down to Alfred Berwick's constant doting over her. She growled in amusement, then straightened and stood. "Witch's hat eh?" she said, as if Sunday had asked something not quite forbidden, but almost. Something not right for young ears.

Sunday nodded, she didn't like Connie, and she was too young to fathom why. Later in life it would occur to her: Connie seemed immune to her skills of manipulation.

"Now then," Connie pulled her own hat from her head. "What do you know about the birds and bees?"

"Lots!" Sunday boasted, looking around the gardens where there were plenty to be seen, suggesting Connie was rather stupid.

"Indeed," she muttered, "just as I thought." The old witch held up her hat, and tapped its cone shaped top. "That's the male aspect."

Sunday just stared at her looking confused.

"The male aspect!" she repeated, hoping the girl would catch on. Then she turned the hat over showing the round opening that was smoothed by years of wear. "The female aspect," she explained solidly.

Sunday's frown deepened. "You're not making sense," she sniped, unable to bring herself to admit she didn't understand.

"You know . . . 'birds & bees'."

"No, I don't know. Would I be asking if I did Miss Walsh?" Even at seven, the young Sunday spoke like a solstice queen.

"Suns & moons?" she tried.

Sunday just gave her a stony look.

"Wands & cups? Pokes & pockets?" Connie persisted, but each suggestion was repaid with a baffled look. "Oak and holly girl!" she groaned, "does King Dick and Queen Fanny mean nothing to you?" She wondered how much more blunt she needed to be.

"There's nobody at Regal-Fox called William or Fanella," Sunday pouted, feeling angry at her own ignorance.

"Yes, well Miss Sunday, maybe it'd be better for Coven-father Berwick to explain that one to you after all." She gave up and sank back into the peas leaving Sunday *with the rattle of grasshoppers, who sounded like they were laughing at something she didn't understand.*

"You look a thousand miles away," Strike interrupted her pleasant memory.

She sighed, "I was thinking of home."

"You said 'Connie'."

"Hmmm, Connie Walsh." Her eyes grew hazy. "What became of them Strike?" she wondered.

"Those that could came to Kolfinnia's coven, those that couldn't . . ."

"Were either killed or caught," she finished. "You know I've been thinking about something." She toyed with her silver necklace as she spoke, avoiding eye contact.

"Yes?" He braced himself, knowing this question had been long in coming.

"With them, we could just march in and take what we wanted."

"But at what cost? Many would be killed," he cautioned. "Not to mention the justice of it."

Just like Connie years ago she failed to comprehend but now she was bold enough to admit it. "I don't follow?"

"What of the men they are? Wouldn't you be making them do things to suit your own plans?"

She recoiled. "That was the old Sunday, things have changed, I assure you," she took a deep breath, "and so that's why I'm going to leave them here. I can't command them to kill on my behalf. I'd be no better than Valgard."

Just then something wet pressed against her hand and she looked around calmly and saw Tawny. He'd come up on them as quietly as a mouse, and even on all fours he towered over her. Again he gently pushed at her hand with his nose. She felt bristles and hot breath against her fingers and she backed up a step. "You can't come with me." She had decided to leave them with the way-beware. They'd be safe, as would the little doll, and others would be safe from them, but Tawny looked to have other ideas. "There'll be fighting," she explained sadly, "and people will die."

He nuzzled her hand again, hard enough to make her rock on her feet.

"No!" she said firmly. "I won't have that on my conscience. I'm not him. I'm not Valgard."

At the name, the huge animal growled and she froze. His two companions ambled right up to her and she noted with a shiver that they seemed to have forgotten the way-beware.

"I'm not your master!" she insisted and stepped back, but a tiny part of her longed to be. She could single-handedly crush the Illuminata with such warriors. "You must remain here with the way-beware, do you understand?"

Tawny simply dropped obediently into the grass at her feet, even so he was still eye level with her. An instant later his two companions did likewise and all three gazed at her expectantly.

Eirik looked at the girl who was Freydis, but wasn't Freydis, and around her he saw billowing fire and overwhelming shadow. This is what she faced if she held her course. He also saw that she intended to leave them and walk alone into that fire, and he knew she would die there. They couldn't let her go alone, not after she had saved them.

"Please," she groaned, "please you cannot. You *must* not come." Here she was again, she despaired, tempted by great powers but knowing it would only bring catastrophe. *Is this my punishment?* she thought. *To repeat the same mistake over and over?*

"Sunday." It was Strike.

She wiped her eyes. "I can't make the wrong choice again, I'd rather have never woken on that beach."

He hopped from the staff, onto her shoulder and whispered, "If your heart's torn, then let someone else decide for you. You've had the courage to believe in signs, I thought it was nonsense, but now I'm going to do the same."

She gave him a searching look.

"Look." He gestured to the air around them.

At first she thought they were dandelion seeds, but one of them landed on Tawny's brow and began to move, then another. She looked closer and saw baby spiders floating past on threads of silk. "Spiders?" She held her hand up and instantly a few snagged against her fingers, but they were so small and fragile she felt nothing.

Strike had thought that following clouds and geese was foolish, but without the way-beware they'd have died. He still couldn't explain how Thorpe's gun had so conveniently misfired and now he told himself it was time to try a little of her faith. "Let fate decide," he suggested.

More tiny spiders drifted by and she watched sunlight glint off silk. "Does this mean something?"

"It does if you want it to."

She watched them scuttle over her hand and decided to be guided by another kind of spider all together. "You're right." She gently blew them from her fingers, and sent them along their way.

"So what will you do?"

She considered this small but enormous question, then without a word she turned and left the bears where they lay, walking away purposefully through the long grass. Immediately Strike peered back over her shoulder and saw all three on their feet, looking agitated. Tawny shambled a few paces after her, stopped, turned, and regarded the way-beware uncertainly. Ash and Silver did likewise. "The choice is theirs now," he whispered, understanding her tactic.

She kept going, taking long determined strides. Tawny roared then lumbered forwards, only to stop again and look back at the way-beware. More tiny spiders floated past and the bears howled mournfully. There came another anguished roar from behind her and in that instant she knew: if they came it was because they *chose* to do so. "I understand now," she smiled at the neatness of his work. "And thank you dear champion." The last howl was the most heart-rending of all and she knew what to do. She turned back to claim them.

"So, we are bound together," Strike realised.

"Together," she agreed and a cold shiver ran up her back. It might have been fear, or excitement, but in truth she knew it was greater than either. It was fate.

They were sleeping peacefully now, but rumbling like dormant volcanoes and she found some time to examine the documents from Thorpe's study. In truth she'd forgotten about them and now they were crumpled and damp.

"Do they help us?"

She looked up. Strike was perched in a hawthorn tree. He said he was keeping watch, but with the berserks sleeping right by her she didn't have a worry in the world. "Curious, come look."

He landed at her side. "What's curious?"

"Here's a clue to a long-standing mystery," she pointed to the paper.

He frowned at the page of text. "Really?"

"Hmm, it's long been known that the Illuminata commission factories to make their krakens, but to the best of my knowledge nobody knew where." She pointed to the papers again.

"And you think you've found them out?"

"Perhaps, listen; *'Harborough & Sons, of Chertfield, West Riding of Yorkshire, dutifully agree to complete the purchaser's requirements to the effect of thirty-two coal-fired SS units, to the sum of twenty-three and half thousand pounds per unit delivered on behalf of Messrs Blake and Crowley of Goldhawk Row, London.'*"

Strike just grunted and shook his head. "So?" He found the wording longwinded but little else.

"This is a bill of sale, and it says here Harborough & Sons are a steel mill in northern England." She tapped the paper.

"And this Blake and Crowley?"

"I'm guessing they're just accountants at Goldhawk, but the important thing is that this tells us who's forging their new krakens."

"Krakens? Where does it say that?"

"Look," she pointed to the words 'coal-fired SS units'.

He looked at her helplessly.

"You're much happier fighting and flying aren't you?" she smiled.

"It shows does it?"

She stroked his brow. "SS units, that's shorthand for 'steam-suits' and that's what krakens are."

"I remember them well." His feathers bristled.

Suddenly she saw herself last October, riding into battle. She punished them hard because in truth she wanted to punish herself. "So do I," she agreed.

"That's a lot of new weaponry."

"And a lot of money."

"Over three quarters of a million pounds," he said matter-of-factly.

She admired him openly.

"What?" he squirmed, looking embarrassed. "You think I was snoozing in my staff while you had your number lessons as well?"

She laughed brightly. "You're right, three quarters of a million. And there's as many as that in London without a crust of bread to call their own."

He looked from the bill in her hand and across to the three sleeping in the grass. He saw a vole scamper under one of their great paws thinking it a safe rock to hide under. When he looked back, he saw her studying him intently. "We're thinking the same thing."

"Destroy them before they're delivered."

"But is it −"

"Don't!" he interrupted. "Fate has decided."

She nodded once. They were going to pay Harborough & Sons a visit and Victor Thorpe would have another reason to hate witches.

George Pratt was twelve years-old. He knew that for a fact because today was his twelfth birthday. He might struggle when it came to reading, he couldn't write more than his own name, and his grasp of numbers was rudimentary, but he was twelve and he knew that clear as crystal.

He walked along carefully because he was barefoot, having lent his own shoes to Thomas his elder brother when his shift at the foundry had ended. Thomas's own, and only, pair of shoes finally died last week and for the time being they had to share until Thomas used his wages to buy a new pair, or at least a good second-hand pair. Harborough & Sons was working double shifts to complete the order and so when George had finished at ten tonight Thomas had gone on. The foundry employed over three hundred men and boys and without it the town of Chertfield in Yorkshire would turn to dust, but no matter how much work the foundry had on its books, the workforce was always bedraggled and poor. Someone was getting rich, but it wasn't the likes of shoe-less George Pratt.

These things didn't concern him right then however. Like most poor folks he took simple pleasures where he found them and he'd waited all day so he could walk home alone and eat his penny's worth of parkin cake. Home comprised two rooms and six siblings, two parents and two grandparents. If he took his treat home, his small slice of parkin wouldn't last any longer than 'an icicle in hell'. This was one of his uncle Darrow's remarks.

"Hell," he said and looked round guiltily. Confident he was alone he tried it again but louder. "Hell!" His mother would thrash him for such language, but here along Back Lane he was alone. The overgrown footpath led from the foundry to Poplars Row, where his own house stood back to back with scores of others. He chose this quiet route to savour his delicacy and save his soles. The damp grass felt heavenly against today's fresh burns. Even with shoes the hot metal could burn clean through and leave blisters. Right now his poor old shoes were working another shift, protecting his brother's feet, but if Thomas didn't get some new ones soon they'd both be without.

He popped a crumb of parkin into his mouth and hummed as he wandered. The night was mild and full of spring promise. He had his birthday and his parkin, and tomorrow was Sunday, which meant church, but at least no work at the foundry. Being in such a good mood he didn't notice the stranger sitting by the wall until she spoke to him.

"Good evening young man."

"Hell!" he blurted and dropped his cake.

"I'm sorry, I didn't mean to startle you," the voice came again.

He bent and retrieved his cake, now garnished with a few blades of grass, and peered into the gloom. A figure appeared, and his first thought was whether it was a neighbour who might tell his fearsome mother he'd cursed. "Beggin' yer forgiveness, I dint mean to curse."

"Don't fret, I've heard plenty worse than that." The stranger drew closer and he saw it was a miss, and a rather comely one at that.

She was dressed as black as the shadows around her, so no wonder he'd not seen her. Her face looked kindly, but just in case, he hid his cake behind his back. It was his birthday and he didn't really want to share today. He didn't recognise her and something about her told him she wasn't the type for mill work. She probably worked at the hospital he thought. "You're 'eading to the infirmary I tek it miss?"

"No, I've business at the mill."

"Arborough & Sons yer mean?" His accent smoothed over the 'H's like a plane.

"Yes," she smiled and he saw she was not just comely, she was regal looking. A 'proper queen' his mother would say, and suddenly he found it hard to think of things to say. "You work there?" she asked, looking troubled.

"Aye miss, and I'm 'eading 'ome." He pointed vaguely up the hill.

"How old are you?"

He straightened. "I'm twelve year old this very day!"

"Then blessings of Oak be on you young man."

He had no idea what she meant, but her remark was sincere. "Many thanks I'm sure miss," he looked at his bare feet, feeling awkward. "Would yer care fer some parkin?" He brought the cake out of hiding.

She beamed at him. "What a charming young man you are George, quite the most gentlemanly fellow I've met in a long while."

He blushed and concealed a polite frown; how did she know his name, he wondered?

"But I tell you what, you keep every last crumb of that cake for yourself, I think you've earned it. You might offer me something other than cake though." She stepped closer, and he caught the scent of flowers, and something funny but nice happened in his belly, something he'd not known since he'd stolen a kiss from Mary Wentworth at Sunday School a year ago.

"'Ave little to offer a lady."

She smiled at his unpractised gallantry. "Directions are all I need. Is the mill down this pathway here?"

"Oh aye miss." He turned and pointed away to where the lights of Harborough & Sons twinkled in the valley bottom. "Place an't shut day or night but for Sunday's for these last eight week."

"You're very busy then?"

"Oh aye miss, plenty busy. Rolling sheet metal, an' pounding, an' scraping out casts an' pits. Soon I'll be old enough to do the same jobs as the menfolk." He sounded proud but she was sad for him.

"You've been such a help," she reached into a bag strung over her shoulder, "and because you've been so polite and offered me what little you have, I want you to have this." She held out a fist.

He seemed uncertain. "Ain't proper to be tekkin gifts from ladies."

"I'm no 'lady' and today's your birthday which makes this is a simple birthday gift." She looked at his weary feet. "Use it wisely."

He looked at her fist. He had no idea what was concealed inside, but he knew it was rude to turn down a gift. He timidly lifted his open palm and she dropped something cold and heavy into his grasp. "Miss?" He held it closer, turning it this way and that. He saw that it was a nugget of silver, probably worth a month's wages for the whole family. "Silver?" he stuttered, "I can't tek this miss, folks'll think I thieved it." He looked up, but she was already walking away down the lane. "Miss!"

She turned back without slowing. "Happy birthday George," she wished him, and then she did something most peculiar, she pulled her scarf up over her face so only her piercing eyes showed.

"Miss!" he called again, but she vanished into the dark. He looked down at the silver in his palm: enough for shoes by the bucket load. As he was considering this, something suddenly rushed overhead and he heard the whoosh of feathers. He had no idea what it was but it seemed huge and he cringed like a frightened rabbit, then came a second, and a third. The sky was blotted out and it felt to George like the reaper's blade had missed his crown by a whisker. He saw three monstrous shadows slice through the darkness, heading in the direction the young woman had gone and if he didn't know better he'd have sworn he heard a deep animal growling. "Am sorry Lord, I dint mean to curse, I swears it!" he sobbed, and turned and fled, parkin in one hand, silver in the other.

He ran from the furnaces of Harborough & Sons as if old Hobb himself were hard on his heels. Suddenly he just wanted to be home and he didn't care if his sisters ate every crumb of his hard earned cake.

CHAPTER TWENTY-ONE

Boys without shoes

'To murder your neighbour is a crime, but to murder a nation is merely war.'
Alice Kale - founding witch of the Ragged-Tower coven, Surrey

Early on Sunday morning, a figure clothed in black watched a steel mill from the surrounding hills. The factory sprawled across the valley floor, veiled in smoke and fed with coal and ore by numerous train tracks. Scores of covered wagons sat idle on the rails, all of them loaded with newly forged krakens, and once in London, the Illuminata would begin assembling them. Sunday had waited for the workforce to leave and now Harborough & Sons was quiet in respect for the Sabbath. She looked at her own army, comprising three great bears lying in the grass. "Boys without shoes," she whispered absently, and toyed with a small bag in her hand, just as she turned her plan over in her mind.

"How will we do this?" Strike hadn't left his staff all night, in order to save his strength.

"They'll deal with the krakens," her eyes went to the waiting bears, "and we'll make sure the wagons never leave here."

"There's something else though, something's got under your skin hasn't it?"

"The train yard is our target," she avoided the question. "The mill has to remain intact, these people need their jobs and we don't want anyone hurt."

"Sunday, tell me."

Boys without shoes, she thought sadly. "Yes, I suppose there's something else."

"Care to share it?"

She unfastened the little bag and behind her she heard Tawny yawn and shift in the grass. "Before Regal-Fox fell I didn't have much to do with the non-magical folk of this land. I had little idea what it was like for them and it's only now I'm starting to wonder," she dipped her hand into the bag and looked reflective, "why is there money for war but not shoes?"

She took out a handful of lamp-soot and began to smear a mask across her eyes. The scarf came next and she pulled it over her face, and when her hat was fixed in place there was little of the old Sunday to be seen. She drew the way-beware from her belt and heard a mellow growling from behind her. "No one is to be hurt!" she called over her shoulder, compelled to say it again. The lightning-staff began to hum and the bears lumbered to their feet. A small flock of finches skimmed past and she counted eight of them. Below her the mill basked in the early morning sun and she counted eight chimneys and eight loaded wagon trains. The signs were unmistakeable. "Thank you dear champion." She touched the scar through her mask. Lastly, she held up the way-beware. "Take some rest," she kissed it and uttered the sleeping-spell. The song became quieter and quieter until it was barely there at all and in response the berserks' growls became louder, but now their strength belonged to her. She pushed the way-beware into her belt and drew hrafn-dimmu. Now she was truly a black witch, just like the witches of propaganda and prejudice. The berserks were just inches from her back and she could almost feel their hot fury. "They want a witch in black – then let them have one," she declared, "For all those who fell at Kittiwake!" She ran through the grass, mounted her staff and flew. Her champions charged down the slope after her with Eirik in the lead, and the closer they drew to the sleeping mill the larger and angrier they became. "BLACKWAND!" she screamed, and the peace of the Sabbath dawn was well and truly broken.

To call it a battle would have been misleading. Her opponents were lifeless machines, but she took vicious pleasure in destroying them. At Kittiwake such machines had killed without pity but now they lay helpless before her and she wasted no time breaking them into molten fragments.

Lightning burns hotter than the sun, and Strike made sure the steel rails and armour suffered greatly. He screamed himself hoarse and delivered blows until he ached and the staff bled sparks, while the solstice queen was no longer a maiden of the sun, but vengeance, and she shrieked with joy as kraken after kraken exploded.

Gorged on rage, Eirik and his brothers became truly immense. Mighty paws hurled wagons from the rails, spilling the armour, then they went to work with their claws, shredding steel as easily as lace, or pounding it flat under their massive weight. Helmets went spinning until the yard was littered with huge severed heads, which stared dumbly up from the mud or lay squashed and humiliated. When the wagons were nothing but matchwood, she put Strike's fire to them, and timbers, canvas, ropes and sleepers were set ablaze. The berserks roared in fury and Sunday screamed along with her warriors, and in the overwhelming joy that comes with victory she didn't hear the church bells ringing out in warning; but then again, would she need to even care?

Folk all over Chertfield came to their windows or ran into the street drawn by the sounds of destruction. They flocked towards Harborough & Sons and saw wagons and mangled krakens being hurled through the air like rag dolls, and heard bestial roars and the shriek of a woman gone mad. The brave folk of Chertfield turned and ran home to slam their doors and shutters, and pray the Lord of the Sabbath day would deliver them.

Her head was spinning and she felt faint after all the adrenaline. She looked around as the berserks finished off the last krakens and then finally she heard the church bells. Time was running out. Soldiers might arrive soon and things would turn bloody. They had to leave. "Strike," she gasped, "there's one last job before we go, the one I told you about."

"Understood."

She climbed on to her staff and steered towards the heart of the mill, where the elusive Harborough & Sons kept their offices.

Eirik looked up, satisfied with his work and contented to have done it on her behalf. Further more, no blood had been spilled. Finally, after so long, here was a victory he could be proud of, a victory that owed nothing to Valgard's depravity. He watched Sunday streak across the ruined yard, towards the mill, and knew their departure was imminent. The final moments of their attack were at hand, and all that remained was Sunday's finishing touch.

George Pratt had seen very little, but even that had been enough. He'd gone to the edge of the pasture to look down on the mill and seen enormous monsters throwing wagons around like toys and a figure in black spreading fire and lightning through the wreckage. He cringed at each flash, somehow believing he was to blame for taking the young woman's silver last night. He felt its weight in his pocket and now wondered if he'd brought this down on Chertfield. He sprinted back up the field and saw his little sister Lilly running towards him. "George!" she sobbed.

"Get back inside Lilly, it int safe!" A roar echoed up from the valley followed by the muffled thump of another explosion.

"But the bells, Mam says its not time for church, so why's the bells ringing?"

"Juss get back in!" He caught her hand and ran back to the house dragging her behind.

"Georgie yer hurtin' me!"

"Dad'll tan yer harder'n me if he finds yer out, now back 'ome!"

"But what's for happening down at the mill?"

"Nowt!" he insisted.

"It's snowing!" she shouted suddenly, and even laughed.

"Don't be daft," he puffed. Poplars Row was just yards away now.

"But it *is* snowing, look!"

Something white swirled past his face and caught in the grass. He stopped, panting hard, and saw that it wasn't snow at all. It was paper, and he gasped when he saw that it was a five pound note.

"It's snowing paper?" Lilly asked timidly.

"It can't be." But she was right, he looked around and saw notes fluttering down all the way along Poplars Row.

"She's making it snow, the lady on the stick!" Lilly pointed.

"Eh?" Bewildered, he looked to the sky and at first he thought it was a large black bird. "It's 'er," he heard himself say, "the silver lady."

"It's a witch!" Lilly clutched his hand, but she sounded excited rather than afraid. "Georgie it's a witch!"

He stared dumbly at the figure tearing across the rooftops. She was laughing and throwing banknotes from a satchel. A fortune was falling from the skies and now more people came out of their homes to see what was happening. He recovered another banknote from the grass and this time it was a ten pound note, more money than he'd see in a year. "Hell," he whispered.

Harborough & Sons' plundered money continued to rain down from the sky. Three quarters of a million pounds in total. Blackwand had very quickly become the most wanted fugitive in Illuminata history.

When Lyle opened his bedroom curtains on Monday morning he almost expected to see storm clouds hovering over London. Victor Thorpe would arrive this afternoon and he knew that if he wasn't careful he'd end up the whipping boy for his fury.

He arrived at Goldhawk just after nine that morning and as he climbed the staircase to his office, his instincts told him something was wrong and he stopped. There was the faint whiff of cigar smoke. "Dear Lord no," he groaned and crept closer, but the smell grew stronger. The man he'd been dreading was already in his office. Suddenly he didn't know what to do. Should he knock at his own door and enter or should he just breeze in and pretend to be surprised? He took a deep breath, fixed a surprised look on his face, grabbed the door knob and entered.

Victor Thorpe was puffing his way through his second cigar. He sat in Lyle's chair with his feet propped on the desk looking more like a gunfighter in a saloon rather than a gentleman in a study. He had been at Goldhawk since eight, having taken the overnight train from York. "Blackwand," he muttered to himself and took a considered draw on the cigar then regarded its glowing tip and imagined pressing it into one of her beautiful eyes and the thrill of hearing her scream. At first he just wanted her dead, but he'd had plenty of time since to plot his vengeance, and the punishments he had in store bordered on the obscene. He just hoped they had the chance to take her alive.

The clock chimed quarter past the hour from its place on the mantel, and Thorpe instinctively knew that Lyle was lurking outside in a muddle. "Show some guts man," he grunted in disgust.

Just then the handle rattled, the door opened and Lyle barged in wearing a rehearsed look of surprise. "Lord Thorpe! I wasn't expecting you until this afternoon. Thank the good Lord you're safely back in London, when I heard about Thorpe Hall I feared the worst sir." His mouth gushed words like a split balloon while his eyes rolled, and magnified by his spectacles he looked even more frightened than he felt.

Thorpe slowly lowered his legs and sat upright, pulled the cigar from his mouth and blew smoke. "I'm touched by your concern," he sneered, "now where's Galen?"

"He's at Hobbs Ash sir. The initial tests have been very promising. The original creature he named 'Vorus' and it shows a strong resistance to magical weapons." He chattered too much, he knew.

Thorpe looked unimpressed. "And any sign of Blackwand?"

"None. Do you think she's gone to ground?"

He smiled. "I'd rather see her under it. Make no mistake: she's on her way. Have the crews at Salisbury been alerted?"

"The staff at Wellesley Hall has been doubled."

"As were the staff at Thorpe Hall," he smiled coldly. "I fear that won't be enough. Wellesley Hall will host the tournament, and if this Blackwand slut arrives and cuts the assembled dignitaries to pieces there'll be a hefty bill of compensation to be settled by us."

"I'll order the local infantry units drafted in sir."

"Never mind. I'm back now and I'll be taking charge of this operation."

"I'll order the garrison at Wellesley Hall bolstered sir, I'll do it right away."

"You better. If she comes they'll need more than guns and troops," he rumbled.

Lyle sensed it was a dangerous question, but couldn't help himself. "What was she like sir?"

He chewed his cigar and bared his teeth. "She has a viper's tongue and a jackal's heart. But magic and monsters weren't her most potent weapons. No, not by a long chalk."

"Sir?"

"She has the power to beguile men."

"A trait of all witches surely sir?"

"Only the beautiful ones," he scoffed. No doubt if Blackwand had been a wrinkled hag then Charles Harrison would still be with them and the slut would have still been tied to that kitchen chair, he thought.

Lyle stood before his own desk, not daring to sit until told. "And these familiars of hers, you said they were demons of a kind?"

"Bears, or very much like them."

"I'm sure Galen's valkyries will be more than a match for them. This creature he's summoned, it appears unstoppable!" He nodded vigorously. "More than a match for Leonhard's forces."

"Galen," he considered the name, then pulled his coat from the back of the chair. "I think it's high time I saw our new champion for myself."

"Right this way sir." Lyle held the door open for him. Thorpe marched past him leaving a trail of stale tobacco odour, and Lyle hoped Galen was ready for his first major inspection.

The journey to Hobbs Ash seemed to take forever. London's streets were strangely busy and the ride was frustratingly slow, which meant Lyle had to make small talk.

Thorpe disregarded his idle chat, and instead glowered out of the windows imagining a shadowy figure on every street corner. Blackwand could be anywhere, perhaps even watching them right now. He held up a hand to stop Lyle's babble. "How many prisoners do we have?"

"Witches sir?"

"Of course bloody witches!"

"At last count sixty-two," he added hastily.

"And how many have you sacrificed to the Vorus creature?"

"Just the one. She wanted more but Galen wouldn't allow it."

"Just as well. We're going to need all the witches we've got."

"Sir?"

"Blackwand might be protected by demons, but her soul is tender. Threats of executing the prisoners will undo her." He looked out of the window, towards the skies and thought of her. "Her compassion will lead her right to us, but first we need to better understand the nature of her demons."

"What if she makes an attempt on rescuing the captives?"

Thorpe drew a fresh cigar from his coat and tapped it to his temple. "Oh I'm counting on it." He actually smiled. "And when she comes, we'll pit her monsters against Galen's. We'll bury the whore then turn our attention to Leonhard and bury that insolent pretender too, along with his mongrel knights."

"Galen's newest creatures are still very weak sir, he recovered them less than two days ago."

"Then we'll have to fatten them up," Thorpe grinned, "just like infants suckle on the teat, we'll let them drink themselves senseless on the red-river."

Red-river? Lyle thought. He'd heard the phrase from Galen, but it sounded peculiar coming from a man like Thorpe.

"That's another reason the captives are precious," Thorpe explained. "Sacrificing them will strengthen the valkyrie creatures."

"Surely there are always inmates from Newgate prison sir?"

"No," he said bluntly. "The condemned must be of witch-blood." He turned back to the window leaving Lyle slightly confused, not to mention disturbed.

How is it you know so much? he wondered, and then realised he didn't want to know.

"Isis and Arctura," Galen read their names from the battered name plaques. The two new krakens, the bull and the eagle, towered over him and Vorus stood in the middle.

"You are pleased my love?" Vorus's voice buzzed in his ear.

"Aye, most pleased, but these new ladies of yours have shown me nought but the most dreadful manners since coming here."

"Galen?"

"They speak with you by means I do not understand, but I'm yet to hear a single word from them. Is this any way to treat their saviour?"

"They are afraid, this world is still very new to them."

"I don't believe her," Elios cautioned.

He glanced at his cane, and for once he was inclined to agree.

"What did it say?" Vorus asked casually. Her voice seemed to float right next to him. "The stunted creature in the stick, she speaks with you Galen just as I speak with my sisters. What is she saying of me?"

Elios growled in response.

"Elios agrees with me," he defended her, "your companions act like shy maids at their first grand ball, but there's more going on than you say."

There was a grinding sound and he looked up to see the huge cherub staring down at him as though he was just an ant. "Galen have pity. They were lost and close to death."

"A fate from which I saved them," he shouted up at her. "Now order them to acknowledge me or I'll have those suits melted down and you'll be an only child again!"

There was a great rumble and a loud clang as Vorus stepped back in shock. "You would do such a thing? How could you be so wicked!"

Elios was afraid. Despite his tough words he was struggling to make an impression on the new valkyries. So far they'd been at Hobbs Ash almost two days and still hadn't spoken a word. Instead, they seemed to view Vorus as their natural leader.

"How dare you speak to me of wicked!" he roared and swiped his cane through the air. "A man died at Smithfield at your behest. A woman was murdered just to be a beacon for your miserable soul, and you yourself crushed a witch under your own machine. If you dare use that word against me again I'll strip you of your kraken and cast you into the gutter!" He stepped forwards, challenging the huge machine.

"My love!" The kraken took a frightened step backwards, and the ones on either side of her did likewise.

"Remind her Galen!" Elios cheered him.

"Now who do you serve? Answer me!"

"Galen, my love for you is unwavering." The cherub cried tears of rust and hung its head in a shower of sparks. "I thought you understood."

"What you fail to realise, all of you, is that an important man is coming here today. If things are not going as he demands, then all of you will be in danger." He swiftly turned his anger at them into concern for their well being. It was so slick that even Elios believed it.

"Galen." A voice none of them recognised boomed through the station and far away he heard horses whinny in fear. All of them turned and looked up at Isis, the bull-headed kraken.

"You spoke my name!" He sounded like a new father and took a step towards it. "Acknowledge me again!"

"Galen," Isis said uncertainly.

He turned to Arctura the eagle. "Now you."

The world was quiet but for the heaving metal suits. At last he was rewarded with the most wonderful word in the world. "Galen," Arctura replied mechanically.

Elios heard not a shred of loyalty in their words, but Galen looked satisfied, and just then an unexpected voice shook them from their private meeting.

"Thrice be the glory of the threefold way."

Galen smelled cigar smoke and the years seemed to yawn wide like an opening book. He took a deep breath and turned to face his past.

Victor Thorpe stood holding a cigar and regarding him impassively. "Galen," he said simply and replaced the cigar between his teeth. He never cast a glance at the three living krakens.

"Thrice be the glory," Galen replied in a shaky voice.

"The Book has waited long for this day." Thorpe dropped the cigar to the floor and crushed the life from it. "I have a carriage waiting. Ride with me."

Vorus watched with acute interest. This new man was like Galen, and not just in appearance. He also had eyes that saw beneath, and now they were leaving to talk privately. She wondered what they might have to discuss and played with the idea of following them, but she had a private conversation of her own to conduct with her sisters. Galen would have to enjoy his reunion with his father in private.

CHAPTER TWENTY-TWO

Hammer and anvil

'When the last of my enemies was dead I wept, for the joy of killing was spent.'
Roskar Michov, 8th century Hapsgort prince

They travelled together on a random course through London, leaving Lyle
bewildered as to why Thorpe had stayed only ten minutes, and without
taking the slightest interest in the valkyries. Thorpe's driver took their
carriage west along the Thames while inside the two occupants enjoyed a
long and very revealing conversation. "It is good to see you again father."
Galen looked down at his knees as if thinking the exact opposite.

"Really?" he huffed. "Was I such a benevolent father that you spent your
exile thinking of me, Matthew?"

Matthew Thorpe, known to the world as Galen, nodded sheepishly. A
day hadn't gone by without thoughts of his father shaping his world. "I
always hoped the Book-of-Nine would one day return to these shores and
step out of hiding."

"And when Krast's ill fated venture shattered the British bloodlines, that
very opportunity presented itself and I called you home." Thorpe lit a
cigar from his seemingly endless supply and the carriage grew heady with
smoke. Matthew Thorpe drank in the smell and it took him back to his
childhood. "You've done well, I ought to congratulate you. Not just one
valkyrie, but three. A towering achievement."

"But it's not enough." He looked up and his eyes gleamed. "I was so close to learning the song of Àeon."

Thorpe's mouth dropped. "The creature can recite it?"

He nodded fervently. "Vorus was about to sing it for me when Lyle spoiled everything."

"Then ask her again!"

"It's not that simple father. I think Vorus is learning man's ways."

"Explain."

"She knows I have a longing to hear the song and so she's calculating a price with which she can bribe me."

His face contorted. "Now listen to me Matthew, these beasts you've recruited from Ruination, it is imperative that they do not set the terms. Do you understand?"

"Oh certainly! And I've resisted all her demands, Elios will corroborate that."

"Elios?" Thorpe scowled. "Ah yes, Elios."

"She has proved indispensable."

He sat back and regarded him coolly. "I must confess when I heard you had your own thunder-sprite I was alarmed. I began to wonder if you'd spent too long with witches."

Galen looked insulted. "I'm an initiate of the great Book, no mere witch impostor!"

He smiled. "You'll have little need of your pet now. I shall direct the experiments with the valkyries."

Inside the cane Elios shivered. This man was colder than Vorus and her sisters put together.

"But without Elios I wouldn't be able to commune with Sophie. Have you forgotten her plight?"

Thorpe tapped cigar ash from the window. "Keep the creature as a pet if you must, but this Elios thing no longer has a role in our plan."

"And what of Sophie?" He was growing angry now and the cane was icy too. "Do we abandon her also?"

Thorpe smiled sadly. "Understand that family history is like a great house Matthew, many of the rooms are open to you but many are locked and without knowing what lies behind them you cannot see the great plan of the Book-of-Nine."

"Father?"

"Sophie was not taken to Ruin," he revealed, "she was delivered there by your great grandfather and I.

The carriage suddenly felt very claustrophobic.

"You lie," he accused, and leaned away.

Thorpe shook his head slowly. "It's time I opened those locked doors for you." He reached into his coat and took out a ring and slipped it easily onto his finger. It was gold and the crest showed a square with a circle at the centre: the symbol of the Book-of-Nine. "Will you allow me to open that door, and will you promise me you'll find the fortitude to look through it?" He held out his hands now and Galen looked down at them as if they were baited hooks.

"Galen no!" Elios tried, but the cane slipped from his fingers and thudded to the floor and he heard her no more.

"Come home Matthew and learn the ways of the family Thorpe." He splayed his fingers, and silently Galen slipped his own hands into them and came home. By skills denied ordinary folk, father and son, master and pupil, shared a secret without words. The first thing Galen saw was a time before his birth when his father was hardly thirteen years old.

After his own parents had been killed in a carriage accident when he was just nine, Victor had left boarding school to be educated by his grandfather at Thorpe Hall. Barlow Thorpe was an enigma but an inspiration to the young and impressionable Victor. At times he could be merry and frivolous and at others he could be wrathful and domineering, and Victor had never learned how to read the man. Barlow spent much time in his study and often mumbled strange things about realms unseen and creatures of the 'threefold path'. Victor was seldom disciplined and so grew without boundaries, believing he could do as he pleased.

After some years at Thorpe Hall the young Victor had taken a fancy to one of the serving maids, named Rachel. Being a lad who'd never learned the art of asking for anything, and seeing all things as his for the taking, he decided upon a plot to take the girl by force. On the day of his thirteenth birthday Victor had waited for Rachel, who was but a youth herself, to come to his bed chamber and change the linen. It was lunch time and she had expected to find the chambers empty, but Victor had skipped his lessons that day and waited for her to arrive.

After she'd entered, he'd sprung from his hiding place and locked the door. At first his advances were restrained, but when she'd refused him he'd flown into a rage and assaulted her, before finally raping her. Rachel's screams drew the household staff and the young Victor was found out, but sadly such events were familiar in the great houses of Britain. Rachel was led away by the matronly cook who dried her tears and dressed her wounds, while Victor was summoned to his grandfather's study for what he thought would be a sound thrashing.

What a day that was for him. The young Victor had his first taste of woman, and his first taste of strong spirit. Barlow hadn't been outraged. Far from it, he was delighted and poured him a tall glass of brandy, handed him an expensive cigar and sat him down to talk with him as an equal for the very first time. That day Victor's life changed and what he learned in Barlow's study was better than the touch of Rachel's body or the taste of drink or tobacco.

Barlow had told him secrets of a mysterious cult known as the Book-of-Nine. Victor knew of the Illuminata, for his own father had been a prominent banker, but the Illuminata and its concerns had all sounded so dull to the thrill-seeking Victor Thorpe. Grandfather Barlow's tales of worlds beyond, and the forbidden creatures that inhabited them however, sounded much more to his liking. Best of all though was the promise of power and domination to those who could learn to control these forces. From that day Victor learned no more Latin, Bible stories or numbers. Barlow declared that he'd proven himself worthy to study from a greater Book by far.

He learned of Ruination. He learned how witches were the foes of the Book-of-Nine and to his amazement he learned how the Illuminata themselves were also their enemies, because they stifled deeper study of Ruin. As a mark of his initiation Barlow gave him his ring embossed with the Book's crest: a square with a circle at the centre.

Victor learned all he could from Barlow and the weeks passed, but soon it became clear that Rachel was pregnant and she was summoned to Barlow's study. The girl stood before the formidable Barlow Thorpe and trembled as he examined her belly for proof of her claim. She was indeed pregnant and Barlow deduced by skills only known to initiates that Rachel carried twins. He ordered her to keep her pregnancy a secret and kept her as a paid but non-working member of the staff to secure her compliance. It was a very generous offer and she eventually, if not willingly, accepted. It was then that Barlow began to hatch a devilish plot to put Rachel's babies to good use, glorious use in fact. Healthy twins were rare and he planned on using them as a tool to further his studies. He ensured Rachel had the best care and never wanted for anything, and all the while he groomed the unwitting young Victor for the terrible deed ahead.

Sophie and Matthew Thorpe were born in the autumn. It was then that things soured between Victor and his grandfather. From out of the blue Barlow suddenly insisted that his initiation was incomplete and that there was one last task ahead, something that might at last offer them a chance of learning Àeon's song. It was the night Victor sold his humanity and Rachel died of grief.

"An opportunity such as this has never arisen before. Healthy twins are so rare, the circumstances are perfect. You must do this!" Barlow insisted.

Victor sat in a chair by the fire and looked towards the bell jar and the crib-robber trapped inside. "It is beyond me to choose."

"The girl, let the girl be taken. Women are more sensitive and she'll forge a stronger link to her brother." Barlow never used the babies' names.

"Sophie," he chewed his lip. "But the girl is all of two days old! She is innocent!"

"We can't delay or the crib-robber will die. Do you know how hard it is to capture such a beast Victor?" Barlow loomed over the youth.

"But Sophie!"

"Once we offer the girl to the creature she will be taken to Ruin, and there I assure you she will be luckier than you or I. She will never die!"

Victor looked towards the creature behind the glass, and again his stomach flipped at the thought of his new-born daughter being wrapped in those writhing arms. He hadn't wanted the children at first but now they were born he felt differently. He even entertained lofty notions of a family life, peace and tranquillity.

"I see your dedication to the Book-of-Nine wavers?" Barlow observed. "Must I remind you what will happen to your claim on this house once I am no more?" There was a long silence in the study, broken only by the crackle of the fire and the rain lashing against the windows.

Victor took a deep breath. "Sophie shall go."

"Good man," Barlow congratulated him.

"And she will be fine you say?"

"I promise. But it must be tonight."

Victor nodded obediently.

"Don't pity her Victor. Once across the threshold the girl will be privy to knowledge that no man has ever seen." He bared his teeth. "How I envy the child!"

"I know my Lord," he wiped the tears from his face.

"And with her brother still earthbound, the two will be linked. She will be our explorer of realms unknown, and he shall see with her eyes and the secrets of Àeon

will be ours!" Barlow was exalted. "Who knows, there might even be a way to
retrieve her once our experiment is a success. She will be a hero, not a martyr."

Victor suddenly looked up. "You really think so?"

"I do." He clutched his shoulder. "One day your daughter will come home."

"Really?" he pleaded.

"Would I suggest this if I thought otherwise?"

Victor nodded solemnly. "Thrice be the glory of the threefold way," he managed.

Barlow's gripped tightened. "You are a fine initiate Victor, now go and make me
proud."

Victor nodded once, and then slid out of the study door and went to send his baby
daughter to realms unknown inside the belly of a monster.

Sophie was taken that night. Rachel's spirit was broken and she succumbed to
illness and died shortly after, and Victor, just like his son in years to come, decided
that guilt could destroy a man and pledged to feel nothing whatsoever from that day
on.

Thorpe withdrew and looked into Galen's troubled eyes. "Now you have
at last come home."

Galen slumped against his seat while Elios cried softly. "Sophie," he
choked, and pressed a hand to his mouth, certain he'd cry if he didn't.

"Forget her Matthew. She was sent to Ruination, but her mission failed."
Thorpe's tone was hard as granite.

"My name is Galen!" he snarled. "You initiated me into your world, and
when the Book-of-Nine was abolished you abandoned me to exile!"

He planted his hands on his knees and leaned forwards. "Understand
that was the only way the teachings of the Book could continue. Be proud
that you alone have kept the cult alive. If I hadn't sent you away the Book
would have been no more."

"I have chased a fantasy all my life. You let me believe that Sophie was
taken, yet it was you that offered her up because, " he stammered, "you
were too cowardly to protect her!"

Without warning Thorpe lashed out and landed a hefty punch. Galen
hit the upholstered seat and bounced forwards again only to find another
fist waiting for him. Thorpe struck another blow and his cigar shot from
his mouth and tumbled to the floor, while Galen's nose erupted in blood.
"The ways of the Book are more important than you or Sophie, or even

the Empire!" He grabbed his collar and hauled him forwards. "You don't think I still wake in sweat and dread for what I did? You think I'm such a monster?" Without waiting for an answer he landed a third punch.

Galen landed hard against the door and slumped back into the seat. He didn't feel the punches or the blood and tears run down his face. He didn't feel anything because his world had collapsed around him. "You bastard," he whimpered.

He was hauled up to face his father again.

"If the Book hadn't been continued by you in exile it would have vanished altogether," he panted, "and for that I am grateful, but mark me now 'Galen', there is still a chance we can get Sophie back, but only if we work together."

He heard words of hope and so he was blinded to the lie. "You promise?"

Thorpe recalled how Barlow had used the very same lie decades before, and the words rolled easily from his lips. "I promise." He pushed Galen back against the seat and smoothed his ruffled lapels. "You've grown into a fine man," he sighed, "Sophie will be proud when she sees you again."

He wiped the blood from his cheek. "All these years father, I've watched her and hoped she'd see me, but she never did."

Thorpe patted his knee affectionately. "Barlow and I hoped the link between twins would let you commune with one another, sadly we were wrong. But you can see her at will can you not?"

"Yes, thanks be to Elios," he nodded weakly, "but it's not enough."

Thorpe retrieved his cigar from the floor, dusted it down and re-lit it. He took a few considered puffs before speaking. "You want your sister and the song of Àeon?"

"Of course!"

"Then heed me carefully. The tournament in June is not just a contest between the Illuminata bloodlines, it's a chance for the Book-of-Nine to at last step out of hiding."

"You mean to declare ourselves?"

"No, better than that. To take control of the Illuminata completely and turn its aims to our own purpose."

Galen looked baffled.

"Imagine," Thorpe elaborated, "imagine the Illuminata's wealth in our hands, you and I, father and son, disciples of the great Book. Imagine how much we could learn of Ruin with that kind of wealth behind us!"

"To bring Sophie home and learn the song of Àeon?" He asked hopefully.

"Indeed," Thorpe growled. "And with such knowledge we could keep our grip on the Illuminata and not slide into old age as every Knight Superior since the beginning. Death is for the poor and the weak, not the likes of you and I and Sophie. Galen," he added gently, and held out his hand. "Work with me to make the Illuminata ours."

Galen looked at his hand warily.

"No trickery this time my son, just a gentleman's agreement. A *father's* agreement. Help me destroy Leonhard and then we'll have all the time and money in the world to bring your beloved sister home."

Beloved sisters coming home, he thought. "And Vorus and her sisters?"

"A marvellous achievement," Thorpe grinned, "and one I haven't fully congratulated you for. We'll keep them compliant until they've beaten Leonhard, and then if they can't or won't divulge the secrets of Ruin we'll kill them."

Galen reached out gingerly and clasped his father's hand. "Agreed."

"Fine boy, fine boy." He gave his hand a crushing squeeze.

"And this Blackwand?"

Thorpe's smile suddenly faded. His hands slid from Galen's and he flopped back against the seat. Outside, the austere War Office building on Pall Mall slid past and Thorpe regarded it moodily. "This is unexpected," he admitted at last. "She is powerful, and something I saw in her makes me believe she has crossed between the mind of existence and the mind of oblivion."

"You mean she's died and been resurrected?" he asked fearfully.

Thorpe shrugged and looked pensive.

"Do you think she's stumbled across the power to live outside time?" Galen refused to believe that a mere witch had discovered the song of Àeon.

"Not at all," he dismissed the notion. "It's something else, it must be."

"Can she be killed?"

"You cannot kill me Mr Thorpe." He suddenly saw her again, defiant, even with his gun pointed at her. At the time he'd thought it a wild boast, then the gun had misfired. Now he wasn't sure what she was capable of. "She can die like any other witch," he reasoned, "but she's protected by demons, and ones that seem immune to bullets and battle. There are forces at work here we need to understand before we can trap her."

Galen dabbed blood from his nose. "Vorus and her sisters are also immune to magic and weapons."

"As I expected, but these demons of hers are not aligned to Ruination."

"Then what on earth could they be?"

"I don't know," Thorpe brooded. "But she's coming, and when she gets to London I want your valkyries ready. Then we'll see how strong she really is."

"Vorus is formidable, she'll kill the witch."

"Last resort." Thorpe shook his head slowly. "I'd much rather she be taken alive."

He might not have seen his father in years, but he knew him well. "Vengeance?"

"Of the most diabolical kind," he gazed dreamily out of the window. "Once she's trapped, we'll let our crazed surgeon Kollip loose on her, we'll remove her limbs . . ." He breathed against the glass and drew a stick figure on the misted surface, then slashed a finger across its arms and legs. "Then we'll compel her to watch her fellows tortured to death while they scream her name as the cause of their agonies. The whore will boil in her own guilt. And when she's seen all the atrocities we can parade before her we'll take her eyes, her ears and her tongue and leave her in a world of sterile darkness."

Galen felt an excitement that was almost carnal.

"And then," Thorpe raised an eyebrow, "we'll bless the Jik with the song of Àeon and bury her alive in an unmarked grave so that she can enjoy her punishment for all eternity." He closed his eyes and let out a long breath.

Galen was thrilled to be working with his father. He reached down and picked his cane up from the floor. "Then we'll have to devise a trap to neutralise her demons."

"You and I will be as a hammer and an anvil. Together we'll enslave her, break her demons, then set our sights on Leonhard. By the end of June the Illuminata will belong to the Book-of-Nine as will the whole Empire."

Galen smiled and wiped blood from his brow as the carriage trundled along Whitehall towards Westminster Bridge. "It's good to be home father."

"Freshen up," he gestured to the blood on his face. "Then we'll inspect these war-birds, these valkyries of yours. I'm filled with anticipation."

Galen couldn't help but smile. He adored his father and promises of them being a family, unbroken and unchanging, filled him with joy. "Have I done well?" he asked mildly.

"Very well," Thorpe beamed.

"Galen?" Elios enquired, at last back in his hands. *"Galen are you quite alright?"*

"Quite so." He closed his eyes and sat back, relishing the smell of tobacco and the gentle rocking of the carriage.

Thorpe watched his son and smiled. He really was very proud of him, and now he was glad that all those years ago he'd chosen Sophie and not Matthew. "God bless you grandfather," he whispered and rested his head against the seat contentedly.

They were still heading south and now only two days from London. Since attacking Chertfield two days ago she'd flown with little caution. Her three warriors were always close by, either as eagles or bears. But she swore she wouldn't grow careless. They sat in the woods around a small fire and Strike listened to a thunder storm rumbling far off and sighed longingly.

"It's a beautiful sound," Sunday complimented.

He nodded without turning, and looked up at the sky through the branches. "I'll be back there one day."

"Yes, when I'm dead," she smiled and continued mending her waistcoat.

"Oh I didn't mean that!" he added. "What I mean is that –"

"I know what you mean," she soothed him, "everyone needs a place to call home." Tawny raised his head sleepily and looked at her. "Even warriors of old need a home," she added, and wondered again how she might help these men find peace. She couldn't roam the world forever using them to fight the Illuminata, although that was a tempting idea. For a while she sewed in silence until at last she was done and she admired her work. "There, Blackwand is a respectable lady again."

Strike stole a glance at her. He loved her more with each passing day, but that meant he also feared for her more. Facing monsters was one thing but men were worse. They were cunning and they had a genius for cruelty. The berserks seemed like kittens in comparison. "We'll soon be in London." He couldn't disguise his melancholy.

"I've been thinking," she lay the waistcoat aside, "perhaps we can cheat a little."

"Cheating?" he grimaced.

"Nothing devious!" she promised, then looked down at her hands, "well not really anyway."

He sat silently waiting for her to explain.

"There's a little experiment I've wanted to try," she added.

"Oh?"

"Yes, all I need are paper and pencil."

"I see." He was relieved, this didn't sound like cheating, not the dangerous kind anyway.

"Well, I thought now would be a good time. We'll be in London soon."

He came and sat closer. "I'm waiting."

She pulled a pencil stub and a sheet of paper from her satchel, while Strike looked on curiously. "This might not work."

"But worth a try," he encouraged, although still no clearer.

She got to her feet and rubbed her back. Tawny lifted his head and growled softly. "It's quite all right, I'm not going far," she soothed, and without thinking she reached down and stroked his ear. She stepped through the three of them and sat in the grass. "I'll need to concentrate Strike."

"I won't say a word I promise."

She picked up the paper and pencil, inhaled deeply, sank into a state of mediation and began. "Dear champion," she whispered, so softly that Strike didn't hear her, but far away another being did and he listened closely.

The Timekeeper set aside the threads he was weaving and listened. He had no name, but someone had called him directly, and there was only one person it could be. Since Sunday escaped Thorpe Hall he'd kept his distance, not wishing to give the assassin reason to strike again. Things had been very quiet for some weeks now and he'd almost begun to hope the assassin had given up. He retrieved her thread and found it safe and sound, closely woven with three incredible threads that he couldn't break even if he wanted to.

"Dear champion." The words drifted through the cosmos and fell on him like petals. He took her thread, delighted to be with her again, and saw that she held a pencil, and understood her intentions precisely. This was an experiment in automatic writing, the skill that some claimed was connection with disembodied spirits, only now this was the real thing.

"Dear champion," the voice asked again.

"Sunday Evelyn Flowers," he acknowledged her, although she couldn't hear him.

"Soon we'll be in London," the voice continued, *"in the heart of the enemy stronghold, and I cannot lie: I'm very afraid. The journey from the black sands to here has been fraught and dangerous, but always I've sensed you close by watching over me, and I implore you now, if it be within your powers, please tell me how to prevail."*

The Timekeeper felt her anguish, but Sunday's request was mammoth. "The weave is soaked in blood," he said scornfully and with that he made his decision. She sat still and silent and with the pencil hovering over the paper waiting for her answer. He manipulated Sunday's thread and in the outside world her hand, the one holding the pencil, began to copy out his answer.

A solitary tear plopped onto the paper and Strike watched as if in a trance as her hand began to twitch and move. She worked the pencil across the paper without looking. Tawny looked up from his place by the fire, as did his brothers, aware that something profound was taking place. Strike heard thunder roll from close by. A storm was heading their way, but he couldn't take his eyes off Sunday. She sat with her eyes shut firm and her left hand feverishly worked the pencil.

Thunder roared again, closer now and the berserks growled in anticipation. Sunday groaned with the effort and at last her hand stopped and eyes snapped open. She looked down at her answer just as the heavens began to spill tears of rain. She had no understanding of it, but the message was repeated over and over until the paper was smothered. The words seemed to scream up at her, and if the

Timekeeper was forbidden to interfere he was clearly desperate to make this tiny scrap of information known.

"Sunday?" Strike ventured. Behind him the berserks were on their feet, concerned.

She looked down at the paper, which crackled as the rain started to fall harder, and tried to make sense of the repeated message. She just looked at Strike and shook her head, then back to the mess of words. There were hundreds of them but they read only one message:

Galen = Matthew Thorpe

The assassin twitched inside its cocoon. It was half transformed now and would soon emerge. The Timekeeper heard the rocks shift and rumble around him, then the cavern grew still again. He couldn't be sure but he guessed that the Patternmaker had sensed his warning message. He wanted to tell her so much more, but it was dangerous. He lay her thread down gently and listened for the assassin, but the glass remained silent. "Luck be with you Sunday," he murmured hopefully, but he knew all too well that luck was a myth and fate ruled with an iron hand.

CHAPTER TWENTY-THREE

A witch in the city

'I wandered the great city until my feet ached and I was parched.
I saw statues of warriors and leaders.
"Where are the tributes to artists, thinkers and healers?" I asked,
but my guide could not answer.'
'Travels in Lands Unknown'
Gishill Baarhan - coven-father of World-Fall coven, Powys

Less than half a mile from Goldhawk, Thorpe had the carriage stop and ordered Galen out. "It's prudent that we seldom be seen together. Once at Goldhawk have a driver take you to Hobbs Ash, I shall meet you there." The door slammed without a farewell and Galen was left slightly breathless on the pavement.

"I need a walk anyhow." He gazed at the departing carriage then lost sight of it amongst the rest of London's traffic.

"Galen, was all that really true?" Elios stung at the accusation of being a redundant pet.

He tapped the cane on the pavement as he thought. "Every word," he said at last, thinking of Sophie and nothing more.

She began to wonder. If Galen had his heart's desire and Sophie came home, what purpose would a crippled thunder-sprite have? *None,* she thought bitterly. The cane became cold in his hand, but her upset failed to touch him. He wiped the blood from his nose and strolled along in a blissful dream, one in which his beloved sister was coming home.

Thorpe arrived at Goldhawk to find a steward waiting with a telegram. The man looked terrified as he handed it over, and then stood rigid waiting for Thorpe to swipe his head from his shoulders. Thorpe scanned the message, once, twice, and then a third and final time. He screwed the paper into a ball and let it drop to the floor. "It's time to feed the war-birds," he whispered hoarsely, forgetting the man was there, then turned and left. Goldhawk's great doors boomed shut and the steward looked down at the crumpled paper wondering what to do next.

"For the third time, he didn't say!" Lyle snapped.

Doulton checked his watch again. It was twelve noon. "You mean he just marched out with Galen, and left? He never even inspected the krakens?" In his book this was something to worry about. "He wasn't impressed?"

"Stop snivelling." Lyle found his anxiety contagious. "As I've pointed out, he didn't stay long enough to gather an opinion."

The two of them loitered outside the barricade. Lyle looked at the guards, welders, and navvies and right then he'd have changed places with any one of them so long as he didn't have to answer to Victor Thorpe. "He'll be back soon, then we can initiate a proper test for him, show him what Vorus can do."

"He's a hard man to please!" someone shouted over the racket of hammers.

They both turned to see Galen pacing their way. His face looked swollen and bruised, but his smile was as broad as the Cheshire cat's.

"Where's Lord Thorpe?" Lyle politely ignored the bruises.

"He's on his way. Wants to see Vorus put through her paces."

"What happened to you?" Doulton asked.

"I came here on foot," he lied, "needed time to think, passed some chaps in a less than respectable part of town and they thought they could roll me for a few shillings."

"I hope you gave the ruffians what for," Lyle said.

"It'll not happen again, let's just say that," he winked, and rested his cane over his shoulder. "So, skates on gentlemen. Lord Thorpe wants a show, let's give him one."

For the first time Lyle felt they were pulling together as a team. "Splendid, that's the spirit. I have a fully working kraken for Vorus to match up against."

"So we can see how she'll fare against Leonhard's knights," Doulton chipped in.

"You!" Lyle beckoned one of the guards. The man came running and was red faced and breathless after just fifty yards. "Lord Thorpe will soon be here, go to the state carriage and make sure the refreshments are ready."

"Not necessary," someone boomed and they all turned.

Victor Thorpe was striding towards them, cigar clenched between his teeth and pulling the jacket off like a man ready to fight.

"Lord Thorpe!" Lyle hurried to greet him. "I was just attending the final details of the kraken test."

"Test has changed." He flung his coat over a crate and began rolling up his shirt sleeves, and Galen knew right away something was wrong, but was careful to remain detached. "This Vorus creature. She won't be pitted against a kraken."

"May I ask why sir?"

"We'll be needing all the ones we have."

"But we'll have the replacements by next week," Lyle blustered.

"Oh?" Thorpe turned on him. "Then why have I just read a telegram telling me that Harborough & Sons has been ransacked and the entire arsenal of krakens destroyed?"

Lyle's jaw drooped and Doulton swayed and staggered. Galen held on to his fixed grin, but only just.

"Sir," he croaked, "I'm sure I don't understand?"

"Let me enlighten you," Thorpe hissed, making the cigar tip glow. "Does the name 'Blackwand' mean anything to you?"

"Dear God," he blubbered. "She destroyed them?"

"All of them. And further more, the thieving harpy raided the safe and let the scum of Chertfield help themselves to our money." Thorpe threw the cigar away, not caring where it landed.

'Just pieces of paper.' Lyle knew he'd fall dead on the spot if he actually said it.

"Valkyries are hand-maidens of the war god Odin are they not Mr Galen?" Thorpe looked his way, pretending to see him at last.

He looked up, as if he hardly knew him. "Indeed my Lord."

"War-birds some call them."

"An apt name my Lord."

"Then we'll feed these birds of yours on blood." He jabbed Lyle in the chest. "Have warden Topp bring me three of those rat-hearted witches."

Doulton watched Lyle actually salute the man then spin on his heels and hurry away, while all of a sudden he felt cold and clammy. They were going to feed Vorus and her sisters.

Twenty minutes later three inmates were brought in: two men and one woman. The men were ordered to halt while the woman was directed through the barricade and into what Doulton had come to think of as the 'killing arena'. None of the captives were armed this time, yet the security was just as tight. This wasn't a test Doulton realised, they were simply 'feeding' the valkyries as a child might enjoy seeing a rat slide down a snake's throat.

The woman was first. She was a middle-aged wretch with a shorn head and a pronounced limp. Thorpe stood way back in the shadows and Galen directed the execution, or test, or experiment or whatever the hell they called it. And Vorus was first to be fed.

All three valkyries lingered at the station's far end where sunlight never reached. The witch known as 7734 was shoved forwards. At first there was only silence, then came the thunder of stomping feet and Vorus emerged from the dark. At the sight of Vorus she backed away, turned and tried to run, but a hail of gunfire stopped her. She flinched and turned all around, looking for some salvation, but her only release lay under the crushing claws of Vorus's kraken.

Galen ordered her to complete her duty, shouting that this was a witch, her enemy, and so Vorus reached down and her fingers closed around 7734 like a cage, drawing sparks from the concrete. Inside the cherub's metal skull, Vorus felt every terrified beat of the condemned's heart.

Then in one swift move the metal fist clenched. Bones crunched and 7743's life ended in a red-river.

The next subject was brought through the screen, and what torments he'd been through was anyone's guess. He must have heard the woman's screams at the end. 1090 was herded forwards like his predecessor and now it was the turn of Isis, the bull-headed valkyrie to be baptised.

By one thirty that afternoon the monsters had been initiated and the test was over. The remains were hosed, swept and scraped away leaving just a pool of tainted water. Lyle was satisfied because Thorpe was delighted and even gifted him with a cigar. He didn't even smoke, but he took it as if it were the greatest honour he'd ever received.

To his relief, Doulton was given new orders; to oversee preparations at Wellesley Hall, the tournament venue on Salisbury Plain. He spent the afternoon at Goldhawk replying to a heap of telegrams about catering, stabling, barracks and a hundred other ordinary duties, and wished he was an ordinary man and not one complicit in murder and torture.

When the sun finally set that day, Hobbs Ash had three fewer witches and although the Illuminata might have virtually no krakens, Thorpe was contented.

He went to the library at Goldhawk and climbed out onto the roof. The weather had been May's finest and the stonework and slates pulsed with heat. To start with, he made notes in his own Book-of-Nine, a tiny affair no bigger than a pocket bible he kept about him at all times. He took a small magnifying lens from his pocket and began to write in tiny letters, and once completed the little book vanished back into his coat.

He sat in his shirtsleeves, overlooking the Thames, and smoking as always. He watched the streets begin to shine as the gaslights were lit. *How mankind hates the darkness,* he thought between puffs and sighed happily. Everything was going well. Vorus was a marvel, the valkyries would destroy Leonhard, then they would answer the ninth chapter's mysteries, and if they refused he would kill them, find fresh valkyries, and torture the answers out of them. The last loose thread was Blackwand, and as the cityscape below grew darker he thought of her more. "Blackwand," he said aloud to himself.

He heard Galen approaching long before he appeared. There came the sound of someone climbing the metal ladder up from the library, and at last his son was with him sitting on the parapet, looking across a city they hoped to claim for themselves. Tellingly, Galen had left his cane under his bunk. "Have I done the Book proud?" They hadn't had chance to speak since that afternoon.

Thorpe grunted an agreement and kept his eyes on the city.

"Is Vorus not all you expected?"

He spat a fleck of tobacco into the dark and sighed. "Vorus is a marvel, I'd be so bold as to say your efforts have excelled those of any initiate in the history of the great Book."

"Yet you seem distracted?"

"I don't like loose threads, Galen."

He felt a lump in his throat at hearing his father use his esoteric name. "Blackwand you mean?"

He huffed a mirthless laugh.

"Vorus will stop her."

"Look at this city." He swept an arm across the labyrinth of streets, bridges and buildings. "Two million souls in the greatest city on Earth. Vorus will stop her, but first she has to find her."

"Vorus and her sisters can patrol the city at night, unseen."

"That means them leaving their krakens," Thorpe argued.

"They're bound to them, they must return or die."

"Hmm," he pondered. "Begin night patrols, take them hunting and have Blackwand taken alive."

"Do you think she's here already?"

"Maybe." Thorpe flicked his stub over the parapet and watched it vanish into the blackness like a broken dream. *You may burn bright Blackwand,* he thought, *but like all things, you'll fall into darkness in the end. Only Ruination lasts forever.*

As it transpired, Blackwand arrived in London three days later. It was Thursday May 26th, and she found London more daunting than battles or volcanoes.

Sunday's original coven was of course Regal-Fox, named for the generations of foxes that had occupied a Saxon king's burial chamber. It lay in the rolling hills between the North and South Downs, in the county of Surrey, and when it came to splendour nobody did it quite like the Foxes. They were known as the most majestic, traditional and haughtiest witches in Britain, and as rumour had it, the richest too.

She was not only born at Regal-Fox but she had lived her whole life there. The nearest village was Crossway, ten miles east, and while London was only a day's journey northwards, she'd never visited. Instead, like most witches, she knew the city as a hive of disease and despair and had always given it a wide berth, until now. The capital of the greatest Empire ever known proved to be everything she feared and more besides and walking through it she felt like a twig washed away in a flood.

"People live in this?" Strike was staggered.

"Some live, some barely make a living at all," she answered from the corner of her mouth. In truth, the conditions shocked her. They followed the flow of people along a road packed with vendors, ringing with the sound of cartwheels and hooves, and stinking of sewers. Strike's complaints made her feel ashamed, as if London's condition was due to her in some way. "Not all of the city's like this," she promised uncertainly.

"Just the nicest parts?"

"I've no idea where we are, this must be one of the poorer parts." They had arrived under cover of night and now she walked London's streets carrying her staff over her shoulder laden with assorted bundles, as was her disguise.

"So now we're here what are we looking for?"

"Trouble."

"You shouldn't have a problem finding that."

"Not just any trouble." She touched the way-beware hidden in her garments and glanced at the sky. Sure enough three dots circled high above. Eirik and his brothers kept constant watch over her. "We're on the look out for Illuminata trouble."

"I was afraid you'd say that."

"That means going to Goldhawk and getting inside."

He hissed as if she'd uttered a curse, and she slipped into a narrow alley roofed with dripping laundry, to speak more easily. One or two unwashed faces stared at her as they passed. *"The Sunday effect?"* he hoped.

"I'd like to think so, but I wonder how many spies are on the streets. News of Chertfield will have reached the capital by now." She retreated into the shadows and watched crowds stream past the alley's opening. "I'd rather go unnoticed."

"Difficult. You're not one of them."

"It shows?"

"Oh yes. There's hope and fire in you, I see precious little of it in them."

"Solstice queen of the wealthiest coven in Britain," she sighed and then knelt and scraped a handful of mud from the cobbles. "That it's come to this," she groaned and then smeared the dirt across her cheeks and chin.

"Isn't mud good for the complexion?"

She sniffed her fingers and wrinkled her nose in disgust. "Not this kind."

"So which way is Goldhawk?"

She leaned against the wall and sighed heavily. A tiny sprig of rose bay was struggling to grow between the cobbles. It looked frail, and it could be stamped or squashed at any moment, much the way she felt herself. "Oddly enough I don't know where Goldhawk is." She shook her head. London seemed so vast and busy that she felt she was losing her direction, and not just physically.

"We could ask?" he ventured.

"No. Goldhawk is too well known, and don't forget they keep paid informants on the streets."

"After Chertfield and Thorpe Hall I'm surprised they don't have your face posted on every street corner."

"It'd brighten the place up a bit," she smiled faintly. "But you're not far wrong. I'll wager they've already got sneaks out looking for us."

"So how do we find it then?"

"We have to get a city map. We'll buy one, or steal one if needed." She wiped the excess mud off her face, fixed her headscarf and readied herself. "Come on."

Together they rejoined the crowds. She kept her head lowered, but her eyes alert. The berserks were too high to be seen, but she knew they were watching and that meant keeping out of trouble. If she was accosted there'd be angry bears beside her in a flash, which was good for her, but less so for the folks of London, or her secret mission. She carried her staff over her shoulder and Strike got a whiff of something rancid.

"What in Oak's name was in that mud?"

"It's not me," she complained. "Look."

To their left was a row of wooden carts and their vendors were selling a range of hot foods, and crying out their wares. As they walked on past the barrow sellers, the shouts and smells changed according to the vendor.

"As spicy as any in all of London!"

"Buy my hot spiced gingerbread, smoking hot!"

"Warm your hands and fill your bellies for only half-a-penny!"

"Nice tripe! nice feet! come buy my trotters!"

"What's tripe?" Strike asked.

"Believe me," she said, "you don't want to know." She hurried past, offended by the smells and sights. Witches believed animals to be living miracles, expressions of the serpent-twins' dream, and now here they were: chopped into mouthfuls of flesh and sold for pennies on filthy street corners. Further down the road she passed a string of children selling frightened birds in tiny cages. Robins, finches and sparrows looked out at her with bewildered eyes and she wondered just who Hethra and Halla's real enemies were: the Illuminata or all mankind? Sunday pushed her way through the crowds, trying to hide her tears. The sight of the caged birds upset her deeply, but there was one bird that took a keen interest in her.

A large crow sat on a roof top with a flock of others, but he was different to them. His name was Harl and he had a duty to witches, and one in particular named Benedict. Just as Neet could see souls, a crow like Harl knew a witch when he saw one. There were at least a dozen witches in the city, maintaining contact through birds like himself, all of them seeking that one chink in the Illuminata's armour.

His fellows broke into a squabble about who had the right to sit on a particular roof tile. Normally he loved such debates, but he had a duty to report this newcomer. He cawed something to his kin then hurled himself from the rooftop and set off to find Benedict.

She found her map, buying it for tuppence from one of the street vendors. The lad was much younger than her and she didn't care for the way he examined her possessions. "New to the city good lady?" he chirped.

There was something oiled about his manner she thought, as if it were a performance.

"I'm visiting an aunt." She clutched the map and pressed a shilling into his palm.

"Where she at, this aunt of yours then? I knows the old city well I do."

"She lives towards the river," she said evasively.

"Oh yeah? What bit then?"

"To the west," she lied and hurried away.

"We need to find a quiet place to study the map," Strike advised.

"And spend the night." She snatched a last look over her shoulder and saw the newspaper lad watching her closely before the crowds swallowed him again. "I hope that was just the Sunday effect," she said quietly.

She skirted the busy pavement and hurried along the gutter, when a cart loaded with barrels thundered past missing her by inches and making her jump back, right into a man wearing a dirty apron and carrying a shoe-shine box. "Bloody watch yer self girl!" he barked, and shoved her aside.

"Sorry," she gasped and staggered on, head down, only to barge into a scrawny man eating from a paper cup.

He choked something and a mouthful of eel and pea soup spurted from his mouth. "Damn your eyes lassie!" he squawked. "Are you blind?"

"Sorry!" This was becoming her stock reply she thought.

"Half wit!" He shouted after her as he mopped soup from his coat front.

"This place is impossible!" Her eyes were everywhere, but all she saw was stone, brick and hard-looking faces. "I've never felt so far from Hethra and Halla." She felt her throat tighten.

"Sunday, people are looking." Strike's tone was hard. *"Save the tears for later."*

"Give me a moment," she asked breathlessly.

Nearby a gang of boys were kneeling on the pavement, playing cards. From their sacks and shovels she reckoned them to be street cleaners, one of the sacks was overflowing with horse manure. "See something you like darlin'?" One of them stuck out his tongue, and the rest laughed.

She moved away quickly followed by a hail of lewd comments.

"Sunday? Are you alright?" Strike was worried now.

She didn't hear him, instead she walked blindly on, past children selling shoelaces from wooden trays and many other hawkers, and one question came to the fore of her mind: What am I doing here?

"Sunday!" he persisted, but she trudged on, bewildered and hardly hearing. *What were you expecting Sunday?* she mocked herself. *Just why in Oak's name did I cross oceans and fight monsters just to arrive in this desolate city?* Despair hung over her like the chimney smoke above. With that thought she looked up and realised she couldn't see the berserks any longer. The buildings were too cramped and the sky too smoky.

"Sunday speak to me!" Strike pleaded.

She cleared her head with a shake. "I'm fine," she pretended.

Faces pressed in, most of them trying to sell her something. "Fat little sparra for yer lady. Sings like a nightingale he does, cos he swears he is one!" Another caged bird was thrust up before her. She pushed the vendor aside, hardly noticing it was just a boy, and too hurt to even look at the sparrow in the tiny cage.

"Penny for six roses!" Someone tugged at her arm.

"Best matches, strikes every time they does!"

Voices bombarded her from all sides.

Ignoring the vendors, she marched onwards. Strike detected her anger rising, even if she couldn't. She smelled yeast, thick and strong, and came upon a crowd gathered around the cart that had missed her only moments before. One of the barrels had fallen off and broken, and ale was jetting from its cracked rim, frightening the horse. The driver was struggling to retrieve the barrel and manage his horse at the same time, and not enjoying much success with either. Golden ale showered up, drawing and thrilling the crowd, most of whom jeered and made a lame joke of holding out their hats to catch the drops.

"Hold steady you mangy nag!" Tom Pollock, the driver, fumbled at the barrel, but it rolled away into the gutter again, hissing ale and sparking yet more laughter. "Hold steady you nag or on my oath it's knackerin' time for yous!" The mare shied away, and exasperated, he drew a length of wood from his belt and lashed at her shoulders. The animal jerked and pulled him to his knees. He landed in a puddle of beer, roared something in anger, scaring the horse even more and making the crowd scream with laughter, then he was back up and flailing with his stick again.

"Sunday," Strike warned, *"remember where we are."* He shared her outrage but this wasn't the time to be a spectacle.

"I know where we are," she growled, drawing her atheme knife, "this is the serpent-twins' realm and these people are vermin."

She walked through the spilled beer and right up to the man. He wore braces over a white collarless shirt and his shoes were curled with age. His broken nose was but a flattened smudge, and his front teeth were missing from fights. One or two onlookers booed, thinking she was going to stop the fun and Tom turned and saw her at last. "Put yer foot on that barrel girl! Don't let it roll away yer thick slut, grab it I said!"

Her eyes went from the mare's bloody neck to the man's reddened face. "Vermin!" she hissed.

"Sunday!" Strike screamed, but too late.

She grabbed his collar, pressed the knife to his belly, and hissed, "You lay a hand on that horse again and I'll gut you where you stand!"

Pollock had fought bare-knuckle fights in every alley in London, but something in the young woman's stare told him such things were meaningless. Her eyes were brilliant blue, and through them she had seen monsters and demons, and bested them all.

"Am I clear? Harm that animal again and I'll string your guts all the way from here to the Thames." She pressed the knife harder, drawing a bead of blood.

Suddenly a shriek went up and Pollock and the stranger were instantly forgotten. "It's a bloody vulture!" someone cried, and the crowd turned into a stampede.

"Oh no!" Strike groaned. *"It's them!"*

Sunday shoved Pollock to the ground, and spun around. "Oh no!" she echoed.

There was a huge eagle sat atop a lamp post; a huge eagle with white tail feathers, a beak like a battle axe and wings spread so wide he looked like a dragon. It was Tawny. He screamed a piercing cry that shattered the lantern and scattered the crowd.

"Sunday, run for it!" Strike yelled.

"I'll be watching you!" she warned Pollock, now lying in a puddle of beer, then she ran. She ran blind, with no idea where she was going but determined to get away from trouble before the berserks tore London down.

Eirik watched her flee and lifted into the air with a great sweep of his wings. The downdraught was strong enough to tip a nearby brazier and scatter its embers, and as he rose up he drew another chorus of screams. Horses reared in panic and people tumbled to the cobbles, convinced they'd be carried off and eaten. Then, he was just a shadow skimming over the crowds and a second later he was gone.

As people crept out from their hiding places, Tom Pollock climbed back onto his cart, but not before looking around nervously. "There there lass, juss jokin'," he patted the mare's neck soothingly.

People babbled and pointed skywards, claiming they'd seen eagles, angels, dragons or demons. A lone police constable patrolled the scene, trying to get some sense out of eyewitnesses. Meanwhile, an inconspicuous newspaper vendor, a lad of only fourteen, scribbled notes onto a scrap of paper, including time, place and date, not to mention a description of the young woman. Later, he'd take it somewhere where a gent would give him a full crown for the information, and he certainly didn't need a map to find Goldhawk Row.

CHAPTER TWENTY-FOUR

A room for the night

'One is the biggest small number.'
Traditional witch saying

The streets grew broader and busier, and the shops more splendid. They were heading into a more prosperous part of the city, but while her disguise was ideal for the poorer districts, here people went around in finer clothes and now she looked conspicuous.

"Where are we?" Strike asked.

She waited until she'd passed a crowd before daring to answer. "I see a sign ahead, hold on," she whispered, and read a street name high on the corner of a building. "George Street, does that answer your question?"

"Oh yes, everything's clear as crystal."

"Sarcasm isn't called for."

"Forget the map, we'll study it later. We just need a secure place to hide for a while."

She turned fully, almost swatting passersby with the staff. "Sorry!" she called. Men in top hats grumbled and women in bonnets turned their noses up.

"Are you determined to be seen!" The episode with the horse had left him angry at her.

"I'm looking for a secure place as you put it," she shot back.

"Rent a room then."

"Certainly not, I want to stay hidden."

"What? By starting fights and making giant eagles drop from the sky!"

More people passed by, casting more curious looks. Again, she waited for them to pass before replying. "Instead of complaining help me find an old building that looks empty." She was angry too by now.

"Very well," he sulked.

She hurried past a police station and came to Regent's Park. *Greenery!* she thought and the world made some sense again. "We'll hide in the park until sundown then find a safe place on the rooftops."

He muttered an agreement and she set off for the small park as if it was the very garden of Eden.

Long after sunset they found an old church close to the park. A candle flickered in the rectory window, but the bell tower was a wreck. She ascended, and less than a minute later she was high above the city and squeezing through the narrow windows and out of sight. The streets below glowed under the gaslights and the occasional cab still trundled past, but she felt secure for the first time since getting to London.

"Welcome home," she said dismally and looked around at the empty tower. There was an ominous looking hole in the floor, covered with planks and looking like a poorly concealed trap. A few pigeons cooed at her presence, but she rated them the friendliest locals she'd met since coming here.

Strike left the staff and enjoyed a good stretch, then landed on the window sill and looked out through the beaten shutters. "Commanding view," he observed.

"We shouldn't be disturbed up here." She began setting out the two little candles and lit them, thinking they'd add some cheer as well as light. The tower began to glow, but all at once she felt vulnerable. "One's enough I think." She pinched the other out, leaving just enough light to see by.

She was setting out her bedroll and meal of bread, fruit and water, when she heard a thump on the slates above, followed by a second and a third.

She crossed the room, careful to avoid the rotten planking, and leaned out of the window. A huge eagle peered down at her and her smile turned into a grin. Somehow everything felt alright again. "Thank you for today. I wish I knew your real name," she greeted him. "If it rains you must come inside, understand?"

Tawny just blinked back at her.

Without thinking she blew the fearsome eagle a kiss, then ducked back into the tower.

"They lived under a glacier for centuries you know, I don't think a little rain's going to bother them," Strike observed.

"That's when they were Valgard's, now it looks like they're mine." She looked down at her feet with a sigh. "I thought I'd know what to do when we got here, and yet I can't even find Goldhawk Row."

"You need some rest," he advised gently.

She looked at her thin blanket on the floor. It was the best she could hope for. "I suppose so," she agreed wearily. She ate without enjoyment, then curled up and tried to sleep.

That night, she sheltered in the tower while her three protectors sat outside and kept watch. Sleep would have been a wonderful release, but she was still awake when a distant bell chimed three and heard the eagle's warning hisses and knew somebody was approaching. She grabbed her staff and jumped to her feet.

"We're found?" Strike had slept no better and he plunged into the staff, ready for whatever.

"Found by chance? Not likely. Nobody on Earth could be 'just passing'". She skipped over the hole in the floor and up to the shutters. When she peered through the cracks she was amazed to see a figure standing on the roof, and holding what looked like a staff of his own. "That's close enough!" she warned.

"Blessings of Oak and Holly be on you sister," the figure called softly.

Outside, she heard the eagles hiss in warning again. If this was the mysterious Galen he was in for a very rude surprise. "Name yourself!" she demanded.

There was a pause. Names were power, and it was dangerous for him to speak his own when he knew so little of her. "Benedict Collins," he said at last.

She jumped as the name fell into place, along with a face; a young man with a short beard and fair hair. "Strike!" she grinned. "He was one of Kolfinnia's witches!"

"May I approach?" their visitor enquired.

"Very well, but slowly." She pushed the shutter open and watched him tiptoe deftly along the ridge. A sound caused her to look up. Tawny had spread his wings in threat. "No!" she reassured him, "this is a friend." He relaxed and looked from her to the approaching figure.

"You're friends don't seem sure of me?" Ben eyed the huge birds nervously.

"Come inside, you're in plain view."

He hurried the last few yards and crawled through the window under Eirik's keen gaze, while Sunday re-lit the candle. He dropped to the floor then turned to face his host. The candle light was dim, but he recognised her right away and his heart juddered and his mouth dried up. Harl had just told him that an unknown witch was newly come to the city. He certainly hadn't been ready for this. She looked more complete somehow, although her cheek was scarred and her clothes were black not white, but she was just as beautiful as he remembered. It was her, the bane and blessing of Kittiwake-coven. It was Sunday.

"Welcome Benedict." Now she had a better look at him she recognised him also. Benedict Collins, one of the many lost witches who rallied to Kolfinnia's call. He'd shaved his beard and his shoulder length hair was tied in a ponytail, but seeing him was like seeing the past come alive.

"I'm sorry," he gasped, noting her own astonishment. "But it's you isn't it? Miss Flowers?"

She blinked back her surprise. "You remember me?"

How could any man forget her? he wondered. At Kittiwake he admired her from afar, and like most of the men and perhaps a few women, he'd been in thrall to her. If Sunday had told them to fly to the moon and back they'd have run to fetch their staffs. "Sunday," he said, collecting himself at last.

"Benedict," she offered him a warm smile.

He held out a hand to make a formal greeting, believing her the same woman he remembered, but she surprised him when she threw her arms around him in a fierce embrace. After a stunned moment his own arms followed suit, and he was hugging her back. "We all believed you dead!" he uttered.

"That was a terrible day Benedict." She surprised herself when from nowhere she began to cry. "The world turned black that day."

"Move you dullards!" Sunday shouted, "this is an evacuation, not a meditation, to the stones!" She was so adamant that they all scrambled to obey. The rescue was rough and ready. Benedict and Betty carried Kolfinnia between them as best they could, and others took Rowan and now the chase was on to get to the stones before the knights.

"Sunday?" Benedict called back. She was walking back towards the coven.

She turned and looked quizzically at him. "Well?"

"You're going the wrong way!" He wondered if she'd taken a knock to the head. "Stones are up there," he jerked his head towards the misty hill.

"I've a last job to do." She took a final look at her dying coven-mother. "Take care of her, and take care of yourselves." Then she turned back to the fight, and left them once and for all.

Months ago he would have given anything to hold her like this, but it felt wrong when she was so upset. "It's over now," he said clumsily, but she showed no sign of wanting to let go.

"But it's not!" she cried against his shoulder. Maybe it was that day's confrontation, or the months of travel, but she said it without thinking, "Benedict, it was all my fault!"

"Nothing's your fault, you fought more bravely than any of us that day. What I'd give just to be half the witch you are." At this she sobbed harder, leaving him wondering if he'd said the wrong thing. He patted her back awkwardly, again feeling guilty because holding her felt so wonderful. "Hethra be praised, we thought you were dead." It was all he could think to say, but he'd never been more earnest.

"It's so good to see you Benedict," she breathed against his ear, and now her closeness was overwhelming.

His awkwardness got the better of him and he reluctantly untangled himself. "And you too."

"I'm sorry, I don't know what came over me." She wiped her eyes, realising that he hadn't understood her confession, and she was ashamed by how relieved she felt.

"Sorry? When Harl told me a witch was in the city I didn't know what to find, but this," he threw his hands in the air, "this is beyond all our hopes!"

She blushed. "Where are my manners? Benedict please sit."

"Only my mother called me Benedict," he joked.

"Ben," she softened, "I've nothing to offer you." She looked around the empty tower.

"You're alive and well, what better gift could there be?" His face was a picture of happiness.

She took his hand and tugged, bidding him sit down on a bundle of clothes, where she joined him. "Let me introduce you to my family. This is Lightning-Strikes-Lonesome-Ash." She offered her staff and Strike appeared and regarded Ben politely. "While the gentlemen outside are my companions."

"Gentlemen?" He arched his eyebrows.

"Their eagle form is a curse, but they're not eagles all of the time," she explained.

No, not all the time, he thought, *sometimes they're great bears aren't they Sunday, or should I say Blackwand?* He'd heard rumblings about Thorpe Hall, and Chertfield, but until now he'd believed the tales were just fantasy.

"Ben?" She saw his mind turning.

"Nothing," he dismissed the thought. "There's so much for us to talk about, I don't know where to start."

She eyed his lightning-staff meaningfully and he took the hint.

"Oh, yes!" he blustered, "this is Fire-Follows-Storm's-Wake."

At that, Wake appeared and hopped down onto the floor. "Glad you remembered me at last," he muttered and shared a bemused glance with Strike. "Just Wake will be sufficient miss."

"Blessings on you for carrying this fine witch Wake," she dipped her head in greeting then turned back to Ben, who was still staring at her.

"Alive," he shook his head in wonder.

She clasped his hand, overjoyed to have the company of another witch, and without realising she reached up and stroked his cheek. "You've had a shave," she smiled.

He coughed nervously and she tactfully withdrew. For a while, the two survivors sat clasping hands, simply taking peace in one another's company. Outside, she heard talons scratch softly against the slates and the sharp 'tick' of a hunting bat. Distant goods trains rumbled past, accompanied by the lonely sound of a steam whistle, and mice scurried through the rafters. "How is she?" Sunday asked at last, and her hands slid from his.

"She?"

"Kolfinnia."

He smiled and began his tale.

From the outset he stressed that he couldn't reveal too much. "Harl's crows know where all the hidden witches are in London, but I've no idea, in case we're caught."

She nodded, and remembered how it felt being tied to that chair at Thorpe Hall.

"And I don't even know where Kolfinnia is now," he continued.

She frowned. "You don't?"

"She moved the coven again, just after we chosen were sent out to London."

"In case you're caught," she realised.

"Harl knows where she is. If we survive this he'll guide us there." He looked down at Wake and smiled faintly. "If," he repeated.

"And Kolfinnia, she's in fine health I trust?"

"She's as stubborn and as wonderful as ever," he smiled, and she saw a different kind of adoration in his face.

Sunday let out a long sigh of relief that had been pent up since Kittiwake.

"And Rowan grows taller by the day I swear it," he added, "at least that's what I remember, I left for London months ago."

"Rowan." The name was like a key to every mystery in the world. "Can she still use her gift?" she asked delicately.

"At Kolfinnia's behest she's learning *not* to. Now she's aware of her talents she often 'looks' and before she knows it she reads others hearts and not all that she finds is pleasant."

"The poor girl," she shivered, and wondered if Rowan had seen her treachery.

"Fret not, she's tougher than she looks. And Kolfinnia's like a sister to her."

"And may I ask what you've learned since coming to London?"

"I'll tell you willingly, because I know you're true at heart."

Her face remained fixed, but her guts tumbled. *If only you knew Ben,* she thought sadly.

"But first there's a mystery that even Rowan couldn't answer."

"There is?"

"Yes!" he laughed. "Such as where in Oak's name have you been all this time?" He had to stop himself taking her hand again, knowing it would be too painful to let go.

"Ahh," she sighed, "now that's a long tale, and one I'm afraid I can't fully explain."

"Start with your friends outside." He twitched his eyebrows upwards.

She took a deep breath. "Let's just say I found myself in a distant land and in debt to a fairy. I agreed to undertake a cleansing, thinking I was banishing monsters, but they're men, cursed warriors from an age ago, and they chose to follow me."

Although amazed, he accepted her every word. "Then they chose wisely. I'd follow you anywhere."

Don't praise me Ben. You've no idea what I've been running away from, she thought.

He sensed her discomfort. "Sunday, I'm sorry, all I meant was that –"

Suddenly her hand rested gently on his, and the world seemed to still. "Ben, I long to tell you everything, but for your own safety . . ."

"I understand," he said dutifully. Her hand slipped from his and the world became grey and confusing once more.

No you don't, she lamented silently. Strike instinctively edged closer and she smoothed a hand over his feathers.

He fought the urge to reach out, or say anything else stupid. "I'm sure you've had a hard road, and I tell you what, once our task here is over, come with me and Harl, come back to Kolfinnia's coven."

Her throat tightened. The idea was wonderful but daunting. "And just what is your task here in London?" she changed the subject.

"The Illuminata," he sneered. "They're rebuilding their order. The whole British bloodline was practically wiped out, but we don't know how the balance of power will shift."

"And you can't ask Rowan because it might harm her?"

"She's still a child, and she deserves a childhood. I wouldn't make such a demand of her and neither would Kolfinnia. So it's up to folks like me to do some grubby spy work," he shrugged.

"Then Kolfinnia chose wisely," she smiled at him, and he was glad she couldn't see him blush in the dim candle light.

"I'm not sure you're right," he admitted, "so far I've learned little."

"Maybe I can be of help there."

"Oh?"

"Do you know of Thorpe Hall?"

He stroked his chin. "There have been rumours."

What kind of rumours I wonder? She bit her lip. "I was there Ben, taken captive."

He stiffened. "They better not have hurt you!"

"I'm fine," she assured him. "It was an awful day, one I don't care to remember, but I came away with my life and information I didn't have before."

"How did you escape?"

She looked upwards and he followed her gaze. The scrape of talons outside told him all.

"Oh," he said simply.

"Brace yourself Ben: the Illuminata are in disarray as you say, so much so that they've initiated a grand tournament to settle the bloodline dispute."

"That's it!" He slapped his brow. "There hasn't been one for centuries, it explains so much." He made to stand right away, but she took his arm and made him sit again.

"Wait, you haven't heard all, the tournament is to be held at Salisbury on the summer solstice."

He blinked rapidly as he processed her incredible news. "I've got to get this information out to the rest without delay. Today's May 27th. Damn it, that gives us less than four weeks."

"You're going right this moment?" She found she didn't want him to leave.

"I have to. The greatest gathering of knights in living memory. Sunday, thank the twins you came when you did!" He pulled her up to her feet and hugged her, and in his excitement he planted a kiss firmly on her cheek.

She smiled against his shoulder, then pulled back. "Thorpe told me lots more, that knights were coming from all across Europe –"

"Later," he interrupted, "dawn's coming and I daren't risk flying by day. I'll come again tonight and you can tell me the rest, but now I have to send a message. Kolfinnia has to know about this."

"But I want to help."

"Oh but you have!" he grinned, and was already at the window and opening the shutters.

"Ben!" She gripped his arm. "They're so frightened. They have some kind of magical specialist helping them, a traitor witch or such like. A name was mentioned, Galen, it might be him."

"Galen?" He suddenly thought of the man in the bowler hat. "Leave that bastard to me."

"Promise me you'll be careful."

"I'll be fine."

"Promise me!"

"I promise," he swore.

"Ben," she began, "I know you can't tell me your plans, but let me help you fight the Illuminata. I can be a torment to them."

"Aren't you already just that . . . Blackwand?"

She stepped back, wary now. "Who told you?"

"Gossip travels fast, and it wasn't hard to work out."

"And what does 'gossip' say?" She felt defensive all of a sudden.

"That an unknown witch put the fear of God into the Knights Illuminata. An estate in the north was burnt down and krakens destroyed before they were even assembled."

She folded her arms and looked away. Why, she didn't know, but she felt embarrassed.

"And chaos on City Road in Shoreditch this morning. Eagles dropping from the sky? I thought it was just nonsense." He studied her. "Sunday, is this true?"

She closed her eyes and nodded. "All true."

There was a long pause before he spoke. "I'd follow you anywhere," he said softly.

"You really wouldn't want to Ben." She remembered Thorpe Hall, and even in the candle light he saw the colour drain from her face. "That was a horrible day. I didn't command them," she looked up at the slates, "but they came to my rescue and lots of men died, and I can't help but wonder if they really deserved it."

His smile vanished. "Would those same men have given you a thought as they carried you away to torture and execution?"

Strike growled an agreement from beside her.

"I have to go," he backed up another step, "but I'll return tonight I promise."

"Make sure you come, because after tonight I'll find another hiding place."

"I'll come."

"But what if you can't, how will you find me? You're the first familiar face I've seen in an age." She tried not to sound too needy.

"Trust Harl, he'll find you for me."

She wanted him to stay and listen to her troubles and her adventures. She wanted to talk with another witch, and to her surprise she found that she wanted to feel his arms around her again. "This is it, we're going to fight again aren't we?" she said finally.

"I wish I could tell you, but –"

"I know. It's not safe." She looked long at him, committing the scene to memory in case he never came back. "Goodnight Ben," she said at last.

"Goodnight," he lifted himself over the sill, "Blackwand." He offered her a playful wink and then vanished from sight.

Above her, she heard talons scrape tiles as Tawny and his brothers watched him go, and then a flap of wings as Strike landed on her shoulder. "He's a handsome devil isn't he?"

"Mmm," she agreed distantly and touched her cheek where he'd kissed her.

"I was talking about Wake."

She gave an embarrassed little cough. "So was I."

He just smiled and let it rest at that.

Eirik looked up from his sleep, suddenly alert. His brothers slept on oblivious. Everything seemed normal, the golden-haired girl slept safely below and the doll sang its soothing song. Night creatures had been drawn to the way-beware and the roof was tiled with thousands of moths, which fluttered away as he stirred. Ben had departed some time ago and now it was dawn and everything seemed so peaceful. But it wasn't.

He raised his head and sniffed. There it was again, that strange and unpleasant odour that had awoken him. It was the whiff of bones and slurry, and of soiled sheets under a dying man. Eirik knew nothing of Ruination, but he knew plenty of death. He turned slowly, scanning the city, scrutinizing everything with raptor's eyes. A flock of pigeons scattered two miles distant. Something had frightened them from their roost. He strained to see better, but whatever had scared them remained out of sight, hidden in London's claustrophobic alleys and forgotten corners. He sat stony, with his stare locked on the distant rooftops, just now revealing themselves as the night withdrew. He stared until fuzzy dots swam before his eyes and at last he saw something move. It looked like a black comet. He caught the merest flicker of it streaking across the roofs, and then it was gone. He sat that way for a further fifteen minutes, waiting, hardly breathing, senses alert and the tingle of battle in his heart, but whatever he'd seen had departed. To be sure he took another sniff. That musty odour, that smell of everything that life wasn't, had gone.

He settled down again, but resisted sleep. His dreams had once been haunted by battle, that was until the golden girl had come and released them. Now though he was afraid to sleep for different reasons. Something in the city was hunting them, or more specifically hunting the girl, and he knew one thing for certain: it was unlike any enemy he'd ever faced. He curled his talons anxiously, scoring grooves in the tiles, and for the first time in an age he thanked Valgard for his curse. There was fighting ahead and he knew it would take a monster to kill a monster.

Chapter Twenty-five

Visitors to the tower

'The sun came out, and though my problems remained, they looked less.'
Traditional witch saying

It was already light when Sunday awoke and sure enough the berserks were gone. She wasn't alarmed though, knowing they'd be circling high above, ever watchful. "We should have left before daybreak," she cursed herself.

"We'll be seen if we fly," Strike checked the view, "the streets are already coming awake."

She packed quickly and climbed down a crooked ladder that dropped from the tower to the floor below where she found a stone stair leading down. The passage was narrow and all along it she feared her footsteps would give her away, but the tower appeared abandoned just as she suspected. If she needed any further proof, the doorway at the bottom was nailed shut and so she climbed out through one of the broken windows. Thankfully her exit was masked by dense laurel bushes, and only minutes after waking she was wandering London's streets once more.

After yesterday's excitement she was determined to lay low. As she walked she mimicked overheard snippets of conversation. She observed the way people asked for goods and the local names for all manner of things. She walked along soaking up London and trying it on for size. She felt less adrift than yesterday and a large part of that was thanks to Ben.

She was determined to be there when he came again tonight, and vowed to stay out of trouble for his sake. There were plenty of things she wanted to know and plenty she had to tell him, but mostly she just wanted to sit with a friendly face and be a witch again.

Excerpt from the Book-of-Nine

The Book-of-Nine is on the verge of recovering Sophie and of taking command of the Illuminata. I have schooled the valkyries in the arts of killing and they have shown a lust to learn. One last obstacle remains however. There has appeared a lone witch by the name of Blackwand, who has pledged to disrupt the tournament. For three nights now I have searched the city with Vorus, and her sisters, but without success. It is imperative we find her soon. My father has devised an exquisitely cruel punishment. When at last caught, her torments will be legendary. However, she possesses three demons that have so far proved unstoppable. But I shall instruct Vorus to summon more valkyries from Smithfield, and when they finally corner Blackwand's demons we shall see just who is the stronger.

There came a loud knock at the door. Galen snapped the Book closed. "Who's there?"

"Message from Mr Lyle sir," a voice came, "he says you're to go to his office this instant."

"I'm on my way." He leapt from the bunk. Perhaps this was it, he thought. Perhaps they finally had a fix on the elusive Blackwand.

"A positive sighting at last!" Lyle waved a paper in the air.

Galen stormed across the room and snatched it from him. "Where?"

"City Road, Shoreditch, on Thursday."

"That was yesterday," he accused, "why weren't we informed sooner?"

"Our street-lads have sharp eyes but little sense of urgency. He was selling newspapers when he met with a young woman by Blackwand's description."

"Could be anyone," he grumbled, thinking it was another false alarm. "This is the eighth sighting in the last three days."

"Oh really?" Lyle said sarcastically. "Then tell me why a very fierce bird appeared when she was in a spot of bother."

"Bother?"

"Cart driver tending his horse. Seems our Blackwand thought he was being a tad rough and confronted him, made quite a spectacle of herself."

"Lord Thorpe was right," he gloated, "her compassion *will* undo her."

"Then when things looked to be turning ugly," Lyle continued, "a bloody huge eagle arrives from nowhere and the crowd panics, Blackwand flees in the commotion."

"So it is her."

"Our lad followed her, but lost her around Pentonville. Last known time, location and description are included in the note. You know your orders Galen, best be about it."

"Time to let the war-birds out of their cages." He tapped his cane to his head and set off.

"Don't come back empty handed this time!" Lyle shouted after him.

He ignored him and once in the corridor he broke into a run. By tonight they'd have Blackwand behind bars and then the real fun would begin.

By seven that night, and after a long but thankfully uneventful day, Sunday was back in the tower and whether Ben came or not it would be her last night. She was apprehensive about lingering too long, but she was even more worried about moving on prematurely and missing him.

Strike sat in the rafters and watched as she tried to make the little room more welcoming. She drew a salt circle around the edge, garnished the floor with cherry blossoms collected in the park, and sprinkled powdered sulphur in the corners for protection. The candle was lit and placed where it couldn't be seen from the window, and she bundled her clothes and blankets into two neat piles. One for each of them to sit on. "He's getting the royal welcome isn't he?"

She jumped, forgetting he was watching, and looked down at her handiwork. "Well, yes, I just wanted to make the place less Spartan."

He said nothing, but watched her prepare the little food she had. There was a selection of fresh fruit, vegetables, bread and baked potatoes, and a currant tart. At last when all was ready she sat with a deep breath and awaited her guest.

The evening dragged on and each sound outside made her jump expectantly. Hours passed and far away she heard a clock ring ten and she told herself not to worry, he'd come, he was fine. She sat in silence, aware of Strike dozing above, listening to her own breathing and the creaking timbers, trying to meditate as she was taught, anything to keep her mind still. Inevitably the distant bells struck eleven and still there was no sign of him. The candle burned away to nothing and she lit the spare. It was her last, but she had a superstitious dread about letting the light die. By midnight she was certain he'd been caught, and by one o'clock in the morning she was sick with worry and a whisker away from packing up her things and setting off out to 'rescue' him.

She stood, unable to bear it any longer and that's when she heard talons grate on the roof. She took a sharp breath and ran to the shutters and peered out. Ben had come at last. Without waiting she flung them open and as soon as he dropped into the room they immediately embraced, and in a manner only those who risk capture and death can understand.

At last they parted and she sat down, worn ragged by waiting but happier than she been in a very long time. Ben took his place beside her and before anything else they said protection spells for Hethra and Halla, then they ate and finally they shared their news.

"I thought you weren't coming," she said softly. "I feared the worst."

"I couldn't leave my hideaway without being seen, I had to wait ages for a boat to leave."

"Boat?" She wanted to ask him where he spent his nights.

"Sorry," he smiled, "it's –"

"Not safe to tell. I know." She looked down at her lap, sad that they had to keep secrets from each other.

He took a breath and sat straighter. "So shall I go first or will you?"

Strike drifted down from the rafters to her side. "Tell him about the black sands and how we almost got eaten, and how I saved the day."

Wake also appeared now and sat beside Ben.

"Very well," Sunday agreed, "we'll begin on the black sands, but remember I can't tell you everything because –"

"It's not safe," he finished.

It's not honourable, she thought sadly. "Not safe," she agreed, wishing that was all.

She told her story. Of waking in a strange land with no idea how she got there, of Neet rescuing them and how they found the enchanted way-beware and used it to free the berserks. She smiled as she recalled their journey across the sea, travelling from island to island like stepping stones, which all seemed like an innocent adventure now. Then came Thorpe Hall and her mood grew serious. She glossed over Strike's capture and praised the berserks, knowing in a roundabout way that they were listening above.

"And what did he tell you, this Lord Thorpe?" He had listened with amazement and admiration, but at this part anger surfaced.

"Lord? How did you know he was a Lord?"

"Who doesn't know him in London. He's a chief at the Bank of England and his name appears regularly in the papers. He loves the limelight." He drummed his finger on his wand-sheath as he thought.

"Bank of England?" she repeated.

"Aye, but never mind that now, what did he tell you?"

"The tournament you already know about, but he also mentioned something called a 'valkyrie'."

"Mythical creature I think," he frowned, picturing that awful Ruinous beast that had attacked him.

"And what about this Galen? I learned that his real name might be Matthew Thorpe, do you think that's possible, that the two are brothers or father and son?"

"Quite possible," he agreed.

"From what you said last night I gather that you know of him – this Galen?"

"Now I think it's my turn to tell you what I know." He shuffled closer to speak confidentially. "If this Galen is the man I'm thinking of, then you're half right about what you said, he's some traitor witch." He didn't notice her discomfort at the wording. "But I don't think he's a witch at all. I think he's some black magic scholar advising the Illuminata."

"Advising them about what?"

"Until I saw you last night all we had were random incidents. At first they seemed unrelated, but after what you told me they fell into place and together they paint a very dark picture." He shuffled closer still, until they were touching, and scanned the tower, and she had the impression that he was afraid of being overheard. "When I came to London I had a contact in the city, a woman with sympathies for witches, although she wasn't a witch herself. She's what we call a 'smoke', a go-between."

"I know the kind of person you mean. She sounds nice, what's her name?"

He looked grim. "Her name was Charlotte Anne Pilling, or Lottie Pilling as I knew her."

"That's the past tense, Ben," she noted ominously.

"Aye," he made ready. "She was murdered."

"Oh, Ben! I'm sorry," she reeled, and before she knew it her hand was on his.

He squeezed gently and continued. "Lottie was murdered, her body dumped at Smithfield. Do you know what that place is?"

She shook her head innocently.

"It'll come clear soon enough," he regretted. "I've spent a lot of time there, and the rumours amongst the traders and locals was that her death was ritualistic. Tellingly I learned that the investigation was given to Goldhawk."

"Goldhawk!" She squeezed his hand tighter.

"That's not all. On at least three occasions I've followed a man from Goldhawk to Smithfield, both before and after the murder, and I'm convinced from what you've told me that this is the mysterious Galen."

"I'm starting to see the picture."

"No, not yet you don't. A few nights ago I was attacked by a night-creature while following this man." His eyes flitted around the room and he leaned closer. "Sunday, it was a creature of Ruin."

"What kind?"

"Unknown. I couldn't see it properly, but it had abilities I'd never heard of before." At this he offered Wake a sympathetic look.

"Such as?"

It was Wake that answered, "I was Ruined miss." Everyone turned to the thunder-sprite, who sat staring at the flickering candle unable to face them. Sprites didn't accept defeat easily.

"Ruined?" she asked gently.

"The magic was drawn from the very air and with it went my hope," he confessed, ". . . and my fire."

Only Strike could fully appreciate what this meant, and he growled faintly.

"We came away with our lives," Ben continued, "but when you put the two together it looks very bad. First a ritual murder, then, a mysterious Ruinous creature at large."

For a moment she couldn't grasp his meaning, or perhaps she didn't want to. "Oh Ben, no!" She withdrew her hand in shock.

"Yes – I think they've broken their own rules about tampering with Ruination."

"No, even *they* wouldn't make such a transgression!"

"Really? When you told me about the tournament I finally understood. The Illuminata are desperate. Winner takes all in June – and they don't have any knights. So, desperate men take desperate action."

"And Smithfield, why's that important?"

His shoulders drooped, and he sighed, "Lottie was a brave and decent woman Sunday." He remembered how she carried on despite the threats and ridicule. Lottie Pilling had dared to show kindness and for that she'd been singled out and murdered. He pulled his knees up to his chest and looked away to conceal his upset.

"Benny!" She eased an arm around his shoulders.

"I *hate* this city," he whispered forcefully, still looking away.

"Benny, please."

"Lottie took what kindness she could to the animals at Smithfield."

She craned over to see him better. "Animals?"

Slowly he composed himself and glanced her way. His eyes were red and he looked both furious and heartbroken at once. "That's the last piece of the puzzle. They needed a place thick with death and fear. And what place better than that?"

"What is it?"

"It's where they've taken them for slaughter for centuries, Sunday."

At last she understood, and her heart felt awash with ice.

"And what do Ruinous creatures thrive on?" he prompted, letting her complete the puzzle.

"Blood and death," she forced herself to answer.

"Aye." He scrubbed at his face, and slid free of her embrace. "Forgive me. Whatever this Galen's plotting is my business, not yours," he warned.

"But I told you, I want to help."

"And you can. In a day or two I expect to hear back from Kolfinnia, and I won't lie. I expect the orders to be hard."

"You think she'll order you to attack the tournament?"

He nodded firmly. "Almost certainly."

"And will you?"

"Without hesitation, she brought us through Kittiwake. Every witch in Britain owes her their allegiance."

"They do," she agreed humbly.

He shifted, looking bashful. "I've a confession," he revealed at last.

"You have?"

"Before the knights came, well, for a while I thought we should make a run for it." He shook his head, ashamed. "I'm not proud of that."

"We've all done thing we're not proud of," she sympathised. *What would you think of my own dark secret?*

"Thank you," he offered her a tired smile.

Eirik and his brothers looked out across the city while Sunday and Ben sat below. He had warned Harger and Karl of what he saw that morning and now they waited for their hunters to come to them. It was only a matter of time.

Sonneday, he thought. He gathered now that her name was Sonneday or such like. *If she's killed, what will become of us?* he pondered. Without her would they revert to Valgard's slaves again? Cold logic told him her death wouldn't mean the return of Valgard's darkness, but there was little that was cold or logical about Eirik. He fought with his heart, and his heart told him that Sonneday was as important as the little doll. He sighed heavily, tired of thinking, and returned to his vigil.

"Ben," she continued, "remember what I said yesterday? About letting me help?"

He chewed his lip. "Sunday, I've thought about this a lot. I even mentioned it in my report to Kolfinnia."

Instantly, she sat back.

"No!" he promised. "Nobody knows who Blackwand is. That part I left out."

"Thank you," she relaxed again.

"But if this goes as I think it might, then every witch on these shores will be busy preparing for battle, and perhaps even covens in Europe. Come the solstice, witches will drop from the sky like rain, but the challenge is huge and time's short."

"Then let me help! Ben, I can —"

"No," he stopped her, "hear me out, please." He gazed intently at her, and she read an unspoken farewell in his eyes. "If the order comes to attack the tournament, then all of us will have to withdraw to make ready, including me."

A coldness rolled over her.

"And that's where you and your special helpers come in." He tried to smile, but without success. "While the covens ready, it's imperative the Illuminata don't guess our plans, and to that end," he paused, considering, "to that end it would be an advantage to have a distraction, to keep their attention fixed on London."

She nodded slowly, understanding what he was asking of her. "Willingly."

"Sunday," he struggled, "this is a very dangerous duty, but already Blackwand is their most hated enemy."

"You know me, I love being the centre of attention," she smiled sweetly, and his heart fluttered despite everything.

"Nothing too serious though, don't think about confronting them, just let them know you're here every once in a while . . . it's not as if you have to rescue prisoners from Hobbs Ash." His smile dropped when he saw the look on her face. "Sunday?"

She regarded Strike and he saw something pass between them.

"Sunday," he stirred, "don't even think about it!"

She shrugged absently. "I can't lie Ben, it was the hope of releasing our captives that brought me to London in the first place."

"Sunday, Hobbs Ash is a fortress, going there will result in death, namely yours!"

"You're forgetting my companions."

"And you're forgetting what you told me about Thorpe Hall, that many men died," he countered.

"Be a distraction you said, and what better distraction than one actually sets free our brothers and sisters?"

"Distraction yes, disaster no. Sunday it's madness to try it alone!"

"Ben, I don't need your leave to serve the serpent-twins in any way I see fit," she stated coldly.

Strike saw the worrying ghost of his old Sunday. He thought Ben made a good point, but Ben didn't understand what drove her on, and the worst part was that she couldn't tell him. Now was just the right time for a little thunder-sprite common sense he thought. "If they want to capture Blackwand, what better bait than her own compassion?" All eyes turned his way. "They would be waiting for us Sunday, and if the Illuminata are desperate enough to break their own rules, they might well possess a Ruinous creature that can even break the berserks." He looked up at his witch, worried for her. "Ben is right. For now our friends must wait."

Last autumn she gave her life to save Kolfinnia. The guilt should have died that day, yet here she was still trying to make amends, and now her goal was denied the wound felt raw all over again. Even death couldn't kill it. "Oh Ben," she cupped her hands to her face.

He pulled her close, and now it was his turn to comfort her. For a while he listened to her soft crying and couldn't think of anything that might help, but then he remembered something. "Farona's quite the hero you know."

She sniffed, and looked up. "Farona?"

"Aye," he smiled, "a hero, and quite popular with the lasses."

She laughed softly and it was like a cloud passing. "You'd better stop, you'll make me jealous."

"I swear it. After all, he's the only witch on Earth to have laid eyes upon *them*." The last word was spoken with great reverence. "Can you imagine how that must feel, to see Hethra and Halla with your own eyes?"

"Farona," she breathed his name, remembering the red-haired youth. "I used to make him clean and press my dresses." She burst out laughing at the irony of it and he joined in, not understanding, but glad to hear her. Something stirred in her. She wanted a family and a coven to call her own. "Tell me more."

"It's just day-to-day things really."

"I don't care just tell me."

"Well, erm, Kolfinnia planted seeds from those trees that sacrificed themselves at Kittiwake so we could have extra lightning-staffs, remember? Flora tends her gardens – and Farona's never far from her, and Clovis keeps everyone fighting fit."

"Clovis? But I thought he was sworn to leave?" Each name made her feel restless.

"He hasn't gone yet, that's for sure."

"Tell me more."

"I can't tell you too much, it's –"

"Not safe," she finished, but he'd said enough. She knew what she wanted again: a home. "Ben, I'll make it my purpose to be a thorn in the Illuminata's side."

"No suicidal rescue attempts?"

"I promise."

"On the serpent-twins themselves?"

"On Oak and Holly themselves," she promised again.

"I'm sorry to hear you say that."

"Why?"

"Because now our business is concluded, and it's time for me to leave."

Suddenly she felt a weight in her chest. "But you'll find us again, Strike and I?"

He hesitated. "If circumstance allows, yes, on my oath."

"And if all goes well, I'll make my way to the tournament, and see you there?"

"Aye, but if Harl doesn't come and find you before the solstice then assume the worst, that we've been found out. If that happens, flee London. Just go and never look back. Get as far away as you can. Start your own coven and enjoy the years you've been blessed with."

"I won't hear of such things, you speak like we've already lost!"

He rubbed at his mane of fair hair. "I'm sorry, there's just so much at stake. I have to say what's in my heart while I can." Without another word he gathered his things and stood. She climbed to her feet without taking her eyes off him, and now each second was more precious than the last.

"Blessings of Oak be on you Ben," she wished him, but struggled to tame her voice.

"And blessings of Holly remain with you all your days, Blackwand."
Gently, he folded his arms around her and it was in the safety of his embrace
that she finally realised her anxiety about him coming tonight wasn't entirely
to do with secrecy, nor was her anticipation all to do with business. Now it
was her turn to feel awkward and she reluctantly disengaged.

"You'd better be off Ben, daylight won't be far away," she sniffed, "and I
reckon its a long way back to the docks."

"You've guessed my hiding place!"

She smiled weakly, "No, you just smell of fish." She patted his shoulder,
finding it an agony trying to be light-heart when her heart was sinking like
a stone.

He laughed softly, almost said something, then checked himself and
turned for the window. She looked down at the battered floorboards and
the remains of their meal, unable to watch in case the sight of him slipping
away was the last she ever saw of him. She heard him clamber onto the
ledge, followed by the creak of slates outside. Then he was gone and
Blackwand was alone in London.

Her heart was in turmoil and so she didn't expect to sleep, but only
minutes after lying down Sunday was dreaming.

Eirik's senses were acute and he could hear her breathing softly. Ben
had left an hour ago and now the sun was not far below the horizon,
which meant they'd soon have to move. He surveyed the city with restless
eyes taking in the park, the railway yard, the canal and the endless forest
of chimneys. *This stillness is not to be trusted,* he thought from nowhere.
Something tickled the back of his nose, a strange and unpleasant smell
like rotten roses. He recognised it immediately as danger, but immediately
wasn't fast enough and the next thing he knew was an explosion of
movement to his left.

Three creatures streaked directly towards them. They were ragged and
horrible, they left trails of living darkness and their screams almost burst
his ears. The valkyries had found them.

Galen heard the screams and looked up. He had been hunting
Blackwand all night and lost track of Vorus and her sisters an hour ago.

He was accompanied by two thuggish minders and a cab for transport, but he seemed to have lost track of them too, and now it was just himself.

He sprinted along Albany Street from the direction of Camden Town, towards the sound of screaming, with his heart pounding and his feet aching. His heart pounded even harder when he caught sight of movement. There was a church overlooking Regent's Park, and on its steep roof he got his first look at one of Blackwand's demons. He stumbled to halt and watched three inky black shadows speed towards what he first took to be statutes of eagles.

"Galen it's one of her demons!" Elios screamed.

He watched with helpless awe as the first valkyrie lunged. If he hadn't seen it with his own eyes he'd have dismissed it as fantasy, but in response, one of the eagles transformed into a monstrous bear and pounced right into the heart of the valkyrie pack. There came another scream and a roar of pain and the battle began.

Eirik saw their enemies speeding towards them and he thrust himself into the air with such force that his talons shattered the stone plinth. Rubble bounced down the roof and sent slates flying like guillotine blades, and a split second later he changed. Feathers turned to fur, talons turned to claws and his bulk increased many fold. And so it was a huge and furious bear, not an eagle, that hammered into the first of the valkyries.

Vorus saw the transformation. She watched in disbelief as the demon engulfed her sister, Arctura, and the two plunged off the roof and hurtled to the street below. But now she had troubles of her own. Enormous birds armed with ripping claws and beaks swooped down on them. She hissed in fury and at her side her sister Isis unleashed a piercing scream. Galen had warned them repeatedly that Blackwand's demons were terrible, but Vorus wasn't afraid. She had the gift of Ruination and Ruin killed all things in the end, even demons like these.

Eirik had never seen a creature like this before. He seized it in a crushing embrace and threw himself from the roof determined to drag the thing to its death, but it writhed in his arms like a wild-cat and tore at him with clawed hands. It was bone-thin, but immensely strong, and clothed in skins and rags through which he glimpsed pale flesh afflicted with sores and boils. Its face was elongated but hooded and it possessed two mouths set side by side. Lips peeled back on both to reveal chisel teeth and she lunged at him repeatedly, while her razor fingers flailed at his muzzle and his neck. He saw the cobbled street racing closer and twisted in mid-air thinking to land on the creature and crush it. The impact came with a mighty jolt and a rumble of masonry, but they kept on falling.

The road was old and the sewers lay only feet below. They easily crashed through and into a world of water and foulness, perfect for a Ruinous creature. Both opponents maintained their deadly grip and landed in a wave of sewage, while rubble, bricks, and even rats, rained down around them. Eirik was doused in a stinking soup of London's filth. The stench burned like acid in his throat and all the while the valkyrie slashed at him.

Arctura lifted her long hind legs and raked his unprotected belly, slicing through his thick hide. The demon's howl echoed around the tunnel and the red-river flowed, but still the bear wouldn't relinquish its hold. Energised by blood and decay she brought her legs up and shoved with one great heave, breaking the demon's grip and hurling it across the tunnel. Eirik slammed into the wall and bricks showered down on him, while Arctura immediately plunged into effluent, soaking up the corruption, and swam right towards her adversary.

Eirik was smacked against the tunnel, punching a crater in the rotten bricks. Blood soaked his lower legs from his wounded gut, but he knew the gift of Valgard would seal those injuries. He roared and pulled himself free, with the urge to kill burning in him like a fever, but the creature was gone and there was nothing to fight. He bellowed in anger and took a blind swipe at the air in frustration.

The river of sludge stilled again and he dropped onto all fours with a splash. A gentle drizzle of dirt and stones continued to rain down, and here and there he sensed scurrying rats, but otherwise the tunnel was empty. He sniffed the air, but the overwhelming stink masked his enemy. He stood motionless and listened to the sound of flowing water and the blood pouring from his gut. *Valgard, be with me now,* he thought darkly.

Suddenly the effluent heaved and Arctura exploded upwards.

Empowered by decay and crazed by the scent of blood she lunged at him from below, catching him right between his front legs and driving for his throat. The impact hurled him backwards. He crashed against the tunnel once more and she sank both sets of teeth into the fur and flesh around his neck and pulled with all her might. The bear roared again, but this time she heard nothing but pain in its call. Spurred on, she shook her head violently, intending to rip its throat open while she raked at his belly, further opening the wound. He snarled and struggled, but the Ruin in her veins seeped into his body like a poison and began to smother that greatest of all weapons: the will.

Eirik was blind with fury. Never had a creature wounded him like this, and for a moment he began to think perhaps Valgard had abandoned them. With that, came a sudden feeling of despair so strong that the strength melted from his limbs. He flopped back against the tunnel with the creature still tearing at his exposed neck, cackling and screaming in victory, but he didn't care and the will to fight flowed away like spilled wine. He didn't care if he was beaten. He didn't care about his brothers. All he wished was to sink into the sludge and rot away to bones and gristle. *Let the creature win,* he thought in defeat. *Life and death, victory and defeat, there is no difference in the end.* That thought was followed an instant later by another. *If the creatures kill us, Sonneday will die.*

Arctura felt his blood flood her throat, overflow, and drench her body. She panted in pleasure, and thrust his head back so she could drink more deeply. The bear's huge arms hung impotent at its side and she was free at last to finish him. She pushed her head into his wounded throat and drank in huge, greedy gulps.

The monster was drinking his life away, but he didn't care. *Sonneday,* he thought calmly. Sonneday had come and given him a second chance, but now these terrible creatures would kill her. "Sonneday," he growled softly.

Arctura barely heard him: she was drunk with blood and pushed deeper, eager for every drop.

"Sonneday!" he growled, louder this time. He had fought Valgard's causes for centuries, but he understood there was a greater cause; redemption, and that thought cut through the despair like a sword through flesh. "Sonneday!" he roared finally, and the tunnel resounded to his cry.

The hopelessness melted away and new strength burst through him. He awoke from his malaise and saw the disgusting thing clinging to his chest, feeding from him.

Arctura sensed her peril, but too late. He lifted his arm and brought it down with immense force. His claws ripped through her shoulder and the joint exploded with a loud crack. Her withered arm was torn away and splashed into the sewage with its clawed fingers still pumping wildly. Suddenly the pressure around his throat vanished and she fell back with a shriek. *"Vorus my sister, please help!"* She landed next to her severed arm with a splash and watched in horror, as the demon roared and then fell on her like a storm.

At last it was Eirik's turn and he threw himself forwards with all his weight. His own huge jaws clamped around her scrawny neck and he found it a pleasing fit. He bit hard, and she screamed.

"Vorus my sister!"

The waters churned as he thrashed her from side to side, shaking her body to bits. She flailed helplessly with her remaining arm, but he was too powerful and in one snap his teeth finally met, severing the neck completely and her scream ended with a gurgling splutter.

"Sisterrrrrr! Pleeeease!"

Her head lolled back, stretching the remaining ligaments like melted cheese, and then it slowly sank into the sewage with a dry gasp. The body twitched and finally stilled. Eirik spat the wretched thing from his mouth, disgusted by the taste. Blood soaked his fur, but already his wounds were sealing themselves. He looked up through the shattered hole in the roof and saw the dawn sky. *Sonneday!* he thought anxiously, and in one huge bound he leapt through it and up towards the daylight.

Vorus and Isis were locked in a battle of their own, so had little time to worry about their sister. Unlike their brother, Harger and Karl fought as eagles and so the battle took to the sky above the church.

Harger found that fighting the creatures was like fighting smoke. They swirled around him and each time he went to snatch at one with his talons it flowed out of reach, before turning and swiping at him.

Vorus lashed at the eagle, intending to bat it to the ground where she could kill it, but its talons were lethal and the pressure wave from its wings was like a gale. She hissed in frustration and tried again, charging head-long at it, but she was forced to dodge at the last moment to avoid its beak, and so careered blindly into the church roof. She used her claws like anchors, scoring lines in the slates and making a terrible screaming noise. As she skidded to a stop she heard a different kind of scream and knew her enemy was swooping down for the kill, and at the last moment she propelled herself forwards, rippling like an eel, and a split-second later she heard a satisfyingly heavy impact as her enemy thundered into the roof.

Harger saw the creature hit the roof and skid across the slates out of control, and he pulled his wings back and stooped into a dive, ready to tear it to shreds. The air whistled past at tremendous speed, but when he was just inches from taking its life the creature tore away and the next thing he knew he crashed clean through the roof and hurtled down into the church followed by a hail of debris.

Vorus circled wide, flowing through the air like a shadow, and came back around to find her opponent had crashed. Perhaps she'd be lucky and Blackwand's demon would break its neck she thought, but for now she could join Isis and together they could finish the last eagle. She screamed in victory and tore through the air towards the last of Blackwand's protectors.

Karl had one of the rotten thing in his sights, but just as he made to rush it he felt something land on his back and grip him with sharp claws. He screamed and rolled in mid air trying to throw this new attacker off. Meanwhile, Isis jumped at her chance. She had been sorely pressed until her sister had come to her aid, but now the odds were much more to her liking and she struck the giant eagle in the chest and plunged her claws through the feathers and into his flesh. Karl screamed again, but both attackers were out of reach of his claws, and the thing clinging to his chest was tucked under his bill. He swiped his head side to side, trying to gouge her, but she was cunning and clung tight, keeping her head low. Then, just like Eirik, he felt an overwhelming sense of futility and his struggles became weaker and weaker.

The valkyries dragged him down to the roof where they could tear him apart. The roof rocked again as the combatants crashed into it, and the trio slid down the slates but stopped where a stout buttress projected above the roof-line like a pointing finger. Karl was pinned and now the sisters set to work. Isis delved her fingers into his chest sensing for a beating heart, the great source of the red-river, while Vorus clutched his skull between her hands and twisted. Karl screamed and snapped his beak, but hurt nothing but air.

"Silence demon!" she hissed, and twisted harder. "Galen warned us of your coming and we made ready. Oh yesss!" She forced his head back, trying to snap his neck, making him scream again.

"When you are dead demon, we shall take Blackwand," Isis gloated, as her fingers continued to probe for his beating heart.

Blackwand, Karl thought faintly. *Blackwand, the girl who brought us out of Valgard's darkness.* He didn't even feel them tearing at him now, he only felt that endless sense of despair. *Blackwand.* The world began to grow dim. *Blackwan . . .*

"BLACKWAND!" someone screamed.

At first he thought it was just another of his confused thoughts, then he saw a figure tearing towards them. A figure in black, flying on a staff.

"BLACKWAND!" Sunday screamed as she charged. She saw the last of the berserks lying against the roof, overwhelmed by two terrible shadows. What they were she couldn't see clearly, but blood and feathers ran into the gutter in a gristly waterfall. Suddenly everything Ben had told her about that strange Ruinous creature came back to her.

"What if it's immune to magic!" Strike warned.

There was no time to reply. She swept past the creatures, lashed out with her wand, and hoped. The rising sun was now just setting the horizon aglow, and she borrowed its strength. "Burn for me, your solstice queen!" she commanded.

Vorus had learned to negate magic, but Isis was immature. Pain ripped through her left eye. It was like seeing the sun, naked and whole in a single instant and she let out a terrifying wail. She slid away from Karl and rolled down the roof and came to a stop at the gutter. The pain circled her head like a crown of nails and it was all she could do to stop herself from falling.

"Sister!" Vorus screamed. She threw the battered eagle aside and took to the air with a howl. Sunday at last had a good look at one of Galen's valkyries.

It was clothed in diseased skins, but she recognised it as distinctly female.

"It's coming!" Strike yelled.

"Not for long!" She dropped neatly onto the roof's gable and held her staff ready. "Come on you stinking hag!" she screamed.

Vorus understood that Blackwand possessed a thunder-sprite's poisonous power. Last time she had endured such an attack her kraken had protect her, but not so now. Torn by uncertainty, she veered away at the last moment with a scream of frustration.

Sunday roared and swung her staff, but the creature went wide and she reached too far, staggered, slipped and fell. A second later she hit the roof, the wind was drummed from her chest and the staff knocked from her grip, and in the next instant she was sliding down the steep incline. "Strike!" she screamed. The world was a blur of sky and slate, and she saw her staff bump down the roof and lodge itself in the gutter. She came next, but she wasn't so lucky and flew off the roof edge.

How she did it she'd never know. Her fingers caught the gutter and gripped fast. The gutter groaned in protest and sagged under her weight, leaving her dangling, with her staff a tantalizing distance away lodged against the buttress. "Strike!" she screamed.

In an instant he exploded from the staff and raced along the gutter towards her. "Hold on! If it comes again I'll see it off!"

She tried to haul herself up, and she might have managed but for Vorus. The creature was crawling along the edge of the roof where the lead flashing was wide and flat. It was coming right towards her, taking its time and evaluating the odds. "Blackwand," it oozed and the word dissolved into childish laughter. "Mighty Blackwand, girl who so terrifies the world of men."

Strike ran a few paces towards it, stopped and flared his wings defiantly.

"Strike no!" Sunday cried.

"This is my witch, you rot-hearted bitch!" he bellowed, "she's mine and you'll not harm her!" He looked puny before Vorus, who clothed herself in dread, and already doubt and terror began to gnaw at his heart.

"Little sprite," she purred, "brave little sprite that at least can fly, not like Galen's crippled pet." She laughed at her own humour. "Why do you think yourself so brave little sprite? Have I not sent sprites back to the skies when I killed their witches? And will you not be there this very day when we take Blackwand? Abandon your witch and flee now little sprite and be spared the indignation." Her words dripped conceit.

It came closer, hunched over and crawling on all fours. Strike saw it was diseased and ragged, but the worst was its face. The head was partially hooded, but he was stunned to see the creature spoke with two mouths, each taking its turn to articulate the speech. He watched in mesmerized horror as Sunday shouted something from far away, but his mind seemed under attack. He felt forgetful and everything seemed so pointless.

"Or maybe little sprite wishes to be with Blackwand, wishes to endure what she endures, wishes for pain everlasting?" Vorus slithered closer.

"Strike just go, run!" Sunday scrabbled at the wall, pushed with her feet and managed to touch her fingertips to her staff.

Strike saw a world of horror waiting for them. He could flee, or he could stand by her and know those horrors forever. *I can't leave you Sunday, I won't leave you,* he thought, but by all the gods of the thunder-heights he was sorely tempted. He tried to stand firm, but he groaned and his proud wings sagged at his side. He heard Sunday scream again, followed by the creature's soft but triumphant laughter. Then he heard a different scream altogether.

"Vorus my sister, please Vorus!"

Strike winced as something called out in terror and then fell silent.

"Sister?" Vorus turned instantly. Arctura was in grave trouble. "Sister I am coming!" She spun around, intending to go to her aid, when something very large and very angry landed on the roof making the whole church shake.

One moment it was an eagle, the next it was a massive bear. Eirik had come to finish what his brothers had started. His claws dug holes in the wrecked roof, and he reared up, towering over the last of their foes. Vorus saw that the tables had turned. She also saw the demon was splattered in her sister's blood and knew Arctura was dead, while Isis was still stunned by Blackwand's attack. It was time to leave. *Next time,* she thought spitefully. Ignoring the huge bear, she burst into flight with a furious scream and skimmed over the roof, caught hold of Isis and fled.

Sunday heard a cry full of terror and pain from the street below. The approaching valkyrie stopped, and at that moment she took her chance and gave one last heave, reached up and grabbed her staff.

As soon as it was back in her hand she heard a terrifying roar and knew it was Tawny. The whole building rocked and she looked up to see him astride the roof, facing down the last of their attackers. But a glimpse was all she got: it took all her strength just to hold onto the crumbling gutter. "Strike!" she ordered, "Strike, get in the staff and let's go!"

"What about the berserks?" He scampered along the gutter, plunged into his staff and powered it up, taking her weight.

She kicked herself away from the church just as the gutter gave way and went crashing to the street below, then she pulled herself up onto the cherished lightning-staff. "They're coming with us," she panted and yanked the staff around and sailed up over the roof. "Blackwand!" she yelled, and this time it wasn't a war cry but a rallying call. They were leaving, and fast.

Eirik roared again, but the valkyries were now just fast receding shadows, tearing across the roof tops.

"Eirik!" It was Harger, he landed heavily besides Karl who lay bleeding and battered on the wrecked roof. "He's hurt!"

"Sonneday will know what to do. Bring him!" Eirik flowed easily from bear to eagle and took to the air, swooping over his wounded brother.

"I can manage!" Karl promised, but he struggled to get airborne and when finally aloft he found flying to be agony.

Sunday raced ahead of them, leading the way, and looked back. The three cruised along behind, but the eagle in the centre was clearly injured.

"Where to?" Strike watched streets and houses flash past, and wondered how far they'd get in broad daylight.

"Five miles west, a common. It'll be safe, and fewer people." Last night she already decided her next stopping point would be Oaks Common, she was drawn to the name but she never thought their departure would be so dramatic and so bloody. Strike shouted something in return then pushed the staff harder, anxious to be out of the city before the sun rose too high. Sunday looked back at her protectors, who flew along with their wounded third in the middle, and she just hoped she could mend whatever damage the valkyries had done.

All of this happened in mere moments, and Galen watched it unfold like the witness to a terrible accident who is powerless to change the inevitable. He stood transfixed by the spectacle, until Elios dragged him back to his senses. *"Blackwand, it's Blackwand!"*

Now he saw what she meant. A figure on a staff had emerged from the church tower to join the fight. "That's her!" he growled, and set off at a sprint. He lost sight of them as he raced past the cavalry barracks. The imposing building blocked his view, but the screams and thunder of falling masonry continued unabated. He ran so fast his vision pulsed and his heart burned and at last came into view of the church again to find a gaping hole in the road and the church looking like it had been hit by a storm.

"Galen, there, she's getting away!" Elios saw the witch heading west across open parkland, followed by three huge birds.

He staggered to a stop. "Vorus!" he screamed, looking around the destruction. "Vorus, the bitch is getting away! Where the hell are you?" As Blackwand shrank into the distance his temper swelled.

"Maybe Vorus is dead?" Elios dared suggest.

"Bitch!" he screamed again and kicked at the air in temper.

"She might be hurt, Galen we must find her so she can explain what happened to Lord Thorpe."

'Thorpe'. The name sobered him. "Aye, find Vorus," he agreed between puffs, and headed for the crater in the road. He reached the hole and from the smell guessed immediately what had happened. He teetered on the edge, careful of the crumbling earth and loose cobbles, and peered down. "Vorus!" he called into the gloom. "Answer me!"

"Galen," the voice was weak, but it was her. She was hiding in the broken sewer. "Galen my sister is dead. Blackwand's demons killed my sister."

He didn't care for the edge of grief in her voice. "We'll mourn her later," he said abruptly, "now be swift, we might still catch up with Blackwand."

"No!" she insisted, and now her voice came from all around him and the air smelled bad, and not just because of the open sewer. "Arctura is dead and Isis is injured, this night has been long and we must return to our krakens." She refused to show herself, which angered him even more.

He turned on the spot, taking in the devastated church and broken slates lying around the street. "But Blackwand was almost in our grasp!" He swung punches through the air. "We must pursue! We must!"

"NO!" her voice came again, hard enough to ruffle his hair and stipple goose-flesh across his neck. "We are weak, we leave for Hobbs Ash." Something like a strong wind rushed past him followed by a rank odour.

"Vorus?" he swiped at the air with his cane. "Vorus! How dare you leave without my say so!"

"Something the matter here?" someone asked impatiently.

Galen turned to see a cavalry officer flanked by two troopers. They had been drawn out of the barracks by all the noise. "This isn't your business gentlemen," he said coldly, "be back to grooming your horses or whatever it is you do for a living."

"Now see here!" The officer took a step forwards.

"This is Goldhawk business," he raised his voice, and at that the officer halted. "Now tell me, does your barracks have a telegraph?"

"It does," he replied cautiously.

Galen regarded the smashed sewer a last time. *Somewhere down there in London's filth lies a dead valkyrie,* he thought, *one of the creatures I've spent my life searching for, drowned like a rat in a river of shit.* Now he had the ability to summon them at will the valkyrie race had lost much of its significance for him. He almost smiled at the irony.

"Sir?" the officer prompted.

He looked again. The sky was empty and Blackwand was gone. "Contact Goldhawk Row," he said without turning, "and tell them Mr Galen needs a ride home."

Chapter Twenty-six

Pieces of paper

'There are two things men will surely fight and die for: flags and money.
Peculiar is it not, to think that the gift of life be so easily
thrown away for mere cloth and paper?'
Sir Jonathan Bowls, former knight turned witch, executed 1629

She'd never been more relieved to see greenery. They followed the Grand Junction canal out of London, towards Oaks Common, an oasis of woodland on the city's western edge. It wasn't perfect, but it was the best she could think of.

"That one in the middle looks really hurt!" Strike dropped in speed so the berserks could keep up.

"We'll be fine once we get to the trees!" she shouted, hoping she was right.

They entered the wood from the canal side. Worryingly, there was a string of narrow-boats, coal barges and dredgers moored along its length, but their chimneys were smokeless, so she desperately hoped that meant nobody was awake yet.

Once on the ground she made sure the eagles had seen her, then ran deeper into the wood. Leaves rustled at her back, followed by the flap of wings, then came heavy feet crunching through the undergrowth and she knew they were bears once more. She pressed on without looking back, deeper into the wood and anxious to be far from people. Oaks Common didn't appear to have many oaks she thought, mostly beech and holly. The ground was thick with young bracken, brambles and foxgloves. A small stream ran through a clearing where bluebells were going to seed. It was clogged with leaves, but the water looked clear enough. "This'll have to do," she decided.

Strike landed on a fallen tree and sniffed the air, but he never spoke. All of them were cautious now. She watched the berserks approach through the wood, with Tawny in the lead as always. The sound of their rumbling breath comforted her, but not so Silver. His fur was bloodstained, his breathing gravelly, and he walked with his massive head hung so low that his nose ploughed a furrow through the grass. At last they came around her and slumped down, and now she could see Tawny was also badly injured.

"Oh no, not you too!" The sight of the dried blood around his throat and belly sent a chill through her. He looked to have been soaked with gallons of the stuff. "Those evil bastards!" she cursed, and knelt between his outstretched front paws. She smoothed her hands along his muzzle and looked into his eyes. His amber gaze looked steady, but tired. "What did they do to you?" she soothed him, and explored his throat tenderly, expecting to find a horrible wound. Her hand slid through fur so thick it reached to her elbow, all of it matted with blood.

He growled something and yawned. Purple lips peeled back to reveal ivory fangs the size of bananas, and a tongue like a carpet flopped out of his cavernous mouth, but she never saw him as anything less than a man.

"What did they do to you?" she appealed again, parting the thick fur to examine his skin beneath. Still she couldn't find anything, not a scratch. "Valgard really does protect you," she said distantly, and he growled in response. Her hands came away sticky with blood, but she seemed not to notice. "You saved me again, and I still don't know your name." She managed a smile and on impulse she stood on tip toes and whispered into that dinner-plate sized ear. "Thank you."

Eirik was tired and battered. His wounds might have mended, but he would remember the pain for a long time yet. Sonneday checked him for injuries, and as always, being close to her and the doll made him feel contented, drowsy even. He yawned as the battle-rage ebbed, leaving him feeling calm and clear once more. The creature in the sewer had almost ripped his throat open and now Sonneday's touch had the opposite effect and his pains melted like ice before the sun. Finally, she whispered something to him, and although her language was a mystery he understood, and if he could have replied he would have promised her the same favour a thousand times over.

"Now for you Silver," she clambered around Tawny's great bulk and to his companion, the warrior she only knew as Silver. He lay on his side in the grass. Blood streaked his flank and neck. Not as much as Tawny, which gave her hope, but his silvery fur betrayed every bloodstain, and it didn't take long to find something amiss. Her fingers brushed against something hard buried in his chest. "Something's broken off here." She leaned closer and parted the dense fur and there, embedded in his chest, was a slender black spike. It was slightly curved, like the tip of scythe.

"What in Oak's name?" Strike whispered. "Is that some broken debris?"

She shook her head. "I don't think anything so ordinary could pierce this hide. I think it's from one of those things." She looked around at him, and Strike saw worry stamped across her face.

"Can you do anything about it?"

"Maybe, but first we need to get it out." She pinched the spike and gave a tentative tug. Silver jerked and growled softly, but it didn't shift. "So long as it's in there he won't heal." She reached for her satchel and took out a handkerchief and the powdered sulphur she'd obtained in Reykjavik.

"Sunday?" he asked.

"Sulphur's part of the spell to banish crib-robbers, if this is what I think it is, then once I get it out I'll need to banish its effect, otherwise the poison will stay in him."

"What is it?" he asked fearfully.

She didn't answer, instead she wrapped the handkerchief around the stump protruding from Silver's chest. "Forgive me," she asked, took a firm hold, and pulled hard. He barked a deep cough and bloody froth erupted from his nose, but the fragment slid free with a slurping sound. "I'm truly sorry my friend," she whispered, then held the black spike up for a closer look.

"It looks like a hook?"

"It's a fingernail."

"From one of those things?"

"What else." She dropped the broken nail into the handkerchief in disgust, poured a generous amount of sulphur over it, then hastily scooped a hollow in the earth and buried it, glad to get the foul thing out of her sight.

In case it's listening, Strike thought from nowhere.

"You called me by name just now didn't you?"

"Did I?" he asked, confused.

"Say my name backwards three times," she reached for hrafn-dimmu.

"What for?"

"Just do it, quick!"

"Yadnus – Yadnus – Yadnus." He looked at her expectantly. "Did I do it right?"

"Fine." She knelt closer to Silver and brushed sulphur into his open wound with the tip of Raven's wand, making each stroke deliberate and purposeful. She muttered the spell and projected her will as she worked. For a while there was only the sound of his deep breathing, the wand rasping through his thick fur and Sunday's whispering. Finally she stopped and gently smoothed a hand over his wound. "Blessed be," she finished.

"Will he be all right?" he asked at last.

"It's the best I can do."

"And the backwards name three times?"

She shook her head. "Just a superstition, not real magic, but you never know. It's supposed to make sure the claw thing can't recall our names," she gave him a chilling look, "in case one day it's found by its original owner."

"Folk-magic," Strike realised, "then we're desperate indeed."

"It was stuck in him all the way from the church, it might have heard everything we said, who knows, it might even let them know where we are."

"What kind of creature can do that?" He stared at the little mound of earth, and shivered.

"Remember what Be–," she stopped herself; "remember what our guest said, 'unknown creature of Ruin'. I think it was one of these things."

"But what are they?"

It was very clear to her now. "Valkyries," she answered and wiped the dirt from her hands,

"It Ruined Wake, his thunder-sprite," Strike evoked, thinking of how empty he felt when the monster was stalking him on the roof. "Come on, let's move away from the wretched thing." /

She looked at their patient and ran a hand over his muzzle. "Can you move?"

Silver opened his eyes and regarded her, then pushed himself upright and ambled slowly across the clearing prompting his brothers to rise and follow. He seemed a little unsteady, but his breathing had eased and to her relief when he lay down, he lay with his head between his paws. She hadn't liked seeing him sprawled in the grass, it was too easy to imagine him dead.

"Come on," she whispered and Strike noticed she wouldn't call him by name. She set off to be with the bears, while he cast a final glance at the mound and it almost felt to whisper to him.

'Maybe little sprite wishes to be with Blackwand, wishes to endure what she endures, wishes for pain everlasting?'

He shivered again and fluttered after Sunday.

She cleansed their fur with water from the stream. She began with Tawny, using a rag to wipe the clotted blood and filth from his neck and shoulders, and she breathed a sigh of relief to find Silver more animated and his wound already healing.

When she was done, the five of them sat in considered silence listening to wind in the trees and the occasional train far off. The bears fell into a kind of wary sleep, while she sat at their centre thinking hard, and Strike kept watch from a tree. The hours passed and she didn't move. She had no appetite for food or chat, instead she brooded and stroked the silver fox around her neck. "Where are you Ben?" she whispered. She really needed to speak to another witch right then. There were big decisions to be made and she didn't want to have to make them alone. "Thorpe," she said under her breath. She knew he was connected to the valkyries in some way, and like it or not, she was locked in a deadly game with a powerful opponent. "I'll be a thorn in their side Ben, but better than that I'll be a dagger in their back when they're least expecting it." Her heart thudded angrily in her chest. They'd come to kill them today, and Thorpe's vile creatures had harmed her friends. Well she wasn't going to stand for that, she thought.

"You'd dare harm my family," she uttered in a low voice. She was unaware of it, but she was breathing in perfect time with the berserks and the four of them together sounded like a well oiled engine. She stared ahead at the trees but she didn't see them, instead she saw London beyond and more significantly she saw Thorpe's jewel: the Bank of England. Already she was reaching for her map and finalising her plans. "I'll be a dagger," she promised again.

Strike looked down at her and could almost hear her mind turning. She'd donned all her war gear, including her black feathers and held her staff across her lap. Worryingly she wore her pointed hat so he couldn't see her face. *Be careful Sunday, now's not the time for rash action,* he thought.

Eirik shifted restlessly. His wounds were gone, but something smelled wrong. His eyes flickered open and he regarded Sonneday. She sat with her back to him, lost in thought and he could tell her thoughts weren't good. It was Sonneday herself who smelled wrong, she smelled of rage and battle and all the things that Valgard coveted. He knew instinctively they were going back into the city, perhaps even tonight, to strike back at their enemies and he couldn't stop himself from growling in anticipation.

Galen requisitioned a carriage and driver from the cavalry barracks and was back at Goldhawk Row an hour later. By now London was coming fully awake and the streets were growing busy. He bounded up the steps intending to grab a few things from his quarters then head straight for Hobbs Ash. He'd lost one valkyrie this morning, another was injured and Vorus was her usual disobedient self, but despite this he was remarkably calm. "Blackwand," he laboured over the name. "I have to hand it to her."

"Do you think Vorus was hurt?" Elios asked as they hurried up to the library.

"I bloody hope so, might teach the monster to be a little more cautious."

"Perhaps it's best to telegraph ahead and learn if she's returned?"

"You worry too much," he scoffed, "she'll be back, and on this occasion I'll bet my neck on it. She's hurt and needs her bloody kraken like a cripple needs a cane." He passed a red-coated steward in the corridor who saw Goldhawk's notorious guest talking to himself again. He gave him a peculiar look and hurried on his way.

When he arrived at the library he knew his father was waiting for him. The smell of tobacco was his herald.

"What will you tell him?" Elios enquired.

"The truth of course," he vowed. "He is a man of the great Book. Would you have me lie to him?"

"Galen, I didn't mean to imply —"

"Enough!" he silenced her.

The cane became still, and she swallowed her words.

"Better," he said abruptly.

The smell of tobacco was stronger now and he stood outside the library a moment, framed himself then entered.

The first thing he saw was his father standing in a haze of cigar smoke with his back to him, wearing dark trousers and a white shirt with the sleeves rolled to the elbows. "Father." He closed the door behind him and locked it.

"How many books are here do you think?" Thorpe asked without turning, staring off into the huge library.

"I'm informed there are almost a million volumes." He wanted to tell his father everything that had happened that morning, not chat about books.

"Hmm," he tipped ash on the floor. "So many pages, so much information, and yet the Jik assassin remains free."

He cringed. His father knew already.

"Well?" Thorpe asked, still staring off into the library.

"The valkyries found her."

"So I hear."

"And they would have caught her, but for her demons."

Thorpe turned. "Are you hurt?"

For a moment he was startled by the question. "No father, I'm fine."

"Best call me 'Lord Thorpe'. Habits are hard to break and can cost a man much."

"Aye, my Lord," Galen sighed, mostly in relief.

"I had an early morning courier from Major Drummond at the cavalry barracks." He thrust a hand into his trouser pocket and looked at the little pile of ash on the floor. "Quite a way to be awoken wouldn't you say, with tales of monsters and witches?"

"You know then."

He just nodded. "I came directly here. To find out for myself." Now he went and sat on the edge of the desk and studied his son closely.

"One of the valkyries is dead," Galen heard himself say. There was a considered silence, and he imagined a pressure boiler building up a dangerous head of steam.

"You haven't slept all night have you?"

He looked up, puzzled. "Well, no as a matter of fact."

Thorpe chuckled. "I think it's time you introduced me to your lady friend."

"My Lord?"

"Vorus," he said simply.

Galen smiled. "I'll call us a cab," he touched the brim of his bowler and swept a hand towards the door. "After you my Lord."

It was peaceful and secure inside the cherub's metal skull. Everything outside sounded muffled and dream-like and Vorus always felt strongest here. Although flying over London hunting their enemies was a thrill, she couldn't sustain it for long and she was only truly protected here. "Sister," she grieved and looked out at the now empty eagle-kraken. The battered machine lay in a heap, with rusty water pooled around it. Countless dead flies and moths, and one or two rats floated in the mire, victims who'd strayed too close.

She thought of Blackwand's demons. Galen had been quite right about how dangerous they were, but she had grown accustomed to her sense of invulnerability and maybe become too confident. The bull-headed kraken also lay in ruins, but it was far from dead. Isis languished inside, weeping softly. "You were careless today sister," Vorus said coldly. "Weep no more. The sound torments me."

"You promised us safety!" she spat.

"Safety must be earned, as must survival. Today's lesson was hard, but do you think Blackwand's magic will still be able to harm you the next time we meet?"

She considered this. "Blackwand's magic will fail?"

"This was your lesson, just as I had mine. Remember sister that all things fail before Ruination."

"But what of her demons?"

Vorus smiled to herself. "No matter, we shall soon outnumber them."

"They killed Arctura," Isis moaned again softly.

"Blackwand," Vorus scraped her nails over the steel helmet, setting sparks, and thinking of the witch who murdered her sister. She stood, impatient to do something about this injustice, and the kraken began to rise. The view from the helmet went from ground level to fifty feet in under a minute as the shattered machine ordered itself upright by her will. Sparks flew and metal screamed, and a handful of frightened men ventured through the barricade then departed just as quickly. "Blackwand," she rumbled and the kraken's gauntlet curled into an angry fist. *Why should we not hunt the magic whore in these towers of steel?* she thought. *If Galen would allow it, we could capture Blackwand without fear of her demons.*

She made up her mind to put this to Galen again. He'd denied her repeatedly so far, but she was sure with Arctura dead he would yield. But where was her devoted Galen, she thought? It troubled her that he hadn't come running, and it occurred to her that perhaps her hold over him wasn't as total as she believed. "I shall make him mine," she said lovingly, and the huge machine reached up and touched the pocket-watch embedded in its skull. "Galen, my saviour," she whispered.

When Galen and Thorpe at last arrived, they found Lyle waiting for them.

"Doesn't that whelp have a home to go to?" Thorpe growled as they drew close. It wasn't even nine o'clock yet. The skies were grey and the first rain had arrived.

"Lord Thorpe, Mr Galen," he greeted them brusquely. "Sir am I to believe the rumour that Blackwand was seen early this morning?"

"Seen and soundly thrashed!" Thorpe pushed past him and into the station. "Is the Vorus creature back in its hideaway?"

"One of the sergeants reported it moving just now sir, yes," Lyle trotted along at his side. "Am I to think I heard you right sir: Blackwand has been defeated?"

Thorpe bristled. "I said thrashed, I said nothing about defeated!"

He cowered and turned to Galen. "You found her then?"

"Aye, but when it came to the fight her protectors proved livelier than expected."

He grasped the picture and unless he wanted to spend the rest of his life sweeping streets he knew it best not to dwell on the matter. "So will you be patrolling London again tonight?" he asked tactfully.

"No, he won't!" Thorpe boomed from up ahead.

Both men swapped curious glances, but only Galen dare ask. "Lord Thorpe?"

He stopped and listened to the rain drum down on the station roof. He found it rather soothing. "No, Mr Galen will not be chasing Jik bandits tonight," he informed Lyle, "he has more important duties."

"Sir," Lyle agreed.

Thorpe looked up at the glass roof, a miracle of engineering in its day, but now it was patched and cracked. *Ruined,* he thought moodily. "Blackwand killed one of the valkyrie creatures," he said simply.

"Dear Lord!" Lyle took a step back.

"So Mr Galen," he looked meaningfully at his son, "will return to Smithfield tonight and find us more of these shadowy phantoms."

Galen saw what his father was driving at. "We must overwhelm her demons with superior numbers."

"Very good," Thorpe smiled.

"But what if Blackwand should strike again before tonight?" Lyle asked timidly.

"She won't," Thorpe blasted. "The Jik will have her own wounds to tend to, trust me she won't do anything tonight but hide in a damp hole and wish she'd never come to London."

"If you're sure sir," Lyle agreed uncertainly.

"Of course I'm sure. Now, I have business to be about. Lyle, draw up a list of the targets she'll most likely attack and have it to me within the hour." He waved him away and turned without waiting for an answer. Together Galen and his father set off to interrogate an eyewitness to this morning's drama: Vorus herself.

Lyle watched the two march into the station, towards the barricade. Thorpe was on the prowl and for the first time he felt sorry for Galen's monster.

The first thing he saw was the cherub's sneering face and the first thing he heard was grinding metal. Vorus turned and looked down at them.

How did he do it? Thorpe marvelled at the giant before him. He checked they were the only ones within the restricted area and stepped forwards. "Vorus," he called up at the machine.

"Galen, you have been away so long!" She ignored him.

"I don't have your skills of flight, more's the pity." He thought of his flightless Elios, and lay his staff across a stack of timber. He didn't want her peeking at his thoughts just now.

"My sister is dead." The giant fell to one knee and the ground rocked. Errant sparks drifted down and were drowned in a pool of gathering rainwater.

"I know my sweet. And I feel your loss, but if you wish to avenge her death then I ask you to set out with me tonight and rescue more of your sisters."

Thorpe watched in fascination. So far he'd only seen the valkyries fed prisoners. He hadn't witnessed this kind of intimacy before and he had the absurd notion that Vorus harboured 'feelings' for his son. *Women*, he thought derisively.

"Red-rivers?" she asked.

"Yes my sweet."

"My sister Isis is wounded also," she toyed with him, "perhaps to taste one of those red-rivers now might restore her fortitude."

He looked up into that deformed face and wondered just what kind of creature sat behind it. "There are none here, but there shall be plenty at Smithfield."

"But have you no care for my sister? Galen, she needs the red-river. Tonight is too long to wait."

He looked over to the bull-headed kraken. It lay in a tangled pile and he suddenly thought of a child feigning illness to win attention, and he smiled cynically. "What have you to say Isis?" He made his way over to her, accompanied by Thorpe and the horrible grating of metal as Vorus turned to watch.

"She was injured today, by the Blackwand witch," Vorus accused.

"I was there," he reminded her, before turning to Isis. "What did that fiend do to you my lass?" He stroked the bull's steel nose and peered into the visor slit. Inside was total darkness.

"Such pain," came a small voice. "Blackwand's spell was agony."

"You have a fine sister Isis, hasn't she told you that spells can be defused, robbed of their sting? Vorus managed it quite well," he glanced at the cherub, "I thought sisters might share these secrets?"

"We risked much for you today Galen." Her voice dropped an octave.

"But as long as Blackwand and her demons live you're at risk, to slay them we must find more of your kin."

"Isis needs the red-river now," she insisted.

Thorpe watched the stand-off with mounting interest.

Galen looked across to his father, who gave him a slight nod. "Perhaps you're right, Isis should be rewarded."

"A witch Galen! Bring her a witch!" The giant loomed over him, and a shower of rusted grains drifted down. Behind him, he heard Isis moan theatrically.

"Alas, we have few prisoners of such calibre left." It was Thorpe. "It can't be a witch."

The disfigured helmet turned his way. "But the red-river is more potent in them, and Isis thirsts so," she said churlishly.

"No," Thorpe decided. "When Blackwand is captured and her demons dead, you can have all the witches you want."

"But the red-river!" she hissed, losing her patience.

"Fret not, you'll have what you want, but the quality might be rougher than you're used to." He dropped the cigar stub into the puddle at his feet. "Rather like tobacco," he said blandly. With that he turned and left.

Galen frowned, then followed, leaving Vorus watching them intently. "What was that all about?" he asked when they were a distance away.

"Didn't you say to give them rewards, train them as one would train a dumb animal?"

"But we can't keep handing over condemned witches at her whim."

"We're not," Thorpe buttoned up his coat as he walked, "have Lyle contact the governor at Newgate prison. Witches might hang from trees, but they don't grow on them. London has plenty of criminals destined for the gallows. They might as well prove of some use in their last moments."

Galen relaxed. "I'm sorry, I didn't mean to question you."

"Never mind. Now return to Goldhawk and get some sleep. That's an order." He glanced back at Vorus, kneeling in a shower of rain, and staring at them. "You've got another long night ahead."

"So I see." Galen picked up his cane again as they passed by. Elios didn't bother to greet him, and he didn't miss her greeting anyway.

Thorpe scowled up at the broken panes and pulled his collar up against the rain. "And tell Lyle to get this bloody roof fixed!"

By chance or providence two people set off that afternoon for the same destination and at the same time. Thorpe chaired a dreary meeting of Illuminata lawyers, listening to their wearisome demands about June's great tournament. When he was done, he left for his chambers at the Bank of England.

Meanwhile, Sunday sat in the woods with her berserks and waited, saving her strength. When the afternoon was drawing to a close and satisfied that the day's banking was ended, she stood and her bears rose to their feet. All of them were rested, healed and ready. She gathered her things and when she was done she left for her mission at the Bank of England, and only chance or providence would decide which of them got there first.

"What's the matter with that bloody horse? The wretched thing lost a leg?" Thorpe banged his cane on the cab roof. They'd been stationary now for ten minutes.

"Apologies sir, some sort of incident further up," his driver shouted down.

Thorpe twisted around to peer along Blackfriars Bridge. At its far end, he could see a crashed carriage leaning at a precarious angle. Knowing the traffic would be held up for some time he resigned himself to a walk. The rain had eased to a light drizzle and the Bank can't have been more than a mile. He swung the door open and climbed down. "Take the cab back to Goldhawk. I'll walk."

"Aye sir."

He buttoned his coat against the wet, set his top hat on his head, and started walking.

She flew high and fast, concealed by the mist and carrying a mental picture of London in her head. There were seven miles between her and her goal and they passed like a condemned prisoner's last moments. She thought of her former home, and of the cursed men flying by her side, of Kolfinnia and Kittiwake, and of Hethra and Halla. But in the closing moments of her short journey she thought of Benedict Collins.

"Please be safe Ben," she asked the wind. The mist thinned and she glimpsed the Thames as it turned eastwards around Waterloo, and then she counted down the bridges knowing the last one was adjacent to her target. "Waterloo, Blackfriars, Southwark," she named them, and at the last one she scoured the city immediately north and saw the wedge-shaped fortress that was the Bank of England. Closer still she saw the bank's vulnerable heart: an open courtyard invisible from the road. *I'll be a dagger,* she thought and began to dive followed by her warriors.

Corporal Patrick Wells arrived at the bank an hour ago, along with five soldiers. Every night without fail they were despatched from the Tower of London to sit watch over sums of money they couldn't even fathom. Like most men in the ranks, Wells knew what a hundred was, and at a stretch he might get his head around thousands, but the idea of a 'million' made his head spin. Right now however the only number important tonight was plain old 'six'. These were relatively peaceful times and a half dozen men was considered sufficient to guard the bank through the night. Wells, stocky and looking older than his mere forty-one, was the man commanding those other five. The guard room was a sombre affair, but it served well enough and mostly they spent the night there drinking tea and playing cards, but right now there was only himself and Private Shaw, a skinny man in his twenties with teeth like a horse and hair to match. "Where's Alcott and Stanley?" Wells asked.

Shaw looked up from polishing his rifle. "Patrollin' down the transfer office."

"And Shipton and Malt?"

"Erm . . down the Lothbury court I think."

Wells nodded, satisfied everything was in order. He picked up a small brown paper bag from the table and looked inside. Just as he suspected it was almost empty: hardly a spoonful of leaves remained. "Oh bloody 'ell Shaw!"

"What!" The younger man looked hurt.

"Did I, or did I not remind you to pick up some tea before we left the Tower?"

He concentrated for a moment, then the memory came back to him and a guilty look spread across his face. "Sorry Corp," he mumbled.

"Well you can tell the rest why we ain't got any tea this night." He grabbed his rifle and headed for the door.

"Where yer goin' Corp?"

"Patrollin'!" he shot back and closed the door with a bang. "Brain like a sieve that one," he grumbled as he stalked along the corridor. His hand absently patted his pocket where a flask of whisky rested. He was a superstitious man and the idea of a night without a mug of tea and a dash of scotch just wasn't right. "God I'd trade all the gold in this place for a cup of tea." It was going to be a long night, unless he nipped down to the servants' rooms and see if he could scrounge some tea from there.

He made his way along corridors and through open courts. The bank was closing for the night, and there weren't many staff left but for the occasional clerk. They looked stern in their black frock coats, and he was always mindful to address them as 'sir', even though he wasn't obliged to, but Wells was an optimist. Being half Irish, half Yorkshire, he took a lot of stick living in London. Sometimes he thought that's why he'd never risen beyond corporal, but he dreamed like any man, and even though his class, his roots, and his age were against him he went on hoping that a dutiful soldier might one day get noticed. Wells was a hopeless romantic, although he'd likely clobber any man who called him such.

He was striding along the corridor adjacent to the Bullion court, with his rifle over his shoulder, daydreaming of being Captain Wells one day, when he heard a faint rumble, like a steam engine gathering pace. He stopped and listened. The only such thing in the building was the great engine that ran the banking machinery, and he knew the sound of that. This was different. The rumbling wasn't regular or purposeful. It was random and chaotic, it sounded more like an engine blowing itself to bits than one running smoothly. Without knowing he slid his rifle from his shoulder.

"Malt? Shipton? Either of yous there?"

The coffee room was directly ahead now, but he'd lost his taste for tea. The rumbling came again, this time a lot closer, and he realised it wasn't an engine of any kind. He heard masonry bomb to the ground and felt tremors roll under his feet. He was fumbling for his whistle when he saw the wall adjoining the coffee room actually bulge like a balloon, as if something was trying to get out. Plaster sloughed away in huge plates and crashed to the marble floor. He put the whistle to his mouth just as the wall ruptured like a burst dam, and through it came not water but the biggest bloody bear he'd ever seen in his life. Corporal Wells blew the whistle, but just like the missing tea, the blasted thing had lost its pea, and all that came out was a dry hiss. No wonder he'd never make more than corporal.

The bear was gigantic, easily as big as an elephant. It shoved its way through the rubble and shook off the debris. As soon as it saw him, it raised its head and bellowed, making his knees weak and his ears ring. He screamed something, raised the rifle and was about to fire when a voice stopped him.

"No! Wait, please!"

Absurdly it was the word 'please' that cut through his panic, and to his amazement a figure stepped through the shattered wall. Right away he determined it was a woman. She looked like a pirate, masked and dressed from head to foot in black, except for a purple band tied around one arm. She carried a staff and even more worryingly she wore a pointed hat. He might not know 'millions' but he knew witches. "Halt right there!" His voice cracked and he sounded like a lad in the throes of puberty.

She advanced, without fear it seemed.

"No closer!" he backed up and waved the rifle. "I shall shoot, on my oath I shall!"

"Please." The stranger stopped just feet away and then slowly and deliberately removed the hat and drew down her mask. A second later a golden plait decorated with black feathers cascaded down, blue eyes sparkled and Sunday unleashed her most potent weapon: she smiled. "Please, there's no need for anyone to get hurt." She smiled again and Wells couldn't help himself. His trigger finger relaxed a fraction.

"Identify yerself!" he demanded.

"Of course, where are my manners. My name is Blackwand."

"Eh?"

"Blackwand. I'm lost," she continued, "and I was hoping you might assist me?" Behind her, that mammoth bear squeezed along the corridor, shrugging the walls aside and bending the heavy light fittings flat against the roof, advancing until it stood over her, growling softly.

Wells just stood there, feeling as flimsy as lace.

"In particular, could you direct me to the bullion room?" She drew her wand and pointed it at him. "Oh, and please lower your rifle," she asked sweetly, and when she smiled again Wells knew he was powerless.

As Thorpe approached the junction of Cannon Street and King William Street he felt an unexpected sense of urgency. Before he even knew it, he picked up his pace and was walking in long strides. The usual things that occupied his mind were brushed aside. He listened to his intuition and in doing so he became Thorpe of the Book-of-Nine, not Thorpe of the city, or the Bank. *Something's wrong,* he perceived, and suddenly his eyes were everywhere, scrutinizing every woman in the street, looking for those unmistakable blue eyes. He marched under shop awnings and ignored their drizzle of rainwater, and barged past pedestrians oblivious to their disgruntled glances. *Something's wrong,* he thought again and knew he had to get back.

Wells marched ahead of the witch and her formidable friend and into the Bullion court, where he stopped. The bear creature came next, smashing the archway into submission as it passed through. Before the rubble had hardly settled, she stepped nimbly past the bear, still pointing her wand at him. Now though he saw she also clutched that long black staff of hers too, and he wondered what manner of nasty thing she could do with that.

"Bullion room is under here," he outlined.

She looked at the rich marble floor.

"There's no way down there!" he added quickly. "Go on young Miss Black, wer, erm?"

"Blackwand," she helped him

"Aye, go on, give it up and be gone while you still can. There'll be more soldiers on their way from the Tower." Why he said this he didn't really know. There was just something appealing about her that went far beyond her appearance.

She smiled, somewhat sadly. "We all have our duties Corporal." Then she turned to her bear, "Can you break it?"

The animal growled and she stepped back, seeming to understand.

"It's hopeless! The floor's three foot thick!" he added, feeling he should at least do something to protect the bank. "Be off now I tells yer!"

"I'd step back if I were you," she advised, and when the bear lumbered into the middle of the court, and lay both its huge front paws on the ground, he did just that.

She watched as Tawny splayed those great paws, scratching ugly grooves in the polished marble, then he pushed hard and reared up, reaching almost to the domed ceiling. When he reached his maximum height he froze momentarily, with his arms hanging before his chest like battering rams, perfectly balanced. Then he dropped with incredible force and his paws came down like hammers.

The floor shook and Wells lurched. The bear immediately reared up and dropped again, harder this time and Wells felt the whole floor rock, making his stomach roll. A marble bust fell from its cornice and smashed and he saw its nose skate across the floor. Worse still, the glass dome overhead shuddered and the iron frame groaned. It sagged and buckled, and glass panes were writhed loose and sailed down. "He'll bring the whole bloody place down!" he yelled.

"We can hope." Sunday stepped back into the cover of the archway.

Falling glass shattered all around, but slid harmlessly off the bear's back. He reared up and lunged a third time, and this time the floor broke like eggshell and his paws plunged into a deep crater. He reared again, clawing a shower of debris out of the floor as he did, and came down with a brutal roar, landing chest-deep in the hole. There followed a deafening rumble from somewhere under their feet and Wells saw fractures open in the marble and zigzag across the room. Water suddenly spurted from ruptured pipes, and dust flew thick and fast. The bear clambered from the ruined floor and Sunday skipped deftly through the wreckage and up to his side.

Wells saw the two meet like friends, and she even teased a shard of glass from his coat and dropped it to the floor. He could have escaped at that point, he could have even reached for his rifle, but he was pinned. Not by fear however: he had to see what happened next.

"Please wait for me, I'll not be long," she asked. The bear growled something that might have been a reply, then she addressed Wells through a cloud of dust. "Please Corporal, let this be a day when only property gets damaged, not people, and so stay just where you are." With that she climbed to the edge of the gaping hole and dropped out of sight.

By the time Thorpe reached the junction where Princess Street and Threadneedle Street joined, he was almost running. Up ahead he could see the Bank of England itself. The building was a huge windowless fortress of smoke-darkened stone surrounded by lethal pointed railings. It rose up like an island in a sea of people and traffic. No force in the world could assail it. He shoved people aside, never taking his eyes off the building. It looked as it always did. There were no flames or gunfire or screaming, it was impassive and solid, so why was he so anxious?

A man stepped out of a tobacconists and walked right into him, barging him with his shoulder. "Bless my soul," he tried to apologise. "I'm frightfully —"

"Out of my bloody way!" He flung him across the pavement. He landed on the seat of his pants, wearing a startled expression, while his hat rolled away under a carriage and his umbrella popped open and landed in the gutter. Dozens of affronted faces turned in Thorpe's direction. A lady pushing a child in pram even shouted for a constable, but he stormed past them all. Everywhere he saw women and men wearing black. Black bonnets, black umbrellas, black coats, hats, dresses and shawls. For all he knew any one of them could be the Jik, watching him, laughing at him.

"I made a fool of you Victor, and burned your house to the ground. And the best of it is that you had me bound and helpless, but that nice Mr Harrison let me go and all because I promised him a kiss," she laughed in his ear.

"Sir! I believe you owe this man an apology!" The lady with the pram shouted after him.

"Go to hell you sanctimonious whore!" he roared back. There was a chorus of gasps, but predictably nobody dared to stop him. "Blackwand!"

His cheeks burned and he started to run.

He arrived at just the same time as reinforcements from the Tower. Dozens of armed soldiers were pouring out of covered wagons while most of the bank's senior officials stood in the rain, either pointing or staring up at the building in alarm. He tried to shove his way through, but was confronted by a police constable. "Can't go in there sir. Dangerous villain on the loose!"

"I'm Lord Thorpe and I practically own this bank." He swatted him away and pushed forwards.

"Lord Thorpe!" It was Jeremiah Bishop, the Deputy Governor. "Lord Thorpe, thank heavens you've come!" Bishop was a frail man in his seventies and from the look of things he'd seen enough excitement for one day. His face was ruddy and his thinning white hair was windblown. Thorpe noted small crumbs of plaster caught in his hair and immediately thought of Blackwand.

"What in God's name happened here?" he continued up the steps, but Bishop pulled him back.

"Lord Thorpe it's not safe, some desperate criminal has struck at the bank and caused much damage. Staff say the culprit's still inside!"

"A criminal?" Maybe it wasn't Blackwand after all he thought.

"Not just that sir, many reported fanciful tales of wild animals on the loose!" Bishop swallowed loudly. "Bears!"

That sealed it. Thorpe bounded up the steps and into the bank.

Wells stood staring at the bear, who stood staring down into the crumbling hole in the floor. He heard movement and turned, hoping to God it wasn't the rest of his troops. If they came there'd be shooting and lots of blood, and it wouldn't belong to any giant bear or mysterious Blackwand. So he felt a strange sense of relief when he saw two more monstrous bears amble into the Bullion court and take their places beside the first one. None of the three paid him any attention, but just surrounded the hole and looked expectantly into it. And a second later Blackwand reappeared.

Less than a minute after entering the bank Thorpe arrived at his chambers, gasping for breath and with a stabbing pain in his side, but when he flung his office door open his heart jumped into his mouth. "NO!" he roared, and ran to his desk, gibbering in rage. All his personal effects had been swept onto the floor and Blackwand had left him a private message chalked on the desk's leather top.

Dear Mr Thorpe, fret not, as you said yourself – 'it's just pieces of paper'

Below that she'd chalked a symbol, which looked like claw marks.

He scrubbed at the message in a frenzy until chalk-dust stained his coat and his palms were ashen, all the while cursing and ranting. He'd find time to be angry later he promised himself, but right now he had more pressing duties. He hastily unlocked the drawer, pulled out a revolver, and grabbed a handful of bullets. "Can't be killed, eh Blackwand? Allow me another try." He loaded the revolver as he ran from the room, leaving a trail of shiny brass bullets.

Her trail was easy to follow. It was one wrecked corridor after another, and he wasn't at all surprised to see the destruction lead towards the Bullion court. Just like Chertfield, he knew what would happen to that money. "Thieving pagan whore!" he snarled as he ran, and how he longed to squeeze that trigger and watch her pretty face vanish in a cloud of blood, but it wasn't the theft that offended him most. He had assured Goldhawk and his own son that she wouldn't strike so soon, and here he was less than twelve hours later caught with his britches down.

Wells whistled softly in admiration as she rose elegantly into view. Blackwand was sitting on her staff, pretty as a picture, but with her face concealed again she was just a dark figure with piercing eyes. "Lads will never believe this," he uttered. He saw she had strung a pair of sacks around her shoulder, which bulged with sovereigns and banknotes.

"You've been such help," she called out and reached into her waistcoat and drew out a bundle of notes. "Take it." She tossed them towards him, where they landed with an enticing thud. "You can always tell them Blackwand took it."

He looked down at the bundle of ten-pound notes. He guessed there were a hundred at least. *A hundred times ten?* he thought dimly, *that's a bloody thousand!* He prodded the bundle with his boot. "This is theft miss, I'll have no part of it!" he shouted, but his mind was already whispering to him how he should spend it.

"And how do you know it wasn't stolen in the first place? Earned from slavery or some other man-made misery?"

"It's theft!" he wavered. "I won't!"

"Then the rich will always be rich, and the poor will always be poor Corporal," she shrugged indifferently, but he could tell she was smiling. Then, the staff and its rider, bearing the Bank of England's gold, began to rise towards the shattered glass dome.

Thorpe was only fifty yards from the Bullion court when he heard voices. He was so close to catching her that he ached with anticipation. He double checked the revolver and crept forwards, stepping carefully through the fallen masonry. "Steady as she goes Victor," he whispered to himself, "steady as she goes."

Wells gazed up at her and so didn't see the bears transform. The next he knew, three huge and frightening birds were rising into view, and the dust around the Bullion court rolled and curled under their wings. He blinked against the grit and coughed on the dust, and for a moment he couldn't see a thing and just when he thought it was all over, the room exploded with gunfire.

Thorpe charged into the court, with the revolver held high, firing round after round at the escaping witch. "WHORE!" he screamed, but hit only the eagles, and bullets were no use against them. He glimpsed something black whisk away, closely followed by the huge birds. The downdraught swept dust and rain across him, and he continued to pull the trigger, even though his six bullets were long gone.

'Click – click – click.' The revolver's fury was spent, but not so Thorpe's. Spying Wells's rifle, he dropped the revolver, snatched it up and began to shoot. The rifle's voice was deeper and deadlier, but it mattered little. Blackwand and her bears were gone. "I'll have your head bitch!" he roared and fired again. The shot echoed around the court and when it finally died away Wells spoke up.

"Lord Thorpe sir?" he trembled.

Thorpe blinked, turned and saw him at last. He was shaking with fury, and for a second, Wells thought he was going to turn the rifle on him. "You let her get away?" he said through bared teeth.

"But, those beasts sir, they were too strong!"

"You let her get away." Thorpe stepped through the debris with long deliberate strides, like a stalking spider. "Your task is to guard the bank Corporal, and you just let that arch-enemy of the Empire walk in here and fill her apron-pockets?" He shook his head in disbelief.

"Sir, those things, they'd have torn every man of us to pieces sir!"

"Then at least you would have died with a shred of honour." He clutched the rifle and his knuckles made crackling sounds.

"Sir, there was little we could do." He swallowed and looked ahead at nothing, and so he didn't see the rifle butt until it hammered into his cheek. Pain exploded across his face and he lurched, missed his footing and dropped to the floor. He scrambled up onto one elbow and looked up to see Thorpe standing over him with the rifle pointed at his head. He met his stare, lay still and waited. *Go on you bastard,* he thought, *go on and kill me, I'm still twice the man you'll ever be.*

Thorpe frowned and his mouth twitched, then he lowered the rifle and mastered his temper. His face never changed, but he reached out and stepped deliberately on Wells's left hand, crushing it against the broken glass on the floor.

He screamed and tried to pull away. "Sir please, there was nothing I could do!"

"Oh I know, Corporal." Thorpe twisted his heel, driving more glass into his palm. "But I've had such a trying day you understand." Wells groaned and wailed, and at last, when he'd had his satisfaction, Thorpe stood back and reached into his coat and took out a cigar. "You're relieved of duty, now get out of my bank." He bit on the cigar, dropped the rifle and turned away, and a minute later the Bullion court was empty but for spraying water and ringing bells.

Wells swallowed hard and pushed himself upright. More stars swam before his eyes and blood trickled down his cheek. He touched the swelling and winced, then crawled to his knees nursing his wounded hand. He could see shards embedded in his flesh where they gleamed like jewels. "You bastard," he glared after him.

As he climbed to his feet, his good hand brushed against something soft. He looked around and saw the bundle of money Blackwand had left, then looked back to his bleeding hand. He was dishonoured and unemployed. *Retirement fund,* he decided, reached out and made it vanish into his battered uniform. He looked up at the broken dome and the rainy sky above. "Good on yer miss," he whispered and despite everything he ended the day with a smile.

Gold and paper make for a heavy load and even a thunder-sprite has his limits. Sunday decided to dump the money, and as luck would have it one of London's poorest districts lay within striking distance. As soon as she saw the landmark of Aldgate Station she flew level with the rooftops along Whitechapel Road, hurling sovereigns until her shoulder ached. She saw coins rain down like comets and disappear into the gloomy streets, bouncing off cabs, gas-lamps, windows, roofs, awnings, shop signs and railings. Sovereigns rolled along the pavements, fell upon opened umbrellas, and under the wheels of carts and barrows. They fell into boxes of fruits and vegetables, or pinged off shop windows. Then she let loose the banknotes, and they fluttered away like leaves in a gale. She laughed and whooped, and screamed her name over and over. "Blackwand! Blackwand! Blackwand!"

Hundreds of faces turned skywards, but she was over and gone in a heartbeat. When the sacks were empty she dropped them too and pulled the staff back, directing Strike higher. Blackwand vanished as quickly as she appeared, back into the gathering gloom of a London evening leaving a fortune behind her.

CHAPTER TWENTY-SEVEN

Elios

"What would you rather have: a lifetime of winter, or one short summer?"
"I don't want you to go," Pelaria replied. "You are my one short summer."
Eliath turned away so she would not see him cry.
Fragment from 'Pelaria and Eliath', a traditional witches' tale
Author unknown

In the last hours of May and the first hours of June, Ben agonised over a special note. It couldn't read more than a few words and it couldn't be too explicit. Each time he thought he had it, it slipped away, and all the while he was conscious of Harl sitting patiently by his side. Kolfinnia's orders had finally come and he was leaving to rally covens across the channel. Namely, L'osier Gris and Le Chemin de Gauche, the Grey Willow and the Left Hand Path. He fervently hoped the witches of Europe would offer their support.

Four days ago, Sunday had begun her campaign to distract the Illuminata, but 'devastate' might be a better word. Ordinarily Ben would have cheered her on, but he was afraid for her. After her audacious raid on the Bank, the press accused the mysterious Blackwand of high treason and demanded the death sentence. Despite their vitriolic articles however, it seemed Blackwand held the hearts and minds of London's poor. He could imagine the Illuminata's outrage at this, but unknown heroes who threw coins to the poor were always going to be popular, even if they were a witch.

To make matters worse Sunday had vanished. Harl had searched far and wide but there was no sign of her in the city. If she'd been caught the news would have been trumpeted all over the papers. His only comfort was his suspicion that she'd withdrawn from the city to wait for the dust to settle.

He put the pencil to the scrap of paper, almost started to write, then stopped. "No that won't do," he sighed and tapped his chin. His impossible note had to say he was leaving and might not see her again. How could he say that in just a few words? The challenge seemed as great as the tournament.

"Just write 'good-bye', she'll understand plain enough," Wake chipped in.

"Fat lot of good you are." He was upset because Wake was basically right, but if he had to write that, he could at least do it with style. He scribbled the note, signed it 'B' and rolled it tight. Harl hopped forwards sensing it was time to go. "Good luck Harl."

Harl took the note, twitched his head in farewell and lifted into the air. Ben followed his progress over the rooftops of Bermondsey until he lost sight of him.

"What did you write?" Wake asked.

Ben looked embarrassed. "I had to make it quick and simple."

"But what did you write?"

He coughed awkwardly. "It was a coded message, only a witch would understand it."

Wake just stared at him.

"Oh all right!" he groaned, "I wrote 'you are my one short summer'. Happy now?"

He looked impressed. "Very poetic, where's it from?"

"Pelaria and Eliath."

He considered. "That's the classic tale of two witches separated by persecution isn't it?"

"Yes," he replied warily. "Just right I thought. She'll understand I had to leave on Kolfinnia's orders."

"Hmm."

"What does 'hmm' mean?" he asked curtly.

"As I understand it the tale is a *romance*. Aren't you afraid she'll understand it a little better than you intended?"

Ben frowned and then it dawned on him what he meant. "Oh bugger!" Now he had something else to worry about.

Excerpt from the Book-of-Nine
Lord Victor Thorpe

June 1st 1887. The solstice month has come at last. This month, the rival Illuminata bloodlines shall be crushed, but June is not merely a month of knights or tournaments. The great Book plays for far higher stakes. When the solstice is done and Britain stands victorious, then we shall learn from our valkyrie creatures the nature of Àeon's song, and if they refuse to divulge it they shall perish. Thus far they have proved formidable yet there is one foe they have so far failed to quell. I speak of the insidious Blackwand and her demons.

"Blackwand," he murmured, and gazed out of the window at Hobbs Ash. He'd come here to make his own secretive notes. The state-carriage was only used for high-level meetings. Everywhere he looked he saw velvet and mahogany, and it reminded him of a very large and very expensive coffin.

"Lord Thorpe?" a voice came.

He looked up to see Galen and quickly closed the Book.

"I'm making ready for tonight's hunt," Galen looked around to make certain they were alone, "father."

Thorpe pressed a finger to his lips. "Let us hope tonight's hunt fares better than the previous five," he criticized.

"She's left the city, I'm sure of it."

"Only for the time being." Thorpe slid the little Book into his jacket.

"I'm sure you're right." He didn't want to remind his father than he had declared Blackwand wouldn't avenge the valkyrie attack. Less than twelve hours later she stole ninety-thousand pounds and dumped it amongst London's gutter-filth.

"And how fare our new orphans?" Thorpe stood and pulled his coat on.

"They're weak and I believe one might be dead."

"We have a full complement now? Nine Ruined kraken and nine valkyries?"

"If this last one survives, but only six of them are fit to hunt."

"If the thing dies, then fetch another from Smithfield." He made it sound like a simple shopping trip.

"There's something else," Galen rubbed at his brow.

He stopped with a hand half-way into his sleeve. "Go on."

"Three is the largest complement I've taken hunting so far. Six might prove a handful."

"You're up to it." He brushed his worries aside.

Galen knew not to trouble him further, although he'd lost sleep over this. Vorus was a powerful influence over her sisters, and although she never openly disobeyed him he was beginning to distrust her. *Perhaps Elios was right?* he worried privately. "And how fare you with your own troublesome devils?" he changed the subject.

Thorpe sneered. "Press and politicians. They're like a pack of street dogs, following whoever barks loudest. Fortunately jubilee celebrations have overshadowed events at the bank, and I've been able to play down the worst of it."

Galen raised his eyebrows, wondering how on Earth anything that serious could be swept aside.

"Threat of loosing one's job ensures newspapers print what they're told," Thorpe explained, guessing his thoughts. "Now, let's see if these war-birds of yours are hungry for tonight's hunt."

Vorus's family had grown. She and her remaining sister Isis had been joined by a total of seven more. Arctura's vacant kraken now had a new mistress, who disturbingly adopted the former valkyrie's name, leaving Galen with the uneasy impression of the dead returning to life.

"Galen!" Vorus pounced on him as soon as he stepped inside the barricade. "My sisters long to hunt Blackwand. When do we leave?"

"At sun down, no sooner." He marched into Vorus's shadow followed by Thorpe. Three new krakens turned and regarded them coolly. The first was a squid-like sea creature representing a real kraken, the next was a wolf, while the last bore a medieval helmet like an upturned bucket with a slit visor. "Vorus the cherub," Galen called up at her, "we'll need to find names for your new sisters."

"I shall name them, Galen."

"Names are of great esoteric importance," Thorpe muttered in warning. "She must not be allowed to take control."

"No need my sweet." Galen thought fast and swept and arm across the three newcomers, starting with the squid-like beast. "I dub thee Neptune the fish, Fenris the wolf, and Void the faceless," he finished with the blank helmet with the slit visor. "Now enough play talk, tonight we hunt."

"And pray you deliver Blackwand," Thorpe added.

The cherub helmet rumbled around to face him. "Lord Thorpe, we cannot possibly fight Blackwand if Galen cannot find her first," she said coldly.

Galen flushed with anger, but bit his tongue.

"As I recall, the last time Mr Galen found Blackwand, her demons proved too strong for you and one of your precious sisters was left a tattered corpse," Thorpe countered.

The air temperature dropped a degree and there came a smell like an opened casket. "There are six sisters now, and three gathering their strength. Nine in total. Blackwand will be yours before this special date you speak of." The huge machine towered over him, breathing menacingly.

"The solstice, yes she'd better be," Thorpe lit a cigar, stringing out the silence, "and if she's not then it pains me to say your usefulness will have expired."

All six swayed a fraction. Metal groaned and the smell of decay grew stronger.

Father! Galen thought worriedly.

Thorpe flicked his spent match towards the giant and then turned to leave.

The cherub's face rolled back towards Galen. "Lord Thorpe is displeased?"

He's always displeased, Galen thought. "Rest, all of you, tonight we hunt."

"And when Blackwand is gone, we find more of my sisters?" Her voice came from right beside his ear and he knew she had slipped from her kraken and was in the ether around him.

Her question was unexpected. "Am I to believe there are yet more like you Vorus?"

"Alas, there will always be lost children of Ruin to rescue." Her voice was like frost against his face.

How many of your kind are lurking at Smithfield? He felt a shiver. Were valkyries really so rare, he wondered? "Alas, we've no more Ruined-krakens to hold your kin." It was hard work keeping the sense of relief out of his voice. He made to go, thinking the conversation ended, when she stopped him in his tracks.

"More can be made my sweet."

All six stared down at him, and finally he understood what it must feel like to be one of the witches they had fed to them over the weeks. "Save your strength, I shall return tonight." He hurried away, unsure if the cold air around him was his imagination, or Vorus watching him like a jealous lover.

Later, before sundown, Elios opened that special window for him once more, and he gazed through the veil. Sophie knelt by that dark river, as always with her back to him, holding something in her arms. *"Little Miss Muffet sat on her tuffet, along came a spider and wove her away."* Her voice was like silk in his ear, but the words disturbed him.

That's not how the rhyme goes? He clutched the staff harder. *What are you doing little twin of mine? All these years what have you been doing?*

She didn't answer, but for an instant she turned. It was nothing more than a twitch, but he caught the curve of her cheek and the suggestion of her nose before she looked away again.

"Sophie!" He gripped the cane even harder. *"It's I, your twin, Matthew. You heard me – I know it!"*

She ignored him, and began singing again, and although he knew the tune the words were all wrong. *"Along came a spider to protect and to guide her, and so she could never be slain."* Now the sky grew black with Ruinous creatures, and Sophie, in her white gown, glimmered like a star in the night. *"The lost children shall soon be whole again, beloved sisters coming home,"* she hummed.

"Sophie?" he tried again. *"You're coming home!"* But the image darkened further, until that glimmering star vanished and all was blackness.

"Galen!" Elios cried out, then suddenly everything was silent.

"Sophie!" he shouted and his eyes flew open and saw only his small bunk-room. "What happened? Elios, where did she go!"

"Galen, the link was broken."

"Broken, by what?"

"Please, I don't know."

He sat nursing the cane and thinking dark thoughts. *Did Sophie block the link, and if so why?* In just a few seconds he convinced himself his sister was plotting against him.

"Galen?"

"Nothing my sweet. You sound weary. Tonight you'll remain here while I hunt Blackwand." He climbed off his bunk, and retrieved his satchel.

"Be careful tonight Galen."

"Blackwand won't get the upper hand again."

"It's not Blackwand that troubles me."

"Get some rest." He patted the cane then shoved it under his bunk and left for Hobbs Ash, still thinking of Sophie's message. *Beloved sisters coming home.*

Nunhead Cemetery proved a good hiding place, but after days without any sign of Harl, Sunday was starting to wonder if it was a little too good. When at last he did come it was the morning of Wednesday June 1st and she hurriedly opened the note. While her fingers worked fast, her imagination worked faster, and she thought about all the things she wanted the note to say, and all the things she didn't. A second later she was reading Ben's message.

It's said that the first thought we have about something is often the purest; that gut instinct that comes in a flash, before a moment later it's swamped by questions, doubts, and hopes. Her first thought was simple: Ben had sent her a love note. The smile was still on her lips when a landslide of following thoughts crushed that fragile first thought, and none of them were good. "Pelaria and Eliath," it dawned on her, and she swallowed a lump of disappointment. "It's just us now Strike." She glanced over to where he was perched on a gravestone watching the cemetery's wide avenues.

"We've managed this far by ourselves. We'll be fine." Although he missed Ben and Wake as much as her.

"But will Ben be fine?" She looked down at the scrap of paper in her hand, realising it might be her last link to him. "My thanks Harl," she turned to the crow, but the bird hopped away. She took his meaning at once. No reply was needed because Ben was no longer in the city. She would either see him on the solstice or never again, it was as simple as that. Harl beat his wings and took to the skies. She watched him go and silently wished him good luck.

"What will we do now?" Strike asked evenly.

The sun was on the rise, and already she could see it was going to be a hot day. Tawny raised his head from the long grass and she smiled to see a spider perched on his nose. The great bear yawned and then sunk back into his sleep.

"Sunday?" Strike persisted.

"The tournament is going ahead, and witches will be readying to attack, there's only one thing we can do."

"Yes?"

She thought of the brief, but wonderful spark she felt at reading his note, and how quickly the darkness had gobbled it up, and then of all the witches who'd undoubtedly die attacking the tournament. Her duty was to them. "The Bank of England was a knife in their back." She folded the little note and put it safely in her waistcoat. "Time to twist that knife I think."

The evening was fine and the crossing promised to be a smooth one. Ben stood watching Britain slide away, and now there were only a few miles between him and France. He could have flown, but these waters were busy and this wasn't a time to be seen, and so he chose the slower but safer route, taking a steamer from Dover.

"You're thinking." Wake stated the obvious.

Ben leaned on his lightning-staff, using it as a crutch again, and even putting a pebble in his shoe to enhance the effect. He watched Britain's shores slowly dwindle. "Yes, I'm thinking," he murmured.

"About London."

"About London," he agreed patiently.

"And about her."

He smiled in exasperation. "You're like a dog with a bone Wake, you know that."

"Is that good?"

"Only sometimes."

"But you are though aren't you?"

"Of course," he admitted, watching the sea roll by. Every so often the ship sounded its horn, while a few gulls sailed past, looking for scraps. *Better luck elsewhere,* Ben thought. Their cargo steamer had nothing to offer hungry gulls. It was carrying iron goods to Calais, and the captain had proudly told him the hold was crammed with twenty-thousand horse shoes. "I'm worried," he confessed at last.

"I know."

"I'm worried they'll find her, and if they do, I can't do a thing to help."

"Help her by breaking this tournament."

"We'll need plenty of luck for that."

"We're sitting on a boat load of luck right here."

He smiled faintly. Britain was almost out of sight now. The ship's horn sounded again and it reminded him of the kraken's battle horns. He thought of the fight at Kittiwake and how much bigger the solstice tournament would be. His last thought he kept for himself, *Lord Hethra, please keep her safe.*

Wake let him have his privacy, but just for good measure he said a silent little prayer of his own. Ben took his leave and hobbled from the rail. Tomorrow would be a long day, and if the covens of Europe said no, then Blackwand would be left truly alone.

Elios lay in a tormented half-sleep. The window into Ruin had never closed before, neither had Sophie ever detected them, and she'd been trying to understand why since Galen left.

"It's your fault you wretched faint-heart, you and your silly dream. You think to be free of me?" The voice was her dead-walk half. *"You are me."*

She curled smaller inside her staff, trying to hide from it, which only made it angrier.

"Come forth and face the consequences worm! Come out and see what harm you've done your beloved Galen, and when he needed you most."

"Leave me be!" She cupped hands over her ears.

"You and your petty jealousy. It was you that broke the link."

"No!" she argued, and scrambled free of the corrupted wood, slipped through the silk and slumped onto the floor. She took a moment to recover her breath, and hopped into the moonlight falling through the open skylight, and looked up at the night sky. *The thunder-heights, my home.* She thought it even before she knew it and then instantly flinched as if having broken a rule. She found the moonlight soothing and sat there for a while, and before long she detected voices outside the window, on the roof itself, and she craned her head and listened.

"Coming here was the most insane thing you've ever talked me into!"

"You've said, at least a dozen times Strike, now shhh!" Sunday crept forwards looking for a way in. Her eagles sat attentive on a chimney stack, scanning for any trace of the valkyries.

"But here of all places! This place is a desert for a fish, a fire for a tree, no witch has come here and left alive!"

"Then we'll be the first," she gave her staff a shake, "now SHHH!"

Goldhawk's roof top world was a vista of towering chimneys, gables, and decorative domes sporting sculpted finials. Weeds sprouted here and there in the gutters, and in places, weathered roof ladders lay against the tiles. She crept forwards hunched over, concealed in black and taking cover behind a low parapet, searching for a suitable window to crawl through.

"What about that one?" Strike suggested.

"Not big enough, you might get through but I wouldn't."

"Then let me go!"

"What!"

"Be fast and silent you said, so let me slip inside and search."

She was upset to find that he made perfect sense, and horrified when she heard herself agree. "Very well, you slip through there," she nodded to an open skylight, "and I'll find another way in. We meet again in twenty minutes."

"Agreed." He slid from her lightning-staff and dropped to the roof.

"Be careful!" She watched him skip lightly up the roof, towards the open skylight. He turned back, gave her a quick nod, slid under the iron frame and out of sight. She quickly slashed five chalk lines on the tiles to mark the right window. "Be careful dear friend," she whispered and then hurried on, looking for her own way into Goldhawk Row.

Strike landed silently on a bare wooden floor. He quickly examined the room and saw a simple bunk with folded blankets. Of all the things he expected to find in the infamous Goldhawk Row, a rustic-looking bedroom wasn't one of them. *Find what we want and go,* he reminded himself, and what Sunday wanted were details of Goldhawk's business associates. The door was ajar, not much, but enough for him to squeeze through, and after a quick look around he bounded across the room towards it.

Elios watched from under the bunk. She couldn't move, she couldn't even think. She forgot about valkyries, Sophie, Ruination, and even her beloved Galen. She watched the thunder-sprite in awe, understanding that this magnificent creature was what she'd always longed to be. A tear glistened and she sniffed.

Strike heard something under the bunk. He froze, and slowly turned back.

Sunday found a larger window and let herself inside. *Goldhawk Row,* she thought as she crept along a dark corridor. Each step was calculated and silent. If she ran into trouble she had no doubt the walls would tumble and three angry bears would be at her side, but this was about stealth not strength, and she prayed to leave unnoticed.

She could spend hours searching, it would take a small miracle to pinpoint what she wanted in the time she had. But just then a small miracle is just what she saw. A large brown spider scuttled out from under one of the doors, detected her, then shot back into hiding. She regarded the door's name plate. "Senior Accountant's Office," she read in a whisper. "Thank you dear champion," she smiled, knowing this was the place. Raven's wand defied the lock and she vanished inside.

There was little time to be selective. She stuffed her pockets with bills and receipts. She was just about done and ready to head back when a voice stopped her.

"So it is true!"

Her heart jumped and she spun around, wand at the ready, but saw nothing. "Who's there?" she hissed.

Something on the desktop moved, and a small fairy dipped out from behind the heavy typewriter. "So it is true," he said again and crawled closer.

She relaxed a fraction. "Who are you, and why show yourself to me?"

The fairy had a large round face and crescent shaped scales. "No harm intended," he assured her. "But you are girl with broken-soul, broom-rider who cleansed the Cold Coast, yes?"

Her mouth dropped and she thought of Neet far away. "Cold Coast," she managed, "yes, I was there. Who are you?"

"A humble moon-fairy is all." He glanced back at the moonlight falling through the window. "But all fairy-kind is alive with tales. I thought it impossible such a girl was to be found, but here you are!" He gazed at something unseen above her head.

"How do you know it was me?"

"Soul-sign tells me so."

"What of my soul-sign?" Now she felt wary, afraid her old treachery was written there.

The moon-fairy lifted into the air and flew closer. "Broken and made whole again, never one like it before. Never one like it again."

"But you're not from the Cold Coast?"

"No matter, tales travel fast. Girl with broken soul."

She backed away, feeling exposed. "I have to leave and so should you, this is a hard place for creatures of magic."

He shrugged. "Yes, sprite told me so, but the moonlight here is seldom harvested."

"What?" She stopped, hand on the door knob. "You said sprite?" *Has he already seen Strike?* she thought.

"Yes, lone thunder-sprite lives here, but with no broom-rider she says." He continued to admire her soul-sign.

For the second time in as many minutes Sunday was dumbfounded. "He," she corrected, "sprites are always *he*. And besides, sprites either travel with witches or remain in their original tree. A sprite can't be here without a witch."

"Not this one, and like it or not, he is a she. She told me so and looked most angry too."

"But that's not possible!"

"Go above, to place of paper and words, and see for yourself."

"A *female* sprite?" She looked to the ceiling, imagining the library beyond.

"I can't, I have to go, and you should too." She turned the knob and let herself out.

The moon-fairy watched her quietly exit. "Everyone tells me that," he muttered, and after harvesting a few souls he made back to the crack in the window through which he'd come.

"Who's under there?" Strike demanded, not realising Sunday was having a similar confrontation downstairs. "I know you're under there, now come out." He heard a soft scraping sound and then saw movement. Another thunder-sprite crept out from under the bunk and he instantly realised this was unlike any sprite he'd met before.

Elios sat staring at him in wonder and trepidation.

"Who are you?" He sniffed cautiously, trying for the stranger's scent.

At first she couldn't speak and just sat there as lifeless as a post.

"Can you talk?" He inched forwards.

She trembled and backed away.

"You're afraid of me?" He thought it senseless that one sprite should be afraid of another, but again his senses told him this was no ordinary sprite.

"You are a thunder-sprite," she said incredulously. Her dead-walk mind would be furious at her for even talking to him, but she was helpless.

"Who are you?"

"I am Elios," she replied.

Strike was fascinated. Clearly this sprite was not male, but it must be. Water was wet, air was invisible, and thunder-sprites were male: except that this one wasn't. This one was unique. He noted how her wings were more slender than his, and her features sharper. "A beautiful name," he complimented, "and I am Strike." Suddenly he felt something strange and unexpected, and remembered Ben's awkwardness around Sunday. "Forgive me, but you're –"

"A flight-less runt," she confessed and backed towards the darkness under the bunk.

"No!" he hopped closer. "No, not at all."

She stopped and looked back, but it hurt. He was a mirror for all the things she had been told she couldn't be.

"You are," he peered at her, thinking of how the way-beware had learned a new song. "You are more evolved."

"Evolved?"

"Aye, sprites are all alike, but not you."

"I am a mistake." Galen knew it, Vorus knew it, she might as well admit it.

"No!" The idea disgusted him and he wondered who'd put such evil in her head.

"No?"

"No. Magic changes with time, it gets better, or so I've heard. So you must be more evolved, more magical." It was the only explanation he could think of.

She had lived her entire life under the command of her dead-walk half. She considered herself to be many things, but evolved wasn't one of them. "I must go," she said, but didn't move. She wanted to speak more with him. She wanted to know about her true self, somehow convinced he could tell her.

"Where is your witch?" He looked around, worried that her witch was a prisoner.

"I have no witch, Galen is my keeper."

He bristled inwardly at the name, but remained impassive. "So this Galen isn't a witch?"

"No, but he found me, and just as well."

"Why so?"

"Because no real witch would have need of a sprite that can't fly."

"Who told you that?" he asked angrily, but knowing already.

"Galen," she flinched, feeling she'd said too much.

"All sprites fly."

She shook her head fiercely.

"Yes they do," he insisted.

"No!" She looked desperately to the dead-walk under the bunk.

"Your home is under there?"

"Please, I have to be back."

"Back to what? What tree were you born in? What place?" He hopped closer still, within touching distance now. "What's your storm name?"

"I can't tell you!"

"What place were you born Elios?" he shouted, heedless of being overheard. "What tree?"

"Please!"

"What tree! Tell me!"

"Dead-walk!" she cried finally.

He hissed in shock and backed away growling.

"You see," she whispered in despair, "I am a mistake."

Sunday heard Strike clearly. He was shouting, and she ran the last flight of steps in a panic. The sound of her footfalls was shocking, but she didn't care. Strike was in peril, she knew it. Voices drew her closer until she at last opened the door to a small room off the library and found not one, but two thunder-sprites. "Hethra's teeth!" She had no idea what she'd stumbled into, but right away she caught the subtle differences. "I never thought I'd see the day I'd meet a *beautiful* thunder-sprite?"

Strike missed the pun in his upset. "Thank Oak you're here! Tell her," he jabbed a finger at Elios, "tell her she's been lied to!"

"Her?" The fairy's words suddenly made sense.

"Her name's Elios," Strike fumed, "and she's been lied to!"

Elios looked up in realisation. This was Blackwand and Strike was hers. "No!" she moaned, "you cannot be here of all places, they will find you and kill you and far, far worse, Galen has such torments in store!"

Sunday instantly sobered at the name. "You know this Galen?"

"Yes," Strike answered for her, "he's the one who insists she can't fly, and that she's a mistake." He'd never set eyes on the man but already he hated him.

"Answer me," she ignored him and glared down at Elios, angry that she would have anything to do with such a fiend.

"Don't be so harsh!" Strike protested.

Elios watched them disagree, all the while conscious that Galen might burst in and catch them.

"How could any sprite have anything to do with witch-hunters and disciples of Ruin?" Sunday shook her head in disgust.

"Because it's not her fault." In one leap Strike landed on the bed post and flared his wings angrily. "Her storm struck a dead-walk!"

Sunday inhaled sharply and her eyes went back to Elios. "Oh dear Hethra, is this true?"

Elios looked up, miserable and confused.

"Then I'm sorry," she knelt and reached out, but Elios shrank from her touch. "Forgive me, I had no idea." Now she understood. Ruin sometimes inverted magic, but for it to produce such an incredible creature as this was so unlikely that she couldn't even begin to comprehend. This wasn't just chance, this was miraculous.

Elios felt like a fairground attraction, or even worse; a traitor for speaking with Galen's arch-enemy. Behind, the dead-walk whispered to her. *"Galen loves you. Remember the days of old, when it was just you and him? Remember how happy you were? Come back to me, lie inside my cold heart and know the joy of despair, come back to me darling Elios."*

"You should go Blackwand," she said sadly, "if they find you, your fate will be awful." She looked down at her small hands, expecting to hear departing footsteps, or some spiteful accusation, but the next thing she knew a soothing hand lay on her wings and she looked up in to the face of their enemy.

"Is it true?" Sunday asked, but the look on Elios's face was answer enough.

"I told you," Strike rumbled, still angry.

"Then come with us," Sunday offered.

Elios gasped in horror and hope, while Strike couldn't hide his delight.

"Elios, Galen has given up everything for you, he needs you!" the dead-walk pleaded.

"I don't know," Elios stammered and looked back into the shadows where her narrow little coffin awaited. "I want to, but . . ."

"But what?" Sunday asked.

"But . . ." She quivered with indecision.

"Go then runt-whore, run away, but remember your happiness will be Galen's heartbreak. He will return to find you gone, and fall dead with his heart in two while you frolic with the enemy."

"Come with us," Sunday urged again. "Come with us and fly."

Fly? Her heart yearned for it, but she groaned and backed away. She was being torn in two.

"Just grab her and let's go!" Strike ordered.

Elios squeaked in horror, and shot back under the bunk.

"Now look what you've done!" Sunday dropped to all fours and peered underneath.

"Reach under and grab her!" Strike flapped.

Sunday was on the brink of doing just that when she heard a thud from outside. She recognised it as a window being closed, perhaps on the floor below, and she guessed the night watch were making their rounds "Elios, come with us now, or not at all. There's no time!"

"Elios, please!" Strike begged.

"Leave me alone," a small voice came from the darkness.

"My faithful little Elios," the dead-walk sighed, *"Galen will be so proud."*

"Please, just go from here Blackwand." She was already crawling under the silk and back into her cane.

Sunday grabbed her staff knowing it was futile. "Strike, we're going."

"But we can't!"

"I know," she empathised, "I know how hard it is to leave those we care about, but we have to go, now!"

He swallowed his despair, shot a last look under the bunk, and vanished into the lightning-staff. Sunday backed away to the door and pulled her face mask up. Just as she did, she heard a small moan from under the bed and it filled her heart with ice.

"The dead-walk is too strong," Elios mourned softly, hardly aware they were there now. "Too strong to fly."

Sunday heard the whisper of silk and then nothing, and the silence made the approaching footsteps even louder. "A lifetime of winter," she murmured, then slipped through the door leaving only a single dark spot on the floorboards where she'd shed a tear for Elios.

Sunday put the stolen documents to good use in the days that followed, and in doing so she learned something disturbing about herself. She *enjoyed* punishing her enemies. She also enjoyed the war waged against her by the press, yet the people still seemed to think her a hero. The most important Illuminata targets were bolstered with troops and fortifications. Banks, residencies, naval yards and steel mills like the one at Chertfield. The major ports and wharfs where the riches of the Empire flooded in were all Illuminata controlled and required full time guards. The expense was enormous, but always Blackwand slipped through and devastated the most obscure targets. The breach of Goldhawk Row went unnoticed and Elios never breathed a word, wishing to forget that terrible yet wonderful night, and so armed with privileged information she tracked down the Illuminata's blackest associates and made them pay. The time for knights and Lords would come at the solstice, but now she brought her wrath against the grubby, the cowardly and greedy. Those men who worked from the shadows, picking the lice of corruption from their master's hide to conceal their crimes. And one such man was Somerset Willoughby Leech.

Leech gave the door to his office an experimental tug, then satisfied it was locked, he left for the night. While the rest of the Illuminata lost sleep to Blackwand, Leech continued with life as always. He was too deeply buried, too obscure, too well protected to be found.

His small office was located in Milk Yard, by the Shadwell Basin. His business and his name were absent from the painted sign outside, which was dusty and faded. It read simply 'Shadwell Export Firm.' He didn't get any passing customers and didn't want any. Leech did his business direct with the men at Goldhawk, and the nature of his exports was children.

He arranged for buyers on the Continent to purchase coven children. Captives as young as two years-old were sold into slavery, hard labour and sometimes much worse, through his network of contacts across Europe, Asia and the Americas.

His office was above a stable block, where he kept all manner of goods, none of which had anything to do with his trade, but provided a believable cover. He left down a flight of stone steps and into the small yard below.

"Mr Leech?" a voice enquired.

Startled, he turned. The gates were locked and the courtyard should have been empty. Behind him, walking down the very steps he'd just used was a young woman dressed in black. She wore a plain bonnet with her hair in a respectable knot, and long black dress. She smiled at him as she gracefully descended and crossed the cobbled yard to where he stood.

"Mr Somerset Willoughby Leech?" she asked again.

"I am he, my dear, and how may I be of assistance to such a pretty young lady?" He spoke like a thug masquerading as a gentleman and she despised him right away.

Sunday swallowed her disgust and returned his smile. She saw he was at least sixty, but still fancied himself as something of a dandy. He wore a black frock coat and immaculately creased slacks, a chestnut-brown hair piece, and powder on his puffy cheeks and even rouge on his lips. When he smiled, the wrinkles looked dusty and deep and his teeth were tea-stained. "Mr Leech, I'd be in your debt if you'd please remove all your attire," she fluttered her eyes at him.

His smile remained fixed, but he blinked rapidly. "My dear?"

"Your clothes Mr Leech, be so good as to take them off, all of them. I want you naked."

He emitted a dusty laugh and regarded her with relish. "My dear child – so bold." He reached up and smoothed the satin bow around his neck.

She smiled benignly and drew a long black stick from the folds of her dress. "Mr Leech, please I shan't ask you again. Either strip down or be torn to strips." She pointed her wand at his chest.

At that he heard a deep growling behind him, and he felt his innards slump like melting snows. He started to turn but she stopped him.

"I wouldn't. They don't like eye contact, it makes them ill tempered."

The growling deepened.

"It's you," he gave a strangled whisper, "Blackwand."

"Yes, it's me. Now strip, you slave-mongering bastard." She reached up and pulled the bonnet from her head.

A shadow fell across him and the growling behind grew louder. He knew without looking what it was and what it could do and his face crumpled. Something warm flooded down his left leg, and he blubbered and grovelled as tears rolled down his powdery cheeks. Slowly, he reached down with his trembling hands and began to unbutton his wet trousers.

Betty Chapman was pushing a barrow full of blankets along Mitre Street, intending to take them to Newcutt Workhouse. They were moth-eaten and old, but they sometimes paid a penny a piece. A flock of pigeons paraded in her wake. They strutted after her cooing and pecking, but they suddenly took to flight in a rapid flutter. She looked around, expecting a cat, or a dog, but what she saw quite stunned her. There was a naked man staggering along the road. "Saints above," she gasped and stepped behind her barrow for protection.

As he drew closer, she reached into her dress for the old chair leg she kept for events such as this. "Keep a distance, there's constables about, yer fiend!" She brandished the chair leg menacingly, hoping a constable would show up right then. One or two windows opened in the tenements opposite and curious faces peeped out. "Don't come no closer!" she warned, and tried to avert her eyes from his groins. What glimpse she did get though had the eels she'd eaten for dinner wobbling in her gut as though they still lived.

He continued forwards, mumbling, and she could see his hands had been tied and there was something hairy stuffed in his mouth. Betty had the horrible idea that it was a half-eaten rat. Strangest of all, there was a board around his neck and a message written in chalk. Betty wasn't the most educated lady in London, but she grasped the words. 'SLAVE MONGER' it said. The man tumbled down beside her barrow, whimpering and moaning, and she lowered her homemade weapon. Now more heads were appearing from windows, and sniggers and mutters drifted up and down the street.

"Is 'ee drunk?" someone shouted.

"Ee ain't even decent!" another cackled.

The naked man looked up at her imploringly. She saw his face was a soggy mess of powder white, and the thing in his mouth was a ragged wig. From the look of his shiny pate she deduced it was his own. Warily, she pulled the wig from his mouth and dropped it to the gutter in disgust. Leech heaved a deep breath. "Blackwand!" he whispered hoarsely.

Betty looked up at the sky and half expected to see a fairytale character up there, a witch riding a broom by all the saints. But the sky was dusky orange and all she saw were gathering rain clouds.

June lengthened and Sunday continued to be a dagger. The berserks' companionship gave her the confidence to execute startling raids, but always it was her intention to avoid bloodshed.

One imposing redbrick house, in exclusive Belgrave Square, was owned by Sir Benjamin Morley, a name very few Londoners would know. But Morley's firm were accountants to key Illuminata business interests. After arriving at midnight and landing silently on the roof, she quickly found what she wanted. There was a healthy growth of ivy sprawling over the front on the house, but a simple spell would make it healthier by far.

Morley was awoken by the sound of creaking wood and grinding brick. "Maud, there's an intruder downstairs!" He groped for his revolver in the bedside cabinet, while his wife groaned in her sleep. There came another crash, closer this time, and just then their bedroom window exploded and something huge and powerful snaked through. He screamed and Maud finally awoke, and immediately screamed as well. There were muscular-looking vines snaking through their bed-chamber, over the ceiling, walls and floor: all of them thickening in seconds and crushing all in their path. "Maud! Rouse the servants!" he screamed as he now fumbled with the lantern. Around him, plaster dropped in crumbling jigsaw pieces, the walls groaned, and timbers complained as if the whole house was being crumpled. There came an ominous rumble from above as the roof began to fall. Maud screamed again and took cover under the blankets, and when her husband finally got the lantern glowing and witnessed the writhing tendrils tearing his house apart, he joined her and the pair clung to one another like frightened children.

Sunday watched from the adjacent building as the humble ivy engulfed the house and literally demolished it. *"I didn't know you had such green fingers,"* Strike admired.

She smiled when she heard the screaming from inside. "Maybe at heart I'm really a gardener-girl after all." They left in a haste, and if not for the chalk marks she left on the roadside, nobody would've known they'd ever been there.

She continued her acts of sabotage and because manpower was diverted to protect the most affluent Illuminata families, these peripheral interests were left vulnerable. Sunday found sensitive information in the documents taken from Goldhawk, and she hunted down the accused with relish. She found where the coal barges that supplied Hobbs Ash were moored and she sank them, she found the small factory that made the meal-biscuits the Illuminata purchased as prison rations, and the mills where they bought their flour. She found the tailors that supplied the soldier's uniforms and the firms that supplied bayonets for their rifles. She found the stables where squires bought foals to train in warfare. She used her skills to freeze the waters of the St Katharine docks where Illuminata merchant vessels were docked. Their days of importing and exporting were put on hold until the freakish June ice was hacked away. She learned which paper mills they purchased from, and imagined how many death warrants were finalised on those innocuous sheets of paper. She found them all and Blackwand sent them a message and everywhere she went she left her mark: five chalk lines like claw marks. The grand bloodlines of the Illuminata sat in their fortified houses across Britain and watched as their army of overlooked merchants began to denounce them. During this turbulent period, Galen and Vorus hunted her by night, but somehow she always managed to stay ahead of them. Galen grew frustrated, Thorpe became ever angrier and Vorus demanded her red-river like a spoiled child.

She promised to be a knife, and she had one target in mind and she left it until the end. It was for Ben and a woman she'd never met: Charlotte Anne Pilling. She made an inspection of the place and found it was everything Ben said it was. It filled her with woe, horror and fury. The place was an obscenity on Hethra's green Earth and she couldn't believe she hadn't been aware of it before now. "How could Ben have endured this place?" she asked Strike later.

"He came here to try and help Lottie," he reminded her, but he couldn't see how anyone, no matter how committed, could change the scale of suffering. *"No wonder they came here to summon demons of carnage."*

She watched the dense crowds below shift and sway. Even from up here the smell was terrible and the sounds of crying animals broke her heart. "Well, they won't come here for much longer."

"We break it?"

"We break it."

"And then they'll not summon any more of those things?"

"No more."

She'd found a safe place to while away the daylight hours. It was the morning of June 14th, the solstice was only a week away, and she promised herself that by June 15th there would only be rubble where Smithfield now stood. "Be safe Ben," she whispered, and huddled smaller behind the chimney stack. Three eagles perched above, all five shielded from unfriendly eyes, all waiting for darkness and the chance to cleanse this wound from Hethra and Halla's world once and for all.

CHAPTER TWENTY-EIGHT

A lifelong lie

James grew angry now, 'What I did, I did so for love!'
Fionelle looked on impassively. 'Yes - love for yourself, not me.'
'The Vagaries of Heaven' - Randolph Taylor James - 1874

"Tell me about Blackwand!" Thorpe roared and swung again, landing another blow to the face. The witch grunted and his head flopped forwards. Thorpe grabbed his neck. "She's a fair-skinned whore with yellow hair and a mark here," he jabbed his left cheek, "a mark like an hourglass. Now tell me about the Jik bitch, tell me her real name!" He landed another punch.

Warden Topp stepped forwards with a small cough of disapproval. Although he didn't want to get in the way of his fists, he couldn't let him beat the prisoner to death. "Sir, I think the lad's telling the truth."

Thorpe ignored him. "What's her bloody name?" He shook the witch by his hair.

"Never 'erd of her," he gasped and gulped back a mouthful of blood.

Thorpe growled something and shoved him back into the corner of his cell. "I'm taking a respite," he flexed his shoulders, "we'll continued later. Topp, have Mr Galen meet me in the state carriage right away." He pushed past him and left.

Topp watched him go and breathed a sigh of relief. Things were getting out of hand and the longer Blackwand evaded capture the nastier Thorpe became. "You heard the man," he ordered his staff, "find Mr Galen." He pulled the cell door closed and locked their prisoner away. "And find the medical officer too and have him take a look at this lad's face."

Thorpe poured himself a scotch, downed it then took a second. "Blackwand," he seethed, "how I wish I'd just shot you in the woods that day."

The carriage door opened and then closed, and Galen entered.

"Doulton telegrammed me from Salisbury last night," Thorpe said without turning, "he tells me Leonhard is thinking of withdrawing from the tournament because we can't secure his safety."

"What!" Galen had hardly sat down when he sprang up again. "But for God's sake the tournament's in one week!"

"Doesn't matter if it's in ten years," he smiled cynically, "they'll leave if Blackwand isn't caught, and that'll give them victory by default. And our hopes to control the Illuminata will be gone."

"I thought the intention was to lure her to us?"

"While she's protected by her demons that simply isn't possible." He swirled his drink and stared at the amber fluid.

"Then we must find how she controls them."

"Indeed," he smiled faintly. "Can you do it?"

He considered for a moment. "If I could find her and watch her, examine the bond between her and those creatures, yes, I believe I could break the link."

Thorpe wiped blood from his knuckles with a handkerchief. "Good. Then I want you to take out all nine valkyries tonight, we need to finish this."

"All nine!"

"I trust you can do this?" he peered at him. "My son," he added for good measure.

"Father," he started, "the hardest part is loosing track of them. It's a severe handicap having to chase on foot while Vorus flies easily over the rooftops."

Thorpe finished his scotch and poured himself a third. When the drink was done he went about the carriage drawing the heavy curtains. "Make it appear," he ordered when all the windows were covered.

"What?"

"Your sprite, make it appear."

He looked down at his cane. "Elios?"

"Yes, Elios or whatever you call it. Make the crippled runt appear."

When he still didn't move, Thorpe snatched the cane, and tossed it on to the table where it landed with a harsh bang, and looked even uglier against the richly polished wood. He took a cigar tube from his coat and undid the lid. It wasn't a cigar inside but salt, and he poured a rough circle around the cane. "Beasts should earn their keep," he said as he worked, "servants must learn their proper place, dogs must learn to hunt or fetch, and sheep should grow fat. Tell me what this Elios has done to earn her keep?"

Galen felt angry. "Without her we'd have no link to Sophie."

"When Sophie's back, we won't need such a creature any longer, so tell me what's she good for?"

Galen just stood there trembling, knowing Elios was aware of their every word.

"As I thought: nothing. So, make it appear." He went and stood at the head of the table, waiting.

Galen reached out, careful not to disturb the salt, and touched the cane. "Elios?" he asked. "Elios, I know you're listening, please come forwards."

The cane rocked gently and an instant later she appeared. Right away Galen saw she was terrified.

Thorpe wasted no time. "You know who I am?"

She nodded.

"And you know how important it is to capture this criminal Blackwand?"

She thought back to that night. *"Come with us, come with us and fly."* Right now she wished she had done. "I understand," she said quietly.

"Then hear me; when Galen commands the valkyries he must be fleet of foot, he must be swift enough to keep up with them. Do you understand?"

She looked to Galen for support, but he was busy staring at his own feet.

"In short, Galen must be mobile." Thorpe stared at her accusingly. "You will carry him."

There was a stunned silence, and Galen heard the ruffle of feathers as she looked between them both, bewildered and afraid. "But, has Galen not said?"

"Elios, please," Galen interrupted, realising a huge lie was about to be revealed.

"I know what he has said!" Thorpe boomed, making her flinch. "But now I'm telling you something different."

"Father please," he tried.

"Silence!" He stalked closer and loomed over the frightened creature. "Galen told you what he needed to tell you, that is all."

She struggled to comprehend, and tried to back away from his anger, but bumped against the salt barrier.

"Father!" Galen tried again.

"Enough!" Thorpe spun around and slapped him across his face. Galen glared at him, but quickly turned his attention back to the floor and Elios was horrified by his look of defeat. He quickly turned his anger back to her. "My son has enjoyed playing 'witch' all these years, and so now you will carry him as a good sprite should."

"But I can't!" she stammered. "I can't fly. I am Ruined!"

"Enough foolish female tricks!" He pounded a fist against the table. "Galen only told you that to keep you as his link to Sophie."

It was out. In plain words. Galen's lifetime lie.

She searched his face for some denial, but he had nothing to offer her. "Galen?"

"I was afraid for you, that's all," he struggled.

"Afraid?" Thorpe sneered. "Be a man and tell the wretched thing the truth."

"Galen?" she choked.

"Elios," he began, "Elios it is true, but I assure you I was afraid for you. What I told you, I did it to keep you safe."

"But the dead-walk," she gasped, "the dead-walk told me I, I . . ." she felt all of its wicked insults down the years. "It told me I couldn't fly," she finished. This was her last shred of pretence, the only thing that might prove his honesty.

"The cane cannot have told you such a thing, because it is not alive," he whispered hoarsely, trying to hide his tears, but from his father not her.

She let out a small groan and slumped to the table.

Thorpe folded his arms. "Do you see now, sprite? What you heard were your own doubts. The dead-walk merely reflected them back to you. You can fly as well as any sprite."

"Galen," she turned to him, but saw only his bowed head.

"All that's Ruinous about you is that sprites are male, you are not," Thorpe concluded. "A novel side-effect of your unusual birth, but one that allowed you to see into the mind of Ruin all these years. It's often said that women are more psychic." He smiled and sneered at this.

Elios heard Thorpe talking, but none of it mattered anymore. 'Evolved,' Strike had called her, 'beautiful' Blackwand had said, yet her own family had lied to her. It was too much, and tried to tuck her head beneath her wing.

Thorpe looked on in disgust. "Will you carry Galen or not?" he demanded.

"Father," Galen tried again.

"Wait!" he held up a hand. "Well?"

Elios sat in silence.

"As I thought, you are of no value. Be out of my sight." He waved a dismissive hand at the cane.

"Elios has kept the link with Sophie all these years," Galen protested. *After you and Barlow sold her to Ruination,* he thought, but dare not say. "At least acknowledge that much." He heard the whisper of feathers and knew Elios had hidden again.

Thorpe smiled. "Keep your pet if you must, just find Blackwand."

"I think I know a way."

"Then take the valkyrie pack and hunt her."

Galen looked to the table. Elios was gone now, hidden again. "No. I'll hunt alone."

"Alone?"

"I can find her without Vorus, without Elios, without the Illuminata."

Thorpe pulled one of the curtains aside and squinted as light flooded in. "And how might you achieve such a miracle?"

He looked at the cane lying on the table and remembered holding a similar stick many years ago and using it to commit his first murder. "Rang-Shaa," he said quietly, then without another word he retrieved his cane and left. There was a long night ahead, but he was confident that by the end of it he'd finally know Blackwand's secret.

Fenomi. It is the spell enabling the worker of magic to project their spirit-self across great distances while the body remains almost lifeless. While travelling in fenomi, the adept sees the world with very different eyes, all traces of magic become visible. Galen hoped that in fenomi he would finally *see* the link between Blackwand and her protectors, and it was one of the few useful things Rang-Shaa taught him.

Thorpe flicked his pocket watch open and noted the time. "Almost nine thirty, it'll be dark soon."

"This is a spell I worked only once before, while mastering the art."

"And you think it will reveal Blackwand's secret?" He had little faith in witch magic.

"If I can at least find her and watch her undetected."

"I note with displeasure that cursed *if* word once again." He made for the door.

"Father?"

They were in Galen's small room at Goldhawk, and he stood in the doorway and turned back.

"It is traditional for the adept to have a second by their side during the journey." He coughed softly, and waited.

Thorpe sighed. "Then I shall second you," he agreed reluctantly and stepped back into the room and closed the door.

"My thanks," he acknowledged. "We begin here," he gestured to the salt circle on the floor. "Both of us inside the circle."

Elios watched sullen and silent from under the bunk. They had no need for her in the ceremony, and now she saw they had no need for her in the bigger picture either. Galen sat cross-legged while Thorpe first lit a paraffin lamp and then lowered himself onto a small foot-stool, propped his elbows on his knees and just sat and stared at his son. She could only guess at what thoughts filled Thorpe's head. He looked waxy and drawn, the last weeks had been hard on him and a tiny part of her was glad. "Be careful Galen," she whispered despite everything.

Galen sat in the darkness behind his closed eyes and remembered the lessons Rang-Shaa had taught him. Just then he felt something pressed into his hands and looked down to see the Book-of-Nine in his grasp and his father wearing a peculiar smile.

"For luck," Thorpe added.

He was touched and he squeezed the book hard and closed his eyes again.

Elios had never seen him perform the spell, and she watched for a minute or two, waiting to see his ether-self rise from his body. As Galen concentrated and settled his breathing, the scene between father and son seemed like a still life waiting for the artist to begin painting. She saw every tiny detail; Thorpe's knotted hands resting between his splayed knees, and the rise and fall of his broad shoulders. For the first time she noticed the silver strands in Galen's hair and even with his eyes closed he looked tired and she saw how Àeon's song was ageing his skin and softening his bones. Killing him slowly as it did all living things. "Please be careful," she wished him again.

Before long she became aware of a third person in the room like a shadow bleeding out of the very walls, and she looked to the corner. Standing there was another Galen, or rather his ether-self. He looked translucent and monochrome, like a living memory. Thorpe continued to stare at his son unaware that he was looking at little more than a soulless mannequin.

Galen regarded his father soberly. It was impossible to hide one's feelings during fenomi, and Elios clearly saw that he both loved and feared his father. She noted sadly that he barely looked her way. "Be careful," she asked again as his spirit lifted like a cloud towards the skylight, but now she couldn't say for sure if she meant him or Blackwand.

Come with us and fly.

"Strike," she murmured without knowing. A second later Galen was gone and she was left with Thorpe and a living corpse that looked exactly like his son.

Galen wasted no time. As soon as he realised he was no longer in his body, he began to ascend, aiming for the skylight. He could pass through solid stone if he so wished but the mind clings to its beliefs and the small pane of glass seemed the natural way to exit Goldhawk Row. He passed through it in a whisper and out into the London night.

Sunday waited in her hiding place above Smithfield and slept. She dreamed of a black river and a weaving spider. *"Let me die, let me sleep forever,"* she pleaded the great spider. But she saw a terrible creature loom up. It crawled from a cocoon within the hourglass and struck down the weaver of fate. The spider fell and this new weaver took up Sunday's thread, but it didn't have guardianship in mind.

"Dear champion!" She tried to reach out to him, but this new creature tugged at her thread, and she understood that from now on everything would turn bad. Her three faithful warriors swooped down to save her but they fell like stones from the sky and lay dazed and feeble, and the assassin laughed.

"Your dear champion will soon be dead Sunday-broken-thread. Fate is absolute and no thread defies the Patternmaker. Now glimpse what is to come and despair."

A new sound filled her ears. She turned to see a mountainous figure, blindfolded and clothed with decaying roses, turning the handle on a grinder and from it poured a song to level all things. Time.

The song continued, but now it was backwards. Instead of age and decay it set her free of time and death, imprisoning her in the now, and her enemies laughed. In the next instant sight, sound and speech vanished and she struggled within the confines of a tiny coffin. She tried to claw at the lid but there were just bloodied stumps where her limbs had once been, and when she tried to scream her severed tongue merely trembled in the dusty socket that was her mouth. This was her fate and it would last forever. Her thread would never break and Thorpe would win. *"Strike!"* she tried to scream, but raised only a dry gasp in a remote and nameless grave.

"Fate is absolute," the assassin whispered again.

"Strike help me please!"

Behind the assassin's warning she heard the horrific sound of the Timekeeper being eaten alive as the new children of fate emerged to enslave freewill. The assassin wove tyranny, and the air filled with the buzz of angry wings.

"Strike!" She awoke, gulping for air and crying.

The night was still and cool.

"You dreamed of death?" a voice asked from close by.

She turned and saw Strike, and heard a bell peal midnight. She felt clammy and feverish and her heart was beating too fast. She glanced around and saw three stoic shadows against the sky. The berserk eagles. They at least grounded her a little and she felt steadier. "I dreamed of the Timekeeper. And he was in great danger." She shivered and remembered the horrible sensation of being entombed alive, and had the awful suspicion that her days of protection were coming to an end.

"What happened in the dream?"

"Something bad," she evaded, and edged closer to the roof to get a better view of Smithfield. "Doesn't this place ever sleep?" Men were still busy herding animals back and forth.

"It's midnight, time to be working," he reminded her.

She looked back to her eagles. "A little longer, maybe an hour."

"Then no more Smithfield."

"And no more valkyries either I hope." She flexed her hands to make sure they were really there. The dream had been so real that for a while she had been there, entombed and mutilated. She swallowed her fear and said nothing, and just waited for the clock to strike one.

Galen sailed over London and saw everything with the eyes of fenomi. The spirit of the Thames was mirrored in the heavens as a huge water dragon, but it looked forlorn and battered, having suffered centuries of abuse. It hung its head like an aged donkey, but he gave it only the merest glance. He saw London's streets as plain as day and each and every soul that travelled through them. Beggars, thieves, gentlemen and ladies: all were as one in fenomi. Even the air around him was thick with souls. Souls of dust and moonlight, dreams and ideas, and insects and pollen and a million other unseen lives. Fays of endless sorts buzzed through the night, gathering souls, gathering news, speeding this way and that, rising in great chattering flocks or trailing alone. Even the stars above showed their souls to him, but none of this moved Galen Thorpe. He was a reductionist. Life was a mechanical process and nothing more. He scanned London with total disregard for its magical citizens looking only for that one special soul.

Show yourself Blackwand. He clenched fists that weren't there. *Show yourself, and the pages of the Book-of-Nine will finally close upon you.* Without knowing why, he was drawn northwards, across the river, to where mortis-fairies hovered over Smithfield. If anything, they were even greater in number than before and Smithfield looked more like a volcano belching ash than a Victorian market building. The dark cloud reached up into the night and in fenomi he finally saw what was hiding at the cloud's centre and he froze in astonishment and dread. There were valkyries. Hundreds of them.

She fastened the scarf around her face, conscious of the way-beware's beautiful song and the berserks' steady heartbeats. They had all gradually become one living magical organism, but tonight her hands trembled and her guts wriggled. *The closer we get to the solstice, the closer they get to me,* she thought as she adjusted the scarf.

"Sunday?" Strike asked for the fourth time.

"Sorry?"

"You were miles away, I said how are we going to do this?"

She looked up to where her three warriors waited. "No blood is to be shed, else all we'll be doing is strengthening the place."

Strike regarded the crowds below and wondered if anything could possibly make this place worse than it already was.

"The berserks will scatter everyone, and we'll make sure there's nothing left standing," she explained.

"This will bring their dark experiments to an end?"

"I can only hope so, if Ben was right and those creatures came from here then we have to stop them." She watched a cart horse plod through the crowds, hauling cages bursting with hens. They were crammed so densely that not a single bird showed, just a mass of feathers. "I had no idea such things existed in the world Strike," she took up her staff, sounding regretful. "If we were brought back for just one thing, let it be this."

"Let it be this." He became one with the staff.

She touched the way-beware and silenced its beautiful song, and behind her she heard the flap of wings in anticipation. "Let it be this," she whispered, and then she stepped out off the rooftop and into thin air.

CHAPTER TWENTY-NINE

The curse of compassion

'It's easy to be cruel. Far harder to be kind.'
'Higher Forms of Magic - a witch's meditations on daily life'
Author unknown

Smithfield never slept. The huge glass lanterns hanging from the market's axis burned with a cold yellow flame both day and night. Everywhere there were drovers and all of them buying, selling or evaluating carcasses hanging from hooks like fishing lures. The carcasses all looked the same; headless and footless, and strung out as if caught mid-gallop, trying to flee. Their ruddy ribs looked like organ pipes and the split bellies grinned inanely at passers by. Even the ironwork roof above looked like ribs and the prevailing odour wasn't manure but iron. Blood iron. All of this commerce and butchery was overseen by one man.

Horatio Bullman was known as 'Bully' amongst Smithfield's market folk. He lived up to the John Bull persona as much as he could, to the point of being something of a tragic celebrity. He always wore a red waistcoat under his long brown overcoat, white knee-length stockings and black trousers, and a battered top hat. The rest of Horatio Bullman didn't need dressing up to match his hero. His plump face was framed by wild sideburns and his gut was broad. He also lived up to the name of Bully by being hard with his stick and hard with his tongue. Smithfield was his kingdom and he marched back and forth enjoying his station as market superintendent and his call was frequently heard above the racket of penned animals, "Make way for the superintendent! Make way!"

A young woman with a large bust and mop of dark curls shoved a barrow loaded with quails' eggs past. He swiped one, cracked it and poured the contents down his throat in one move. "As sweet as ever I did taste Maggie," he laughed.

"Ay! These is Billy Whistler's, they ain't fer the likes of you master Bully." She tried to sound indignant but clearly she adored him.

He clamped a hand against her broad backside and squeezed. "And, erm, might this be more for the likes of the superintendent, me sweetness?"

"Thems are pounds and ounces way beyond your purse Bully!" She shook with laughter and he saw the way her breasts quivered and his already overworked heart gave an extra thud. She gave him a sharp prod with her elbow and pushed her barrow off, but not before he snatched another egg. He drank it down and wiped the yoke from his chin with a lacy handkerchief that spilled out of his top pocket.

"Make way!" he roared, setting off again, waving his stick and poking his nose into everything and anything.

It was now 1am but Smithfield was as busy as ever. He had worked this market for almost thirty years and had seen all it had to offer. He knew every call of every animal, he could tell the mood of cattle, or whether a ewe was with lamb or just lame, and so as soon as he heard it he knew something was wrong. All the animals began a low moaning sound. An instant later there came a scream, but not just a lone cry. This sounded like a whole choir exercising their lungs. Trouble was brewing, and it was time for him to step in. "Make way for the superintendent!" He waved his stick with purpose and pulled men aside, heading towards the sound of trouble.

"It's a murderin'!"

Bully looked around and saw Tommy Clegg, a Smithfield regular. "You say what?"

"It's the Sheep-Lady, it's him what done her, he's come back an' gone an' done another un!" Tommy looked animated.

"A murder?" Bully tried to peer ahead through the crowd, all of them moving towards the sounds of screaming.

Tommy was a lithe man and he pressed his way through the crush and out of sight. Just then the screaming intensified and the next peculiar thing happened. Some natural law states that people will first flock to danger out of curiosity, then just as fast run in panic from it. It was this second natural law that now came into play.

Bully sensed the crowds around him slowing. "Let me through, damn your eyes, market business, market business!" He waved his stick, but the mood was such that hardly anyone noticed. Close by, he heard pigs begin to squeal and he detected terror in their calls. A bull bellowed uneasily and he heard hooves kick at partitions. The folk of Smithfield might not be bright enough to know when death came calling, but the animals did.

"It's a bloody monster!" someone screamed from the front, and Bully looked up aghast to see Tommy, fighting his way back through the crowd, with his flat cap askew and his eyes wide. "A bloody monster!" He screamed as he struggled past.

"Talk sense man! What's up there?" Bully snatched at his sleeve.

"Juss bloody run!"

From ahead, came the sound of an animal growling and it echoed down the cavernous market. The crowd fell silent for a confused second, then as if on cue, everyone began to scream and barge back the direction they'd come.

"Damn yer wretches!" Bully shouted as they jostled past him. "Damn yer and make way!" He seemed to carry very little weight now, other than around his middle. The screams were suddenly blotted out by an almighty roar and Bully understood that he was listening to an animal that had never graced Smithfield market before. Whatever it was, it was a predator and they were now the meat. He was knocked to his knees and splashed into a puddle of slurry and his top hat was swept from his head as people flooded past. "Curse yers all to Sodom!" he screamed and heard his fingers crack as someone crunched them underfoot. His cedar stick was the next thing to go, kicked away and lost.

The mob scattered and the screaming grew even louder and more desperate, and now the animals joined it, squawking, bleating and bellowing. Bully clambered to his feet, dripping with filth and nursing broken fingers. He stood transfixed and watched the last terrified people stream past him and in the grand arcade ahead he saw the impossible sight of a huge bear towering over the frightened crowd.

"It's a monster!" he heard Tommy yell again as he fled, and Bully had to agree: it really was.

Galen circled Smithfield but kept a distance. *"I shall hunt alone tonight,"* he had told Vorus that afternoon.

"I beg you not to travel in such a way, it is dangerous!" she had said. *"Allow me and my sisters to find Blackwand."*

Now he understood why Vorus had been so concerned about his coming here in fenomi. There were valkyries waiting at Smithfield, many of them. *You were right Elios!* he gasped, Vorus was not to be trusted.

Worse still, now he saw them naked, and they were grotesque. Under their robes they looked like wizened old women, he even saw how their breasts looked perished and mummified, and their abdomens spewed loops of intestine like waving anemone tentacles. Their limbs were impossibly long, and at last he saw their likeness, the face that had spoken to him from inside those Ruined krakens all this time, and his ether-self flushed blue with horror. They were each like living tribal masks, formed with two mouths and no eyes, and many sported symbolic horns or huge domed heads or wore ragged blindfolds. *She's going to bring them through in force!* He understood now: the Book-of-Nine had been used for her purpose.

He was still reeling at all of this when he saw a brilliant spark in the darkness below. Blackwand had arrived. With a last look at the valkyries, he turned to the huge market building. He would deal with Vorus later, but now at last Blackwand was in his grasp. He flew like a spear downwards into the darkness where men and animals were screaming.

Her plan was simple. She would assault at the building's northern end, break open the pens and the berserks would terrify the animals into a stampede. Many would be rounded up again, and all of them would be bewildered and frightened, but a slim chance of escape was better than none at all.

She crashed through the roof, and dropped into the heart of Smithfield followed by the eagles. Even before they landed they reverted to bears and the ground shook as they thundered into it. The first to realise that all wasn't right were the animals, and they erupted into a deafening chorus.

Sunday landed on the concrete followed by a shower of broken glass, and whirled around. She saw a sea of hostile faces blur past and in the next moment her bears were at her side and Tawny let out an ear-splitting roar. A scream went up and resounded through the vast building, cattle bellowed, dogs howled and bells began to clatter. Blackwand had arrived. "Strike, the gates!" she ordered and immediately set to work.

She ran at the nearest stalls where sheep screamed and bucked, and broke the heavy fastenings with her lightning-staff. The bolts exploded and she hauled the gates wide. She didn't stop to see if the penned animals knew what to do, she moved on to the next and then the next. Sheep, cows, pigs, bullocks and bulls began to pour out into market, where they fled in terror from Tawny and his brothers.

She released more and more of them, destroying locks, fences and pens, and set about driving them down Smithfield's Grand Avenue. The scale was overwhelming, but she knew she couldn't leave a single soul captive. "Away all of you!" she roared, and her message was meant equally for the two-legged animals at Smithfield. "This place will burn, run or burn with it!" The berserks proved her threat with a fierce roar, and flanked her protectively. They barged down the market, flinging carcasses to the ground, shattering pens and terrifying everyone into a headlong rush for the south gate.

She watched heifers and goats leap and kick. Geese, hens and ducks flapped through the air, crashing into people. She stepped over a shattered barrow and its pile of spilled lambs' heads with their snow-white fleeces stained with blood and dung. "Run damn you, run you filth!" she screamed, and in her rage she sent a bolt of lightning over the crowd, which drilled into the largest lantern above and shattered it. The gas ignited and shot a plume of fire above the throng and a fresh cry of terror went up.

More lightning arced overhead. Glass shattered and girders groaned. Lanterns ruptured and breathed fire like a host of dragons. Still she continued in a blind rage, heaving gates open, even dragging the stunned animals out and sending them on their way with a slap on the rump.

"Run damn you!" she screamed to anything that would listen.

A cage of conies was liberated and its occupants raced away through the maze of legs, both human and animal. She found birds destined for the feather trade and in no time at all there were robins, finches, tits and starlings darting through the air. Terrified cockerels and partridges swooped over the crowds, sending down showers of droppings. Dogs leapt up to snatch them down, and Smithfield's traders continued their blind rush towards the south gate, fisting and dragging one another out of the way, slipping and grovelling in the river of manure and urine left by the stampeding animals.

Blackwand had come and everyone knew where ever she went destruction followed. The bears howled, the building quaked and Sunday put her fire to the mountains of filthy bedding, sealing Smithfield's fate. She would burn this cursed place from the face of Hethra's green earth. Prisoners had been executed here, animals had endured the unthinkable, and the Illuminata had summoned their demons here, but she swore by the black sands where she started her life anew that these atrocities were ended.

"YOU!" a man screamed and she turned to see a filthy figure staggering towards her waving a stick. "You dare come 'ere to my kingdom!" Bully was brown from head to foot, and he'd retrieved his stick and his hat, but it sat crooked on his head and had been flattened from a passing hoof. He coughed and gagged on the gathering smoke and was crying in rage. The sight of fire spreading through his kingdom gave him a courage he'd never known. "You bloody whore!" His teeth flashed white in his muddy face and he swung his stick threateningly.

Sunday turned her cold stare on him and watched him approach, and for a moment she considered just killing him.

"Remember, no blood to be spilled," Strike warned.

"I'm getting tired of being called a whore." She raised her staff, ready.

Behind her, the berserks formed a wall of muscle and fangs and watched the tiny figure approach.

"Miserable black-hearted slut!" he spat, stumbling towards her over smashed cages and carts.

I could kill him without a second thought. The idea was so satisfying that it startled her.

"Don't! You were right about Thorpe that day, don't sink to this," Strike pleaded.

"A man's kingdom this is, you slut, you 'ear me, a man's kingdom? And I'm the bloody king!" He finished the last twenty yards at a run.

Behind her she heard Tawny step forwards.

"No!" she commanded, "I'll take care of this myself."

Bully raised his stick with a savage cry. "Yer trespassing toad, be out of my kingdom!"

It was so easy she felt ashamed. She jabbed the staff into his gut and sent him flying. He was thrown screaming through the air and landed in one of the mash pits and sent up a wave of effluent. "Long live the king," she muttered disdainfully. She turned from the sight of Smithfield's king splashing around in the slurry and watched the flames spread through the vacant pens, devouring the hay as it went.

"Fire will only do half the job," Strike reminded her.

"You're right." She lifted her staff and her bears lumbered over.

The market had drained of people now, and even Bully had dragged himself spluttering from the mire and was crawling away, leaving a glistening trail like a slug.

Tawny drew close and she looked into his eyes. "Will you help me once more?" Something in his gaze troubled her. He seemed to regard her sorrowfully, as if he knew their time together was coming to an end, and she shivered, remembering her awful dream. "Remember the sewer, those awful things that tried to kill us?" She reached up and ran a hand over his muzzle. "There'll be more of them if we don't break this place."

Eirik looked down at Sonneday. He saw the darkness around her had become almost total and he knew that soon they'd face their greatest challenge, one that even berserks might not survive. He remembered how she cleaned his wounds that day. He and his brothers loved her and whatever she asked they would give her freely even if it be their very lives.

Sunday knew none of this, but Tawny growled in response and shuffled back. The fire was raging along the whole east side of the market now and she could hear angry shouts from the crowds outside not to mention a multitude of animal calls.

The great bear settled his flank against one of the roof pillars and with a single shoved he sent the thing crashing to the ground. It flopped against a row of stalls sending burning straw up in a glowing cloud and the iron clanged mournfully before shattering. His brothers did likewise and before long the whole east side of the market was starting to sag. Sunday watched in awe as the vast roof began to droop, and shattered glass rained down as girders crumpled. The berserks might shrug off the collapsing building, but she wouldn't.

"Time to leave unless you want to be buried here," Strike advised.

"Buried," she echoed.

"And so this is how you stole the war god's champions and turned them to your own purpose." For an instant she thought a voice had whispered right by her ear, then she dismissed it.

"One last thing!" she shouted over the din, and took out her chalk and left her sign in marks ten feet long on the market floor. They would never be found but that wasn't important. "You're avenged Lottie. Walk Evermore in peace."

A massive section of roof crashed down and she rocked on her feet. Now the air was thick with smoke and the smell of roasting meat. Slates exploded and somewhere a water tank collapsed and hissed in the inferno.

"You'll be joining her unless we leave right now!" Strike nagged.

"I wish you were here to see this Ben." She mounted her staff and called to her bears. They watched her rise up from the burning wreck of Smithfield and rose to follow her, no longer bears but eagles. Blackwand and her protectors slipped away, even as the walls began to tumble and the glass roof plunged down.

Galen watched as a spectre from her side, close enough to reach out and touch her. *Lost warriors of Valgard rescuing dumb beasts. So at last the great Book knows your secret,* he smiled to himself. *Your own compassion has undone you.* Fenomi stripped away the veils and he finally saw the way-beware in all its magical glory. *"And so this is how you stole the war god's champions and turned them to your own purpose,"* he whispered right against her ear. She twitched, and for a second he thought she detected him. She took a piece of chalk from her clothes and began to scrawl on the floor.

So much trouble you've caused us little one, he thought, and reached out with spectral fingers and caressed the way-beware. Blackwand was ordering her bears to demolish the market now, and he coiled around her wishing he could just crush her right there. *Plenty of trouble, but not for much longer I think. Your champions might be unbreakable, but is your maestro?*

He'd been so absorbed in her methods that he'd barely given her a glance, but now he looked her over and his human eyes saw a woman of great beauty, but his fenomi eyes saw much more. Above her head floated a soul sign the likes of which he'd never seen. And it terrified him. *No, it's not possible!* He floated away, suddenly afraid. *No mortal can cheat death!*

Her soul had been severed and rejoined. His father's suspicions were correct: Blackwand had somehow achieved something none of the Book-of-Nine's greatest initiates ever had.

Anger festered in him as he watched her escape, flying gracefully through the collapsing roof followed by her berserks. Flaming wreckage crashed down over him, but he hardly registered it. In fenomi he was immune to the destruction, but in his heart an equal catastrophe was happening. *"Fly as fast as you like Blackwand,"* he seethed, *"but your days of freedom are over."*

Chapter Thirty

To catch a witch

'The tender heart is easy to predict, easy to manipulate, and easy to break.'
Abraham Kessel, 17th century Knight Superior

"Blackwand!" he gasped, "she has a broken soul!" Galen flopped into his father's arms, fighting for breath as the effort of fenomi finally crashed in on him.

Thorpe hardly noticed his condition. "Impossible!" He clutched his shoulder and shook him.

"I saw it, and the demons, they're champions of the war god," he spluttered.

Thorpe felt something unexpected and it took him a while to realise that he was afraid. "Then it is little wonder we couldn't defeat her." His hands slid from his shoulder and he rose to his feet.

"Not for long though." Galen's breathing was steadying. "I saw how she controls them."

Thorpe glared down at him. "Then out with it!"

He wiped a hand over his sweaty face, and from under the bunk he was aware of Elios listening. "She possesses a spell-doll. It sings a song that enchants the warriors."

Thorpe rattled a dry laugh, "A *doll* has thwarted us all this time?"

He nodded.

Thorpe considered this. "Where did you encounter her?"

"Smithfield."

His brow furrowed. "You think she knows?"

"Without doubt, she burned the place to the ground!"

Thorpe looked to the skylight and sure enough the sky to the north glowed faintly. He drew a cigar from his waistcoat and his face remained impassive. "Blackwand has a taste for fire."

Galen got to his feet and rocked unsteadily. "That's not all. I saw valkyries there."

"One or two more would be useful." Thorpe lit a match.

"One or two? Father I saw hundreds!"

The match stopped inches from the cigar tip. He gave his son a freezing stare. "It appears that Vorus has been less than honest with you."

Galen noted the word *you* and not *us*. "What do we do?" He stepped carefully over the salt circle and slumped down on the bed.

Thorpe watched the sky glow brighter in the north. Smithfield would be well ablaze by now. "The fire will purify the place, the valkyries there must surely perish."

"She never breathed a word of their true numbers." He couldn't believe she had lied so convincingly. "She's been plotting all this time."

"Vorus might be a creature of Ruin, but at heart the thing is like every other female," he sneered. "Deceit is their nature."

"But what do we do about her!"

"Do nothing for now."

"But more of her kind will come, something is happening beyond the veil in Ruination." He had the urge to grab his cane and see Sophie.

"Right now we have nine valkyries under our control, enough to defeat Leonhard. After the solstice we learn what we want from them, then kill them." Thorpe now also stepped over the salt circle. "But Blackwand is our principal concern."

"And what do we do about her?" he insisted.

"Do?" Thorpe grinned. "We invite her to Hobbs Ash of course."

"Invite?"

"This spell-doll you saw, you believe Vorus can Ruin its magic?"

He nodded in understanding.

Thorpe checked his watch, it was now 1:42 am, there was still time to make the morning papers. "Then it's time we sent Blackwand a message." He went to collect his coat and hat.

"Father?" He stood and immediately felt dizzy. "Where are you going?"

He buttoned his coat. "Fleet Street, and I assure you that within two days Blackwand will be ours." He slammed the door on the way out and Galen shuffled over to the window and watched the sky glow where Smithfield was burning. Elios came and sat close to him, relieved that he was safely back, but he didn't even look her way.

ARCH-CRIMINAL ONCE AGAIN
STRIKES TERROR INTO HEART OF THE CITY

London Amalgamated Post. Wednesday June 15th 1887

In the early hours of June 15th, the long sought mastermind of terror known as Blackwand again subjected the capital to a night of destruction and calamity. The historic site of Smithfield with its splendid market hall, which was completed only in 1868, was destroyed by a tumultuous fire started by the traitor's hand and it is clear that many thousands of beasts and hundreds of innocent market workers have perished in the fire, which spread to a neighbouring tenement block where many more innocents also perished. Wounded survivors have been taken to St Bartholomew's Hospital where provision has been made for their grievous injuries, and many women and their infants were counted among the dead and maimed. The Queen-Empress has expressed her sympathy for those affected by the wrong-doer's evil plot, but has assured the Empire that it shall not darken the jubilee ceremony next week.

But there is more sterling news to lighten this tragedy. Mr Virgil Lyle, chief in the hunt for the notorious Blackwand, has made it clear to the press that a number of her accomplices were caught last night. They have been taken under heavy security to a compound at Hobbs Ash where they will face immediate execution and so provide a resounding example to all those who raise a hand against Britannia. The condemned will be hanged at noon on Friday June the 17th so as not to sully the Queen's anticipated week of jubilee celebrations beginning on Monday June 20th.

The article continued in the same tone for a whole page.

"It's all lies, you must see that?" Strike dismissed the propaganda.

"I know." But Sunday sounded doubtful.

"The place was empty, we saw that with our own eyes."

"I know," she repeated, but still the article did its nasty work. She looked down at the headline again, then in a fit of anger she crumpled the newspaper into ball and hurled it away. "Bastards! And those condemned to hang," she groaned with her head in her hands.

"It's a trap," he said evenly.

It was now the evening of the 15th and they'd been cooped up inside the cellars of the Orphans' Institute at Kentish Town for hours with only a single candle for light. The building was derelict but the cellars were alive with scurrying rats. The berserks lurked on the floor above, being too large to squeeze down the cellar stairs. "In less than two days they'll execute prisoners and I'm the reason." She felt utterly wretched. "I have to do something."

"Ben warned you not to go there, and you promised."

"If he knew what was going to happen he'd agree."

"But you promised!"

"I have to try and save them."

He surrendered with a sigh. Both of them knew they had no choice but to walk into a trap. "So how will we make our move?" he asked despondently.

She looked up at the cellar roof, thinking of the berserks and wondering what kind of fiendish weapons they had in store that could harm such beings. To make sure of it, she touched the way-beware and for the first time felt anxious for the innocent creature. Suddenly she didn't want to linger in this dirty cellar any longer, she didn't care if they were seen. "Come on, I need some fresh air."

She slowly collected her things, aware that every step she took from this moment on was dictated by Thorpe's blackmail. The words in the newspaper were like a cord reeling her in, and she could do nothing to stop herself. Strike flapped on to her shoulder and together they climbed the narrow stairs away from the dereliction. If she had less than two days of life and freedom remaining, she would spend it in the open and with the few souls who mattered to her. If fate was exceptionally kind she might see Ben once more, but she hardly had the strength to hope. *Please gather the covens Ben, please just come.* She touched her waistcoat where she kept his note. *'You are my one short summer.'* She thought it might be a very short summer indeed if Thorpe prevailed on the 17th.

As she left, carrying her candle, the cellar returned to pitch blackness and she took a last look back and thought of her awful dream; of endless darkness in an unmarked grave.

The Timekeeper felt her torment. He had watched over her constantly and he knew full well her enemies' plans. If it was in his power he'd ensure she triumphed at Hobbs Ash, but he saw that Victor Thorpe had schemes that could disarm even berserks. Many dangerous threads were coming together in a strangling knot around Sunday Flowers, but he was still hopeful that he could see her safely through. "Fear not Sunday, fate does not yet control all." He sighed heavily and the webs of fate waved gently in response.

Behind him, silent and unseen, another creature listened intently. *Fate does not yet control all?* it thought derisively. *The thread should have remained broken, yet you returned her to the weave and so the great Patternmaker will punish her like no thread has ever been punished before, and she will wish for all the aeons it takes for the sand in this timer to expire that you had indeed let her die.* A tiny tear appeared in the assassin's cocoon and it peered out from behind the silk. It was ready to emerge and fight. The moment was less than two days away, and then the universe would see whether fate controlled all or not.

It was noon on June 16th and it was baking hot. The heat crashed against London and bounced off in shimmering waves, while the Thames seemed to have ground to a halt and now it sat there festering and sullen. The entire city felt to be holding its breath.

Outwardly Hobbs Ash looked deserted, but it was only pretence. Secretive preparations were being made under cover of the station. Inside a workforce toiled, while outside remained an empty wasteland scoured by hungry gulls and pounded by the sun. A few sentries were left on patrol, but they looked like soldiers lost in the wilderness.

Doulton had been summoned back from Wellesley Hall because tomorrow they expected to close the net around Blackwand and needed all the men they had. Everyone knew it was going to be one hell of a fight.

He tugged at his collar feeling breathless in the heat, and his shirt was pasted to his torso. It was hot, even for June and the Hobbs Station with its glass roof was like a greenhouse, which made the Ruined krakens smell even more fusty.

"Who have you selected?"

Doulton turned to see his counterpart Lyle, who looked equally uncomfortable. "I have ten good squires in mind, they'll pilot the machines as well as any knight." He gestured to the reserve krakens. "I just pray they survive."

"Lord Thorpe doesn't mean for them to fight, just to be a presence tomorrow so Blackwand doesn't get wind of the valkyries waiting to spring the trap."

"Thorpe's keeping things close to his chest, I have literally no idea what's going to happen."

"He's rightly cautious, afraid the enemy might be spying." His eyes flicked back and forth as if Blackwand was with them right there.

A long wooden platform was being erected at the mouth of Hobbs Station and a line of gallows sprang from it, thirteen in all. Doulton knew that somewhere ropes were being knotted into nooses. This might be a feint, but it looked convincing enough to made him shiver. "It looks so real," he muttered.

"It has to look real."

"I'm sure the wretches they string up there'll think it's real enough." He wanted Lyle to assure him this was all part of the ruse, that they weren't really going to execute thirteen men and women tomorrow.

"They'll come to no real harm," Lyle said caustically. "Besides, it's no more than they deserve. They're criminals after all."

Doulton ran a finger around his collar and puffed in the heat. "Where's Galen?" He changed the subject.

"Where do you think?"

He looked towards the barricade at the rear of the station and imagined him in there with his sinister cane and a horde of valkyries. He was relieved not to have been at Hobbs for some time.

"What's he like?" Lyle asked from nowhere. "Count Leonhard?"

"He's confident."

He huffed, "He won't be soon."

Doulton's look said otherwise. "Really? He's gathered a huge European army. For acres around Wellesley there are camps, squires, infantry and knights."

"Galen will prevail," Lyle preached.

"I wonder," he sighed, "they might be adept at fighting a lone witch, but how will they fare against steel and gunpowder?"

Lyle thought on this for a while and now it was his turn to change the subject. "I hear the arrogant Prussian gas-bag has even brought his retinue of concubines."

"As I say, he's confident."

Lyle regarded the deserted plain outside. He could almost imagine her out there answering their challenge, a lone witch in black who seemed to cheat death itself. They had valkyries, infantry and krakens, but still he felt vulnerable. "I have duties," he said moodily and stalked away.

Doulton watched him go, knowing full well which duties. Someone had to choose thirteen prisoners to be their bait tomorrow.

Galen ran a hand across the cherub's brow, letting his fingers stroke his pocket watch embedded in the metal and listening to the sound of breathing from within. It sounded like two creatures in there, two sets of lungs drawing air at the same time. Again, he caught himself thinking of what he'd seen at Smithfield, but remembered to guard his thoughts. He'd been play-acting around her since, and now he found it had to bear her presence. *Dishonest viper,* he thought, sounding so like his father. Elios was weak while Vorus was fickle, he reflected. It seemed that all the females in his life were fatally flawed. *Once we know Aeon's song, once Sophie is back we'll burn you and your bloody sisters.*

"Galen?" Her voice reverberated through the helmet.

"Vorus!" he smiled, snatching his hand away. "I thought you were sleeping."

"I heard you."

He froze.

"I heard you breathing, you sound troubled."

He relaxed again. "Aye," he admitted, "tomorrow is likely to be a day of consequence."

"My sisters and I know what must be done."

He looked at the eight others. Steam rose in gentle plumes and flies buzzed around them as if they were organic, not mineral. They all smelled of damp and rust. "I know you've waited long for this."

"Since Blackwand murdered my sister, yes I have waited and thought of nothing else."

He looked into the cherub's eyes and wondered again at her secrets. "Once Blackwand is removed, you shall enjoy all the trappings of the tournament. I'll warrant your defeat of Leonhard will be the talk of Europe for generations to come."

"He has machines like ours you say?"

He heard eager scratching sounds from inside the helmet. "Many," he said. She asked this often, and it appeared to hold a special fascination for her.

"We shall Ruin them my dearest."

He smiled woodenly and turned to go, but she wasn't finished.

"And they shall bear more of my sisters."

He stopped and looked back at the mound of living metal. "Vorus?"

"I promised you more could be made," she purred.

He understood now. Leonhard's krakens wouldn't just be destroyed: they'd be Ruined. Perfect vessels for more valkyries. "Sweet Vorus always keeps her promises." He fixed a smile and hoped it looked convincing.

"Anything for you my love," she hummed.

He continued on his way, letting his numb legs do the walking and trying to ignore the bile rising in his gut. The Book-of-Nine was playing a very dangerous game and he had to speak to his father right away.

"She has plans to take over, I'm certain."

Thorpe drummed his fingers on the table. They were meeting in the state carriage again. "It was always likely," he contemplated.

"But now it's happening, we must intercede."

He looked up, clearly shocked. "Kill her? Before Blackwand is vanquished, before the tournament, before the song of Àeon is ours?" He shook his head. "You overestimate her reach my faint-hearted son."

He flushed and clutched his satchel tighter.

"Calm yourself, that rotten harpy will get what she deserves, but only after she's given us what she owes us." He leaned back in the chair and laced his hands over his middle.

"The longer we allow her to plot, the stronger she gets."

"So she might believe, but remember Smithfield," Thorpe cracked a smile. "You haven't told the thing?"

"No, but it's hard keeping news from her."

"Just so long as she believes Smithfield still stands and her kind still thrive there."

"We're playing against the Illuminata *and* the valkyries now, it's becoming too much."

Thorpe regarded him scornfully. "Five days until the tournament. Once Leonhard's forces lie in dust, the Illuminata will be ours. Then, and only then, do we dispatch Vorus and her vixens." He stood and came over. "Don't falter now, we've come too far, and remember," he rested a hand on his shoulder, "Sophie is waiting."

Galen nodded his compliance.

Thorpe took a cigar from the box on the table and lit it. He regarded the match as it shrivelled slowly in the flame and thought of Blackwand and the destruction at Thorpe Hall. "You'll be the one burning tomorrow," he murmured.

Galen looked out at the baking wastes of Hobbs Ash as the comforting smell of cigar smoke filled the carriage. *Many things will burn tomorrow,* he thought.

Sunday spent her last night of freedom in the overgrown grounds of the Orphans' Institute. There was a cluster of tumbled down stables and barns and it gave them some privacy. In a strange way she felt oddly liberated, knowing that whatever happened tomorrow she wouldn't have to run and hide anymore. She also knew in some instinctive way that even if she was spotted tonight she wouldn't be challenged, Thorpe needed her at Hobbs Ash and nowhere else. She threw another stick on the small fire and thought about tomorrow.

"Who would you most like to see again?"

She turned to Strike. He was sitting on an old chimney pot buried in

the grass. Around her the berserks slept peacefully. Now they were more
like docile dogs and she wondered again if using them was morally right.

"Out of the Regal-Foxes, who do you miss the most?" he asked again.

"Well, coven-father Berwick of course," she smiled.

"Perhaps he was one of the ones who escaped."

She thought of what Ben had said about some huge breakout last
autumn. "Let's hope we don't see him tomorrow then."

"Let's hope."

Silence fell between them and they thought of the thirteen witches facing
the gallows in their name, and whether they could do anything to stop it.
She took a bite of her apple. Her appetite was zero, but she ate for the sake
of routine.

"Hrafn-dimmu is prepared?" He'd asked her at least three times already.

"Raven's wand is ready, yes." She stroked the sheath where it rested.
She'd made the parting spell with hrafn-dimmu in case they were beaten
tomorrow.

"Valonia would be proud," he nodded.

"I hope so."

He couldn't think of anything further to say. She thought of her time
at Regal-Fox, of her position as solstice queen and Alfred making her
unofficial coven-mother in waiting, to take his place when he stepped
down. That would have made her the youngest coven-head in Britain,
until Kolfinnia had come along that is, but she saw now that all of those
things were just trappings.

"What will you say when you see him again?" Again, he shook her from
her thoughts.

"I'll thank him, for all the years he gave me. For being as good as
a father to me. And I hope he'll see me as a better person than I was
before."

"Very noble, but I didn't mean coven-father Berwick."

"Oh?"

"I meant Ben."

Her heart floated and she smiled. "Why would I have anything special to
say to Ben?" His crafty smile made her blush and for a heavenly moment
everything was as it should be.

By the fire Tawny stretched his huge limbs and without thinking she went and knelt beside him, and buried her face in his fur and reached her arms around his neck. Raw strength radiated from him and his pelt felt like a silken meadow. The great bear opened his eyes a notch and regarded her. "It's a long way from that cave on the Cold Coast," she whispered.

He hummed a deep growl that quivered her bones. Beside him, both Silver and Ash looked up. All three of them looked mournful tonight, and suddenly she was fighting not to cry.

"What will happen to them?" Strike asked sadly.

If they were killed tomorrow would Tawny and his kin revert to savagery or simply fall dead? She had no idea. "Only Valgard knows that," she replied.

Moths fluttered around them, drawn by the fire's glow. The night steadily deepened and Sunday firmly believed she's seen her last sunset. Months ago, on a desolate shore, she'd not wanted to awaken from death, and now just as she was ready to embrace life again it was about to be taken from her. Fate was cruel, but she swore to face it as a witch should: she would be proud and regal as Alfred Berwick had always taught her.

'You are my one short summer.' Ben couldn't have chosen a better message.

She pressed her face deeper into Tawny's fur, to hide her upset from Strike.

Eirik felt Sonneday's tears falling and felt her hands clutch at him. He thought back to the moment she walked into their tomb and freed them, but despite his love for her, Valgard still lurked at the edge of his mind, ready with the shackles of rage.

"When the girl and her singer lie dead, I shall be there Eirik Thorvaldson," Valgard whispered from across the universe. *"You and your brothers will be mine again and you will spill an ocean of blood in my name."*

He curled closer to Sonneday, while above him the first stars began to shine, and the brightest were those of the great bear. *Lucky stars shine for all of us tomorrow,* he prayed.

CHAPTER THIRTY-ONE

Broken wand

Leaves like scales of red and green, clothe me when they rest my soul.
Limbs that hold the world aloft, cradle me when I at last come home.
Verse from 'The Ballad of Oak and Holly'

June 17th was even hotter than its predecessor. Thorpe watched the air
swirl in baking eddies over Hobbs Ash. If the heat continued like this, ash
is all that would remain. He took a long draw on his cigar and strolled out
from the station mouth, past the row of gallows and onto the expanse of
industrial waste. A hundred paces later he stopped and checked his watch.
It was eleven-thirty.

He stood alone and surveyed the horizon, turning full circle as he did.
The fortified embankments of the Thames rolled by followed by Hobbs
Station itself. Outside, ten pristine krakens stood in two rows of five either
side of the gallows. Even their furnace smoke was listless, and it crawled
skywards in thin trails. The krakens' war banners hung breathless and
limp, and he didn't envy the squires sat inside the helmets. The gallows
dripped ominous nooses and in ten minutes they'd bring the prisoners out
and stand them in full view. It was the perfect bait. Inside Hobbs Station
a thousand infantry waited, artillery batteries were hidden around the
perimeter, and of course there was Vorus and her sisters.

He caught sight of Lyle waiting anxiously in the station, and even from this distance he could see he was wringing his hands. Behind him, there were rows of disciplined soldiers. The trap was set. He looked up and saw nothing but an empty blue sky, then checked his watch again. It was now eleven thirty-two. "First deal with Blackwand, then Leonhard, then Vorus," he promised himself. Cigar ash drifted down across his waistcoat. He squinted at the empty horizon, but saw only heat ripples dance through the air. "Come on you black-hearted bitch," he whispered. In his suit pocket he toyed with his special ring, the one bearing the Book-of-Nine's crest: the crest Galen's krakens would bear as their banner on June 21st.

Alfred Berwick might have been locked away for over nine months, but he sensed something significant was going to happen today, and so when he heard keys rattle in his cell door, he knew it wasn't about the usual yard privileges. The door opened and Topp looked in. He could tell right away the man was troubled. "Mr Berwick," he swallowed.

The coven-father of Regal-Fox slowly rose to his feet. He was a tall man and his head almost touched the ceiling. "Mr Topp," Berwick acknowledged in his mellow voice.

"Special duties today Mr Berwick," he pretended.

He looks regretful, Berwick thought. Perhaps after months of incarceration they finally had a use for him, or had run out of uses for him. Either way he knew it wasn't good. He straightened his shabby clothes and smoothed his long beard. "Lead on," he held a hand out.

He stepped back inviting Berwick to exit. Sunday's beloved mentor stepped over the threshold and into the narrow corridor flanked by guards, and was led away.

Doulton watched uneasily as thirteen dishevelled prisoners were marched through the station. They selected older witches thinking them easier to handle if they panicked. The company of condemned was led by Topp and surrounded by a mass of guards. Doulton saw thirteen grim faces. "Dear God," he whispered to himself.

Lyle coughed disapprovingly at his side.

The prison party halted behind a screen, just out of view of their destination, and perhaps that was just as well. It was now seventeen minutes before noon and Thorpe marched into view. He crushed a cigar stub under his foot and began issuing orders. Topp slowly organised his troops and all of them swung rifles from their backs and began to usher the prisoners forward. Doulton could almost taste the moment they caught sight of the gallows and the air raced from his chest. Suddenly he was sweating too much.

"It's not real," Lyle assured him impatiently.

Not real, Doulton told himself. If he baulked at a fake execution he'd lose his rank. "*They* don't know that."

"Neither will Blackwand, remember our foe has skills we do not. They must think it real for her to sense the same," Lyle reasoned.

Doulton watched as the prisoners were jostled up the steps towards the platform and the last long drop. "Not real," he said under his breath.

Galen checked his watch. It was ten minutes before noon. He turned and looked at the mangled cherub. It seemed to be wearing a lover's smile. *Just until the 21st,* he gripped his cane, *then we'll burn you and all your sisters you treacherous gutter-rat.*

Elios heard him plain and clear, and although she agreed wholeheartedly her thoughts were with Blackwand and Strike.

Inside her metal chamber Vorus regarded her dear Galen. She had changed over the last weeks through her contact with man, she had evolved. She sighed at the sight of him and promised herself never to let any harm come to him. She would keep him safe forever.

Galen frowned at the cherub. Something was different about it but he couldn't say. He shrugged the idea away and checked his watch. Eight minutes to noon.

Alfred Berwick stood stony and resolute. His hands were bound, and the rope around his neck was rough. He looked down at his feet and saw the trapdoor and wondered at how such a simple device could have such profound consequences. He fought the urge to scream. He'd long taught his witches that magic should be regal, and although there were none from

Regal-Fox here, he still lived by his own example. None of his witches had taken that lesson to heart more than Sunday. He'd raised her as his own and it gladdened his heart to know she'd escaped and was still out there, he hoped, free and regal.

To his left, one of the condemned witches began to sing softly. He recognised it at once as the ballad of Oak and Holly and he took up the melody, singing through numb lips and gazing ahead at the empty horizon. Before his first tear of pride fell, the whole row of thirteen were singing.

The Timekeeper was immune to the effects of time, but those last minutes before Sunday arrived gave him an insight into how mortals must live, and it was awful. He read her thread, taking it up with exquisite care and he understood how she planned to attack. He observed the countless other threads gathering around her, and perceived their plots and counter plots. She flew onwards to the fight, and far away he heard her call.

"Dear champion," she wished him.

He tensed, ready to weave as he never had before, and vowed the Patternmaker wouldn't punish her for his crimes.

William Digby was a squire without a Lord. He wasn't unique, after last year's dire assault there were plenty of Lord-less squires, but he never thought that one day he'd be sitting *inside* a kraken. He wanted to admire the walnut panels and the gleaming brass controls, but there was work ahead.

He scanned the empty plain, waiting for the Blackwand witch. He checked the kraken's chronograph for the tenth time. Less than five minutes to noon. If she was coming she was cutting it fine. The knights had taken a beating last year, but he lost a good few friends also, and their own squire-superior Bertrand Hathwell had vanished, presumed lost in action. "Come on," he growled, anxious for retribution.

The chronograph now read four minutes to noon. The pressure gauges hovered over optimum and the whole machine vibrated at just the right pitch. He could have all one hundred and twenty tons plunging into battle in the wink of an eye.

"Cowardly Jik scum," he simmered, and leaned forwards to peer through the visor. The heat made the horizon waver and he saw black spots come and go. Any one of them could be Blackwand. At one point he reached up to sound the horn, convinced she was really there, then he swallowed his relief and disappointment. "Come on," he growled again . . . and at three minutes before noon, she finally did.

Digby saw something impossible five hundred yards away at the Thames embankment. It took his terrified mind a second to register the spectacle and a further second for his flailing hand to grab the chain and sound the horn.

Blackwand had come.

Doulton heard the foremost kraken sound its battle horn. "God save us, this is it!" he yelled and reached for his revolver. A thousand soldiers took up his warning, but all of them were drowned out as all ten krakens suddenly sounded their battle horns and their furnaces began to rumble. Thorpe dropped his unlit cigar to the dust and reached for his own revolver. Behind the barricade Galen kissed the black cane and Elios bid him good luck, while Vorus thought of her slain sister and waited for Thorpe's special sign.

The forward batteries never stood a chance. They expected attack from above. Intelligence reported that Blackwand's demons were able to transform into eagles, and so they never expected an assault from the river. None of them thought to scour the Thames for signs, but even if they had they'd have had scant warning. The river exploded in a huge wave that easily engulfed the embankment. Three gigantic killer-whales hurtled up from the depths and at their centre flew a witch dressed in black.

In a second they became bears and landed in a tide of earth and water. Engorged by rage they were almost as large as the opposing krakens. Sunday led them, tearing through the air on her staff, right towards Hobbs Station, drawn by the sight of the gallows exactly as Thorpe had planned.

Digby forgot his orders in his anger and advanced. The kraken lumbered forwards. Piston clashed and chimneys gushed torrents of smoke. Inside it he felt utterly invulnerable.

The first of Blackwand's demons was hurtling across Hobbs Ash. It looked to Digby like a gigantic bear. Its claws scooped deep trenches in the earth as it galloped towards him, and weaving between the three massive animals was Blackwand herself. Doulton's orders blared through the communicare but in his excitement he ignored them. *"Digby fall back in line, fall back!"* the voice crackled.

"This is for my fallen Lord!" he proclaimed, and the kraken raised an arm bearing a heavy scissoring claw. He'd heard the tales, he'd been briefed, but he still stubbornly believed steel could beat flesh any day. He was wrong.

Eirik crashed against the machine and sank his teeth through plate steel. The kraken slowly tilted backwards taking the bear with it. Digby screamed and flailed the kraken's ponderous arms. They spun like a windmill, but tore at nothing other than air, while Eirik continued to maul its chest and throat. Huge paws hammered the furnace plate and its blazing contents erupted like a volcano, then the kraken dropped onto its back and thunder rolled across London. Eirik reared up from the wreckage and shook the twisted metal from his muzzle and charged on, leaving one destroyed kraken and Digby screaming in the cockpit in sheer terror.

"Order them up!" Thorpe roared, and Doulton signalled the remaining krakens to advance. Men ran in disciplined formations and suddenly there were at least two hundred rifles lining the mouth of Hobbs Station. Behind them, the bewildered prisoners stood just inches from death, but even this fact was eclipsed. They might have been incarcerated, but they'd heard the stories. This was Blackwand, scourge of the Illuminata. "FIRE!" Thorpe roared and two hundred soldiers all fired at once.

It ought to have ended there. Witch or no witch, it requires serious magic to survive two hundred bullets and even Sunday wasn't that strong.

Far away in his hourglass the Timekeeper wove in a blinding frenzy. Two hundred threads, each one aiming a rifle at her. He worked with lighting speed, playing each like a puppet master, making eyes deceive their owner and fingers squeeze triggers at just the wrong moment. He sent a gust of wind and bullets were minutely diverted and so whisked harmlessly past her. Somewhere at her back, Digby's kraken exploded and the Timekeeper even found a use for its death throes. Flying shrapnel whirled through the air and by impossible chance debris swatted bullets from the air. They even glanced off one another and span away on hopeless trajectories, smoke from the barrage wafted back along the line obscuring the target.

"Fate does not control all!" He was breathless with anger and effort. His legs blurred through the air as he un-wove the deadly knot that was trying to strangle Sunday's thread. At last the final bullet sailed past only inches from her head, and Sunday charged onwards, unaware that in the last few seconds he'd saved her life two hundred times over. "Fate does not control all!"

Behind him the cocoon, buried deep in the tangled silk, twitched. The assassin thrust a leg through and slowly and silently began to slice its way free.

Thorpe watched expressionless and impassive. The Jik and her demons were half way across Hobbs and the first infantry volley hadn't even scratched her. For a brief moment the smoke cleared and he had the vision of three monstrous bears and a streaking black shadow at their centre. Now though, there were nine krakens to compete with. He settled back, confident he couldn't lose. *Welcome back Blackwand, I'm so looking forward to meeting you again,* he thought, and smiled coldly.

"Tawny, to the right!" she screamed. Three krakens had outflanked them in the smoke.

Eirik wheeled left and pounced on the first of the challengers. This time the squire was ready and he rammed a clawed fist forwards and caught the bear by the neck. Thousands of pound of pressure tightened around Eirik's throat. He swiped with his claws, raking trenches in the earth, but he was too far away to inflict any damage. He roared and tried to push forwards again and saw the kraken's fist looming into view. It struck him on the brow, hard enough to shatter steel, and for a moment Eirik was blinded by pain.

The pilot managed a grim smile, but it didn't last long, as seconds later both Eirik's brothers landed on him like a mountain and began tearing in a frenzy, ripping great chunks out of the kraken.

The garrison at Hobbs Station saw only fire and smoke on the plain outside. Inside, the stink of sweat peaked and somewhere someone was screaming.

The ground shook under the battle and the timber gallows creaked ominously. Alfred Berwick heard his fellow captives crying. He swallowed his fears and stared at the smoke in awe, trying to fathom what was going on. Somewhere out there in that calamity was the lone witch everyone had come to know as Blackwand. He had no idea who she was or what kind of beasts protected her, but in all his days he'd never seen anything that made him feel as proud to be a witch as he did right then.

"Second volley!" Thorpe ordered and two hundred guns again aimed at the wall of smoke. "Fire!" he bellowed, and bared his teeth in a wild grin. He was enjoying this so much.

The Timekeeper again whirled and danced and sent their bullets off course, but the effort was enormous. Bullets streaked by, many sent wild by his efforts, but not all, and a good number of the bullets that missed her were sheer bad shots. He groaned with the strain, pushed to bursting point, and so he didn't hear the sound of insect legs rustling through the silk in his hourglass, or the angry buzz of wings creeping closer and closer.

Eirik looked up from the devastated kraken. Four more had come to support their beleaguered fellow and soon they'd be surrounded. Just then he heard a shriek and saw Sunday whiz past. She lashed at the foremost kraken with her wand, and the water in its furnace pipes suddenly froze. It was a simple enough spell, but the effect was dramatic. Fire and ice met and its armoured chest heaved as if it was choking to death. Rivets flew like popcorn and then the furnace exploded.

Behind her, the berserks were again hunting in a pack and had brought another kraken to its knees. They flocked over it gnawing and ripping until it bled boiling water and vomited coals from its ruptured torso, before exploding in a ball of black smoke. Fire and debris engulfed Eirik and his brothers, but they passed through unscathed and angrier than ever.

She flew onwards into the teeth of a second volley. Bullets whistled past her ears and everything happened so fast she didn't even have time to wonder how on Earth she'd survived. The smoke cleared and she briefly glimpsed the heart-stopping sight of witches on the gallows. Behind them,

Hobbs Station was crammed with soldiers and she knew Thorpe would be amongst them. "BLACKWAND!" she screamed, charging with Ráven's wand held like a sword.

Thorpe ordered a third volley, right into the thick of the fighting not caring whether it hit berserks, krakens or witches. The Timekeeper pulled at the mesh of threads, sending bullets spinning away, but he was tiring and he only had milliseconds to make countless unfathomable calculations. Two hundred bullets, two hundred threads all in the blink of an eye. If Thorpe added even just one extra man to the volley he wouldn't be able to keep her safe.

"Fate does not control all!" His joints ached and his eight eyes throbbed. "No!" he defied, and he heard his master's furious voice echo around the cavern. "Fate shall not control all!" The sand timer shook under his rage and then at last he heard it; the sound of danger, the whisper of silk right at his back, but too late.

The assassin struck.

Sunday saw the gap closing and heard the pounding of her berserks. Ahead, standing naked and vulgar against Hobbs Station was a line of gallows. Now she was close enough to see some of the captives, knowing she was their last hope. "Faster Strike!" she screamed, leaned over the staff and accelerated.

The Timekeeper was hit from behind and sent hurtling against the glass. He crashed into it and flipped himself upright, recovering with incredible speed, but his assailant was on him in a second and finally he saw the intruder that had haunted his glass these last months. She was a jet black wasp armed with a vicious stinger and blade-like wings.

He pounced at her, aiming for her abdomen, but she flitted aside effortlessly and all he hit was a net of threads. He thrashed against the silk, hissing and cursing and she landed on his back and pinned him with her needle legs. He bucked furiously as he tried to dislodge her, and looked up to see her snap at him with her fearsome mandibles. He flinched and tried to twist away, but her jaws caught one of his eyes and it burst, splattering ooze against the glass. He roared in pain and pushed with all his strength, but she thrust downwards and sank that lethal stinger through his exoskeleton and injected a dose of paralysing venom. He screamed in anger, but even that was cut short as her toxins rapidly began to cripple him. "Tell me traitor?" she buzzed against his head, "does fate control all now?"

His cry drained away to a mumble and finally a gasp. He contorted in pain and curled into a crumpled knot, twitching and juddering. She scuttled down and contemptuously flicked his body aside, and the great Timekeeper rolled away, belly up amongst the threads. *Sunday, flee while you can!* he pleaded silently, and struggled furiously, but not a single muscle moved.

"Fate has chosen a new weaver." She surmounted his helpless body and tapped her stinger against his underside, leaving drips of venom. "But you have been shown mercy by the Lord of Fate. He will grant you one last great purpose." He sensed everything around him, but lay there utterly immobile. "You shall be the first meal for my young, the children of fate," she finished.

The Timekeeper had his own thread, one that couldn't be broken or manipulated. It was his alone, a perfect circle of silk he kept close to his heart at all times and that's exactly what she was looking for. She searched his frozen body sensing with her fluttering antennae and gently plucked her prize from his upturned belly. As long as she possessed it he would be in her power, with or without her venom coursing through his body.

No! he thought in despair. *No Sunday I've failed you, turn back, turn back, the valkyries are coming!*

Keeping his unique thread pinned, she reached down and claimed her greatest prize. She lifted Sunday's thread high for him to see and gave it a gentle tug. "Does fate control all?" she asked again and her wings trembled with pleasure. "I think it does 'dear champion'."

He watched paralysed and impotent as she finally set about punishing Sunday Flowers for his act of mercy.

Thorpe watched Blackwand close in and knew the time had come. It was time for the signal. Amid the explosions and gunfire a bell rang out at Hobbs Station, and Vorus and her sisters heard the call to fight.

Finish her Galen, he thought anxiously, but his hands were now moist and his breathing too fast. He'd seen her fly through three volleys unscathed. Something more profound than just cursed warriors protected her, and he realised with shame that he was terrified. If Vorus failed they were finished.

Galen heard the clanging bell and jumped to his feet. "Your hour is at hand!"

Vorus and her sisters had waited for this moment and they raced from their krakens as phantoms, knowing what to do. Vorus came first, leaving a trail of foetid air in her wake. Behind, came her eight sisters. They passed over the infantry as fast and silent as shadows. She thought of her dead sister and crackled with vengeance, aiming directly for the way-beware.

The way-beware sang softly, lulled by Sunday's spell. It wasn't aware of berserks or battles, and it probably had little care for such things. All it knew was that its special song ended the loneliness it had endured so long. Vorus closed in, wishing she could kill Blackwand right there, but Galen had been adamant. The doll was their real enemy, but as she drew closer she heard its beautiful song in her ears and for an instant she wavered.

For the first time since being stranded on Earth, she saw clearly. She saw the true nature of her being. She saw her beloved father Àeon and remembered why he'd given birth to her kind and why the girl Sophie was like a mother to them. She saw her innumerable sisters and their divine and original purpose, the incredible song stilled her and just like Eirik she remembered who she really was, but then, she also remembered how Àeon had abandoned her. With that came fresh anger, which blotted out all else and she plunged forwards with renewed hatred, claws outstretched. Blackwand didn't sense her as she streaked past, reached out and snatched the doll away.

The way-beware was Ruined in a heartbeat.

Its true self died that instant, but it did not stop singing. Its pure motives were spoiled and turned upside down and now it screamed and howled. The song changed from one of comfort and companionship to one of possession and control, smothering rather than soothing.

Eirik charged on at Sunday's side, but suddenly something changed.

He heard the way-beware's Ruined song in his ears like a shrill whistle. The noise drilled into his brain, and where there'd just been clarity and purpose, there was only confusion and domination. The song told him love was possession and control. It screamed in his ears and battered his head until he began to stagger, uncertain now of where he was. Around him his brothers lurched uncertainly, while he ambled on blindly, swinging his huge head from side to side in distress. The song dominated his will until finally he fell with a crash into the dust. His brothers fell by his side and all three of them lay on the moonscape of Hobbs Ash in stunned despair. One doll had achieved what armies couldn't.

Sunday Flowers almost prevailed that day. Victory was so close, but fate had other ideas. The first sign of something wrong came from Strike. *"Sunday, it's them!"* he cried.

She dodged another collapsing kraken, not grasping his warning. "Hold fast!" she screamed. *We can do this, we might really do this!* She dared to hope they could win. She saw the gallows in striking detail and the condemned watching in awe.

"SUNDAY!" Strike shrieked, and suddenly the power just vanished from her lightning-staff. She caught the whiff of rotten flowers and spoiled meat. Something invisible tore past and snatched at her clothing, and she understood now the valkyries had come, but it was too late. Vorus and her sisters pounced on her like a pack of dogs.

Strike was Ruined and only fifty yards from Hobbs Station her staff ploughed into the dirt like a broken arrow, sending her rolling. She skidded over the ground, grazing her face and chin. The wind was knocked from her and dust stung her eyes. "Strike!" she choked, and pulled her face mask down. Gagging and coughing she picked herself up, drew her wand and turned to see the horrible sight of her bears lurching drunkenly. One by one they dropped down, making the earth tremble and vanishing in a cloud of dust. "No! Tawny!" She staggered back to him, bruised and bleeding and trailing her useless lightning-staff in one hand. "Tawny, Silver, Ash!"

"Remember my sister Blackwand," something hissed in her ear.

"Damn you!" She whirled her staff, but it was no more use than a twig now.

Around her, she smelled corruption and heard mocking laughter. Strike moaned inside the staff, and now he sounded feeble and incoherent.

"Blackwand and little sprite wish to spend eternity in darkness, is that why they so foolishly came?" The voice came again.

She screamed in fury and lashed out again, but hit nothing. Valkyries swirled around her unseen, mocking and taunting, but still Sunday pressed on to her beloved bears, all of them lying in the dirt, limbs twitching, tongues lolling. "Tawny! Silver, Ash, please get up, please hear me!" She reached to her belt for the way-beware, and that's when she realised in horror that it was gone.

Eirik looked up, but his vision was blurred and the image wavered. The darkness around her was total now, and he knew it would entomb her. And although he vaguely felt something for the golden-haired girl he couldn't remember what it might be or even her name. He just wanted to turn to stone and let that shrill screaming burn away his soul.

"Tawny, please, what have they done to you!" She tried to haul his great head off the ground, but it was like trying to lift a whale. "Please!" Tears cascaded down and only then did she realise that the fighting had stopped. Hobbs Ash was silent. The stink of decay vanished and she understood the valkyries or whatever they were, had stolen the way-beware.

She turned, and through the dust she saw the condemned still standing on the gallows less than fifty yards away, watching her wide eyed. Around them, endless soldiers now advanced out of Hobbs Station led by Victor Thorpe.

She pulled her wand from its sheath and advanced towards him. Somewhere behind she heard another explosion from the burning krakens, but she walked on, directly towards Thorpe.

Another man pushed his way through the soldiers and stood at Thorpe's side. He carried a black cane and wore a tatty army coat and a bowler hat, he looked breathless, but satisfied, and she knew right away that this was Galen. In his other hand he now held the corrupted way-beware. She heard its twisted new melody in her ears and it sounded like the symphony to a tragedy. *Pelaria and Eliath,* she thought from nowhere, and wished with all her heart that Ben was there.

When she was less than twenty paces away the soldiers all raised their rifles. She half hoped they'd fire, but she knew they wouldn't. But while she had breath left in her she would try to kill the tyrant. Trembling, bleeding and sweating, she gripped her wand tighter and walked straight towards Thorpe.

Thorpe watched in satisfaction. It had been a close run thing and their opponents formidable, but in the end the great Book had prevailed. "Blessed be Àeon," he whispered under his breath, and in his pocket he toyed with his golden ring.

"Blessed be Àeon," Galen added quietly and looked down at the way-beware in his hand. It was such a small thing, but it was Blackwand's undoing. The soldiers began to mutter as she drew closer and he heard someone on the gallows weeping softly, while another was still singing quietly.

They were almost eye to eye now and Sunday felt she'd never hated anything more. She crunched over the last few yards and stood facing him and raised her wand. Around her, hundreds of rifles quivered and fingers tightened on triggers. Men moaned and whispered, but Thorpe just stared at her in amusement. "I'm delighted to meet you again my dear," he crooned.

"Die, you bastard!" She'd never stooped to a curse before, but there was always a first time. She jabbed the wand at him, but nothing happened and he just smiled back at her sympathetically. "Die!" she cried again and thrust the wand, but still nothing. In truth she wasn't surprised to find it was also Ruined.

Around her, frightened whispers turned to sniggers.

"I'm afraid your wand is no longer any use." He stepped forwards and slapped it from her hand, sending it spinning.

She instantly reached for her atheme. When spells failed there was always steel and she grabbed the knife from its sheath and lunged with a scream.

He had plenty of time to see it coming and snatched at her wrist, swung her around and threw her to her knees while wrenching her arm behind her back. She screamed in pain as he twisted her arm, while the atheme clattered harmlessly to the floor. In his pocket he slipped the Book-of-Nine ring onto his finger and made a fist.

"I'll kill you, you bastard," she snarled and twisted around to face him, just as he hoped. He drew his fist back and landed a blow against her face.

The ring gouged the skin from her cheek, and with it went her delicate scar. She saw stars for a second and pain filled her head. Blood ran hot and sticky and she intuitively knew that even the great spider himself was in danger. *Dear champion!* she moaned.

"Mr Galen, if you will," Thorpe indicated the fallen wand.

He collected it and held it up for all to see. Whispers of amazement rippled through the ranks.

"Behold the enemy's black wand," Thorpe announced and everyone fell silent. "The wand that almost crippled the Illuminata, the wand that sent many innocent souls to their graves." He twisted her arm again for effect, making her cry out. "Now break it," he commanded.

"NO!" she screamed and tried to stand, but he shoved her down again.

Galen brought Raven's wand down across his knee and a sharp crack split the air. The witches gasped in horror and even the soldiers recognised that something irreversible had happened. He tossed the two broken halves down in front of her and she stared down at them in abject horror. The black wand was dead.

"Now, what was the last thing you said to me?" Thorpe gloated. "Something about one of us being dead upon our next meeting?"

"Bastard!" she writhed.

He leaned closer and breathed right by her ear. "Which of us looks closest to death now? And if you're not sure what death looks like, let me remind you." He tore her hat from her head, giving everyone their first clear look at Blackwand, then he took hold of her plait and dragged her around to face the row of condemned.

She looked up at a forest of bayonets and behind them thirteen terrified faces staring down at her. They saw their last and only hope broken and bleeding. *I'm sorry,* she pleaded silently, *forgive me, I'm so sorry.*

When Blackwand's hat was torn from her head Alfred Berwick had to bite his tongue to stop himself calling out her name. Despite everything, joy surged through him. It was her. His solstice queen. It was Sunday.

"This is what death looks like," Thorpe explained and signalled to Topp.

Somewhere close by Doulton had a dreadful moment of precognition. "No," he protested, "he can't, it's not supposed to be real!"

Sunday knew what was about to happen and looked helplessly at the lost witches. One of them, a tall man in his seventies, was staring at her so intently that she felt his stare like a presence and when she turned to regard him she suddenly understood. "Alfred?" she whispered.

Sunday, he mouthed silently. He couldn't name her, but he could still tell her how proud he was of her. "Never in all my days have I ever seen a witch so regal and so proud," he declared in a loud clear voice.

All faces turned his way, even Thorpe.

"Long live Blackwand!" Berwick shouted, "Long live Blackwand!"

His voice carried long and far across Hobbs Ash and one by one all of the witches took up the chant. Alfred Berwick locked eyes with the young woman he loved as a daughter and smiled in farewell.

"Long live Blackwand!" they chanted over and over and beside her she heard Thorpe snarl in frustration.

"They love me Mr Thorpe," she smiled defiantly, even as she cried. "Can you claim anyone on this Earth feels the same for you?"

"Long live Blackwand!" they cheered on regardless.

"Release them!" Thorpe raged and seized her hair, forcing her to watch.

Topp pulled the lever, and thirteen trapdoors opened and thirteen witches fell forever.

CHAPTER THIRTY-TWO

A secret in the attic

Initiate: Why does the Illuminata's arms bear magical beasts?
Knight: We take witches' coveted emblems of magic and make them our own,
to invert their meaning and power. Thus their cherished dragon and unicorn
are now ours.
'Ways of the Illuminata Knighthood' 2nd century document.
Author, Alexandrus Marrium, Knight Superior

Salisbury's so called Roman-field hadn't seen a battle since legionaries fought Britons centuries before, but all that was about to change. It took its name from the artefacts discovered there but it wasn't a field, rather a five hundred acre plain. It was here, in view of Wellesley Hall, that the Illuminata would fight their tournament.

Wellesley Hall was surrounded by fertile land occupied by tenant farmers, all of whom had been sent to London to enjoy the Jubilee, whether they wished to or not. When the krakens finally fought, the Illuminata wanted the spectacle to remain private. With the tenants cleared out there wasn't a soul in a ten mile radius around Wellesley who wasn't either a noble or a soldier. This strategy also made it impossible for witches to attack without first crossing miles of open land, where lookouts were more common than rabbit holes. Roman-field was fringed by temporary barracks while the lords and knights found accommodation in the Hall itself. Leonhard and his forces had arrived two weeks previous to oversee the assembly of their krakens and draw up their plans, and as eleven powerful bloodlines from across Europe had gathered under his banner, there was much to coordinate. Wellesley was filled with knights, dignitaries, lords, ladies, courtiers, solicitors, industrialists and translators. These elite, from Germany, Spain, Portugal, France, Holland, Italy, Poland, Hungary and Austria were engaged in a kind of tournament of their own, attending elaborate dances to wage society battles over music and fine dining.

The British had only the Hall's restricted north wing to call their own, and they looked rather like poor relations to their European cousins. It was common knowledge that while Leonhard could field at least three hundred krakens, the sum British total was less than a dozen. Leonhard and his allies openly mocked them, and the overall feeling was that this effort and expense was utterly wasted and that on June 21st the British might as well just hand over the title of Knight Superior and spare themselves the shame of a resounding defeat. The British had set up their kraken depot a long way from their competitors, and for good reason. Inside the cavernous hanger stood nine krakens that were more living creatures than machines. Thorpe and his retinue endured the mockery, knowing when the time came those nine krakens would change the face of the world map.

In the skies above this pomp floated a fleet of airships, both Leonhard's and London's. The huge hydrogen vessels had lifted all the equipment here from afar, and the largest of them was Leonhard's command ship named Echelon, which hovered higher than all the others. From two-thousand feet, its pilots could watch every man coming and going, take notes and report back. Echelon was like a great eye in the heavens scrutinizing everything.

All of this was familiar to Doulton who had spent most of June at Wellesley supervising the proceedings, but Lyle hadn't, and he was bowled over by the scale of the event. "Even London's Jubilee celebrations fall short of this!" he admired.

Doulton sauntered along without answering. Everywhere there were horses, soldiers and devisers from Europe's mightiest families. A few knights strutted around the infantry like peacocks amongst sparrows.

"Didn't you hear me?" Lyle asked.

"Beg pardon, a lot on my mind." He couldn't forget events of two days ago.

"All's well that ends well," he dismissed the matter. "The last challenge now is to beat Leonhard."

Doulton looked around at the Polish garrison as they passed. Twenty gleaming krakens all bearing helmets like boars. "Why am I the only one who doesn't think Leonhard will be beaten so easily?"

"Don't fancy our chances eh? Just two more days and we'll wipe the smiles from their faces."

"I've no more liking for Leonhard's bragging than you, but I've been uneasy about Galen all along, I don't have to remind you of that."

"Lord Thorpe assures me once the tournament is done, the creatures will be of no more use. Galen will dispatch them."

"Thorpe told you that?"

"He did." He brushed the matter aside. "And once this is over then we can finally get back to normal. The young Knight Superior needs a mentor." He puffed a sigh, sounding like a man waking from a bad dream.

Everything back to normal, Doulton thought sardonically. *If only that were true.*

The new keeper of fate looked down at the Timekeeper's very own thread. As long as she held it, she held him. She glanced over to the helpless spider, then returned to her work. The world revolved as always but one special thread in the glass was blessed with her undivided attention. The wasp teased Sunday's thread, stretching it gently. "No thread defies the weave," she called without turning. Her voice echoed around the hourglass and the Timekeeper tried again to move, but although her toxins had long gone, she now controlled his thread and he'd never so much as twitch a muscle again unless she commanded it. "She is waiting 'dear champion'," she taunted, "waiting to see what they will do to her. The fear is building inside her, I can taste it. Do you know what they will do to her?"

The Timekeeper lay still while a storm raged inside him.

"I think you do," she teased. "She is calling to you, far away, frightened and alone, she is calling out to you for help." The wasp rocked with silent laughter. "But no answer will come will it 'dear champion'?"

The Timekeeper pictured his thread, pinned by one of her legs. If he could just reach it he thought, and tried to flex again, but nothing happened. *Sunday!* he agonised. A droplet splashed against the glass from the cave roof, and he was aware of the stalactites growing painfully slowly, yet even they moved faster than he hoped to. *Sunday, I have failed you.*

Close to Wellesley Hall were the remains of an abandoned village called Morden Vale. All that stood there now was a roofless Norman church, a barn, and a row of cottages which were now little more than humps overgrown with ivy. Trees had invaded the extinct village and grew where sculleries and courtyards once stood. The trees in turn had been strangled by ivy, until all of Morden Vale was a forest of leafy columns. Little sunlight penetrated and little wildlife made its home here. All was dark and still, but Morden Vale had found a new lease of life, and now lords and ladies walked arm in arm along the narrow paths, swinging walking canes or twirling parasols. They ambled along, laughing and chatting, following their armed escorts through the neglected woods to witness the tournament's star attraction: Blackwand and her demons.

Thorpe had proudly announced Blackwand's defeat, and that she was being kept at Morden Vale as an exhibit. The great Illuminata families were keen to see this evil avenger for themselves, and pay handsomely for the privilege. He hoped to recoup enough by selling her to rebuild Thorpe Hall, thinking it delightfully fitting.

Lord and Lady Cartwright were one such couple. They followed their guide, duty-warden Topp, from the sumptuous grandeur of Wellesley Hall and through the ornamental gardens. In celebration of the Jubilee, rarities had been gathered from across the Empire. There was a caged elephant, a tiger and a giraffe, all inside the confines of the tropical house. Lord and Lady Cartwright first thrilled at the wild beasts, then left behind the hothouse that smelled of warm earth, and entered the woods along seldom trod paths lined with nettles. They were leaving the world of man and venturing into the embrace of the wildwood. They pretended that this wasn't just some sideshow, but the real thing, and so for Amelia Cartwright, a witch or malign spirit lurked behind every tree. The distant roar of the caged tiger added to the effect. They followed Topp deeper into the woods, sometimes passing other dignitaries, imagining the wildwood watching as they drew ever closer to where Blackwand, queen of witches, lay captive. Lady Cartwright fanned her face. The woods were humid and the air was musty. "How much further?" she demanded.

"Just around the corner my Lady," Topp replied without turning.

"And these demons of hers, I believe they're on display too?" Lord Cartwright enquired.

"Indeed sir, large as life, in the barn next to the church."

"And am I to understand the fee paid will afford us a glimpse of these monsters also?" Cartwright wanted his money's worth.

"Right after you set eyes upon their former mistress my Lord."

At that instant they came into view of Morden church and Lady Cartwright hung back a step.

"My dear?" her husband enquired.

"The witch-queen's in there?" She gazed at the stout, roof-less walls and the square tower with its blunt battlements. Now the adventure seemed a little too real. Lord Cartwright took his young wife's arm and steadied her. Another step along the path, and she saw the first of the soldiers forming a ring around the ruined church. "Richard?" she whispered fearfully.

"It's quite alright Amelia, the fiend is under guard."

"But can't you sense it?" She worked her fan harder. "The evil of *her*."

"She is powerless, Lord Thorpe himself captured her."

"Powerless for sure," Topp added confidently.

"They should have put her to death and had done with it." She clung to her husband's side.

"They will, I'm sure." He'd paid one hundred pounds to see Blackwand and he wasn't going to let her waste his money.

Lady Cartwright peeped out from behind her husband and saw soldiers everywhere, guarding the church, empty but for one solitary prisoner. Other dignitaries came and went, and servants wandered around with refreshments. All looked normal but she remained edgy. "I don't want to go Richard," she decided, afraid of the ivy-clad walls and thinking of the murderous hag inside.

He groaned and pulled his arm from hers. "Fine, remain here then."

"Be careful!" she called after him.

"Just here sir," Topp ushered him to one of the windows. Either side, couples were spying on the queen of witches through similar openings. "Take this sir, as a precaution." He handed him a plain mask, the kind used at fancy dress balls to conceal the eyes.

"Whatever for?"

"It's not safe to let the witch see you sir. It's reputed she could kill with one look."

Impressed, he took the mask, held it to his face and then gingerly stepped up to the window to see. Cartwright had heard that Blackwand was so ugly that she could turn a man to stone, and that she filed her teeth to points to better eat children and nip her demons to keep them in order. Everyone knew she rode a stick through the skies that could spit lightning, and most chilling her black wand was somehow alive and told her the secrets of dark magic. Cartwright took a deep breath and leaned forwards. At first he saw only the church's empty innards. The floor was a mosaic of recumbent headstones worn smooth by years of passing feet and in the centre stood a stone like a monolith. Mounted at the top was a sign.

BLACKWAND

THE BLACK-HEARTED QUEEN OF WITCHES

The stone was dark with age, so dark in fact that at first he didn't see the chained figure resting against it. Then he caught the glint of golden hair and a face that could have been the image of grace itself. "Dear Lord," he gasped, "this is Blackwand?" At the name, the young woman turned and stared at him defiantly. He looked full into her face and backed away.

"Part of her glamour," Topp explained quietly. "Lord Thorpe says her trickery makes men see a woman of great beauty."

Cartwright looked back again, feasting his eyes as he grew bolder. The queen of witches was exquisite, despite a bruised cheek. "Then what does she really look like?" he asked faintly.

"Best no man should see her true face my Lord."

"Really." Although he knew some shrunken hag lurked under that perfect exterior, he couldn't stop himself imagining her in his bedchamber. His cheeks flushed and when she stared at him again he felt sure she knew his every thought and he decided he'd seen enough. He turned back to Amelia, but now he thought his wife looked dull in comparison. He felt the harlot's spell work in his loins and cursed himself for coming here. Thorpe was right: Blackwand was very dangerous.

"My dear?" She thought he looked pale.

"Let us be away," he tugged at her elbow.

"But you saw her did you not?"

"I saw her," he said stiffly.

"What did she look like? Richard do tell!"

"A vile hag," he shook his head, "best you don't see." He hurried on, dragging his astonished wife behind him, all the while thinking things a good husband ought not think.

Sunday reached out again for the Timekeeper, but now there was just an overwhelming silence. *"Dear champion!"* she asked for the hundredth time, but her only answer was a furious animal roar from far off. It sounded like a lion, but how she wished it was Tawny.

Trees towered over the roofless church and even they seemed to be watching her. She felt like an insect in a jar and on all sides masked faces came and went, staring in at her. Nobody set foot inside, but the whispers and laughter continued unabated. She sat against the stone, under that mocking sign and stared ahead at nothing. *Queen of witches,* she thought bitterly. *Queen of the solstice.*

She wanted to bury her head and hide, but then the crowds would gloat. Alfred Berwick had taught her that magic was regal, and so for his sake she fixed a defiant expression and endured. Hour after hour they came to ridicule her, and she thought of the animals at Smithfield.

"This is Blackwand?" someone murmured to her left.

She looked around at yet another masked face, and stared him down. After a moment she saw him withdraw and drag his wife away before she even got a glimpse. A second later a new face peered through, but the murmurs and giggles were all the same.

Despite all of this, two things gave her hope and she thought of nothing else. Firstly, hrafn-dimmu, the black wand she named herself for, *wasn't* dead. "Blackwand lives," she whispered and smiled secretly.

Before her ill-fated attack she cast hrafn-dimmu into the Thames with orders to find its original owner, and prayed that Hethra would guide it home along rivers and streams until it found Valonia's heir. The wand Galen had broken was her own painted black, a sleight of hand she hadn't even shared with Strike. A great loss for sure, but hers was merely a wand, not a living thing like hrafn-dimmu. "Safe journey black wand," she sighed, "tell them about me if all goes bad." She rubbed at her eyes to suppress the tears, rattling her chains as she did.

If rescue failed to come she hoped that hrafn-dimmu would tell its finder of her fate. If she was to be subjected to Thorpe's obscene vengeance then perhaps someday a witch might come and find her, and out of mercy kill her. It was her last desperate hope, but one she didn't dwell on, not while there was still Ben.

"Ben," she smiled. Along with hrafn-dimmu, this was her other great shining hope. There was still a chance he might come and bring the covens with him. "You are my one short summer," she recited under her breath, and again imagined his note wasn't a cryptic warning, but a love letter. The innocent daydream blotted out her prison, and Hethra knew she needed all the help she could get, even from a hopeless fantasy.

This is how she endured mockery and imprisonment, this is how she survived when memories of dear Alfred Berwick threatened to drown her. She imagined the fabled black wand sailing freely through the world, making its way back to Kolfinnia and she held a secret, fictional conversation with it.

"Will Ben's army come hrafn-dimmu?"

"The future is unwritten Sunday," Raven's wand seemed to say.

"You sound like a friend of mine," she thought of the Timekeeper. "What's become of him?"

"He resurrected you and Strike, and protected you all along, and now he is being punished for that pity."

"Punished by who or what?"

"The Patternmaker, the Lord of the Weave."

"What kind of creator despises pity?"

"One that fears to lose control."

Someone threw a stone at her through the window. She heard laughter and clenched her fists.

"Hold fast Sunday, the future is not written, for if it were the Patternmaker himself would be redundant."

She imagined Raven's wand gliding along in a clear stream, with London far behind it and hope ahead of it. "I wish Ben were here." She lowered her head and touched her swollen cheek where her special scar had once been and where he'd kissed her, but now where there was only a bloody scab. "Can there possibly be a happy end to all of this?" Tears threatened again, but she swore she wouldn't cry.

"The future is not written," the wand promised and vanished into the darkness, borne along in a fast flowing stream, going home.

"Don't go," she whispered.

"Remember Sunday . . . Blackwand lives," the wand whispered back, sliding from her imagination, leaving her chained amongst her enemies.

"You are my one short summer," she said to nobody. Tomorrow was the 21st and either Ben would come, the battle would rage and she would shine once more as solstice queen, or her star would fall into Thorpe's darkness and her last hope would be for release in death.

Doulton was nervous. Not only was his plan unorthodox, but right now he was within touching distance of one of Blackwand's bears. He made his way to Sunday's prison, past the derelict barn where her beasts were kept. Getting them here had been no mean feat and now all three lay in the overgrown ruins along with her sinister flying staff, fastened with chains staked into the ground. At first they were terrified of the monsters, even after Galen assured them they were practically dead. The sinister doll had crushed their will, and for good measure it now stood at the centre of the three where it continued to subdue them. Now the bears' prowess was all but a memory and men had ridiculed them until they were bored with their cruel games and went about the cosy task of escorting Lords and Ladies.

Doulton hurried past the closest animal. It was tawny brown and its mouth was large enough to swallow a boar. He saw massive fangs glint under the rubbery lips, while its eyes were partially lidded and only the whites showed. Galen was right, they were utterly senseless.

He tried to look calm as he weaved through the crowds. He passed a woman wearing a bonnet, leading several young ladies giggling at their handsome escort, a soldier barely in his twenties with an immaculate uniform. Waiters carried silver trays loaded with champagne and roasted meat, while porters carried parasols for their masters. It was all a long way from the fury of Hobbs Ash two days ago, and it was the matter of executions that brought him here. He had something he had to say to Blackwand.

"The prisoner's to be kept isolated sir," a sergeant stepped up, not recognising him.

"I'm Doulton, the squires-marshal."

"Apologies sir, but still," he looked uncertain.

"I was there when she was caught," he explained.

The sergeant nodded and lowered his rifle. "Just a few minutes won't hurt I suppose."

"Thank you." Doulton edged past, through the archway bristling with ivy, and into the church.

Sunday heard approaching footsteps but didn't move. A moment later a tall man in his early thirties stepped into view. He stood before her with his hands clasped behind his back, his posture looked confident but his expression was worried.

Doulton wasn't sure how to start. "Miss Blackwand?"

She made a play of looking about her. "She's gone to the privy, may I be of assistance?"

He coughed and began his prepared speech, which wasn't easy; his words were difficult and she was something of a distraction. "My name's Doulton, I was at Hobbs Ash."

"Then you witnessed the execution of my kin," she stung him.

"That's the matter I came to speak about." His eyes flicked side to side and she knew he was putting himself at risk by coming here. "While I deplore your actions and do not lament your capture, I concede that what was done was improper."

"Improper?" she sneered. "In the same way a lady might show an ankle in public?"

"It was against the rules of engagement, and I for one am not proud of it." This was the point where he intended to march away feeling renewed, but her gaze held him. Even chained in the dust she looked regal.

"Then be at peace Mr Doulton," she said scathingly, "I'm sure they died a cleaner death than Charlotte Anne Pilling."

He swallowed his shock. "I don't know what you mean."

"You had her killed in a manner befitting your aims did you not?"

"I've never heard of the woman."

She leaned back against the stone and regarded him. "This is only the beginning, you know that don't you?"

"Your meaning?"

"When tomorrow dawns, Europe's Illuminata will see your dark secret will they not? A valkyrie I think you call it."

"How can you know this?" he demanded, terrified she'd read his mind.

"You'll win this tournament through Galen's dark arts won't you?" she smiled dangerously.

He stood looking down at her, while his tongue flopped around his mouth like a dying fish, groping for words, but she spoke first.

"Shall I shout it aloud? Shall I tell them their chivalrous knights face creatures of Ruin tomorrow and that this whole tournament is a trap?"

"Lower your voice!" he hissed and knelt to speak in private. To the on-lookers he seemed to be kneeling in reverence. "How do you know this?"

"Blackwand has her ways Mr Doulton. But as I say, this is only the beginning."

"Explain."

"You mean you can't see the obvious?"

"Just bloody spit it out!"

"When your enemies are beaten and go home to lick their wounds, what do you think they'll do?"

"Recognise our supremacy of course," he sniffed.

"And you really think it'll stop there?"

He frowned, lost for an answer.

"They'll know you've broken an age-long pact and they'll summon their own Ruinous creatures to combat yours. The age of knights will be over. Wars will be fought with armies of demons. Tomorrow the world changes forever. You've opened a door that can't be closed."

The revelation was like being woken from sleep to find a burning house.

He loathed to admit it but she was right. "We're in full control of the matter," he pretended.

"By 'we' you mean Victor Thorpe. Do you trust him?"

"Implicitly!" he lied.

"Have you stopped to consider that perhaps the Illuminata themselves are being sacrificed, just like those innocents on the gallows? That someone is using you for their own ends?"

"Who?"

"Who do you think."

He eyed her suspiciously and snatched at the only explanation that made sense, anything else was too horrible to contemplate. "Oh, I see your game," he smiled uncertainly, "you are cunning aren't you. You poison men's hearts with your beguiling looks and crafted words." He stood and took a steady breath.

"You don't believe me?"

"Why should I. You're a witch, spells and words are your power." She just looked up at him and a few seconds of her stare was all he could stand. "What happened at Hobbs Ash was regrettable. I came to set the record straight, I believe I've done that," he insisted and turned.

"Then tell me," she called, loud enough for the crowds to hear.

He stopped and looked back.

"Why has Thorpe kept Galen's true name a secret?" she added softly.

The blood in his veins crawled to a stop. "What do you mean?"

She thought of the Timekeeper's note, *'Galen = Matthew Thorpe'*. Now it all made sense. "Ask Thorpe why he keeps his son's name so secret." She gave him a smouldering smile to ruffle him further.

Son? Is that possible? The earth seemed to wobble under his feet.

"Ask him Mr Doulton," she provoked.

"Ever the witch, ever the trickster," he said offhandedly, but now he was shaking.

"Someone is indeed playing tricks, but it's not I."

"That remains to be seen." He left, trying not to run and all the while wishing just like Lord Cartwright, that he hadn't come here.

Sunday touched the silver fox around her neck and managed a small smile. Even without Strike, berserks, or a wand, Blackwand still had teeth.

Galen had taken the attic room in the Hall's north wing as his own. The cramped space held tea-chests and cobwebs but little else and it roasted in the heat. Tonight was the tournament's grand opening ball and he'd be expected to attend, but first he had to see Sophie again.

The evening was hot and so he was topless. Sweat glistened across his back and he sat cross-legged on his blanket holding his cane. Inside, Elios obediently showed him the mind of Ruin, but the effort was very hard, as if something was denying them. *"Where are you?"* Ahead of him was a silvery mist, nothing more. No Sophie, no Àeon, no landscape of dark wonders. *"What is going on here?"*

"She's close," Elios insisted.

"She's hiding more like. Why would she do this to me?" Some part of him understood that she was indeed aware of him after all. He should have been overjoyed, but he was angry.

"She's listening," Elios warned.

"Sophie!" His call resounded through Ruination. *"Sophie answer me!"*

"Beloved sisters coming home," a voice replied. *"The threads of fate are closing around the girl with the broken soul."*

"Damn you, show yourself!"

The mist swirled. Elios hissed, and he saw a figure approaching. It drew closer until it stood only yards away and now he could make out that it was a child, cloaked and hooded.

"Sophie?" he asked, suddenly fearful. *"Is that you?"*

"Sophie's crib is empty now the robber's belly is full," the figure sang softly. *"Along came a spider to protect and to guide her, and so she could never be slain,"* it continued, but now the sweet voice sounded twinned, like two throats speaking at once, and he caught the whiff of decay.

In Ruination his mind froze, while in the stuffy attic his body oozed sweat. *"I never knew what Barlow did to you, believe me."*

"Beloved sisters coming home," Sophie repeated and went to lower her hood.

On his blanket, Galen smiled weakly, believing she was finally acknowledging him. But his smile turned to a grimace of terror when the hood fell away. He expected Sophie's solemn face. What he saw instead was a horror bearing two mouths, devoid of eyes and looking more like a tribal mask than a flesh and blood thing. *"Àeon is watching,"* the two mouths said, *"and he is most displeased with his disciples."*

He screamed and scrambled back, dropping the cane and breaking the link. He collapsed against the rough floorboards and lay there fighting for breath. "Sophie," he panted.

"The mind of Ruin is disturbed I see," someone said gravely.

He gulped hard, and looked up to see his father standing over him. "Father?" He slithered upright and rubbed at his pounding head. "How long were you there?"

"Long enough."

"She saw me," he groaned.

He nodded as if this was expected. "Everything is speeding up, even the song of Àeon, time itself. Many fates are wrapping themselves together and tomorrow on the longest day they'll meet at last."

"And then?"

"Then beloved sisters shall come home." He looked at his old hands and thought of his daughter. "Now go and get changed and have a shave, the opening ceremony begins in one hour."

"Who can think about bloody dancing at a time like this?"

"You don't have to think about it, just be there. We have to keep up the pretence."

Galen reached for his cane and climbed to his feet. "There's something else, Sophie spoke of Blackwand."

His eyes narrowed. "She's aware of our world then?"

"She must be. Something's happening beyond in Ruination, but she's hiding it."

He smiled. "Sophie's playing with us? My cunning little girl's growing up."

"Father, what's happening?" He clutched at one of the roof beams.

"I don't know," he sighed at last.

For a few seconds both of them stood lost in thought, listening to the muffled sounds of guests below and the creak of roof tiles cooling in the evening still.

"Torture the answers out of Blackwand," Galen demanded at last, "ask her how Sophie knows of her."

"Not yet. Until the Book-of-Nine has control of the Illuminata we must treat Blackwand just like any other prisoner," he reminded him.

"Bury her you said, mutilate her you said!" he enthused, "why must we wait?"

"Because those are the punishments of the great Book, not the Illuminata! Can you imagine a better way to draw attention to ourselves?"

Galen hung his head and mumbled an apology.

"Just a while longer, after the solstice the Illuminata will be commanded by us." He clasped his son's shoulder. "Then, and only then do we make Blackwand pay."

Galen smiled, "And then put that bitch Vorus in her place."

"Perhaps she can share a grave with Blackwand, bed fellows for eternity." Thorpe squeezed his arm and gave a scratchy laugh.

There came the sound of a soft click and both men turned to see Doulton step out from the shadows with a revolver trained on them, and Galen could almost feel the webs of fate knot themselves into a noose. Now things were going to get very nasty.

"Mr Doulton, got lost on your way to the powder room did you?" Thorpe growled.

"I've been waiting here all afternoon," he replied coolly. "Waiting in the stifling heat for you and Galen to meet in private, or should I say Matthew Thorpe."

Galen gasped faintly.

"Well, well," Thorpe chuckled, "Lyle and I were wrong about you. You have the makings of a man after all." He reached into his coat.

"Keep your hand where I can see it Thorpe!" he ordered, aiming the revolver. "It would be regrettable if I had to shoot you, but I will if I must. I only need one of you alive for interrogation."

"It seems I was very wrong about you," Thorpe conceded, and slowly brought his hand from his coat where he was now holding a cigar. "Would you deny a condemned man a last smoke?"

"Save it. You can enjoy it on the gallows before they hang you, traitor."

"Father," Galen growled and took a step forwards.

"That's close enough," Doulton swung the revolver towards him. "I knew you were a sham the moment I set eyes on you," he jeered.

Galen smiled coldly. "It's a hard case to prove; Lord Thorpe an enemy of the Illuminata. Sure you're up to it son?"

"I'd be ashamed to be a son of yours," he retorted. "What I've heard tonight will be sufficient to postpone the tournament, close down your experiments and send you both to the noose. Now both of you, down on your knees." He fished in his pocket and brought out the first pair of wrist-irons.

Galen saw that Doulton was far bolder than he'd guessed. The revolver was steady and he'd clearly thought this through. *But has he reckoned on Elios?* he thought. *"Elios, Ruin the man,"* he demanded silently.

"Galen I won't! I refuse to murder when it suits you!"

"I'll throw the cane. When it touches him, kill his heart," he ignored her.

"You can't make me kill again."

Doulton stepped closer, revolver steady, eyes cool. "On your knees traitors," he demanded.

"Kill the bastard or I'll break this cane and cast you out!"

"Galen!" she pleaded, but she didn't finish because just then he hurled the cane.

Doulton saw it spin towards him. Without thinking he fired, aiming for Galen. There was a loud crack, but the cane glanced off the muzzle and sent the shot wide.

"No!" Elios made her decision.

The cane hit Doulton's chest, and dropped harmlessly to the floor.

Treacherous runt disobeyed me! Galen had time to think, just as his father hurtled past him. He'd seen his feint and wasted no time. Doulton and Thorpe crashed to the floor and Galen heard the revolver roar a second time followed by a scream. His father had been hit.

"Traitors!" Doulton roared, and tried to raise the gun, but Thorpe had him pinned.

"Nobody stands before the great Book," he bellowed and landed crushing blows, despite his wounded shoulder.

"Father!" Galen ploughed into the confusion and brought his foot down hard on Doulton's throat. There was a wet smacking sound, like a paper bag being burst, and he began to cough and retch. The revolver roared a third time and a roof tile shattered before Galen prised it from his grip and hurled it away.

Doulton fought for breath and tried to climb up, but father and son fought dirty. He had come to put things right, but he would pay dearly for his sense of duty. Lyle was right, he was an idealist and he still couldn't believe that wrong would prevail today. *Can't let them win!* he thought as they rained blows down on him, but he knew they could and would. His faith in innate justice had abandoned him, and now too did hope of victory. *You were right Blackwand.* It was his final thought.

The disciples of the Book-of-Nine kicked and pummelled until he was bloodied and unconscious, then, when confident he wouldn't get up again, the two stood gasping and bleeding looking down at their victim. The attic was hazed with gun smoke, and Galen's ears rang from the shots. He heard a rough sawing sound and realised it was his father's breathing. "You're hit!" he exclaimed. He'd been shot just under the right collar bone and now the white shirt was scarlet.

"Never mind that, finish the bastard," he panted.

Galen retrieved his cane and felt Elios trembling inside. "You let me down," he said stonily.

"I won't kill for you any longer."

"She says she won't help us," he relayed to his father.

"What did you expect?" Thorpe sneered and clamped a hand to his bleeding shoulder.

"After all I've done for you?" Galen shook his head.

"After all you've done to me. I am a thunder-sprite, not a mistake, and Blackwand and her kind are more a family to me than you ever will be." She couldn't believe she was finally saying these things, neither could she believe how right they felt.

He rocked on his feet and looked down at Doulton's battered face. He was still breathing, the job was only half done. "You won't help us?"

"I won't."

"What's the thing saying?" Thorpe slumped down on a tea chest, nursing his limp arm.

"Elios will aid us no further."

"Typical bloody woman," he huffed, and reached down for Doulton's revolver. "Then we do things the old fashioned way."

Galen hardly heard him. "Sophie, Vorus and now Elios. All of them betrayed me," he said in a broken voice and dropped the cane to the floor.

"The female heart is poison." His father spat blood from a split lip and took aim at Doulton's chest. "And so are spying little cowards," he added, took aim and finished the job with a single shot. The revolver blazed a fourth and final time. Doulton jerked, his eyes even fluttered open for a second and then closed again. There was a smoking hole where his heart lay, but now he struggled for breath no more. "Cleaner end for the spy-rat than he deserved," Thorpe tossed the revolver down in disgust.

"Father, what are we going to do?" Galen wrung his hands, wanting to hold his cane for comfort but knowing there was none to be found there.

"Do?" He wiped his face. "Get a surgeon for me, and tell all of Wellesley that we shot a witch-spy, that's what we do."

"And Elios?"

"Burn the cane with the crippled whore in it for all I care."

Galen looked down at the black cane next to a growing pool of Doulton's blood. He touched it with his toe, to see if she had anything further to say, but it was as silent as the man lying on the floor. *"Goodbye Elios,"* he accused silently, but she said nothing.

The night drew in and the ball was enjoyed with great pomp. News spread that a witch-spy had been killed by Lord Thorpe and all of Wellesley was alight with tales of his valour, and with renewed fears of a witch attack tomorrow. Lyle was stunned, but readily accepted Thorpe's fiction, after all he'd seen Doulton's reaction to the executions at Hobbs Ash with his own eyes. Clearly the man had sympathies with witches. Maybe he thought his good turn would secure him a place in Blackwand's bed, instead it sent him to a shameful grave.

Morden Vale was lit by a hundred sentries carrying lanterns. Sunday sat in the glare of sodium lamps as brilliant as daylight, watched by a hundred pairs of eyes. Close by, Eirik and his brothers lay in a tangled heap, all enslaved by the Ruined way-beware. Her lightning-staff had been unceremoniously tossed onto the piled bodies, and Strike was imprisoned within, powerless and numb.

The Echelon command ship floated high above Wellesley Hall, and from its control deck it would have been hard to believe treachery and murder were rife below. The Hall and the surrounding encampments glowed comfortingly with a thousand lanterns, looking like a town at peace, but one man knew better. His name was Williams, he was about fifty years-old and had a metal knee as a result of an old war wound. He'd managed to wangle his way on to the Echelon's flight crew two weeks ago after his predecessor fell sick, or at least that was his cover story. There were numerous English mercenaries in Leonhard's ranks and so nobody suspected Williams to be a fraud. He stood adjusting controls to keep the huge vessel steady, and trying to keep a low profile. The bridge was manned by a skeleton crew comprising him and three other pilots, one French and two German, although in truth he wasn't a pilot and Williams wasn't his real name. He was a squire. In fact, at one time he'd been Knight Superior Krast's squire.

One of the crew was inspecting a row of gauges. "We seem to be heavy again, compensate for it Williams," he ordered in a thick German accent.

"Aye sir." Williams adjusted the hydrogen flow a fraction. He wasn't a pilot, but he knew enough to blend in.

"Echelon's been getting heavier all evening," the crew man grumbled. His name was Hansa and he was the first officer.

"Heavy cold air sweeping across the plain sir," Williams lied, "cools the ship and weighs it down."

"Never has such a thing happened in Germany," he smiled wryly.

"Britain's a strange place," he smiled back. In truth he liked Hansa and certainly didn't want to have to kill him, although he would if he had to, but only if he *really* had to he told himself.

Hansa relayed orders in German to a subordinate, probably still wondering why the Echelon seemed to be taking more power than usual to keep aloft, but Williams knew why, and his task tonight was to make sure nobody else found out.

This is going to be a bloody long night, he sighed. Williams, whose real name was Bertrand Hathwell, busied himself with the controls and thought of the witches so very close by and one in particular called Hilda. Beyond the thousands of cubic metres of hydrogen gas, outside on the Echelon's huge domed surface, an army was gathering, but without him they might all be caught before daybreak.

Williams, better known as Hathwell, was right about one thing. At two-thousand feet the June air was much cooler, and the clear skies didn't help, although Ben thought the view was spectacular. No airship rode higher than Echelon and so it was the perfect place to gather in secret, on top of the top-most vessel at the whole tournament. Who could possibly see them?

Senior witches were known as Wards, and Ben looked over at their Ward now. Her name was Swanhilda Saxon, although everyone knew her as Hilda, or Hilly, and he'd met her in France but she hailed from Wildwood. Kolfinnia talked about her a lot, and for good reason. She was strong in witchcraft and the fact that any witches had come to this infernal place was mostly due to her persuasion and leadership. He hovered close enough to hear her breathing. She was a striking woman for mid-fifty with pale eyes and a plait of long dark hair. No wonder Hathwell adored her, such thoughts set him thinking of Sunday again. "I wish I knew what was going on down there," he murmured.

She watched a shooting star twinkle overhead. "You're sure about these creatures of Ruin?"

He sighed. "How many they've got and what they really are is unknown, all I know is they've been experimenting."

"I never thought they'd resort to such tactics, not even them."

"And if they have?"

She listened to the faint sound of firecrackers and laughter far below. It sounded like ancient memories.

"Hilda?" he leaned closer.

"Then we'll have to deal with them as well. We can't let them get loose."

"Then Oak be with us," he added.

Hilda shared a private moment with her thunder-sprite and Ben could tell her thoughts were dark.

"Tell me more about Kolfinnia," he asked, trying to lighten the mood.

She adjusted her cloak against the cold and thought. Meanwhile he took a moment to survey their forces. Five hundred witches from Britain and covens across Europe, floating on their staffs above the Echelon. They took turns to alight on the airship and give their tired thunder-sprites a rest. That's why the vessel seemed heavy to Hansa, and that's why they needed

Hathwell to cover for them. He just hoped the former squire could weave a convincing fiction until tomorrow. "She was always the most untidy little witch," she said at last.

"Kolfinnia, untidy? But she's so organised."

"Many's the time she'd turn up for her spell lessons and hadn't even run a comb through her hair," she smiled, thinking of Wildwood. "She was always happiest in the garden, mud and Kolfinnia loved one another."

He shared her brief happiness. "You'll be seeing her again soon, at her new coven."

"I hear she's a coven-mother now and has quite a reputation."

"Aye. She spoke of you often, but feared you were dead."

"I would've been if not for Hathwell."

"Are you and he —"

"No," she said abruptly.

He retreated and began again. "Whatever happens tomorrow Hilda, well done."

He saw her eyes twinkle in the moonlight. "For what?"

"For making this possible." He jerked his head towards the ragged army spread through the night, all of them counting down the hours until tomorrow.

She smiled craftily. "Hathwell rescued me from Kittiwake and smuggled me to France. You gave me a good reason to come home." She shifted on her staff as a moth fluttered past her ear. "Tell me more about this Blackwand. She sounds like a once in a lifetime lady."

"Oh she is," he agreed, and went on to tell her of Blackwand's courage, but not her true name, that was his special secret. As he talked he imagined her sublime face in every detail right down to the delicate hourglass scar. "And now she's a captive," he rounded off, and his face felt hot.

"Only for now," she assured him. "And I was captive too remember, and here I am."

He grunted a reply, too upset to speak. *One short summer,* he thought, *it'll be a bloody short summer indeed if things go bad tomorrow.* Tomorrow was the solstice, and one way or another this business would finally be concluded.

CHAPTER THIRTY-THREE

The longest day begins

'Some days we do what we want, others we do what fate tells us.'
'Higher Forms of Magic - a witch's meditations on daily life'
Author unknown

The witch in her knew when midnight had come and June 21st came with it. It was the day she'd been named for, Sun-Day, her day as solstice queen and now her 21st birthday. Today Alfred Berwick was to have announced her as coven-mother in waiting, and one day Regal-Fox was to have been hers. Now though, she'd trade all that for one last moment with him. "The longest day," she sighed and from nowhere a strange thought welled up. *Beloved sisters are coming home.* She had no idea what it meant, but she looked to the dark sky and knew before this day was done she'd find out.

Galen was sleeping, but he had to take a draught of hemlock and hensbane to earn that sleep and his dreams were disturbing. He lay on his sweaty blankets next to his cane, which was now his burden rather than his companion. He had etched Elios's name into the wood to keep her restrained, having all but disowned her.

In his dream the mist cleared and there was Sophie as always, aloof, turned away, holding something in her arms, something out of his sight. *"Sophie."* Now he didn't know if he loved or hated her.

"You've come here many times," she replied without turning.

"All my life." In that dream state when all things seem possible he didn't feel any surprise that she at last acknowledged him.

"Since you found your sweet Elios and she showed you the way."

"Yes."

"But I have watched you from the day I came here." Her arm moved regularly, and he guessed she was stroking whatever she cradled in her arms. *"Lord Àeon has been watching you too."*

"What have you been doing these endless years?" he asked dreamily.

"Àeon's children needed a guardian."

"It was wrong of grandfather to send you here like this," he apologised.

"But if he hadn't, the beloved sisters wouldn't have had a mother to care for them."

"Beloved sisters, I don't understand?" He always assumed this referred to herself, his beloved sister.

"Àeon's children," she sighed mournfully, *"but many of them are hurt and lost."*

"Then let me help you find them." He took a step towards her, anxious to see what she was doing.

"You already did brother," she said icily. *"You found them and corrupted them.'*

The accusation burned. *"Explain yourself!"*

She sighed again. *"Àeon saw his children lost to the world of man, barghests, latchers, thelling-horsts, bloat-goblins. They came to Earth by accident and found a sea of woe made by man's wounded heart, and they changed brother."* He noticed the sky was darkening as Ruinous creatures in their thousands came to pay their respects. He'd been right, she was beloved of Ruination. *"They changed and became twisted by the evil in the world. Monsters you called them, and monsters they became and forgot the song of Àeon. And so Àeon created a new race of children stronger than the rest. He made shepherds of Ruin, beloved sisters, to keep the family together, but one of them also strayed."*

"Vorus!" he gasped in understanding.

"That is your vulgar name for her. To Àeon she is a special daughter, but one who can never come home."

"Never? But why?"

"She flew too close to the horrors of man like a moth to the flame and found the walls of Earth would not allow her passage back home. She has lingered in the world ever since, corrupted by its horror."

"But Vorus thrives on horror!" he scoffed.

She shook her head. *"Àeon's children thrive on death and decay, not cruelty and horror, those are the traits of men."*

"Then take her and rid me of the harlot!"

"She is too corrupted now."

He laughed scornfully, *"How could Vorus become more of a monster than she already is?"*

"Because finally she met you dear brother, and learned the joy of killing. Out of spite to hurt her father Àeon, she lured the shepherds away and corrupted them. But these other beloved sisters, these shepherds, are still redeemable and they are coming home."

"How dare you lecture me!" Now he decided he hated her and he wanted to throttle the life from his sanctimonious sister.

She stood slowly and turned. He steeled himself to see her at last, and when he did he saw not a hideous valkyrie, but the real Sophie, and there was the radiant likeness of his mother in her features.

"I've given my life to find you," he accused.

"But I was never lost," she corrected. Now he saw what she'd been protecting all these years. She held an infant valkyrie in her arms, a shepherd to bring the lost home, but here in Ruination, untainted by man, it was serene and ethereal. *"Lord Àeon has no regard for those who hurt his children. Thank the merciful stars for Blackwand."*

"Blackwand?" he recoiled.

She said nothing, but smiled coldly and looked down at the beautiful being in her arms and then began to sing again. *"Along came a spider to protect and to guide her . . ."*

He turned and ran, cursing and screaming, but now everything was black and he couldn't see his way. He felt the sensation of falling, falling forever like witches on the gallows, and awoke on his blanket drenched in sweat, and with his heart galloping in his chest. He groaned and held his head in his hands.

Imprisoned in her cane, Elios listened, thinking he sounded more and more lost with each passing day.

It promised to be a beautiful day, but Thorpe had more on his mind than weather as he marched along accompanied by his honour guard. His duty was to invite each family to take their place on Roman-field ready for the trials to begin. He walked tall, wearing a black suit and a top hat, and with his right arm in a sling. Lyle walked ahead while Galen skulked at his father's side. He'd submitted to wearing a smart uniform for the occasion, but he still carried his satchel and his now silent cane.

"You look half dead," Thorpe growled quietly to his son.

"Bad dreams," he mumbled.

"Are Vorus and her brood ready?"

"I spoke with her at dawn, she's excited."

"Then she better make the most of it, as soon as the tournament's won and we have the song of Àeon I want the thing and her ghastly sisters put down."

"Nothing would please me more." He thought of his strange dream. *Not a valkyrie, but a shepherd?* He wondered if he should tell his father, and decided against it.

"Then we'll have our long overdue meeting with Blackwand, see how pretty her eyes look lying on a silver plate," he chuckled.

Galen felt a rush of anticipation and despite his sore head he managed a smile.

Leonhard held court in a small pavilion in the gardens. It was a gaudy affair decorated with swathes of red and yellow silk. A host of decorative peacocks strutted around it while red and yellow banners flew above, each showing a water-dragon and crossed lances. Even his krakens, known as the castle-guard, had helmets fashioned like watery serpents. Leonhard was languishing on a velvet couch with Hieder at his side and backed by a wall of generals. All of them looked up as Thorpe's party approached. Hieder stepped forwards but Leonhard remained recumbent and sullen.

"Lord Thorpe. You are better I trust?" Hieder indicated his wounded arm.

"Rude with health Mr Hieder."

"It was a lucky escape you had."

"I put my faith in the good Book and it has never failed to protect me."

"Quite so." Being a devout man Hieder clearly approved, while Galen stifled a smile. "The English summer is all you boasted," he complimented.

"And how does the Count find Salisbury and our English summer?" He turned to Leonhard, who resembled a bulldog with an aversion to the sun.

His English was excellent, but he seldom spoke it.

"Count Leonhard is overjoyed to be here," Hieder explained.

Thorpe smiled at the Count's sour expression. "And it shows," he flattered him. "And now I'm honoured to invite the Count and his allies to begin taking their places on Roman-field, the first contest shall begin at one o'clock sharp."

Leonhard grunted something while Hieder clicked his heels and stood straight. "May victory go to the most worthy, for the glory of the Illuminata."

"For the glory of the Illuminata," Thorpe echoed, then checked his pocket watch. "Then I shall see you on the field of honour in precisely two hours."

Leonhard pushed himself upright. "When six hundred years of history shall be overturned!" he rumbled.

Thorpe looked at him directly. "Many things might fall today your Grace."

Leonhard looked puzzled, then pouted indifferently.

"Until then gentlemen," he finished and was reaching for a cigar before he'd even turned away.

Galen went to see Vorus and check last minute details.

"The uniform is becoming on you," she complimented.

"Kind of you to notice." He looked down at the dark blue uniform and its gold trim, wondering what was going on in her strange head. "Your sisters are hungry?"

"They shall free the red-rivers as you taught us, these knights are of noble blood you say?"

"The richest in Europe. Rich and thick it'll be." He patted the cherub's cheek, and heard a sad sigh from inside. "You sound troubled my lass?"

"We have come far, you and I Galen," she said tenderly. "I was lost, but you found me."

He regarded the battered helmet with his pocket watch ticking away in the forehead, and for a moment he felt regretful that they had to kill her. "Make me proud today my sweet."

"My sisters and I owe you so very much." She sounded uncharacteristically humble.

Hidden in the cane, Elios pricked her ears. She wanted to remind him that Vorus was a liar, but the gulf between them was now too great.

"Do you think more of your kind might come one day?" he asked carefully, thinking of the many valkyries hidden at Smithfield.

"Alas we are a dying race," she lamented.

Crafty bitch, he thought, as he smiled lovingly. "Mind your sisters today Vorus, you will be as a shepherd to them." Perhaps it was his imagination, but the air temperature felt to drop a degree.

"Just as you are a father to us," she countered.

He imagined two separate mouths speaking at once, truth and lies, light and dark, life and death. "Thrice be the glory of the threefold way," he muttered, then tapped the cane to his brow in salute and took his leave.

Vorus watched him until he was out of sight. She had indeed been on Earth too long, because now just like man she understood jealousy and possession, and like so many she mistook these things for love. "Mine forever," she promised and a solitary tear of rust dripped from the cherub's blank eye.

Twenty-one cannons announced the solstice noon and their thunder rolled across Roman-field. There was now one hour left to go. Leonhard's retinue took their places under a huge canvas pavilion large enough to seat hundreds of guests, while endless carriages trundled past adding ever more spectators to the throng. Roman-field was fringed with pavilions, barracks, soldiers and of course rank after rank of gleaming krakens. From where Thorpe stood at the British camp, the horizon was a sea of flags and banners. The atmosphere was leisurely and regal, and he wondered how the jubilee celebrations were going in London. "Six hundred years is a long time," he mused as he regarded the enemy through his field glasses.

"The last time a tournament took place men fought with swords and shields." Lyle clasped his hands behind his back to contain his anxiety.

"It'll be a day to remember for sure." He jammed a cigar in his mouth and quick as a flash Lyle was making to light it.

"I trust my Lord still needs a mentor for the young Knight Superior?" he asked nervously.

Thorpe sucked on the cigar then blew smoke. "Don't worry Lyle, you'll get your share of the spoils." He shifted the glasses and studied Leonhard's krakens. "Impressive toys wouldn't you say."

"Indeed." In reply, Lyle regarded the ill-equipped British garrison, who looked like pirates amongst princes.

"Don't fancy our chances eh?" Thorpe noticed.

He swallowed and forced a smile.

"You'll change your tune by five minutes after one," Galen came and joined them, "and by one thirty Leonhard will be begging to surrender."

"That's the spirit Mr Galen," Thorpe handed him the glasses.

"The Dutch contingent look to form the bulk of Leonhard's allies," Galen noted after a careful examination.

"The Dutch have always hated us," Thorpe grunted.

"I've heard he's fielding the Dutch first, saving his own castle-guard for the last," Lyle said and took a pinch of snuff.

"How many's he permitted to field?" Galen realised he had little idea how the tournament was to be officially conducted.

"Each family is allowed to field one champion, per contest" Lyle said between sniffles. "And there are eleven bloodlines, so eleven knights."

"In succession?"

"According to the rules they have the right to field them all at once," Thorpe smiled.

Galen's face dropped. "So our first valkyrie faces a possible eleven foes!"

"That's about the measure of it, yes." Thorpe took the glasses back. "Of course it would be fairer if all the British bloodlines were here, a champion a piece for each of them, but of course if they hadn't been wiped out we wouldn't be in this mess in the first place would we?" he concluded cheerily.

"But eleven?" Galen wondered if Vorus knew the odds. "No wonder they've been laughing at us all this time."

"She'll be more than a match for them Mr Galen," Thorpe assured him.

Galen and Lyle swapped worried glances and then both turned back to the depot where Vorus and her sisters waited. "Nine against three hundred," Lyle whispered, and this time he forgot his snuff and went straight for his hip-flask.

Bertrand Hathwell, known as Williams to the Echelon's crew, had endured a tough night making small talk with men who spoke little English, kept propped up by endless cups of black coffee and all the while terrified of being found out. The Echelon remained stable, if heavy, and when he heard the cannons he knew there was only one more hour to play out this charade, then he'd make his escape. The descent from the Echelon involved a windlass chair and a two thousand foot drop, but the alternative was to stay here and perhaps go down with the ship. One way or another things were going to get rough.

He gazed at the steadily growing crowds, and spotted the tell-tale smoke from kraken chimneys as the great machines were fired up ready to fight. "Just like old times," he reminisced and then took another sip of his cold coffee and hoped his hands weren't shaking too much.

Vorus sensed the tension grow steadily thicker. She sat in her kraken breathing calmly, savouring a secret only she and her sisters knew. Unbeknown to all, there were hundreds of valkyries circling Wellesley Hall, more than enough to take control of every kraken there. By nightfall she would command an army of her own. "Galen," she sighed with a smile. Today she would show him just how much she loved him. She curled into a ball and slept the remaining hour away without a care in the world.

He saw shadows come and go. Sometimes they threw stones at him, but Eirik felt nothing. No pain, no hope, no time. There was only the way-beware's melody, which scoured away his will and left him numb. He just wanted to turn to stone and give up, and perhaps he had, for even when he thought of a special woman with golden hair he couldn't remember her name, and he felt no more for her than a stranger in a crowd. Somewhere cannons fired and there came the sound of a tiger's fierce roar. It was so brutal it almost awoke a spark in him, but then it was gone and Eirik Thorvaldson, just like his brothers, was as stone once more.

Ben heard the cannons, but hiding above the Echelon all he could see were acres of grey fabric. He turned to Hilda, who looked weather-beaten and weary. None of them had slept and now there was a day's fighting ahead. Everywhere he looked he saw tired but resolute faces.

"It's noon," Hilda explained the cannon, "one hour to go, then they'll fight."

"And we wait until they've knocked the stuffing out of each other," he finished.

"Just the small matter of those Ruinous creatures you spoke of," she said ominously.

"Maybe they'll just kill each other and we can go home?" he hoped.

"Just a pity we can't see it from here."

He looked away and puffed a huge sigh.

"She'll be fine – I promise," she pledged, noting his anxiety.

He gave up pretending, even to himself. "She's very important to me."

"Maybe it's not my place to say so dear, but I think she'd like to hear that from you next time you see her."

He just smiled, and promised himself he would.

Outside Morden Vale, guards continued to circle, but now there were no visitors enjoying Sunday's imprisonment. They were waiting for something far more important. She looked up, but it wasn't the cannons or the tiger's wretched roar that distracted her. For some reason, she looked to the hovering airships hoping to see witches in flight, but there was no sign of help. "Ben?" she wondered, but her only answer was a chattering magpie. "Nobody's coming," she whispered. It seemed her hope was as dead as the names on the graves around her.

The wasp saw all of this in perfect detail. "As it should be," she approved and looked to the great spider. "Are you listening traitor?" She jabbed at his thread for good measure. Agony flooded through him, but he couldn't even flinch. "I shall let you watch as the threads of fate come together in this special weave, never again to be repeated." She turned so he could see the torments in store for Sunday. "And after this special knot is woven, you have fatherly duties to attend to," she buzzed righteously.

He saw her abdomen swollen with eggs and knew what their first meal would be when they hatched. *Sunday!* he despaired, and tried again to move.

"The time is at hand. No thread defies the Patternmaker," she hissed and began to weave.

A single cannon fired at one o'clock, and Leonhard's knights entered the field.

"He's sending his full complement!" Lyle gasped, looking through his field glasses. "Eleven krakens of the Dutch regiment."

"Didn't I say he would! Who's our first champion?" Thorpe demanded.

"Vorus my Lord." Galen maintained the façade even at this late hour.

"But eleven against one." Lyle hadn't really believed Leonhard would exercise his right. "That's hardly sporting!"

"Come now, did you think this would be a church picnic?" Thorpe said flatly. "I for one commend the man, it's exactly what I'd have done."

Lyle watched eleven immaculate krakens march onto the field, heralded by a rider on a white stallion carrying their flag. The regiment was known as the Soaring Eagles, and their blue banner showed just that. Each kraken was painted blue and white, and bore an eagle helmet.

"He's keeping the Castle-Guard to the end," Galen observed.

Lyle swung his glasses to where Leonhard's serpent-headed krakens stood at the rear. His greatest fighters and strongest unit. "He thinks our contingent will either be beaten by then or fatally weakened. He's using the rest of the European families like cannon fodder."

"Wise man," Galen muttered.

"He doesn't have a clue what he's facing yet!" Thorpe emitted a husky laugh. "I wish I could see his face when Vorus takes the field." He turned to his son, "Mr Galen, if you would."

Galen saluted and set off to lead their first champion onto the field: Vorus of the Book-of-Nine.

"This is the hour," Lyle chattered nervously. "Eleven against one."

"It's going to be a hot afternoon." Thorpe removed his top hat and shrugged his coat from his shoulders, he let both fall to the floor like a disguise that had outlived its purpose. "I think the Eagles are about to have their wings clipped," he smiled, bit on another cigar and waited for Lyle to light it.

The kraken depot opened slowly. The doors screamed in complaint, and everyone in the British barracks turned to the huge dark oblong and waited for their equally dark champion to appear.

At first it was silent, then came the thud of marching feet. Lyle stared at the opening and saw sparks flicker in the darkness from her Ruined armour. Sweat glistened across his brow, every man there fell silent, and even at this distance he smelled spoilage and felt a sense of despair. The sound of grinding metal grew louder until at last she emerged from the shadows. Her kraken was painted black and a huge banner flew from her back, also black. The giant flag carried a strange symbol, Lyle had no idea what it was and it hadn't struck him as important, but there it was; a square set at an angle with a circle in the centre, the symbol of the Book-of-Nine. "Vorus," he whispered, and for the first time he shared Doulton's sense of something forbidden, but now of course it was far too late.

It was normal for a standard bearer to lead knights onto the field, but horses shied away from the sinister kraken and so Vorus was led by Galen alone. Men parted to let them pass, more from fear than reverence. Galen stared blankly ahead and Thorpe dipped him a small bow as he passed. He headed towards Roman-field followed by the huge metal giant, to where the valkyrie would bathe in the red-rivers.

Leonhard watched through his field glasses. The Dutch knights stood in the centre of the plain some quarter of a mile distant and all that remained was for the British champion to take the field.

"There," Hieder looked through his own glasses.

Leonhard saw a black kraken being led onto the field, not by a rider, but a lone man on foot. "They can't even afford horses!" he laughed.

"They have a total of nine, if this first one falls we can expect only eight other challengers." Hieder noted the time. It was ten past one.

"This should be concluded by mid afternoon," Leonhard sipped at his wine.

"Where upon you shall be the new Knight Superior my Lord," he finished, but he was distracted, the enemy kraken flew no banner he was familiar with.

"What regiment is that?" Leonhard spotted it also, and felt affronted. "That's not even an official regiment! Are they sending mercenaries against us?"

Hieder squinted through his glasses and saw a black banner with a white square and a circle at the centre. "Unusual, but not illegal my Lord."

Still, there was something sinister about the black kraken and for the briefest moment he felt a twinge of worry.

The Dutch herald waited on his stallion before the gathered knights watching the lone kraken approach. His horse whinnied and he felt it tremble under him. "Easy boy," he patted its neck affectionately.

As the challenger advanced he saw it in better detail and instantly the sun felt to lose its warmth. It had a staring, but misshapen cherub's face, it limbs and torso were just compacted scrap seemingly crushed into the crude impression of a body, and where as all krakens were powered by coal there wasn't a single furnace-stack along its shoulders. It walked like a living thing, swinging its arms and moving with a fluid grace no mere machine could match. Above that cruel face flew a huge black banner, as ragged as the reaper's cloak and the symbol on it made him shudder even though he didn't know why. "God be merciful," he reached up and touched the little crucifix around his neck. The kraken and its herald, a man on foot, halted two hundred yards away and waited for their Dutch counterpart to make his declaration of combat.

"There are so many," Vorus observed her enemies.

"Break them as I showed you," Galen rested his hand against the metal and heard her thoughts.

"And my sisters?"

"They'll get their chance, they'll keep sending knights against us until we're defeated, at least that's the idea. You can rest while one of your sisters takes the field."

"They'll not defeat us my love," she sighed.

"You must take this seriously Vorus," he insisted, "if we do not prevail today I will be banished and you can say farewell to your refuge."

"They'll not defeat us," she repeated.

He wondered if she understood the gravity of the day, or knew something he didn't. Either way he didn't have time to find out because the Dutch herald was parading before his line of knights. The first contest was about to begin. "I must leave you now Vorus," he patted the kraken, "make us proud." He set off back to the British garrison, half hoping Vorus would be killed. He stole a look back and saw her single kraken facing a line of eleven foes. "Àeon's blessing on you," he muttered, "may you rot in Ruination with Sophie and Elios and every other traitor."

The Dutch herald began to trot along the line of knights. The earth rumbled under their furnaces and he heard steam hissing through pipes and their banners whipping high above. They looked invulnerable and omnipotent, so why did the lone challenger unsettle him he wondered?

As he rode along the line with the Soaring Eagle's banner trailing out behind him, the crowds broke into ecstatic cheers knowing the moment was at hand. As he drew level with the black kraken however, he caught the whiff of rotten flowers and sealed rooms thick with shame and decay, and he felt icy cold. He spurred his agitated horse on and when at last he reached the end of the line he thrust the banner into the ground with a sigh of relief.

This was the sign they'd all waited for. The field now belonged to the knights alone and as one the Soaring Eagles started towards their enemy to the wild applause of many thousands.

"Now we'll see," Thorpe watched intently through his glasses.

Galen came back to his father's side and watched his creation standing alone, waiting for her enemies to come to her.

"Do you think she'll stand against eleven?" Lyle looked from Thorpe to Galen and back again, desperate for reassurance, but was ignored by both.

Vorus sat inside her kraken and listened to the hundreds of valkyries circling above like a great flock of vultures. They whispered and sang, but only she could hear them. She had lured them with false promises, to the consternation of Àeon himself. Galen wanted her to defeat their enemies, but she had far more noble plans. She would Ruin their krakens to provide refuges for the circling multitude. This wasn't war: it was a rescue. "Beloved sisters coming home," she rejoiced. With that she willed the machine forwards, ready to slaughter in the name of mercy.

"She's begun." Galen gripped his cane, aware of Elios observing closely. *I wish we could have enjoyed this moment together,* he lamented quietly.

"Watch and take heart Lyle, today you see Europe brought to its knees," Thorpe said with the cigar still clamped between his teeth.

Lyle did indeed watch, but he didn't take heart. He saw a solitary kraken charge eleven foes. "Bloody hell," he whispered.

Halven, the Dutch captain, led the charge. He pulled on the steam horn, pushed the machine ahead of his fellows and drew back the kraken's massive sword. The crowds roared and there was nothing genteel about it. They were like a gladiatorial mob baying for blood and death. He saw his opponent loom closer and had a moment to puzzle the strange way it moved, not like a machine but a man. He experienced a brief but overwhelming sense of hopelessness, then it vanished and he swung the sword with a furious roar, aiming for the cherub helmet.

"Fool doesn't even had a sword!" Leonhard chuckled, knowing Halven's weapon put him within striking distance before his opponent. "What an embarrassing day for these English eh? They are like kings too feeble to carry their own crowns any longer!"

"This whole tournament has been a farce from the start," Hieder smiled, and watched through his glasses as Halven pulled back to land a killer blow.

Halven saw the massive blade swing towards the cherub's neck, content that in a moment its head would be lying on the floor and he'd crush the knight inside to death. He screamed a war cry as the sword rammed home. He expected his machine to shudder with the impact and hear the glorious sound of breaking armour, but instead his sword exploded in a shower of rusted fragments and all that was left was a stump protruding from the hilt. "Holy God!" he cried in outrage.

Why the sword had failed he didn't have time to think, he just pulled on the controls, making to land a punch before his opponent could take advantage and close the gap. As the deformed cherub closed in however, he felt a wave of despair so real it threatened to swallow him. "No!" he screamed, and drove an armoured fist directly at its sneering mouth.

Vorus was utterly confident. She realised that men made their machines walk with levers and cables, while hers was an extension of her body. She saw the fist coming and dodged it in a way no mechanical thing could or should. The ground rocked, the blow went wide and Halven's kraken spun in an about-turn under the momentum, now presenting its back to her.

She wasted no time and lunged for the helmet, clawing the flapping banner from its crown first and dropping it like a rag, and then sinking her metal fingers into the polished steel dome. She literally ripped the kraken's skull open, tearing the thing apart. It dropped to its knees with a thunderous crash, sending up soil and grass and bleeding jets of steam. The furnace-stacks coughed smoke as the machine fought its doom and around Roman-field cheers turned to shouts of outrage. Halven's kraken was on its knees and Vorus plunged her hands into the helmet, looking like a ghoul engaged in brain surgery.

Halven screamed as the cockpit was ripped open, and Vorus smelled the red-river so close and so hot. She reached inside and dragged the screaming knight from his chair, breaking his limbs in the process.

"Please, no!" He wriggled and sobbed as she closed her fist around him. *The red-river,* she anticipated with a shiver.

There was a sickening crunch, a scream, and then a sticky warmth. The feel of his life draining through her fingers made her dizzy and now she craved to open the rest and wash herself with their terror.

The first of Halven's knights now closed in on her, mad with rage at seeing their captain so ruthlessly killed. Swords were drawn back and ten krakens now crashed into the scarred cherub and Roman-field shook with battle.

Thorpe exploded with laughter and could hardly keep the glasses steady. "Oh, but the saucy bitch has a flair for killing! Well done Mr Galen, very well done!"

"Thrice be the glory . . ." Galen couldn't finish, he watched in horror and awe as first she slaughtered the Dutch captain and then was herself surrounded by enraged knights. The black kraken vanished behind a wall of enemies, smoke and clouded soil. He saw swords rise and hack repeatedly and felt the clash of metal rumble through the earth.

Lyle looked on in stunned silence and now he knew Doulton had been right, this Vorus thing wasn't just going to roll over and die when Galen was done with it, and he found himself half hoping Leonhard would win the day. He lifted the hip-flask to his mouth again, but he'd long since drunk it dry.

They hacked and chopped at her, but the black kraken moved faster than any machine they'd ever seen, first twisting away from their swords, then snatching at the blades and warping or snapping them between its fists. "It's not a machine!" Dien, the foremost knight screamed into his communicare, but all he got back was static and dials in the cockpit whirled haywire. Something was wrecking his instruments. A pressure hose ruptured and rivets sprung loose, and not from battle damage. The cockpit walls bled rust and the air stank like a crypt in summer.

"The machine is alive!" he screamed again, just as his kraken was hit by a terrific blow. He was jolted in his seat and thrown violently forwards, only to be snapped back by his harness, and through the visor he saw the cherub bearing down on him as if trying to deliver a kiss, while behind it, his comrades were raining blows, but without much effect. "Repeat, the black kraken is alive with witchcraft!" he spluttered and felt his machine begin to fall sideways as Vorus wrestled it to the ground. He heard the furnace roar in protest and metal scrape outside the helmet and knew it wanted to drag him out and crush him just like his captain. "Emergency, emergency!" he pleaded.

Suddenly the sensation of falling and stink of rot became too much, and he vomited down his uniform. The next thing he knew his kraken toppled sideways, and ploughed into the earth and the furnace exploded.

Vorus delighted in the destruction. She dragged another knight to the ground even as the rest swarmed across her, slashing and pounding at her, but as soon as they ripped chunks of Ruined metal away they merely skittered back into place like filings attracted to a magnet.

Her opponent fell. His kraken hit the ground and she landed astride it in a dreadfully intimate pose. The furnace split and spewed boiling water and white hot coals. Fire engulfed them both, and inside his kraken Dien began to choke and roast alive. He fumbled at the seat harness, hoping to bail out, but just then there was a horrible noise followed by sudden daylight as the helmet was torn open like a tin can. Vorus leaned over the impotent machine and began fish for the contents of its skull. "Emergency!" he raved over and over, and tried to scramble free of the pilot chair. The cherub's deformed face slid into view and peered down at him. He saw a universe of futility hiding behind those eyes. "Please, no!" he sobbed as she reached in and wrapped her talons around him. He was still crying when those metal fingers curled tight, and his life ended with a gruesome scream and a fountain of scarlet. She had learned well from Smithfield.

The remaining Dutch knights were incensed with fury, but it seemed that not only was this mysterious kraken highly resistant, it had a disturbing effect on their machines. The knights of the Soaring Eagles didn't know it, but their grand krakens were slowly being Ruined.

Vorus clawed at another one, raking a gaping wound across its chest, popping the furnace plate clean off and dropping it to its knees where she eagerly plunged her fingers into its head and ripped the helmet open, possessed by the stink of fear from within. Ignoring the screams, she feasted on the man, absorbing his terror just as she'd suckled the animals' terrors at Smithfield.

The rest saw that communications were somehow scrambled and fighting was futile. They tried to turn their machines, but now their judgement and courage was clouded by Ruination, and they lumbered around aimlessly and she easily picked them off one after another.

Leonhard struggled up from his couch. "English scum are cheating!" he roared, but it was hard to hear him over the screams and shouts of dismay from the crowd.

"My Lord, you must send in reinforcements!" It was Colonel Treven, the Dutch commander.

Leonhard was on his feet shouting his orders. "Hieder, take a platoon of soldiers, go to the English, arrest that bastard Thorpe!"

Hieder looked around in and shock as the grand tournament slid into a confused panic. "On what charges my Lord?" he faltered.

"I don't give a damn, invent something, just stop this!" He didn't know who or what that black kraken was, but from the look of it, it could take on every knight he had and still come out on top. "Just stop this infernal contest!" He shoved Hieder into action, who scuttled away just as the Dutch commander relayed more bad news.

"My Lord, my company is all but beaten!" Treven beheld Roman-field, which was now cloaked in smoke and fire.

"No single knight can beat eleven!" Leonhard snatched his glasses and joined scores of generals and commanders, all scrutinising the so called 'field of honour'.

"There my Lord!" A Polish commander saw it first.

Leonhard swung around just in time to see a battered kraken stagger out of the smoke, a moment later it was seized upon by Thorpe's demonic champion and they all watched in horror as it dragged their knight to the ground and ripped the helmet open, and then reached inside. Leonhard had seen enough. Something was very wrong here. "Commanders! Take to the field, kill that thing and then go to the British barracks, destroy it and bring me Thorpe!"

Europe's allied commanders ran to their posts without even bothering to salute, and very soon there would be at least three hundred knights on Roman-field.

"What the hell do we do now? That bloody valkyrie thing's gone mad!" Lyle panicked, and for once Galen had to agree with him.

Thorpe rounded on him looking exalted, "This is exactly as it was meant to be!"

Lyle stared at him in horror, only now understanding.

"I'll tell you a secret that doesn't appear in any Illuminata history," Thorpe pressed his face right into his. "When the last tournament was fought six-centuries ago it was carnage, a free for all, the British butchered their enemies, even their families, then roasted them and ate their hearts."

"I don't believe you," he blubbered.

"The bloodlines of the Illuminata are built on just that: blood," he snarled, and turned to his son. "Mr Galen, order the rest of the valkyries forward."

"My Lord?" he stammered.

"Leonhard's going to throw every knight he has onto Roman-field, I dare say he's already sending troops to take us captive."

"No!" Lyle pressed his hands against his cheeks and looked like a dismayed old woman.

"Send in the rest of the valkyries Mr Galen," Thorpe laughed.

Galen was almost about to say 'no', that Vorus was out of control and throwing her sisters into the mix would only make things worse. He wanted to challenge his father's judgement, but just then the decision was made for him. The kraken depot rocked in its foundations, and everyone turned to see the huge doors buckle as the monsters inside began to hammer it open.

One way or another, Vorus's sisters were coming to enjoy the tournament and it appeared the valkyries weren't taking orders any longer.

Vorus stood in the midst of the fire and chaos, utterly happy. Blood and tattered flesh dripped from the kraken's claws, but still she wanted more. She looked to the skies and saw what mortal men couldn't; her sisters waiting above, and now she called to them. They descended in a great flock and a cold wind swept across Roman-field carrying the scent of spoilage. At first there were relatively few krakens for them to inhabit, but Vorus would soon see to that. They would Ruin every knight on Salisbury plain and her army would grow. It would be her wedding gift for Galen.

The huge doors finally shattered and timbers fell like straws. First to Vorus's aid was Isis the bull-headed, and she led her sisters through the disordered British barracks, heading for Roman-field, where they knew exactly what to do. "Father!" Galen screamed.

Lyle watched Isis bulldoze her way through their soldiers and horses until Galen's shout at last sank in. *Father?* he thought, and almost swallowed his tongue in shock. *Father!* Thorpe and Galen were father and son.

Galen grabbed his father's wounded arm, who was so shocked he hardly felt the pain. "They're taking over just as I said!"

Thorpe stared in disbelief at the eight krakens, all black, all bearing the Book-of-Nine banner. They waded through the makeshift camp, crushing the barracks and terrifying horses. Soldiers began to fire on them and suddenly the air whistled with bullets.

"Father!" he screamed again, directly into his face. "What do we do?" Galen panicked and looked around, now Lyle was nowhere to be seen either.

"Let them go," he clamped his shoulder and squeezed hard, "let them finish Leonhard!"

"Are you mad? We have to stop them now!"

"No! Britain must win this tournament if we are to seize the Illuminata, then we can start again, begin our experiments into Ruination afresh!" he ranted.

"You're not making sense! There isn't a bloody tournament any more, it's a bloody war!" Just then, as if to prove it, Isis broke through the barracks and an ammunition supply wagon exploded close by. The gunfire intensified as soldiers fought in vain to regain control.

Thorpe grabbed him by the collar. "Go kill Blackwand."

"What?" he gasped.

"She knows our plans, imagine what Leonhard would do to us if she told them, by God they might even pardon the slut for betraying us!"

Galen suddenly saw the truth of it. If they lost they'd be exposed and hunted down by every bloodline on the globe. "Give me your gun," he said finally.

"I was so looking forward to our vengeance," he said regretfully and pressed his revolver into his hand, "make it as painful as you like, but just make sure she's dead at the end of it." He turned, intending to salvage something from the unfolding disaster.

"Where are you going?"

"To do what we came here for – to kill Leonhard and his pretenders." He vanished into the turmoil and Galen watched him go, then turned and ran back towards the little overgrown church of Morden Vale where he would kill Blackwand once and for all.

LOVE IS ETERNAL

CHAPTER THIRTY-FOUR

Above and below

*'Darkness deepened, but I was not afraid. The dark became my shield,
and through it I moved unseen to strike back at my enemies.'*
Sunday Flowers - solstice queen, Regal-Fox coven, Surrey

Lyle wasn't stupid. He realised now that Thorpe and Galen were guilty of treason and he'd be tarred by their treachery, so he was making a run for it. "And I'll wager they murdered Doulton because he found out!" he flapped, then it occurred to him they'd kill him too if they realised he knew, and he ran faster. He charged through the gardens at Wellesley Hall, which were strangely deserted, intending to flee back to Goldhawk where he had a tidy sum in gold stashed away. He'd take it and run for the continent. Behind him on Roman-field he heard distant gunfire, cannons, the crash of metal and worst of all, terrible screaming.

Leonhard kept vigil through his glasses while his troops began evacuating guests and mounting an offensive against the British. He watched the smoke clear before rolling in again, and all the while that lone kraken stood at the centre of the destruction, like a lightning rod awaiting the storm.

"My Lord, knights are ready." It was Cass, his Spanish general.

"Then send them in!" Leonhard demanded.

"How many sir?"

"All of them you oaf!" He waved him away and went back to his glasses.

"Wait, Cass come see this!"

The grizzled Spaniard halted.

"To the west," he passed the glasses, "tell me what you see."

Cass saw it immediately. One of their krakens was struggling to right itself. "Impossible," he breathed. The machine had a hole in its head big enough to drive a horse through. The black kraken marched over and he expected it to smash the remaining life out of it, but it didn't. Instead it stooped and helped it to stand. "What in the name of God?"

Leonhard snatched his glasses back. The destroyed kraken was on its feet again, swaying drunkenly, but upright, and then the smoke obscured his view again. "Damn it," he cursed.

"Something ungodly happens here," Cass muttered.

"Lead the knights onto the field Cass, and the infantry, and artillery, everything we have."

Cass saluted and ran.

Leonhard looked again. Soldiers were flooding from the Polish and French barracks on to the field, and gun teams were priming their cannons. Closer to the pavilion, Lords and Ladies forgot their breeding and shoved their way back to their carriages. He saw fallen serving trays, top hats, parasols, and even a few peacocks racing around in panic, dodging the stampeding feet. "You'll pay for this Thorpe, you English bastard," he vowed and turned back to the battle. At first he didn't believe what he was seeing. He dropped the glasses, rubbed his eyes, and looked again. "Witchery!" he gasped. On Roman-field, the Dutch krakens, whose knights had been killed, were starting to rise up. All of them.

Vorus watched her new sisters descend and slide into the machines, become one with them and discover their strength. A kraken clambered up, still on fire, and turned its mangled face towards her. Another regarded its new hands, and flexed them, tasting their power, and one by one the dead machines climbed to their feet trailing shredded banners and twisted metal. The grass beneath them withered and died as their forces grew. They looked formidable, but Vorus had a large family and she needed more. *"All our sisters need a safe refuge,"* she ordered, *"follow me, Ruin them so our family may grow."*

More valkyries circled her like a vapour, waiting for their chance, as Isis and the rest now marched towards her through the smoke.

"Sister," Isis acknowledged. Her voice was empty and dead.

Vorus gazed through the smoke and saw the incredible spectacle of Leonhard's hundreds of krakens marching towards them, while soldiers in their thousands advanced at their feet. The original valkyries from Hobbs Ash now formed a rank behind their mistress, all of them black, all of them flying black banners, while behind them the new ones did likewise. Together they formed a force of twenty, but Vorus had greater ambitions. *"For Galen,"* she declared and they advanced, while around them the first artillery barrage from Leonhard's approaching army hit home.

General Cass was a knight of Spain's infamous Vow-of-Silence regiment, and his scarlet kraken was fashioned like a stallion baring its teeth. He barked orders in perfect English through the communicare as each stride brought him closer to the valkyries. "Valdez, Rosseu, bring your knights up with me, we meet them headlong. Schiller, Pindello, take the left and right flanks." He didn't wait for his commanders to reply, instead he pressed the furnace hard and the kraken accelerated.

He saw the barrage send up plumes of ruptured earth before them, creeping towards the enemy. Shells drilled down, but the strange black krakens seemed hardly to care. A swift look through the rearward periscope showed him hundreds of knights on the march and a sea of banners. He'd never seen so many war machines in one place. The spectacle took his breath away and even coaxed a tear.

They were close enough for visual identification now. The enemy krakens included a cherub, a bull, a wolf, and something like a sea-creature, all of them black, while the rest were obscured by smoke. Their construction was bizarre, but it was the way they moved that truly disturbed him. They didn't jerk and lurch, instead they strode like living things, and neither could he see any exhaust fumes. "Saints protect us," he muttered, "what are these things?"

The sinister cherub broke rank and powered its way towards him, its black banner was so huge it looked like a galleon's sail. Cass roared and pushed his own machine in reply, and the two champions spearheaded their forces towards a stupendous showdown.

Ben listened to cannons and screaming from below and when a murmur of disquiet rippled through the ranks he knew the time had come. "What's going on down there!" It sounded like a war, not a society event.

Hilda glided over. "Some double-cross or other, all the European knights are marching against the British."

"So what does that mean for our plans?" He looked around and saw witches forming into ranks, readying to dive.

"Same as before," she pulled her scarf over her mouth, "there's probably every war machine in Europe down there, we break them, it'll take years to rebuild, then deal with their Ruinous allies, find Blackwand and get out before they settle their differences and turn on us." She signalled to her Wards and a dozen fighters waved back.

"You make it sound so simple."

"It is," she winked. "WILDWOOD!" she cried suddenly, loud enough to make him jump, and then banked her lightning-staff and streaked away down the curve of the Echelon.

The Wards echoed her cry, and right behind that came the roar of five hundred witches so loud it made his ears pop and drowned out the battle below, and then they all moved out as one. "Come on Wake!" he cried.

They set off after her down the Echelon's bulk. Grey fabric flashed by at dizzying speed, and more and more of Roman-field became visible as they dived. The tournament was in chaos.

"They've all gone berserk down there!" Wake gaped.

Ben liked the choice of words. "Blackwand!" he screamed and tore vertically downwards, gripping his staff for dear life. Below him, he saw the flash of cannon fire, a sea of billowing banners and an army of krakens on the march. The wind screamed past his ears and tears streaked from his eyes, his vision blurred and blood pounded in his head like a war drum. Either side of him hundreds of witches hurtled down in an unstoppable wave, ready for whatever dangers awaited below.

The Echelon crew had more to think about now than a weighty airship. Hansa ran around shouting orders in German while Hathwell watched the chaos unfold below. He hadn't a clue what was happening down there but he knew it wasn't good, and he might not speak the language, but when he heard Hansa's blunt exclamation he didn't need an interpreter. He spun around knowing what he'd see even before he saw it. The crew were staring out of the windows, frozen with horror. People were dropping from the sky like bullets, people riding staffs. "Witches!" Hansa screamed again.

Hilda, Hathwell thought. This was his moment. It was time to bail out.

Hansa grabbed the communicare, but all he heard back was the rumble of cannon fire and confused snatches of conversation. "Witches!" he roared repeatedly, "the tournament is under attack!" His eyes rolled towards the windows and now there wasn't just a shower of them, there was a downpour. He saw grim faces flash past, and each looked more savage than the last. "Williams," he shouted, "Williams alert the gun crews, we'll shoot the bastards down!" He rushed to the helm, aiming to turn the airship and give the gunners a better view. He jostled with a crew member, fumbled with the controls, and screamed more commands. "Williams, you hear me?" he twisted around, still clutching the aft engine lever, but when he looked he saw Williams was gone, and the rearward escape hatch swinging open.

Hathwell didn't like heights and he screamed until his throat ached, as the windlass chair rocketed downwards, not knowing if he was terrified or exhilarated. He looked up and saw the Echelon's broad underbelly receding at incredible speed, while a wave of black specks showered down from it, and he knew each one was a witch. The Echelon's guns rattled into life and poured death from the sky, while below, he saw krakens race towards one another. There was danger everywhere, and he was trapped in the middle. Three hundred feet from the ground he reached for the brake and heaved. Sparks flew, cables shrieked and the chair swung like a pendulum. The battle below loomed closer, and he just screwed his eyes tight and hoped.

General Cass saw the black cherub was within striking distance and he swung his great sword towards its leering face and screamed in hate. Before the blade even made contact he smelled rotten flowers. For a split second he saw the lifeless face of his mother Isabella, who'd drowned when he was only a boy, and he relived the grief all over again. His war cry turned into a mournful howl as Ruination washed over him, and when his sword struck the cherub it crumbled to dust.

Vorus hardly budged as the sword Ruined against her. Broken fragments rained down and after a considered moment she smashed a well-aimed fist right into Cass's helmet. The impact flattened the stallion's face and the whole machine staggered back, crashing into the kraken behind. Vorus lunged again, stepping into the punch and this time hitting so hard that her fist ploughed clean through the helmet. Cass was split at the waist, metal screamed all around him and black smoke mushroomed up from the furnace. His blood mingled with oil from the dying machine, but all he felt was endless grief. He lay trapped in the mangled cockpit even as one of Vorus's fledgling sisters swooped down to claim it. "Isabella," he moaned, "mother."

A shadow fell over him as the valkyrie crept inside and the stink of corruption became so thick it blinded him. He gibbered incoherently as she plunged her fingers into his chest and was still babbling when those fingers wrapped around his struggling heart and stilled it forever, and a new kraken joined the ranks of the Book-of-Nine.

Colonel Patoria saw Cass fall. Immediately the hateful cherub shouldered his defeated general aside and marched on. "English bastards!" he screamed, pulled on the controls and swung a massive fist.

He was lucky, and the fist crashed into the side of the cherub's head. Sparks flew like spittle and the helmet spun a full circle. That alone should have severed the main turret drive, but when the cherub's face rolled back into view it looked even nastier then before. It lashed out with horrible speed and clamped a gauntlet on his shoulder, held him fast and pumped a fist towards its chest furnace.

"Oh no my English bastard friend!" He saw it coming and swept her arm aside hard enough to shatter it at the elbow.

Vorus watched as her severed arm dropped to the ground and exploded into fragments.

"Now *I* bury *you!*" He pumped his forty-foot long sword right into her guts. "Die!" he laughed.

Distracted, she didn't have time to Ruin his sword and it impaled her, driving up through her chest until the entire blade was embedded to the hilt.

"Now we see if your friends die so easy too, eh?" Patoria, yanked the sword free, expecting the machine to topple, but what he saw left him insensible. The broken arm was reordering itself. "Witchcraft!" he realised, and reached for his communicare. He had to send an urgent warning to his commanders, but now Vorus was virtually whole again and suddenly his mouth dried up and his heart felt as heavy as lead. "Witchcraft!" he groaned again. The air in the cockpit curdled, he retched and cried at the same time. "Evil magic," he croaked one last time, but nobody heard him. A moment later Vorus's fist hammered into him, grinding him into the wreckage and sending up a fireball. Colonel Patoria's kraken slumped to its knees with its helmet and banners ablaze, and Vorus brushed it contemptuously aside and marched on.

She pressed on and when enemies challenged her they quailed and their courage faded. Isis and her sisters followed in her wake, and behind them came the Soaring Eagles, now possessed by valkyries. They crashed into Leonhard's army like a wedge, splitting it down the middle, slaughtering everything in their path and trampling them under. Soldiers fled, cannons fired and krakens shook the earth with huge blows, but nothing could stop them. On and on the black wedge drove deeper. Resplendent krakens were decapitated, gutted and torn open. Brightly coloured banners fell from sight to be shredded and humiliated. The air around them was cursed and foul.

Above this sea of carnage, Leonhard saw the black banners of the Book-of-Nine pressing onwards, and in response the banners of Europe's mightiest bloodlines fell before them like trees in a storm. "Find that bastard Thorpe!" he screamed again to anybody that would listen.

At the very rear of Leonhard's forces, knights of lesser rank followed their leaders unaware of the danger ahead. One such knight was Philip DeMont. The sun beat down and he sat sweltering inside his kraken with little to do. "Blast this miserable country," he cursed, and pressed his eye against the periscope as the machine lumbered along. Still, all he could see were hundreds of banners and smoke in the distance. His kraken was hardly moving and he wished he was closer to the action. Some battle charge, he thought sourly. He had hoped to impress a particular young countess at tonight's closing ball, but tales of waiting in line were hardly going to set her pulse racing. His little daydream ended when the adjacent kraken sounded its horn, almost scaring him out of his skin.

He reached up to the periscope again as more krakens took up the alarm. Metal boomed to his left, and he looked and saw his neighbour making an about-turn. The huge machine struggled to turn fast and tight, a dangerous manoeuvre saved for extreme situations. "About turn? But the enemy are up ahead?" He whirled the periscope around to the rear. At first he saw nothing, which alone troubled him, then he saw movement, but it wasn't British knights. "Shit!" he cried, and heaved on the controls.

The sky behind them was black with witches.

Mayhem and damage. The cost of rebuilding will cripple them, Hilda promised herself. The krakens were their targets, not their knights, and so they would wreck the machines and let fate decide whether their pilots lived or died. It was the best compromise she could come up with. They dropped from two-thousand feet and came wide across the plain. The field looked to be in utter chaos with the heaviest fighting to the east of Wellesley Hall, while at the rear, Leonhard's knights were almost at a standstill. *The perfect targets,* she thought coldly.

She saw the formal gardens sail past, where guests were running through them in panic. She briefly glimpsed a small wood where a church tower poked up through the trees, then the great Hall itself rushed by and was gone in a blink. Ahead, were krakens in their hundreds and the sky above them was black with smoke while infantry and cavalry swarmed around them like ants. When she heard the distant boom of a battle horn she knew they'd finally been spotted. "Just like old times Valonia!" she shouted, reached to her back and drew her second lightning-staff.

She heard the crack of rifle fire. Soldiers screamed in alarm and bullets peppered the air, a wall of krakens lay ahead, all of them blind to this surprise assault. The nearest of them was trying to turn, but too late. She drew her staff, leaned low and screamed. "WILDWOOD!"

She swung at its shoulder and the thunder-sprite did the rest. There was a brilliant flash and a deafening boom. Its torso exploded, catapulting the furnace plate from its hinges, then the machine flopped backwards into its fellows bleeding smoke from its ruptured gut. She didn't see it though, she was already streaking away over the krakens, weaving through their banners for cover. "For Valonia!" She made another strike and the explosion almost knocked her from her staff. Krakens whizzed by as she slalomed through their banners, and then she heard a terrible but glorious noise behind her: the war cry of five hundred witches. It sounded like the heavens were falling, a split-second later multiple explosions buffeted the air and shrapnel whirled like snow. She chanced a look behind and saw a wall of fire, and then an army of broom-riders burst through it and everywhere banners were swooning in flames.

"Blackwand!" someone screamed.

She looked to see Ben streaking along beside her, teeth bared and face blackened with soot. "Blackwand!" she cheered back.

The infantry now turned their weapons to the heavens and opened fired as five hundred witches charged into the heart of the battle, towards the ominous black banners that flapped like sails, knowing these would be krakens unlike any others.

Vorus clawed the face from another foe, shredding the knight inside. Around her the world was fire, death, and red-rivers. She stamped men and horses into pulp, while her sisters slaughtered kraken after kraken and bathed in their terror. Her ranks continued to swell, but something was wrong. Through the smoke and stench of war she smelled something unexpected: the smell of magic. *Broom-riders?* She remembered how wicked Galen had said they were, and she turned and looked eastwards.

"Vorus?" It was Isis, her lieutenant.

"Isis, lead the sisters, do not let the broom-riders kill the knights." She knew a kraken downed by magic wouldn't hold a valkyrie, and she needed all the machines she could get.

"And you?" Isis ground another helpless soldier into the mud.

"Hold the broom-riders, I must go and find Galen." She didn't wait for a reply, instead she left her precious kraken and flew like a wraith, speeding over the battlefield, hunting for her lost love before it was too late. If the witches dared to take her Galen then they would have her to pass first.

The distant noise and trembling earth told Sunday that all wasn't well.

She struggled with her chains attempting to weaken them with spells, even without her wand. "Break damn you!" she hissed, keeping her hands between her knees out of sight. There was a rash of excited chatter from the sentries and she looked up to see Galen approaching. He was wearing a smart uniform and carrying a revolver and his cane. He marched past them, ignoring their confused questions, and into the church. *Something's very wrong,* she thought, and backed up against the stone.

He stood before her, regarding her with loathing. "Firstly, my apologies. We had such delights planned for you. But those plans have changed."

She knew he was here to kill her and a small part of her was glad. "Witches spoiled your plans?" she hoped.

He laughed, ignorant of Hilda's attack. "There are no witches coming to save you Blackwand. You've been left to rot."

Ben's not coming, she realised.

He saw her despair, smiled, and lifted the revolver. "Now where shall we start? A bullet to the gut? I'm told that's particularly painful."

I'm coming Alfred, she braced herself against the stone.

"It wouldn't be fitting to kill you quickly, not after the trouble you've put us through." His grin melted and now he looked furious and scared. "Payment's in order."

"They've outwitted you haven't they?" she blurted, stalling just as she had at Thorpe Hall. "The valkyries are refusing to obey." His mouth twitched and she saw she was right. "Did you think they'd follow you like lost lambs?" Now it was her turn to smile. "Have your plans been Ruined Galen?"

"Ruined?" He glared down at her.

"Let me guess, you want me to help you stop them?" She might as well laugh at death rather than cringe before it.

"I know you have a broken soul," he sneered, "that you went to death and returned – but you won't come back a second time, I promise." He pointed the revolver at her head, when a shout from outside stopped him.

"Witches on Roman-field, hundreds of 'em!"

He whirled around and saw the soldiers outside descend into panic.

Ben! she thought and her heart galloped. "This'll be one short summer for you Galen," she laughed and tried to rise against her chains.

He looked from the stricken soldiers and back to her. There was no time for fun and games. He'd shoot her between the eyes and have done with it. "Sleep forever with your precious dragon-worms, Blackwand," he finished, raised the gun and fired.

'Evolved' Strike had called her. What kind of evolved being could stand by and permit murder? Elios heard his every word and knew what to do. She summoned enough strength to break the bonds he'd set on her, and sent a burst of power through the cane.

The gun retorted just as the cane stung his hand. He jerked, sending the bullet wide and it hit the stone above Sunday's head and she screamed. "Elios!" he roared, and flung the cane to the ground. It landed on Sunday's blind side and she twisted to see better.

Elios had lived her whole life under his lies and even now it was hard to disbelieve them, but she put her faith in Blackwand, threw herself against his restraints and burst free. There was a brilliant flash and a faint rumble of thunder, and she stood there angry and independent at last. "I'll not live with your lies any longer!" She spread her wings in defiance.

"Elios?" Sunday struggled, but couldn't see no matter how she writhed. "Elios no, he'll kill you!"

Now Galen understood why his father hated the female heart so much. All of them betrayed man in the end. He regarded the brave little sprite with a mixture of loss and hate. "Judas slut, just like the rest," he accused, raised the gun and without a second thought he fired.

Elios was hit in the chest and flung backwards across the graves leaving a trail of blood and feathers.

"Bastard! You bloody bastard!" Sunday screamed. She heaved on the chains and spat curses, but Galen didn't hear them, he was distracted. Suddenly the air around him smelled 'wrong'.

Sunday smelled it too, the odour of decaying roses. Ruination. The distant sound of battle continued, but now she realised that the soldiers outside the church were silent, in fact all of Morden Vale was silent, even the birds in the trees. She heard a succession of muffled thuds, and turned slowly to see. Outside, she saw the last of the guards drop down dead. *Valkyries are here,* she understood instantly. The air grew heavier and now it smelled like sun-baked afterbirth and liquefied remains. Vorus was with them.

"Vorus?" Galen turned full circle, waving the gun, but she wouldn't show herself. "Where are you?" His voice was as shaky as the revolver.

Vorus hovered over Elios, watching the dying thunder-sprite trying to crawl to Blackwand's side, marvelling at the creature's devotion. *Galen has cast her out to make room for me alone in his heart,* she thought, delighted that her rival was dying. *So this is love, Galen does love me after all.* At last, the greatest mystery of man's world revealed itself.

"Show yourself!" he demanded and fired a wild shot. The bullet struck a column and sparks danced.

Vorus swirled around him and the smell of rot thickened. *"The broom-riders have come to kill you Galen, but I shall save you fear not."*

"Get back to your position," he snarled, "have you forgotten your duty?"

She floated unseen, convinced love was jealousy. *"Tell me who you really are dearest Galen, and then I shall slay your foes and we shall be as one forever,"* she promised.

"Who are you to make bargains? You follow orders, you don't wield them!"

"Tell me."

"Curse your black heart!"

"Confide in me my love."

"You're a maggot wriggling in the devil's dung!" He fired again but hit nothing. Far away there came a rumble of gunfire as the battle intensified.

"Tell me your secret my sweet." Like all blinded by love, she heard only tenderness in his words. *"Tell me and together we'll lead my hundreds of sisters across this world and Ruin it."*

"Treacherous bitch!" he roared and fired again, and all the while Vorus tightened her loops around him.

Elios lay between life and death and watched as if through a misty veil and saw another figure . . . a young girl with dark hair. Nobody seemed to notice, not Galen, Vorus or Blackwand, but she knew her right away. It was Sophie.

"You are tired little sprite, worn by a life of lies," Sophie said gently, "but I'd ask one last act of bravery of you." She looked purposefully to where Sunday was struggling with her chains.

"I understand," Elios said weakly.

"And then you might at last go home."

"Ruination?" she asked fearfully.

Sophie smiled. "Ruin is part of you, but it is not your true home. In your heart you have always known this."

She thought of Strike and gazed up at the beckoning sky. "The thunder-heights?" she asked hopefully, but when she looked, Sophie was gone. "Strike," she gasped. She knew what to do now, and she dragged herself over the graves and their forgotten names, towards Blackwand.

Sophie's appearance was brief, but it *was* noticed by one other. A wasp inside an hourglass. "What is this?" The wasp watched in a state of confused worry. "A thread out of place and out of time? This is not possible, the Lord of the Weave did not command this." Sophie had penetrated the veil and disrupted the weave. In that stunned moment, the Patternmaker's assassin inadvertently relaxed her hold on the Timekeeper's thread and for an instant he was free.

The spider twitched and the words *'dear champion'* blazed through his mind. He felt his old strength crash through him like a tidal wave and wasted not a second. He righted himself with blinding speed and pounced, roaring with fury.

Sunday tried to block out the mayhem around her and concentrate on escaping. Galen was behind her now, shouting nonsense and she guessed the valkyrie was taunting him. The gun was spent and she heard dry clicks as he continued to fire at nothing. *He's losing his mind,* she thought in a panic.

"I am Galen!" he roared.

To Sunday he sounded like a lying child having a furious conversation with himself. The air stank as bad as Smithfield now, but still the valkyrie wouldn't reveal itself.

"I am Galen, now return to Roman-field!" The gun clicked again.

Suddenly she understood. He was protecting his true identity and the answer was in the Timekeeper's strange note. She had no idea if the great spider still lived, but she knew what to do. She took a deep breath and screamed, "GALEN IS MATTHEW THORPE!"

Everything stopped.

Galen froze, the air stilled and Vorus caught her breath. Silence reigned, punctuated by the cry of a few startled birds, distant cannon fire and Galen's panicked breathing, then came a chilling voice.

"Matthew?"

He turned and saw her in all her glory. Vorus was crouched at the rear of the church, inside the dilapidated tower, now holding his cane, stroking the Ruined wood with her bony fingers.

"My cane," he gasped, trying not to look at her.

"Oh yes," she agreed, "your cane this shall be." She kissed it gently, first with one mouth then the other then she crept out of the shadows.

He saw her limbs were bony and a clot of intestines dangled from her split chest like tangled yarn. Her face was like a living tribal mask, a testament to the visceral powers that undo all creation. She was Ruin incarnate. He staggered back, horrified by his first clear look at her. "Vorus?" he whispered.

"My love," her mouths smiled sweetly, and inside he saw hooked teeth like a lamprey's. "My dear, sweet Galen, my dear sweet *Matthew*," she finished almost shyly, making his flesh crawl.

Sunday sat petrified wondering what nightmare was unfolding behind her. The creature was so close that life itself seemed as insubstantial as the names on the graves. *Strike where are you!* she begged, but it was another thunder-sprite that saved her. She caught the glint of blue feathers and Elios crawled into view.

"Blackwand," she groaned, and dragged herself closer.

"Matthew," Vorus said again. She knew his real name now and she spoke it like a summons and she leaned on his cane, driving the tip between the gravestones.

"I am Galen," he lied, but he felt a horrible tugging sensation in his belly and he turned to run. He didn't get far before some invisible force tumbled him to the ground, and instantly he was being dragged towards her. He slithered over the stones, bumping over their uneven edges, while raking at them for purchase. "Elios!" he screamed. His fingernails scraped over the eroded words *'love is eternal'* and he twisted around to see Vorus waiting for him with her skeletal hands planted firmly on the cane, and now the dead-walk wood gaped just as the terrible trees had done in

Iceland. He saw its fleshy inner pulsing like a womb ready to receive him and he screamed again, "Elios!"

"You cast out Elios," Vorus sighed adoringly, "you have proven your love Matthew." He was dragged bodily towards the cane screaming and thrashing, while she watched trembling with excitement.

Sunday tried not to listen to his ghastly screams.

"He has what he wanted," Elios slumped against the padlock.

"You're hurt," Sunday sobbed, "come with us, witches can help." Elios's feathers were dull and her eyes glassy, she doubted any magic on Earth could stop her dying.

"He wanted life outside time," she gripped the padlock tight, "and now he shall have it."

She had no idea what Elios was talking about. "We have to find help, maybe Strike knows what to do, yes, we've got to find him!"

Elios curled around the padlock and collected her last spark, behind her Galen screamed again, but she only felt pity for him. "Remember me to Strike," she asked, and then she breathed her last reserves into the lock.

There was a flash and Sunday flinched. The padlock flicked open and instantly the chains around her slackened. "Elios!" She wriggled free and snatched the wounded sprite up into her arms. "Elios I'm going to save you." She was on her feet in a second and she ran without looking back, she ran away from Galen's terrified screams as fast as she could, with Elios lying limp in her arms.

His foot was first to go. It vanished into the cane and the wood tightened around him like a snake swallowing its prey. "Bitch!" He screamed and kicked, but the magic was too strong and the next thing he knew both his legs sank into the cane, up to the knees. "Bitch!" he shrieked.

He raved and cursed, but the cane continued to swallow him down, sucking him right out of his clothes. Bones cracked and gristle creaked as his limbs were contorted. The cane wrapped itself tight around him. His heart was crushed to the size of a plum stone, but it still stubbornly beat. He tried to scream again, but his lungs were pressed tissue-thin and all he could manage were a few dry croaks.

Vorus watched him vanish inch by inch, feeling the cane come alive again as he entered it, knowing he would be hers forever. She saw his hands

vanish into his coat cuffs and his agonised face sink beneath his collar
leaving his splendid uniform as just an empty heap. The cane had no need
for them, neither had it any need for his hope or joy. It spat them all out
and in their place infused him with despair and grief, like an embalming
fluid as it packed and folded him away. His eyes bulged and his tongue
turned purple as he desperately tried to scream. "Be still my love," she
comforted him.

The cane continued to eat him, and his head was last to go. It hung limp
from the fleshy opening and his eyes were wide and aware. The Book-
of-Nine ring around his neck fell in a coiled heap and pinged against the
headstones. A mournful groan escaped his lips and then the dead-walk
began to close over his upturned face like stage curtains being drawn.
He re-entered the womb and the last thing Matthew Thorpe saw was the
upside down view of Morden church, then blackness crept over his staring
eyes and he was Ruined.

The Timekeeper rammed his foe. She shrieked in surprise and crashed
against the glass, dropping Sunday's thread, and he landed on top of her,
while her stinger stabbed vainly at nothing.

"Traitor!" She flailed blindly. "Fate has promised me dominion!"

"Fate does not control all!" He plunged his fangs downwards, just
behind her head. There was a brittle 'crack' as her exoskeleton broke and
she screamed.

"I was promised!" she struggled, but now his toxins coursed through
her. "I was promised," she gurgled but her words became incoherent and
slurred. "Promised," she gasped one last time then slowly she stilled.
Her legs and wings twitched randomly, and she finally convulsed and
died. He dropped her body in disgust and backed away, breathless and
furious.

"Is this the first of many assassins?" he shouted, and scanned the
darkness with his remaining seven eyes. "If you dare attack my realm
again I shall tell all humanity your deepest secret, the one you hide even
from yourself." He listened for any response, angrier than he'd ever been.
"What would happen to your precious weave if souls learned the truth of
you?" He was threatening the very universe.

Around him the cavern seemed to shrink, and after what might have been centuries or seconds his answer came. The cavern groaned as something vast shifted in dread.

The Timekeeper listened. "A compromise?"

The ground trembled in answer and the Timekeeper slumped down in disbelief, aware that the universe had just evolved, and all because of one solitary witch.

Vorus lifted the cane to her lips and kissed it tenderly, feeling him preserved inside. "I was lost Matthew, and you found me." She looked down at the empty clothes. In the middle of them lay his satchel containing his cherished Book-of-Nine. Now there was one last task; she would kill Blackwand as vengeance for her slain sister, then she would seize every kraken on Roman-field before the broom-riders spoiled her plans. She stalked over to the stone where Blackwand was restrained, but when she got there all she found was a pile of chains, some bloody smears and feathers, and part of a fallen sign reading *'queen of witches'*. The witch had escaped.

Eirik's senses had once been so acute he could hear a butterfly's wings, now all he knew was the way-beware's Ruined song. He wasn't even aware of Sunday by his side. "Tawny, I don't even know your real name." She gently stroked his brow and then lay Elios in the grass. Her chest hardly moved and her feathers were matted with blood. "Strike'll know." She stepped through the tangled bodies towards the way-beware, knowing what *she* had to do and feeling like an executioner. "I've no other choice," she told herself and the doll seemed to look up at her in miserable agreement.

"I sang because I was lonely," it seemed to say.

"I'm sorry little singer." She knelt by the doll, understanding that it suffered from a disease she couldn't fix.

"This is not the song I wanted to sing."

"Please forgive me." She drew it from the earth.

"Will I be lonely on the spiral?" She didn't know if it was the way-beware, or her conscience.

"No, you'll never be lonely again," she promised, swallowed her grief and then in one swift move she broke the doll in two.

If it had screamed she would have gone mad with despair, but she was spared that at least. It fell silent immediately, leaving nothing but the distant rumble of guns, then she broke down, realising what she'd done. "Damn you Thorpe!" She clutched the broken way-beware to her chest and wept uncontrollably. "I killed it," she sobbed.

"You did what you must," a voice said.

She turned to see Strike. He was sitting in the middle of the berserks, who were now climbing to their feet, effortlessly shaking off their chains as they did. All of them looked stiff and groggy, like animals awaking from hibernation. "Strike?" she smiled weakly.

He hopped over to her and regarded the doll in her hands. It was silent now, just wood. "You did what you must," he repeated.

She wiped her eyes, not wanting to think about the way-beware's fate, and went to Elios's side. The sprite was curled in the grass, hardly breathing. "Can you do anything for her Strike, as one sprite to another?"

A single look at Elios told him the worst, and he shook his head once.

"But she saved me," Sunday broke down. First the unique way-beware and now a unique sprite, Thorpe and Galen had a lot to answer for she thought.

"I can't save her, but I can help her." Now he was fighting the tears. "A moment alone please."

She withdrew and went to Tawny, where she wrapped her arms around his neck, feeling safer already.

Strike took a moment then leaned closer and whispered against her ear. "Elios?"

Her eyes fluttered half-open. "Strike?"

"You never told me your storm name," he tried to smile.

"Never had one." Her voice was tiny.

"You'll need one if you're to go home," he explained and he took her hand. "Home?"

"The thunder-heights."

"The thunder-heights," she echoed happily.

"Take my name, you'll be of my clan and when you get there remember to speak it as loud as thunder." He squeezed her hand and leaned closer so none of the others would hear, and then he told her his storm-name, the one even Sunday didn't know.

"A beautiful name," she whispered.

"Promise you'll remember it."

"I'll speak it as loud as thunder." She managed a last smile and then she melted away from him.

He stepped back and waited, a second later there was a delicate flash of lightning and Elios returned to the thunder-heights.

Sunday's heart was in pieces. "Strike?"

At first he was silent. "Where is that bastard?" he asked without turning.

"The valkyrie took him."

"Then good riddance." He turned and she saw he was furious.

"Strike, Ben's come," she stood, "there are witches here, fighting right now." As if to prove it cannons rumbled far off.

"Are you ready to fly then," his eyes flashed, "Blackwand?"

Tawny growled at her side and his brothers joined him until it felt like an earthquake.

She picked up her staff. "Let's finish what we started."

A second later a witch on a black staff erupted from the woods around Morden Vale, screaming in rage. She was closely followed by three mighty bears, whose talisman was no longer an enchanted doll, but their devotion to her. They raced to their friends on Roman-field and the ground shook under them.

Wellesley Hall was utter Pandemonium. Out on the battlefield the valkyries were claiming kraken after kraken, not that anyone could tell through the smoke. Soldiers and horses ran around in panic below the metal giants and random shells continued to fall, adding to the calamity.

Hieder had gone to arrest Thorpe, but the villain was nowhere to be seen and after an ugly showdown with the British commander, the next thing he knew the British soldiers opened fire.

Hieder screamed and ran for cover as the inevitable ensued and a second battle front opened up with the combined European infantry now fighting the scant British forces. It seemed there was no shortage of bullets or guns at Wellesley, and now cannons on all sides began to pummel the house and surrounding gardens. The greenhouse was hit and glass and palm leaves rained down along with rare blooms and even a few bananas. Leonhard's soldiers advanced through neatly clipped gardens, hoping to outflank the British, but they were pushed back with heavy cannon fire which turned the Hall's east wing into rubble. In the midst of this confusion was the surreal spectacle of a terrified elephant. It had escaped from its enclosure and now it charged around blindly crushing men as it went.

"Find Thorpe!" Hieder shrieked repeatedly, but his soldiers had more immediate worries, like avoiding the British counter attack and a rampaging elephant.

Ornamental trees were hit and flopped over, the hedge-maze was trampled by cavalry and even set ablaze as some fool in the Hungarian ranks ordered the use of incendiaries. Not to be outdone the British responded likewise and fires began to rage across Wellesley Hall. Guests and serving staff fled, taking their possessions or in some cases whatever loot they could lay their hands on. Never let it be said that the Illuminata elite were so rich that they failed to seize an opportunity when they saw one.

Hilda thought she was ready for anything, even death, but events on Roman-field left her stunned. She saw the black krakens at a distance and right away she knew these were the creatures Ben had warned her of. "Ben!" she screamed.

"That's got to be them!" he shouted back, indicating the huge black banners.

"There's so many . . ." She saw European krakens in their ranks and couldn't grasp what was happening.

Both of them dodged a salvo of gunfire, while an explosion to their left scorched and buffeted them.

"They're taking them over!" he yelled.

Another explosion drowned him out and Hilda swerved to avoid a sweeping sword blow.

"What?" She drew level again.

"The Ruined krakens, they're taking the others over!" He stabbed a finger at the black banners.

Think Hilda, think! She snatched a look back and saw her Wards in close pursuit and the occasional flash of lightning as a witch was killed and their sprite rocketed skywards. *What would Valonia do?*

"Hilda!" he roared.

"I'm thinking!" Burning banners whizzed by and tracers rained down from the sky. She looked up at the Echelon through the haze and thought of Hathwell and it was his words that came back to her, something he'd told her about his days as a squire.

'The biggest threat isn't always the strongest enemy.'

Suddenly it made sense. "Forget the Ruined krakens!"

"What?" He ducked to avoid a shower of shrapnel.

"Forget them. Destroy the others before the Ruined ones get to them, it's the only way to stop their numbers growing."

Now he understood: break them with magic before they were Ruined. "Understood!" His throat was hoarse from screaming. "Then find Blackwand?"

"Then Blackwand!" Immediately she dropped back to relay these new orders to her Wards.

Ben charged onwards, knowing they somehow had to isolate the valkyries. That meant getting up close and personal with the monstrous things again.

"Remember the one we met in London," Wake cautioned. *"Magic won't stop them."*

He remembered it all too well. "How in Oak's name do you fight monsters immune to magic!" He watched the black banners draw closer, all the while wishing desperately that Sunday was there.

Hundreds of witches raced to where the valkyries were hammering Leonhard's forces, although now Vorus's ranks included a good many assimilated machines.

Some two hundred yards from them, Ben landed on one of Leonhard's krakens. He could see the black banners ahead through the smoke and the noise of battle was deafening. Leonhard's knights here were so densely packed that there was hardly room for foot soldiers, but shells still screamed down from the sky. He stood upright on the lumbering machine, balancing as best he could, and struck the furnace stack, looking away at the last instant. Hot metal peppered his back and the explosion boomed in his ears.

To either side of him he saw hundreds of witches drop down to attack Leonhard's knights, and after each attack they leap-frogged to the next and steadily the krakens stacked up against one another like broken toy soldiers, creating a barricade and preventing the valkyries from Ruining further machines. Lightning flashed, knights bailed out, banners burned and smoke churned upwards like distress signals. "This might really work!" Ben gritted his teeth as the machine lurched.

"I get the point, now shift!" Wake ordered.

Together they set off for another target. Ben swerved to miss another witch, a French girl barely an adolescent. In the next horrible instant she was hit. He saw a puff of blood erupt from her temple, then she tumbled into the chaos below and her thunder-sprite shot skywards. "God-Oak!" he howled.

"There's nothing you can do," Wake yelled, *"now pick a knight and wreck it!"*

Still in shock, he dropped astride another, this one with a serpent's head and emerald banners, and stabbed his staff like a harpoon. In his fury he aimed for the helmet, not caring if he killed the knight. The staff discharged and the serpent's face ballooned in the explosion, popping a shower of rivets as it did.

"Now the next!"

He wasted no time, and still thinking of the young girl, he mounted his staff and left the burning machine behind.

Isis ripped open another kraken. Boiling steam bathed her armour like blood, while searing coals sent up pretty sparks, but a series of unexpected explosions caused her to turn and she suddenly forgot her pleasure. The witches were making a concerted attack and she saw their intention right away.

They're taking what is rightfully ours. They're wicked and sly, just as Vorus warned. Alert now, she looked around at her own forces, but Vorus still hadn't returned. She shoved the wrecked kraken aside and screamed a warning to her sisters, those on the battlefield and those waiting for their chance to descend.

A terrible shriek rang out across the plain, and for a moment the fighting lulled. Witches and knights alike looked up to see the valkyries standing motionless. At their front stood a bull-headed giant with fire all around it.

Ben stood on top of a wrecked machine bearing a boar's head, he could hear the knight inside coughing and groaning. Flames licked upwards from the shattered furnace, but he felt cold despite that. "They know," he whispered, transfixed, "they know what we're doing."

Around him he heard witches mutter prayers in a host of languages. He turned and saw countless wrecked war-suits with hundreds of witches surmounting them, and all of them holding their staffs at the ready, watching the enemy. It was June, but he saw his breath and the sunlight felt cold. "Oak protect us," he prayed.

"They're forming rank behind us," someone muttered. He turned and saw Hilda standing on another battered helmet just yards away, but she was looking back. "The Illuminata behind, Ruination in front," she elaborated.

He followed her gaze and saw Leonhard's remaining knights were squaring up on the other side of the barricade they'd created. "We'll be caught in the middle," he realised and suddenly he felt scared, like a child lost in the dark.

"Steady Ben," she warned.

"What do we do Wake?" Now his limbs were shaking.

"It's Ruination! Fight it."

"Fight it Ben," Hilda repeated, but even she sounded uncertain.

He heard gentle crying and turned to see a witch, a young Dutch lad, in tears. "We should go from here, we cannot win," he stuttered in poor English, then began to sob openly.

He's right, Ben thought, *what the hell are we thinking? We can't win against these things!*

Hilda felt it too, like a lullaby bringing endless sleep because there was no point in being alive. "Steady Hilly," she told herself, and looked around at her fighters. All of them looked shell-shocked. "We *can* win!" she shouted.

Frightened faces turned her way, but doubt was stronger than hope.

Ahead, Ben saw a tide of rust creeping slowly over the destroyed krakens and even at this distance he smelled mildew as their banners crumpled and decayed. It swept onwards engulfing everything; insignia began to blister, water pipes clogged with slime, furnaces gasped their last, and coals flickered and died. He watched everything turn red with rust, or was it blood, he couldn't be sure? It was all the same though in the end. *We can't win*, he thought. He heard a clatter and saw the Dutch lad had dropped his lightning-staff and covered his face with his hands. Around him he heard whispers of doubt. *We can't win*.

"Fight it!" Hilda commanded.

He wanted to, but the voice in his head said otherwise and it sounded so rational. *We can't win*. The feeling of defeat roused awful images. He saw people saying empty prayers for loved ones who would never return, memoirs burned without ever being read, and worst of all he saw that death had no secrets: it was just the end of everything. "Nothing escapes death." His voice was empty and old.

A hundred yards ahead, a knight emerged from his broken machine. His uniform was ripped and his face bloody. He climbed into view and stood uncertainly. Ben, along with everyone else, saw him stagger over the jumbled wreckage and into the shadow of the bull-headed kraken. He stood there for a second, like a tiny lighthouse before a tsunami and when Ben saw him reach for his belt he knew what was going to happen, and worse still he agreed. *Yes, you might as well, because we can't win.*

The knight took his revolver and pressed it to his head. The giant bull regarded him almost approvingly, and then Ben heard the gun fire. The knight jerked, then flopped down and vanished from view, and the bull head slowly screeched upwards and returned its gaze to the army of witches. *You see,* it seemed to say.

"We can't win," Ben realised.

"Fight it, Ben! Bloody fight it!" Hilda tried to rally, and she turned to face them all. "Fight it!" she ordered, but in answer she heard a noise like a landslide and whirled around to see the valkyries advancing. Shattered krakens, helmets and limbs were hurled aside as now the valkyries marched with intent, forming a wall of darkness heading right towards them.

Isis glared at her enemies. *The red-river inside each broom-rider is worth a hundred commoners,* she goaded her sisters. They would kill them, then plough through the worthless metal to reach the pristine krakens beyond and Ruin them. She shrieked in victory and her sisters took up the chant.

"Fight it!" Hilda screamed.

The rust had now crept level with Ben's feet and into his soul, Ruining hope. "Can't fight," he slurred, feeling heavy and lethargic. "Can't fight . . ."

There is no purpose or salvation, there is only Ruination.

"Can't fight . . ."

Hope is torment, oblivion is peace.

"Can't fight . . . can't –"

"FIGHT!" someone roared, "FIGHT THEM!"

A lone witch flew overhead and her war-cry swept through them like a hurricane, breaking the spell of Ruin. Three eagles swooped down to flank her and changed to enormous bears in the blink of an eye. "FIGHT!" Sunday screamed again and the bears roared loud enough to split the earth.

"Sunday?" Ben gasped.

Blackwand? Isis stopped in her tracks, remembering that day in the London sewers. *But she is dead, Vorus said she was dead!* Now it was her turn to be afraid, and she screamed in hatred as berserks and valkyries met in battle one last time.

CHAPTER THIRTY-FIVE

One short summary

'Bloodlines are sacred. Family, before all else.'
Illuminata Knighthood

Hilda had seen many incredible things over the years, but never the likes of Blackwand. "Oak Endures!" she praised, not sure who was the most fearful: berserks or valkyries. "Ben, take half the witches and keep Leonhard's knights back."

"Where are you going?"

"To help Blackwand." She signalled her Wards, and everyone seemed to be waking from a bad dream now.

"But I want to go with you!"

"Just do as I say," she argued, already on her staff with witches forming up behind her.

"Ben, the knights, they're advancing," Wake warned.

"Not for long," he promised, then addressed the others. "You heard her, there's still plenty of knights left to break!" He jumped down and took flight, and they gave a furious cheer and made to follow. Now their forces split. One half followed Hilda, while the rest joined Ben, but despite the danger he wore a huge grin. Sunday was free.

"Dear Mother Goddess, there's more than ever!" Strike saw an army of possessed krakens, with the nastiest right up front.

Sunday counted eight from Galen's original experiment, the rest were newly spawned. "Let the berserks handle the originals, we'll concentrate on the others."

"But the curse of Ruination?"

"The newborn won't know how to withstand magical attacks yet."

"I hope you're right."

"Trust me." She accelerated, intending to pass the black krakens and strike the vulnerable newborn behind. The bull-headed valkyrie swung at her as she tore past. For an instant the downdraught swirled her hair and the air became bitterly cold, then she was past and faced with a wall of lumbering krakens that had been driven by living men not long ago. These were the newborn, and she just hoped they were slow learners because she had a hard lesson to teach them.

Isis powered a sweeping blow at Blackwand, but the nimble witch slipped by unhurt. She screamed in frustration, but her scream turned to one of fear when she saw her next opponents: Blackwand's demons.

The way-beware's song had been like a dam holding back Valgard's fury, but now with that gone, it flooded through him and only his loyalty to Sunday kept it in check. Now he used that rage to increase his size and ferocity until he was almost as large as a kraken himself. He remembered that day in the sewers when a valkyrie had almost killed him, but now he understood how to fight their despair. He had evolved, it just remained to be seen if the valkyries had too.

He hurled himself at her, sailing over the last fifty yards without touching the ground; claws outstretched, teeth bared, and roaring like a storm. Isis screamed from inside her helmet.

The two giants collided, metal against flesh. Eirik sank his claws into her shoulders and clamped his jaws around her throat, thinking to drag the worm from her helmet and grind her between his teeth. Isis struggled for balance, but the kraken was already falling and it dropped onto its back. He landed on top of her, thrashing his head side to side, trying to wrench the helmet free. It would have ended there if her sisters hadn't come to her aid.

Suddenly, mechanical claws seized him and he spun around to find three opponents; Fenris the wolf-headed, one like an eagle and another like a sea monster. He swung a fist at the latter and raked a massive chunk from its midsection, leaving it disembowelled. Cables dangled like split guts, but it lurched forwards doggedly. He was about to finish it when he was assailed from behind as Isis righted herself and joined the fray. "This is for my fallen sister!" she screamed and sank her claws into his skull and forced his head back, causing him to roar in pain.

Fenris swung her claws like knives, intending to slice his throat, but Eirik shoved backwards against Isis, sending her stumbling, and Fenris's blow went whistling through the air, missing him completely. Isis and Eirik fell for a second time and her kraken shattered under his weight, she screamed, he roared and thunder rolled across the battlefield.

Either side of him his brothers battled two valkyries each, but Eirik was still outnumbered four to one, although it would be wrong to say he didn't relish the odds. Isis's machine was shattered, but unless he dragged her from her armour and killed her she would quickly reform. He scrambled in her grip, rolled over and came face to face with that staring bull's head. He could smell the worm inside and all its fear and rot. *Now we finish this.* He bared his teeth and lunged, only to be dragged away again. Fenris took hold of one arm, while her sisters grabbed his other and they began a horrible tug of war with him in the centre. He roared and bellowed and fought against them, all the while conscious that Isis was slowly reordering herself.

Smoke and blood were perfume to Valgard and the delicious smell coaxed his gaze away from Earth's other innumerable conflicts. He watched in fascination as his berserks fought against a strange and powerful foe and briefly toyed with the idea of taking back the berserker rage right then. It was in his nature to be fickle, and granting victory to the undeserving or striking down the mighty was what pleased him most. The idea amused him, but so did the battle and so he decided to wait just a while longer. Then he'd take back what was his.

None of the newborn had been fed sacrificial prisoners like Vorus and her sisters, and until they learned the nature of magic they were going to remain vulnerable. And the first witch they faced that day was Blackwand herself.

Sunday heard the calamity behind, snatched a glance back and saw Tawny wrestling with one of the black krakens. "Oak and Holly be with you," she blessed him, and selected a target of her own, which wasn't hard: there were at least forty newborn to deal with. "That one!" she screamed and Strike saw it right away.

"That's disgusting, even for a knight!"

The newborn that stomped towards her had a helmet that had been split down the middle, leaving an ugly cleft from which the knight still dangled. His corpse rocked and flopped with each step and Sunday thought it looked like the machine's brains had spilled out and her stomach flipped.

"That's just disgusting," Strike repeated.

"Then he shouldn't have come here," she said coldly and landed right on top of the helmet. Instantly she felt a profound sense of despair and she wavered.

"Just hit it while you still can!"

She shook her head clear and lifted the staff.

"What are you waiting for?"

Something hissed like a snake. She looked down into the damaged helmet and saw something moving inside.

"Just kill it!" Strike was starting to feel it too, a sense of heaviness that slowed his heart.

A gruesome face stared up from inside and she shuffled back a step. It had two mouths and it bared its teeth and the hiss escalated to a deafening scream.

"Hethra and Halla!" she screamed back, and stabbed downward through the crack. For a second the cockpit was illuminated like the sun, sparks shot upwards, and its scream became an agonised cry. Unprotected and inexperienced, it died instantly.

With the lightning's after image still in her eyes she flitted away to land on another. This one also had an eagle helmet, but there was no handy gap to attack through. Without thinking she simply struck it as hard as she could. Strike roared and the staff blazed. The kraken rocked and Sunday clung on for dear life, but the armour held and the valkyrie survived, and now it had tasted its first dose of thunder-sprite. If they didn't kill it with the next blow it would almost certainly become immune. Sunday was desperately trying to think of something when Strike suddenly roared, *"Look out!"*

Without thinking, she twisted aside just as its gauntlet raked at her, sending up sparks, and she heard the valkyrie's furious screams from inside. "It'll become immune if we don't finish it. Maybe one witch isn't enough?" That despair seemed to be returning. "Strike, what if one witch isn't enough?"

"Then two might be better Blackwand!"

Sunday jumped.

"Two's better Blackwand!" Hilda grinned, brandishing her own staff.

"Call me Sunday." Together they took aim and struck. The explosion rushed past them and both flinched away. Sunday smelled singed hair and felt molten grains burn her neck. The valkyrie's scream ceased abruptly and the giant machine began to slide sideways.

"Ben sends his regards by the way," Hilda shouted, and without hesitating, she swept away on her staff.

"Ben?" Sunday followed with a running jump just before the kraken flopped like a demolished mill chimney. Blinding smoke billowed up, but she pushed the staff hard and shot through into clear air beyond. That's when she saw that the sky was full of witches.

Everywhere Sunday looked she saw witches swarming across the newborn, but although these krakens were vulnerable they weren't helpless. Wands broke, spells decayed, and while thunder-sprites did their best some of the valkyries were already adapting. *They're evolving!* she realised.

She saw a man and a youth struggling, and rushed to help them. Although she saw multiple lightning-strikes, the kraken reached up with terrible speed and clawed one of the attackers from its face. She witnessed the man vanish inside its fist and blood and lightning erupt from between the fingers, as witch and sprite were killed. The youth, who couldn't have been much more than fifteen, screamed and attacked in a frenzy.

"NO!" She landed hard, stumbled on the kraken's shoulder plates, found her balance and went to grab him. "No, look out!" She caught his arm and pulled, but a fraction too late. That massive fist, still dripping blood, dropped on him like a cage and clenched. She heard a sickening crunch and he became one with his late father. Warm blood showered across her face and she staggered back in horror, now holding the lad's severed arm. "You evil bitch!" she howled, and charged without thinking.

By sheer chance, or fate, her staff slid clean through the visor and rammed into the valkyrie within. Lightning blazed inside the cockpit and the valkyrie died with a shriek. *"They're getting stronger,"* Strike gasped. *"The Ruin'll be too much for us soon."*

"Can you still fly?" She swayed as the kraken lolled sideways.

"Jump and see!"

She didn't have to jump. She literally fell as the machine toppled. For a second her belly rolled as she dropped, then Strike took her weight and the staff lifted higher. She wiped the blood from her face and rejoined the battle, and what she saw wasn't good. While some krakens had fallen, others fought back, clawing and snatching at witches as they struggled to get close enough to attack. Worse still, behind them across Roman-field defeated krakens were struggling to rise up, Vorus's army was still growing and there were still plenty of valkyries waiting to descend. She had time to wonder if the defeated ones would simply be inhabited by another valkyrie, if so they would have to fight them all over again. "Tawny, please hurry!" She looked back and saw the berserks engaged in a stupendous fight with the most vicious valkyries of all, Isis and her sisters.

"We can't fight them alone, we need the berserks!" Strike emphasised.

"All we can do is fight." She selected another and raced towards it screaming her name. "Blackwand!"

While Sunday and the berserks fought Ruinous enemies, Ben streaked towards flesh and blood foes, but they were no less dangerous for that. If they stood any chance of getting to Leonhard's krakens, they'd have to fly through thousands of bullets first. The krakens looked like a mountain range on the move, and around their legs he saw rifle-flashes dance in their thousands.

"Nice welcoming committee," Wake groaned.

"We'll never get close enough!" Ben despaired.

"Keep it fast!"

"I know how to bloody fly!" He twisted around and saw at least two hundred witches strung out behind him.

"There!" Wake shouted.

"Which one?"

"The pig-faced bastard with the drooping banners."

He saw it now; a kraken with a boar's head and sagging banners that were obscuring its view. "Here goes." He curled low, just as the first bullets whistled past.

For the last hundred yards he experienced a strange sense of peace, understanding he would either reach the enemy or he wouldn't. He became aware of countless sensations around him, expecting any one to be his last. The wind rushed in his ears, he smelled sulphur and earth, heard distant cannons and even a regimental piper playing a tune. He watched his target grow larger and listened to bullets whine through the air. "This is for Lottie Pilling," he reached for his wand just as the kraken's banners flapped away, and the knight finally saw the threat.

The huge machine raised its arms, but Ben was already too close. Just as he dropped down on to the helmet, he heard a huge cheer followed by a series of explosions and he looked to see witches flashing by, scoring hits as they passed. The line of krakens erupted in flames and now they looked more like volcanoes than mountains, but the charge cost them. The gun fire became crazed. Bullets rang against the krakens and witches fell like stones. He counted over thirty casualties. Another few runs like this and there'd be no witches left. "Now for yours Lottie," he remembered his own target.

"Ben, look out!" Wake cried.

The cockpit banged open and a very scared, and very angry Polish knight reared up waving a revolver and began shooting. Without thinking Ben rammed the staff into his chest. There was a loud crack and a tiny flash and it was over. He sank back with smoke curling up from between his lips and Ben felt an profound sense of shame. It was easier to kill krakens than their knights. He stared around at the destruction and death. "God Oak? Is there any difference between any of us?"

"You're talking like Ruin again," Wake growled, *"get moving!"*

He did just that, and set off after the others, who were now regrouping in the tree cover, readying for a second run.

The age of krakens was over. The witches had proven again that they were too vulnerable to small mobile opponents. Leonhard's krakens had entered Roman-field as impressive giants, but would leave it as obsolete scrap. He watched one after another fall and with each one he felt another bite taken out of his treasury. "Where's that bastard Thorpe, I ordered him arrested an hour ago!" he screamed.

One of his Austrian commanders stepped up, looking bloodied and breathless. "Sir, the British garrison is all but beaten, but there's no sign of Thorpe."

"He tricked us, he let that Blackwand devil loose to wreck us!" He pointed a trembling finger. "This whole tournament was a trap!" There came another explosion, another expensive machine destroyed and Leonhard whimpered with fury.

"That being so sir, I respectfully suggest we retreat. The contest is void."

"Europe will support my claim to be Knight Superior?" he seized the opportunity.

They all nodded eagerly, anything to be away from here.

"Thorpe has betrayed even the British bloodlines," the Austrian calculated, "they'll hunt him down, they cannot possibly deny you the right to be Knight Superior now. I say withdraw and save what we can."

There was a chorus of restrained approval, after all, nobody wanted to look like a coward, while outside there were more explosions and screams. Leonhard considered a moment. "We go!" he barked at last. "Ready the Echelon. I am leaving!"

A tangible wave of relief rushed through the pavilion and men hurried to carry out his orders. Leonhard flopped back into his chair and sighed heavily. He didn't want to think about the cost of this disaster, socially or financially, but at least they were going home and he would be Knight Superior.

Every fit of madness has some method at its heart and Thorpe's method in all this chaos was to find Leonhard and kill him. If he died, the European alliance would crumble and the Book-of-Nine might still salvage something from this day.

He'd spent the last hour waiting in Leonhard's quarters in the west wing. When he'd broken in the servant girl had tried to raise the alarm and he'd been forced to shoot her. He dragged the body into the dressing room and dumped it under some heavy drapes, then waited in the drawing room for Leonhard to return. He knew the crafty Hun kept valuables and important documents in a small safe and whatever happened today he'd come back for them.

He took cover behind a screen decorated with Chinese characters, crouched down and waited. Outside, the battle raged and he wondered who was winning, but found that he no longer cared. Waiting like this he remembered waiting for Rachel in his bedchamber that day. The memory excited him and he felt a shiver at the prospect of killing Leonhard, while the Hall rocked faintly with cannon fire. "Pity about Wellesley Hall," he smiled and settled down to wait.

He must have dozed off. A soft thud awoke him and he snatched at the gun in his lap, cursing himself and wincing at the pain in his wounded arm. He heard the bedclothes rustle and the springs creak and smiled. *Time to put you to bed forever Leonhard,* he thought, and confident the German was his, he stepped out from hiding with the gun raised.

The bed was empty.

He stiffened, and took in the whole room. The door was closed and he was alone, but he saw that the bed wasn't entirely empty. There was something lying on the cover: a black cane. He recognised it right away and for some reason it scared him. "Galen?" he hissed, "Matthew?"

His reply was a smell of rotten flowers so strong that he gagged and pressed his arm across his mouth.

"Matthew?" he coughed and scanned the room, gun at the ready. He couldn't say why, but his gaze was drawn back to the cane, lying against the white cotton it looked like a knife wound. "Rachel," the name fell from his lips without him knowing he'd spoken.

He heard something, a slithering sound, and he whirled around to see the screen wobble, as if something had just disturbed it.

"Vorus?" His eyes rolled but he saw nothing. "Ought you be with your sisters on Roman-field? And I mean *all* your sisters. Yes, I've known your plans for some time," he taunted her. "And of course you'll need your precious kraken. How would you feel if I were to have all the Ruined machines melted down, would you like to go back to skulking in cesspools?"

Vorus lingered against the ceiling, watching closely. He had a gun and could kill her if she appeared, but to complete her plan she had to get physically close to him. Her timing must be absolute. She waited for her moment, ready to claim her new home.

"Come out you diseased crone," he growled, scanning the room, but again it was the cane on the bed that tugged at his gaze. "I said come out!"

She saw the opening she was looking for and lunged. He felt a breeze against his cheek and smelled decay, and without thinking he raised the revolver and fired. She changed from ether to solid just as the bullet whizzed through her, rupturing her gut, and she screamed in pain.

"Got you, whore!" he roared in triumph, but she crashed into him and knocked him to the floor sending the gun spinning. His bullet had drilled through her abdomen, and she knew death was certain if she didn't finish what she started.

She had him pinned, but he was strong, even with a wounded arm and he reached up and clamped a hand around her scrawny throat while he rammed his fingers into the open wound aiming to rip her open. "Die you bitch!" he leered up at her, twisting his hand and enjoying her pain.

Vorus screamed. She could have slashed his throat open and finished him right then, but she must not damage him. Instead she repaid his gesture and jabbed a finger at his wounded shoulder, into the hole left by Doulton's bullet. This was the special opening she needed.

"DIE!" he roared and shoved back harder, forcing his fist deep into her gut and once inside he grabbed something soft and squirming, seized with a murderous grip and pulled with all his might.

She wailed in agony as he disembowelled her, but there was still time for her one last secret. She pushed her fingers deeper into his wound, ignoring the way he was unravelling her innards, and began worming her way into his body.

First her hand and then her whole arm sank inside, while Thorpe continued to laugh like a lunatic, thinking he'd got the upper hand. As she penetrated him, she became a vapour racing through his system and claiming it. Only when she crawled into his brain did he register the threat.

"NO! Damn you, you whore, get off me!"

Vorus panted and shoved. She was inside him up to the shoulder now, and continued to pour herself into him like a funnel. Her breathing was desperate and rapid, if she didn't find refuge soon she would die. She *had* to get inside him.

He felt her fingers begin to grope his deepest memories, memories of Rachel and Barlow. "GET OUT OF ME WHORE!" he screamed in terror and began lashing at her with his fists.

She lowered her head and began to inject the last of herself into Doulton's bullet hole. He'd sworn to take Thorpe down and in a peculiar way he had, it went some way to pay for his brutal murder. She pushed her face against the wound, smelling the blood and feeling its warmth, and then she burrowed into him like a hungry tick and sailed along with his bloodstream, navigating the red-river.

He screamed until his throat almost burst, and clawed at her until his nails were ragged. He howled a hundred different curses, but she continued to slide into him like an eel and now her entire upper body was buried leaving her spindly legs dangling free and scrambling for purchase. Now he felt vague and forgetful and his body was icy cold and a thought came to him from nowhere, *This is how Rachel felt that day.*

That was his last thought of freewill. Her legs slithered into the wound, followed by a string of her damaged intestine, and then they vanished with a smacking sound and she was at last inside her new home.

Thorpe mumbled gibberish and his body twitched as something inside wriggled into a comfortable position. A groan escaped his lips, he convulsed and then lay still and his eyes became glassy.

She flowed through his body touching every cell, making them hers. Inside his brain she found his storehouse of secrets and read them at will, knowing all he knew, but Victor Thorpe was far from dead. As she claimed more and more of him, he shrank smaller and smaller. She had no use for him, he was like the packaging that might conceal a pretty new frock, but it pleased her to keep him close because she knew how much Matthew loved his father. How delighted he would be to know they were all together as one family, she thought.

Thorpe was left as a tiny thought drifting somewhere in the empty universe that used to be his own mind. He watched his life's achievements stolen one by one, until he was just an echo of his own name. He shrivelled to a memory with no use, lost in the endless black inside his own skull.

The figure on the carpet jerked and coughed, before blinking a few times and breathing again. She took a moment to feel the beating heart in her chest and the way her ribs heaved with each breath, which was gritty with years of cigar smoke. *I am alive?* Vorus wondered, and began to push herself upright.

She looked around with stolen eyes and then slowly climbed to her feet, feeling shaky and unsure. She reached up and touched the bullet hole in her shoulder and winced. It had all but closed now and she was safely sealed inside Thorpe's body. This had been her last secret. She had learned how to survive without some cumbersome machine. She had evolved. As long as she knew the song of Àeon, Thorpe's body would not be Ruined and she could keep it forever. "It worked," she uttered, stunned to hear herself speak with his voice. "It worked!" she said louder, and half walked, half staggered over to the bed and snatched up the cane. Immediately she felt whole again. "We are one, the new family Thorpe."

One of Thorpe's stolen thoughts occurred to her and it seemed very fitting. *Bloodlines are sacred, family comes first, before all else.*

"I quite agree," she sighed. The building rocked to another explosion, but she didn't hear it. She pressed the cane to her cheek and shed her first tear of joy.

One minute he was surrounded by generals making a hurried retreat, then came a huge explosion and a kraken toppled down in front of them, throwing him from his horse and scattering his guards. He fled in panic and now he was lost and running blind, and Leonhard wasn't the running type.

"English pig filth!" he spat, gasping for breath. Everything looked different in the smoke, but when glass crunched underfoot and he saw the skeletal ruin of the tropical house, he at last had his bearings. "Hieder!" he shouted, "anyone?" Fire crackled through the Hall's portico, it looked like the whole building would soon go up in flames, and he heard something crash through the undergrowth to his left. He loosened his tunic, fighting for breath and feeling faint. He hated exercise. "Hieder?" Something in the laurel bushes moved again. "Who's there!" he demanded, drawing his revolver. His reply was a deep growling, and he immediately thought of giant bears. In a panic he fired aimlessly, just as something powerful sprang from cover and charged at him in a flash of orange and black. *A tiger?* he had time to think.

The tiger probably didn't know about 'vengeance' but after weeks of being taunted in a cage it felt good to be free again. It pounced with terrible grace and landed on Leonhard and put its teeth and claws to the test and found they were still very efficient. The Illuminata's new Knight Superior screamed and begged, but of course to the tiger all his fuss was just a rusty gate.

Eirik struggled against three enemies and Sunday couldn't stand it any longer and she disengaged to help him. She dropped to the ground and dodged immense steel feet, and weaved between them aiming to land a blow. Killing it was unlikely, but she might at least distract it. The ground was pummelled and blackened, and stones rained down where claws ripped up the earth, while around her the roars and screams of battle sounded like the apocalypse. Tawny was drenched in blood and although his wounds healed as fast as they opened, the pain remained and his blood was still precious, now it rained down and misted the ground.

"Blackwand!" She charged and rammed her staff against the kraken's ankle. Lightning flashed and thunder boomed.

Fenris felt the broom-rider's magic wash over her. She had endured this at Hobbs Ash and understood it couldn't harm her, but she made the mistake of looking away. *Blackwand!* she thought hatefully.

Sonneday? Eirik took advantage and lunged, clamped his jaws around the wolf helmet and bit hard. The steel split open and they both tumbled down, and even before the debris had fallen he hooked his claws into the crack and prised the helmet wide like a clam. Fenris's shrill screams only inflamed him and he forced his head into the crack lacerating his muzzle, and dragged her out between his jaws.

"Vorus!" she howled.

He shook her until her bones were powder and her limbs dangled by gristle, then he spat the corpse to the ground and pounded his enemy flat, before bellowing in triumph. The valkyrie was dead.

Her death-scream brought a brief lull to the madness. One of the original nine was dead, and spurred on Eirik turned his attention to Isis.

He swatted the bull-helmet from its shoulders with one swipe. It fell and rolled a little way before coming to rest like a bowl, while the rest of the kraken slumped down and shattered. Isis immediately crawled free like a worm from an apple, and Eirik batted her to the ground crushing her left arm and leg, but before he could finish the job he was attacked from behind once more.

She dragged herself away, spluttering blood and wailing in pain. *Vorus?* she despaired, *Vorus knows the demons are too strong and she has abandoned us.* She saw it plainly now; her treacherous sister had promised them so much, but ultimately left them all to die. *Vorus!* she raged, but now she was crippled and if the demons didn't kill her time would. She crawled away sobbing pitifully and curled up under the defeated Book-of-Nine banner like a shroud where she waited to die. She listened to the sound of thunder, roaring bears and screaming witches, and thought Ruination the most blessed and peaceful realm in comparison to this terrible place.

Karl finally toppled one of his opponents and ripped the head wide open. The valkyrie slashed at him until his muzzle was bloodied, but at last he caught her between his teeth and bit hard. Her lower half dropped from his jaws, while her head and upper body remained wedged in his mouth, and through it all she was still screaming, still clawing at him. He shook her free, then pinned her down and swiped her bulbous head from her shoulders. It went spinning and only when it landed with a thud did the screaming stop.

Harger meanwhile heaved one of them up off the ground and slammed it down head first. Its black banner crumpled first and the helmet soon followed, instantly killing the valkyrie and without it the machine exploded into fragments. He crashed into the wreckage, then righted himself and shook the debris from his back with a victorious roar.

Sunday continued doing what she could; running, dodging and striking until her chest felt like fire. The stink of decay and blood was all around her, the air was ice cold and the sky was thick with smoke. It could have been January for all she knew. Suddenly the sky was blotted out as another kraken fell. She screamed and ran while the earth heaved and the berserk's roar filled her ears. She fell to her knees and curled up against a wave of debris. *How much longer can we do this?* she despaired.

She crawled to her feet again, and saw Tawny with his deadly paws either side of a helmet, trying to wrench it free, while the kraken's gauntlets gouged bloody furrows in his shoulders.

"Tawny!" Without thinking she set off running through craters and crumpled metal. Tears washed her vision and when she reached them she swung the staff blindly with a scream. "LEAVE HIM BE!"

Even Strike's best wasn't sufficient against one of the nine, and now his power was all but spent, but it was still just enough for Sunday's purpose. The kraken rocked, and in the lull Eirik finally dragged it to the ground where he ripped the head free before reaching inside to crack the valkyrie between his jaws. Rancid blood flooded his mouth once more and made him want to retch.

For a second she locked eyes with him and both of them knew. If the newborn became as strong as the nine they would be fighting until doomsday. "I'm sorry," she croaked, "I'm sorry I brought you here." She didn't see a monster or a warrior, she saw a man who had saved her over and over and she didn't even know his name. She ran to him and threw her arms around his muzzle, which was split by countless wounds, and looked into one of those huge brown eyes and saw only fatigue and pain. "I'm sorry I brought you here," she cried again.

Eirik was racked by pain, but not entirely unhappy. His strange sense of peace came from knowing the end was approaching. He felt Sonneday's arms around him and briefly imagined how it would feel to hold his own wife again, and despite the horror and the Ruin he smiled, knowing it would be soon.

Of the original nine, only three remained and they were in a sorry state, missing limbs and swaying unsteadily. Now they staggered back to regroup, while behind them, their newborn sisters came to reinforce them. The berserks themselves looked little better, and as the valkyries retreated, the three brothers lumbered to stand shoulder to shoulder. All of them steamed with sweat, and their fur was dark with blood. The two opposing forces regarded each other across a field of destruction, waiting for the final showdown. As if this was their signal, Hilda's forces withdrew to regroup and before long tired and bloodied witches were dropping from the sky to stand alongside the berserks.

"Blackwand!" someone called.

Sunday turned to see Hilda hurrying towards her. Her hair was a mess and her nose was bloodied. "I told you, call me Sunday," she smiled wearily.

All the surviving witches were gathering now, drawn to the berserk's power. The three huge warriors stood towering over them, daring the valkyries to attack, but all were breathing and bleeding heavily. Hilda saw how the valkyries were clustering together, while on the far side of Roman-field she heard endless rifle fire from Ben's assault. She cast an eye over her remaining witches, who looked scared and exhausted.

"We can't let a single valkyrie leave this place," Sunday said softly.

"I know," Hilda nodded solemnly. "It would have been so nice to see Kolfinnia again."

Sunday saw something flinty in her eyes. "Keep everyone behind me and the berserks."

She acknowledged with a nod. "Form up in ranks!" she called to them. Tired witches began to make files, facing the valkyries, expecting a charge very soon. The berserks moved into position with Eirik in front at Sunday's side. "I won't leave you," she pledged, and pressed a hand to his leg. From high above she heard him rumble something, and she smiled. "Ready Strike?"

"Ready for what though, that's the question."

"Maybe we'll wake on a beach somewhere, and we can begin again."

"Let's hope it's a warm beach this time."

She touched the strip of purple cloth around her arm. "I won't fail you again Kolfinnia," she swore. Through the smoke ahead she saw valkyries forming their own ranks, and their numbers were still growing. "I hope you burn for what you've done Thorpe." She wiped tears and blood from her face, held her staff with pride and waited to die a second time. Somewhere behind her she could hear Hilda issuing her commands. Suddenly a terrible scream came at them through the smoke. "This is it!"

"At last!" Strike sounded relieved.

She heard the clash of metal as they began to advance. "Hold fast!" she shouted, but in reply she heard witches groan in fear.

"Oak save us!" someone cried in despair.

"We're losing them Strike," she moaned, "we're losing them and I don't blame them for a minute."

"What can we do though?"

"I wish I knew," she whispered.

There came more alarmed cries from behind. The witches were on the brink of running.

It was Eirik that showed them the way. Sensing their fear he rose up on his hind legs, threw back his head and bellowed. His war-cry carried clear across Roman-field and all who heard were either inspired or intimidated. His brothers immediately joined him and the three roared until the earth quaked and the air was splitting. Their roar drowned out the approaching valkyries, the cannons, even the despair. It reverberated through flesh and blood, rock and soil, and everyone felt new strength return to tired limbs and kindle fresh fires in wavering hearts. Sunday looked up at him lovingly and raised her staff and joined them. Hundreds of witches screamed and roared with animal fury and all of them briefly tasted what it meant to be a berserk.

This was the hour. Offer them hope, then snatch it away, it was cruel, it was hard, it was perfect. Valgard rumbled with laughter and the lake of blood around him surged. He was pleased. His champions had provided him much entertainment and now he would repay them with death. It was the least he could do. He reached down and claimed back the berserker rage, just when they needed it most.

Smoke rolled in from nowhere and Sunday lost sight of the enemy. Behind her Tawny roared again, but now it sounded wrong, she could almost discern words and she realised he wasn't roaring, he was shouting. The ground rocked as something large collapsed, and she turned back, forgetting the valkyries, forgetting everything, and fearing the worst. "Tawny!" She ran to him through the smoke, but it wasn't a bear she found lying in the mud, it was a man, and right away she knew he was dying. "Tawny!" She dropped to his side.

He had fair hair and a strong face, and at first she had the awful idea it was Ben lying there, the similarity was painful. He wore clothes of the Norse era; an open-neck shirt and woollen trousers, but whatever wounds he suffered as a berserk remained and now they wouldn't heal. She saw blood soak his clothes from the injuries underneath. It began as blotches and quickly spread until he was bathed in the stuff and she knew his wounds must be terrible and she was glad she couldn't see them. "Tawny!" she sobbed. It sounded trite now, but it was the only name she'd ever had for him. His eyes found hers and he muttered something and she leaned closer.

"Eirik," he breathed against her ear.

At last she knew his name, just moments before he had to leave her. "Sunday," she replied and caressed his cheek.

He reached up and pressed something into her hand, anxious for her to keep it. She looked down and saw a small silver hammer. "Sunday," he sighed contentedly.

She couldn't stop the tears then, and she kissed his brow and held him tighter. "Eirik, don't go."

At hearing his own name he smiled, realising it was what he'd wanted to hear from her all along. Somewhere close by he knew his brothers were also free. He wanted to stay with her and fight, but Evermore was calling and so was Freydis. He was going home. Sunday buried her face against his neck and he thought her tears felt as warm as summer roses.

She heard metal feet marching closer and the dismay of frightened witches, but none of that seemed important anymore. "Eirik," she murmured in praise and loss, and when she looked once more she saw that he looked profoundly content, like a man who has come to the end of a gruelling journey, and it took a second for her to realise that he had died. "Walk Evermore in peace," she kissed him farewell, then collapsed across him crying hard, no longer caring if the valkyries won this day or not.

"We can't make another run!"

Ben turned to the French witch who'd addressed him. "I know," he agreed. They had just attacked Leonhard's forces a third time. The first was their best, after that their casualties became heavier. Ben took stock; one hundred fighters, fifty wounded and at least the same killed. "We've done all we can here." Muttered agreements and translations circled the group. "Those too wounded to fight should leave now," he added, "Harl's crows will guide you to safe territory." More chatter, more whispered translation.

"Look!" someone shouted, and Ben groaned thinking the worst.

Bloody hell what now? He ran to the tree line and looked out. Leonhard's remaining krakens were either moving off, or their pilots were abandoning them.

"They're givin' up!" came a gruff Yorkshire voice.

Ben turned to a hulking man with a flat nose. "They can't be?"

"Nay, look! Knights are bailin' out," he pointed. "Just soldiers guardin' them krakens now, and yer know 'ow much they get paid don't yer?"

Ben shook his head.

"Not enuff to die guardin' empty machines, that's what!"

The rest looked confused and closed in, trying to see what was happening. Ben saw what he meant. "So if we pass over again, they'll break and run?"

"Call me a liar if they don't."

"I call you a bastard if they don't," he muttered.

"That's the spirit, now are we off?"

"It'll be a pleasure, Mr erm?"

"Braker," he finished. "Tom Braker – Black Rabbit coven, Yorkshire."

Ben took a deep breath. "Everyone . . . one last run." He eyed the krakens. *Let's hope you live up to your name Mr Braker,* he thought, grabbed his staff and set off to Sunday's rescue.

Sunday knelt beside Eirik, still holding his hand, while around her, witches began to lose their cohesion, but she didn't react or care. It didn't matter any more. Maybe it was the creeping veil of despair emanating from the valkyries, or maybe it was just that she'd lost another friend.

"They're almost on us," Strike said softly.

She looked up and saw the three originals had been joined by countless newborn. "Thank you for all your years of friendship."

"Don't mention it." He hopped back towards his staff. "One last fight?"

"One last fight," she smiled wearily.

"It was a short summer after all."

She smiled again, but this time it was genuine. "Still better than a lifetime of winter."

Strike vanished into his staff, she picked it up, stood slowly, and turned to face an enemy that couldn't be beaten.

It was Isis who lay dying under the tattered Book-of-Nine banner that heard it first. A child's voice drifting through the racket of battle, and a deeply buried part of her recognised it. She pawed the fabric aside and looked out on to a world of smoke, death and betrayal, but there was something more. A girl walked through the smoke towards her. She had no rightful place on a battlefield, but she was calm and unafraid. "They named you Isis didn't they?" The girl knelt by her side, and Isis recognised her and only then realised that she had forgotten her, in fact she had forgotten a great deal.

"Forgive me my Lady," she uttered. "Yes, I am Isis."

"No you are not," the girl said firmly.

"I am not?"

"Do you know who I am?"

"Yes my Lady. You are Sophie, beloved of Ruination, chosen of Lord Àeon." The name seemed to unlock something deep inside the dying valkyrie and she began to weep with shame.

"Shhh," Sophie comforted her, "you are coming home, all the beloved sisters are coming home."

"Me? But I'm unworthy to return to Àeon's side."

"You are not a valkyrie, you are not Isis," she sneered at the names, "Lord Àeon made you and your sisters as divine shepherds."

She remembered now. The lost creatures of Ruin that found themselves stranded and alone on Earth, it was up to her and her kin to bring them home. "Not a valkyrie?" she repeated, then more certainly, "not a valkyrie."

"Not a valkyrie."

"And Vorus?"

Sophie looked sad. "She can never come home, but the beloved sisters can, and you also."

"Am I worthy, my Lady?" Isis had indulged in many terrible things since being tempted away from Ruination.

Sophie reached out and stroked her hideous face, angry that this world had turned beautiful creatures into living horrors. "Your name is not Isis," she repeated, "your real name is the roar of a falling mountain, the last beat of an ageing heart. Wherever Ruin brings change, that is your name."

She remembered now. They were not valkyries or tools to be used, they were shepherds and their task was divine and great. "Beloved sisters coming home," she sighed hopefully.

Sophie smiled, "So let us begin shall we?"

"Form line!" Hilda shouted, and the remaining witches formed a file behind her. She saw Sunday standing proud of the line, some hundred yards ahead. From here she looked like she was facing the oncoming valkyries alone. "Blackwand?" she shouted, "the berserks are gone, you must join the line!"

Sunday looked back, raised a hand then turned away again, but she didn't shift.

Hilda understood. "Oak bless you," she wished her quietly. Witches formed up alongside Hilda, staffs and wands at the ready, but without the berserks they were already beaten. "Make ready and good luck!" Hilda roared over the sound of marching feet. The valkyrie-krakens marched onwards, right towards them. *Good luck to you too Hathwell,* she thought, and hoped she hadn't been too hard on him. When she'd awoken from the battle of Kittiwake she'd been disgusted to find who her rescuer was, but he wasn't such a bad man for a squire. Maybe she ought to have told him that? "Too late," she muttered regretfully.

Sunday stood proud of the line refusing to leave Eirik and his brothers' side, and the ground rocked in time to the valkyrie's marching feet. The pulse was almost hypnotic and it thudded like an angry heart. She counted the beats and felt them grow stronger until the giants emerged from the smoke and battered helmets stared down at her with cold eyes.

Thud – thud – thud. She thought it sounded like a judge's gavel.

"Oak, let us die well," she prayed quietly.

Thud – thud – thud. It seemed to go on forever, then it suddenly stopped. She juddered back a step and looked up, the valkyries halted and the earth became still.

"What's this?" Strike wondered.

Then she smelled it; earth after a flood, a charred forest after a fire, decaying leaves in autumn. Finally came a voice, that of a young girl, "Not all Ruination is your enemy, Blackwand."

Sunday took another step back. "Who's there?"

"Ruin is death and change, not evil and cruelty, that is the domain of man," the girl said sadly.

"Who are you?" she challenged.

A figure walked towards her out of the smoke: a girl wearing a long cream dress. Her hair was black and her eyes were pale just like Galen's. She looked young but her words were as old as time itself. "I am Sophie." She came closer and Sunday saw that she cradled an infant in her arms, but what it was she couldn't say, she'd never seen its like before. It was beautiful but frightening, and its body was like that of an embryo shark, while its face was hauntingly child-like. Gossamer wings sprouted from its shoulders and it was illuminated by an inner radiance. "This was Isis," Sophie looked down lovingly at the young shepherd in her arms. "All the beloved sisters are coming home."

Now Sunday detected figures moving through the smoke, all of them gathering around Sophie. They hobbled, limped and crawled towards the girl, and she saw they were valkyries, perhaps hundreds of them, all the ones Vorus had deceived.

"I have something for you before I go." Sophie stepped back. At her feet lay a black book. "Put it to good use." She smiled at the infant in her arms again, then turned to leave.

Sunday looked down. It was Galen's Book-of-Nine. "Sophie, wait!" she called, but the girl walked on and the valkyries clustered around her thicker and thicker until she was lost amongst them.

"Along came a spider to help and to hide her," Sophie's gentle song receded into the mist.

"Sophie!" Sunday stumbled on a few paces. "Sophie, please!"

"She's gone," Strike finished.

One of the valkyries looked back and Sunday saw its degenerate shell falling away revealing a creature just like the one Sophie cradled. It regarded her for a moment with bottomless shark's eyes, then turned and sailed away back to realms both dreadful and wondrous. "Beloved sisters coming home." Now she understood and watched the last of the shepherds vanish into the smoke following Sophie back to Àeon's side. "Good luck," she whispered after them, and in reply she briefly heard what sounded like a child's laughter, or perhaps that was just her imagination.

The Ruined krakens began to collapse then. All across Roman-field they fell down dead and useless and the last to fall stood way at the rear; a black kraken with a sinister cherub's head. Its strange pilot had abandoned it to look for her beloved, and now it crumbled to scrap until it was just an unrecognisable heap. The last piece was the helmet. It dropped with a hefty clang leaving the cherub staring across a field of defeat and looking somewhat sullen, that is until a ragged banner drifted down across its face, and then the cherub saw nothing at all.

"Hilda!" Ben hit the ground running. They had attacked Leonhard's abandoned krakens on the way and left most of them flaming like candles. "Hilda, where's Blackwand?" he rushed.

"She's up ahead," Hilda gestured in Sunday's direction.

"Then what are you doing! We've got to bloody help her!" he made to go, but she restrained him.

"Ben, listen!"

All he could hear was his thudding heart. "Listen to what?"

"It's silent," she explained, "the valkyries are gone."

"What?"

"Trust me," she smiled and tapped her brow. "I'm a witch."

"Then where's Blackwand?"

She pointed off into the smoke. "Go and see for yourself."

He grinned and sprinted away.

"The rest of you," Hilda shouted, "make ready, I want everyone away from here in ten minutes!" As if he'd been waiting for that very order, a shiny crow alighted on her shoulder. "Harl!" she beamed, "delightful to see you again." Dozens more crows landed around her. This land was a strange place to many of these witches and they all needed an escort to safety. "If you're looking for Ben, he's gone that way, I'll find another to guide my way," Hilda nodded in his direction. "But first I have to find an old squire with a bad knee," she decided.

The Timekeeper stared at the mound of severed threads, hundreds of them in all, and sank down with a sigh. "It's over," he said to nobody. He'd been through a battle himself. He was drained and weak, and there were still countless threads to be commanded, but he was determined to finish this properly. He selected two special threads, just to give them a helping hand and brought them closer until they touched. "Well done Sunday," he smiled inwardly, "not many souls can claim to have changed the universe."

"Sunday?" he called, running blindly through the wreckage. "Sunday?"

"There!" Wake spotted her.

He saw a figure in the smoke and ran for all his worth. "Sunday!" She turned and he saw her face. She was dirty and bloodied and her hair was wild, but he'd know her anywhere.

"Ben!" Her expression blossomed. "Ben!"

He dropped his staff and threw his arms around her, half believing he was dead and this was the after-life. "Did we really live through that?"

"We did!" she cried and laughed against his cheek. "We did!"

"This is a summer to remember," he held her even tighter.

"Better than a lifetime of winter?" She pulled back a little and gave him a searching look.

He remembered his note. It was only three weeks ago, but the whole world had changed since. "You got my message?" he smiled.

"I did, and my reply is long overdue." She leaned closer and kissed him fully.

Somewhere far off another kraken exploded, but neither of them heard it. The hated Illuminata lay in ruins, Sunday was safe, and Ben wondered if he hadn't died and gone to paradise after all.

CHAPTER THIRTY-SIX

Loose threads

'Long thread, short thread, sew and weave, the Keeper spins our destiny.'
Traditional witch's nursery rhyme

Tired looking flags hung from shops, railings and lampposts. Five days after the solstice and London was still recovering from its Jubilee hangover, and the streets around Cadogan Place in Pimlico, lined with lime trees and elegant houses, were no exception.

The weather was warm, but one man loitering on the street wore a long coat and bowler hat, attire more suited to winter than late June. He actually lived in this affluent area although you might not think so considering his rumpled clothes and the stubble on his chin. Instead, he looked like he'd been sleeping rough for the last few nights, which is exactly what Virgil Lyle had been doing. "Don't they ever give up?" he groaned as he passed a discreet distance from his house. The door was still ajar and he knew the Goldhawk men were there searching. "Bloody Thorpe!" He must have cursed the man a thousand times in the last five days, he just hoped the maniac was dead and it'd taken a long time. "Treacherous bastard."

He hurried past his own house and decided to try again later. He'd been hanging around all morning and people might grow suspicious.

He found what he wanted at Goldhawk, having raced back there before news of the disaster spread, and taken a substantial amount in gold. His luck soured though when he arrived at his own home later that night. There were Goldhawk men standing guard outside. The bad news must have followed faster than he anticipated. He planned to lie low, hoping they would assume that he had been killed at Wellesley, and so he'd come back each night since, but there was always someone there. *Give it up, and go back and tell them Thorpe was a traitor.* He'd lost count of the number of times he set off, only to lose his nerve and scurry back into hiding. "They'd never take my word over Thorpe's, even if the evil bastard's dead, they'd never take my word," he fretted as he left his hiding place in the grounds of the Royal Hospital. It was now well past midnight and he'd made his mind up that come hell or high water he'd get what he came for. There was a fortune in bonds in the safe as well as sensitive documents he could offer rival families as blackmail material in return for protection. By tomorrow evening he could be living in France safe from British wrath.

When he got back, the house was dark and empty. He took his chance, but once at his own front door he was shaking so much he needed both hands to hold the key steady. A cat mewed at him from the bushes and he shooed it off, fearful any slight noise might give him away. The key turned and he crept into his own house like a thief. Thanks to his innate fussiness he knew every inch of his home and so didn't need a light to slip into the study, locate the safe and open it. He was fishing his important documents out when a voice came out of the dark behind him.

"Mr Virgil Lyle?"

"Christ!" He spun around and banged his head on the safe door. He clutched his head and saw a faint glow and wondered if he was seeing stars, then realised it was a lantern.

A figure stepped forwards from the shadows and turned the lantern up. "Mr Virgil Lyle?" he asked again, and another man stepped up to join him.

He didn't recognise either of them. *Not Goldhawk men,* he thought and calmed down a little. "Who the hell are you and what are you doing in my house?"

"Do you live here sir?" The stranger approached and turned the light up full.

Lyle saw two men he almost recognised. Both were wearing standard London overcoats and black bowler hats. "Explain yourself," he demanded.

"Forgive me sir, Detective Inspector Frank Lord, of Scotland Yard."

Lyle's stomach churned like a whirlpool. *Shit! this is about Smithfield,* he thought with dismay. "Of course Inspector, how may I help you?" He used his most civil tone now.

"Perhaps you recall the Pilling case back in April?"

"Ah yes, terrible business Inspector. The investigation is still on-going." *Bloody Yardies,* he thought. They were subordinate to Goldhawk. Under normal circumstances he'd have him thrown out of his job. "I can't make comment," he elaborated, "besides, it's hardly proper to be conducting interviews in the dead of night is it?"

"It's hardly proper to be slipping into one's own home in the dead of night and opening the safe with all the lights off either is it sir?" Lord pondered.

"What I do in my own home is my affair."

"You're a hard man to track down Mr Lyle," Lord ignored him, "we came by earlier, but the men from Goldhawk wouldn't let us near the place."

"The Yard is subordinate to Goldhawk, need I remind you of that?"

"I know my place sir, but when it comes to justice I might be old fashioned but I believe no man, and no institution, is above the law."

"And what is it you are so desperate to speak with me about that you'd commit trespass?" He started to wonder if he could get to his revolver in the top drawer.

"Barclay," Lord snapped his fingers and his colleague passed him a piece of paper. "Tell me sir, if you've seen this letter before?" He handed it over and Lyle took it tentatively, fixed his glasses and read it.

It was the letter luring Charlotte Anne Pilling to Smithfield.

Shit! he thought, *keep it cool old chap, keep it cool.* "Never seen it in my life," he lied, "and this should have been surrendered to Goldhawk right away, I could have you charged with withholding evidence."

"If you like evidence you'll appreciate this next piece I'm sure." He reached inside his coat and drew out a battered old book. "This was posted anonymously to Scotland Yard, it arrived this morning." He held it up for Lyle to see.

It was a black book and someone had slashed five chalk lines across the cover like the claws of a bear. He knew the book and he knew those marks. His eyes were drawn back to the desk where his revolver was waiting, thinking he had no choice now.

"There was a marker drawing my attention to a particular page sir, if you'll indulge me." Lord's tone was calm and polite. "Light please, Barclay."

Barclay raised the lantern.

Lord thumbed to the right place, cleared his throat and read aloud, *"Mr Lyle of Goldhawk arranged the timely demise of one Charlotte Anne Pilling, in the shape of a note luring her to Smithfield. Once there, Francis-Joseph Kollip, whose life is embittered by addiction to opium, did what many men would quail at and ended her life."* He closed the book and stared expectantly at Lyle. "A curious thing to write – can you explain this sir?"

Lyle stood in stunned silence, wondering how the hell Blackwand had turned the tables on them all.

"Sir?" he pressed.

"It's a deranged fiction."

"Kollip says not, we arrested him earlier. He says you and another fellow put him up to it. He's ready to testify to that."

Suddenly it seemed he couldn't breathe, tremors gripped him, and his eyes went from Lord to the drawer and back again.

Lord should have seen it coming, but Lyle was faster than his age suggested. He lunged for the drawer and pulled the revolver out in one frantic move.

"No!" Lord saw the barrel point his way, when just then Barclay hurtled past and landed a fist against Lyle's nose. There was a small yelp and meaty thud as Lyle landed in a heap. He lay there with his glasses askew, groaning and nursing a bleeding nose, and Barclay wrenched the weapon from his grip. "It was Doulton," he lied, "Doulton set it up and Thorpe as well!"

Lord breathed a sigh of gratitude. "Nice work constable."

"Thanks sir." Barclay rubbed at his sore knuckles.

Lord came and stood over him, and now he sounded merciless. "Virgil Lyle, you are under arrest for the murder of Charlotte Anne Pilling. Have you anything to say for yourself?" The room was quiet except for Lyle's soft crying. "I thought so. Take him out Barclay," he concluded.

"Aye sir." Barclay pulled him up by the scruff and shoved him towards the door, leaving his fallen glasses on the carpet.

Lord waited for the footfalls to fade, and regarded the room one last time. "No institution is above the law." He said it as a challenge to the likes of Goldhawk, but mostly he said it for Charlotte's sake. "Thank you, whoever you are." He looked down at the mysterious book. Without it, the investigation would have died as surely as Charlotte herself. Then he slipped it back into his coat and left, closing the door behind him.

Lyle might have missed the boat to France, but there was one other 'loose thread' that had no such trouble. The steamer Forget-Me-Not skimmed the waves bound for France and a lone figure stood by the rail watching Southampton's lights shrink away.

On outwardly appearances the distinguished looking man was alone, but appearances can be deceptive and nothing about this picture is what it seems. For starters this was no 'man' despite the tall frame and bristling moustache, in fact this wasn't really a human at all. In fact 'he' was a female, and neither was she really alone. She carried a black cane and inside was her beloved, preserved forever so they might be a couple always, but that was not her only companion. Hidden away in the depths of her skull buzzed the shrivelled essence of the man whose body this had once been.

The lone figure was in fact three individuals, a whole family indeed, and a closer and happier family you'd be hard pressed to find. Or at least that's what Vorus believed. Her sisters might have abandoned her and returned to her hateful father Àeon. Sophie might have come and wrecked her plans and Blackwand might have prevailed, but she had her beloved Matthew to make these injustices bearable.

She hummed softly to herself. It was a strange melody nobody on Earth had ever heard, although many had gone mad searching for it. It was the song of Àeon and as long as she remembered it Thorpe's body wouldn't be Ruined and she could live inside him forever with Matthew by her side. She sighed contentedly and drew a cigar from her coat. She'd developed quite a taste for these of late and this body offered her countless other experiences her old one hadn't, even the lingering pain in her wounded shoulder held a fascination for her. The match took some lighting, but eventually the cigar tip glowed red and she flicked the spent match into the waves.

She stood that way for some time, smoking and humming to herself until finally Southampton was gone, as was the cigar. "It's getting cold Matthew," she stroked the cane as she spoke, "let's retire to our cabin." The family Thorpe made its way along the deserted deck and out of the wind as the first stars twinkled above.

* * * * *

From high above, Roman-field resembled a huge wound. Fire glowed bloody red and smoke stained the sky like a bruise. It was an awful sight and an awful place, but part of her didn't want to leave. Eirik still lay there along with his brothers and a good many witches, but escape took priority now.

She flew fast and hard. Strike was exhausted but they had to put a good distance between them and Wellesley. No matter how fast they flew though, the sadness kept up. Tears blurred her view of Ben up ahead and of Harl beyond him. Together they were heading to Kolfinnia's secret coven. She blinked the tears away but when she looked again Ben and Harl were gone, and now it was night and she was flying alone and lost. "Ben?" she called him over and over, but he'd left her behind and she was alone in the darkness, just as it had always been. 'Happiness isn't for you Sunday,' she told herself.

She jumped awake. The dream was familiar now. She had endured it every night since escaping Wellesley nine days ago. It was Thursday June 30th, and although barely perceptible the balance of day and night was tipping towards the latter. They'd been following Harl for days. The first night they pushed hard and camped close to a ruined castle at Avebury. Most of the time they travelled on foot, first passing out of Wiltshire and then heading north west to Gloucester. Along the way she imagined the village names were trying to tell her something; Oakland, Haresfield, Crowhill, and Foxhole, and also along the way she inevitably grew closer to Ben.

She rubbed the sleep from her eyes, took a moment to gather her thoughts and looked to where he was lying sound asleep besides the campfire. A few cinders still glowed and the sky was warming as dawn approached. She wanted to wake him and tell him about her distressing dream, but he needed his sleep and he had enough worries of his own. She whispered his name without waking him, still amazed that they'd found one another again. "I need a wash," she decided and slid out from under her cloak. "Watch him for me Harl."

The crow blinked drowsily and looked from her to Ben and back again. She took her boots and quietly slipped away to the stream to bathe and start a new day.

The day had been extremely hot and they'd flown right through the early dawn until the rising sun made flying too risky. For the rest of the day they followed Harl on foot before making camp at dusk. It was still hot, and they sat by a stream on the warm rocks and cooled their feet in the waters.

"Do you remember Clovis's miracle?" Ben asked her from nowhere.

Kittiwake, she thought with a pang. Clovis had shown them a glimpse of Evermore so they wouldn't be afraid. "I chose not to look Ben," she said sadly, and stared at her feet under the stream's surface.

"You didn't?"

She just shook her head.

"Were you afraid of something?"

Again, she shook her head, and this time he knew not to badger her. He assumed it was fear, but Sunday knew better and wished with all her heart she could tell him.

He listened to the stream's soothing melody and decided now might be a good time. "Here, a late solstice offering." He handed over a small packet with a smile.

"For me?"

"You're a solstice queen who missed her day in the sun. I thought it'd be a bit of normality."

She looked down at the brown paper packet. Solstice had come and gone and they'd all been so busy fighting that nobody had remembered its real significance. "Thank you," she smiled. He watched her closely feeling slightly nervous. It seemed each word and gesture carried more significance as they grew closer. The wrapping fell away to reveal a beautiful comb fashioned from rosewood, inlaid with silver and carved with, what else, but a fox. She brightened, "Oh, Ben it's beautiful!"

"I'm glad you like it. I traded with a Spanish witch for it."

She knew he must have parted with something rare to obtain it. She traced the silver whorls with a finger and stroked the fox head. "It's perfect, just perfect." She reached around his neck and kissed him. "Will you do the honours?" She held the comb out and he took it gladly.

They climbed out of the stream and onto the banking. She sat between his splayed legs with her back to him, and he began to gently comb her hair. "That feels wonderful," she praised him.

"They say our lives are like threads." He watched the comb slide through that sea of gold, smoothing and restoring as it went.

She murmured an agreement. The late hour, his touch and the comb's stroking rhythm were making her feel drowsy.

"I wish our lives could be so easily untangled," he added.

"Would they be better though?" she sighed.

"Simpler."

"Simpler's not always better, maybe we need a few tangles to make life interesting."

"Then I'll leave these in," he joked and gently tugged at her hair.

"No, don't stop."

"I'm too rough?"

"Hardly, you're sending me to sleep."

"You mean I'm dreary company?"

"You know what I mean." She listened to the comb sigh through her hair. Each stroke was followed by a smoothing hand.

"You've got some twigs in here," he smiled.

"Don't spoil the moment," she whispered, almost asleep.

The comb continued to glide through her hair, from her crown to its tips, then back again sounding like soft breathing and each stroke felt to brush away a little more hurt. Lulled by the warm rocks and the touch of his hands, she felt light enough to drift away. He continued, top to bottom, top to bottom. Her mind untangled, her breathing fell in step with each stroke and the noises around her melted away until she was left with only a profound sense of peace.

"Sunday?"

"Don't stop," she murmured.

"Sunday." The voice was insistent.

"Ben, shhh!!"

"Sunday."

"Ben!" she groaned and forced her eyes open, but when she looked he was gone and so were the woods and the stream.

"Sunday, see this moment before it's gone for all time," someone told her.

She was standing on a spiral of stone stairs that wound on forever, lined with doors and lit by the souls of the departed and yet to be born. One of them she recognised at once, even with his back to her. It was Eirik.

He walked upwards along the spiral and as he did, a woman rose from her place on the steps to greet him. She had waited a thousand years for him, but what is time when you have forever on your side?

Sunday watched the two embrace and felt something mended in the world. "Eirik," she whispered his name and touched the silver hammer around her neck. He looked back, thinking someone had called him, but he didn't see her. He took Freydis by the hand and together they walked on. Sunday watched them until they were lost in the throng of souls. He'd found his way home and her heart felt less tangled for it, and she knew who to thank for this vision. "Dear champion," she smiled.

"Sunday?"

She awoke in Ben's arms.

"You fell asleep," he explained.

"I did?" She rubbed at her eyes.

"And you were talking."

"Really?" Suddenly she felt vulnerable, and she sat upright.

He looked regretful for a moment. "I don't suppose I'm your 'dear champion'?"

"You're one of them, yes," she promised and ran a hand through her hair, which was now like a river of silk. "You're very thorough."

"Did I get them all?"

She thought of that one last tangle in her heart, the guilt over Kittiwake, and wondered whether he could straighten it. "You got them all, for now." She offered him a mysterious smile and brushed a kiss against his cheek, then climbed to her feet. She decided there and then that she would risk it, she would tell him, but not just yet.

July came and both of them felt the pages close on a harrowing chapter and June would never seem the same again. The evening of July 1st they made camp by the entrance to a small limestone cave overgrown with yew and larch, and they decided to go no further that day.

"Do you think Hilda will get there before us, to Kolfinnia's coven I mean?" Sunday looked forward to meeting her again.

"That depends, her friend Hathwell doesn't have a staff. They'll have to make the whole journey on foot, and only Harl's crows know how far that is." He looked to where Harl was perched on a rock, while both thunder-sprites were sitting in the grass preening their feathers.

"Hilda's friend?" she quizzed him gently. "Like you and I are friends?"

He thought back and remembered the sheer relief on Hathwell's face at finding Hilda alive, while she had looked rather unmoved, or maybe that's only how she wanted to appear. "No, I don't think they're friends like us." He couldn't help but feel a little sorry for Hathwell, already he couldn't imagine life without Sunday.

She studied his face, liking everything she saw there. "I'm glad we're, well . . ." she trailed off.

"I'm glad we are too," he agreed simply.

They shared a lingering look, which might have gone on all evening if Strike hadn't interrupted them. "Thunder's coming," he said plainly.

Reluctantly, they looked away from each other and to the sky, although neither of them needed to check. If sprites knew anything it was storms. "Then best we shift into the cave mouth eh?" Ben reached down for an armful of firewood, intending to take it under cover, and sure enough no sooner had they moved than they heard the rumble of distant thunder.

Strike wasn't wrong. The storm rolled over them like an angry giant and lasted well into the night. Ben fell sound asleep long before the little fire had died, but Sunday lay awake and listened to the thunder roll and the rain beat down. Both thunder-sprites had gone out to bask in the storm and listen to their ancestors speak. She could just see Wake sitting by the cave mouth. Occasionally he was silhouetted by a flash of lightning, but she couldn't see Strike. Worried, she retrieved her cloak, pulled it over her head and went out to check on him. "Where's Strike?" she asked over the rain.

Wake was sitting on a rock gazing reverentially up at the storm. "Just up ahead, he's sad so I left him be."

She was taken aback, and ignoring the sodden grass and pounding rain she braved the storm and went to find him.

"Strike?" She knelt beside him, cloak held tight, while around her the rain hissed and the trees groaned. He was staring at the heavens just like Wake, but he didn't look serene, he looked desperately sad. Rain cascaded down his feathers and his upturned face and he didn't seem to hear her. "Strike?"

He turned to regard her and she didn't know if it was the rain or whether he'd been crying. "I heard my name."

"Yes, I came to find you."

"No, the one I only told her."

Suddenly she knew and she looked up, thinking of Elios.

"I heard my name shouted as loud as thunder," he proclaimed. "She remembered."

"She's gone home?"

"In style." Thunder rumbled again and he pricked his ears.

She saw him sigh and his shoulders slump. "Come inside Strike, there's nothing more you can do." She ran a hand over his wings.

"You go, I'll wait."

She looked up at the blackness, squinting against the falling rain. *Magic evolves,* she thought, and wondered if Strike had become the first sprite to fall in love, but looking at his sad face she wasn't sure if that was such a wonderful thing. "I'll be waiting for you," she promised.

"I know," he said and turned skyward again.

She left him then and went back to the shelter of the cave, staring out to where he sat. Outside remained utterly black, but every so often the lightning flashed and she saw her lonely sprite silhouetted against the dark, listening as Elios shouted his name as loud as thunder.

They continued north-west, crossing the river Severn in Gloucester. Sunday found herself staring into its calm waters and wondering where hrafn-dimmu was right then. Wherever it was she hoped it was steadily making its way to Kolfinnia, its rightful keeper. "Safe journey dark-raven," she wished it.

In Gloucester they spied a market man selling caged song birds. Fortunately the market was busy and Sunday charmed the trader while Ben quietly opened the cages. After she had teased him long enough she drifted away and he turned to find finches, tits and robins fluttering through the crowds.

"I see the 'Sunday-effect' is still as potent as ever," Strike observed, listening to the man spit and curse.

"Long live Blackwand," she replied contentedly.

Eventually Harl turned westwards and Ben saw their route was taking them to the border with Wales. Over the next few days they all felt it grow stronger, witches and sprites alike; an expectancy, like a constant tremor in the earth. Their journey was coming to an end. On the night of Tuesday July 5th they camped close to the village of Ross-on-Wye while Harl scouted ahead. Late that night, Sunday lay next to the fire and watched the shadows dance and wondered why she felt so confused. "Ben?"

"Hmm?" his voice came out of the dark.

"Are you excited about going home?"

"Aren't you?"

"Yes and no."

She heard movement and a moment later he came and lay behind her. "Confused?"

"I feel so many different things," she stroked her cheek where the Timekeeper's special mark had once been.

"You've endured a lot. It's only natural to feel confused."

"I suppose so."

They lay belly to back, and he circled an arm around her protectively. She clasped his hand and together they stared into the dying fire. "Mostly I think of all those left behind," she confessed and her hand strayed to Eirik's silver hammer around her neck.

"And I'm sure they're thinking of you. The departed watch over us."

She was quiet for a while before speaking again. "I haven't had a home since Regal-Fox. What if I don't fit in?"

"Afraid it'll all be too much for you?"

"Something like that," she admitted.

"You'll always have me, and Strike, not to mention the adoration of witches far and wide."

She looked over her shoulder at him and frowned. "In what way?"

He gave her a crafty smile. "They were telling tales of Blackwand in France even before I got there. Get used to being a hero." He leaned over and kissed her, "Now go to sleep Blackwand, we'll be there soon. Another day, two at most, then we'll be home."

"Home," she echoed.

"Home." He squeezed her hand.

She pressed herself closer to him, took his advice and surrendered to sleep.

Later she awoke with the distinct feeling of being watched. She came fully alert, lay still and waited, and after a few minutes a small figure crept into the firelight – an oak-fairy. It regarded her with something like awe. *My soul sign,* she realised with a smile, thinking of Neet, and lay perfectly still so as not to scare it away.

It sniffed and blinked, shook its leaf shaped wings and crept closer. "Broom-rider with broken soul," it said to itself, "so the tales are true." It regarded her a few seconds more, then backed away with its head bowed until it vanished into the darkness. It seemed tales of Blackwand were spreading amongst fairies as well as witches.

Broken soul? She snuggled closer to Ben who remained blissfully asleep. *Not broken any more,* she smiled and briefly allowed herself to believe that she deserved happiness after all.

Harl returned at dawn and at first Ben thought the sombre bird would simply lead them on as he had for over two weeks, but he was full of news and couldn't resist sharing it.

"Stormwood!" Ben grinned at her over their sparse breakfast.

She shook her head, mystified.

"That's Kolfinnia's new coven, Harl just got back and he told me."

Strike and Wake both came close to listen.

"Stormwood?" She liked the name, it sounded elemental and savage.

"She named it for the wood at Kittiwake," Ben explained, "where trees surrendered their lives so we could have more lightning-staffs, remember?"

"All too well," Strike chipped in.

"What a storm *that* was," Wake added.

"Stormwood-coven," she tried the name again and smiled broadly, realising it was her new home. "How far?"

"Another two days, one if we push it, but that would mean arriving at night." He watched her closely.

Suddenly she lost her appetite with the excitement. She lay down her bread, stood and looked westwards. *Only one day's walk beyond those trees lays Kolfinnia's coven.* It was a chance to start again, and the thought made her dizzy.

"We can be there tomorrow," he added soberly.

She saw all of them were waiting for her reply, as if this was her expedition. "Tomorrow it is then."

Harl agreed with a rough croak and that sealed it. Tomorrow they would at last go home.

That night was the last night of their journey. They spent it only four miles from the border where Herefordshire gave way to the Black Mountains of Wales and somewhere in their forested peaks lay Stormwood-coven. "Black mountains, black wands," Sunday reflected, thinking that all those little coincidences built up to a much bigger picture.

"She certainly likes out of the way places," Ben passed her a mug of mint tea. The distant hills were just a dark ridge against the sky now.

"Thank you," she sipped her drink lost in thought. "Ben, have you got a pencil," she asked at last.

He fished around in his pockets and brought out a stub no bigger than his thumb. "Ready for anything, what's it for?"

"Nothing really," she tucked it away in her waistcoat, "but you'll get it back, I promise."

He couldn't hide his amusement. "Always full of secrets."

"I am not!"

"Really? Tell me a secret then."

She looked pensive for a moment, and then smiled. "Very well. It was when I was just a girl. I hadn't been paying attention in spell lessons and I'd forgotten how poisonous the yew is. When Alfred found me I had an apron full of yew berries, he was very angry and demanded to know if I'd eaten any, but I was so afraid I couldn't answer. He feared the worst and so dragged me off to Geraldine Mead, the coven herbalist, and she made me drink something that made me sick until there was nothing left in my belly." She smiled and shook her head at the memory. "I cried and cried. Alfred was so worried he put me in the bunk right next to his and watched me all night. I'd never felt so poorly, but at the same time I'd never felt safer."

He gazed at her, feeling he was seeing someone emerge after a lifetime of hiding. It was like watching a flower bloom. "You never told anyone that?"

"Not the part about how safe I felt." She shook her head. "Never that part."

"You certainly never told me," Strike complained.

"Wait until you hear the rest of the things I never told anyone," she said with relish.

They spent their last evening sharing secrets. Eventually they settled down for the night with the dwindling fire for company. As sleep overtook them, Ben confided his last secret. It was hardly a whisper because he didn't want her to hear it, not yet anyway. "I love you," he said.

Sunday slept on unaware, and dreamed of home.

They found the first of Stormwood's way-bewares hidden in the bracken. It was the early evening of Thursday July 7th, Thor's Day appropriately enough, and they had arrived at their destination. Ben stepped through them and offered his hand. "Welcome home," he said sincerely.

"Home." She clasped his hand and took the last step of her journey, the one that had started on the black sands of Iceland, and stood by his side. "Home!" she cheered, then grabbed him in a celebratory hug which went on for a long time.

They walked along sedately for another two miles with Harl leading the way. They threaded their way through woodland surrounded by birdsong until the trees thinned and they found themselves overlooking a small sheltered valley. *That's Stormwood,* she understood, and her heart jumped.

She saw people down there, and she heard the distant echo of someone chopping wood and the faint sound of children's laughter. A silvery flash drew her attention, and she saw a river winding its way across the valley bottom, with fruit and vegetable gardens along its margins. Wisps of smoke spiralled up from thatched huts and when she looked closer she saw tree-houses linked by rope bridges resting in the branches. She nodded appreciatively, and all of a sudden she just wanted to be there and any doubts she harboured simply vanished. This was right.

"What are we waiting for?" Ben grinned and pulled her forwards, but she held back, knowing there was one last task. "Sunday?" He saw the cogs turning in her mind.

"Go ahead Ben, I just need a moment."

She looked reflective, sad almost, but he knew better than to intrude. "Just don't be long, I know there'll be plenty of people waiting to meet you, Kolfinnia amongst them."

Harl croaked in agreement, and Wake nodded sagely.

"I'm coming," she promised and squeezed his hand.

He let go reluctantly, gave her one last smile then set off down the slope through the heather and foxgloves with Harl flapping ahead and Wake perched on his shoulder. He walked like a man without a care and even began to whistle a tune. Sunday recognised it at once as the ballad of Pelaria and Eliath and couldn't help but smile. She watched him go until he dipped out of sight, heading down to where Kolfinnia's coven awaited.

The Timekeeper listened to the thoughts whirring through her thread and knew her intentions. "Home at last Sunday," he said in satisfaction. The past months had been hard. As Sunday reflected on all that had happened, so too did he. He could have left her thread broken last autumn, but he didn't. He could have broken her thread again as ordered, but he resisted, and he might have died and let the assassin bury Sunday alive, but he prevailed. Perhaps he had earned the title of 'dear champion' after all, he thought. As Sunday made ready to finish what she started in his cave last year, he surveyed his realm of perfect blackness, alive with the sound of running water. "The time is at hand my Lord, the Flowering of Fate has come." He addressed fate as if there had never been a word of dispute between them.

A distant star erupted as a violent super-nova in reply, but despite his show of anger the Patternmaker was powerless to keep his word, like it or not.

"We have our bargain my Lord, you gave your word," the Timekeeper rebuked him, and he had no need to remind the overlord of fate what would happen if he want back on that bargain. The Timekeeper thought of the Patternmaker's great secret, the one that had finally forced an end to their duel. In reality it seemed such a small secret to the great spider, but like all tyrants the Patternmaker lived in constant fear of being found out. *'There can be only one God,'* was his overriding command, and only the Timekeeper really knew why that was so. But this was a secret he was bound to keep for the sake of their truce. Suddenly the thread in his grasp twitched. "She is beginning," he announced.

"Home," Strike looked bewildered but happy. "We're actually home."

"Not quite." She took Ben's pencil from her waistcoat and pulled a sheet of tatty paper from her other pocket. It had been there since she'd taken it from Thorpe's study weeks ago. The edges were frayed and the ink blurred, but the document was still legible. It was a purchase bill for prison rations at Hobbs Ash. She didn't know it then, but the greatest artefact in witchdom, one with the power to set humanity free, was about to be written on a prison document. Fate had a sense of humour after all it seemed, albeit a very dark one.

She sat in the grass and smoothed the paper across her thigh. Strike sat close, waiting while she gathered her thoughts, pencil poised, wondering how to begin. A dragonfly hummed past, a grasshopper rattled, and dandelion seeds drifted against her cheek feeling like spider silks and she smiled. "Dear champion, something tells me our business isn't quite finished yet," she sighed, closed her eyes and waited.

Strike watched in respectful silence as she copied out the Timekeeper's reply and he thought of that dark cave far away and the river of fate that flowed through it. The pencil scribbled and scratched its way across the paper without her looking, writing line after line in her delicate script and just when Strike thought she'd run out of space her hand stopped and she let out a long breath. "Sunday?" he asked.

She opened her eyes and blinked away the vagueness, looked down at the letter in her hands and read it for the very first time.

In the years that followed, the Timekeeper's message became known as the Flowering of Fate and was rightly regarded as a hallowed relic: the voice of creation. Tales grew up of those witches who braved incredible danger just to set eyes on it, and such stories could fill a library of their own, yet it was addressed to Sunday and Strike and it was they who had the honour of reading it first.

"What does it say?" Strike whispered, almost afraid to find out.

She cleared her throat and carefully read aloud, knowing this moment could never happen again.

Sunday Evelyn Flowers and Lightning-Strikes-Lonesome-Ash. I have watched over you both, and for a time I believed your threads would be broken once more. In the end however, pity prevailed, and the Patternmaker yielded. But the legacy your courage has forged shall be this; the Patternmaker concedes individuals shall be free to determine their own fates, providing they believe ardently enough. Earth has needed such a Flowering of Fate for a very long time, and only your sacrifice and love made it possible. I would watch you further Sunday, but it appears fate has brought you a new protector. May your days with Ben be long and happy, until at last your thread is woven no more.

She held his letter in trembling hands, knowing its significance was beyond price. "The Flowering of Fate," she uttered.

"Maybe something good did come from that note of yours?" Strike ventured, understanding it was a very dark subject for her.

"Maybe," she wondered, before finally slipping the priceless letter into her coat. "Thank you dear champion," she said.

"Thank you," Strike echoed.

"Last task," she promised, and took a small bundle from her coat and unwrapped it.

"I'm glad you didn't leave it there," Strike said.

"Me too, it deserved so much better." The cloth fell open and she gently retrieved the contents. As soon as she saw it again she felt sad. The broken way-beware looked up at her. Its humble life and beautiful song were gone, but she hadn't wanted to leave it at Wellesley Hall. "Galen would have prevailed if not for the song of one small way-beware." She regarded it for a while longer knowing this was goodbye at last, then she knelt and scooped out a hollow in the earth, placed it gently inside and whispered a prayer before covering it over. "Sleep little singer, may Oak and Holly watch over you always."

"Be at peace," Strike added.

She brushed the soil from her hands and a tear from her eye then stood and looked down upon Stormwood, the evening wasn't far off and Ben was out of sight now. "Come on Strike," she smiled, "let's go home."

"Home." He fluttered onto her shoulder. "Lead the way, Blackwand."

She picked up her staff and they set off after Ben, to where good company and a good supper awaited.

Blackwands

Richard Dunnock had only been a police constable for eight months, but he was already tired of the job. He was also tired of his nick name at the station; Dickie Dunnock didn't sound too flattering to his ears. Maybe he should have become a Methodist preacher as his father had wanted, he thought. To make matters worse it had snowed, then thawed and frozen and now the streets were hard with rutted mud and the pavements slick with ice. "Three more days, just three more bloody days," he grumbled.

It was December 21st and in three days he'd enjoy Christmas with his family. Perhaps it was the cold or maybe London was experiencing a bout of Christmas cheer, but the streets seemed unusually quiet tonight he thought. He walked briskly to keep warm, passing under a succession of gaslights, coming and going in the islands of light they cast.

Something cracked underfoot and right away he knew it wasn't ice. He looked down to see a sliver of broken glass. "Someone's been up to no good then?" He held his lantern up and saw a shop with a broken window. At first he thought 'theft' and almost reached for his whistle, but then he saw the symbol chalked on the brickwork, five lines like claw marks, and he took a step backwards. "Blackwand," he muttered and suddenly felt even colder. All of London remembered her reign of terror, although many still hailed her as a saint. Dunnock couldn't make his mind up, but he knew Blackwand was dead, it had said so in the papers. She was caught in June and hanged and he knew the papers didn't lie, but dead or not it seemed Blackwand had inspired folks. Since her execution small acts of criminal damage had been reported all over London, just like the one he was looking at now. Hanging in the window, were a dozen fat Christmas geese, but now the window was broken. "Merry bloody Christmas," he grumbled and reached for his note book to log the incident.

He didn't understand crimes like this, there was no gain to it as far as he could see, but such crimes were becoming more common. Unpopular parliamentarians had their gates daubed in paint, and wealthy mills suffered vandalism in the name of better wages, and it clearly wasn't just one person. Something was happening out there on London's streets, something that compelled folks to take matters into their own hands. 'Crimes of quiet dissent,' the newspapers called them and they were always accompanied by those five chalk lines, like the claws of a bear. Dunnock finished his notes with a weary sigh, kicked the glass safely into the gutter and continued his beat, wondering what the world was coming to.

ABOUT THE AUTHOR

STEVE HUTTON

Steve attained first a BA then later an MA in illustration. As a freelance illustrator he has worked for the National Trust and created character concepts for film and TV, most notably 'The Golden Compass'.

After years of illustrating for established writers, Steve decided it was time to tell his own stories. Taking his love of rugged northern lands, their legends and folklore, and combining them with other diverse interests, the resulting narrative is *The Dark Raven Chronicles*.

Steve owes as much to modern classics, like 'Watership Down', and Mary Stewart's 'Hollow Hills' trilogy, for their inspiration as he does to the 'Icelandic Sagas' and 'Beowulf'.

The *Dark Raven Chronicles* is a fantasy series blending historical facts with wild fiction to create a unique world, enhanced and enriched by Steve's own illustrations.

RAVEN'S WAND ALMANAC

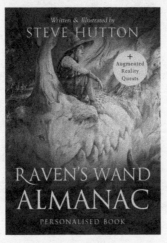

Text and illustrations © Steve Hutton

The *Raven's Wand Almanac* is full of images selected by you - just for you, making it a unique personalised picture book.

The *Raven's Wand Almanac* will take you through the beliefs, traditions and legends of the world of *Raven's Wand*. Steep yourself in the life and values of the witches and discover the Sign of your Birth & the Season you relate to.

Walk through your year in the Wildwood and learn about the characters you are most drawn to by creating your very own picture book of Steve Hutton's incredible artwork.

Visit

www.DarkRavenChronicles.com

Facebook: Dark Raven Chronicles